I0706167

THE
OBSIDIAN
BLAZE

ALSO BY BEKA WESTRUP

WINGED SPIRITS TRILOGY

The Seldom Wings

The Obsidian Blaze

Book #3 (TBA)

THE ETERNAL BRIDES SERIES

Demons and Roses

Book #2 (TBA)

SALT AND EARTH DUOLOGY

Blood in the Tea Leaves (Prequel Novella)

Beneath the Bloody Aurora

Book # 2 (TBA)

STANDALONES

Song of Dark Tides

THE
OBSIDIAN
BLAZE

BY BEKA WESTRUP

First published in the United States of America September 2024 by Beka Westrup

Cataloging-in-Publication Data is on file with the Library of Congress.

ISBN: 979-8-9863087-7-7 (paperback), 979-8-9863087-6-0 (e-book)

Author website: https://www.bekawestrup.com

Editor: Alexa Thomas (The Fiction Fix)

Map Design: Eternal Geekery

Cover Design: Fay Lane

Internal Art (character art): MsMorbid (@msmorbid on Twitter, @msmorbid.art on Instagram)

AUTHOR'S NOTE

This dark fantasy trilogy features a morally gray FMC who doesn't always do the right thing, or even the wrong thing for good reasons. She's complicated and has a lot of growing to do. If you aren't one for "difficult to love" women, then this probably isn't the book for you.

Also, please note that this book does end on a cliffhanger.

Content Warnings:

- Explicit sexual content
- Bondage
- Themes of grief and death
- Themes of war
- Graphic torture
- Substance/alcohol use
- Mention of rape
- Mention of infertility

PLAYLIST

1. Who's Afraid of Little Old Me? - Taylor Swift
2. scary part of me - Sody
3. MISTAKE - NF
4. Stay - Kygo
5. Mess It Up - Gracie Abrams
6. Call You Mine - The Chainsmokers
7. The Albatross - Taylor Swift
8. Wrecking Ball - Miley Cyrus
9. I'm Her - Natalie Jane
10. Dying Breed - The Killers
11. Geronimo - Sheppard
12. Heavenly Kind Of State Of Mind - Lewis Capaldi
13. Real Problems - Kyd the Band & TAELA
14. Vicious - Bohnes
15. gold rush - Taylor Swift
16. Little Did I Know - Julia Michaels
17. Falling - Harry Styles
18. Waiting in the Dark - Cathartic Fall
19. Can You Hold Me - NF
20. The Last Time (Taylor's Version) - Taylor Swift
21. Masterpiece - Cloudy June
22. Free - Florence + The Machine
23. Nightshift - MOTHICA
24. Euclid - Sleep Token
25. Risk - Gracie Abrams

ANNEX

(NEED A REMINDER?)

SERAPHIM

Cockatriz — wings come in varying hues of green, hazel eyes with luminous streaks of emerald, gifts: "energy devourers" and charming sight

Fenix — wings come in varying hues of gold, golden and light brown eyes, gifts: creation/manipulation of flames and the power of combustion

Great Ravens — wings come in varying hues of black, black eyes, gifts: possession of nature

Halcyon — wings come in varying hues of gray and white, blue eyes, gifts: hoarfrost, storm magic,
*when the Halcyon is born more spirit than human, they may possess the ability to lull others to sleep

Harpies — wings come in varying hues of brown, brown eyes, gifts: air manipulation, born with extra limbs and third eyes, heightened senses

Impundulu — wings come in varying hues of red and copper, red and dark brown eyes, gifts: lightning, blood thirst, memory absorption

Malforian — wings come in varying hues of pink, green eyes, gifts: emotion amplification and/or manipulation

Quintessentials — wings come in varying hues of blue, blue eyes, gifts: Materie (ether) manipulation

Sphinx — gossamer wings that glisten with the faint sheen of any color, yellow eyes, gifts: light creation/manipulation

Stymphalian — wings made of iron and/or otherworldly metal, silver eyes, gifts: manipulation of metals

Serpents - the primary population of beings that live in the ocean of this world
Elves - the primary population of beings that live in the alternate dimension of this world
Sutilis (singular usage) / Sutilus (plural usage) - otherworldly monsters that harvest organs from living creatures for eternal life

IMPUNDULU
THE GNASHING FOREST
LANDMARKS
STYMPHALIAN
HARPIES
SPHINX
FENIX

HALCYON
MALFORIAN
QUINTESSENTIALS
COCKATRIZ
N
W
OTHANA

To the pieces of my heart I have lost but still remember...

I love you, James.
Thank you for everything.

CHAPTER 1

SIA

Poppy smoke filled the room, clouding my mind.
Red flooded my vision, the faerie orbs overhead spinning with each slow blink, reminding me of precisely just how many seeds I'd burned through in the last hour—a significant amount.

Lust was a heady presence in my veins, strong enough to drown out the anger that had consumed me since arriving back home. Days, I'd been drowning in it, and I would continue to rest in this blissful haze a little while longer.

Planes of flesh stretched beneath me, feline smiles and curves slick with arousal. Sphinx wings fluttered in my periphery, the transparent feathers gleaming with yellow light as I drove the creature underneath me to the razor-edge of ecstasy.

This female was new to the castle pleasure chambers, a courtesan still bursting with enthusiasm and wonder, with an eagerness to explore what the Fenix court had to offer.

She hadn't anticipated *me*.

As she cried out, I smiled against her, my tongue flicking the tender flesh between her legs. She came moaning my

"

name, her hands ripping at the orange satin sheets. The sound echoed through the cavernous room, somewhat lessening my gratification. *Sabrina.* I was always Sabrina up here. I bit at her clit to make her stop saying it, delighting in the garbled sob that erupted from her mouth instead.

My core throbbed.

Goddess, my need was practically seeping down my thighs now. Maybe I should have intruded on my brother's side of the pleasure chambers sooner. Sex like this, with beautiful women like her, always satisfied me. Kahem had good taste. This one was delicious, like salted caramel and cream.

Warmth encroached on my back, dainty nails grazing my waist and hips. Wet kisses caressed my spine as a finger drifted down to my aching core.

I twisted to grab the second female, tugging her down onto the mattress with me beside the first. *This* female I knew.

Elena smirked as I turned and settled her on top of me, secretly glad I put my wings away before my arrival. It made rolling around on these hard beds much easier.

Father always preferred for me to paint my wings before coming to this side of the palace anyway, and I didn't want to go through the trouble today. I hated the paint. It got everywhere at the first hint of moisture and smelled terrible. I'd rather everyone think I was ashamed of my wings.

And wasn't I? Ashamed?

Father had certainly tried to make me feel that way.

Elena's single pale pink set twitched above me, the small flecks of gold threaded through her feathers glinting in the low light. Malforian were the prettiest of seraphim in my opinion, all joy and laughter and tricksters of feeling. The humans liked to call them Honey Thieves, angels of blood and jealousy, and they weren't wrong.

Her small breasts brushed against mine, every inch of the pebbled skin between us heightening my desire. She leaned down to kiss me, and I welcomed her soft lips and prodding tongue, sighing as she stroked between my legs. She wanted me to come, wanted to be the one responsible for relieving me, but I wasn't ready yet.

I grabbed her waist and pulled her forward, nipping at her red-washed skin when she tried to fight my generosity.

There was no fighting me in here.

I settled her on top of my face, wringing pleasure from her as she gripped the headboard. My body was tingling, my cunt clenching, driving me toward that precipice of light as she rode my face until we were both gasping.

Another set of hands seized my thighs, squeezing, teasing my sensitive skin.

The sphinx beside us had recovered, and now she wanted to feast on me.

Before she could lower her mouth to my slit, I gripped Elena's ass and lifted her off my mouth as I threaded a hand in the new girl's hair. "No," I snapped.

She blinked, her ghostly wings going still behind her, in fear or disappointment, I couldn't be sure.

I grimaced, reasoning with myself. The newcomer didn't know my rules yet. "I want to feel your sex against mine," I rasped, pulling her forward by her hair.

Her eyes flashed in surprise and then delight as she crawled over me. She straddled my hips without hesitation, though I could tell by the way she slowly arranged herself that this position was new to her. She was still learning. Elena had been assigned as her teacher, but I didn't mind teaching her a thing or two myself.

I nodded when she looked to me for approval. "So good, sweetheart."

As she lowered her body to mine, I groaned. Her slickness mixed with mine, our heated flesh rubbing together. She laughed airily, the power of her position hitting her as she started moving with purpose. I met her grinding thrusts with a desperation of my own, and my fingers dug into Elena's hip as I brought her back to my mouth.

Within a few minutes, we were coming in such perfect synchrony that I swear I kissed the stars.

As I came down, harsh reality crept back in. My mind swirled with the dulling edge of the poppy seeds, losing the haze as my heart thundered away, life dragging me down with each echoing thump.

Elena collapsed, the sphinx falling with her as they curled up together beside me.

I wiped my mouth with the back of my hand, keeping my eyes on the ceiling as it came into clearer focus. The constellations etched into the white molding glimmered faintly, the golden fillings lit up by small red orbs revolving above us.

Frowning, I lifted my wrists to look at the magical cuffs my father imprisoned me with.

My freedom had never felt so much like a faded dream.

When my pleasure faded to a slight tremble in my bones, I rolled upright, slipping my feet off the side of the mattress. The room was an avalanche of crimson curtains and orange silk, every surface upholstered in red velvet and golden trim. It wasn't my favorite room in the pleasure hall. It wasn't even one I liked. How could it be with these nauseating colors? But this was Elena's favorite room, and I liked to make her happy when I visited.

I stood and scooped my gown off a nearby chair, pulling it over my head in a quick motion.

Once I donned my matching purple robe, I returned to the bed and the two winged women cuddling in the center of it. I lit a bowl of poppy seeds as I settled against the headboard, sucking smoke deep into my lungs through the golden pipe. Anything to get this churning abyss in my gut to go away.

The sphinx rolled over and laid her head on my lap. I stiffened for a moment, worried she might try to taste me again, but she didn't.

It was too intimate, in my opinion, to let someone touch me like that. Spread me open. Drink me in. I would much rather do it to someone else than have it done to me.

I forced myself to smile down at the sphinx and run an affectionate hand through her hair.

Elena met my gaze as I handed her the pipe, and a sly smile touched her lips. My seasoned bed-mate had already updated me on the comings and goings of the pleasure hall. After a few years, I'd expected some change.

By the time I was old enough to come here myself, I'd learned the real purpose of the courtesans and why my father and brother visited them so often. It was more than sex. It was intimacy, companionship, friendship.

This was a place to lay down one's burdens and frustrations, to strip naked beyond the body and be held for a while. The men and women here were confided in by the nobles of our city about all manner of things, great and small. They listened and comforted. It was a vital part of their duty, perhaps even more vital than their ability to please and distract.

They all took it very, very seriously—most of the time.

Elena was my brother's favorite; everyone knew that, but I knew she loved me just a little bit more. It wasn't conceited of me to think that—it was simply the truth.

I'd been quietly mining information from her for years.

Every female and male who occupied this pleasure hall served because they loved the work, the sex, the luxury of palace life. They chose this world and all the benefits it offered. If you were a courtesan, you could permanently settle in any clan you desired, if the royalty there found you pretty enough to accept your service.

Our territory was a popular option, for obvious reasons.

No other territory possessed floating cities in a state of perpetual summer.

Courtesans lived in a special hall at the palace, nurturing relationships of passion or friendship or something in between. My brother was a frequent visitor, keeping several females and a few males on rotation. There were one or two females who lingered in this wing for my father, though his rare form of loneliness didn't bring him here very often. In reality, the majority of courtesans were those who had formed relationships with the dukes and duchesses of our city.

They were cherished lovers of the nobility.

Since nobles most often married for power, extramarital lovers were essential to the well-being of our city.

The sphinx purring like a sated cat in my lap was my brother's newest fascination, which meant she, more than anyone else, had been confided in by my brother over the last few weeks, more so than even Elena.

He certainly hadn't been confiding in me...

Both Kahem and Father shunned me upon my return. No matter how often I hounded their rooms, requested audiences, or scoured the grounds, I couldn't get more than a brief moment in passing. Maybe that was my punishment for rejecting Alezandral on the front steps of the palace, for my continued refusal to move forward with our betrothal.

But I wasn't past his betrayal, and I couldn't see a day when I would be.

Alezandral... *Lee*. I knew who he truly was now. He wasn't a human detective or a Halcyon spy. He was the prince I bound myself to at the meek age of seven.

And he'd made a fool of me.

"You poor little dear, so needy for touch," I muttered, running my fingers through the Sphinx's strawberry-blonde hair. "How could my brother have abandoned such a pretty thing like you?"

A furrow formed between her thin eyebrows. "He hasn't abandoned me."

"No?" I twirled a lock of her hair around my finger, tugging slightly to make her look up at me.

She bit her lip, thinking. "The prince is busy. He warned me that his trips to the Impundulu would take up his time for a while."

I glanced up at Elena. "Kahem always has loved the biters."

Elena smiled, taking another hit off the poppy pipe.

The sphinx's eyes widened as she sat up, blinking rapidly.

Reaching forward, Elena pulled the sphinx's hair back, caressing a brown finger across her pale pink collar. One touch, and an overwhelming wave of emotion surged into the air, radiating out of Elena's skin. The sphinx didn't think to shield herself from it, from the viscous jealousy she felt now. Though it had little to do with her true feelings. Courtesans were carefully trained *not* to be jealous, after all.

That was the true beauty of a Malforian—the ability to exploit and manipulate even the faintest threads of emotion.

"You don't really think he's there for another female, do you?" The sphinx's blue eyes searched my amber.

I shrugged again, offering her a compassionate smile. "I don't know, sweetheart. I know nothing of my brother's dealings with the Impundulu, but he does have to find a suitable bride eventually. Why else would he be spending so much time there?"

The sphinx closed her eyes against glittering tears.

Elena chuckled to herself behind the sphinx's back, baring her teeth as she bit the end of the pipe, reddish smoke curling out of the corners of her mouth.

I brushed away the first tear that slid down the sphinx's cheek. Leaning in to capture her gaze, I whispered, "But if you tell me a little more about what's going on with them, maybe I could help you determine the truth of the matter."

Just like that, the sphinx broke wide open and told us everything she knew.

My brother was working with the Impundulu—the territory north of us—to place traps along the mountain borders. Every trap was imbued with a magic that would burn trespassers to ash. At least they had listened to me when I told them of the sutilis' susceptibility to flame. Those rotten, stitched-together creatures couldn't withstand daylight—or any measure of heat—without falling apart.

Aside from the traps, patrols were being sent out to monitor the coastline regularly, but all was quiet so far.

I knew better than to press for details about what my brother and father had in mind for safe-guarding the human city, and I knew better than to assume they had anything planned at all. My father promised to keep the continent safe, but there was plenty of room for negligence. Father could very well wait for a second invasion before he involved himself with the humans.

I'd managed to kill a small army of those creatures, perhaps a majority of their forces, when I'd boiled the human city's bay. That battle had left the city in shambles, though, and the humans were panicked.

When the sphinx finished speaking, I returned to the pipe, and Elena occupied the sphinx's mouth with her own.

Amidst the loneliness of the palace, at least *here*, I felt understood, my darkness noticed and soothed. Elena's friendship ensured that. She was always willing to help me, always eager to make me feel important, because she thought I deserved to know the things my family kept from me. It made me wonder if Elena lingered here the same way my father's lovers still did for him, as if she always knew I'd be back. My mind spun with that thought, the poppy smoke ripping apart my coherence.

A knock brought me back to reality.

The women in bed beside me jerked apart, turning to face the voice that sang beyond the bronze door, disembodied through my brain haze. The voice was calling the sphinx's name. "*Meranda... Are you playing in there without me?*"

I grinned, recognizing the voice, and stood from the bed, gliding across the room like a sail treading water. My legs were heavy, and my hand seemed a million sizes too small as I grasped the doorknob. As I swung the door open, my brother's eyes fell on me.

His smile faded, and those thick auburn brows pulled together. "What are *you* doing here?"

"That's not any way to greet your sister." I pouted, leaning heavily on the edge of the door. I'd fall over otherwise. "And I think the better question is: why are *you*," I booped the tip of his nose, "interrupting my fun?"

Kahem leaned forward, craning his neck to look into the room.

The women in bed waved to him.

He squeezed his eyes shut and sighed, slowly withdrawing a step. Then, he leveled a glare at me. "Must you always steal my favorites?"

"It's not my fault you can't hold their fascination."

He rolled his eyes. "You just have a foul, golden tongue."

Yes. It was the only thing golden about me.

I huffed a laugh. "If you and Father didn't avoid me so thoroughly, maybe I wouldn't feel the need to seek out other company."

"If you're feeling *lonely*," he replied evenly, "maybe you should entertain your betrothed. He's only a door away."

My upper lip curled. "I'd rather—"

"Live in squalor with human filth?" he interrupted with a smirk. "You've been there, done that. It's time to grow up and fulfill your duty, and you know it."

Heat cut through my poppy high, simmering in my hands

as I fisted them. The metal was already warming around my wrists; I had to be careful not to lose my temper. I already had scars from where they'd burned me before, in that river down in the gnashing forest.

Kahem wouldn't care about the humans I met, the joy and goodness I found among them. There wasn't a point in defending the mortals.

And yet...

My brother turned and waved for me to follow him. "Come on, then. I'm assuming you won't stop bothering me until we talk." He assumed right.

I staggered after him down the dimly-lit corridor into the greater west wing, forcing awareness back into my body. I sighed in relief as the red faerie orbs on the ceiling were overwhelmed by natural light from a wall of windows to our right.

The city bustled below, shops and parks thriving in the afternoon sun.

A breeze flowed in through the cracked windows, sobering me enough to organize my thoughts. I'd gotten what I wanted—my brother's undivided attention. Now, I just had to get through to him.

Kahem glanced at me over his shoulder, ensuring I wasn't too far behind. His golden earrings twinkled, and his loose cream shirt billowed with every long stride. His pants were burnt orange velvet, rustling loudly with each step. As he passed a pair of guards, he stopped one and leaned over to whisper into the gilded helmet, my brother's red hair grazing the guard's golden chest plate before he pulled back.

The guard's dark eyes snapped to me as they nodded, and then my brother released them to continue on our way.

I fell into place beside Kahem, my bare feet slapping and his boots thumping against the tile. "I heard about what you're doing to the northern borders," I said without further preamble. "The flaming swords."

His expression didn't shift, as if he'd expected me to figure it out. "What about it?"

"Don't you think that effort is better spent elsewhere?"

Kahem shrugged. "The Impundulu are disturbed."

"The entire *coast* is disturbed," I retorted. "The Impundulu have better natural defenses than most of the country. The human city is defenseless."

"We're doing what we can, Sia. Our resources are stretched thin as it is."

We turned out of the wing into the belly of the palace. The windows fell away, and we plunged back beneath a wave of warm-toned orbs. My chest tightened; I couldn't walk fast enough to the corridor on the other end of the antechamber.

"Are we really doing everything we can?" I murmured bitterly. "I would think our long-suffered hospitality of the Halcyon prince entitles us to some assistance should we need it."

Kahem laughed without humor. "Just yesterday, you were chasing me around the palace, lobbying for Alezandral's removal, and now you wish to benefit off him? You've refused to even speak with him."

I held up a hand. "I don't want to talk about him."

"I'm not the one who brought him up," Kahem countered.

I bit my lower lip, trying to keep myself from arguing. There was no point in arguing.

We finally passed into the next wing—*my wing*. There were no windows down this hall, no lights. That was how I liked it. I'd rather amble through the dark than stomach those bloody orbs in any space of my own. They reflected the remnants of the Baron's mansion I'd left burning in the smog. They reminded me too much of the death below us, of the people who continued to suffer while we lived in this blissful ignorance.

I wasn't ignorant anymore.

I wondered if anyone mourned them—the Baron's men. *Brimley.* I grieved what I did to him, often as I laid in my bed at night and begged oblivion to come for me through the poppy high.

For half a second, less time than it took to blink, I swore I could make out his silhouette in the darkened recesses of the corridor. A shadow of a memory.

I quickly forced my eyes forward, letting the darkness meld into nothing once again.

"Look," Kahem sighed again, walking nearer to me in the hall until our arms brushed, "I'm aware of how angry you are. Keenly, painfully aware. Alezandral is aware of it too. I don't think you understand how fortunate you are that this bad attitude of yours has done little more than amuse him—but you're playing this all wrong. Father will never let you sit in on any of our meetings if you keep this up. Alezandral *wants* you to be involved, Sia. You need to stop ignoring him."

I tensed. "You two have been meeting with Alezandral about this? Without me?"

Kahem inclined his head. "We have meals together frequently, and we break fast with Father daily in his guest room."

That explained how Alezandral had caught on to my schedule so quickly, how he'd discovered all the quiet havens that I loved to retreat to. The library. The kitchens. The gardens. He was always *there,* and it exhausted me, trying to dodge him at every turn.

"I refuse to waste my time with him," I grumbled, fisting my brother's sleeve. I'd dealt with Alezandral long enough in the human lands, with all his lies and silence where there should have been honesty. "Please, Kahem, just talk to me, listen to me. I'm not useless."

Kahem's face softened, a crack in the cool façade he'd

maintained since my return. "I never thought you were useless."

I ignored the warmth blooming in my chest. "The water gates along the coast are perfect conductors for magic," I explained quickly. "If we can convince Father to recruit a witch and cast a warding using the Fenix flames, it could prevent anything beneath the surface from getting into the bay."

Kahem's golden wings and eyes practically glowed in the dark.

I wondered what he saw as he studied me, with my hair back to its natural dark shade and shorn to my shoulders, blending in with the dim of the hall, my eyes flickering with amber light as I held my breath.

A mere shadow of his brilliance.

Did he see his sister, or the destructive flame Father always hoped to hide? A flame Father now hoped to slowly snuff out.

That was what these bracelets were: a way to keep me contained, to starve me of oxygen until I was small and quiet. It was working. The only way I could endure this was by smoking enough poppy that I didn't feel my magic anymore. My family liked me better when I was high and docile. Always had. That was why they had provided the seeds to me since adolescence, despite Father's disdain for the drug run.

Kahem pursed his lips and glanced down the corridor, running a hand over his jaw as he finally muttered, "We would need to place our people on the gates. I don't think the human government would appreciate our interference."

"I think they'd appreciate a second invasion even less," I countered.

Kahem's lips twitched. "I suppose that's true."

"I can send a letter to Gwaith—the Lord there can help us

convince the other Houses. And I know a witch in the city, Peppi, who might assist us in the warding."

After another moment of contemplation, he shook his head. "You know that even if I *did* think this was a good idea, Father wouldn't listen. Collaborating with witches and humans? It'll take more than me to persuade him."

He'd rather not get involved was what he *really* meant to say.

I'd always felt a curious connection to my brother. It was like we were constantly trying to hold onto each other, even as we burned alive. There was an ocean of uncertainty spanning the distance between us, of all the things we'd left unsaid and unfelt, our betrayal and jealousy, and just enough love to drown out the bitterness. All we needed to do was snuff out our flames for a while, to just dive in and find each other in the middle of the waves somewhere... but we both knew the ocean was a harrowing place, and neither of us had ever been brave enough to cross it.

I wasn't sure if that connection was real anymore or simply a figment of my imagination.

Sometimes, I wished he could be brave enough for the both of us, because I'd long ago lost the courage to face it on my own.

"However," he murmured, meeting my despondent gaze with a hidden smile that loosened my chest, "if you do one little thing for me, I might be able to help."

"What?"

He gestured to the door to my room. "We should discuss this in private."

"What trouble did you get yourself into now?" I laughed. "Don't tell me Father's finally talked you into an engagement of your own." I threw open the door, taking a few steps inside my sitting room before tripping to a stop.

Someone was here.

I saw the scar first, illuminated by the sun pouring through the balcony doors behind him, the wicked length of twisted flesh stretching from his ear to the nape of his neck. My visitor's head turned, and vibrant blue eyes met mine.

Alezandral was lounging patiently on the arm of my couch.

I didn't need to wonder who had encouraged him to lie in wait; I should have been suspicious the moment Kahem stopped that guard in the hall. I turned to my brother with a black flame dancing on the tip of my tongue. "I hate you," I spat, the fire quickly dissipating, too weak from the shackles to reach him.

Kahem leaned over the threshold and grasped the doorknob, smiling at Alezandral and then me. "Terror for terror, you little brat. Have fun getting out of this one."

Without another word, he wrenched the door shut and left me alone with my heart-bonded adversary.

CHAPTER 2

I was way too fucking sober, and yet, not sober enough for this. Not as my heart raced and the floor undulated under my feet, and Alezandral looked at me like… like I was some sort of wild animal.

Close enough. I felt entirely caged and rabid standing this close to him.

I tore my gaze from his perch on the blue couch and headed for the opposite end of the room, where a set of glass doors opened to the balcony. The sheer white curtains dancing in the wind to either side didn't help my balance problem. I fell with each step, barely feeling my legs as I staggered onto the veranda where my moon dais stood.

Alezandral said my name; not in greeting, but rather a quiet sort of warning.

I dunked my face into the shallow, pedestaled bowl, and the chill of the water bit into my skin, anchoring me. By the time I pulled myself out, my lungs were screaming, and I was marginally more coherent. I gasped for air as I flipped my black hair out of my face, the wet sheet slapping against my thinly clothed back, soaking the purple satin.

Alezandral now stood on the balcony beside me, watching me wick the excess water out of my eyes.

"You smell like sex," he pointed out.

I squinted at him. The strands of his blond hair gleamed in the sun, but not nearly as bright as his white wings. It hurt my head to look at him.

"That's because I've been having a lot of it," I slurred.

His navy tunic was unbuttoned halfway down his chest, displaying his extensive black markings. The loose sleeves of his shirt were rolled up to his elbows, his pants black and thin enough to cling to every edge of his muscled legs.

He looked like he'd just rolled out of bed, which was odd, considering it was past noon. But then again, I was still in a nightgown too, wasn't I?

Alezandral must have reported here straight away when he received my brother's summons, not wasting even a moment to change. My room was just across the hall from his, and Father placed a charmed door in our rooms that connected them directly.

I kept my side of the door locked, with a chair barricaded in front of it for good measure.

Alezandral frowned, his eyes narrowing as he took a step closer. "Are you high right now, Sia?"

I crossed my arms. "So what if I am?"

"You told me you didn't smoke that shit anymore."

I laughed bitterly. "And you told me I could trust you. I guess we're both liars."

Alezandral assessed me, the deep blue of his eyes piercing my skin like an invisible blade. I shifted on my feet. His eyes slid past me, looking over my shoulder, and his frown deepened. A thickness coated my mouth and throat as the smell of poppies filled my lungs, the scent going straight to my head. I felt dizzy again. My legs started to shake. Then, Alezandral was closing in on me, cutting me off from my room.

I retreated until the stone parapet dug into my lower back.

On instinct, my hands flew out and gripped the front of his tunic in both fists as he leaned over me. I couldn't breathe. My vision swam as the effects of his magic sapped my strength away. There was no kindness in his voice as he said, "If you wished for mindlessness, you could have come to me. I would have given you rest. I would have given you release. Could have saved yourself and the poppy dealer all that hassle."

His power swept through me, scraping my insides, turning my thoughts inside out until all I could focus on were his eyes. And even *they* were hazy, like looking up at the moon on a cloudy night. A few moments more, and I'd pass out.

Why did he care so much about this lie when he'd kept so many more from me?

I clung to him like the veranda was about to fall beneath me. "Stop it," I whispered.

He didn't. "Where are your wings, Sia? Why have you put them away again?" His voice was impassioned and vicious.

My head spun faster, distorting my vision, forcing me to close my eyes. The scent of burning poppy grew so strong, I was sure I would be sick.

"It's easier that way," I forced out.

"Bullshit."

I glared at him through my blurry vision, clenching my jaw. "What do you know?" I bit out, slapping weakly at his chest. I tried to push him away, but he didn't budge. "You don't know *anything* about me and what my life is like here."

His eyes flicked back and forth between mine as he listened intently.

That only made me angrier. My voice lifted until I was shouting, the words thundering in my head along with his magic. "Don't pretend like you suddenly care what I do with my wings or what I use to escape this nightmare. You had years to come for me, to be here for me, and you didn't fucking bother."

"I'm here now," he retorted.

His grip on my arms was the only thing holding me up, but I didn't care. I dug my nails into his chest. "That's not enough," I snarled.

Our faces were so close, my eyes caught on every freckle and scar on his cheeks. Brutally handsome. How had I ever convinced myself he was human? His breathing was staggered, and mine wasn't much better, but I could feel his magic weakening inside me, *hesitating*.

"Then tell me what would be enough," he pleaded, his voice soft. "Tell me what I must do to earn your forgiveness."

My heart squeezed.

I hated him for making me feel *anything*, especially sadness, especially pity… but I did. Damn my traitorous heart. I knew every effort I made to avoid him, to keep this betrothal at bay, was in vain. How could I fight this heart bond tugging at me with every breath? This thing that pulled us toward each other?

What more would he take of me? What more would I give?

I would always be treated like a female to be painted and paraded, then forgotten about once the curtains were drawn. A female to be kept *under control*.

I couldn't let him use me.

"You can't," I whispered. "Now let me go."

Frowning, Alezandral guided me away from the balcony's ledge before releasing me, and the scent of poppies vanished in the wind. Water coursed down my back, chilled to needlepoints along my spine thanks to his hoarfrost. The magic he'd used against me left behind a painful sobriety in its departure.

A familiar pressure in my chest roared for release. *My flame*, awake and desperate.

Alezandral's eyes softened, fluttering with what looked almost like remorse as he stepped away, allowing me access to my rooms.

I shot past him, withdrawal already rearing its ugly head in my chest. I collapsed on top of the couch and grabbed a blanket, pulling it tight around my shoulders in an attempt to stave off my trembling.

Alezandral followed me, pausing to pull the double doors shut against the breeze before he turned back around. He remained at a distance, giving me my space, but the air between us vibrated. There were a thousand things he could say, could *do*, now that he'd shown me just how powerless I was. As if I'd needed any reminding.

But Alezandral simply crossed his arms and looked around the room, studying it. "Your quarters are so different from the rest of the palace," he muttered.

I peered at him from the corner of my eye.

"All the pale blues and browns," Alezandral mused, still admiring the room instead of meeting my stare. "It's refreshing."

"I hate red," I admitted.

Alezandral nodded, his gaze catching on my hair. "Darkness suits you better."

My stomach rumbled, and I turned my gaze to the glass tabletop in front of me. "Leave me alone."

"I will leave if that's what you really want, but we need to talk eventually."

I snorted. "We've done that already. It gets us nowhere."

"Because you prefer to exchange pain instead of words," he countered sharply. "You need to let me explain, Sia. I promised you back in the smog that I would."

Yes. Back when he'd offered friendship and I had wanted it. Goddess, I'd wanted him so badly in that witch's shop. My heart had shattered when that sutilis stabbed him. Now that I knew of his betrayal, I was ready to stab him myself.

"I don't need to let you do *anything*," I growled, my limbs shaking so hard that my knees slapped together. "Whatever debt you think exists between us isn't there. It isn't real. Just like this connection between our hearts—it's a lie." His eyes darkened. "You want to talk? You want my words? Let's start with how you tricked a seven-year-old child into a bond of forever. Did you use your magic on me then? Did you lull me into a false sense of calm before you handed me the blade?"

There. It was out in the open—the fear that plagued me when I was sober enough to entertain the worst.

Alezandral stopped breathing.

We were so young when we pledged that heart bond. I'd felt lost and forgotten, and it would have been easy for someone to take advantage of me. He'd been a child too, but I couldn't remember much, not enough to trust him.

"That's what you truly think of me?" A defense was rising in him, sharp and sudden, a storm cloud shifting to block out the sun.

The scar over my heart prickled, like the Goddess herself was clicking her tongue at me. "What am I supposed to think?" I asked. "Why did you keep me in the dark when I deserved to know who you were? Why come for me now, when your absence made it clear you have no interest in the friendship we supposedly formed? You have no interest in who I am or why I do the things I do, not really. You plan to use me, just like everyone else does, and I'm not fucking doing that anymore." I couldn't stop my voice from cracking.

He lumbered forward a step.

I shrank from him, and he paused.

Alezandral lifted his palms up in supplication. "The moment I bound myself to you, Sia, you became a part of me, and I became a part of you. What happened afterward, the consequences of it…" He gasped for a moment, as if the context of that sentence stole all the air from his lungs. "They didn't matter. The time, the space, the waiting and silence, it was inconsequential. I *knew* why we walked into those birch trees together, and I remembered it coming out. I'm not here to use you. I am here to be whatever you need me to be, just so long as you don't ask me to be your enemy."

I saw what he left unspoken, that the memory of that day had left a mark on his skin, in his blood and bone, beyond the scar on his chest. He felt it too. *The pain.*

I wanted to believe him, but even a heart of ice could be capable of faking love. "We were lonely children left to our own devices. You are a stranger to me, Alezandral, and you may remember what happened the day of our heart bond, but I certainly do not. I don't trust you."

"Don't or won't?" he demanded. He had asked me a similar question in ink and paper once, when I'd been grieving my first love. When he'd been no one.

I shook my head. He had his answer—the only one I was capable of anyway.

But Alezandral padded across the room and sat down beside me anyway. "I was wrong to keep secrets from you," he whispered. "But I'm done with them, with anything that could separate us, from here on out. In all those years apart, you never reached out to me either. How was I supposed to act? What was I supposed to do? I was afraid to tell you who I was. The only thing I want now is to honor this promise, because we need each other."

"I don't need anyone," I said coldly, glaring at the wall across from us.

Alezandral was silent for a moment.

"You're right."

I slid my eyes to his, and he returned my stare without

blinking, without shame. I saw the dark circles under his eyes, the redness.

"Maybe it is I who needs you," he confessed.

My anger hesitated, and my breath caught in my chest.

His words were pretty, but they weren't true. They weren't fair. I knew Alezandral would do whatever was necessary to keep us together, whether I agreed to it or not. The cuffs on my wrists were proof of that.

They were working against me, all three of them.

I shoved the bracelets into his face. "You say you want to honor the promise between us, but it's not honor if it's forced."

His gaze dropped to the shackles. "What are those?"

"As if you don't know," I sneered.

"Who put these on you?" he said sharply, reaching for them, but I stood from the couch, prepared to end this discussion even if I had to set the whole damn room on fire.

And yet, I kept talking. "It might as well have been you. You're the reason they exist."

Before I could blink, Alezandral had his hands on me, on my wrists, his gaze scouring the bracelets, and I misplaced my resolve for a moment. He was trembling. When he lifted his gaze to mine, I saw fury in his eyes, the blue unyielding and frosted over by a thousand winters.

"Why?" he bit out.

A humorless laugh crackled out of me. "Because I'm a flight risk, obviously."

"Why haven't you burned them off?" he snapped, a confused look in his eyes now.

I was struck silent again, reeling from his raised voice. Was he mad at *me*? What the fuck did *I* do wrong? I tried to jerk my wrists out of his grip, but he held fast.

"If I could have, I already *would* have, asshole," I growled, pouring all my resentment into the words. "But my dear father went above and beyond this time—the stone is immune to all flame, even mine. I'm not here because I want to be. I never wanted *any* of this—not my wings, not my family, and definitely not *you.*"

Alezandral flinched.

I almost let myself regret those words, but what point was there in regretting the truth? To his credit, Alezandral recovered in the next instant and tugged me closer.

"Coat the metal in your flame."

I gave him a scorching look. "Did you not listen to anything I just said?"

"What's the harm? It's not as if you can hurt me."

"That's the last thing I'm worried about."

And the hell I can't.

He inclined his head toward the shackles. "Good. Then spark up."

With a snide smile, I grasped his forearms and released a portion of the pressure in my chest. He was holding the metal in his hands; if I burned this time, he would burn with me. Darkness licked to life in my palms, surging with hunger in every direction.

Alezandral didn't blink.

Frost already glazed his hands, snuffing the black fire as it bit at his skin, spreading frost over my wrists as well. My dark flames on the cuffs blazed against it, but my wrists were cold, the joints rigid as the frost formed a barrier between me and the vibrating metal.

The bracelets suddenly started morphing, expanding.

"Close your eyes, darling."

I opened my mouth to tell Alezandral not to order me around, but the metal imploded. I recoiled, shutting my eyes against the small shards that flew toward me.

Then, I looked down at what he'd done.

Twin rings of smoking metal sat in his hands, the cuffs

broken at the seams where magic had sealed them shut. "How—"

"You said they're immune to flame," he explained, "but even molten glass will shatter when exposed to rivaling extremes."

"You shocked the atoms apart," I realized.

My appreciative tone made him smile. "Every magic has a snapping point." Alezandral slipped the broken cuffs into his pocket.

I didn't know what he was going to do with them, but I didn't much care. I could *leave*.

My plan to ward the city would be more than a hope if I flew straight there. With Peppi's help, I could find a way to imbue my own flame into the iron gates, and then I could return to the elven realm, to Ehlark. He had to have some answers about my origin by now.

I'd have to return to my father's city and Alezandral eventually. I certainly didn't want to stay away too long and invite that pain from my scar to return—but this would give me enough time to finish what I'd started, to figure out what I really was.

"There. All better." Alezandral took my wrists and brushed his thumbs across the scarred skin, sealing me back in the present as a growl rumbled in the back of his throat.

I tore away from his gentle touch. "This doesn't change anything for me."

His eyes softened, and a sad smile flickered over his lips. "Then consider yourself free from all of it."

Alezandral stood and stalked to the door leading into the hall, ignoring the charmed one across the room. Each footstep resonated in my scar tissue. He swung the door open but then paused on the threshold, his fingertips bracing the door as he glanced back. "I will not be your prison, Sia. Not today or any day to come."

CHAPTER 3

The sun was setting when I left my room.

I wore only a green fleece dress and a short cloak to fend off the evening chill. All I allowed myself to carry away from the palace were my daggers and a replenished coin purse. I would need money for the coast, to bribe any reticent Houses to agree to my plan for the water gate.

I'd freed my largest set of wings from my back and painted them gold. It would cover my feathers well enough for a few hours, so long as it didn't rain.

My walk through the palace and side yard felt like drifting through a memory. I left at dusk last time too, many years ago. I'd felt so sure of myself then. I had seen so much potential in the world. Now that I knew what the world was really like, I didn't feel anything, nothing but the tepid wind.

Winter never truly touched this island.

Magical braziers were placed around the circumference of the floating city, between the water wheels, radiating a gentle heat that swept across the surface. Any ice or snow that fell from the sky melted before it reached us. The lily pad ponds would never freeze, the grasses never dying. Even the trees rarely changed, every plant adapted to eternal summer. I loved the sun, but when I was here, I missed the seasons.

Once I'd ducked under a pair of weeping willows at the edge of palace grounds and settled onto the cobblestone path leading into the city, I pulled my hood down over my brow.

Every fall, these hidden groves were cleaned and trimmed, prepared for revelries to celebrate the days of harvest. Right now, no one cared to admire their beauty, making them the perfect exit route. Small coves made of stone lined either side of the path. Runes of fertility were hewn above each threshold, curtains whipping in the breeze, dancing into the aisle to caress my sides with crimson fingers, as if they wanted to snatch me into the shadows and keep me forever.

That was going to happen eventually.

I'd soon be stuck in a loveless marriage, in a land I hadn't seen since I was a child myself. I would be trapped, so I had to make sure I was my own best company. The best possible version of myself, with all the knowledge that went along with it.

That thought alone urged me forward, down the winding path, until I heard a scuffle up ahead accompanied by two male voices.

People still walked these paths sometimes, couples mostly.

I ducked quickly into a nearby cove as two shadows crept around the next bend. I tucked myself into the corner of the rutting space, hidden by the rocky walls.

The voices grew clearer as they drew closer, and no sooner had I recognized who they belonged to than a flurry of movement appeared. Two male bodies collided with my stone cove, and debris fell above me, tiny pebbles raining down on my shoulders and head.

In the fading twilight, I made out my brother and Alezandral.

My betrothed had Kahem pinned by the throat against the

front of the cove. For a moment, I couldn't move, couldn't breathe. *What the fuck is going on?*

Kahem spoke through gritted teeth, his hands bracketing Alezandral's arms. "I'm going to kill you for this, Halcyon."

Alezandral laughed, a heartless sound that brushed down my spine and made my skin crawl. "Don't think I wouldn't relish in tearing you apart, little Fenix, but this isn't an attack. It's a threat." Then he smiled, as if that wasn't the worst thing I'd ever heard him say.

My wings twitched.

He was threatening my brother; I needed to do something. The second I tried to step forward, though, my bones turned to lead. My head spun. My lungs screamed for air I could not give it. Under my dress, the scar over my heart was *burning*.

If I interceded, Kahem was going to hurt Alezandral.

I'll never let anyone else hurt you again. Anything that hurt Lee would hurt me. I felt the agony of that truth in my heart, a phantom ache, my body warning me against getting involved.

Orange and red flames erupted between them—my brother's magic—but it was snuffed in the next breath by ice-blue frost. That brief moment of flame managed to singe my betrothed's tunic, leaving red welts across his chest, but he didn't so much as flinch.

My stomach twisted as an echo of that burn seared through my scar and into my chest.

I swallowed a whimper as I inched backward, leaning against the stone wall. I hated that my instinct was to protect Alezandral, that I wasn't strong enough to overcome it.

The air froze around me, and I knew no new flame would spark in it.

Alezandral was taking precautions now.

His magic overpowered my brother's, and that unsettled me. It wasn't as if Kahem lacked power himself. They were both borne of spirit, both carried three sets of wings on their back, just like I did. It should have been a fair fight, but for whatever reason, it wasn't.

Kahem's voice was hoarse as he spat, "A warning? For what purpose?"

"I saw the cuffs your father placed on Sabrina. Is that how you Fenix treat your kin? With force and neglect?"

I shivered at the anger in his voice.

Alezandral didn't know. He truly had no idea what they'd done to get me here. Suddenly, I wasn't struggling against the promise anymore, wasn't interested in stopping this. Despite my reservations, I was… *curious*.

Kahem scoffed, and that plucked a weak, fraying string in my heart. "The cuffs are for her own good. It's not like we're beating her within an inch of her life to teach her obedience." A layer of spite laced those words—my brother knew exactly what he was saying, and so did I.

He was referring to Alezandral's father, what he'd done.

Alezandral leaned in close, his lips curling back to bare his teeth, his body pulled taut. "All purposeful mistreatment is abuse, no matter how gentle."

My heart thundered as something warm curled tight around my ribs, stealing my breath. I couldn't believe Alezandral had said that. It was what I had thought to myself a million times but never had the courage to say aloud.

"Where did it come from?" Alezandral growled. "Where did your father find the stone?"

Kahem's brow creased. "Some mountain far from here. Why does it matter?"

Alezandral smiled again. "Because I'm going to eviscerate it. I'm going to ensure no one collars her ever again."

Tears welled in my vision like a black veil.

"You can't do that," Kahem sniped. "It's a fucking mountain."

Alezandral's hand tightened, and my brother frantically

scratched at his arm as his feet left the ground. Kahem kicked the air and the stone wall behind him, trying to gain enough leverage to keep on breathing. Every scratch he gave Alezandral echoed in my skin, but I barely felt it. No, the look in Alezandral's eyes consumed me.

"It could be the sky and I would still tear it down for her," Alezandral swore. "You'll tell me where the mountain is, or I can knock you unconscious and we'll continue this discussion somewhere no one will hear your screams."

Just when I thought my brother might pass out, Alezandral lowered him back to the ground, loosening his grip enough for Kahem to respond. For a moment, all my brother could do was cough and gasp for air. Alezandral had used all the magic in his possession to bring my brother to heel. I could smell it —poppy seeds burning in the distance. My brother's eyes drooped, his body trembling as he struggled to remain upright.

"What… is wrong with you?" he eventually rasped. "You know this is enough for the Fenix to declare war, you frosty fucker."

"You would compromise your sister's bond?" Alezandral countered. "You would risk giving her wings and mind rot because of the broken promises between us? That doesn't sound like you care for her at all. If you loved your sister, you would protect her, not chain her up and supply her with drugs to make her compliant."

I bit back a shudder as his words settled over me. I didn't know how he'd figured it out, but he knew the part my brother played in my imprisonment.

As I watched them glare at each other, I noticed something.

I didn't realize until this moment just how terrible Alezandral looked. The circles under his eyes were darker now, the skin sunken. His wings were tucked in tight behind him, and they were *trembling*. When I first saw them in front of the palace, they'd seemed so large, so strong. He was barely holding them up off the ground now.

You would risk giving her wings and mind rot?

His words were threaded with real fear, because that was already happening to Alezandral. The promise he made to me was turning on him, all because he'd left me alone. That was why he was being so aggressive, so impulsive. What use was there in being civilized when his body was rotting from the inside? Pain made people do horrible things.

Perhaps Alezandral thought he had nothing more to lose, and that was a very dangerous state of mind.

Kahem, thankfully, didn't push him any further. "Fine," he ground out. "I'll show you."

"Is that a promise?" Alezandral prompted.

"Yes," my brother spat. "I promise to show you where the mountain is."

Alezandral's body uncoiled, but I saw the tension lingering just beneath the surface. He would find no true relief without my help. "Perfect," he drawled, releasing Kahem's throat to slap him on the arm. "No hard feelings, right, brother? Let's go find a map."

As Alezandral took a step back, my brother elbowed past him, stalking up the trail toward the palace.

Once Kahem turned his back, the smug mask fell from Alezandral's face. Guilt and exhaustion filled the void, and I saw such overwhelming sorrow in his blue eyes as he took another step back. Then, those eyes flicked up and met mine.

It was as if his heart had known where I was, even if his mind didn't.

He stiffened as his gaze slid to the wings behind me. Understanding fluttered across his face as he realized what I was doing, that I was leaving. He didn't seem angry about it, though. He didn't seem to feel anything more than his initial surprise.

Before I could say anything, he inclined his head in a shallow bow, and I could almost hear the unspoken words in my head: *Goodbye Sia.*

Then he turned and walked away.

I didn't leave the cove until his footsteps had faded down the path.

No argument. No fight. He just… left.

My steps were stilted as I continued towards the city, but I wasn't moving nearly as quick as I had been before. There was too much on my mind, on my conscience.

Alezandral believed our promises were being broken, that I was going to abandon our heart bond. Belief was all our bodies needed to begin breaking down. In my room, he told me I was freed from all of it. Freed from the heart bond. Freed from him. It wasn't even a promise, yet he was following through with it, even if he had to be the one to face the consequences.

Alezandral didn't realize the heart bond weighed on me too, didn't know that I was plagued by the same pain. He didn't understand that I was coming back.

The agony was deeper for him. It was taking him faster, because he saw no hope.

No one had ever fought for me like that before, stood up and defended me, demanded the best for me despite the consequences. Alezandral was sick and suffering, but he'd still put me first, even though I was partially to blame.

Maybe it is I who needs you, he had said.

Was I really going to leave now and let him think I'd abandoned him? With the way he looked, I worried he wouldn't last more than a few days before snapping altogether. What would he destroy once he did? Would he become as volatile and cruel as his father? Would he become a mad prince to match the mad king?

He had intended to spend his last threads of sanity getting rid of that mountain for me.

I slowed to a stop on the path. "*Shit*," I hissed at the darkening sky.

My mind was already changed. Alezandral had wiggled his way in and ruined my plans. I wasn't going to leave the city without him. He told me he wanted to be whatever I needed from him, and now... I believed it.

How much would he take from me? How much would I give? Too damn much.

And now, I knew I would give it all up freely.

Maybe I was still a little angry with Alezandral, because I let him stew in his room for the rest of the night. I let him *think* I'd left.

A few more hours couldn't hurt him too badly, but just in case it did, I removed the chair from the charmed door connecting our rooms. I unlocked it, dared to open it just a crack. Alezandral didn't notice. He didn't so much as glance in the door's direction the entire night, which made me think he purposefully kept his eyes from straying to it.

I watched him pace his front room with a map in hand, watched him write letters with his enchanted quill and send them away, responding to the messages that were hastily returned, more and more of them as the night drew on, until he eventually retired to his bedroom. He didn't get much sleep though, and neither did I.

Which was to be expected, considering I refused to leave the door for more than a handful of minutes at a time. I sat there in my reading chair, watching, waiting for morning. Waiting for my father to arrive for breakfast.

Palace staff came in first and filled the dining table in the front room with food just before daybreak. Alezandral was already awake by then. He sat in a chair, sipping straight from a whiskey bottle as the servants siphoned in and out of the room. The sight made me smile; this palace had a way of driving me to the bottle too.

But I stopped smiling when I remembered what had driven Alezandral there—me.

His white wings shuddered in pain every time they rubbed against the leather cushion of his seat, so he didn't move much. He just glared at everyone. Drank. Glared some more. All while spinning one of my broken shackles between his fingers.

I could feel his tension, his simmering anger, and I hated to admit it, but I *liked* knowing he was upset because of what had been done to me. He was in pain, but he was also furious. I shifted impatiently on my side of the door, chewing my nails to the quick as I paced.

Alezandral was reserving all his fury for my father, and I wasn't sure how to feel about that. Half of me wanted to step in and protect my family, but the other half wanted to know what Alezandral would do, what he would say.

I wasn't used to having someone on my side in rooms I wasn't in.

Finally, a knock resounded through Alezandral's quarters. The door to his room opened, and Spiro entered first, wearing red military velvets. He inclined his head to Alezandral, who sat motionless in his chair. "Good morning, your Highness. His Majesty, King Herbert." He stepped to the side, gesturing behind him as Father appeared. "And His Highness, Prince Kahem."

Father was wearing his morning robes, layers of luxurious, burnt orange silk that draped generously to the ground and dragged behind him between his gilded wings. He entered with a smile, walking to the table as his eyes scanned the room for Alezandral.

Kahem followed Father in, taking his seat at the table without looking up. His countenance was quiet, humbled—a far cry from the brother I was used to.

A small spark of worry stirred in my belly. If Kahem told Father what Alezandral did to him last night, there would be serious consequences for the Halcyon prince. But then... Kahem wouldn't be acting like *this* if he had—like he was ashamed.

My father's smile faltered when he realized Alezandral was in no hurry to stand and bow in greeting.

"Grand rising to you, Alezandral," Father offered kindly, continuing to the head of the table and gracefully sitting.

So Kahem definitely hadn't told Father about last night. *Why not?*

Alezandral didn't say a word in response to Father's greeting. He only took another swig of whiskey before slamming the bottle down on the wooden surface next to his chair. Then he rose and walked swiftly across the room to join Father for breakfast, taking a seat on the opposite end of the dining table.

The guards who entered the room behind Father and Kahem were already on alert. They could sense Alezandral's hostility, Spiro too. The Raven sat in the chair across from Kahem and kept a sharp eye on my betrothed as the king filled his plate. If my father felt threatened, he didn't show it. Apparently, he was going to ignore Alezandral's sour mood the same way he ignored everything he didn't readily like or understand.

At least I wasn't on the receiving end of his dismissal this time.

Alezandral didn't touch his plate. His fingers rapped impatiently on the table, the red cloth beneath his hand growing particles of frost where his fingertips touched, again and again. The room fluctuated in temperature; I could feel it, even through the cracked door. It would drop a few degrees and rise again in the next heartbeat.

He and Father were silently battling for control.

From the outside looking in, it would appear as if nothing was happening, only eating and glaring. Except I knew where to look to see the truth.

I saw the slight feathering of Alezandral's jaw, the brief, sharp glances Father made across the table as he diligently worked through the protein on his plate.

Surprisingly, Kahem didn't touch the food either. He only sat in his chair, spine straight and stiff, watching Father and Alezandral warily. With a jolt, I realized that Kahem was wearing the same clothes he wore yesterday. I wasn't sure I'd ever seen him repeat an outfit, much less two days in a row. What did Alezandral make him do last night?

Father grew tired of the silence first.

"We have a lovely spread this morning, don't we?" he commented, pointing with his knife to the overflowing bowl of fruit in the center of the table. "This will likely be the last harvest from our citrus groves before we force the trees to rest for winter. Perhaps you would like to take a few saplings to the Halcyon territory for Sabrina when you two depart. She loves the groves. I imagine she'll miss them."

Alezandral slapped his hand against the table, and white frost spread like a spider web straight to Father's plate. The porcelain broke in half with an audible crack, and Father's steak froze through instantly, capturing his fork and knife mid-cut in a thick layer of ice.

Kahem grimaced.

Spiro's eyes widened.

The guards looked at one another, unsure of what to do, if they should intervene.

A sharp huff of air left my nostrils as I held my laughter in, and my breath clouded white in front of me. If I didn't already feel inclined to forgive Alezandral for his actions in the human lands, I might have done so just for that.

Father sighed and let go of his utensils, threading his hands together on top of the table as he returned his eyes to my betrothed. "Is something wrong, Alezandral?"

Alezandral's eyes narrowed as a bitter smile cloaked his face. "Why would anything be wrong, *Your Majesty?*" The venom in those last two words were potent enough to make my knees buckle.

No one spoke to my father like that.

Well, no one but me.

My father leaned back in his chair and said, "I heard you visited with my daughter yesterday. I'm sorry if she was unpleasant to you. She can be difficult to manage sometimes, but she will come around. You'll see."

My stomach churned with heat and bile. Father *would* say something like that. I bet he believed it too.

Alezandral's smile faltered. "Did you say you *manage* her, Your Majesty?"

Kahem closed his eyes, as if in pain. Soft reluctance flickered across his features. Even if he disagreed with Father, he would never confess it. He had resigned himself to silent obedience a long time ago, and I often wondered if he carried guilt over the way he let Father treat me. Seeing his reaction to Father's lecture now, I started to believe he might.

"I must," Father asserted, forcing me to tear my gaze away from Kahem. "Eventually, you will learn how to do the same. She is special and extraordinarily beautiful, as I know you've noticed, but she's also a sensitive spirit. Delicate, really."

Liquid iron trickled down my spine, hardening me as it embraced the chilly air. *Delicate?* I bit my lower lip to keep from scoffing.

Alezandral laughed, though it came out as something closer to a growl. "Please, go on," he rumbled. "I'd love to understand exactly what you mean by that."

The guards inched closer. They heard the veiled threat in Alezandral's voice, and they were prepared to step in should Alezandral do something stupid, like attack. He knew better than that, though. He had to.

My hand closed around the doorknob, but I didn't go in. Not yet.

This was the most I'd heard Father say about me in years. Some pitiful, lonely part of me wanted to hear more, even if it hurt. It was better to be angry than sad. At least I could do something with the anger. At least the anger pardoned me from caring so damn much.

Father thought for a moment, his eyes scouring Alezandral. "Sabrina can be… mercurial, to put it lightly, prone to isolation and spiteful words, much like her mother. She needs stability, Alezandral. She needs some semblance of *control*."

He was comparing me to my mother? That was another small miracle. I was both elated and miserable to hear him mention her. She had willingly entered into the heart bond with Father, and so I'd assumed they made each other happy, but perhaps I should have known better.

Father leaned forward, resting his forearms on the table. "Don't let it get to you, Alezandral. It never lasts. I have every confidence that she will soon come to her senses and apologize for her recent behavior. We just need to be patient." He smiled encouragingly and reached for his golden goblet. He wanted the conversation to be over. I knew he did.

Alezandral steepled his hands in front of his mouth. "What exactly do you think is to blame for these moods of hers? Why do you think she pushes everyone away?"

Father only murmured, "I do not imagine I will ever know."

Alezandral's eyes flashed with anger. "Because you've made her feel *ashamed* of her power. You've suffocated her," he roared. Without even looking, he pointed a finger at the door connecting our rooms, and I shrunk back from the opening. "This female who single-handedly saved an entire human city and wiped out an army of monsters that even our ancestors could not overcome—you wish to weaken her. You wish to make her feel helpless. *Why?*"

Luckily, Father didn't look in my direction either. But then, he never had.

Kahem did, though. My brother raised his golden eyes to my door and saw me, and his jaw slackened in surprise. The remorse he felt unraveled between us, cutting me deeply.

I quickly lifted a finger to my lips, willing him to remain quiet, willing him not to give me away. *Protect me, just this once. Please.*

Kahem nodded once, a shallow tilt of his chin, then forced his gaze away from me.

My chest loosened in relief, but it was a fleeting satisfaction.

Father was rubbing a palm over his mouth and jaw as his eyes took on a glassy sheen. "What I have done for my daughter is not about shame; it is about *protection*. My daughter is powerful, yes—but that is a dangerous thing to be when you are the only one of your kind. Think carefully, Alezandral. I hoped you would understand, seeing that you were born as unique as my Sabrina."

My eyebrows stitched together. What did *that* mean? I didn't have time to analyze that admission, though, because Father continued talking.

"But I can see that you are blinded by your feelings for her, by your bond. So I will lay it out for you plainly. *Your* origin is understood, Prince Alezandral. It is accepted by all—our treaty ensures that. My daughter was not so lucky. You wish to know why I have kept her gifts a secret since she was a babe? It's simple. She would have been seen as a threat. She would have been targeted, even amongst our own people. She is something unknown, and I feared for her. I feared *losing* her." My father's voice thinned, conveying more emotion than I ever thought him capable of. "To me, it was better for her to be suffocated than extinguished entirely."

Alezandral's anger didn't subside. If anything, it became more apparent. "And now," he replied tightly, "she doesn't have faith in herself or the power that runs through her veins. She does not know herself."

Father shrugged. "At least she is alive and strong enough now to find what she needs."

"I hope for your sake that she does." Alezandral pushed his chair away from the dining table and stood as tall as he could manage in his weakened state, thousands of tiny ice particles twirling in the air around him as the guards moved to crowd the king's side of the table.

But Alezandral was already withdrawing something from his pocket. He slammed my broken shackles down on the table in front of him.

Father's eyes locked on the black stone, and he pushed to his feet. "Where did you get those?" he demanded.

Alezandral only smiled, his frost angrily creeping across the floor beneath him and the ceiling above.

Kahem grinned too, but his was knowing as his golden gaze flicked to me.

"Where is my daughter?" Father roared. Without waiting for the response he knew Alezandral wouldn't give, he turned to his sentinels. "Check the princess' quarters and lock down the city. *Now!*"

I flung the door open.

"I'm right here, Father. Calm down," I said as I sauntered in.

Everyone froze, and my father's eyes widened as he drank in my presence. Every trace of tension fled from the room, and weighty relief took its place. Even Alezandral went a bit boneless, dropping into his chair as his chill evaporated from the air.

His frost drew back, returning to him.

I followed Alezandral's retreating magic, approaching his chair. Every step I took toward him made his skin seem paler, his eyes redder. My heart clenched. My scar throbbed.

Without so much as glancing in my father's direction, I reached forward and braced my hands on the armrests of Alezandral's chair, then twisted my body to sit nimbly on his lap. His bright blue eyes weren't glaring anymore, so that was something, but he was stiff as a board. He gasped as I wrapped my arms around his shoulders, my fingertips grazing his top wings. They twitched forward, yearning for more of my touch.

I knew it would be a relief to his body—my proximity.

"Good morning, Alezandral," I whispered, smiling at him.

His chest fought for a deep breath as he returned my stare. Already, I could tell his pain was lessening, his wings lifting off the floor. He dropped his hands to the armrests on either side of me, and I finally noticed the gloves he was wearing.

In fact, I couldn't remember seeing him without those gloves since I rejected him on the front steps of the palace last week.

After a moment, Alezandral managed a quiet, "Grand rising, darling."

My father studied the two of us, his eyebrows delicately raised.

"Will you excuse us, please?" I implored sweetly. "I'd like to have breakfast with my betrothed this morning. Alone."

Father looked between the two of us once more, his gaze dropping briefly to the broken shackles on the table. "Of course, little love. A grand rising to you both." Then he stood, abandoning his frozen breakfast.

My brother shot me a wink before standing too.

They swept out of the room, Spiro and the guards at their heels. The instant the door closed, my smile fell, and I turned back to Alezandral.

"We need to talk."

"Look," he muttered quickly, "if this is about what you saw last night—"

I shook my head. "I'm not here to talk about what happened between you and my brother," I told him. "To be completely honest, Kahem deserves to have his ass handed to him once in a while. I knew you weren't going to kill him."

Alezandral's eyes met mine, hardening as he tilted his head. "Do not underestimate the lengths I will go to in my fury, Sia. Especially when it comes to you." There he went again, saying things that sounded like promises.

"I would've never forgiven you."

"You were leaving," he countered. "Forgiveness wasn't on my mind."

A weak smile tugged at my lips. "No, I suppose it wasn't."

Alezandral blinked, his eyebrows pulling together. He didn't understand why I was still here, why I hadn't left, and honestly, I wasn't sure I fully understood either.

I lifted a hand to brush a tendril of hair from his face but stopped short when he flinched. *Right.* He didn't like being touched. I probably shouldn't be sitting in his lap either, but he needed this. Touch. His body needed to understand that I was here, that I was safe. The dark circles under his eyes were already fading. There was some color in his cheeks again, blooming pink under his sunny freckles. He was recovering.

My heart knew what he needed better than he did, and that scared me.

I wondered if he carried the same intuition for me. I

wondered if that was why he sent me those letters in the gnashing forest, if that was why he came searching for me in the smog. Maybe he knew I'd needed it. Maybe someday, I would be brave enough to ask.

I clasped my hands together in my lap, squeezing tightly enough to lose feeling in my fingers, but that was better than attempting to touch him again when I knew he didn't like it. "I saw you. You were hurting," I said slowly. "You're suffering because of me, because of this thing between us, so I decided to stay. I'm here to make it right."

Alezandral's throat bobbed. "You don't know what you're talking about. I'm fine."

"You're *fine*?" I repeated, my voice taking on a challenging lilt.

His eyes narrowed. "Yes, that's what I said," he bit out.

I lifted my hands to his shirt, moving with deft swiftness to undo the first few buttons on it, and Alezandral immediately stiffened. His eyes dropped to what I was doing, a look of utter shock crossing his face. Then his hands wrapped around my wrists as he tried to gently pull my fingers off his shirt, but I fought against his grip, continuing my task, lifting the shirt away so I didn't accidentally touch his skin.

"What are you doing?" he demanded tremulously.

His gloved hands tightened around my wrists, so I quickly hooked my hands in either side of his shirt and ripped it open enough to expose his scar.

Once we could both see it, I let him tear my hands away.

The skin of his scar was irritated, purpling and swollen. Even through that last week I spent in the human lands, when my scar was giving me the most trouble, it had never looked like *this*. A little redness was the most I noticed.

Our seraphic bodies punished us to the measure we believed. That was how our promises worked. That was why I never felt his pain when he was on the other side of the continent—because I could not see his pain, I could not feel it. I didn't know when someone else hurt him. I only felt our promise down in the smog because, deep down, I knew Lee was him. The whole time, I knew, even if I'd initially refused to accept it.

And in the same way, Alezandral had never known how lonely I was here.

Judging from the state of his scar, he must blame himself for it now, for my leaving yesterday. He blamed himself for our broken bond.

He was far too hard on himself, and I wouldn't allow that anymore.

I smirked. "*Fine,* you were saying?"

Alezandral let go of my wrists and dropped his hands to my waist, gently but firmly pushing me off his lap. I backed away, stopping only when my ass hit the ledge of the dining table. It gave Alezandral enough room to stand, and he shook his head as he straightened, towering a foot or so over me.

"Just stop," he said, pulling the shirt closed to cover his scar. "I don't want you to stay because you feel guilty."

I crossed my arms over my chest. "And I don't want you to tell me to go because *you* feel guilty. It's the right thing for me to stay. You have to realize that the bond will take me too. It doesn't matter if you let it consume you first. We are equals in this."

Alezandral's eyes softened. My betrothed didn't say a word in reply, but he didn't need to. I knew I'd gotten through to him.

A spinning white light swept through my mind, filling me in one moment and vanishing the next, leaving behind a handful of words.

You and I are equals in everything.

"That's what I thought," I murmured, stepping away from the table. "I'm staying, so stop arguing with me about it. You know, I thought you'd be more appreciative, but I see you're as difficult to please as you were when we were children."

A flash of warm surprise lit Alezandral's eyes. He walked to me, gently taking my hands in his. "You're right. I should be expressing my gratitude. Thank you, Sia."

Heat crept into my cheeks. Now that I had his appreciation, I wasn't sure what to do with it. I pulled my hands out of his and turned away, walking to the dining table to pluck a citrus fruit from the bowl. "It's no trouble," I declared, hopping up onto the table so my legs could swing beneath me. "I already have a plan to get us out of this."

Alezandral's brow furrowed. "A plan?"

I tore the citrus peel open, nodding. "We only need to stay together long enough to get rid of the heart bond, and then we'll be free to go our separate ways." The golden peel piled up beside me, and after a moment of silence, I met Alezandral's gaze, but I couldn't quite read it.

"I see," he said tightly.

"That's the best option, isn't it?" I urged.

He blinked. "What if I don't want that?"

There was no anger in the question, but it made me feel defensive anyway. I slid off the table and shrugged. "How can you know what you really want? Neither of us understood what we were doing when we made this bond. We were children. We couldn't mean it in the way it bound us, not for forever. Anything we feel for each other now is likely muddled by the bond. It's counterfeit."

Alezandral scoffed and turned on his heel, strolling to the table he'd left his whisky on. He grabbed it and continued to the small liquor cabinet behind the chair, reaching in to retrieve two glasses from the shelf. Then, he poured two drinks—one for each of us—and folded himself back into the large chair, nursing the crystal rocker against his chest.

After swallowing the knuckle of liquid in his glass, he

smacked his lips and said to the floor between us, "How disappointing the reality of our situation must be for you."

I ambled my way to his chair, the fruit sitting forgotten in my hand.

Perching myself on the arm of the couch across from him, I said, "This has become a prison for both of us, Alezandral. Your recent condition is proof of that. There has to be a way out of it; we can't be the first ones to ever make this grave of a mistake."

Alezandral leaned forward to brace both elbows on his knees, the empty glass hanging between them, his smile cutting me like a blade. "Alright, I'll bite, darling. How exactly do you intend on getting us out of this *mistake*? Think it's as easy as burning away the scar? Cutting it out? My father tried both."

My stomach flipped, not only because of the cruelty he'd been subjected to, but because of the way he spoke about it. He had said it so easily.

Something wet trickled down my leg.

I glanced down and realized that I'd been clenching my fists, and the citrus in my hand was now pulverized. Dropping the fruit, I stood, reaching for the liquor Alezandral had poured for me. I gulped it down, ignoring the burn in my throat as I set the glass back down.

Then I considered Alezandral. The promise on his chest. The scar on his neck. I wanted to ask him where that other scar came from, because maybe he'd be willing to tell me this time...but I didn't. That knowledge seemed too intimate now.

"Once we move forward with the engagement, we have to take our tour," I explained. "We have to meet with the Wight. And if anything knows how to break this bond, or if we even *can*, it's that thing."

Meeting with the Wight was a tradition for seraphim, an honor. All royal matches sought its wisdom before marrying.

Alezandral dropped his gaze to the empty cup in his hands then glanced at the crushed citrus on the floor. "What if there's no way to break it, Sia?"

I shrugged again, even though he wasn't looking at me. "We'll explore that sky when we get to it." Then, I stepped closer, sliding into place in front of him, and waited for him to look up at me. When he did, his eyes were darkened by the whiskey and his lack of sleep, but at least he seemed more in control of his body. "Until then, let's just focus on coexisting. You told me yesterday you wished to earn my forgiveness. Is that still true?"

"Without question," he replied.

I smiled and took a steadying breath. "Good. Because there's something important I must do, and I want you to help me."

CHAPTER 5

Later that afternoon, I returned to Alezandral's quarters, dressed warm enough for travel outside of the city. It was bound to be chilly, even in an elven realm.

I had donned brown leather pants and a matching tunic that cinched tightly around my waist. It was long-sleeved and lined with soft satin, paneled carefully around my shoulders to completely enclose the base of my wings. An extra foot or so of the tunic hung straight behind me from my hips to my knees, like the tails of a trench coat, and tapered up to my pelvis in the front, framing my thick thighs. I was relieved to be wearing clothes like this again. Luxurious. Tailored for my wings and curves.

I knew how fucking good I looked—because it was as good as I felt. I had found a way forward and my father's shackles were gone. There wasn't much more I could ask for.

Alezandral's front room was empty when I walked in. The doors to his balcony were wide open, letting dappled sunshine filter in, though I could see he wasn't standing out there. He must be in the bedroom. The double doors on that side of the room were half closed, and I could only see a flicker of candlelight coming from within.

He didn't seem to like the red faerie orbs either. He'd covered them.

I left the door between our quarters unlocked the entire day, but he hadn't so much as knocked on it since I left after breakfast. I got the feeling he wouldn't be bothering me much now that we'd come to our agreement.

"Are you ready?" I called.

Alezandral's reply was muffled by the doors. "Almost. I'll be just a moment."

I heard movement in the bedroom, then watched Alezandral's bare torso appear in the open doorway. Luckily, he was wearing pants, but they hung low on his hips, the ties not yet tightened in the front. Candlelight traveled across his back as he walked past, a golden glow silhouetting his chiseled form and illuminating the scar on his neck. That trail of mangled flesh continued across his shoulder and back, all the way down between his wings. A few inches to either side, and whatever had caused that scar would have injured his wings, possibly even severing them.

He wasn't just a memory anymore. He could be hurt. He *had* been hurt.

Who had done that to him?

My eyes barely got the chance to follow the scar down to where it curled around Alezandral's waist before he disappeared again.

Water started running in the bathroom. The sink.

That was another thing I had missed about home—the access to running water at the turn of a knob. The water was pulled from nearby rivers by magic and heated by a Fenix charm. I still preferred to use moon water to wash my face and hair when I had the patience for it, but the dais I set up in the gnashing forest had never collected enough rain to bathe in, and it was never warm.

I listened to Alezandral move around the bathroom. Unable to stop myself, I inched closer until I was standing at his bedroom doors, and I could see his profile through the bathroom mirror.

His stomach flexed as he gathered water from the faucet and ran his fingers through his hair, soothing the blond, tangled mess. He looked better, the darkness under his eyes only faint shadows of what they had been this morning.

Alezandral couldn't see me without looking over his shoulder, but he knew I was here. He didn't seem uncomfortable with my watching, so I kept doing it. There was comfort in seeing him like this—performing ordinary tasks without his gloves and the navy tunic that usually covered so much of his markings.

That massive scar wound through half of his mark, twisting it into something unrecognizable, but the other side was stunning in its clarity. Whorls of ebony and curling mist stretched from his collar across his shoulders, the bottom edge as jagged and sharp as shattered glass.

I wanted to see if his wounds were as deep as mine. I would feel more at ease around him if I knew they were.

Alezandral turned off the sink and exited the bathroom, and I quickly averted my eyes. It didn't matter though, because Alezandral didn't glance my way—he simply reached for the tunic laid out on his bed and started donning it.

A strange tension mounted between us. All the things we had said and done to each other in past weeks.

"What were you doing down in the smog?" I asked.

Alezandral's fingers fumbled with a button on his tunic, but he didn't lift his gaze from the task.

"I mean, I understand why you came to collect me," I continued. "But I don't understand why you lied to me about who you were. I don't know why you stayed there with me instead of trying to bring me back home. Why involve yourself in the problems of a human city?"

His brow furrowed as he continued securing his tunic.

"You were as much a stranger to me as I was to you," he eventually said. "All I had were whispers of what you had done across the continent and our notes back and forth. That wasn't enough to understand who you were, what you were like. I was trying to prepare myself."

I could hardly believe it…

He'd been nervous about reuniting with me too.

"When I entered that city and followed our bond's tug to that flower market, I wasn't even sure if I would introduce myself yet. And if I did, I had every intention of telling you who I was. But then, I saw you with that little girl, and… I realized there was so much more to you that I did not understand, more to the city and why you were there. I wanted to know more. I wanted to help you."

He paused, huffing a quiet laugh as he glanced up at me.

"Though I'll be honest, I also suspected that if I told you who I was, you might run. So I stayed and played the part you had already assumed for me—a human detective—because it was too easy. It was too tempting. I could get to know you without our current circumstances weighing on us. I didn't mind waiting. At the time, I was content with waiting for you to approach me, thinking you might eventually feel the same pull I felt toward you… but then you didn't.

"And then it became clear to me that the city—and, in fact, our entire fucking continent—was facing down something serious, something eerily *familiar*. The Halcyon Elders who fought in the war on your islands have been recounting their war stories my whole life, and I recognized the pieces without seeing the whole."

Alezandral started tightening the strings on his pants, his

jaw feathering before he added, "I figured it out when I found the sutilis blade in that massacred House, the one you hid from me in. I knew then that you refused to see me as anything but your enemy, and I didn't have time to explain the truth. I'd realized they were coming in from the ocean and that an invasion would be imminent. So, I left you there.

"I called in some reinforcements, but one of those rotted fuckers was waiting for us on the beach. They knew I'd been meeting with members of my court there. They'd been watching me. It attacked my cousin and harvested his wings right in front of me."

He finished the last knot on his pants with a sharp jerk of his hand and lifted his gaze to the wall across from him, his blue eyes burning bright.

That male on the beach had been Alezandral's cousin? Suddenly, it all made sense. That seraph had asked Alezandral to put him out of his misery, and my betrothed had done it without hesitation because they were *family*.

I would have done the same for my brother. I would have done anything he asked as he was losing his wings.

Judging from the fury in Alezandral's eyes, I knew it had hurt him to do it, more than he would ever let on. I hadn't considered what Alezandral lost by coming for me. I had only lost my freedom, but he'd lost so much more.

Inhaling, I found that my lungs were too tight to get a deep breath.

"From that point on, my involvement was extremely personal," Alezandral seethed. "I tracked down another sutilis that very same night—that dead one you saw in my tent. I needed answers, and I got them. But it was too late."

"I'm sorry about your cousin, Alezandral," I whispered.

He turned away from me, reaching for the sheathed sword on his bedside table. "Yeah," he said as he cinched the weapon belt around his hips, "me too."

I fought against a sudden wave of dizziness, my hand bracing the door frame as I forced the next breath into my lungs. My mouth welled with bitterness, and I prayed to the Goddess and all her many spirits that I wouldn't get sick here.

There was nothing I could do now. His cousin was gone.

He blamed me for it, surely. Or worse—he blamed himself. I hoped he didn't blame himself. There was too much left to be addressed, to be taken care of, and none of it could afford to be waylaid by guilt.

Cursing myself for what I was about to do, I watched as Alezandral sat on the edge of his bed and started pulling on his boots. "I need to talk to you about the human city."

"Go ahead," he replied, working the laces of his boots.

"We can't leave it unprotected," I started, swallowing the stiff lump in my throat. "The warning I gave the sutilus by boiling the bay will only last for so long, but then they'll come back. They'll take the city. My father will send his soldiers in to help too late, and when he does, we both know the humans will only see them as a threat. They'll feel trapped. If we don't get the Houses on board now, there will be confusion and unnecessary bloodshed. There won't be a city left to protect by the time it's all over. I was thinking that maybe…*we* could write a letter to Gwaith. You and I, together. We could offer each of the Houses a generous stipend to ensure their cooperation. And maybe you could lend my father some soldiers to relieve the ones we've sent to the Impundulu so we can send those with flame in to monitor the city's water gates? That's what they need."

My heart was pounding so hard, I could barely hear my own thoughts. This plan only worked if Alezandral was on board. Father would never entertain the idea if he thought it was coming from me, and I couldn't trust my brother to convince him either. Alezandral would have to be my shield.

He could take all the glory for it if that was what he wanted. I didn't care. I just wanted the city to be protected.

Alezandral stood from the bed and turned to me, his eyes meeting mine. They were glowing a soft, radiant blue, and I suddenly wished to know what he was feeling, what he was thinking. What had made his eyes glow?

"You're asking for my money and soldiers?" He spoke clearly, evenly, nothing in his voice but the question.

I slowly nodded. "Yes."

He crossed his arms, dropping his gaze to the floor as he mulled it over. When he lifted his eyes back to mine, the glow was gone. "Alright."

My dizziness returned, and I lost the ability to breathe for a moment.

It couldn't be that simple, could it?

Alezandral smiled, walking across the room to me. As he reached for one side of the doors and pulled it open, joining me on the threshold, I remembered how to speak.

"Alright?" I repeated. "That's it?"

Alezandral leaned against the doorway, stuffing his hands in his pockets as his wings splayed behind him. "Yeah. That's it. I trust you, Sia. I believe you when you say you know what they need." His eyes drilled into mine. "I'll give you whatever you ask for."

I raised a hand without thinking and squeezed his arm as the weight in my chest lifted. "Thank you," I said.

I realized a moment too late that I was touching him. He didn't return the touch by any means, but at least he hadn't reacted too severely this time. I wondered if that meant he was okay with it, or if he was better at hiding his discomfort now that he was in his right mind.

As I dropped my hand and took a step back, Alezandral pushed off the doorframe and followed me, bringing his face mere inches from mine.

His eyes flicked all over my face, as if he was mapping constellations in my skin. "You don't need to thank me for doing my part to protect our continent," he said.

Then, he was gone, walking into the front room as I stared at the empty doorframe he left behind, gasping for breath.

His mere presence was intoxicating.

I wished I could blame his magic for it, but there was no scent of poppies in the air, and I was more awake than I had ever been. It was this promise, pulling us toward each other.

"The longer we can hold off another invasion, the better," Alezandral said behind my back. "At least until we can figure out what's happening in the ocean."

I slowly turned to face him.

He was pulling on his gloves at the dining table.

"The ocean? How do you plan on doing that?"

"My country is dealing with it."

I crossed my arms and glared at him until he returned my stare. "You've reached out to the serpent king," I guessed.

With a sigh, he leaned against the dining table, his gloved hands gripping the edge. "We're trying to, yes, but he hasn't responded to any of our summons. I wouldn't be surprised if the serpents ignore us entirely."

"Even with the treaty your father made with them?" I asked.

Alezandral's eyes flashed with anger. "That treaty is barely worth the paper it was written on. It offers my country and I nothing but heartache."

Isn't that interesting...

"Why?"

Alezandral's jaw clenched. As his gaze traveled the length of my body, it caught on some point around my head, and his eyes narrowed.

"What?" I braced my hands on my hips. "Why are you looking at me like that?"

He shook his head and set his sights on the balcony, walking right past me again. "You're beautiful, Sia."

I strode after him as he stepped out onto the stone platform. Red and gray palace turrets marked the landscape around us, with dips and valleys where the towers led into corridors. There were a few seraphim flying in the distance, out in the city. No one was in the sky here; very few places in the palace required flight to access.

Where we were going did, though.

Alezandral approached the railing and unlatched the large iron gate in the center of it, swinging the panels in to allow us to walk up to the edge together.

"You weren't looking at me like you thought I was beautiful," I argued. "You looked at me like I had upset you somehow."

Alezandral snorted. "You've done nothing wrong. Let's just get moving before the sun runs out on us, alright?" He jerked his head toward the maze of towers. "Tell you what: I'll even race you there."

My brow furrowed. "I don't think that's—"

"Wise?" he interjected. "Why? Worried I'm still faster than you?"

My mouth dropped open, even as the corners of his lips twitched upwards. "I happen to recall that I kept up with you just fine when we were children, Alezandral. You couldn't even win a game of tag when you thought I was going to turn into a serpent and eat you."

He laughed brashly, his amusement echoing off the towers. "Because you *cheated*," he countered. "That's your favorite way to beat me at anything from what I can tell."

My mouth puckered.

Under my thick clothes, my body was starting to sweat. Had I let him get under my skin so easily, or was I actually *excited*? I'd be the first to admit there was very little in my father's palace that challenged me, people included.

"I can beat you," I took a step toward him, "*without* cheating, if I wanted to."

He smirked and met me with a step of his own. Quicker than I could see it coming, his right hand flew up and tugged sharply on one of my braids. "Prove it," he purred.

I lifted my hands to push him away, but he was already spinning, falling backwards off the edge of the balcony with a wink. He had done that to provoke me.

Alezandral liked me on fire.

I stalked up to the edge, startling as Alezandral reappeared, the air whistling through his wings as he shot upwards on a frigid breeze. His wings flared as he circled to face me.

"Look at that, darling—you're already falling behind," he taunted. Then, he pulled his wings in and dove, angling himself toward the low roof across from us. At the last second, he extended his wings, using forward momentum to veer upwards and crest the beveled peak.

I flung myself off the balcony after him.

He had a head start, but I would have no trouble catching up. I'd been flying here my entire life; I knew the palace better than anyone, had been left alone to explore it until I had every inch memorized.

Alezandral weaved through the towers leading to the southern wing of the palace, dodging the short spires appearing before him, more and more of them coming the farther ahead he flew.

This part of the castle was reserved for the *Academy*—an assembly of scholars and inventors the palace supported, alongside their families. They were encouraged to spend their lives dedicated to all manner of intellectual pursuits. Without them, we wouldn't have this hovering city and its many advancements. Magic and science were two sides of the same coin; one could not exist without the other. It was all a matter of belief in the impossible.

Alezandral was swift, I could concede that—impressively so. It probably had to do with the length of his wings, but that also prevented him from squeezing into narrow spaces with any kind of agility. I could, however, because I knew where to take risks, where it would be safe to twist and glide vertically, where there were broken tower windows I could fly through.

Within a few minutes, I was right on top of him.

I laughed, knowing he would hear it. We were nearing our destination—the southernmost tower. It was the tallest point of the palace, rising steeply to leave behind the fabricated warmth of the island and spear through the clouds.

The box at the top wasn't visible from here. We'd have to blindly follow the column up.

I emerged from the surrounding rooftops before Alezandral and shot up into the clouds, knowing the tower was straight above. Circling the column, I scanned the mist as I ascended. I couldn't see Alezandral anymore, couldn't tell if I was still in the lead. Continuing to spiral, I turned my attention to the empty mist above me.

A heartbeat later, the clouds shifted above me. It was strange, like watching milk pour into water, thickening the air, but they didn't move as I rose toward them.

There was no way I had reached the box yet.

I slowed in my confusion, reaching a hand out to touch what it was, and thank the Goddess I did slow down, because my fingers connected with a solid pane of ice. "What the fuck?" I breathed.

A chill raked down my back at the same time I heard Alezandral whisper, "See? I can cheat too *if I want.*"

I spun around with a growl, but my fists met another solid plane of ice. I was boxed in. He'd formed a cage of ice around me in less than an instant. When he taunted me a second ago,

I could tell there had been nothing between us, but now there was.

His form was a blur on the other side of the ice, but I swore I saw the smirk he flashed before shooting upwards.

Heat flushed my body as I pounded on the ice, screaming in frustration as the sheet barely fissured. He fucking *trapped* me. He had to know how that would make me feel. The chill of the ice sank under my clothes, caressing my overheated skin. Anger welled in my eyes, but I refused to let the tears fall. I wouldn't cry for him, even if it was only because he infuriated me beyond the bounds of my sanity.

A flame does not conquer that way.

My breath hitched as that thought glimmered softly in the back of my mind.

He hadn't trapped me, not really. Ice couldn't do that to fire. I quickly raised both hands to the ice. Molten obsidian erupted from my palms, and the box shook violently, sizzling as I burned my way out in a matter of seconds. The instant I'd melted a hole large enough to fly through, I was squeezing through it.

My eyes locked onto a figure hovering in the mist nearby. Alezandral had stopped. He'd been waiting for me.

Fucking asshole.

By the time I could see his eyes again, I already had another black flame in my hand. I flung it at his stupid, smirking face. With a laugh, he dodged the attack and flew away, circling the tower as he continued his ascension. I chased him, tossing flame after flame at his heels.

He kept laughing.

Eventually, I managed to throw a flame around the opposite side of the tower, and it caught him off guard. He brought up a shield of frost at the last second, but his surprise cost him valuable seconds. I caught up with him.

My hands twisted in his tunic, and I wrenched him toward

me, not knowing exactly what I would do—only knowing that it would maim us both.

His hands grabbed me back, our momentums merging and causing us to spin out, and I realized too late that we weren't in the mist anymore—we'd flown into the opening at the bottom of the tower box. Black walls replaced the white sky, and I was grappling blind in the dark. There was only the sensation of Alezandral's hands wrapped around my arms, the burning in my skin.

Then we collided with something, and it sent us tumbling.

My wings tucked in on instinct, protecting the inner tendons from damage, but that didn't lessen the bruising my back took as we rolled across the hard floor. I shoved away from Alezandral as we came to a stop, collapsing at his side, catching my breath instead of setting him on fire.

I didn't want to do that *here*.

I simply laid there for a long moment, blinking up at the ceiling lit with millions of fake, glittering stars.

We had arrived at the planetarium.

CHAPTER 6

"*Your Highness*, are you alright?" a soft voice exclaimed.

Delicate hands helped me sit up as the stars swirled above us. I looked over and saw the astrologist on shift staring at me with dark golden, doe-like eyes.

I forced a polite smile. "Yes, Aida. I'm fine."

After patting her hands to let her know she could let go, I quickly got to my feet and ran my palms over my tunic, smoothing the crinkles.

The planetarium looked nearly identical to the last time I saw it. We stood in the outer room—a place for the astrologists to study, write, and read. A thousand or more scrolls hovered in mid-air against the walls; records of the sky, organized and stored chronologically. Torches were erected throughout the room, most unlit, chairs and tables arranged in small groups between them.

We had indeed collided with one of the tables moments ago. The mahogany surface was lying on its side a few feet from us, the chairs toppled.

Alezandral peeled himself off the floor, his gaze drilling into the side of my face.

Aida saw him then, and practically leapt out of her gilded feathers. "Oh, and *Your Highness*." She curtsied again, low, her eyes bulging. "Goddess beside us, this *is* an honor. I did not expect any visitors today. If I had known, I would have lit more torches. My apologies for the low visibility upon arrival." Her hand flicked up, and the torches around us lit with persimmon flames.

She was a Fenix through and through, but she only had one set of wings. Her flames were likely limited to about what it took to light all the torches, but she was brilliant all the same. Aida was the daughter of a mathematician. She grew up in the palace, in the Academy, and she would probably live here the rest of her life. I met her as a child, and instantly admired her. I spent a lot of nights here, listening to her talk about the stars and planets, science, all the magic one might find in the sky.

But as I grew older, I started to envy her. She had the privilege of choosing her studies, deciding her own future.

Alezandral appeared at my side. "Not to worry." He smiled at Aida. "Our tumble wasn't your fault in the slightest. We were quite distracted."

I folded my arms over my chest. "Distracted? Is that what you're calling it?"

He glanced at me sidelong, a subtle smirk digging into his cheek. "Well, I suppose *you* were rather focused, but on the wrong thing. You still lost, by the way."

"We both lost," I retorted.

Leaning toward me, he whispered, "Or perhaps we both won and now must share the victory. Just tell me how you'd like to celebrate, darling."

His eyes twinkled with mischief.

I averted my gaze. "I'd rather have lost."

Aida shifted on her feet, her wings tucked in tight behind her. "Is there something I can do for you?" she asked.

"We'd like to send you home for the night," Alezandral replied, sliding his hand into the dip of my waist and holding me close. My skin tingled in discomfort, but I forced myself not to shrug him off. This was the role I had to play.

"Excuse me?" Aida's brow furrowed.

Alezandral gestured to the opening in the floor behind us. "You may go."

Her golden eyes flicked to mine. "Am I in trouble? Have I done something wrong?"

"Not at all," Alezandral assured her with a charming smile. "I just have some Halcyon business to attend to and the Fenix King has given me permission to utilize any equipment I need while I'm here. I'm sure you can understand why I would want some privacy for that."

Aida looked at me again, but I didn't say a word.

We'd decided before I left Alezandral's room this morning that he would take the lead today. Anything we did, he would take ownership for. That way, my father wouldn't be able to intervene on my behalf.

"What could you possibly need the planetarium for?" Aida muttered. She wouldn't be so easily dismissed. The plane-tarium was more than stars, after all, more than the sky. This was her life.

She'd also been taught to question everything and everyone who came here, even royalty.

The Academy followed its own rules.

I stepped forward. "I'm sorry, but we're in a hurry, Aida. You could go see my father if you wish, but I doubt he would appreciate being bothered during supper. I'm right here, watching over everything, and I'm telling you to head on home. You can return for your usual shift tomorrow night." I smiled, trying to put her at ease.

Aida was obviously suspicious, but she lowered herself into a shallow curtsy. "As you command, Your Highness. Would you like me to prepare the inner room before I go?"

"That won't be necessary," Alezandral interjected. "I know how to do it."

I shot him a glare, but he was already walking toward the massive golden door on the curved inner wall behind Aida. She gave him a wide berth, her eyes traveling over his white wings as the corners of her mouth turned downward in disapproval.

He couldn't see the change in her expression, but I did. Because he was Halcyon. I wondered if everyone in my territory looked at him like that behind his back. I wondered if he noticed, if he cared.

I didn't like it.

When I cleared my throat, Aida startled, plastering a smile on her face. I walked up to her and whispered, "Alezandral wanted to inspect the planetarium's equipment to see what might need an upgrade. He plans on contributing to the Academy as his engagement present to me."

Aida's doe eyes widened. *"Really?"* Her gaze shifted to Alezandral's departing figure, wonder and surprise shining there instead of mistrust.

I nodded, a sly grin tugging at my lips.

It was a lie, but if we were going to move forward with the engagement, even if it was just pretend, presents were still expected, weren't they?

Father would expect it.

The Fenix Academy was still rebuilding after the loss of our home island, behind the other territories in terms of equipment and supplies. We did the best with what we brought over and what we could find in the human lands beneath us. The seraphic territories didn't share resources easily. The merging of species through marriage was one of the few exceptions where it was expected.

Because marriage wasn't just a merging of two seraphim; it was a combining of families, and families shared everything.

I might as well ask for an engagement present that would benefit the Fenix. That way, once Alezandral and I went our separate ways, my family would still be better off for it.

And besides, this would help the Fenix warm up to him while he lingered here.

"Darling?" Alezandral called from the threshold of the inner room. He braced the heavy gold door open with one hand as he looked between the two of us.

He hadn't heard me give away another drop of his country's enormous fortune, but he saw the shift in Aida's countenance. Her shoulders were loose, wings open, and a genuine smile transformed her face as she glanced at him.

"Everything alright?" he asked cautiously.

He kept me in the dark about who he was for weeks. He could deal with being left there for a night. "Very," I said brightly.

Then, bringing a single finger to my lips to convey that I'd told Aida a precious secret, I winked at her and turned to follow Alezandral. The moment she arrived home, word would spread through the Academy, and it would hit the city within hours. Everyone would know about Alezandral's generosity by morning.

They would know before he did.

Alezandral held the edge of the door for me as I crossed the threshold into the inner room. The torches weren't lit in here either, but they often weren't. The stars on the sloping ceiling were brighter here, illuminating the room in a blueish-silver light. Thin, metallic gold lines crisscrossed above us, all of them leading to a large pillar in the center of the room. The pillar was made of copper cylinders and glass spheres, the contents glittering with contained lightning.

I smiled, breathing in its beauty.

"I always forget how incredible this room is," I murmured.

Alezandral made a grunting noise behind me. When I looked at him, he was closer than I expected. He gazed down at me, close enough to feel the great exhale he expelled, hot against my cheek.

"You know, you make me feel like even more of a freak when you stare like that," I informed him.

"Your hair is stunning under the starlight."

The simplicity of that response made me rock back.

His eyes shifted, catching on the wings directly behind my head, and he frowned. "Your wings would look beautiful too, if you hadn't covered them up." Those words were sharp.

Alezandral turned away and stalked to the control panel before I could even think about responding.

I followed him to the pedestal, looking over the buttons and cranks for the planetarium's machinery. My wings suddenly felt a hundred pounds heavier, the gold paint a physical itch I wanted to scratch. "They have to be painted," I finally managed.

Alezandral read the scattered runes on the panel, familiarizing himself with the layout of the buttons, his hair hanging in front of his eyes. It had grown at least an inch since I met him in that flower market. I liked it grown out; there was something so youthful about it, so careless.

"You're angry with me," I ventured.

His head whipped up, those bright blue eyes flying to mine, emotion burning in them. Maybe not anger, but something close to it. His hands clutched either edge of the control panel, his knuckles turning white. "Why are you still allowing your father to hide the truth? Why are you pretending to be something you're not?"

I blinked at him as his words sank in. "So that's why you were glaring at me in your room. This is about the paint on my wings?"

He shrugged, releasing the control panel to cross his arms. "To begin with, yes."

I scoffed, falling back a few steps, needing some space from that piercing stare. Mirroring his crossed arms, I said, "I don't know what I am, Alezandral. If I allow my territory to see my true power, they will have questions, ones I don't know how to answer. My father was right to keep it a secret. It's better if everyone believes I'm Fenix. My people will not understand; they might not accept me."

"I do," he replied without hesitation. "I accept you completely, and if your family doesn't do the same, then they are not your people. What you look like, where you come from—those things are trivial. Are you supposed to hide your true colors your entire life?"

I swallowed hard. "If I have to."

He huffed a humorless laugh. "You *don't* have to. You are the same person you have always been, and if *I* have to, I will stand between you and every territory. You and the entire world. I will ensure that no harm comes to you."

There was truth in his words. He seemed to believe them, even if I didn't.

"You can't ensure that," I told him with a frown. "You're not that powerful."

Alezandral smirked. *We'll see about that.*

My spine prickled, and I forced myself to quickly look away, nodding at the panel in front of him. "Do you really know how to work this thing?"

"It's just about the most rudimentary control board I've ever seen. A child could work it." I smiled, knowing he would be eating his words later when I explained to him that he would be installing a new, more advanced one.

He started pressing buttons; the first lit up the control panel, and the next few made the pillar in the center of the room rumble.

Lightning snapped and crackled in its container as the glass spheres opened and electricity was allowed to travel up and down the pillar, striking either end of the cylinder with loud claps. I tore my gaze from the pillar long enough to see Alezandral typing out Ehlark's name using the archaic alphabet. After he confirmed the input, the sound of metal scraping together came from the pillar.

We both turned to watch a panel on the outside of the pillar slide away, revealing raw lightning and a small black rock shard hanging in midair, a conduit. It would convert the lightning into a form of unstable magic.

Unstable magic could be forced to take the shape of anything; even, Goddess spare us, a portal.

Alezandral waved a hand toward it, and several darts of his crystalline frost speared into the strands of lightning. An ear-splitting screech filled the room, accompanied by a flash of light. I barely had time to blink before the light disappeared.

There, hovering like a sideways pond in front of the pillar, stood a gateway to the elven realm.

My stomach flipped.

Would it hurt, passing through? It was made from lightning, after all. How different could it be from the staircase portals? There were no woodland spirits or nightmares hiding in the shadows, but that didn't mean we would be passing through safely. These portals were uncharted territory.

Alezandral turned to face me, and I wiped the worry off my face before he could see it. He gestured to the portal, bowing at the waist with a grin as his beautiful blond hair fell into his eyes again. "After you, darling."

Heavy dread twirled in my stomach.

There was no way I would back down, though. I decided weeks ago that I was done letting fear keep me from who I could be. Who I *should* be.

Lifting my chin, I sauntered forward, keeping my eyes straight ahead as I passed through the shimmering surface.

CHAPTER 7

Walking through the portal felt like passing through mist, cool and wet, and my eyes fluttered as I emerged from the blur.

This elven realm was darker than I remembered it. The glowing mushrooms were dim. The black trees didn't shimmer with green veins. Every color was muted. The sky was dark too, clouded over with charcoal-gray clouds as rain sprinkled through the canopy. No sprites flew in to greet me. Everything magical had gone into hiding.

Alezandral emerged from the portal and ran straight into my back. I stumbled forward, but he caught my arm, steadying me.

Turning around to face him, I whispered, "This isn't right."

He shook his head, his gaze scouring our dreary surroundings. "No, it's not." He had likely seen the way it was before, when he entered the staircase portal to retrieve me back in the human lands.

I pulled away from Alezandral and ran into the trees, searching for that worn foot path. Something terrible had happened since I was last here, and I just knew that it was my fault. I had come searching for him. I had asked him for help and he'd agreed, but at what cost?

It took me longer than I would have liked to find my way to his tree house, and when I did, I saw that there was no sign of light or life in Ehlark's grand home either. It wept without radiance, the hanging tendrils dark and dripping with rainwater.

Before I even hit the stairs leading down into Ehlark's living quarters, I felt the shifting atmosphere.

Invisible drifts of energy washed over me, caress after caress. I leapt over the short steps, skidding to a stop just beyond the entryway.

Ehlark wasn't here.

There was a staleness in the air, an emptiness despite the warmth radiating from the center of the room where his alchemy table had been destroyed. The glass pipes and vials had been shattered, the boiler hung in pieces, and inky droplets of some kind flecked the surface of everything.

Alezandral finally caught up with me, rushing down the steps behind me, but I couldn't look at him.

Above the table, a jagged scar pulsed in mid-air, weeping watery gray light. My heart stopped dead in my chest when I saw it. It was the length of my forearm, and the center of the scar seemed to curl inward, as if something was tugging on it from the other side.

"Goddess spare us, it's a rift," I whispered.

Alezandral wandered forward, his eyes trained on the fissure. He was coming to terms with the same thing I had: that gray light was responsible for the darkness around us.

"How?" he breathed. "What could have caused a *rift* to open up *here*?"

It felt like my ribs were collapsing.

The elven realm wasn't a solid enough place to handle the weight of a rift. Realms like this only barely existed, squeezed between worlds like horizontal railroad slats, holding the more substantial lines apart, and it was the same for whatever realm the passing occurred in. The veil. The Goddess's realm. There was no rift in which the dead could return to us and no way to create one. No way I knew of, at least.

Rifts didn't happen in a place between worlds. They only served to connect two separate worlds to one another—until now.

My gaze drifted lower, to the broken vial of blood on the ground. *My* blood.

"Me. It was me," I choked out.

Alezandral's eyes narrowed. "What?"

Swallowing the rock in my throat, I explained, "I gave Ehlark a vial of my blood. I asked him to run tests on it, to see what he could learn from it—"

"You think your blood did this?" he interrupted, pointing at the rift without looking away from me. I couldn't interpret his tone. I'd anticipated a reaction, maybe anger or fear, even judgment, but I didn't perceive any of those things.

Somehow, that made me feel better, *calmer*.

"I think whatever he did with my blood caused it, yes," I clarified. "Why else would the rift be hovering over this table? Something must have gone wrong while he was experimenting with it."

Alezandral ran a hand through his hair and turned away. He started pacing, his eyes shifting nervously around the room, the gears visibly turning in his head.

I was reminded of the rift that opened in the river when I was bathing just days ago, and how I had seen a flash of green eyes through it. Had that been real? Had I seen Ehlark? If I had, then that could mean...

It had been *days*.

My stomach churned. "Do you think he—" My voice cracked, and the rest came out strangled as I stumbled toward the rift. "Goddess, could he be trapped in there because of me?"

Alezandral's arm caught me around the waist. "I don't know," he said into my ear, "but let's think through what we're going to do."

I shoved out of his arms and faced him. My vision wavered around the edges, filling with a dark film. "I can't just leave him there. This is *my fault.*"

His hands fisted as I backed away, but he didn't come after me again. I felt the waves of heat getting stronger the closer I inched to the rift. "We don't know what's beyond the rift, Sia," he said. "We can't go in after him."

"Says who? You?" I huffed a menacing laugh. "I don't care what you do for me or how important you think you are—you will *never* order me around."

Alezandral glared at me. "That wasn't my intention."

"My father had the best intentions too, in his mind, but that doesn't change the truth."

His blue eyes flashed as the muscles around his jaw tightened, tugging at the scar on his neck. "Compare me to your father one more time, Sia, and I'll make sure you never think of him when you look my way again." His voice was deceitfully soft.

I raised an eyebrow at him. "Oh yeah? How?"

Alezandral smirked. The air between us shifted, heating as his gaze slid down to trace the curves of my body. I felt his answer fizzle under my skin like bubbly wine.

I scoffed.

As if I would let him seduce me. There was nothing about him that tempted me, even if I now found myself mildly fascinated by the gloves on his hands and the cold look he got in his eyes whenever I pissed him off. I wanted to explore his anger more, but that was mere curiosity at best.

"Only in your dreams, Alezandral," I sneered.

His chuckle sent a thrill rolling up my spine. "Want to place bets on how long it'll take for me to wiggle my way into yours?" His brow lifted, daring me to play along.

I wouldn't.

He was trying to distract me.

My heart thundered as I fell back a step, shifting my weight to the balls of my feet. The heat of the rift was curling possessively around my shoulders.

Portals were different from rifts. Portals were simply passages that connected places in the same universe, connected dimensions that already touched each other. No one traveled through the rifts. They bridged gaps between *worlds*. There was no way of knowing where they led, and no way of controlling them.

Our winged spirits traveled through these rifts, and we'd been warned by them that the worlds they fled were uninhabitable. But what if there *was* something on the other side?

I owed it to Ehlark to at least look.

Alezandral knew what I was planning before I did it. He lurched forward, his gloved hand reaching for me in the same moment I threw myself toward the scar in the sky, lifting off the ground entirely with a flap of my wings.

"No, Sia," he screamed, but it was too late.

My fingertips grazed the rift, and the atmosphere exploded around me in a burst of blinding light.

CHAPTER 8

A high-pitched ringing sang in my ears, deafening me. I was on my stomach, my cheek pressed against soft dirt, and I couldn't quite remember how I got there. A burnt flavor filled my mouth as I inhaled, and hot air curled brightly in my lungs until I was coughing, yearning for a deeper breath—but the next one I took was no easier.

It felt like something was wrapped around my chest, like a corset pulled too tight.

The rift, I suddenly remembered. I'd gone through the rift.

A violent shudder rolled through my body, and goose-bumps spidered across my skin. It was sweltering here, wherever *here* was. I lifted my head, my vision wavering.

Burning pillars surrounded me, and I squinted through the haze of heat. Goddess divine, they were *trees*. They towered over me, spearing into a starless night sky, the bark seemingly carved from crystallized honey. Liquid shadows oozed from the black flames flickering on their boughs, coursing down the trunks like wax from a burning candle.

Shadows curled at the roots, billowing in place, watching me as I watched them.

The ground hummed beneath my palms, and I dropped my gaze to it, then threw myself back with a gasp when I realized it wasn't dirt at all. The ground was a thick layer of ash, and as I crawled backwards, it oscillated like warm, live flesh. Like it was *breathing.*

What the fuck?

Movement caught my attention, and I stilled, my gaze focusing on a tree in front of me as something peeled away from its bark. A figure took on the shadows like a soldier would a set of armor, growing taller than any creature I'd ever seen and absurdly thin. It built and built until it was taller than even the trees. The limbs were as slender as blades, and I watched it turn to look at me, teetering on its needle-like legs.

If it had a face, I couldn't see it, but I felt its malicious intent spill into the air.

The atmosphere shook as light erupted behind me.

I twisted in time to see Alezandral falling from the rift that was now substantially larger than it had been only moments ago, at least a foot wider in either direction. Alezandral tumbled across the ground, his arms curling inward to take the brunt of the fall.

He really came in after me. No sensible person would have done that.

Perhaps his scar had demanded it.

Somehow, Alezandral remained conscious. As he rose to his knees and lifted his head, I saw that his eyes were glassy, his skin red. Veins bulged all over his body as he scratched at his neck, his mouth gaping in a silent cry. He couldn't breathe.

I wanted to run to him, but shock and fear paralyzed me.

No *person* was hurting him, so our promise sat dormant in my chest, but I suddenly decided I would have rather felt the pain.

A roar pierced the air, powerful enough to make the ground tremble, and I glanced over my shoulder at the source

—the massive creature that had emerged from the tree. Its roar disrupted the forest, and I looked around frantically, marking every small shift around us.

Sparks shook free from the trees and caught in Alezandral's wings, attempting to set him on fire.

Alezandral reached back to put out the embers, but his frost refused to spread, only gathering in his hand to swiftly melt away. His magic wasn't working here either. If we didn't get back home soon, he was going to die, either by flame or asphyxiation—or at the hands of the creature now approaching on spindly legs.

Something surged in the distance, between the shadowy trees. Figures coalesced, and I would have recognized that faint clicking anywhere. *Sutilus.* The rift had sent us to their world.

I needed to snap out of it. I needed to—

Alezandral's panicked eyes met mine. *Move!*

I scrambled toward him on my hands and knees, barely getting my feet beneath me before I hefted his solid body upright by sheer adrenaline. Setting my sights on the rift, I took on as much of Alezandral's weight as I could and ran. My wings flapped behind us, helping carry us forward, Alezandral's feet stumbling as he tried to keep up with me without tripping us both. His lungs were wheezing against my shoulder, though I held Alezandral so tightly, he probably wouldn't have been able to breathe if his lungs *were* working.

I couldn't lose someone like this again.

Not again. *Not again.*

The ground rocked beneath my feet. That needle-limbed creature was breathing down my back, but it wouldn't catch us. I wouldn't let it.

I leapt for the rift, my wings fluttering, extending a hand toward that luminous sliver of life beyond it.

A second otherworldly roar split the air behind me, loud enough to make my hearing pop. Something sharp slashed across my calf and right lower wing, and I knew it must have cut me deep, but the pain didn't register. Not yet.

I hoped I wouldn't feel it until we were at least back in the planetarium and the portal was closed, but I wasn't holding my breath.

I didn't trust the Goddess to be that forgiving.

My fingertips finally made contact with the rift and an explosion of light wrapped around us.

Bzzzzzzzzzzz.

My ears were screaming, bubbling. They might have been bleeding. My head rocked against a hard surface, my whole body jostled by a hand on my shoulder.

"Sia. We have to go!" The voice was so faint, it could have been a thought.

We had to go—go where? It was important. I forced my eyes open, every millimeter a battle. I looked above me, expecting to see the person who spoke, but instead, I saw nothing. There was only what seemed to be a blanket of silver undulating in front of me.

Something moved beyond it. A woman's silhouette. Then another.

Two women stood on the other side of the silver sky, their features unseen, beings unknown. They touched the sky, and silver clung to their delicate fingers like liquid metal, outlining their hands in a gray shadow as they pressed deeper. As the sky stretched, I realized they were reaching for *me*. What did they want?

The voice came again, and this time, I recognized it. "Wake up, darling!"

Squeezing my eyes shut, I battled for control of my mind. I wasn't seeing things right. I wasn't awake yet. I lifted my heavy arms and started shoving at the presence above me, my hands tingling as I touched something hard, something real. As I fluttered my eyes open, streaks of color filled my vision, then crystal clarity as Alezandral's face came into focus, his blue eyes bright as he glanced at something on my other side.

I followed his gaze to the rift.

The scar in the atmosphere was now a gaping wound, those waxy black shadows pouring through, pooling on the floor below it.

The open gash rumbled, and then a burst of light assaulted the room. I lifted a hand to shield my eyes, squinting through the brilliance as a long, blade-like limb shot through the rift. The rift continued to glow as the creature's other leg tore through, stretching the scar, the air all around us shuddering.

Luminous veins of light skittered to either side of the rift, lengthening it.

My travel through the rift must have made the opening big enough for this monster to squeeze its way through, to use its massive limbs as leverage.

Alezandral cursed under his breath and wrenched me to my feet, and I didn't fight him, his hand a brand on my lower back as we ran for the entrance. The sprinkle of rain that greeted us upon our arrival had become a torrential downpour. An endless curtain of crystalline droplets glimmered against the dark forest, the steps leading out of Ehlark's home slick with it.

As my foot came up to meet the second step rising out of his home, the wound on my calf screamed in protest. My other boot slipped out from beneath me and twisted my ankle at an odd angle, triggering another lash of agony in my leg.

I flexed my wings in an attempt to right myself, but a searing pain there made me gasp.

Alezandral was there, his hand supporting my elbow as I tried to stand up. I cried out as I put pressure on my ankle. If it wasn't broken, it was at least sprained. I glanced back at the rift, my heart skipping when I saw it had opened to the width of a carriage, and the large creature pursuing us wasn't the only thing pushing its way through.

The blackish, oozing bodies of sutilus crawled through around the creatures' long limbs.

My eyes flew to Alezandral's.

I couldn't fly. I couldn't run.

Before I could even say a word, he reached for me.

As he grasped my hips, ice-cold magic trickled down my spine, pulling at the ligaments around my wings. In a split second, my wings were tucked away into my back. It was as if they just… *snapped* there.

Alezandral's wings were gone now too.

A thick black mist clung to his back, but it faded as he threw me over his shoulder and started sprinting for the tree line, back in the direction of the portal we'd opened. The scent of earth filled my nostrils.

What the fuck happened to my wings?

What was that black mist?

I pressed my palms into Alezandral's back and craned my neck to look at the rift. The sutilus pouring through were worse off than the ones we'd faced in the city. These were half-rotted, missing limbs, their stitches barely holding them together. The clicking and horrifying smiles were the same, though. They fell free from the rift as the spindly creature above them tore another foot of atmosphere open.

The soldiers brandished their glowing blades and chased after us.

"Alezandral?" I said nervously.

They were gaining on us, and we were without wings, without weapons. What were we going to do?

As if replying to the question in my head, Alezandral yelled, "Set them ablaze, darling. *Now!*"

Forcing my spine as straight as I could, I lifted myself away from Alezandral's back, raising my hands to the impending horde. Rain turned to vapor as I released my flame.

A black flood of heat erupted from my palms and crashed into the first line of sutilus. In the distance, I saw the head of that tall, spindly creature finally emerge from Ehlark's home, its razor-thin limbs sweeping through the forest between us, falling several of the elder trees at once.

A few sutilus broke away from the rest, veering into the forest to either side of us.

I threw a hand out to follow the ones on my right, engulfing the forest in black fire as my attention was pulled in too many directions.

"They're trying to surround us," I shouted. "On your right."

Alezandral's arm tightened around my thighs, and in the next moment, I watched the rain to his right turn into shards of ice, ripping into the decaying bodies, through their flesh and softened bone until they were nothing but ribbons of death. It bought us the time we needed to reach the portal.

I felt the mist swallow my lower half first, and then my vision blurred as we emerged on the other side, back in the planetarium.

Bringing both hands in front of me, I kept my fire burning, directing it through the portal, where I could see an undulating reflection of the sutilus fast approaching. I could barely see through my flames but the sutilus seemed to be falling on the other side, gaining ever so slowly as they trampled on top of each other to reach us.

In one smooth motion, Alezandral deposited me on the ground in front of the portal, ducking under my outstretched arms. "Don't stop," he gasped before leaping toward the control panel.

I fought the urge to roll my eyes. As if I would stop *now*.

He frantically clicked the keys on the control board as I sat mere feet from the portal. The smell of the sutilus drifted through—rot and magic, stale and bitter. A thin sheet of sweat gathered on my brow from the pain in my wing and leg, the exertion of my power, my flames quickly raising the temperature of the room.

One of the sutilus breached the portal, and I caught a glimpse of its arm, a hand holding one of those curved blades.

Seething with anger, I bared my teeth and leaned into my magic, tucking my legs awkwardly beneath me as I shifted to my knees. I tapped into that raging inferno swirling in my belly, the one that was always there. I gave the portal all I had, pushing the sutilus on the other side away from this plane, away from my home.

They couldn't have it.

They couldn't have us.

A guttural cry tore out of my mouth.

"Almost there, darling," Alezandral called. "Just hold on."

For the first time since I boiled the bay, I felt the ceiling of my power. I was quickly closing in on it, and while I knew enough to understand that ceilings could be lifted through training, seeing as I'd had almost none, my endurance wasn't what it could be, what it *should* be for a seraph my age. Adrenaline could only carry me so far.

I pushed myself, digging deeper.

Alezandral once said that I could do anything, but I knew now that anything worth doing required time and patience I did not allow myself. That changed today, this second. I would do what I needed to make myself strong, to make myself proud.

Sweat coursed down my chest, and my sides started to ache.

At last, the portal trembled, its surface solidifying with static lightning as the road between realms closed.

CHAPTER 9

Collapsing, I let my black flames dissipate as I caught myself on my hands and knees. The sudden darkness was alleviated only by the twinkling stars above us, the ceiling spooling silver light across the scorch marks I'd left on the floor. I raked in a deep breath, and my chest shook as I held the air in my lungs for a moment.

That was too close. I'd nearly brought the sutilus *here*, to my people, who had fought so hard to escape them. I had opened a door. I had opened a *rift*.

Finally, I lifted my head.

Alezandral was pacing in front of the control panel. He stared at the floor of the planetarium without seeing it, his arms crossed and one gloved hand gripping his jaw so tightly, I wouldn't be surprised if his fingers left bruises beneath the dusting of golden stubble on his face.

I lowered my ass to the floor and scooted backwards toward the couch in this room.

I bit back a groan as I used my sprained ankle as leverage. At least it wasn't broken. Everything in my body ached, from my head to my toes, even the things that hadn't been directly injured.

Alezandral continued pacing, lost in thought—or perhaps he was ignoring me. Maybe he didn't want to look at me. I wouldn't.

Now he knew the depths of my wrongness.

I was the one to blame for this. I had been stupid and reckless to give an elf my blood like that. And now we saw what had become of it.

Darkness. Suffocation. Almost-death.

I leaned against the couch and pulled my leg in to examine it. The deep cut was puckered with hot pink tissue, weeping blood down my calf and onto the floor.

Alezandral turned to me, and his eyes felt like red hot irons against my skin.

"Sia," he rumbled, "what happened back there wasn't your fault."

My head snapped up to find his eyes soft, even as he clenched his hands into fists, arms straining against the material of his tunic. He was upset, but not in the way I thought he'd be. How could he believe this wasn't my fault? Either he was delusional, or he was lying to me.

"Yes, it is," I argued. "*I'm* the one who went there in the first place. I'm the one who asked Ehlark for help. Something terrible has happened to him because of *my* blood, because of what I asked him to do with it. What if he—" My throat tightened too much to finish that thought, that worry, that fear. I closed my eyes briefly and waited for the tears to recede.

I wouldn't cry. I had no right to cry.

Steeling myself, I returned Alezandral's piercing stare. "I am responsible for opening that rift, Alezandral, and I'm the reason those creatures have taken Ehlark's home. It *is* my fault." My voice lifted, filling the room. "I have no idea how I did it, and what's even worse is that I don't know how to stop it. So please, don't give me false comforts. They won't fix this. They won't make me feel better. If you want to give me *anything* at this point, give me a fucking solution, because I don't know where to go from here."

Alezandral's eyes burned into mine, twin rings of blue pulsing through the dark.

I could almost feel the phantom wisps of his frost stretching toward me. I'd give anything to feel it now. I was sweaty, and the cut on my leg throbbed like hell.

Without a word, Alezandral turned and stalked out of the room.

As the heavy door shut behind him, my heart sank. The blood in my veins thickened, slowing my thoughts and cooling my temper. He walked away. I didn't know why that hurt so much, or why I expected anything more, but I didn't want to examine the pain too closely.

Certainly, it had something to do with how much time I spent alone here as a child, how much time I *felt* alone.

It was fine. I was used to this.

I braced my feet flat against the floor, ignoring the retaliatory spike of pain in my ankle, but then the door to the inner room opened again before I could push myself up onto the couch. Alezandral walked in holding a cloth and the small bottle of liquor that Aida kept in the cloakroom.

I'd drained that bottle more times than I could count; I'd laid right here on this couch, getting drunk under these manufactured stars.

Waving the cloth at me, he said, "Turn around and lay down on the floor. We should clean that wound before it heals over. Your wing, too. Those blades were as foul as the hands holding them."

I would heal quickly enough without any assistance, but he was right: I didn't want anything from that strange world getting trapped under my skin.

He didn't leave me.

Warmth slithered through my veins, and I frowned at myself. Was it because of the promise between us, or did he really want to take care of me? He didn't know me, not really. He'd admitted as much earlier today. Alezandral came looking for me in that smog, and this was what he found. Whether he liked it or not, we were connected, so of course he was going to take care of me. When a limb was infected, you cured it or cut it off. Otherwise, the infection spread.

That was why I had to find a way to break this bond. I would always be the infection that needed treatment, and it wasn't fair to him. It wasn't fair to anyone.

I reached for the items in his hand. "I can do it," I murmured.

Alezandral lifted them out of my reach. "For fuck's sake, Sia, just lay down. I'll get it done faster than you will."

I tried to glare at him, but it was useless.

He just smirked at me, lifting one eyebrow, and I knew I wouldn't win.

With a huff, I wiggled away from the couch and flipped over onto my stomach. I could *feel* the weight of his gaze as he knelt at my thigh. My skin crawled in anticipation as I waited for the alcohol to hit my wound, but instead, I heard a soft slap and looked over to see that he'd taken off his gloves, discarding them next to my head. Then, the sensation of melting ice crept across my ankle, spreading upward to the gash on my leg, soothing the inflamed tissues.

A small moan escaped me. That felt so good.

Alezandral's frost intensified, numbing my skin as it sank deeper, numbing my nerves.

"Thank you," I exhaled.

I felt faint pressure as he touched me, his fingers walking along my swollen ankle, assessing for a break I already knew wasn't there. Maybe I should have told him it wasn't, but this felt nice, being touched by him.

"I hope you weren't attached to these pants," Alezandral muttered.

Before I could reply, he gripped either edge of the pant leg, and my lower body jostled as he ripped them apart, giving himself access to the wound. I heard the tell-tale pop of a cork being pulled, and then pain pierced through the numbed skin of my leg as Alezandral doused it. As he ran the cloth over the cut, I could tell exactly how deep it was, because it felt like he was scraping needles through the muscle.

Whimpering, I pressed my forehead against the floor.

"Keep breathing. Nearly done with this one," he whispered before pouring more alcohol on my leg.

His words made the next pass of cloth hurt a little less.

Dread gathered low in my belly, knowing that my wing was going to hurt even worse. I could feel the cut on my upper dorsal, even with my wings burrowed deep within my back. I would let them out after he was done with my leg. I should have let them out the moment Alezandral set me down —their absence only contributed to my exhaustion, kneecapping my power—but just the thought of pushing them out right now made me want to cry.

How had Alezandral done it earlier? How had he made my wings disappear...well, not disappear exactly, but *moved* somewhere else?

I opened my mouth to ask, but he interrupted me.

"I have to tell you something. I didn't think it was important before, but now..."

I waited, and when he didn't continue, I snapped, "What? What is it?"

He sighed, crawling forward until he was just within my line of sight. The bloody cloth was clutched tightly in his fist, and worry danced in his eyes. "Do you remember the sutilis I chased down back in the city?"

My heart started pounding. "The one that stabbed you?"

"The very same. I brought it back here, alive, as a prisoner."

I pushed myself up on my forearms, halting only when the bend in my back made the wing inside ache. "You did *what*?" I ground out.

"That's why I left the city so abruptly," he said in a rush, running a hand through his blond hair, my blood leaving behind a red streak. "I held onto it when we fell off the roof. I decided in that moment that we needed a survivor, something to keep as leverage, someone to interrogate."

Interrogate, one of those *things?* That was the reason he let me think he'd died?

"And how is that working out for you?" I said wryly.

He avoided my accusing gaze. "They can speak," he murmured. "When they want to."

Well, *that* was a surprise. I'd assumed all that clicking was their sole method of communication.

Alezandral finally looked at me with large eyes, and tension coiled in my limbs. He had more to tell me. The imprisoned sutilis wasn't the end of it.

"Why are you telling me this?" I demanded.

He hesitated. "Because the sutilis I captured asked for you. It recognized you down in the bay. It called you a..." The word caught in his throat.

What the fuck was his problem? *Just spit it out.*

"Say it," I hissed.

Alezandral closed his eyes. "It called you a world ripper."

The world spun slower somehow, and I was caught between this moment and the next. I managed to choke out, "What does that mean?"

"I don't know." Alezandral twisted the cloth in his hands, my blood smearing across his knuckles.

"When?" I pressed. "When did the sutilis ask for me?"

"The morning after the invasion."

Heat crawled up my neck. "And you waited until *now* to tell me?" I could hear the accusation in my voice before I even made the conscious decision to blame him. I couldn't take it back now. It was already hanging between us.

The gentleness fell away from Alezandral's face as he returned my glare. "You were avoiding me like a plague, Sia. How could I have told you *anything*?"

"You could have mentioned it this morning."

"You've been a bit demanding today, darling. It slipped my mind."

"No. It's just another secret you've been keeping," I snapped back. "How much more are you hiding from me?"

Alezandral just stared at me for a moment, a muscle in his jaw ticking.

I crossed my arms over my chest.

"Nothing more that concerns you," he said tersely.

There were definitely more secrets…

"What you did to my wings concerns me," I countered.

He blinked a few times, his features softening. "Right."

His gaze dropped to the cloth in his hands, then to the bottle of liquor sitting on the floor beside him. Lifting his hand palm-up between us, he narrowed his eyes at the bottle, his brow creasing in concentration.

I felt the shift first, the displacement of the atmosphere, as if the energy all around us was being pressurized.

Alezandral blinked, and the vessel disappeared from the floor before reappearing in his hand with a burst of dark mist. There was no delay from one place to the other. It was as if the bottle had always been there, in his hand, except I knew it hadn't. The dark mist told me it hadn't. The mist fell beneath his hand—settling in a thin layer of dust on the floor.

My eyes bulged, a delighted smile tugging at my lips.

Hoarfrost wasn't his only gift. He had the blessing of ether manipulation too.

"How?" I breathed.

He nodded once, and my wings were released from my back, unfurling to either side of me. I hissed as the wound on my wing was exposed to the open air and the dust of his controlled ether.

Alezandral crawled forward, arranging himself behind the injury. He gripped the peak on my wing with the cloth as his frost swept in, but it did little to mask the pain as the alcohol hit my wound.

A strangled cry hissed through my teeth.

My body instinctually leaned forward, my wings curling in an attempt to break free, but Alezandral kept a fierce grip on me. There was nothing to do but endure it as he swept the cloth over the cut. "Just a few more moments," he said encouragingly.

"Are you going to answer my question, or is that one of the secrets you plan on keeping?" I asked.

He didn't respond until he'd finished cleaning my wound.

"Can you stretch it?" Alezandral tapped the tip of my wing, and I lengthened it, showing him that I could with a little effort.

Glancing over my shoulder, I watched him examine my shifting muscles, his fingertips tracing the slope of my wing and making me shiver. "Alezandral?"

His gaze snapped to mine, and his hand fell away.

Anchoring my eyes to his, I conveyed that question again as I willed him to get rid of this secret, *every* secret.

In a small voice, he said, "My mother was half Quintessential. I have Materie, but a very negligible amount, so negligible that it's barely worth mentioning. I can move items the size of my hand or smaller across a room with ease, or larger things the distance of a few feet."

My brow furrowed.

In theory, his explanation made sense. Quintessentials alone carried the gift of Materie—the ability to manipulate the energetic fabric of the universe to transport items from one place to another, to control the ether of our world.

But if he was Halcyon, how could he be part Quintessential too? Especially when he was spirit-borne?

"I don't understand," I admitted. "You have six wings."

His eyes swirled with bitterness. "My mother was a willing sacrifice, the same as yours. The only difference is that mine survived the reckoning, and believe me when I say that my entire country suffered dearly for it."

Alezandral stood then, sitting on the edge of the couch beside me, running both hands through his hair. His eyes slid shut, and he remained like that for a long while, his hands fisting his hair and elbows resting on his knees.

Alezandral's mother... had been a *seraph* sacrificed to the Winged Spirits?

I'd never heard of such a thing happening before. Humans were sacrificed, not our fellow seraphim. I had so many questions. It was clear that Alezandral had no interest in discussing it at length, though, and I wouldn't ask him to.

"I should talk to the sutilis you captured, shouldn't I?" I asked instead.

He opened his tired eyes, nodding slowly as he leaned away from me. "Yes. We'll go once you're healed up."

CHAPTER 10

The dungeons were beneath the Fenix palace, carved into the rocky underbelly of my father's floating island—where it was musky, wet, and dim.

Orange faerie orbs flickered in small hollows dug into the stone, but they were weak and sporadically placed. This area of the palace was not maintained as well as what sat above the surface. Few ever saw this area of the city, and those who did were usually staying a while. Imprisonment was reserved for the most heinous of crimes. As a seraph, there was no greater punishment than being grounded for years, unable to fly higher than the ceiling of a small cell—save for losing one's wings entirely.

I didn't want to know what the prisoners here had done to earn time in this place. They called to us as we passed through, reached between the bars and clutched at nothing.

Every step Alezandral and I took down the staircase echoed off the damp walls, alerting the guards on every level to our presence as we approached the lowest level of the cavern. They saw us, but they didn't intervene.

Alezandral had permission to be here.

When we finally readied to leave the planetarium, after he'd retrieved some hastening serum from the hospital wing to help my wounds close, Alezandral informed me that the sutilis he captured was chained to the pit of the island. No one but Alezandral was allowed to enter the sutilis' cell. Nothing was given or said in its presence that could alert the creature to where we were, because there was no way of knowing what it was capable of, if it had ways of communicating with the rest of its army by whatever magic held them together.

The way they had organized and moved so seamlessly in the city suggested a horde mind, like the shared mind of lycanthropes and the nymphs of the forest, so we had to be cautious.

I descended the final curve of the spiral steps and entered the enormous hall at the bottom of the cave system, Alezandral at my heels. He fell into place at my side as we approached the only cell on this level.

There were four armed sentinels standing outside the door who sprang to attention.

Two of the guards walked forward to meet us. One of Father's highly favored, Alldrich, stared me down. He was the seraph Destin shot back at Gwaith House, and he was looking as sour as ever as his gaze caught on my wings. The rain had made the gold paint on them run, and I didn't bother returning to my room to recover them before coming here.

Every staff member and soldier assigned to the central palace was sworn to secrecy about my *condition*, those in the dungeons included. Promises weighed on their tongues, preventing them from sharing what they saw within the palace walls—not with their families, and not even with each other. Many of the oldest soldiers already knew about my wings, Alldrich included.

"What is *she* doing here?" he demanded.

He wasn't even addressing me directly. Nice.

I crossed my arms and gave him a saccharine grin. "Is that any way to speak to your princess?"

He barely glanced at me. "I'm not talking to you."

"You are *now*."

Turning back to Alezandral, he said, "Princess Sabrina is not permitted in the dungeons, Your Highness."

Alezandral smirked. "What makes you say that?"

"King's orders. She's never been allowed down here. It's too dangerous," he explained.

"I see." Alezandral's wings ruffled. "Tell me something. Has Princess Sabrina ever been accompanied to the dungeons by the prince who plans to make her a *queen*?"

My gaze snapped to Alezandral's face.

His arrogant smirk made my heart swell. That one sentence shouldn't make me feel like this, shouldn't make me want to smile, but it did. This was more than a declaration of his title and authority. It was a declaration of *mine*.

A queen. He could just as easily have said *his* queen. There was a difference. At least to me there was.

Alldrich looked between the two of us, and then his eyes flicked around the room to assess the reaction of the other guards. They were noticeably distracted by the floor. His throat bobbed as he returned Alezandral's stare and replied, "No, Your Highness. She hasn't."

The dry amusement faded from Alezandral's features as he bit out, "Then I suppose you could say circumstances change, can't you?"

He jerked his head to one side, dismissing the sentinels. His impatience was an invisible flurry bearing down on the cavern. I could sense it building beneath his skin, even while his voice remained as cool as ice. "Now, step aside."

Alldrich stared wide-eyed at him, stunned. When he realized Alezandral had every intention of plowing through him if he didn't move, he fell back a few steps, allowing my betrothed to cut a path for us straight to the cell door.

I smirked at the sentinels as we passed, and they wisely averted their eyes.

Perhaps I'd gotten it wrong before. Alezandral wasn't acting as my shield; he was acting as my equal, and that was a far more powerful move, for me especially. I wasn't sure what *he* got out of this. He had to be gaining *something*, but I would have to worry about what it was later.

Alezandral glanced over his shoulder as his hand closed around the cell's barricade. "Clear the level. We'll retrieve you once we're finished."

Without waiting for a response, he lifted the wooden barricade away and opened the cell door, ushering me through in front of him. As it slammed shut behind us, I looked around the room. It was smaller than I'd anticipated, maybe a hundred square feet at the most. The tip of my wings grazed the ceiling.

It was never intended to be a cell. This was the source of the island's power, the reason it could float, static in the sky even in the face of the greatest winds and storms.

The pit in the center of this room held a Fenix flame, encapsulated by a sheer triangular vessel. I'd heard of it before, but this was my first time seeing it. The orange flames slammed viciously against their magical boundaries, ricocheting from one corner to the next, lighting up the walls with energy. That energy snaked up the length of the triangle to its peak, funneling into a vibrating metal rod that disappeared through a hole in the ceiling.

My mouth dried. It was so hot in here, my skin erupted with gooseflesh beneath my winter clothes.

A few of the Fenix elders who survived the initial invasion gave their lives to create this flame when they arrived on this continent, the same way my father's sisters had given their lives to burn the rest of the sutilus on their island. The elders' spirits were trapped within that glass vessel, where they could provide safety for our people forever. I'd been taught to respect their sacrifice growing up, but secretly, I thought it was a horrible way to die. Because it wasn't really death; it was an endless state of *dying* until the time came when their spirits were released and allowed to rest.

That time might never come.

Weak clicking brought me out of my thoughts, echoing from the other side of the triangle, and Alezandral urged me onward with a tilt of his head, allowing me to take the lead.

Skirting the edge of the room, the sutilis slowly came into view. It was bound by iron chains around each limb, each ankle and elbow and wrist, and more were wrapped tightly around its neck. An anchor-like weapon protruded from its stomach, connected to more chains, holding the creature in place against the triangular vessel. If it tried to remove itself, its body would rip in half.

Flames burned into the sutilis' back, and I could smell the char, overwhelming even the pungent scent of rot seeping from between its weakening stitches. There were cuts all over it, shallow enough to see gummy muscle but not enough to make it bleed out.

It looked like a brutalized, horrifying rag doll.

Alezandral paused just beyond the other side of the trian- gle, his arms crossed and one hand raising to cradle his jaw, out of view of the sutilis but close enough to watch me interact with it.

The sutilis lifted its head, and its drooping, mismatched eyes peeling open: one brown, one blue, both bloodshot. When they landed on me, the creature smiled. My stomach rolled; its teeth were sharp and yellow, the gums around them black and bloody, and I caught a glimpse of the black thread wiring them in. It was grinning at me with the teeth it had helped massacre a pack of lycan-thropes for.

"Why, hello, little one," it said in a dulcet, echoing voice. "I thought I smelled you."

It didn't seem right for such a lovely voice to come from a creature like this. If I was to close my eyes, it could have been a woman. It could have been *human*. I fought a shudder, lifting my chin as I met its hollow gaze.

It had stolen that voice too.

"You asked for me to see you. Why?"

Clicking erupted from its throat. A laugh, I abruptly realized. Had they been laughing the entire time they invaded the human city? As they killed?

The creature tilted its head, those mismatched eyes drilling into me. "I wanted to *meet* you, of course, and what an honor it is. You are even more stunning when you are *not* killing our brethren. You have grown well, little one."

My spine prickled.

I didn't like the way it said that, like it was trying to insinuate something. "Why do I matter to you?" I demanded.

"You have always mattered to us. We have been watching you for a long time, me and our kin," it replied. "We know everything about you."

I clenched my hands to keep my flames contained. "You don't know anything."

"Oh, we know more than you do, I guarantee it."

"Prove it," I countered.

Another sonorous clicking. "Come closer, little one, for it is a secret."

Alezandral strode forward. "Don't get close to it, Sia. You can't trust it not to try something."

The clicking intensified, reverberating through the room as the sutilis looked at Alezandral. It wasn't smiling anymore, instead baring its teeth like a hound. "What do you know of us, ice bird? You may be powerful in this world, but you would be nothing in ours. You felt it for yourself. Were it not for the mercy of our little spirit, you would be ash and broken bones trampled beneath our feet. *That* is your rightful place."

Alezandral paled. The sutilis was referring to the events earlier this evening, when he'd nearly died in their universe.

My gaze whipped back to the sutilis. "How do you know about that?"

The sutilis beamed, its long, rotten tongue sweeping hungrily over its teeth. "I told you, we know everything about you—all that you do, all that you *are*." More clicking. It was taunting me, toying with me, but I had no interest in playing games.

I stalked forward.

There was a slight dip in the stone floor around the triangle, where luminous runes were carved into the rock, and as I entered the circle, I felt the hot embrace of the pit envelop me. It was near-blistering, and the heat made my vision blur.

Alezandral said my name, but I ignored him.

I took one more step toward the creature and crossed my arms, holding back a hiss as the leather of my tunic pressed more firmly against my skin. "*What* do you know?"

I was close enough now that I could count the stitches in its chest. There weren't many left; flaps of rotten skin peeled away from its ribs, giving a glimpse into the inner workings of its abdomen.

"You have the death of our kind on your hands again," it accused quietly. "I can smell their ashes."

At first, I thought it was another attempt at dodging the question, but there was a twinkle in its eyes that made me hesitant, made me think harder about what it said.

Our kind, it had said.

"They're your kind," I told it, "not ours."

The stitches in its face tore through desiccating skin as its smile grew. "Ah," it mused, "but we are the same."

I shook my head.

The sutilis leaned forward, the anchor in its stomach ripping it open a bit more, but it didn't seem to care. It was too eager to explain. "My blood sang the instant I saw you," it crooned. "I know what you are, *World Ripper.* Your spirit belonged to a god—*my* god. Before it abandoned us, that is. You are simply their newest creation."

It couldn't be true. If that was the truth, then I was... I was—

"I'm nothing like you," I snarled.

My throat swelled, choking me. Maybe it was because of the heat, but I couldn't quite convince myself, and I wasn't convincing the sutilis either.

The creature tsked. "So the birdie does not like what's inside of her? That is a pity."

My heart felt like it was going to burst. There was arrogance and amusement in the sutilis' voice, and I knew what that meant. It wasn't lying. At the very least, it truly believed what it was telling me.

"If I may offer you a piece of advice, from one sister to another," the sutilis purred. "There are many things you can change about yourself, but *this* is not one of them. The blood in your veins is eternal, and it is the same as mine. Rotten. *Dying.* Eventually, you will realize you are the only one who can ensure your own survival, your own happiness, and you will do what you must to bend the world to your will. You will realize you are exactly like me, like us. You know it's true."

Every word hit me like a punch, and I felt myself curving inward, crumbling under the weight of it. My withered husk of a heart clenched.

I forgot myself and staggered forward until I was mere

inches from the sutilis. The sutilis leaned in too, its teeth gnashing in excitement. The heat of the Fenix flame was scorching my cheeks, but I didn't care. The only thing that mattered right now was silencing these horrific thoughts in my head, the ones assailing me like arrows, fast and fierce.

All you're capable of is destruction.

Everyone knew it from the moment you were born.

It's in your blood.

You can run, but you can't escape.

I had resisted them the best I could—but they were so loud now that they found something real to cling to.

With all the strength I could manage, I rasped, "Even if what you say is true, I will never claim any part of what you are. You are not my family. *This* is my world, my people, even if my flame doesn't burn the same as theirs."

The sutilis' smile fell, but not in offense.

No, something was very wrong about the way it looked at me then. Its glassy eyes flicked to either side of us, then up at the ceiling. When its body slumped against the pit, the wounds on its back sizzled anew.

"Fascinating," it finally mused, grinning sharply. "Is that where I've been all this time? I wondered why I felt so...*high.*" That last word was almost unintelligible through the subsequent clicking.

My heart dropped. It knew. It knew where we were.

"No." I took a step forward but bent over at the waist as pain ripped across my mind. My vision went white, and music echoed just beyond my reach—that same ethereal song I'd first heard in the city. A few dozen voices clambered on top of it, drowning out the lovely lilting notes in a cacophony of words I couldn't quite understand.

As my vision cleared, that whisper of a song disappeared with it. Those voices remained, though, as did the dull ache rattling like rusty wheels in my head.

Alezandral's hands wrapped around my arms as he crouched in front of me, staring at me with eyes as bright as an icy sea.

I forced myself upright and turned my attention to the sutilis. Its eyes had gone distant, staring into nothing, as if it was... preoccupied. Squeezing my eyes shut, I turned to the racket in my head. I heard its voice, speaking in a different language with the others, having a *conversation*. The hive mind. The horde. Somehow, I was listening in on it.

The sutilis was showing me just how true its claim was.

No one could join a hive mind unless they were connected to it, either through the bloodline of a species or by a spirit bond. A new voice rumbled through my head like a blade, slicing through every thought, *demanding* my attention.

Hello, little one. It's about time we met.

My eyes snapped open, and I turned to Alezandral. The pain pushed me beyond words. I couldn't think. I couldn't *breathe*.

The sutilis laughed.

"The rest of our kin is not so far away, little spirit. They'll be so excited to see you, especially now that our dearest king Cravet is free. First, he will conquer your pitiful family, and then he will conquer *you*. Do not fear. You will make a fine breeding mare for this new world."

I felt the king's essence stretching toward me through the horde mind, reaching across oceans to dig his claws into the back of my neck. I fought back, pushing against that voice, against the heavy blanket wrapped around my awareness. I ripped and tore and slashed at the covering with all my might until the haze started to part.

"Alezandral, it's telling them where we are," I choked out, continuing to claw my way out of the hive, inch by inch, voice by voice. "You have to stop it."

My vision recovered in time to see Alezandral lift a hand

to the sutilis. Every inch of his body was covered in frost, a shield against the Fenix flame. He'd coated me too.

The sutilis jerked in its bindings, and the hive mind ripped away from my thoughts as I fell to my knees, gasping for air.

Frost spilled from the open sores on the sutilis' face. Ice crystallized over its eyes, hardening into glass-like shards that pierced them through, taking away its sight. The creature writhed and convulsed as it screamed, and a slow shiver walked up my back.

"What are you doing?" I asked breathlessly.

Alezandral responded without a speck of inflection. "It can't communicate telepathically without a brain."

Sharp tips of bloody-black ice started erupting from the sutilis' head, like a thousand horns emerging from its skull.

The sutilis stopped screaming, stopping fighting, and with hair-raising calmness, it dropped its chin to stare at me with those ice-crusted, mismatched eyes, giving me one last smile. *It doesn't matter, little one. I've already done my part, and so will you.*

My hand found the hilt of Alezandral's sword and wrenched it from the sheath, then I spun around to slash the blade across the sutilis' neck.

As the head rolled away, I realized I had beheaded it, though I couldn't remember deciding to. I was left reeling in the aftermath of what I had done. Mold and blood speckled my body. My wrist ached from the weight of the sword. Every inch of my body shook, and my mind was no steadier.

"*Sia?* Hey," Alezandral said from somewhere far away. "Are you okay?"

I dropped the sword and ran.

Shoving through the cell door, I was grateful for the empty level, because I was sprinting across it to reach the staircase. Stone enveloped me as I ascended swiftly towards the second level. I needed to get out from beneath this suffocating stone.

I needed the sky. Lights flickered above me as I neared the second floor, but I didn't make it there.

Alezandral's broad hand wrapped around my forearm, halting me. "Slow down. Talk to me, Sia."

I tried to pull away, but his grip was iron. The walls closed in. My lungs caught short, shrinking smaller and smaller with every breath I attempted. My head was cloudy from lack of oxygen, and when Alezandral pulled me closer, I was too weak to stop it.

"I can't," I gasped. "I can't—*can't breathe.*"

Alezandral's hands slid behind my back and pressed me firmly against his chest.

I lethargically fought him. "Don't," I whimpered. "I'm covered in blood."

"I don't give a fuck about that," he growled. His frost skittered across my back, spreading out from his palms and around to the front of my torso.

It shocked my senses enough that I swallowed a deep breath, and then I managed another one.

Alezandral's chest rose and fell, his even breaths as luminous as the moon. I couldn't fight him anymore, not even if I wanted to. My fingers twisted in the sides of his tunic as I dragged myself even closer, my face burrowing in his shoulder as I allowed his body to tame mine. His chill spread over every inch of me, slipping beneath my clothes and caressing my skin. By the time I calmed down enough to make full sense of the world again, I realized we were sitting on the staircase together and… I had started nuzzling him.

He was returning the affection, albeit warily.

I hadn't received this sort of affection from anyone since I was a child, and a young one at that. It was comforting to seraphim, drawing close to someone and nestling into them. Gentle, *nurturing* comfort. The streets above our heads were filled with it. Mothers and children. Friends and lovers.

This heart bond really had a mind of its own.

As I stopped nuzzling his neck, he turned his head and whispered against my temple, "It's okay. You're okay, darling." There was a ripple in my mind. Words materialized in the darkness, where I could feel his voice but not quite hear it. *Just keep breathing.*

"We're going to figure this out," he swore. "I'm going to help you." *You're not alone.*

My heart pounded hard in sudden understanding.

Alezandral wasn't surprised when I told him I could hear the sutilis in my head; he had simply reacted. I was teetering on the edge of something, a revelation, and I wanted so desperately to turn a blind eye to it, but I couldn't. All those times I thought I could read the thoughts in Alezandral's gaze, in his smile—had it been more?

His voice continued to whisper into both my ear and mind. He spoke with such sweetness, but the familiar feeling of betrayal curdled them beyond recognition.

Was this yet another thing he had withheld from me? Something he planned to use against me when he saw fit?

I pushed four words to the forefront of my mind.

Can you hear me?

"Of course I can," Alezandral murmured.

I wrenched away, my gaze searching his for the answer to my next question.

His white wings curled protectively around us, his eyes soft and preemptively apologetic. He'd need to voice that apology and a thousand more if what I suspected was true.

Are we speaking to one another in our heads? I thought.

Yes.

Shaking my head, I breathed, "How?"

He smiled, reaching up to brush back a lock of hair that had come loose from my braid. "It's the bond, darling. It connects us in more ways than our hearts. I *am* sorry this comes as a shock to you, but I figured you would've known this. It's not a secret. Haven't you done any research about our bond at all?"

I felt my brow furrow. No, I hadn't. How foolish was *that*? All this time I'd spent getting high in my room, avoiding my problems, and never once had I opened a book.

I couldn't expect Alezandral to coddle me through this bond when I hadn't bothered to educate myself on the details of what it really meant, what it entailed. I should have assumed a mind link was involved. We were bound beyond a promise of words, bound in blood and spirit, bound by our innermost beings.

Alezandral sat patiently, watching, letting me work through my scattered thoughts. His stare was unexpectedly comforting.

Damn him for making me like *him.*

Alezandral smirked, and I knew he'd heard me think that.

I pushed a few other choice words into the forefront of my mind. They were crude, and he laughed.

Sighing, I let go of my anger, the heat in my palms slipping away. Somehow, in the circle of Alezandral's wings, I felt safe enough to release, to rest. The darkness was cool and silent. Alezandral felt no inclination to fill the emptiness with words, and I loved that. I could think more clearly in the quiet. I could breathe easier too.

He'd known exactly what I needed, *again*.

Before I could formulate a proper sentence, a familiar voice boomed through the staircase around us. "Prince Alezandral, am I to understand that you've brought my daughter into the dungeons knowing full well she isn't allowed?"

Alezandral's wings pulled back, and I saw my father standing a few steps above us, his head haloed with bright red flames. He was furious, his upper lip doing that lopsided curl it always did when he shooed me away from important business.

"You agreed to respect my rules when you stowed that creature here," my father growled. "Don't make me regret helping you."

Alezandral helped me to my feet before he replied, "There's no need to fret, Your Majesty. The creature is dead now, so you may consider our agreement null and void." Then, in a stunning move of arrogance that made me smile from ear to ear, Alezandral slid past me and started climbing the staircase, tugging me along behind him.

My father sidestepped, cutting off our path. His golden eyes simmered orange around the edges. "You're coming dangerously close to trouble with me, Alezandral."

It was my turn to intervene. "Careful, Father. That's my future husband you're threatening."

Father's eyes narrowed, his nose flaring as he looked between the two of us.

I smiled, leaning my temple against Alezandral's arm and nuzzling it gently. Alezandral's hand tightened around mine as the rest of his body stiffened. I knew how touch-adverse he was. This whole night must have been a nightmare to him.

After a moment, my father shook his head, letting go of the staircase railing so we could retreat up the steps. His voice followed us. "I suppose you two should retire to your beds and get some rest. You'll need it for the coming week."

I paused, disliking the intent in his words. "Why?"

"The preparations for your engagement party, little love. You've made it clear that you're finished stalling."

CHAPTER 11

Once, when I was nine years old, I held my breath so long that I fainted. I had collapsed on the platform I was standing on now.

Once was enough.

My party dress had been ruined. I was careful after that, only holding my breath for a minute at a time, sometimes two if the painter was working on the feathers nearest my face. I wore a light robe during our sessions now too; no stains, no evidence of my father's deception.

My entire childhood had been a lesson in how to manipulate my appearance, but looking at myself today, I wasn't sure how anyone didn't see right through me—through the paint on my wings, the feigned smiles and the eyes that weren't quite golden. Most people could be tricked into believing anything given very little evidence to support it, as long as the lie they were told gave them comfort in one way or another.

I often wondered how much of the world understood that.

There was so much foul trickery that went undetected in the human lands, and surely in the other seraphic settlements too. I couldn't be the only secret, but I was still alone.

There was a stool on the platform behind me, but I didn't use it.

That stool was a reminder of the treatment I'd always been given here: the incessant and fearful coddling. It was a reminder of what they all thought of me. I was the strange and temperamental princess. They wanted me to feel delicate, because they feared what I might do to them if I knew I wasn't. They feared the princess they had created, the version of me that I had sometimes validated with my fiery, emotional outbursts.

I knew what I wasn't now, but I stood here anyway, letting them mask my wings all over again.

The palace painter had been gilding my wings for events since I was old enough to attend them, and he'd invented a handheld device that utilized his affinity for wind to spray the paint across my feathers in a fine mist. It provided better coverage and durability than when I dipped them, but it still smelled awful.

My lungs were screaming as Hollund finished spraying my upper left wing, the feathers closest to my root joint.

I shuddered. That was an especially sensitive spot, and his wind always tickled a little anyway. The paint drenched the robe around my wing panels, slowly seeping down my ribs as Hollund released the trigger on his device and backed away to analyze his work. I exhaled my spent air and raked in some more, grimacing at the metallic odor.

Hollund was a hybrid of Harpie and Fenix. Creamy, smooth skin. Dark red hair. Brown eyes with brilliant gold flecks sparkling in them, his wings golden with dark brown dappling. The air around him wavered, the skin of his face glowing with a colorless light.

Air always shifted around him, but I knew this particular glow was from the charm he'd cast over his appearance.

Harpies were born from wind terrors. *Twisters*. As a result, the seraphim who came from those sacrifices were truly unique. They were often born with a second set of arms and several eyes, as if the Goddess and her ever-present vision was being lovingly laid into the species. It made their faces a bit terrifying to look at, though, so most Harpies wore charms outside their territory.

Hollund was born here a few decades ago, after his Harpie father moved here to marry one of our nobles.

It had to be exhausting for him to always hide his true face. Would I face a similar discomfort in the Halcyon territory, if I were to marry Alezandral?

The thought intruded on my mind, even as I tried with all my might to shove it down. The question lingered as I recalled that empty palace. Would the rest of the country be more of the same? That would be terribly lonely. Lonelier than here. Lonelier than the gnashing forest. Lonelier than Gwaith House, filled with all its smog and sadness.

I miss Erlene.

Her sweet smile and innocent eyes. Her voice. The feel of her small hand tugging on my skirt. She had always been there, and now she wasn't. It felt like I was missing a limb. And if Destin had anything to say about it, I would never see her again.

Another crushing, penetrative thought.

My stomach churned and, with a shake of my head, I pushed away that dark spiral. I focused instead on Hollund as he refilled the paint reservoir with his second right hand.

My father brought him into my room a couple hours ago. I had already been awake, watching the maids filing in and out with clothing and fragrant soaps and oils to prepare me for the engagement party. I didn't bother arguing with any of their choices; I was too exhausted to care. This last week had seemed endless to me, and Alezandral was conveniently called away from the palace the morning after we killed that sutilis in the dungeons. I hadn't seen him since.

My teeth ground together remembering it all. The frosty bastard up and disappeared on me, leaving me to face a dozen of my father's overzealous party planners on my own.

What a waste all this planning would be if I killed the groom, I thought with a smirk.

After the first thousand questions, I told my father's staff to do whatever they wanted with the decorations as long as they didn't bother me again.

The party was being held in the southern courtyard, where several citrus trees and koi ponds were arranged in a garden-like fashion. There were tulle-laden white tables and ribbons tied in the trees showcasing a variety of fiery shades, the emblem of the Fenix stamped everywhere it possibly could be. Father always displayed it proudly.

A special dye had been stirred into the koi ponds and the adjacent fountains to make the water bluer in honor of the Halcyon colors, which I thought was a relatively nice touch on my part. There were benches and a few larger trees on the outskirts of the yard to offer shaded seating, and several footpaths led back to the grand patio and the southern sunrooms that I loved so well.

The southern courtyard was one of my favorite places in the castle, but today, it would become my nightmare.

Royalty and nobility from the adjacent colonies had been invited—the Impundulu to the North and the Stymphalian to the South—and most of our own nobility would be in attendance as well, both the Halcyon and Fenix. I was fairly certain that was the reason Alezandral had disappeared. He was accompanying his father here. Crossing the entire gnashing forest took a while, and he had to do it twice.

I only had to get through this one day with my father.

Afterward, Alezandral and I would leave on our tour of the

seraphic settlements, and at the end of it, the Wight would tell us how to go our separate ways. Then, I would figure out what to do about the sutilus in Ehlark's home. There was no sense in dragging Alezandral into this mess any more than I already had. We got lucky that night. He could have died, and it would have been my fault.

It was my responsibility to make all of this right again… somehow.

Hollund returned to the rose quartz platform I was standing on—the one he always brought along with him. It was easy to move solid stone when one could lift it with wind.

The painter's second set of hands swept through the air to gather wind into his palms, preparing his bronze and silver invention for my second set of wings. I filled my lungs with a fresh breath, but before he could pull the trigger, someone knocked on the door to my room.

We both twisted toward the door as it swung open and Alezandral rushed in.

My betrothed shut the door behind him, locked it, then turned to face us. His eyes locked on my wings and widened slightly, then his gaze flashed to the painter beside me, a small muscle feathering in his jaw. He made it back in time for the party. How considerate of him.

I crossed my arms, glaring as I said, "Usually the purpose of knocking is to allow the person *inside* the room to let you in."

Alezandral crossed the room to me with swift, forceful strides. "You would have shut the door in my face, darling," he replied curtly before turning to Hollund. "Leave us to speak in private."

Hollund's brow furrowed at the same time mine did, his lips parting mutely as he glanced at the door Alezandral had just locked.

"Wait in my quarters," Alezandral ordered, gesturing to the

door on the adjacent wall, the one I had left open, waiting for him to return. "Close the door behind you. I'll fetch you after."

Hollund looked around in confusion, his hands covered in paint.

"After what?" I asked.

"Go!" Alezandral snapped at Hollund, pointing at the door again.

The painter leapt off the platform and huffed quietly to himself as he carried his machine into the other room.

By the time Alezandral twisted to face me, I was seething. "What the fuck is your problem?" I stepped forward, my hands tingling with heat. My voice resounded through the room as I shouted, "You can't just barge in here and demand—"

He pounced on me without warning, slapping a hand over my mouth. His other hand wrapped around the back of my neck, holding me firmly in place against him, and I was so shocked, I froze. I should have bit him or pushed him away, but I didn't do those things.

Because before I could get my bearings, he growled, "Stop yelling, Sia. You can't let him hear you."

I didn't think I had ever seen a version of Alezandral that could be considered "well-rested," but there was a tiredness in his eyes right now that demanded my attention.

Who? I demanded in my head.

Was he talking about his father?

"No," he bit out, answering the question I hadn't intended him to hear. Alezandral slowly dropped his hand from my mouth and explained in a frantic murmur, "Listen to me, because I don't have much time. If we're doing this, then I need you to swear to me we're going to be convincing about it, at least until we know whether we have a way out or not."

I didn't have time to process that before someone started knocking on my bedroom door.

"Fuck," Alezandral grumbled as he glanced over his shoulder. "The ancient relic is faster than I thought he'd be."

My thoughts spun with what he'd said before. *We had to be convincing.* Convincing about what?

"I'm not sure I understand what you're asking for," I admitted quietly.

The knocking came again, more insistent as the temperature dropped around us. Frost grew on the crystal platform beneath my feet, and I knew without asking that Alezandral wasn't the one causing it. This chill didn't feel like him; it was biting and impatient, without the hesitation that so often accompanied Alezandral's touches.

He leaned into me, as close as when he'd had his hand over my mouth, only now, there was nothing between us, and I couldn't stop myself from looking at his lips, at the way he licked them before he started talking.

"You and me," he whispered. "When we're in public, like at this party, this engagement has to seem real. We have to look like we care for each other, like we *want* to be married. And it has to start right now, this very second, for the male on the other side of that door."

If this wasn't his father, then who was it? Who could possibly be so important to him? "Why?"

The doorknob started rattling, fighting the lock.

Alezandral shook his head and took my hands in his. He wasn't wearing his gloves, and his skin was surprisingly warm. "Just trust me in this. *Please.*"

There was a faint crackling sound, and then the door to my room burst open like someone had set off a small explosion in the lock.

A male sauntered in—the ancient relic, as Alezandral called him. Seraphim didn't age as humans did, not noticeably. He had shoulder-length, silvery-blue hair, but that was not uncommon amongst our kind, especially for the Halcyon. His four stark white wings flared stiffly behind him, and his pale face crinkled with a smile as his gaze fell upon us.

Alezandral turned slightly, moving to shield half my body with his wings.

Alright, I told him in my head. *But if I pretend to like you, you can't let it go to your head.*

His right hand reached back to blindly grip mine, and I allowed it. We were playing our parts now. We would be playing them all day. *Technically,* he thought, *doesn't everything about you go straight to my head now, whether you want it to or not?*

I shook my head, biting back a smile.

The stranger strolled across my room, his eyes scanning the furniture and the open terrace, his left hand holding a pocket watch. The behavior might have unsettled me more if Alezandral's presence wasn't still sitting in my head.

The ease with which he invaded my mind scared me a little bit.

It exhilarated me, too.

We were merged so completely. He'd turned into an extension of me. His consciousness leapt forward and caressed mine like a gentle wave, and I felt myself crash over him in return. An ocean with two shores.

I knew this wasn't the best time to discuss my limits, but I would have to address them soon. I was done leaving doors open when it came to my commitments, my promises. I had made a mess with Destin because I let him walk right into my heart like he belonged there. I'd played with him and allowed him to play with me in return, and that had been a mistake. He got the wrong ideas about us, the wrong feelings. When he looked at me, he saw everything he wanted and none of who I really was. Until the end.

Then he saw the truth, and he rightfully despised me for it.

I couldn't let this thing with Alezandral get out of control. This time, I was keeping a tight rein on my horny, traitorous heart.

I'm not going to sleep with you, Alezandral.

There was a soft rumble in my head that I knew must be laughter, and his hand tightened around mine. *Your loss, darling. I would have made you scream.*

It was a joke. Had to be a joke.

In terror, maybe, I sniped back.

The transfer of thoughts was instantaneous. We didn't need to waste time forming the words with our mouths, and there was little chance of misunderstanding each other.

There was another soft rumble through my head as Alezandral replied, *Well, I can't argue with that.*

I physically reeled before I could stop myself, meeting his gaze as he smirked. What the hell did that mean?

Wouldn't you like to know, he purred.

Alezandral pulled away from my mind, shifting his attention to the Halcyon in front of us. The male ambled to a stop in front of my platform and cocked his head, his dark blue eyes sliding forward to meet mine.

"Well?" the stranger chirped. "Aren't you going to introduce us, Alezandral?"

Alezandral's fingers twitched around mine. "Sia, this is my father's right hand, General Abaddon. He currently trains and commands our military."

I didn't miss the nuance in that *currently.*

The general offered him a slimy smile. "You insult me by guarding her like that," he crooned. "Move aside. Let me see our future queen."

Alezandral glared at him down the line of his nose. "You can see plenty."

This would get nowhere quickly. I rolled a smile over my features and ducked under Alezandral's wing to sidle up beside him. My left wing was still shielded by his right. We were tucked extremely close together. I brought my hand up to his chest. His heart raced under my palm, and he was barely breathing. That made my anger toward him soften, feeling the effects of his fear. He needed me, this.

Looking into Abaddon's eyes, I said, "It's lovely to make your acquaintance, General. I didn't expect a visit, or I would have summoned some refreshments for you. Would you like me to call for some now?" *Please, for the love of the Goddess and all her spirits, don't say yes.*

The sneer on Abaddon's face faded under the weight of my hospitality.

Then he smiled. "I'm sorry, my dear. I can see that we've interrupted your primping, so I won't stay long. I only wanted to see you before the party. Make sure you were indeed… *willing.* Festivities can make such introductions harried and insufficient." His gaze traveled over my painted wings. "What a lovely shade of gold you're being dressed with. Under different circumstances, I think it would have fooled even me."

"The paint was her father's decision." Alezandral interjected. He hesitated a moment before adding, "I personally think we should consider making her true origins known soon. *Publicly.*"

My eyes widened, sliding to Alezandral even though his gaze remained trained on Abaddon. "What?"

"I don't think that would be prudent, Alezandral. There's no point in making waves with this alliance, especially if it still might not happen."

I squinted at Abaddon. "And what makes you think it's not going to happen?"

The General's lips twitched. "After all this time apart, you expect me to believe that you two even *remember* each other, much less wish to be joined together forevermore? Weren't you missing only weeks ago, Princess? *Running* from this marriage?"

My feathers bristled. "You have no idea why I have been gone."

"Oh, sure," he replied, nonplussed. "I'm sure you have wonderful excuses, but they won't convince me, and they certainly won't convince our king." His voice and eyes hardened. "Alezandral is the Halcyon's only heir. We need to be sure his marriage will produce strong children, and considering your," his gaze traveled up and down my body, "*uniqueness*, we have no assurance that you even have the ability to bear them naturally."

"Excuse me?" I gasped.

This was about my ability to have children? That was positively primeval. And how did he know anything about my *uniqueness* in the first place?

My father has known the truth about you from the beginning, Alezandral explained in my head, *so Abaddom knows as well. On the day of our heart bond, he saw your flames.*

I swallowed my disappointment. *Great.*

"This would not be such a concern to us," Abaddon continued, "if Alezandral had not opposed the idea of letting you copulate with our Winged Spirit instead."

Dread coiled low in my gut.

Alezandral's father wanted *me* to be a sacrifice?

"That's never going to happen," Alezandral snapped, letting go of my hand to cross his arm over my abdomen, though that did little to shield me with our wings tucked together. "Not to her or anyone else in our territory again."

Abaddon's eyes anchored in mine.

"You see, my dear." I wanted to rip his tongue out for calling me that. He clasped his hands together in front of his stomach, his head tilting. "So just know we're keeping a very close eye on you. If you do *anything* to jeopardize Alezandral or the Halcyon crown, you will face the consequences. We will end this connection of yours by any means necessary."

A growl curled through Alezandral's chest, his arm freezing against my robe. "Tread lightly, Abaddon."

"Or what, child?" He laughed. "What could you possibly do to me that your father wouldn't hear about? That he wouldn't punish you for? Don't forget who you are talking to."

Alezandral's jaw clenched, but he didn't say anything in return. Instead, he reached out to me, mind to mind.

I'm sorry, Sia. Were I able, he'd be dead already.

What happens to seraphim who are sacrificed? I asked.

He didn't answer me. There was now nothing on his end of our connection, as if he was shutting me out. I had to learn how to do that. Though, half of me wanted to learn how to burrow my way into his mind anyway, to find answers, but I knew that wasn't fair.

Didn't he do that to me, though?

"All of this hostility is unneeded, and frankly, unwelcome," I said. "This should be a *happy* day, Alezandral. Try to be agreeable."

His blue eyes flashed to mine.

I turned to our guest. "General Abaddon, I wouldn't dream of hurting my betrothed. You have nothing to worry about."

"I am glad to hear that." Abaddon smiled tightly and reached into his pocket. "I have a gift for you, Princess, from the king. You may consider it an offering of our goodwill."

What a fucking farce.

He presented me with a small blue box, and I knew what would be inside. I didn't reach for it, and neither did Alezandral.

I pursed my lips. "And might I ask why your king didn't give it to me himself?"

"The king is not here, of course. He has no interest in wearisome travel and silly parties. They are beneath him."

The Halcyon king didn't come?

This was his only son's engagement party, and he wasn't here. *Why?*

I was not the only carefully-kept secret, indeed. It seemed the Halcyon had a few of their own, and I was suddenly dying to figure them out. "Ah," I replied cheerily. "So he sends *you* to deal with what is beneath him. Got it."

Abaddon's eyes darkened.

With a grimace, he tossed the ring box at Alezandral, who caught it out of the air with ease. The Halcyon General glanced down at his watch and grunted when he saw the time. Then, he lifted his head to glare into my eyes. "He sends me to safeguard our country's future when he cannot, Princess. And believe me, I take that duty seriously."

CHAPTER 12

Navigating the winding corridors toward the southern wing, I studied my gift.

I didn't like it. Not the ring, and certainly not the way it was given to me. Still, I stared at it, trying to intimidate it the way I would an opponent. That was all I *could* do, really; its entire purpose was to intimidate *me*, and if I destroyed it, Abaddon would know he had succeeded.

The ring didn't sparkle as I walked past the large windows looking out over the city. It was old, its silver band tarnished and the gems dull. A dark blue sapphire was set in the center, the largest I'd ever seen, and it was surrounded by clusters of cloudy diamonds. It might have been pretty at one time, but it was clear this hadn't been designed to last. I would have expected more from a *king*. I expected more from Alezandral, actually, but I also hadn't expected a ring in the first place, considering our arrangement, so I would keep my complaints to myself.

A storm had unexpectedly blown in with the eastern winds, and the sky was snowing in earnest, though the flurry was a mere drizzle within the warm embrace of the island.

There wasn't much to see through the endless curtain of rain, but I knew the streets below must be bustling, *humming* with excitement. The citizens were preparing their own celebrations to honor my engagement.

I wished I was out there instead of here. There would be less pressure to behave. More ale, too.

After Abaddon's visit, Alezandral had opened the box and presented the ring to me before wordlessly retreating to his room and locking the door between us. He didn't even stick around to watch me put it on.

It fit well enough, though it was snug and surprisingly heavy. I knew it had been forged with someone else in mind before I even saw the inscription.

The words *"mine to crown"* were carved into the silver band.

It was, perhaps, the most *un*romantic and *un*original engraving I'd ever seen. Those were the vows made when seraphic kings married their sacrifices. I could only assume this ring belonged to Alezandral's mother.

That would explain the look on Alezandral's face when he opened the box, the dejection and mild irritation, the swiftness with which he left my quarters.

He didn't like talking about her, his Quintessential mother, but that made me infinitely more curious about what happened to her. Maybe it wasn't right of me to want to know, but then, my betrothed and I were long past what was right and wrong. He'd asked me to play a game of pretend, and I couldn't help but think back to the day we first met, when I'd chased him through his palace and called him a silly swan, when I'd shown him just how good I was at pretending.

It was incredibly sad to think about it now, our brief friendship, especially now that I knew Alezandral had been punished for it.

Punished because of me.

His father had tried to burn his scar away, tried to tear it out. My own scar tingled at the reminder. I didn't want to think about what he'd been through beyond a passing acknowledgment. It made me feel too much. And I certainly didn't want to remember what happened after our fathers found us amongst the birch trees. The blood. The screaming. My losing control. That was a memory I would bury over and over again if I had to.

My eyes slid back to the ring.

The Halcyon king had offered his wife up for sacrifice. A fellow seraph. There was no precedent for that, no way of knowing if she would have survived the encounter, so why did she agree to it?

Perhaps the same reason any human would agree, I reasoned.

Honor, comfort, adoration.

Sacrificed queens were treated well, not only because they were pregnant during the majority of their reign, but because they carried the most power anyone in this realm ever saw. For a few short months, they were capable of astonishing magic, more so than even their children carried.

I'd heard the stories—legends, really.

There was so little we understood about what those women were truly capable of, because they were usually dead by the time they learned to wield that magic with any confidence. That was another way in which Alezandral's mother was different, a way in which my mother had been different too. They'd already had magic before the sacrifice, but then, Alezandral's mother had also survived the birth.

Did the magic she gained during pregnancy endure too? Was that what had ultimately killed her?

Magic could overwhelm the strongest of creatures, could be lethal if the body was not strong enough to carry it. I'd seen it claim many in the gnashing forest.

As I neared the main foyer, I heard the clamor of our

guests. I glided toward the doors leading into the receiving hall. I was bound by our little ruse now.

Time to pretend.

As I opened the door to the foyer, the commotion hit me at full force, overlapping voices and bright orbs filling my senses as I left the corridor behind. Nearly taking a bronze wing to the face, I sidestepped out of the way of an Impundulu who was trying to wrangle two young children. They were playing tag, darting around his legs faster than he could catch them and disappearing into the crowd ahead of us. When he twisted to face me, the blood drained from his face, forcing his freckles to stand out all the more.

"Princess Sabrina—ah, Your Highness—my sincerest apologies." He bent at the waist. His crimson eyes scanned me head to toe, and then he looked around at the seraphim to either side of us.

"It's quite alright," I soothed him. "I could see you had your hands full."

"I do," he exhaled, bracing his hands on his hips and smiling. "The storm has made the children restless, I'm afraid."

As I nodded, though, his words hit me. My stomach sank as I realized something that should have occurred to me sooner. *The rain...*

The rain would ruin the paint on my wings.

"Not to worry, though, Your Highness," the Impundulu added quickly, reacting to my worried expression. "I can sense the brunt of it passing already. The weather shouldn't put too much of a damper on your happy day. Besides, it's a bit of good luck, isn't it? Snow. Or rain, rather, in this particular case," he rambled on, and I tried my best to act like I was listening.

I grimaced at the skylight above us.

The drizzle outside had lightened, but not *enough*. Good omen or not, I was feeling pretty screwed.

It was hard enough to keep people from seeing the truth in the sunlight. Father had to be raving mad at me, considering I was already late to the sun rooms by an hour and a half. I sucked in a breath to excuse myself, but before I could utter the words, the crowd parted behind him, revealing the Queens of Impundulu.

They were walking hand in hand, their court and a few of their eldest children trailing behind them.

The male at my side bowed. "Majesties."

"There you are, Zachary. Lost the children again?" The Queen with straight brown hair and deep burgundy eyes was the one to address him, a teasing lilt in her voice.

Zachary—the Impundulu's newest Royal child-keeper, I suddenly realized—turned a bit red in the face. "Not lost, no. Of course not. They're just... getting ahead of me, Your Majesty, for a game. I'm giving them a head start."

Those must have been the Queens' twins he just lost.

The Queens didn't seem to buy Zachary's explanation, but they didn't seem upset with him either, so I could only assume the twins were always this rowdy.

Queen Mizel—the one born into the Royal bloodline—caught sight of me and beamed. "Well, look at our luck, Lanier! We get to be the first to give our congratulations to the bride." Mizel was pretty, with curly brown hair and vermillion red eyes, freckles all over, and a sweet, button nose.

Her wife, Lanier, smiled indulgently and gave me a curt nod. "And our sincerest condolences too, of course."

I knew it was a joke, so I chuckled along, but I felt more like crying..

The children accompanying them peered at me around their bronze wings. The Queens had a hearty dozen. I hadn't met all of them yet—and I was sure it would prove difficult to remember each of them if I had—but I recognized the crown prince as their troop spread out around me. I'd met *him* several years ago. We fooled around in a closet once, a mere month before I met Tova. I met their oldest daughter then too, when she walked in on us.

I grinned at the Queens. "Thank you for coming."

A deafening crack interrupted us, and we turned to face the source. The entire room fell silent as static filled the air, raising hair on several heads. Smoke curled through the open doors into the sun rooms, and I would bet anything that the children's game of tag had just come to a dramatic end.

No one was screaming or crying, though, so chances were, no one had been hurt.

"I'll go fetch them," Zachary squeaked before dashing away.

As the room resumed its frenzy of voices and movement, Queen Lanier grimaced, pulling her arm out of her wife's. "I'm going to help him. Goddess knows he needs it." She kissed Mizel on the cheek and gave me a small nod farewell before disappearing into the crowd.

I'd never admit it out loud, but I admired the Impundulu, if for nothing else but how unconventional their current reign was.

Both Queens carried only two sets of wings. The last spirit-borne in their territory —those heirs born from a mortal woman and Winged Spirit—had been the previous King. His daughter, Mizel, decided not to participate in sacrificial marriage.

She married a noble lady instead, married for love.

That wasn't unheard of. A royal could marry anyone they pleased if they were not already promised to another. However, in those situations, arrangements were often made to ensure powerful heirs. For those territories that desired more spirit-borne, it was recommended that the kings and queens took their human wives first, before marrying a fellow seraph. Then, if that eternal partner could not bear further children, conjugal visits could be arranged with a noble the court approved of. Or, if it was a matter of sexual orientation, there were more experimental means to produce children, medicinal treatments that were growing more successful in recent years.

Rumor was, the Queens tried the medicinal treatments decades ago. When it didn't work for them, they adopted their heir.

They were the first royals to go against the wisdom of their elders and find happiness apart from tradition and the pursuit of power. While I'd overheard all manner of vitriol aimed at them for it, I thought it was a beautiful thing they'd done, a beautiful family they'd created. It was no less a family than my own, of *any* child formed in the womb by the Winged Spirits.

The life the Impundulu Queens had, the love they shared… I envied it.

If I married Alezandral, I would not get a choice in how we built our family. I would be a consort Queen, which wasn't much of anything. Consorts had no authority. They had no voice. Alezandral would never make me his true equal the way the Impundulu Queen had her wife, the way my father had done for my human mother. No. Abaddon made it clear that legitimate heirs would be the sole purpose of our marriage and, if I was being totally honest, a small sore part of me yearned for more—that part of me that would never be satisfied with anything less than a passionate love affair.

Perhaps I wasn't suited for marriage at all.

The confessions of the dead sutilis echoed in my head, each word a bit of shrapnel embedded in my skull. I could turn from it, but the words were still there. If I was truly like them, if that kind of evil was festering inside of me some-where, then I was better off alone.

"Have you just arrived?" I asked Queen Mizel.

"We were here before the Stymphalian." She nodded at a group of metal-winged seraphim huddled close by. "But your father suggested we all remain within palace walls until the darkest storm clouds pass. He said it was tempting disaster with all this metal."

Because of the Impundulu's affinity with lightning.

Her smile remained pleasant, but her eyes flicked to the ceiling briefly—as close to an eye roll as she would allow herself.

"I'll speak with him," I replied with a sigh. "I don't see any reason why you should have to sit on top of each other in here —the yard has been prepared for hours. Except," I fought a smile, "perhaps the children should play inside a little while longer."

Queen Mizel laughed, her red eyes glittering. "That sounds more than fair."

She stepped to the side and beckoned her older children forward. "Speaking of children, I don't believe I've had a chance to introduce you to our future king and his sisters."

Traditionally, I wouldn't get these kinds of introductions until Alezandral and I went on our engagement tour. That was the time for us to become familiar with our allies and them with us. In theory, we ruled alongside the royal families of each settlement, ruled the continent together, and so we were meant to develop friendships with them, or at the very least, mutual respect.

Queen Mizel must have decided she already liked me.

She gestured to her son first. "This is Edmin."

Ah, yes, that was his name. I acknowledged him with a nod. "A pleasure," I muttered.

He bent at the waist ever so briefly, his gaze clashing with mine before it ricocheted away. His eyes landed on the sister clinging to his arm, the one who had walked in on us.

I bit my tongue.

Clearly, our tryst was a secret, and I wouldn't upset anyone by spilling it.

"And these are my two eldest daughters, Tonia and," Queen Mizel waved at the one clinging to Edmin, then her brow furrowed as she craned her neck, searching the crowd behind them, "Korinna, dearest, step away from the puffs and come meet Sabrina."

Edmin and Tonia shuffled to the side, revealing a young female with a mouthful of pastry and a set of scarlet eyes framed by cinnamon curls.

I recognized her instantly.

Korinna… but she'd told me her name was Kori when we met.

It was the Impundulu from the city—the one the sutilis had charmed into doing their bidding. Terror curled in the pit of my stomach. If the sutilus could take a royal from the highest-guarded mountain pass on this side of the continent, then they could take *anyone.* There was no way to reach that pass without flying in.

Did that mean some of the sutilus… had wings?

They'd tried to take Alezandral's cousin's wings on the beach. Perhaps that hadn't been the first time they targeted one of us for that purpose. And if they *could* fly, what was stopping them from reaching us here, on my father's island?

Nothing.

Tonia swept forward to grasp my forearm and curtsied. I barely felt my legs as I mirrored the gesture. Then, Queen Miza nudged Kori forward.

Kori's strides were stiff as she struggled to swallow the food in her mouth.

I extended my hand and wasn't surprised when she hesitated to take it. Her mother's eyes flicked between the two of us, confusion etched into her brow. "Korinna? What's wrong?"

Kori didn't blink. She just stood there, petrified, and I

knew our last encounter was to blame. *Get away from me. What have you done to me?* There was no sign of that mania in her mind now, but I saw the memory of it in her eyes. When she drank my blood.

What had she seen that day? Had she seen the monster inside of me?

I grimaced, dropping my outstretched hand and turning to the Queen. "Kori and I…" The rest of that sentence lodged in my throat as I felt a hand grip my arm.

Kori's entire body trembled as she curtsied, and before I could react, she released my arm and fell back a step. "What a lovely dress you're wearing. Is that organza silk?" Her voice was breathless, high-pitched and lined with forced enthusiasm.

My hands flew to my hips, clutching fistfuls of the gruesome orange fabric. I hadn't thought it was lovely at all. "Oh, uh. I don't know. It might be?"

"It is, I think," she said.

I rolled my dry tongue against the roof of my mouth. She was keeping our meeting a secret too, it would seem. "That's… nice," I murmured, clasping my hands in front of my stomach as I returned my gaze to her mother.

Queen Mizel huffed a laugh, shifting on her feet as she watched the two of us try not to stare at each other. "Korinna has an interest in clothing, you see," she offered in explanation, "so she has a keen eye for fabrics."

As she said that, her eyes lit up with an idea.

She reached forward to take both my hands in hers. "You know, if you haven't set your heart on any particular wedding gown, you should consider letting my Korinna design one for you. She has a stack of sketches at home that would look *beautiful* on you. You have the perfect figure for them, blessed be."

Kori cleared her throat. "I'm sure she already has a dress, Mum. Leave her alone."

"Oh, I have no idea what I'm going to wear for the wedding, actually," I interjected. "Haven't given it a thought."

Kori looked at me again, some of the fear fading from her eyes. "You haven't?" Her brow pinched, a mirror of her mother's shock, and I realized that any eager bride would have at least *thought* about the dress by now.

I scrambled for a reply. "I mean, the wedding is still a few weeks away."

Kori scoffed. "What kind of wedding dress do you plan on having made *here* within a matter of a couple weeks? A burlap sack?"

My eyes widened in surprise, but a smile teased the corners of my mouth. I liked her.

"*Kori,*" Queen Mizel scolded her.

"No, it's alright," I said quickly. "Truth be told, I completely forgot about the wedding dress until you brought it up. I wouldn't mind a little help with it, if Kori has the time." I looked at Kori, trying to convey that she could decline if she wished to.

Queen Mizel clapped her hands, bouncing in place as she said, "Splendid! Kori would *love* to help. She's been dying to get out of the mountains a bit more."

I felt my eyebrows raise.

Queen Mizel obviously had no idea that her daughter was charmed by a sutilis, and now everything about this little interaction made perfect sense.

I smiled at Kori. "Well, I'm coming to your city in a couple days for the tour. How about we look through your sketches then?"

Her lips parted in surprise, but she said nothing.

A large hand slid into place on my lower back, and I immediately bristled, but Alezandral's voice poured over me in the next breath, soothing my nerves. "What are we talking about over here, ladies?"

"Dresses," I said. "Did you have something to contribute to the conversation?"

I craned my neck and found Alezandral smirking down at me, his face inches from mine. His musky pine scent filled my nostrils. My wing was tucked under his, but I didn't dare pull away and give away how angry I was with him.

He took my hand and pressed a kiss to the back of my palm.

"Only that you would look beautiful in anything," he murmured. His eyes flashed to Kori. "Even a burlap sack."

Kori grew impossibly paler, but Alezandral only chuckled and turned to Queen Mizel.

"I'm afraid I have to steal my bride away from you. She's needed elsewhere."

Queen Mizel inclined her head. "Until we meet again."

Alezandral bowed and I curtsied, and then he was tugging me away, cutting a path to the sun rooms. We passed Queen Lanier and her teary-eyed twins in the crowd, Zachary trailing close behind them with a broken tiara clutched in his hands.

The doors to the sun room were closed and guarded by sentinels, but the moment the guards saw Alezandral and I coming, they opened them and ushered us through.

The sounds of rain enveloped us as we walked inside.

To the right, I saw the casualty we'd heard earlier: lightning had struck the ceiling, and there was now a hole that wept profusely from the storm. This particular sun room was vacant. It was more of a hallway than a room, really, with doors on the other end that led into the larger botany rooms.

The door shut behind us, sealing us in privacy, and I spun to a stop. I pulled my hand out of Alezandral's. "She's *royalty*."

Alezandral sighed. "I know."

"You *know*? How long have you known that?"

He shrugged and crossed his arms. "Since I got a good look at her face down in the city."

"And you said nothing?"

"I didn't need to."

I gaped at him. "Okay, we really need to work on your communication."

Alezandral piqued an eyebrow, then dropped his hands to his hips in that dominant way males so often do. "The minute *you* start being forthcoming, Sabrina, I'll do the same."

"You wiggle your way into my head all the time."

He rolled his eyes, which made me want to smack him. "You think I *try* to hear your thoughts all the time, Sia? I really don't. I would much rather have a real conversation with you, but you keep everything locked up in your head. I'm starting to doubt you've ever spoken your true feelings out loud."

I pursed my lips, and when I couldn't find the words to argue with him, I crossed my arms.

He was right, of course. My head was such a loud place, I sometimes forgot that I was the only one inside it. Instead of denying the truth, I shrugged and said some of the loudest thoughts I'd ever had. "What's the use in saying what I feel if no one cares to listen? Talking won't change anything. It doesn't change me or you or the bond between us. It won't bring back the people we've lost. Words are *nothing*."

His eyes softened, and I hated him for that. It felt too much like pity.

But then he said, "That's not true and you know it. Words *bind* us. You and me to each other, us to the universe. Maybe you should take a chance on me one of these days. You'd be surprised by how much I care."

Did he? Care?

And what did it matter if he did?

We'd already established that we weren't going to do this. This engagement wasn't real. It couldn't be.

Yet, I couldn't deny the squeeze in my heart as he studied me. It was such a small thing to ask for—my thoughts. It felt like the most intimate request in the world. I looked away from him. "I'm assuming my father sent you to fetch me."

Alezandral walked past me, heading for the door at the end of the hallway. "Your father is angry and impatient and wearing on my last Goddess-damned nerve, but no, I wasn't sent by anyone. I came looking for you myself. I think it's time we got this party started."

Glancing up at the rain-streaked glass, I muttered, "I think that'll be difficult, considering this storm."

I followed Alezandral to the door straight ahead.

When we reached it, Alezandral wrapped his hand around the knob and smirked over his shoulder at me. "Don't worry about the storm, darling. I'm the one who summoned it."

CHAPTER 13

Alezandral was exceedingly proud of himself for the storm. He walked into the sun room where my father waited with a grin that would put shame to the sun. That smile fell a moment later, when he saw my father had enlisted the help of a witch to conjure floating umbrellas for the guests, and an *extra* large one for me.

My chest tightened when I saw the witch at our disposal.

Peppi.

She was scowling at the lot of us.

I had told Kahem her name, and it seemed he had passed it along to our father, who was now exploiting her after I informed him of my newfound agreement with Alezandral.

Soldiers had been sent down to the human city. I also sent Destin a letter explaining our plan, but I hadn't received a response. I doubted I ever would. The ease with which our seraphim were able to enter the city told me he'd received my correspondence, though, and that our bribery had worked on the Houses.

Father would summon Peppi every chance he could just to spite me, to teach me a lesson about staying in my place.

"I can't even begin to tell you how sorry I am about this," I whispered to her.

She rolled her eyes and grabbed my arm, shoving the orange gossamer fabric up to draw a rune on my skin with charcoal. "Apologies won't send me back to my shop," she mumbled. Her touch was gentle despite her irritation, and that only made me feel worse.

This was why witches didn't share their names. They could be summoned with it, to anywhere, and they could be implored upon to share a bit of the world's magic.

It was the world's magic that made a summoning possible, that same magic which pumped through their veins, which chose their wielders based on the condition of their hearts and the strength of their minds. That magic *wanted* to be shared, but, as my father confirmed today, it could be used for selfish means if placed in the wrong hands, and I had been the irresponsible fool to drop it.

"I'll make sure you're well compensated for your time, I swear it."

She drew the largest umbrella toward her, white magic glimmering like a string from the umbrella to her fingertips. After marking the umbrella with the same rune on my skin, she released it. It snapped into place above me, wide enough to protect the length of my wings if I kept them tucked in tight. "Your father has already paid me," she murmured. "I don't want your gold. I want to be forgotten. I've helped you enough for a lifetime, of that even my magic agrees."

I could feel the truth of that in the magic wrapped around my forearm, in the rune. It didn't cause me *pain* exactly, but its presence was uncomfortable. "I will ensure he never calls for you again, Peppi. *I promise.*"

Whatever the cost.

I knew Father was sure to ask for something wholly

absurd in return, but Peppi's magic seemed to settle a little at my promise. She waved me away without another word.

Guests were brought into the sun room, and I was ushered outside with Alezandral. He'd rejected his umbrella. Instead, he walked beside me, half of him under my shelter and the other half being sprinkled with rain. The storm had ebbed significantly, and now the dark clouds above us were simply a side effect of his soured mood.

"Did you really think the storm would make my father call off the party?" I asked as we approached the red dais. We'd be the center of attention for a while as everyone filed in and offered us congratulations.

Alezandral scoffed. "That wasn't my intention."

"What was your intention, then?"

He ducked out from under the umbrella and vaulted onto the dais, turning back to offer me a hand up. Icy rain pebbled over my skin as I placed my palm in his. He was wearing his gloves again, the black leather slick and smooth against my palm. I really should remember to ask him about that at some point.

Why did he wear them so often?

"I was trying to prove a point," he said as he hauled me up next to him, pulling me close enough that we were nose-to-nose under the umbrella. "That this ruse of yours is unsustainable. The painted wings. These clothes you hate. You have never been under this kind of scrutiny before, Sia, and by so many at once. This party is only the beginning. Sooner or later, the truth will get out, and it's better for all of us if we're in control of the timing."

He'd been thinking about this for a long time, I could tell, and the bunching of his brow told me exactly how worried he was about it.

I knew he was right. If the settlements learned the truth about me during our tour, it would reflect badly on the both of us. Our families. Our countries. And I knew things would be bad enough for my family once everyone found out this engagement was a sham.

"I'm not disagreeing with you," I said carefully, "but I don't know how we could possibly go about this. It is not as easy as announcing it. My father will intervene the instant we try. Your father's Hand too."

Alezandral pressed his lips together, his lapis lazuli eyes swirling.

I wanted to reach for his mind, but I kept a tight rein on that impulse. If he wasn't actively trying to read my thoughts, I wouldn't dig for his. It was tempting, though. It suddenly felt like an untouched, unshaped skill, and a piece of me so badly wanted to learn how to wield it.

I wanted to be able to read him.

Voices echoed toward us as the guests poured into the courtyard.

I turned to smile at the Stymphalian royals headed our direction, ignoring the fact that Alezandral was still staring at me like I was a puzzle to be solved.

"I'll think of something," he said eventually, loosening his hold on my waist just enough to face forward.

The Stymphalian royals approached the dais, the king with his six iron wings and the queen with her four. Every inch of them gleamed in the dour light. The queen wore a form-fitting chainmail dress that complemented her russet brown skin perfectly. Dozens of delicate silver strands glittered through her plum-purple hair. The king wore a tunic the same shade of silvery-white, his shoulders cuffed in some dark metal that matched his trousers. His bright gray eyes were trained on Alezandral as they came to a stop in front of the dais.

"It is good to see you again, and so soon at that, Prince," the Stymphalian King said, smiling with warmth.

I didn't see any children behind them, so they must have left theirs at home. The King had taken a few sacrificial wives over the course of his reign, before he met his current wife and crowned her. He was also one of the oldest royals currently ruling, cresting his thousandth year.

That was how the Stymphalian had always ruled. While many of our kings and queens chose to relinquish their titles as soon their children were old enough to handle the task, the Stymphalian preferred longer reigns, with abdication only when the heir was of a significant age.

Old, wise rulers were what they liked.

I had visited their land a handful of times, and I still remembered the grassy cliffs and valleys they settled on. The intimate townships. The iron torches that flickered in the streets at all hours of the night, beckoning passersby into the guilds that sat on every corner.

These seraphim who carried such sharp wings on their back, whose hands created the most formidable weapons known to our kind…they lived softly.

Alezandral leaned into me, seeming to sense that I was lost to my thoughts. "It's good to see you too, Vilhelm."

I peered up at Alezandral from the corner of my eye. Had he just addressed the Stymphalian King by his first name? Very informal of him.

"I'm thankful it's under better circumstances this time," he added solemnly.

King Vilhelm grimaced. "Indeed."

I looked between the two of them. "You've seen each other recently?"

The Stymphalian King nodded, clearing his throat. "Yes, Princess. Unfortunately, we've been experiencing the loss of a great many elders recently—they're disappearing from our capital at night. Alezandral stumbled upon the body of one a few weeks ago and brought it home to us."

It suddenly dawned on me that we were talking about the Stymphalian I'd discovered in the human city. The one that had been murdered near the docks.

I'd completely forgotten about them.

Alezandral had taken care of them, taken them home. My chest felt like it was going to cave in as I scrambled for a response. "My—I am," I fought to get control of my trembling voice, "*so* sorry, Your Majesties. If you need anything—truly, anything at all—know that I will do everything in my power to help."

King Vilhelm exchanged a sharp look with his wife, and she took his hand.

"Your betrothed said the same thing when we last saw him, Princess, and I will admit, we were hesitant to ask for assistance. However, our situation has become... quite dire. May we speak more about this during your tour?"

Alezandral and I nodded.

"Excellent," King Vilhelm said. "And, of course, you have our hearty congratulations on your engagement. May you find joy in this promise and true contentment in your marriage."

With a small bow, he and his queen turned to leave.

A rowdy line was forming behind them already. The metal-winged seraphim—their court and relatives, no more than probably a dozen in total—were eagerly waiting for their turn to speak with us... and already, I wanted to fold in on myself and disappear.

No one should have to meet this many people in one day.

The Stymphalian Queen broke away from her husband and returned to my side of the dais. "I'd like to introduce myself to you now instead of later, Princess Sabrina. If I may?" She gestured to the edge of the platform in front of her.

"Oh, of course."

I knelt to bring myself level with her and took the hand she extended to me.

"My name is Marketa," she said, her delicate hand squeezing mine.

"It's a pleasure to meet you, Queen Marketa."

Her brow furrowed, and a small smirk quirked her mauve lips. "Please, just call me Marketa. Or Mark, for short. Us consorts grow quite familiar with each other at court functions."

I acknowledged her request with a shallow nod, and she drew even closer, leaning in to whisper, "I just want you to know that I am beyond honored to be witness to this match." Her eyes flicked to Alezandral briefly and then returned to me, something I couldn't quite read swirling in her silver eyes. "You two will accomplish great things together, my heart is sure of it."

I forced a smile, even as her words fell like stones in the pit of my stomach. "Thank you."

Marketa curtsied, then returned to her husband.

Alezandral's hair was dripping now, damp and sandy brown, by the time I settled back into place beside him. Alezandral slid his hand over my lower back and took up the next introductions, but I was too busy thinking of the Stymphalian, of what they'd just admitted to us.

Their elders were going missing, and I could guess what was behind it.

I hoped I was wrong.

Peering over at Alezandral, I felt that path between our minds open. It was as if he'd opened the door for me and was patiently waiting on the other side.

Do you think we'll be able to help them? I wondered.

There was a long pause as Alezandral said farewell to the seraph in front of us, and then he replied, *We'll find a way. There will be additional security tagging along with us for the tour, so that's a start. My father may be open to an exchange of some sort; perhaps he will station some of our military there if they agree to provide us with more advanced weaponry. I'll just have to make sure whatever agreement we come to is in no way dependent on our marriage. Let me think on it.*

His hand remained on my lower back through the rest of the congratulatory train, his thumb brushing against my spine almost absentmindedly.

After the Stymphalian, we greeted the Impundulu Queens again and their rambunctious pack of children, then the handful of Halcyon nobles Alezandral's father had sent in his stead. The Fenix came at the end of the line as the host territory, and the stream of golden wings seemed never-ending.

Alezandral started glancing at some point beyond the line. He shifted impatiently, from one foot to the other. His behavior stirred my curiosity, and when I followed his gaze, I saw that not all the Halcyon had been in line after all.

There were two unfamiliar faces watching us from the other side of the courtyard, where refreshments had been set out under a few stationary umbrellas. They ducked their heads when they saw I'd spotted them. One was a female, wearing a pale blue gown and carrying four silver-speckled, white wings. The other was a male in uniform leathers with olive-toned skin and a single set of dark gray wings—not a noble. How interesting.

I reached blindly for my connection to Alezandral, grasping at the sheer veil that rippled between our minds.

Are they yours? I asked.

The next Fenix stepped forward, and Alezandral loudly greeted them. But into my mind, he said, *They are my dearest friends, and they're eager to meet you, but I told them to wait until we approached them. I didn't want to overwhelm you.*

I fought a frown. *What does that mean?*

Alezandral shifted on his feet. *They will have... expectations.*

Expectations that the rest of this party won't have. For now, they believe the same as everyone else, that our engagement is real.

I prickled internally. *And you think I'm going to disappoint them?*

Alezandral's eyes slashed to mine. "No," he said out loud. The Fenix before us stopped talking, her brow creasing in confusion. Alezandral throat bobbed before he said, "My apologies, Madame. We have to move on now. I'm sure you understand."

She strode away in a huff, and the line moved forward.

My head fell eerily silent for a moment, and then Alezandral responded with, *I'm worried I will be the one to disappoint them. They will quickly fall in love with you, Sia, and when you leave, they will blame me for it.*

My heart rammed against the base of my throat.

I wanted to say something, anything to make him feel better because, when it came right down to it, it *wasn't* his fault. It was mine.

We aren't getting married, but that doesn't mean we can't remain friends, I offered.

He chuckled under his breath. *Is that what we are?*

I thought we were getting there.

You have a strange way of talking to your friends.

My eyes flicked up to the cloudy sky. *I didn't say we were* there *yet. And besides, I don't have much experience in the realm of platonic relationships. I usually end up fucking them, one way or the other.*

There was a long silence, but when I glanced at him, I could see that he was trying hard not to laugh out loud.

That wasn't a joke, I told him.

Oh, no, I know. I'm just curious what this "other" way of yours is. I'm certain I can guess at the first.

A memory surfaced against my will, of when I'd plunged that dagger into Brimley's stomach. It was pitiful that I had ever considered him a friend. I had been drifting down there, in Gwaith House and in the gnashing forest. I'd been isolated, feared, often hated.

Honestly, it was a miracle I hadn't lost my mind.

My stomach churned, and I shoved the memory away before it made me vomit all over the dais.

Alezandral went still, every trace of his humor fading.

This connection between us was a sword, a defense as well as a weapon. It would swing the wrong way sometimes and hurt us as easily as it drew us together, and I'd be a fool to think that anyone would want to be my friend after seeing my darkest thoughts.

I was a fool.

We reached the end of the line, and I didn't even realize it until my father stepped forward and cleared his throat. He was wearing a red tunic the shade of blood. Spiro flew close by in the same military suit he always wore, watching, considering.

Father nodded. "Well done, you two. Now, go have a little fun." His eyes slid to me. "But not too much."

"Thank fuck," I mumbled as I crossed the dais.

I needed a dozen or so glasses of fizzy wine to make the rest of this party bearable. If I was quick about it, I could be drunkenly raiding the food table in a handful of minutes.

Someone grabbed my wrist.

Alezandral turned me around, drawing me towards him. His eyes were wholly sincere as he said into my mind, *You are still good to me, Sia.*

I couldn't breathe.

Why would he say that after what he'd seen, what I'd done? How could he mean it? My heart thundered as I pulled my hand out of his. *Then you have a really shitty sense of character,* I retorted, walking away.

CHAPTER 14

My tongue was on fire, but I didn't mind. This was my favorite way to burn—with the taste of chili filling my mouth, wine in my belly, and the cream of a spiced pastry soothing my taste buds just enough to lean in for another bite.

Nobody talks to you when you're eating. It isn't polite.

I was working those good manners to my advantage as I perched on the edge of the food table, a plate of appetizers on my lap and my sixth glass of fizzy wine bubbling in my hand. All I was missing was music. That was the best part about attending these events, in my opinion. That and the dancing.

Father had sent the orchestra I hired—the one thing I'd actually taken pleasure in planning for today—away from the courtyard because of the storm.

So I was brooding a bit.

Alezandral charmed our guests well enough for the both of us. He maneuvered the crowd with endless laughter and a poise that I could only achieve in my dreariest of dreams. He was *vibrant*.

For someone who seemed to feel so much disdain for my father's deceit, he was very good at pretending. Pretending to be happy. Pretending to be in love. Every time he looked at me, I felt the entire party look along with him.

I was careful not to let myself scowl in return. The chewing helped.

My brother appeared up ahead, striding purposefully out of the crowd with his golden eyes trained on me. He was dressed as casually as tradition allowed. A red jacket and cream tunic folded open at the collar. His neck and ears were dripping with gold. A gilded crown sat on his head.

I caught a glimpse of the female following him, then—the noble daughter he'd been dodging at court festivities for years now. She was very persistent. And Father approved of her a little too much, which only made Kahem *more* uncomfortable around her.

"Save me," he pleaded as soon as I was within hearing distance. He glanced over his shoulder and cursed when he saw she was following him over to the table.

He bounced on the balls of his feet, nervous energy emanating from his skin.

I scoffed, idly picking at a pastry. "Why should I, *traitor?*"

I was still pissed at him, though my ire was significantly less after witnessing his guilt at that breakfast with Father.

Kahem ate up the last few steps between us, seizing my hand and forcing me to look at him. "*Please*, Sia. She's relentless." He pouted, his eyes round and lower lip large.

I resented that he thought that would persuade me. Because it did.

Wrenching my hand out of his, I removed the plate from my lap and slid off the edge of the table. "Fine," I sighed, "but you owe me."

"Whatever you want."

I hooked my arm in his. "Perfect." I tugged him toward the opposite end of the table.

The noble girl following him slowed, but she didn't stop. I hadn't expected her to be deterred by my presence, and that was why I was dragging Kahem toward a cluster of Impundulu speaking amongst themselves.

"Princess Kori!" I shouted, waving at her.

Kori met my gaze immediately. I was certain she hadn't lost sight of me from the moment she entered the courtyard. She'd been carefully avoiding me.

"Come here," I called to her. "I want to introduce you to my brother."

Kori looked at her mothers, and they encouraged her with warm grins and a cursory wave at us, then the princess strolled toward us with a strained smile.

Kahem elbowed me in the ribs. "What are you *doing?*" he seethed.

I shushed him, nodding at the noble girl who had finally staggered to the stop a few yards away. She frowned at us when she spotted Kori. Finally, she turned away. Kahem sighed in relief as I dragged him forward, meeting Kori in front of the nearest garden trail.

"Your Highnesses," Kori muttered, curtsying.

I pulled my arm out of Kahem's and gestured between the two of them. "Kori, this is my brother, Kahem. Kahem, this is my new friend, Princess Kori of the Impundulu territory."

Their gazes met, and locked. The atmosphere seemed to electrify, raising the hair on the nape of my neck. And there was something about the way they stared at each other.

Did they know each other somehow?

My brother offered her his hand. "Yes, I believe I've seen you around the palace on my recent visit to your territory."

"I do believe you're right," she said, pinching his hand with her fingertips the way someone might hold a used hand-kerchief.

I felt my eyebrows shoot skyward.

My brother chuckled. "Lovely to see you again."

"Likewise." But it didn't sound like Kori thought it was lovely, not even a little.

My brother folded his hands behind his back and turned to me with an arrogant smile. "Did I hear you say you've actually made *friends* with this girl?" He glanced at Kori sidelong. "How'd she rope you into that, gorgeous?"

Her eyes narrowed.

I cleared my throat, attempting to break the tension. "Yes, our first meeting was quite the act of fate. I think we're destined to be very close."

Kori's gaze slashed to me, her face paling.

My brother's smile grew, and he tilted his head toward me without taking his eyes off Kori. "Oh? Is that so?"

I opened my mouth to lie, but Kori surged forward and placed a trembling hand on Kahem's arm, her eyes large and desperate. "I'm anxious to take a walk through the groves now that the storm has passed," she announced breathlessly. "Would you like to join me, Prince Kahem?"

Eager was an understatement.

Kahem's smile fell. Something like disappointment crossed his face, and he gently removed her hand from his tunic. "No."

Then, he turned to me and whispered not all that quietly, "You were supposed to help me evade father's matchmaking schemes, not trap me with one of your own instead."

Kori's brow furrowed.

She had no idea that "taking a walk through the groves" was code for far more lecherous activities, especially where my brother was involved. I knew that hadn't been her inten-tion. She'd simply said the first thing she could think of, trying to end this conversation before I spilled her little secret. She thought I was going to tell him about how we met.

My brother didn't know this, and he was self-centered enough to jump to conclusions.

I rolled my eyes. "*Please.* She would have to actually be *interested* in you for this to be a scheme, Kahem." I twisted to address her. "Kori, do you want to marry my brother?"

Her head rocked back, her nose wrinkling in disgust. "What? No!"

My brother blinked, looking a little bit offended.

"You see," I said cheekily. "The only reason she asked to take a stroll with *you* was because she wanted to get away from *me.*"

His offense faded. "Why? What did you do to her?"

It stung a little, I had to admit. Even my brother thought the worst of me.

I swallowed the pain. "That's precisely what I plan on finding out. Now, say thank you and flutter away. Oh, and as for the favor I'm owed—you need to get Father to agree to never summon that witch again. Peppi is off limits."

Kahem gave me an incredulous look. "That's not going to be easy to accomplish, Sia."

"Does it look like I care?" I deadpanned. "You already agreed to a favor of my choosing, and that is what I want." *What I need.*

He growled in frustration, scrubbing a hand over his face. "You're the worst."

"I know." I grinned at him.

As he disappeared into the crowd, I caught Kori trying to sneak away. "Where are you going?"

She froze, her wings ruffling as she slowly twisted back around. "You must be eager to speak with the rest of your guests, Your Highness," she offered.

"Not at all. Come, *I'll* show you the groves."

I beckoned her toward the trail and, after casting a longing look at the party over her shoulder, Kori followed me.

The garden trails snaked all over the courtyard, but this particular path had direct access to the citrus groves south of the palace. It wasn't a long walk. Taking the trail with Kori certainly made it feel long, though. She stared intently on the path in front of her feet, her steps jilted as she struggled to walk in line with me. I could tell she wanted to run, to get far away from me, and it was taking all her willpower not to. She was frightened of me.

"Kori?"

She flinched at the sound of my voice but lifted her face to meet my gaze. "Yes, Your Highness?"

Again, she forced herself to smile, but it looked downright *painful* for her, like she was biting down on razor blades and rock salt. So I got right to the point.

"I'm sorry for what happened in the witch's shop," I said, keeping my voice soft. "I didn't mean to hurt you."

I managed one step toward her before she shook her head, backing up until she collided with a citrus tree. Blood bloomed in her cheeks—she was either embarrassed or angry or both.

"Please don't be afraid of me," I whispered. "This is uncharted territory for me too. I've never—no Impundulu has ever...with me. I didn't *know*—" I failed to find the right words.

"You didn't hurt me," she said softly.

My heart skipped a beat. "I frightened you, though," I countered. "A lot, from the looks of it."

She took a deep breath and nodded. "Yes."

Another short silence stretched between us as we stood there, awkwardly watching each other. I cleared my throat. "If I had known, I wouldn't have given you my blood," I told her. "My error was in ignorance, I swear, but I am deeply sorry for whatever you suffered as a result."

"I-I figured it might have been a mistake," she murmured, "once I came to my senses."

My throat tightened. "Did it take long for you to recover?"

"Just a day or so, the length of time it took for your blood to absorb into mine. I stopped… seeing things then."

I remembered that. She had screamed at me to go away, for *them* to go away. What had she seen?

"I have to know what you saw," I said gently.

She shook her head, her breath coming faster again. "No."

I took a small step toward her, and Kori burst into motion, slipping between the trees and bee-lining for the party.

"Wait—" I called after her, trying to follow her along the path, unable to catch up to her because of the large umbrella above me. It brushed against the wet leaves, and droplets of water flew at me. I knew I couldn't inch any closer, or I would risk my wings bleeding gold. As I jogged beside her, the draping collar of my dress got caught on a branch and stopped me, the iridescent material ripping away from my shoulder. "Shit."

With a snarl, I ripped the material from the branch's grasp. There was no way I would catch up to Kori now, so I gave up and tugged on the limp piece of fabric hanging off my arm.

"*Stupid. Fucking. Dress,*" I seethed. "As if you weren't already the ugliest fucking thing I've ever laid eyes on." Insulting the dress made me feel better, even if it didn't fix anything.

"What is even the *purpose* of this?" I smacked a stiff loop of fabric bulging from my hip.

I was inches from burning the entire thing to ash and returning to the party naked. I'd look better that way, I was certain of it.

Footsteps sounded up ahead on the path, and I looked up to find that Kori had turned around, watching me curiously, her eyes scouring the tear in my gown.

I sighed and offered a small, helpless shrug. "I hate this dress," I admitted.

"Yes, I can see that." Her fingers were rubbing together at her sides. Then, as if she'd finally resolved something in her head, she strode up to me, reaching down to fiddle with the layers of her own gown. As Kori ambled to a stop, she withdrew a small needle and silver thread from her skirt.

She saw the question on my face and explained, "Us females should always be equipped for repairs. May I?"

I acquiesced with a curt nod.

Kori stepped closer, her eyes training on the material. She seemed steadier now that she had a task. Her fingers didn't tremble, her breathing didn't catch. It was sweet of her to turn back and help me, all things considered, so I didn't stare at her as she fixed my dress. I didn't demand answers.

After a minute of silence, she cleared her throat.

The moment our eyes met, I saw that something had shifted. Her eyes flicked back to the dress as she whispered, "I saw the dead, back in the witch's shop."

My skin prickled.

"After I drank your blood, I saw them standing in the room all around us, screaming at us," she added. "They were begging for help, and once they realized I could see them, they crowded me. They tried to grab at me, *touch* me, and it was like your blood made it so I could nearly feel them."

Kori shuddered at the memory. "It was horrible, and I'm frightened to talk about it, to even think about it, because what if they're still around? What if they hear me talking about them and they continue to touch me, but I just can't see them do it now? That feels worse, somehow." She finished repairing the tear and nimbly tied it off.

I examined her stitches. I couldn't tell that a tear had ever been there.

"Were they human spirits?" I dared to ask.

She frowned, occupying herself with pinning the needle back within the folds of her dress. "Most were human, yes."

Then she crossed her arms over her stomach and lifted her chin, her red eyes anchoring in mine. "But I saw other creatures there too. Wolves and elves and... *faceless* things. Creatures I've never seen before. Creatures I don't even think exist in our world. I think I..." The princess hesitated, her face pinching as she confessed, "I think I saw into The Veil."

CHAPTER 15

"You paint your wings," Kori pointed out.

We were nearing the end of the garden trail. I led us onto a perpendicular path, extending our walk for another couple minutes so I could answer without anyone at the party eavesdropping. We strolled shoulder to shoulder, but Kori seemed more at ease with my proximity now that she'd told me what my blood did to her.

"My father." That was the most succinct explanation I was capable of.

Luckily, that was enough for Kori. She nodded slowly, then her eyes scanned me from head to toe as she started chewing on her lower lip. "You would look beautiful in purple, I think. A deep, rich amethyst. You know… if you ever decide to put the Fenix colors behind you. Maybe for your wedding gown?"

I knew what she was really asking: whether I had any intention of showing the world my true colors. I didn't know yet.

Alezandral wanted me to, but I didn't know what that would mean, what my life would look like once everyone knew the truth. I was unprepared, and scared. Her comment about my family's colors startled me because she was right. If the truth was to come out, it would be well within my rights to break away from Fenix traditions. I could create my own.

Amethyst… I liked that idea.

For a brief moment, I actually considered it. My mind raced with all the benefits my coming out would offer me, the freedoms, so long as the colonies were willing to draw up a new treaty to include me. They would do that, wouldn't they?

Maybe not.

It didn't matter, I reminded myself—because once I found a way to separate from Alezandral, I would be leaving the settlements altogether. I'd become one of the exiles traveling from town to town, or maybe I'd establish a more permanent home for myself on the coast or in a mountain range near here, somewhere I could keep an eye on Erlene from a healthy distance.

Kori couldn't know those plans, so I simply said, "It would be worlds better than orange and red, that's for certain."

The path we were walking opened up to the party again, and this time, we emerged from it. Above us, the clouds were breaking apart, and the sun shone in thin rays across the party, reflecting off the scattered wine glasses and the wet brick under everyone's feet. To our right, a photographer was setting up his camera, fiddling with the light bulb as koi ponds bubbled in the background.

Photographs were all the rage for events like this—and in fact, many of the pictures found their way down to the human lands, sold off like precious artifacts to newspapers that entertained curious mortals.

I could just imagine that human woman I'd seduced down in the smog reading about my engagement in a few days' time.

To our left, the party was alive and well.

I smiled when I saw that a few string musicians had

returned to the palace with their instruments now that it wasn't raining anymore. They played a plucky, energetic melody, and my body started to relax as I scanned the crowd.

I spotted Alezandral not too far away.

He was steeped in conversation with the Halcyon who'd been watching us earlier, all three of them standing close together. The female was very pretty, with silvery-blonde hair and bright blue eyes. She looked familiar to me, but I couldn't quite place the reason.

"What are you looking at?" Kori muttered.

I tore my gaze away to find Kori staring at me expectantly, waiting with her arms crossed over her chest.

"Sorry—I just..." I trailed off, looking again in my betrothed's direction. I took a deep breath and asked, "Do you know the female standing next to Prince Alezandral?"

She smiled. "Why? Feeling some kind of way about her?"

I scoffed, shaking my head. "No. He just... He didn't want me to meet her right away, and I'd like to know who it is."

"That's his cousin, Lana. Not only is she family, but she's also a member of his silent court. You'll be spending plenty of time with her soon enough."

Silent courts were council members waiting to rise to the throne along with the crown royal. The crown royal often built their court from a pool of previous court members, elders, and family.

Something loosened in my lungs knowing Lana was family. My relief was brief, though, because then Kori nodded at the male standing on Alezandral's other side and added, "If you're looking for someone who has warmed your betrothed's bed, that would be the General. Augustus Bruns."

My heart squeezed as I looked at the male again.

Augustus was classically handsome, with cropped brown hair that was shaved on either side of his scalp and soft, brown eyes. A few scars peppered his square face. He was the same height as Alezandral, but with an extra inch or so of muscle lining his silhouette. Augustus leaned in to say something to my betrothed, his hand wrapped around Alezandral's elbow as if that was the most natural thing in the world for him to do. Maybe it was.

Alezandral didn't flinch or pull away from the touch—he only laughed at whatever his General said and leaned over to respond.

I didn't know why this came as such a surprise to me. I certainly hadn't saved myself for my marriage to Alezandral. Why would he abstain?

And yet, the ground swayed beneath me. I glanced over at Kori, searching for some kind of anchor. "Truly?"

She nodded, placing a hand on my forearm, either to steady or comfort me. "Truly. The rumors are years old, though. I don't know if anything is going on between them anymore, but they're still close. Prince Alezandral can't give him the official title of General until he ascends the throne, but the intention is there. He wouldn't be tagging along to court festivities otherwise, since... well, you can see that he's—"

"Not a noble," I finished in a murmur. "How do you know all of this?"

Kori smirked before glancing around us, then leaned in to whisper, "Why do you think the Impundulu can only feed off each other?"

I shook my head, at a loss for what to think.

I'd always assumed the Impundulu fed off each other because it was too dangerous for them to feed outside their own species, that it would open the door to too many messy inter-territory conflicts. I'd seen firsthand how Kori got carried away feeding on me. Maybe it was my blood to blame, but everything my father had told me about their species suggested otherwise.

Kori whispered the truth to me now, pride in her eyes. "Because we can read the memories of anyone we feed on."

The blood drained from my face.

That would mean... *oh Goddess.*

"So, you read *my*—"

"Thoughts?" she cut me off. "Yes. And let me tell you, I think your memories offered enough excitement to last me the rest of this decade."

"You saw *everything?*"

Kori shrugged. "It doesn't take long, and you let me feed for a while."

"I wouldn't have let you feed on me if I'd known what you were really doing," I mumbled, more to myself than her. My mind wasn't the most pleasant place in the world.

She squeezed my arm. "It's okay. We're keeping each other's secrets now."

My gaze strayed to Alezandral and his two companions. I suddenly wanted to ask Kori to feed off Augustus, because I wanted to know everything. How had he and Alezandral met? How had a singularly-blessed seraph risen to the highest military rank of the Halcyon territory? Did Alezandral love him?

Kori nudged me with her elbow. "You're glaring again."

I was. I was watching them like a total creep, but I couldn't help myself.

Alezandral's gaze unexpectedly slid to mine, and the other two Halcyon followed suit. I spun away, facing Kori, but it was too late. I knew they'd seen me. "Shit," I hissed, squeezing my eyes shut. "They caught me."

Kori chuckled, patting my arm. "Well, you weren't exactly subtle about it."

I peeled one eye open. "Are they still looking?"

She glanced over my shoulder and smirked. "Oh, they're more than looking."

I didn't have to ask what she meant by that. I could *feel* him.

Alezandral's presence moved like silken ice across my back, and I barely had the time to compose myself before his hand hooked on my bare waist and tugged me toward him. "We've been waiting for you, darling."

I smiled at Alezandral before directing my attention to the Halcyon who had followed him over. "Were you? That's nice."

Augustus grinned at me, the tan skin around his eyes crinkling in delight while Lana carefully looked me over. I reached for Kori's wrist, trying to pull her into the circle beside me. For some reason, it made me feel better that she was still here.

"I was just showing Princess Kori the garden trail," I explained.

Kori offered the circle an apologetic look before she turned to me. "I had a lovely time, Your Highness, but I think my mothers might be wondering where I am. Please excuse me." She curtsied, and I let go of her. It wouldn't be fair to force her to stay, so I let her walk away, bracing myself to face these introductions alone.

Alezandral's hand squeezed my soft flesh. *Alright, so maybe not totally alone.* His fingertips swirled over my skin in slow caresses, and I bit down on a shiver.

He gestured to Lana with his free hand. "Sia, this is my cousin, Lana. She's my Hand. Lana, this is Sia."

Lana stepped forward and clasped my forearm in greeting.

"General Augustus isn't your Hand?" I asked, the words escaping me before I could stop them.

Usually, the role of Hand was taken by each territory's General. But Alezandral only piqued a brow at me. Augustus chuckled, shaking his head. Lana cleared her throat, and I realized with a pang of guilt that I was partially ignoring her.

I gave her a small smile in apology.

Her blue eyes were dappled with the faintest threads of silver. "No, our court is a little more complex than that."

"Lana took up the mantle of Hand when her brother, Lenz, passed into The Veil last month," Alezandral explained.

I blinked, glancing at my betrothed, but his eyes were trained on his cousin.

That was when it dawned on me. The seraph from the beach, the one he'd stabbed in the heart with a dagger... that had been his Hand?

Tears glimmered in Lana's eyes as she tried to pull her hand from mine, but I caught her fingertips, stilling her. "I'm sorry," I told her. "It wasn't right—what happened. I consider it an honor to have met him, despite the horrific circumstances. He seemed like a good male."

Lana's gaze softened. "He was. Thank you, Sia."

She took a step back, and Augustus immediately took her place, extending a hand without waiting for Alezandral to introduce us. "It's so good to finally meet you, Sia." His voice was deep but gentle, filled with enthusiasm.

I placed my hand in his. "Likewise, Augustus."

"You can call me Gus," he told me with a wink. "All my dearest friends do."

My hand tingled as he kissed the back of it.

I was still reeling with the knowledge of what he was to Alezandral and the fact that he seemed happy to meet me anyway. I didn't want to say the wrong thing, so instead, I offered him the kindest smile I could muster before pulling my hand from his.

The warmth of Alezandral's body crowded me, his hand returning to my hip.

Alezandral had lost so much since our reunion—his cousin, Lenz, and Legend, that magnificent winged beast. If it wasn't for me, he'd still have them both. Lana would still have her brother. Gus and Alezandral would have had each other for a while longer too, at least until Alezandral's father demanded he marry some other female and produce heirs for the Halcyon crown.

The thought settled heavily in my stomach.

It could have easily been another female standing here, wearing his mother's ring.

I glanced over my shoulder at Alezandral, but he only squeezed my side and offered a small, sweet quirk of his lips intended just for me. A secret.

But then, he kept a lot of those, didn't he?

Cheering spared us from the tense silence, and our circle turned to look at koi ponds, where the photographer had finally finished prepping his camera.

The first couple in line stepped forward and arranged themselves in front of the pond as the Sphinx technician ducked under the black velvet to take their picture. He raised a brown hand from beneath the curtain, and the bulb on the camera flashed with blinding brilliance before the line cheered again.

A smile tugged at my lips. It was such a small thing—the photos—and yet, so joyful.

Alezandral noticed my smile and took my hand. "Come on, let's go cut the line. It's our party." He tugged me toward the koi ponds, and I realized he wanted to get a photo *together*.

It was our party, wasn't it? I could count the number of times I'd had my picture taken on one hand, and none of the copies had survived long. I'd burned them before I left home. I hadn't wanted my father to give my exact likeness to his bounty hunters... not that it mattered in the end.

As we approached the camera, Alezandral waved the technician down, and the family in front of his lens quickly retreated as we took their place.

There were a few bags in our way that we had to step over,

and I tripped over one, nearly tumbling head-first into the koi pond, but Alezandral caught me at the last second.

I blew out a sharp chuckle and glanced up to thank him, but the words snagged in my throat when I saw his face.

His eyes were glowing as he stared intently at the pond, his brow furrowed in thought. I looked over my shoulder, but all I saw were fluorescent fish wiggling beneath the surface.

"What is it?" I asked.

He blinked, seeming to come back to himself. "Nothing." Then he tugged me toward the camera.

The technician welcomed us warmly, coming around to direct us into our places. His transparent wings fluttered eagerly behind him as he pushed us close together and arranged Alezandral's hands on my body.

Alezandral smiled down at me. His hair was damp from the rain, a deep, dusky gold. The scent of him wrapped around me as his wing pressed against mine. He smelled like pine and sweet peppermint and that musk all males seemed to carry to some measure. It was all-consuming.

My body reacted without my permission, leaning in.

When the technician had managed us to his liking, he leapt back behind his camera and directed us to look into the lens.

I was too aware of myself.

I was too aware of *Alezandral*—the even cadence of his lungs under my hand and the way his fingertips played notes against my skin. Why did he have to touch me like this? Why bother, when we both knew this was only a ruse and his lover was watching from across the courtyard?

Unless they weren't lovers anymore... but I wasn't going to ask.

The Sphinx took a series of pictures, directing us which way to look and when to smile. Alezandral held me tighter and tighter with each flash of the bulb. He shifted on his feet, and I followed him as he inched backward. It made me wonder if the flashes were bothering him. Every time they flashed, he recoiled.

The photographer told us to stare at each other for the last picture, and I looked up into Alezandral's face, searching his features for any sign of discomfort.

He seemed perfectly at ease, though. The crooked smile he gave me was practically giddy.

"What are you so happy about?" I murmured, even though I was grinning now too.

Alezandral shrugged. "I have a beautiful female in my arms, and she isn't threatening me the way she usually does."

"I can remedy that if you'd like."

His cheeks creased around a soft smile. His fingers dug into the dip of my waist, making me jolt and giggle as the camera flashed again. Then he leaned in and whispered, "I like making you smile more."

My cheeks radiated heat as he pulled back, looking into my eyes.

Alezandral glanced at the photographer. "One more."

"How about a kiss?" a seraph called out from the line.

The Sphinx's eyes lit up. "Yes, that's an excellent idea. A kiss between the future King and Queen Consort of Halcyon is front-page worthy material. The papers will go crazy for it."

The weight of everyone's attention landed on us, even those who weren't in line. I should have anticipated this. They all believed we were getting married, so of course they would expect us to kiss.

Alezandral grimaced and said, "I don't think a kiss is necessary."

Everyone within hearing distance gave him a confused look, including me. A few seraphim voiced their disappointment from the line. What was he thinking? We weren't in a position to refuse something as simple as a kiss. There were too many other things to worry about—huge, world-altering things. A kiss was nothing. I didn't even care if he was thinking about Augustus right now. We had a fucking agreement, sans the fucking.

I whispered into his mind, *Do you want to convince the party that this is real or not?*

Alezandral's fingers twitched against my lower back.

"It's okay, Alezandral, you don't have to say no for my sake," I said sweetly. I gave the crowd around us a timid smile, let them think I was shy. Alezandral's eyes glimmered with understanding. "I don't mind kissing for the camera. It is our engagement party, after all."

Then I leaned into him, and several seraphim whooped their approval.

Alezandral shook his head, the movement so negligible, no one else could see it. *Such a pretty liar you are.*

So I've been told.

Alezandral hooked a finger under my chin, his thumb pressing into the center of my chin as he tilted my face toward his. I didn't close my eyes; that was too dangerous. At least if I watched him kiss me, I could focus on the reality of it all. This wasn't a real kiss. It was a performance.

He brushed his lips over mine. So brief a touch, I barely felt it; just the tiniest spark jumping from my mouth to his.

We both pulled away before the camera bulb flashed. There was no way the lens had captured that kiss, but it didn't really matter to me in that moment. I could tell that he had felt it too, the hint of power surging between us.

A faint rumble echoed around us, and it took me a moment to recognize it for what it was: the party reacting to us. The photographer's voice cut through the clamor. "You'll need to hold the kiss a lot longer than that, Highnesses."

"Just get it over with," I exhaled.

Alezandral's eyes narrowed, a muscle in his jaw feathering

before he whispered back, "Close your damn eyes this time, darling, and I will."

I forced myself to obey.

As my eyes fluttered shut, whirls of cool air slid over my cheeks, trailing down the sides of my neck like invisible fingers. Alezandral kissed me again, and I had no choice but to surrender to the sensations of it. His lips were soft and firm, moving against mine persuasively. If he belonged to someone else, I couldn't taste them. I couldn't taste anything but him. I tried not to give in, but that was like telling my lungs not to breathe, like telling the sun not to shine.

I wasn't really in control anymore. He was water, and I was thirst.

The scar over my heart throbbed as if it suddenly had a pulse of its own... and that wasn't the only thing throbbing. I think the bulb of the camera flashed, but I couldn't be sure. I was lost in him. It had only been a week since I last visited the pleasure chambers. I shouldn't be this desperate for release, not from a single kiss and a couple platonic caresses. Even in my youth, when my desires were brand new and everything was still exciting, I hadn't felt this way. Not even with *Tova*.

That realization struck like lightning.

She was dead now, and I was still alive. Everything was broken between us, all my promises to her and *especially* the love I had felt. I'd moved on, and happiness seemed so possible as I kissed Alezandral. Now that I was feeling warmth and want beyond my past, I hoped that meant I would have a future worth fighting for.

Feeling *anything* made me real again, made me significant.

Alezandral's voice tickled the edge of my mind, hovering on the threshold of my thoughts. *Do you trust me?*

That question sobered me.

Absolutely not. The simple fact that he was asking such a question made me uneasy.

When I tried to pull away, he wouldn't let me.

A chuckle rumbled against my mouth as he pressed me harder against him, crushing me to his chest, and my spine started tingling. Something wasn't right. *Then you should probably hold your breath*, he said into my mind.

What—

Before I could complete that thought, he stumbled backwards and pitched himself into the koi pond, pulling me in along with him.

CHAPTER 16

Betrayal dug its talons into my heart as the water enveloped us.

This couldn't be happening. We couldn't be falling into the koi pond as everyone watched. Dread hardened in the pit of my stomach as my lungs screamed for air. It was a miracle I didn't sink all the way to the bottom of the pool.

Well… if Alezandral's arms could be considered a miracle. I knew better, though. They were responsible for this.

Alezandral held me tightly as he scrambled to get his feet beneath him, launching us back through the surface. The pond was shallow enough that we could stand in it.

I held onto Alezandral's shoulders until I found my own footing, then I pushed against him roughly so he would set me down.

"You okay?" Alezandral whispered as I swiped the excess water out of my eyes.

Shame burned in my cheeks as I shoved away, staggering backwards as the several layers of my dress clung to my legs and threatened to trip me all over again. I didn't want to touch Alezandral right now. I didn't want *him* to touch me. Why did he do that? How could he—

My gaze caught on the golden paint trailing after me on the surface of the water. *My wings.*

He exposed my wings.

Alezandral extended a hand to me. "Come and smile for the camera, darling." He stepped toward me, but I stilled him with a vicious look.

The photographer was frantically preparing for the next capture, trying to capture *this*. I was sure I looked like a mess. I didn't need a mirror to feel the kohl stinging my eyes and streaking down my cheeks.

"Fuck you, Alezandral," I said quietly.

His grin turned brittle as he swiftly closed the distance between us. "They're watching us, so either smile for the picture, or I'm going to kiss you again to hide your frown."

I glared at him, my upper lip curling. *You wouldn't dare.*

That sounds like a challenge, he thought with a smirk.

I didn't trust the look in his eyes; if I let him get too close again, there was no way of knowing what would happen next, what I might discover he was willing to do for this little ruse. Begrudgingly, I smiled, allowing him to tug me toward the ledge of the stone pond.

It'll be alright, he said into my mind. *Just follow my lead.*

He pulled himself out of the pond first, then turned to help me. It was a struggle to move in my wet dress, but Alezandral's hands were strong as they wrapped around my waist and hoisted me out of the pool.

I made the mistake of looking around.

The party was awestruck, utterly transfixed by me. I knew how to act when everyone thought I was Fenix. I had something to imitate. This? Being whatever the hell I truly was? I didn't know what that meant, how much to show of myself and how much to hide. Now it felt like I was breathing wrong, like I was *existing* wrong.

I receded, detaching to protect my shivering heart. I was still there, holding Alezandral's hand as he pulled me forward, but I wasn't present.

The bulb on the camera flashed, and I didn't even blink. I could only assume I was still smiling, because Alezandral didn't kiss me again. Thank the Goddess for that.

Then, a glass of wine was being handed to me.

Alezandral's voice anchored me back in reality. We were on the dais again, his hand settled into place on my lower back as he addressed the party. "We were going to wait until the end of the festivities to make this announcement, but I suppose fate had other plans," he said with a breathless laugh.

A few seraphim chuckled along, but almost everyone in the audience wore some shade of worry or concern on their face, though Alezandral pretended not to see it.

"Everyone raise your glasses to the future Queen of Halcyon, a flawless jewel hidden no longer. A remarkable blessing from our generous Goddess." He turned to me with bright eyes, raising his glass. "Here's to building a new world with you, my darling."

My back prickled, wings spreading as his words sank in.

It suddenly dawned on me why he had *really* wanted this. The truth was so obvious to me at that moment.

I hadn't realized what he stood to gain from making my origins known before... but now, seeing him smile at the crowd, I understood. We were bonded. When we were children, our hearts and souls had recognized each other as perfect equals, so even while I was alone in my power, there was still a match for me in this world. *Him.*

And now everyone knew exactly how extraordinary I was, and therefore, how extraordinary he was by comparison.

My origin had strengthened him. It should have strengthened *me* too—but I had never felt so weak as I did when I looked at the crowd gathered around us.

I wanted to run.

And why shouldn't I?

My ears were ringing loud enough to drown out the party as Alezandral tapped his glass to mine. I lifted the flute to my lips and drained it. Then I pushed my glass into Alezandral's chest and turned to address the crowd myself. "If you'll excuse me, I need to change out of this dress now. Thank you all for coming, and now you can leave."

I leapt off the dais and took to the skies, not caring that I was rude, not caring that the paint on my wings was now sprinkling the party beneath me.

They could choke on it for all I cared.

Landing in one of the open alcoves of the palace, I let go of the tension I was holding in. Sparks erupted from my fingertips, licking the ground around my feet, skittering across the marble with every step I took toward my wing of the palace. When I reached the stairs, I flew right over them, veering into my private hallway.

I immediately collided with a solid wall of muscle.

Alezandral wasn't finished terrorizing me, it would seem. He grabbed my arm as I attempted to weave past him. "Sia, why did you storm off like that?"

Alezandral was playing with fire. *My* fire. Much more of this, and he was going to burn.

I pushed him away, my hand leaving a scorch mark on his tunic, but he didn't seem to care. He only summoned his hoarfrost, chilling the air around us and his hand as it grabbed at me again. My sparks flew out in retaliation, but there was nothing for them to catch on. My family knew better than to allow anything too flammable in my wing of the palace.

The only thing I could do damage to right now was Alezandral.

Welts appeared on his face where my sparks hit his skin, and I felt the echo of them, my promise to him. Right now, it didn't matter if I hurt myself as well. This was the only thing making me feel better. Or, at least, good in this moment. I knew it wouldn't last. Regret was already building beneath the pain, eager to overcome me. I couldn't let it in. I couldn't let any of it in, any of *him*.

"What. Is. Going. On?" His voice rattled through me. He was the thunder and the lightning, the snow and the ice, and my sparks faltered at the authority in his voice.

I glared at him. "I wanted to get away from *you*. Now let me go."

"You want to be left alone? Fine, but you're going to tell me what's wrong first. You're not running away to suffer in silence. Not again. Scream at me if you have to, bite and scratch and hurt me." He was almost shaking my entire body now, his hands bruising my upper arms. "Just *talk to me*."

There was such desperation in his voice, my heart skipped a beat. Then, my cheeks filled with more heat, more rage. How dare he.

"You can't be serious right now," I hissed. "Take a wild fucking guess, Alezandral."

I tried to wrench my arm away from him, but only succeeded in ripping the other sleeve of my horrid orange dress. I pushed at his chest a second time, but it was like slapping a glacier. He was ready for my violence. A thin sheet of frost covered him from head to toe.

"Stop, please," he begged. "I can see I made an error in judgment. You're upset about the pond?"

I laughed, and it was a terrifying sound, even to my own ears.

"No, I'm *angry*," I said. And a little embarrassed, but I

wouldn't admit that to him. This was the first party I'd attended since my return, and I was walking out of it like *this*. My feelings weren't making sense, even to me. I didn't *like* parties. This shouldn't mean anything to me—I shouldn't *care* this much, but I did. Somehow, it meant something to me, and *he* was the one who ruined it.

My anger grew and spread, burning in my palms as I stepped into him.

"But that's only because I let myself believe you were actually on my side. That you were looking out for me. That you *cared*. I didn't think you would use me for some impulsive political move, but trust me, I won't make *that* error again."

His hand tightened on my wrist, his other hand lost somewhere to my side, hovering but not touching. "Sia," he said my name like a plea. "I didn't intend to hurt you. I thought we were on the same page about telling everyone the truth. I thought you were ready. The pond, the pictures—I was only trying to remedy the situation. That's why I fell in *with* you. We did it together."

"And yet, I'm the only one they looked at like a freak. I'm the one who lost something today."

Alezandral huffed a frustrated sigh, his eyes narrowing. "Give me a fucking break, Sia. You lost nothing but a lie that was fragile to begin with."

"A lie that was mine to shatter," I insisted. "I would have liked to do it with some semblance of control." I had too little control over my life as it was.

Alezandral blinked, dropping my wrist, and I spun on my heel to stalk up the corridor to my room. He didn't follow me; he remained rooted to the spot, even as I paused to open my door and shot him a nasty look before walking in.

My anger bled away almost instantly.

He shouldn't be allowed to look at me like that, to look so *fucking devastated*. It stole my anger and pointed me to the

source, reminded me that I was hurting only because, somewhere along the way, my heart had become invested in this
friendship. And despite my foolishness, despite his mistakes,
it still was.

My stupid, miserable heart.

CHAPTER 17

The instant I closed the door to my room, I tore at the dress, peeling it away from my skin until it landed in a soaked pile at my feet.

My sparks returned, flowing out of me like rain from an overburdened cloud. I was the one storming now.

I kicked the dress away then ripped my undergarments off and added them to the pile before setting the whole thing on fire. My anger poured out on the gaudy material. Water fizzled. Heavy ribbons of steam twirled toward the ceiling, and it took everything in me not to send flames flying up with it. I forced myself to keep my eyes on the burning pile. *Sight serves as my guide.* Alezandral taught me that little trick, and I hated that I was still grateful to him for it.

I just wanted to *breathe*.

It was good to talk to him about what I was feeling, even if he had to shake it out of me. There was so much more I wanted to say, wanted to explain. My entire childhood raced through my head in flashes of shadow and light. I searched for my family in it, but...what family? I relived the fearful disdain and wide-eyed stares, all the times I'd hoped for better, hoped for change, and only wound up sorely disappointed. I saw my past cracking like glass and the future I thought I'd have crumbling like sand. Why did it feel like I suddenly had *nothing*? Like I *was* nothing?

I always knew I was something other, but now, everyone else knew too. Now, it was *real*.

My origins, the sutilis, these black wings on my back—they were real, and there was no going back. No more hiding from it, or from myself. So, I kept burning, kept seething. I didn't want to think about it anymore. What I felt. What he said. I *refused* to think about him. None of it would matter once I was gone.

I took a deep breath and leaned into my reserve of power, draining it as the marble floor blackened.

I wasn't thinking about it…

But how did Alezandral *expect* me to react after what happened back there? Did he expect me to thank him for shoving me into the koi pond? Well… for *pulling* me in. I remember his grip on my waist, the taste of him on my lips, the way he looked at me after we surfaced.

My skin tingled at the memory: him lifting his glass, his eyes a smoldering blue beneath thick brown lashes, his soft voice. *Here's to building a new world with you, my darling.*

My darling.

That one little addition to his usual antagonism made my head spin.

My fire sputtered out.

I couldn't *not* think about Alezandral right now. His presence was here in the room with me. My skin was so cold without the flames, and it might as well have been his hoarfrost. The air smelled of char and sadness.

My body longed to be touched.

Retrieving my robe from the bathroom, I wrapped the silk around me and pulled the summoning rope hanging next to my bed. A minute later, someone knocked on the door to my chambers. I told the maid what I needed, ignoring her bewildered stare, and then I walked to the balcony and threw open the doors, attempting to clear out the smoke before my guest arrived. He appeared in the doorway as I was pouring moon water over the blackened embers of my dress.

He was shorter than I would have liked, but pretty enough to serve his purpose, lean and blond. One of my brother's courtesans. He eyed the mess I'd made. "Good afternoon, Princess. Is this a bad time?"

I dropped the stone bowl, and we both flinched at the heavy thud.

My heart was hammering, blood rushing powerfully through my ears. Why was I so nervous? Somehow, it felt wrong to have him here, but that was ridiculous.

I had no reason to feel bad for needing to be touched, for needing distraction.

Even so, Alezandral's words from last week returned to me. *If you wished for mindlessness, you could have come to me instead. I would have given you rest. I would have given you release.*

But I couldn't go to him. Not for this.

I stepped over the stone bowl, sensually pulling the sash loose on the front of my robe. "It's the perfect time, as long as you like what you see?" It was only polite to make sure. All courtesans had the right to say no, even to needy princesses without a home.

As I pulled my robe open, the courtesan's gaze dropped to peruse my body. He licked his lips. "Certainly."

I closed the space between us and spread a hand over his chest, over his heart. His skin was so perfect there, unmarred... and right now, that was the best I could do. I gently pushed him in the direction of the couch until he collapsed onto the cushion. I nodded at his lap, and he took the hint, starting to untie his pants.

Quick and hard, that was all I wanted. Something to cleanse my body of this tension.

The question left my lips before I even realized I was thinking it. "Are they talking about me?"

He nodded, his expression sobering. "They are." Then he smiled gently, his eyes flicking to my ruined wings. "How could they not when you are this beautiful?"

Without uttering another word, I straddled him. I buried my fingers through his golden hair, closed my eyes, and lowered myself onto his lap. Then, I started moving.

Nothing special. Those words burrowed their way into my head as I rode him. *This is nothing, nothing at all.* His groans warmed my ear. My fingers tightened in his hair. He returned every thrust, but my belly burned for more, and it didn't matter how much more I took. This wasn't enough.

Anger rose like a tide in my chest, swift and painful.

"Highness," the courtesan choked out. "I'm sorry, I'm going to come."

There were rules I had to observe now that I was engaged to a crown prince. No one was allowed to come inside me except for *him*, and every courtesan was sworn to honor that. If they didn't, they were sworn to turn themselves in and face the consequences.

We would *both* face the consequences.

Growling in frustration, I braced my hands against the back of the couch, shifting the angle at which our hips met... but that only intensified the edge I was dancing on without any promise of release.

I wasn't going to come. I wasn't even close.

"Princess?" The courtesan's voice was panicked now, his gray wings shuddering.

I pulled myself up and staggered away from the couch, my

chest heaving. The courtesan grabbed his cock, catching himself as he came, but that wasn't where my eyes drifted.

Alezandral and Lana watched us from the magical threshold connecting my private room to my betrothed's.

A needling tingle swept across my neck.

For a moment, I couldn't react. I could only catalog the rage on Lana's face, her small nose wrinkling and her eyes narrowing to slits.

Alezandral seemed to be frozen in shock, the same as me, his gaze hollow.

The courtesan cursed, snapping me out of my daze.

I scrambled to retie my robe, and the courtesan put himself away before launching off the couch. He bowed and headed for the door, and I let him go in silence. There were no words in me right now, only the weight of my regret. I should have told him to go the moment he got here. I should have trusted my gut.

The door slammed shut, and I winced.

Alezandral turned to Lana, leaning to whisper something in her ear. Her gaze slid up to meet his, but her expression remained terrifyingly severe as she nodded and handed him the black box in her hands.

My stomach churned. Had she brought me a *present*?

Lana strode to the door the courtesan exited through, following him into the hallway.

After the door snapped shut, I turned to Alezandral. All evidence of feeling had disappeared from his features. "Sorry for interrupting," he said tersely.

"Then why did you?"

Alezandral lifted the box between us. "We wanted to surprise you."

"Well, you certainly succeeded in that, didn't you?"

"It's an engagement present, Sia. Do you want it or not?" His patience was wearing thin, and I knew I had two choices.

I could tell him to go, or I could ask him to stay. I wasn't sure which one he wanted.

I reached for his thoughts, but there was nothing available for me to pilfer. He was locking me out again.

Probably for the best.

I gestured for him to sit with me on the couch.

He sat on the table across from me instead and set the heavy box on my lap. "We were going to give it to you at the party, before I screwed everything up," he muttered.

My throat swelled.

"I don't have a gift for you."

Alezandral shrugged. "You don't need to give me anything. This isn't a real engagement."

"Then what's your reason for this?"

He grimaced. "I had something to give. Just open it, okay?"

I lowered my attention to the package and lifted the lid, my heart hiccuping when I saw what sat inside: two black daggers. The blades weren't straight, exactly; they were narrow at the razor-sharp tip, growing thicker as they gradually curved toward the leather-bound hilt, the cross guards carved into flared wings.

This was made from the same material my father shackled me with.

My eyes flew up to mark Alezandral's expression, but it was as unreadable as stone. "What do you expect me to do with this?" I whispered.

His gaze dropped to my mouth for the briefest heartbeat.

"Let that which has hurt you become your weapon, Sia. *Conquer it.*"

Tears pricked my eyes, and I looked down at the blades before they could fall, blinking the threatening darkness away. They were beautiful, sharp and wicked, with runes of strength elegantly carved across each blade.

"I don't know what to say," I croaked.

Except *I'm sorry.*

Except *I wish you hadn't seen me riding a courtesan that looked like you, because that was exactly what I asked for.*

Alezandral sighed and reached over to pluck a dagger from its satin bed. "Lana's grandmother carries Stymphalian blood," he explained. "She helped me design these and found a way to forge them for me. The blades should hold your flame. I charmed the leather on the hilts to protect your hands, so no worries there. I know they aren't what you're used to, but I'll help you train with them, if you want. I've been wanting to bring up training together for a while. I figure, if we only have a couple months before you leave, I'd like to spend some of that time getting you more comfortable with your magic."

I bit my lip. "I don't know if that's a good idea."

"Why not?" His suddenly sharp tone had my wings ruffling. *Pushy asshole.*

I glared at him. "I'm dangerous."

He scoffed. "So what? I can be dangerous too."

"Not like this," I insisted.

Alezandral only smirked, setting the hilt of my new blade in the center of my palm. It fit comfortably, *perfectly.* "I will take you on any day, darling. And until you learn how to master yourself, I'll beat you every single time."

The tension between us unraveled.

My body responded to his arrogance, relaxing into the embrace of our familiar bickering. "I guess we'll see about that, but don't come crying to me when I burn you alive."

"I wouldn't dare," he laughed.

A chuckle weaved its way through my chest too. Then, we just sat there, staring at each other for a long moment. Everything was fine again. It was as if the party never happened.

All too quickly, his grin wavered.

"It was better that we showed everyone the truth today. You have to know that. You have to understand."

I leaned away from him, shoving the blades off my lap and onto the cushion so I could stand up.

"Stay out of my head."

His eyes followed me across the room. "I'm not in your head, Sia. I'm miles from it, I promise."

His promise was a pleasurable tickle down my spine.

I twisted to face him, crossing my arms. "I understand that we needed to do something. I just wish you would have told me your plan beforehand."

Alezandral wrung his hands between his knees. "I *couldn't.* We needed to convince your father it was an accident, and I didn't want to ask you to deceive him to do it. I didn't want to risk him seeing through us. This way, there's no reason for him to punish you," he reasoned.

I sighed. "He wouldn't have hurt me, Alezandral."

"At least not in a way anyone could see, right?" I recoiled a step from his venomous tone, and his eyes softened in remorse. He sighed. "You're right. I made a decision that hurt you, and you had every right to know beforehand. I'm sorry. I suppose I'm… I'm a little paranoid when it comes to court dealings, but it's for good reason. If you ever visit my territory again, you'll understand. You just have to trust me."

I ventured closer to him, perching on the arm of the couch. "If you want me to trust you, then *earn* it," I said quietly. "Stop keeping things from me. You can trust me too."

His eyes hardened, and I knew I'd said something wrong.

"No, I can't trust you," he eventually whispered.

My heart plummeted.

He continued in a thick voice, "I care for you, Sia. If you believe nothing else I say tonight, I hope you at least believe that. This complicates *everything,* you and me. If we were following through with this marriage, if you were really going to be my wife, then maybe things could be different. I *want* to look out for you, but there are other people I have to look out for too. There are things I must do, decisions I *have* to make for my country, and I can't think of you when I make them. Pretty soon, you'll have what you've been searching for, you'll go, and they will be the only thing I have left. I have to protect them. It's my duty, my honor."

All the warmth seeped out of my limbs, leaving me cold. I'd never felt so… *unwanted.*

"Then we know exactly where we stand with each other. You're a king." I shrugged, unable to put a label on what I was. The thought was in my head, though. *I will always be alone.* I shook my head to get it out. "Just know that the next time you keep me in the dark like that, it'll come to blows between us."

How wonderful it must be for him, I thought, *to have a whole country to keep him company.*

It was a terrible thought. A jealous one.

In my heart, I knew it wasn't that simple, but the hurt in my chest twisted what he said into something I could more easily bear. It gave me animosity to cling to, more anger. Because beneath that, all I felt was sadness, and I didn't want to feel that over something that had never been mine in the first place. It was wrong to want anything from Alezandral. Not companionship. Not a purpose. Not a crown.

After what he just walked in on, he had to know I would never be a suitable queen for him anyway. Even if I wanted him, which I didn't, I'd ruined any chance of marrying him.

And that was for the best.

"How about next time, instead of assuming anything about my intentions, you just ask me?" Alezandral offered. "And, while we're setting our expectations at ground level, you probably shouldn't invite a courtesan to your room either. Our situation is delicate. There's about a thousand guests in this castle right now, and you didn't even secure the servant's silence before you sent him away."

"I didn't need to," I said tightly, a little irritated by his judgmental tone. "They're sworn to speak of nothing pertaining to the Fenix royals." Nothing to anyone outside of the royal family, at least.

Alezandral gave me a pitying look. "But you aren't Fenix, Sia, and now everyone knows it."

I stopped breathing, because he was right. There was nothing stopping that courtesan from telling the entire city about what I'd done. "*Shit.*"

I stumbled my way towards the door.

Alezandral stood and caught my upper arm. "Don't worry. I sent Lana after him; she'll make sure he doesn't talk."

"Are you sure about that? She looked ready to maul me before she left. I don't think my reputation is high up on her list of concerns."

"Lana's loyal to me," he replied with a grimace. "She knows what this could do to our country if it got out. We'd *all* be screwed. Just please, be more discreet from here on out."

I wrenched my arm out of his hand, my chest burning around a caustic laugh. "You're telling *me* to be discreet? *You* invited one of your bedmates to our engagement party. You gave him a permanent seat in your court, influence over your soldiers. How is what I did any worse? At least I entertained mine in the privacy of my room." The words were really flowing now. Like a fucking river.

And I'd really pissed him off.

Alezandral's smile was violent, his eyes glowing like blue fire. "I'm sorry, Sia. I didn't realize I fucked Augustus in the middle of the party where everyone could see. What a burden that must have been to you."

I ground my teeth together to hide a wince.

"Besides," he added. "I'm not sleeping with Gus anymore. He's just my General."

"I don't care," I said evenly.

He laughed, some of his anger dissolving into levity. "Sure

you don't," he purred. "That's why you didn't bring him up, right?"

"Fuck you."

He backtracked to his bedroom door. "You already established we wouldn't be doing that, remember? Changing your mind already? How *mercurial* you are."

"*Never.*"

Alezandral smirked over his shoulder at me. "Mighty strong words for a female who didn't come today."

"What makes you think you could make me come any easier than he did?" I hoped he wasn't listening to my thoughts, because they were being traitorous whores right now to match my traitorous heart.

He looked me up and down. "I don't know. It's just this feeling I get when I look at you."

"Maybe you should stop looking."

"Maybe I should." He didn't look away, though. He kept staring, a smile slowly blooming across his full lips.

I pulled the robe tighter around me. "I'm tired," I growled.

Alezandral faced forward with a chuckle. "Have a good night, Sia. I'll see you bright and early in the training room. Don't be late. " He turned to close the door behind him, and a flash of vulnerability crossed his face as he did, as if he'd dropped his mask just a second too soon.

I called for him, and the door halted a mere inch away from the latch.

When he looked up at me, I said, "I didn't mean for you to see that." Because he needed to know. I hadn't wanted to hurt him that brutally. I hadn't wanted him to *see*.

There was a brief, chilling silence.

"I know," he muttered. "I'll knock next time. You'd have to do a lot more than sleep with someone else to turn me against you anyway."

Then, he closed and locked his side of the door.

CHAPTER 18

The training arena was in the east wing of the palace, near the courtesan hall. It felt strange to walk into it, and even stranger to see it so empty.

When I was younger, I used to sneak up to the door of this room and watch my brother train. I would study his form and technique, and then I would return to my bedroom and practice by myself, with nothing but a mirror to assist me.

That was as close as my father ever let me get. The door.

Alezandral had sent me a note last night insisting we meet here before dawn, and when I sent a message back asking why he wished to torture me so, he didn't respond. I didn't feel like tracking him down to argue about it, so here I was.

There were no glass windows in this space, but on the far wall of the room, a series of shifting panels could be opened to the outside. A handful were in that position right now.

The cool morning air was the first thing to greet me as I stepped across the threshold.

Runes were carved into the marble floor in the center of the room. I'd seen enough from a distance to know that they were charms to turn the marble more malleable in the training ring, to soften falls. Dummies of all shapes and sizes were clustered together into the corners of the room, and the weapons…

My eyes gorged on the silvery iron, my nostrils flaring at the overwhelming scent of leather and steel.

Alezandral looked up from where he stood at the far end of the room, fiddling with the straps on his gloves. They were different from the ones he usually wore—these were designed for blade wielding, the fingers cut off at the first joint to help with his grip. My betrothed was shirtless, because *of course* he was. The Goddess had already made it perfectly clear that she planned on testing me at every turn nowadays.

Judging from the sweat shining all over Alezandral, he'd been awake for a while already.

"Grand Rising, Sia," he said, his dark blue eyes flicking over my leathers as he walked past. The greeting felt cold, even if his voice had been polite.

He approached a collection of swords on the wall.

My back prickled as he picked up a long blade and a wicked-looking dagger. The sword he chose would have required me to use two hands to wield it, but the weight didn't seem to bother him.

"Ready?" he asked, walking into the training ring without giving me a second glance.

Alezandral was clearly in some kind of mood. Or perhaps I'd pushed him over the edge yesterday, and this was the male behind his many masks. Curt. Frigid. Bored.

When he reached the center of the training ring, Alezandral turned to face me, beckoning me towards him with the dagger. "Come on, then. Show me what you can do." There was no inflection in his words—just pure, impenetrable will.

A heat feathered low in my stomach.

I wasn't sure if I liked him like this. It was a surprise to realize that I had liked him before.

I joined Alezandral in the ring.

As I pulled my daggers from their sheathes, they sat heavily in my hands, but not in a negative way. I felt the magic embedded in them—the charm Alezandral had applied to protect my palms and the leather from melting around the metal. It was a comforting tingle.

But that wasn't enough to calm my racing heart as I faced off with Alezandral.

The instant I stepped over the runes into the circle, his eyes trained on me, assessing critically. Every inch of his body was deceitfully docile, but I didn't let my guard down for even a heartbeat, not when I could feel his heart thundering alongside mine. It was an alarming awareness, but looking into his eyes, I couldn't shake it.

I could feel him decide to strike before he even moved.

His blades slashed at me, and I barely ducked out of the way in time to miss his long sword. He lashed out again with his dagger, moving so quickly that my heart stopped for a moment. He growled under his breath as I stopped his next blow, and the next. Every inch of his body was coiled, and I saw no mercy in his eyes. I wasn't expecting this... this *frenzy*.

I slammed the hilt of my blade into his chest to push him back a step. My defensive blow barely gave me enough space to whip under his arm and escape toward the other side of the ring, but I took it. I backed away slowly, watching as he turned toward me with a furious look on his face. My limbs were shaking.

My heart ached. I felt the place where I hit him, a small bruise forming over my right breast. How was I supposed to fight him with this promise between us?

Alezandral didn't chase after me.

He paused, clicking his tongue against the roof of his mouth. "Pitiful work. Where's your spark hiding today, Sia?"

My fingers pulsed around my daggers as I tried to plan my

next move. He was too quick to fool, too lean to outmaneuver. Mind whirling, my hands fell into their old habits, and I flicked my daggers over my knuckles, the hot metal grazing my skin and sharpening my thoughts.

I wasn't so sure I could beat him anymore. I couldn't see the way to it.

Alezandral's eyes snapped to my hands, marking my tic. Then, his gaze leisurely traveled up the length of my body before settling on my frown.

An amused smirk tugged at his lips. "Cute."

That single word scraped over my skin, and I launched myself at him. I didn't want to hurt him. I just wanted to punish him for making my heart flutter the way it did, for making me want to hear him say that word again.

We collided in a flurry of steel and feathers, and for a brief moment, there was nothing but us, nothing but our blades.

His defense was as unforgiving as his attack, and soon, I was the one being advanced on again, conceding step after step to him as I tried to keep my blades from slicing his skin.

He didn't seem to feel that same hesitation.

My fear earned me a few minor cuts on my face and my knuckles. Still, he advanced. It wasn't until I had staggered outside of the ring that he finally stopped. He lowered his blades and glared at me as I bent over at the waist to catch my breath. "You can be more vicious than that," he murmured. "Let that flame out. Try to really hurt me."

I scoffed. "You know I can't do that. If I hurt you, I hurt myself."

He rolled his eyes. "Do you remember the way you phrased your promise to me, Sia? Because *I* do."

I only stared at him.

"You said you would never let anyone *else* hurt me," he clarified. "So twist the words however you need to in your head to allow us to really train. Anyone *else* can mean anyone *other* than you, can't it? You can be the exception to our promise."

He *wanted* me to be able to hurt him?

After yesterday, he should be protecting himself from me *more*, not less. How could he be so trusting?

I wasn't going to let this happen. I wasn't going to let him sacrifice the only thing that protected him from me, not when I was capable of terrible things.

"Maybe I could," I muttered, "but why would I choose to believe that? I'm not a frozen-hearted Halcyon like you."

Such hurtful words, words I wasn't sure I believed anymore.

Alezandral stiffened, but after a moment, he huffed a chuckle, his body liquefying as he replied, "But aren't you still *angry* with me, Sia? I've pissed you off so often in the last few weeks, surely you can find enough fault to damn me. I mean, that's what you do, isn't it? You pluck a few humans from the world to obsess over and leave the rest of them behind to rot. In some cases, you even kill them yourself. It's great population control, I suppose." His voice was a honey-coated blade, cutting right to the heart of me.

"Stop it," I whispered, my fingers tightening around the daggers.

His eyes glittered as he stepped back, giving me space to enter the ring again, practically *daring* me to. "Stop what? Telling you the truth?"

"You're trying to get under my skin."

His eyes trailed down the length of my body again, scorching me from the inside out. I wished he would stop doing that. His gaze was a heavy weight to bear.

When his eyes met mine, he purred, "I'm not trying. I'm *succeeding*. Do you know what the humans are making in their factories, Sia?"

The nerves all over my body sprang to attention.

In my silence, Alezandral continued, "You forgot about that, didn't you? You were so eager to send supplies and money down to your mother's city, but you can't see the poison in the water because your eyes are closed. Your head is foggy from all the poppy you smoked to forget about them."

My chest prickled as I stalked forward into the ring, and Alezandral's smile widened, victorious and arrogant as ever.

"That's not how it was," I growled.

Alezandral shrugged. "I won't tell them how easily you abandoned them—not that they'd care. I can tell you what they're cooking down there, though. Aren't you curious? I was."

When the only thing I offered in response was my glare, he laughed again, dark and bitter.

"They're making *nothing* in those factories. They're running machinery all day and night for the goddess-damned smoke. They're killing themselves to keep the beasts of the forest off their doorsteps, to keep the spirits away from their homes. They are *dying* because your father drove away everyone and everything who used to protect them before your island settled above them, and all *you* do is look down and commiserate from afar. How are you any different from the rest of the Fenix, Sia? It sounds like you're as frozen-hearted as me, maybe more so."

My flames sparked to life, wrapping around my hands, enveloping my blades.

Damn him.

"Shut your fucking mouth," I seethed. "As if your people are any better. I've seen your empty palace, or did you forget?"

Pain swept across his expression. I'd hit a nerve. "The emptiness of my palace is trivial. Our human towns aren't dying in droves, Sia. They aren't being *invaded.* So maybe I know a tad bit more than you about protecting the parts of my country that need it. What have *you* been doing? Need I remind you? Hiding from your responsibilities, meddling with forest folk, pretending to be mortal and caring for a child that is not yours while hundreds suffer in your willing ignorance?"

Once again, I was on the receiving end of that terrible helplessness between us. I could feel it inside me. Bubbling. Ripping and shredding. Forcing me to act.

I no longer cared if he was doing it on purpose.

I attacked him.

This time, I didn't hold back. I let his advice free me of my promise to him—I allowed him to make me dangerous, to make me the only person who could hurt him. And I wanted to right now. I wanted him to hurt as badly as I did.

Our blades collided, every clang met with a sparkle of black embers, and it took me a lot longer than it should have to realize that the air swirled with particles of frost too.

He made me feel safe to lash out, safe to *be*.

My anger grew, because why did it have to be *him?* Why was he the only person who could do this for me?

It should have been my family. I should be able to fucking *control* this by now.

The adrenaline pumping through my veins was enough to cut through his defenses. One moment, I was connecting with steel, and then I sheared through something softer.

The instant I saw his blood, I stopped.

I pushed away from him and staggered back, watching as he blinked in shock and lifted a hand to the weeping slice across his face.

Alezandral huffed a chuckle as his fingers came away red.

When he looked at me, his eyes were bright. "Atta girl. Didn't feel a thing this time, did you?"

He stalked forward and forced me to block another blow, then his next. I didn't retreat, though I desperately wanted to. This was how things were going to be with him, here in training. He was going to force me to face the things I wanted to hide from.

The fury inside me twisted itself into knots, until suddenly, it looked different. It *felt* different.

Before I even realized what was on my mind, I was voicing it. "You think I don't realize exactly how wrong I am in this world, Lee?" My voice was rough and warped by exertion, but it was mine, more mine than it ever had been.

Right now, he wasn't Alezandral to me. He was Lee, and I could tell him anything.

Lee's eyes glowed behind the steel between us.

"You think I don't feel my potential?" Every word was punctuated with the clash and zing of our blades. The air grew colder, and I wasn't sure if it was because Lee thought I needed more of him, or if it was my own flame that was dimming. In this moment, it didn't matter.

"You want to know why I stand still? Why I hide?" My voice was barely audible. "It's because I prefer to be too weak to change this world. If I tried, I'd only ruin it. I've known that since I was old enough to burn."

I'd pushed Lee so far that we were at the edge of the ring again, and when those words left my mouth, he stepped outside of it.

"What did you just say?" He gazed at me with compassion.

"I shouldn't have said that," I whispered. I turned away, hiding my tears.

His body heat crowded my side, and I knew I wasn't succeeding in hiding anything. Not from him. Not anymore. A callused finger hooked beneath my chin and lifted my face. When I realized he wasn't going to let me off the hook, I let myself look at him.

His gaze was tender. "No. I think that was precisely what you needed, darling."

"You don't know what I need."

Before I could take a full step away, his hand cupped the back of my neck and brought me back in. The gentleness of his touch kept me from reacting. "I may not yet, but I will. I'm collecting glimmers of you, darling, every bit and piece of your darkness that you let me see. Eventually, I'll see all of it. It's only a matter of time."

I was letting him get too close. Every line I'd drawn between us was suddenly blurring, and that frightened me.

But he was in the ring again, wasn't he?

I flipped the daggers around in my palms and threw a punch.

Even unexpected, he managed to catch the blow. His long sword fell, though, and I was already lashing out with my other fist. The rest of our weapons dropped as we fell into hand-to-hand.

We were a tangle of hands and desperate fingers, harried gasps as we did one another damage beyond the physical.

At least, that was how it felt to me. Every touch was more.

Then his hands found purchase somehow, on my arms and my waist, and the floor fell out from under me. The room spun, and suddenly, I was pinned against him, my back to his chest, my wings tucked uncomfortably between us.

All I could do was catch my breath in his arms.

How had he done that?

When I found my voice again, I whispered, "That was incredible."

His chin rested on my shoulder, and as he chuckled, it stirred the loose hair around my ear. "Are you flirting with me, Sia?"

I jerked in his arms and he let me go. I scrambled away, twisting to face him with a grimace. "Definitely not. If I was flirting with you, you'd know it."

He clicked his tongue, one side of his mouth twitching downward in disappointment. "Shame."

I stepped closer. "How did you do that? Did you use your —" I made a general wave in his direction.

"No, it wasn't my Materie. I'm not a cheat like you, darling," he teased.

"Then how? How did you pin my wings like that?"

"If you want to find out, come here and pay closer attention," he taunted with a smirk.

Goddess damn the both of us.

I walked up to him, raising my hands in a defensive position. The moment I was close enough to strike, he surged forward, pulling me under the next wave of violence and skin-to-skin. My body simmered.

It felt too near to longing, but there was nothing I could do to change that.

Then, just like the last time, as he knocked one of my wrists away from his face, he continued that sweep of his hand until it was level with my waist. He held me firmly as he crouched, dodging the fist hurtling for his face, letting me swing into empty air. I felt his palm slide around the back of my leg. His fingers dug into my thigh as he wrenched me forward, pushing me into the missed punch. My wings instinctually tucked behind me, attempting to restore my balance, and that was when Lee caught me in his arms, successfully pinning me to his chest.

Huh. I might learn a thing or two from him after all.

I tried to peel myself out of his arms, but he lifted a hand and bracketed my jaw, turning my face toward his. For whatever reason, I allowed him to keep me for a moment more.

"I need you to hear this," he whispered. "You aren't wrong in this world, Sia, and you aren't weak, regardless of what you do to make yourself that way. What you are is untouched. Where you come from doesn't mean anything unless you *want* it to. *You* choose who you become. That's a decision each of us make for ourselves, and it's just about the only thing you *can* control."

Everything within me quivered.

"What if I don't know who to be anymore?" It was such a reckless thing to admit, and yet...

A sad smile tugged at his lips. "Then you take it one mountain at a time. One day—one hour, if you must. We'll go on our tour. We'll train. And when the time comes, I will help you learn the truth of *every* matter."

"Just so long as I pretend to love you while we do it, right?"

His smile fell.

"Remind me why we need to pretend like that again?" I pleaded.

He sighed and let me go. When I twisted to face him, he was pacing the edge of the ring, running a hand through his messy, golden hair.

"Only because that's what our countries and families expect of us. Between you and me, there are no expectations, not for the marriage or the training, not any of it." He glided to a halt and looked at me. "If I've learned anything about you, Sia, it's that you're a spectacular liar. So in front of everyone else, you just need to keep on doing that. We *both* do. My country is wary of this union, wary of me as a ruler—they believe the very worst. They believe the poison my father has spread about your family. In their eyes, I'm still a child, even though I've been running the country in my father's stead since I was seventeen."

That little morsel of information was a surprise.

I knew his father was sick, but I didn't realize his condition had deteriorated that much. My surprise must have been evident, because Lee abandoned his pacing and strode up to me, his expression more open than I'd seen it in weeks. "I came for you, Sia, because I made a promise to you. And I know you hate me for it, but, please, for *my* sake, my people need a reason to stand with us. They need to approve of this bond until we know for certain that we can break it. You aren't losing anything by helping me."

I wasn't losing anything in this scheme he'd concocted, but what was he risking? A broken engagement. A broken bond. That had to be just as bad for his rule as a discontented union.

Unless…

"Oh, I see now." I scoffed, crossing my arms. "When we go our separate ways, you'll turn me into the villain who abandoned you."

Offense burned brightly in his eyes. With a slow shake of his head, he murmured, "No, darling. When you go, I will be the foolish king who loved a wandering heart."

Those words struck my heart with a resounding clash. I felt the echoes of it travel through my body, ruffling my feathers and scoring pain through my chest. I suddenly wanted to ask if he truly believed that. And if he did, I wanted to tell him he was wrong.

Because it *felt* wrong.

It knew it wouldn't matter what he believed, though, in the end. Instead of picking a fight I'd lose, I took a deep breath and squared my shoulders. We would go on our tour. We would train. We would find the answers—together.

I stepped closer, waving him forward. "Show me again."

CHAPTER 19

The Impundulu territory was beautiful in the winter, with its landscape of mountainous pines and endless, snowy-laden peaks. Their palace sat upon one of those peaks, nestled close to the northernmost coast of our continent. Mountains guarded the city on every side, with only a single pass leading down to the ocean.

There was no other way to get to this city but from the sky.

As I emerged from the carriage, I drew the fur shawl tighter around my shoulders, the cold a shocking contrast to the humidity of my father's city.

My breath billowed thickly in front of me as I stalked away from the landing strip, eager to keep moving, my legs tingling as cold air seeped up underneath my dress. As I approached the gathering of tents up ahead with their canvas glowing with the promise of fire and warmth, I allowed my gaze to wander.

Seraphim were flying in the distance, giving away the position of the city. The palace was situated slightly higher up on the mountain, but not so far that it wasn't easily accessible to the citizens. It was less opulent than the one on my father's floating island, but just as beautiful. Strong and tall, built from the stone and minerals harvested from the mines beneath.

The Impundulu tended to mines throughout this mountain range and hoarded deep reserves of lightning that served to power their city year-round.

Instead of faerie orbs, they had electricity. That contraption in the Fenix observatory was powered by them too. They had little need for anything that couldn't be sourced from their own territory, so much so that sometimes, I pondered why they bothered with alliances at all.

As staff emerged from the tents to retrieve my luggage, they greeted me with pleasant smiles and nods, but I didn't miss the way their gazes caught on my wings... and lingered.

A different kind of shiver crawled up my spine.

Was this going to be my fate for the rest of the tour? Would I be a walking spectacle for the next couple months? I sighed in resignation. Could I really expect anything less?

Entering the main tent, I was immediately enveloped by a large, overhead light. I blinked, my vision acclimating as heat wrapped around me. The warmth emanated from several iron pillars erected throughout the room. I could hear the faint hum of electricity vibrating within them.

Otherwise, the room was simple: a worn stone floor and wooden furniture.

My eyes landed on a few sentinels sitting around a table near a staircase descending into the mountain. Seeing me, they straightened, their bronze wings tucking in as they exchanged a look, as if trying to decide which one was supposed to greet me.

I smiled, equal parts confused and amused by their surprise. "I didn't think I was *that* early. Aren't you expecting me?"

A voice echoed up the staircase, accompanied by urgent

footsteps. "I'm coming, I'm here." Then, a head emerged from the dark—a crown of iron and diamond set upon brown curls. Queen Mizel herself was here to welcome me to her territory.

The sentinels scrambled out of their seats and bowed, but she only waved a dismissive hand in their direction. They quickly relaxed into their seats.

She gave me a bright smile as she crested the final step, and her gaze slid right past my wings. I wondered if she had any idea how much that comforted me. Just her mere *presence* soothed my nerves. My returning grin was effortless, and as I curtsied, there was no resistance to it. I wanted to bow for her. I *respected* her, as a queen and a mother and a female.

I suddenly felt extremely grateful this territory was the first stop on our tour.

"I'm sorry. If I had known you were wanting to greet us, I would have arrived at the right time." I had been too eager to leave my father's island, eager to get out of the consistent rain and humid heat. I hadn't meant to inconvenience her.

Queen Mizel took my hands in hers. "Don't be sorry, my dear. I am delighted to see you; you are welcome anytime."

My heart hummed under her motherly kindness.

She craned her neck to look behind me. "Is it just you who has arrived?"

"Yes, for now. Alezandral is running an hour or so behind me." His luggage was still being loaded when my carriage left. I hadn't seen him yet today. We didn't train this morning, which was also why I left a little earlier than we'd planned. I had a well of nervous energy that I couldn't expel.

Alezandral and I were *expected* to take separate carriages, just as my brother and my father were. I was only a little surprised that my betrothed had agreed to it.

In the days between our engagement party and the start of our tour, we'd become practically inseparable. Early morning training led us to having breakfast together—after I got dizzy during our second morning and he realized I wasn't eating to his satisfaction. After that, we shared nearly every meal in the same room. He brought me books to read that ranged from war strategy to old archives he thought might be useful in our search for my origin. Some of them I'd read before, but most I hadn't. Quite a few of the volumes were from other territories, stamped with the other colonies' coat of arms. How he got his hands on them, I wasn't entirely sure. Maybe he was closer to the other royals than I knew, or maybe he was "borrowing" them with the help of his Materie. I didn't ask.

We discussed the books over dinner each evening, and I started to understand just how much Alezandral read in his spare time. I didn't know how he found the time to sleep.

He was an overbearing jackass most of the time, but he was also brilliant. Every day, I learned something new. Every day, I felt a little stronger, a little more confident in using my flame. As the mornings passed, he demanded more from me. His masterful control of hoarfrost was near impenetrable, and I soon forgot why I was ever afraid to hurt him.

The simple fact of the matter was that I couldn't.

I walked away from our sessions sore and sweaty and frustrated, but I felt alive. And best of all, I had a purpose again. I had a goal. Someday, I would get the upper hand on Alezandral in that training ring, and I couldn't fucking *wait*.

So I could admit I wasn't entirely opposed to sharing a carriage with him. His company was comfortable now.

"Well, then," Queen Mizel said, pulling me away from my thoughts. "Let's get you to your room so you can settle in. We have a few hours before the commencement." She looped her arm in mine and guided me down the staircase.

The stairs led into a tunnel lit by warm yellow bulbs, lined on either side with more of those iron pillars.

It was clean but suffocating.

Thankfully, it was a short walk to the staircase on the

other end, and Queen Mizel distracted me with easy conversation. When we ascended into a spiraling tower, I breathed a sigh of relief, and Queen Mizel tossed me a knowing smile as she gave my arm a pat.

I couldn't imagine walking tunnels like that every day. They were smaller than the dungeons beneath my father's palace. But the mines had to be a thousand times worse.

The Impundulu were *used to this.*

Maybe their relationship with nature made them feel more at home surrounded by raw stone? Either way, I was glad to have some space to breathe again, glad to see the outside world through panes of frosty glass.

I admired the old halls as she led me through them. There was a striking sense of history to the family portraits and all the aged crimson banners. Did my father's family have this once? On that island the Fenix left behind? My heart ached for what was lost, even if it was never meant to be mine. Even if I wasn't Fenix in my blood.

"I hope you'll be at ease here," Queen Mizel murmured when she caught me staring. "I know it's not as bright and warm as the home you're used to—"

"No, this is lovely," I replied quickly.

If only she knew what I was used to, the dark places I had been.

Queen Mizel led us with more purpose down the next corridor. Leaving my side, she opened a door on the right and ushered me into a large room with massive windows and a wide bed with white downy bedding. The rugs scattered throughout the room were threaded with silver and gold. A stone fireplace crackled on the far end, next to a pair of double doors that led into a dim bathroom, not a trace of red to be seen. That seemed odd to me, considering the Impundulu colors were red and black.

But then, I hadn't spent a lot of time in other territories.

Perhaps my father held more tightly to his heritage because of what he'd been forced to leave behind. Perhaps embedding red and orange into every inch of his home was the only way to feel close to it. That realization brought with it a deep sadness, similar to the aching, but a little different. A little harder to ignore.

Queen Mizel turned to face me, and seeing the pain in my eyes, she lifted a hand to my cheek.

"I know this is all overwhelming—it was when my Lanier and I went through it—but I want you to know I'm here to listen if ever you need an ear."

"Thank you, Your Majesty."

Her eyes sparkled as she leaned in and whispered, "And I'm sure you want some time alone with your betrothed when he gets here. I'll have the staff leave his bags outside the door."

My breath caught in my throat like a thorn.

I hadn't given a thought to sleeping arrangements yet, but her insinuation was clear. Alezandral and I would be sharing this room. *Goddess beside us…*

We would be sharing a bed for the next three months.

Queen Mizel chuckled, clearly mistaking my petrified expression for shyness, and slid around me to leave. And as the door shut behind her, I finally remembered how to exhale.

CHAPTER 20

Two hours later, I was still standing alone in our temporary bedroom.

Where is he?

We needed to talk about this. This… sleeping in the same room business.

I couldn't even sit down, I was so wired. I paced the length of the room in my robe, my gaze flicking from the door to the gaudy red dress laid out for me on our bed. The bed we were apparently *sharing*. It seemed so intimate to sleep together, even if there wasn't anything physical involved. To listen to his breathing. To wake up beside him and look into his eyes as sleep lingered between us. I bet he was beautiful like that. I could practically see it now—his soft gaze and wicked smirk, those long fingers of his twisted in our sheets.

I shook my head, flinging those thoughts away before they changed my mind.

We couldn't sleep in the same bed. It wasn't a good idea. I needed to tell him that I was willing to take turns sleeping on the floor if we had to—but he wasn't *here*, and there was no explanation for why he wasn't.

I tripped to a stop on one of the silver rugs as a terrible thought gripped me.

No, his carriage couldn't possibly have been intercepted. My heart thundered as the possibility sank its claws into my mind. Someone would have found out by now if it had. Someone would have told me. They would have told me, right? Unless there were no survivors.

Now, I was spiraling, drowning in waves of panic.

This area was wrought with rebels and assassins hired by the human royals. We were too close to the smog, too close to the human epicenter, the palace just beyond these mountain ranges and across the sea to the east. If the human royals knew we were traveling nearby, they might have done something about it. Taking out the only heir of a seraphic crown might have been too tempting to resist.

My early arrival could have tipped them off, if they were watching. I didn't wait for him. I didn't even say goodbye. Chest tight and eyes burning, I stalked across the room. I would search for him myself.

I had to, before I lost my entire mind to worry.

When I tore open the door and stepped into the hall, my entire body went cold. His luggage was here. At first, I felt a burst of relief, a loosening of my entire body as I slumped against the doorframe. He was safe.

Then that relief bled into anger and disappointment, and another vicious raw emotion I didn't have a name for.

He was here, but he wasn't *here*. Why hadn't he come to the room? Did he not want to see me? If he wasn't here, what was he doing? Who was he with?

He told me Gus had returned to the Halcyon territory, but perhaps he'd lied.

With a snarl, I turned to retreat into the room, pausing when I saw the woman approaching from the other end of the hall. "Oh my. You look upset," Kori said with a laugh, her arms overflowing with a thick black bag and a stack of loose parchment. "What's wrong?"

I smoothed my expression. "Nothing at all."

She laughed again. "I don't believe that for a moment."

The Impundulu princess seemed far more relaxed today than she had been at the engagement party. Her cinnamon hair was twisted into a loose bundle on top of her head, and her cheeks were rosy and full. I'd be willing to bet she fed recently. Her skin had taken on that same hue from when she fed from me down in the human city.

I didn't know how to respond, so I didn't.

In my silence, she nodded at the door to my room. "Do you mind?"

With a start, I realized that the bundle in her arms was intended for *me,* and I pushed the door open for her. She shuffled into the bedroom and dropped the items onto my bed—*our* bed—with a tired huff. Then she turned to me with a smile and brushed the hair out of her face. "I have some sketches for you to look at," she informed me. "And also, a present. You don't have to accept it if you don't like it."

I joined her at the edge of the bed, eyeing the pile she'd deposited on top of my red dress. "Alright..."

Kori scooped up the papers and shoved them into my hands.

My eyes scanned the charcoal smudging, the sweeping lines of a dress she'd designed. *My wedding dress.* Divine Mother... I'd forgotten about it again. My curiosity won out, and I started sifting through the sketches, my eyes widening as I realized just how talented Kori was. Every dress was as elegant as it was unique, with asymmetrical layers and long, flowing trains. Some had beautiful detailing, others stunning in their simplicity, and all for nothing.

I wasn't going to get the chance to wear any of these.

"These are beautiful, Kori," I murmured, because there was

nothing else I could say. There was no way to explain the sinking sensation in my stomach, even to myself.

She gave me a wide, breathtaking smile. "Hold onto them for a while so you can think about what you like best. Just make sure to let me know your decision before you leave next week so I can get the dress finished before the end of your tour."

I set the papers aside and nodded at the black bag. "And what's that?"

Shyness crept back into her expression. "It's a dress. For today, if you want it. Don't feel obligated, though."

"For today?" I echoed.

She shifted on her feet. "Yes, I thought you might like to wear something more... *you* for the tour. Something special."

I just stared at her for a moment, my chest warming. I couldn't believe she would do something so thoughtful for me. After I scared her. After I chased her down at the party. She'd made a dress for me simply because she knew how uncomfortable I was in my father's colors, and that was a gesture I couldn't reject, despite how unworthy I felt.

"Let me see it."

Kori spun around and stretched the bag out on the bed, loosening the ties holding it closed. As she tugged the bag open, a small gasp fell from my lips.

Amethyst crystals shimmered across the bodice of the dress, with sheer lavender backing flowing into a voluminous skirt cinched at the waist. The short sleeves were angled, designed to wrap around my arms just past the shoulders. Several shades of purple were sewn into the stitch-work, and they coalesced into a magnificent symphony of color.

I exhaled sharply, shaking my head in disbelief. "Kori..."

"Here," she held it up to my body. "Put it on. I can make adjustments while you wear it."

I removed my robe and allowed her to pull it up over my

hips. It was nearly perfect already, and I silently cherished the way she seemed to understand every curve of my body as she retrieved a set of pins from the bag and went to work on eliminating every inch of extra material. By the time she was finished, it fit like a glove.

When she tugged me toward the large mirror in the bathroom, I saw myself, and it felt… *right*.

The jewel tones brought out the blue sheen in my wings. My dark hair stood out against the vibrant purples. My amber eyes were brightened with hope and comfort, and I realized this was exactly what I needed. A color just for me.

"I have other dresses for you to take on the tour as well," she said, admiring my reflection in the mirror. Her voice was soft, nervous about admitting such a kind deed. "I'll admit, I went a little stir-crazy after your engagement party last week."

Before I could second-guess the urge, I grabbed her by the arms and pulled her into a hug.

She stiffened, but I held fast. I wanted her to know how much this meant to me. "Thank you," I whispered, my throat burning with unshed tears.

"You're welcome, Sia. But, uh—you're sticking me with a pin right now."

I laughed and let her go, stepping back so she could continue her work. She saw the dampness in my eyes and smiled gently, looking so much like her mother in that moment that, even though I knew they weren't related by blood, it made me believe for a heartbeat that what Lee said to me in the training ring was true.

We could choose who we were and where we belonged.

* * *

Kori and I walked in companionable silence toward the front of the palace, where, apparently, there was a balcony prepared for Alezandral and I. We would emerge there and allow the citizens waiting in the courtyard below to welcome us. Then, there would be a dinner with the nobility and a series of other activities the Queens had scheduled for us over the course of the next week.

The goal was to become familiar with the royal family, to form bonds that would strengthen our future alliances.

While I was eager to get to know the Impundulu better, I was also nervous about subjecting myself to their scrutiny. It wasn't about secrets anymore. It was them seeing me as I truly was. We'd be spending time in the city as well, and I didn't know what to expect from the general public. Queen Mizel and her daughter accepted me well enough, but the rest of the territory didn't have to.

Naturally, I was prepared for the worst.

I wished Alezandral was walking to the commencement beside me. That would have made me feel better. He always seemed to know exactly what to do or say to get me out of my head, even if he had to wiggle his way in and push me out by force.

As Kori led me into the grand hall, my gaze skipped across the crowd of nobles, and I found him instantly.

Alezandral stood beside a pair of walnut doors that rose nearly to the ceiling. He wore a stiff tunic threaded with shades of blue, the Halcyon coat of arms gleaming silvery-white over his heart. This was the first time I'd ever seen him in a crown. It was a simple, hardy ring of silver, and I thought it suited him well.

His blond hair was swept to one side beneath it, a few soft golden tendrils hanging down over his brow.

I'd forgone the ruby crown my father sent with me. Instead, Kori had let me borrow a diamond hairpiece to take its place, but I would have to find a proper replacement soon. Especially when Alezandral looked like *that* in his.

As if sensing my eyes, Alezandral lifted his gaze to the room. When he saw me, his jaw slackened. His eyes roamed the length of my body, drinking me in, and a little spark of pride set fire to my nerves.

Kori snickered. "I think he likes it."

We crossed the room together, and I realized as Kori broke away to join her mothers that the Impundulu Queens were also waiting by the doors.

Alezandral hadn't so much as blinked, his eyes trained on my dress as I closed the distance between us. Before I could reach him, someone called my name.

"Princess Sabrina."

I turned to see Edmin, crown prince of the Impundulu, extending a hand to me.

His eyes were alight with interest, and his thin mouth spread to reveal sharp, white teeth. This welcome was a stark contrast to our brief greeting at my engagement party. He was smiling like he was happy to see me. He took my hand, pressing a kiss to the back of my palm. "You look absolutely beautiful today, Your Highness."

I tugged my hand back when he didn't immediately let it go.

He folded his arms behind his back and leaned in. "I do apologize for my coldness the last time I saw you. I figured you would rather no one know of our familiarity."

I narrowed my eyes. "What familiarity?"

I knew he was talking about our hour-long fling a decade ago, but his tone irritated me. He was acting like we had kept this secret from everyone on purpose, and I hadn't. We didn't know each other.

Confusion flashed across his features, but then he threw his head back and laughed. "Yes. Precisely."

Clearly, he assumed I was agreeing with him, admitting I wanted to keep our tryst a secret. So I said, "I couldn't give less of a fuck, if I'm being honest. I figured your sister would have told people about it by now. Why didn't she, by the way?"

I gave him a small smile—one that told him exactly what else I wanted to know. *Why did his sister walk in on us in the first place?* Edmin had been alone in that corridor when I stumbled across him for the first time, but maybe he'd been waiting for someone. Why hadn't Edmin or his sister been promised in marriage yet? Why did they cling to one another?

It could be a coincidence, but I didn't think so.

His sister glared at me now from where she stood next to her other siblings. I was right about them, I just knew I was.

Edmin was momentarily taken aback by my accusation, but he smoothed his expression with an evasive grin. Somehow, he seemed to be *more* interested in me after subtly threatening to expose his secret. "My *sister* is discreet."

A throat cleared behind me, and I sighed in relief as I was given an excuse to pull away from Edmin.

Alezandral had walked up on us while we were talking. He didn't touch me, but I felt him all the same. His gaze staked a claim that Edmin instantly recognized. When the Impundulu prince backed away another step, I beamed.

But Alezandral didn't see that.

He simply kept glaring at Edmin until the prince cleared his throat and gave a shallow bow, excusing himself.

I turned to my betrothed, and his gaze finally shifted to me, admiring my dress again. I waited for him to compliment it, but all he gave me was silence.

"Well," I prompted, "aren't you going to say anything?"

"Prince Edmin beat me to it," he murmured, quiet enough that I knew no one else could hear it. "He told you *precisely* how beautiful you look."

I bit my lip.

This was the first time I'd ever seen Alezandral jealous—

blatantly, petulantly jealous. He was visibly stiff, shifting uncomfortably on his feet. His eyes were hard.

It stroked a sweet pleasure deep in my belly, knowing he felt even the slightest bit possessive over me, but I decided to put an end to this before it ruined our day. I wrapped my hand around the inside of his arm and inched closer. "He's not someone I want compliments from. I already had a taste of Edmin in my youth and have no desire to revisit that memory. He kisses like a chicken."

Peck, peck, pecker, I added in my mind, wrinkling my nose in disgust.

Lee's lips twitched, but he quickly pursed them, masking his amusement. He stepped toward me, and my body lit up with electric tingles as a full, warm smile bloomed on his face. With one gloved finger, he brushed a tendril of hair out of my eyes. "You are stunning, my darling."

I knew he was only calling me his darling because the guests around us were listening in, but it sent a shock racing up my spine anyway.

Damn my traitorous heart and my traitorous body, my traitorous fucking mind. All I could think about right now were his lips. It had been too long since I last felt them, last kissed them. I suddenly wanted to know what they felt like on the soft skin of my belly, on my plush inner thighs. I wanted them *everywhere*.

But that was a really, really terrible idea.

Unfortunately, I knew just how much I loved flirting with terrible ideas. That was how I always managed to make a mess of things, so I couldn't indulge this one. Not ever.

Queen Lanier turned to us as we walked to the royal family. "Great, you both are here. Let's hurry and get the commencement out of the way so we can eat." She tugged on her wife's hand, pulling her toward the doors, and Queen Mizel laughed.

"Always starving, my love," she teased, resisting her pull.

Queen Lanier gave her an exasperated look, and I couldn't help but laugh a little too.

When Queen Lanier tugged her forward again, Queen Mizel went willingly, and a pair of sentinels surged forward to open the doors for them. The doors swung wide with a heavy groan, and a flood of gray winter light drenched the four of us. The queens stepped out onto the balcony.

A thunderous roar erupted from the crowd below.

Alezandral's hand found mine as we walked up to the threshold together, pausing as we waited for the crowd to quiet enough for introductions.

As Queen Mizel approached a narrow pole near the stone railing, I noticed a thick rope was attached to the star-like pendant at its peak. I could hear the electric current emanating from it. When she spoke, her voice crackled all around us, projected through a speaker system set up on the balcony. "Welcome, all. Thank you for joining us this evening to receive two very special guests into our territory."

The crowd roared again, and I could *feel* their voices rumbling under my feet.

Alezandral squeezed my fingers, and I gave a tight squeeze in return. Even though I knew better than to draw comfort from him, the gesture succeeded in soothing me.

The bronze-winged queen laughed, leaning away from the microphone as she waited for the cheers to die down. "It is a momentous day, indeed. We are honored to be hosting the future Halcyon king and his extraordinary bride on the first stop of their engagement tour, and I hope you will give them a welcome worthy of the lightning running through our veins."

She stepped to the side and swept a hand toward us, and the crowd went wild.

They were stomping now, clapping and shouting in a rhythmic beat. The reverberations slammed into me, and it was an effort not to stagger backwards into the relative silence of the grand hall.

Alezandral glanced over at me. "Ready?"

"As ever," I exhaled.

We walked as one over the threshold, and as the crowd crept into view, everything inside of me quivered. I could no longer feel my feet; Alezandral's hand alone continued to pull me forward.

My hesitation wasn't because of the crowd itself—it was what I saw there.

A little girl sat on her father's shoulders, her little bronze wings smeared with charcoal. Then, my gaze caught on others. Males, females, and children alike bore those black streaks all over their wings. Their cheers intensified as we peered over the railing, and it struck me suddenly that their eyes were on *me*, not Alezandral.

For a moment, I couldn't quite understand, and then it hit me, the realization as loud and overwhelming as their cries. It knocked the air out of my lungs.

They had painted their bronze feathers to look like *mine*. They *liked* them.

I blinked rapidly, fighting the sudden sting in my eyes.

You see? Lee whispered into my head. *They want the real you, just as I do.*

I glanced at him, my vision blurring. There were no words in my head for him. There was only a storm of emotion I had no power over, and it had nothing to do with my flame or my rocky self-control. This… I didn't know what to do with it.

Alezandral tugged me closer. *I'm going to kiss you now.*

When he leaned down to press his warm lips to mine, a small, vicious thing inside me uncurled, blooming under his kiss. I wrapped my arms around his neck, surrendering to the embrace. And, despite my best efforts to hold my betrothed at a distance thus far, I found myself foolishly hoping that this moment between us wasn't just for show.

CHAPTER 21

On the first morning after arriving in the Stymphalian territory, I woke in a fit of agony.

A deep, vicious ache had settled into my lower back, and I could barely turn over in the bed with the sharp needles digging into my belly. My stomach churned, and I moaned into the pillow as I curled into a ball, my wings twitching behind me.

It hurt to even breathe too deeply.

Winter had seized the hills and valleys of the Stymphalian territory, and I could see frost kissing the dark windows across the room. An eternal flame crackled in a clay fireplace nearby, and the blankets tangled around my body were thick wool, but I was still shivering.

When I reached for the flame inside me, it twisted away, unwilling to surface.

We'd arrived at the Stymphalian territory late last night, and we'd yet to commence the tour here. We were supposed to do that this morning. In fact, if the lightening of the sky was any indication of the time, I should be moving around already, preparing to meet Alezandral in the training area.

But there was no way I was getting out of this bed right now.

Had I gotten sick? What a foreign notion.

For a brief moment, I worried that this feeling was connected to the bond Alezandral and I shared, but when I placed a hand over my heart, it was beating slow and steady. My scar didn't hurt. This must be something else.

Alezandral and I had spent the previous week in the Impundulu territory.

The Impundulu were an enthusiastic people, friendly and warm and a little bit wild in the best way. I'd loved spending time in their city, loved their expansive art galleries and the world of music that came to life in their streets at night.

Even though we were visiting for our engagement, Alezandral and I didn't spend much time together, save for our continued training every morning and the daily meals. My panic over sharing a bed with him had been a waste of worry. Every evening, he walked me to our room, dressed down for the night, and promptly left. I wasn't sure where he was sleeping, but it wasn't at my side.

Writhing there on the bed, I watched as the sky outside brightened to a soft, welcoming blue. I could see the rooftops of the town spread out around my little cabin.

Another twinge of pain dug into my lower abdomen, and I squeezed my eyes shut with a whimper, wondering if I might be able to sleep off whatever this was.

A knock against the door to the cabin shattered that hope.

"Sia?" Alezandral's voice rumbled through the room.

I groaned, turning my face fully against the pillow.

"I know you're in there, Sia. If you think I'm going to let you skip out on even one training without warning, you're sorely mistaken. Open the door."

"Go away," I growled, my voice sounding weaker than I wanted it to.

There was a moment of silence, and then Alezandral asked, "What's wrong?"

"Nothing," I sighed, wincing at another sharp stab. "I'm not feeling up to training today. Please, just leave."

"Open the door and let me see you."

I clenched my jaw, which really didn't help with the ache between my temples. "Fuck off, Alezandral."

When the doorknob jiggled, I glanced over my shoulder at it, relieved that I had remembered to lock the door last night. That didn't stop him from using his Materie to jump right inside the room, though.

It took a moment to school my expression as the mist appeared.

I had forgotten about his Materie but, in my defense, he never mentioned he could move *himself* places with it. He was quite a bit larger than a bottle or a set of wings.

The billowing black wisps fell and curled along the floor, sparkling like a night sky, swiftly parting to reveal Alezandral in the center. He was wearing his training leathers, a navy tunic gaping down the front of his chest, a thin layer of sweat glimmering over his skin.

Of course he wasn't going to let me be.

His royal jackassiness wouldn't allow it.

Alezandral's eyes narrowed at my contorted position on the mattress. "What's wrong with you, Sia? Why are you still in bed?"

Anger surged through me, and I twisted toward him, ignoring the clench of my stomach. "It's none of your business. Why can't you just listen and leave me alone?"

He stalked forward, his brow furrowed. "*Because* you're being incredibly stub—"

Alezandral stopped abruptly half-way across the room, his nostrils flaring slightly. Some of the tension in his shoulders loosened and his eyes fluttered, warm compassion dancing over his features. "You're bleeding, Sia."

I pushed back the blankets and saw that he was right. Bright red blood stained the sheet beneath me.

"Oh," I breathed. "So I am."

My bleeds were finally here. I had known they were imminent, of course. Twenty-five was the average starting age for seraphim, but I was secretly hoping I'd have another year or two without them. Bleeds were a sign that, at least in function, my body was now capable of bearing children, but I had no interest in finding out for certain.

Lee stood there, keeping his distance, his hands fisting at his sides. "It's your first bleed, I'm guessing?"

I swallowed my embarrassment. "Yes. I'm sorry, I should've known what it was."

Alezandral shrugged. "How could you?"

"I thought I was sick," I admitted.

"Of course you did. The first bleed is the hardest. Why didn't you call for someone?" He nodded at the summoning rope hanging next to the door.

I rolled my eyes. "We've barely arrived here, Alezandral. I didn't want to inconvenience anyone with my stomachache."

Alezandral's jaw hardened before he turned on his heel and walked to the door, pulling on the charmed rope with a decisive jerk. A tinkle echoed through the room. Without another glance in my direction, he crossed to the bathroom and disappeared through the door.

The faerie orbs inside flickered to life, glowing white over the threshold as Alezandral's boots stomped across the tile.

I stared at the bathroom in confusion as the faucet to the tub turned on. With a bit of effort, I managed to sit up, twisting my fingers in the sheets pooled around my hips. I could feel the blood between my thighs now, unpleasantly slick. I didn't want to sit in it much longer, but I also didn't want to stand up and risk Alezandral seeing it. I'd never felt like this before, so shy and uncertain about my body. So, I waited there, hoping Alezandral would be quick about washing up so I could use the bathroom after he left.

Except he wasn't closing the door like he usually did.

When he emerged from the bathroom still fully dressed and approached the bed, my heart raced. He reached for me as if he intended to scoop me up, but I shoved his arms away. "What are you doing? Stop."

Alezandral glared at me and pressed his fists into the edge of the bed. "I'm taking care of you, whether you want it or not. This is my responsibility."

I shook my head. "We aren't really getting married. You don't have to."

"Just accept a little bit of help when you need it, Sia. Doing so doesn't make you weak."

Heart hammering, my lips parted to give him a response, but I was unable to find a single word.

"You couldn't even walk to the door to call for help," he pressed. "Do you really think you can make it into the bathroom right now without collapsing? You think you can get into the tub without slipping and hurting yourself?"

I squinted at him, my pride preventing me from admitting that the answer was no.

My whole body trembled from the effort it took to sit up. If I stood, there wasn't a doubt in my mind that my legs would give out, but I'd rather crawl to the tub than tell him how weak I was feeling.

When he reached for me again, though, I surrendered with a small sigh.

Alezandral peeled the blankets down my legs, and as he wrapped his arms under my knees and around my back, I felt his Materie tingle down my spine as his magic folded my wings into place beneath my back.

"It'll be easier to clean up without them," he explained as he lifted me off the bed.

My wings added pressure around my spine, which surprisingly helped with the ache in my back. The pain in my belly intensified, though.

Gritting my teeth, I focused on breathing through it.

He carried me to the bathroom and set me down on the raised latrine. When his fingers grasped at the hem of my nightgown, a fresh wave of insecurity rippled over me.

I caught his wrists. "Wait—"

Alezandral settled his gaze on my face. "I won't look," he swore. "I just want to help you into the tub before the physician gets here. The hot water will help."

I had no idea how he knew so much about female cycles, but I nodded, letting go of his wrists. "Okay."

He peeled the gown over my head and tossed it toward the bedroom, and then his arms were around me again. He carried me to the tub and lowered me into it. True to his word, his eyes didn't stray from my face. When the hot water enveloped my lower body, I couldn't hold back my moan as the ache in my hips lessened.

Alezandral's body stiffened, but he screwed his eyes shut before pulling away.

"Thank you," I muttered.

With a sharp nod, he turned and exited the bathroom, pulling the door nearly shut behind him. I wondered why he didn't close it completely, but when I heard a knock at the front of the cabin, I realized that was probably why.

His steps clipped over the floor, and the faint rumble of voices drifted into the bathroom. They were too quiet to make out much, but a minute later, I heard the door shut and then Alezandral's measured steps back to the bathroom. A sliver of his body appeared beyond the threshold. "The physician is on her way. It'll just be a few minutes."

"Alright."

Silence stretched between us as he lingered.

"Is there something more you need from me?" I asked.

He cleared his throat. "I found another book. It looks promising." Another tense silence, and then he added, "I can read some of it to you while we wait."

I huffed a laugh. "You want to read to me while I sit in the bath?"

"Yes. I'll stay right here. I just figured… it's worse when you have to suffer alone." His voice seemed so small to me in that moment, like a child's.

My heart kicked hard against my ribs.

The water was brimming past my chest now, swirling with lavender soap and shiny bubbles. He hadn't just turned on the faucet for me. He'd prepared a *bubble bath*. My body was mostly concealed, and that gave me a sense of confidence again. A sense of safety.

Besides, I sort of liked having him nearby, in our room. "I'll listen to you read."

He walked away and returned a minute later, lowering himself to the floor right outside the bathroom door. As he started reading, I leaned forward and turned off the faucet, then melted against the slope of the tub, allowing the water to envelop me up to my chin. I closed my eyes and let his voice lull me into something like a trance. He described the habits of Winged Spirits, how they gravitated towards terrain that most resembled their home worlds, how they could migrate from one place to another if disturbed.

Alezandral couldn't have read more than a couple pages before he paused.

He fell silent, humming thoughtfully. "I wonder if…"

"What?"

"Your father says that the Fenix spirit traveled to the continent with your people," he started, but the statement felt like a question.

"Yes. Both my brother's and my conception happened on the mainland."

"In the same place?"

I shrugged. "As far as I know. They happened in a crater somewhere between the Impundulu and my father's island. I visited it once, but there was nothing there, just a deep, dark chasm."

"Interesting," he murmured.

"Why? What are you thinking?"

"I just—" He sighed. "I've been thinking about what the sutilis said to you. I think the Fenix spirit might have been there for your brother, but then maybe it moved, and whatever spirit came from the sutilus' world, maybe that took its place... until your mother was sacrificed. If we can figure out where it migrated to afterward, we can go to it. We can see it. You could talk to it."

My body stiffened.

Visiting a Winged Spirit wasn't unheard of. In ancient times, the seraphim did it often, to better understand their origins and powers. But me? Seeking out the spirit responsible for my life and potentially the lives of those rotting, vicious creatures that rip the weak into pieces?

It was daunting.

And it might be the best idea we'd had yet.

I cleared my throat. "How could we figure out where it migrated to, Alezandral? We might spend our whole lives searching for it, and there's no guarantee we'd find it. If it moved once, it might have moved a dozen or more times since my conception."

"We could ask the Wight where it is now."

That was... true. We *could* do that.

Another knock sounded on the cabin door, interrupting us

before I could formulate a response. As Alezandral jumped up to receive the physician and direct her to the bathroom, my mind spun with the possibility. The Wight was still months away. We had plenty of time to decide what exactly to ask it.

We only had two questions, one for each of us.

Mine was reserved for our heart bond, to figure out a way to break it, so maybe Alezandral was suggesting that we use his to find my Winged Spirit.

When the Stymphalian physician entered the bathroom, I forced myself to put away those thoughts. She was one of the Stymphalian elders. I could tell from the way she walked, slow and graceful, and from the way her iron wings dragged along the ground behind her, as if the effort it would take to hold them up was the least of her concerns. Her dark brown skin looked as soft as silk under the faerie orbs, and a few luminous silver streaks glistened in her hair. She carried a small basket in and shut the bathroom door behind her.

"I hear we have your first cycle to deal with today," she said as she glided across the room.

I nodded, scooting myself higher up on the slope of the tub.

Despite her age, she knelt beside me. She pulled small glass vials from the basket and placed them along the flat edge of the tub. "Motherwort, dizasil, restoration bloom, and the concentrated juice of nightsage berries," she explained. "A small sip of the first three will lessen your pains. You may repeat that three times a day, as needed. Nightsage in the evening will help you sleep. The first night can prove difficult for even the toughest of females, so don't force yourself to suffer through it, understand?"

She leveled a serious stare at me.

"I understand, Elder," I said.

Elders were honored in every seraphic settlement, but especially here, in the Stymphalian territory, because here, there were many. Regardless of the number of wings on their back, if a seraph aged past a century, their magic started to grow again, to change. Most of our kind weren't hardy enough to endure the test of time, surrendering themselves to the Divine Mother by the time they turned 800. Those who endured discovered that a little of the world's magic found its way to them. They became our protectors, our guides.

The healer gave me an encouraging smile, nodding toward the herbs.

I picked up the first vial and took a small sip, grimacing at its bitter earthiness as the thick liquid slid down my throat. Then I quickly sipped from the next two, doing my best not to discern their taste.

"Very good," she hummed.

She withdrew a stack of clean cotton rags from the basket and set them on the counter. "These should last you through to the end of your cycle. Change them frequently. I've brought you a bag to place the used cloth in. Before bed, summon a maid to take them, and they will provide you with a new bag for the next day. I also suggest putting a towel on the bed beneath you as you sleep, at least for the first few nights. Your bleed should lighten dramatically after that, Goddess willing."

It was strange listening to her gentle instruction, knowing that if my mother was still alive, she would be the one telling me this. It was a reminder of what I had lost to my father's legacy, to the sacred tradition of my kind, a tradition that made my existence possible.

And yet, I felt enough regret for us all.

By the time I left the bath, I was feeling much better. The ache was still there in my lower back and hips and tops of my thighs, but the pain was no longer turning my legs to jelly. I dried off then donned the clothing the healer retrieved from my room. It took a little while to figure out the right way to fold the cloth into my undergarments, and it was a little uncomfortable when I walked, but not unbearable.

As I returned to the bedroom, I was shocked to find Alezandral standing with the elder at the foot of the bed, studying the contents of her basket with a furrowed brow.

"I didn't think you would still be here."

Alezandral's head whipped up at the sound of my voice, and as his eyes landed on me, they crinkled in a smile. "You aren't getting rid of me that easily, darling."

The elder stepped forward. "My work with you isn't done yet. If you'd please lie down." She beckoned me toward the bed and plucked a vial of golden liquid from the basket.

Alezandral tracked the movement with a grimace.

"Lie down?" I repeated, shifting uncomfortably. "For what?"

"Acupressure. It helps with any lingering aches."

"Meaning…"

She smiled patiently. "I'll be massaging a few pressure points on your legs."

That didn't sound appealing at all. The idea of anyone touching my body was downright repulsive. "Oh, that's really not necessary."

The Stymphalian opened her mouth to argue with me, but Alezandral set the basket down on the bed and reached for the vial in the physician's hand. "I can take care of her from here. Thank you for your time, Elder."

The elder shot him a surprised look. Thank the Goddess and all her spirits, Alezandral was sparing me.

I nodded eagerly. "Yes, we'll be fine now. Thank you."

Luckily, the physician didn't take any offense. She only

bowed her head to each of us and retreated across the room. As the door to the cabin clasped shut, I sighed in relief.

"Thank you for getting me out of that," I muttered.

Alezandral turned to me, his eyes narrowing. "You didn't get out of anything, Sia. Lie down on the bed."

Hold on, he was being *serious*? *He* wanted to be the one to rub that oil on my legs?

I fell back a step, shaking my head. "No way."

His lips tightened, and he crossed his arms in front of his chest the way he always did when he got bossy. "*Now*, Sia. Before I wrestle you down onto it myself."

My jaw dropped, and for a moment, I just stared at him, trying to determine how successful he'd be. I was feeling a lot stronger now, but not fully recovered.

It wouldn't be worth the struggle. He'd win.

I stomped over to the bed.

The sheets and blankets had already been changed; someone must have done it while I was bathing. I found it hard to be grateful as I dropped down onto the mattress. I shot a vicious glare at Alezandral and grumbled, "You're so fucking infuriating sometimes."

He beamed, climbing onto the bed near my feet.

I briefly considered kicking him in the face, but then he said, "You can be as angry with me as you need to be, darling. I'll still be here." And for some reason, that cut my anger off at the knees.

Alezandral shifted on the mattress, and I felt every press of his body jostling the bed. He glanced at me, lying there as stiff as a board, and chuckled. "Get comfortable. This is going to take a while."

"Don't antagonize me right now."

He shook his head. "I'm not trying to antagonize you. I just need you to relax." He reached for something in the basket and tossed it at me.

A bundle of burlap cloth landed heavily next to my fist.

"There, clever girl," he purred. "Eat a little of that."

I unwrapped the bundle and found a slab of chocolate. Begrudgingly, I started sucking on one corner, glaring at him as he poured a drizzle of oil into his palm. He wrapped a hand around my calf and inched closer until my foot was resting on his thigh. When he pressed the heel of his hand into my soft skin and dragged it upward toward my knee, I forgot my irritation.

A moan crawled out of my throat.

The pressure was both agony and pleasure. It was as if he'd found a muscle in my calf that led straight to the source of my aching. He rubbed the same spot again, dragging a long line from my ankle to the valley beneath my knee. It felt good— *really* good. Almost better than sex.

I brought the chocolate back to my lips, if only to keep myself from crying out again.

After a few long strokes, he shifted his grip and worked another tight muscle loose. I whimpered; that one was more tender. "How are you so good at this?" I gasped.

He smirked. "You didn't think I was the type of male who would allow my bride to endure her cycle alone, did you?"

"That's not what I mean. You've done this before, for someone else. I can tell." I'd been thinking that since he carried me into the bathroom.

Alezandral nodded. "I have."

I didn't know what to make of the heaviness that settled over me. He'd had someone else. Someone other than Augustus. Someone other than me. *Not that I wanted him to have me that way*, I reminded myself.

"What are you thinking?" he murmured.

I looked up to find Alezandral watching the emotions bend and dance across my face. "Nothing."

He set my leg down on the mattress and crawled forward

between my thighs. My heart leapt, pumping harder as he pressed his hands into the blankets to either side of my head, hovering over me the way he had in his tent when I snuck in to kill him in his sleep.

That felt like a lifetime ago.

"What are you—"

He shook his head, and the words died in my throat.

"Everything and everyone leading to this was only practice for me, Sia, preparation for the role I would take when I found my way back to you."

I couldn't breathe. He was so close, so large and overwhelming.

"And maybe it was cruel of me to be with anyone in an intimate capacity," he admitted quietly, "knowing you were coming. Maybe it was cruel to them, and to you, but that's just the way it happened."

What was he saying? That he felt *bad* for touching someone else like this? Because of *me*? So what?

He'd been with other people. I already knew that. And sure, it didn't feel great to talk about it, or to think about it, but I was in no position to complain. I *wasn't* complaining. I didn't know why I bothered to bring it up. I refused to harbor jealousy over his past relationships. Because I shouldn't.

I turned my head to look out the window. "It's fine, Alezandral. It's not as if I was celibate in our separation either." *And we aren't getting married, so it doesn't matter.*

When he remained there, staring down at me instead of backing off, I rolled my eyes and met his stare.

Alezandral was smiling, his eyes bright and chest shaking with silent laughter.

"*What?*" I growled, breaking off a piece of chocolate and imagining it was his arm I'd just snapped.

He bit his lip, trying to bring his amusement under

control. "Would it make you feel any better if I told you it was my *cousin* who taught me about cycles?"

I felt my eyebrows raise. "Well, I'm certainly curious as to how that came about."

"It wasn't one of my better moments, I'll admit," he said with a wince. "I lost a bet to Lana when I was seventeen after teasing her about all the time she spent in bed every couple of months. She held it over me for *years*; every time her cycle came around, I had to wait on her hand and foot. I never realized how miserable it could be before that."

I glared at him again, but it lacked conviction this time. "You're lucky I'm not your cousin, because I would have set you on fire."

He laughed. "If Lana could have, I'm sure she would've tried."

Tsking, I shook my head at him. "Pitiful behavior, Alezandral." I said it with the same chastising tone he gave me during training, and his eyes darkened.

Quick as a strike of lightning, his head whipped to the side, and his mouth closed over my fingers. His tongue swept between them, stealing the half-melted piece of chocolate there before he peeled away from me with a victorious smile.

My chest rattled like a train rail.

Without thinking, I brought those fingers to my mouth, licking away the melted chocolate and that barest trace of himself he'd left behind, the whisper of mint and pine.

Alezandral's smile fell as he watched me suck my fingers clean. Without breaking my stare, his hand dropped to my other leg as he hooked my ankle over his shoulder. Before I could react, he curled his finger into a loose fist and pressed his knuckles into the taut muscle.

I yelped, trying to pull away, but he held on tight.

When he spoke, it was in a voice as dark and soft as ash.

"You know what else I've heard makes cycles more bearable? Something I *haven't* done for my cousin?"

I swallowed my nerves. "Do tell."

He grinned fiendishly. "Orgasms." His fingers teasingly rapped against my inner thigh, stroking toward the ache between my legs, and I quickly slapped his hand away.

"You're disgusting," I said, unable to keep the laughter out of my voice.

He returned his fingers to safer ground. "I never figured you for the type of female to be turned off by a little mess."

I bit my lip. I didn't think it was disgusting. In fact, now that the pain was fading, my ache had transfigured, shifting lower. There was nothing more appealing than the chance to scratch this new, very particular itch, but he was the one person I shouldn't be sleeping with. We'd already agreed.

Unfortunately, he was also the only person I wanted to be with that way now.

I turned my head to the side again, pretending to watch something on the other side of the window.

After Alezandral finished massaging my leg, he gently returned it to the bed and sat back. "Would you like me to continue reading to you for a while?" he asked.

My gaze snapped back to him, and he smiled.

"Don't you have better things to do than keep me company in this bed all day?"

"No," he replied. "I don't have to be a king today. All I want is to be your friend." Those words stirred up a whole mess of emotions. Fear and excitement and happiness, and a little bit of disappointment too.

What the fuck was this male doing to me?

I nestled my face into the pillow and let it muffle my answer. "I'd like that."

CHAPTER 22

The next day, I felt well enough to leave the cabin. Alezandral retrieved me in the morning for commencement. It wasn't nearly as wild as our welcome from the Impundulu, but that was to be expected.

The Stymphalian capital city was more of a village. They liked living in intimate communities spread out across their land, with the only seraphim who lived in *this* one being elders and nobles.

After the commencement, King Vilhelm and his consort walked us through their township. They gave us a tour of the forge guilds and the libraries that cornered every street. The last time I'd been here, I was only a child, and I'd forgotten how it felt to walk these cobblestone roads. Despite the snow falling all around us, I was warm.

I loved the close-knit buildings.

Yellow orbs of light flickered in streetlamps to either side of the road, a stark contrast to the gray sky above us. They were like miniature suns. Not faerie orbs, though they looked similar from a distance. I knew these spheres of light belonged to the Sphinx—the other species of seraphim driven from the islands, who had created a temporary home here with the Stymphalian.

Both species roamed the streets together—light and iron—smiling at us as we passed by.

Alezandral kept an arm around my back, his thick coat brushing my wing with every step. His fingers dug possessively into my waist the whole walk. I both loved and hated the feeling. I hated it because I liked it too much.

We soon arrived at the Stymphalian palace, where we would have dinner with the royal families.

Their home stood a story above the rest of the township, with iron filigree clinging to old windows and the porous silvery stone. A sentinel opened the heavy walnut door to usher us in, and firelight and blissful heat enveloped us. I eagerly wiggled my way out of Alezandral's grasp to remove my winter wear.

The entry hall was an oval room with a small brazier burning in the center made of pure iron, embedded halfway below the gray marble floor.

As the staff stepped forward and took our coats, Alezandral's hand found my waist again before we were led into a room on our right.

An oblong dining table had been prepared for us, with a female sitting in one of the five iron chairs placed around its circular edge. Her six sheer, phantom-like wings were relaxed, hanging limp down either side of the chair as yellow light twirled lazily around her shoulders.

It was the Sphinx queen, Valentina, and she was halfway through her second bottle of wine from the looks of it.

As we entered, she lifted her delicately painted, pensive eyes to consider us. Her brown fingers traced the mouth of her goblet, around and around, but she made no move to rise and greet us. She only gave us a shallow nod of acknowledgement.

Alezandral and I met her briefly at the engagement party, and even then, she wore this cool expression.

Valentina lost more in the war than anyone, and nearly her own life as well. Seeing the scars peppered across her face and on the skin beneath her plunging neckline was enough to make my stomach churn. It was impossible not to think of the sutilus blades, to think of how painful it must have been to be carved into like that.

My gaze caught on the light swirling around her other forearm. She lost flesh and bone in the war. Now, transparent threads of light shimmered there in the illusion of a hand.

But those scars were nothing compared to the pain of losing her heart mate.

She survived, but at the cost of living the rest of her time without him. She never remarried, never bonded her heart to another. She was only a queen and a mother as far as the world was concerned.

Judging from the number of chairs in front of us, none of the children would be joining us tonight.

By the time we had settled in our seats, the wine was poured and dinner was being eaten, and I realized why they didn't. There was an expectancy in the royals' stares, an air of secrecy between them. Valentina glared at King Vilhelm, as if silently demanding he speak.

This wasn't just dinner. This was a round-table meeting.

Vilhelm twirled the base of his goblet as he turned to Alezandral. "We lost another elder last week."

Alezandral's eyes flicked to mine. I was sitting between the Stymphalian king and his consort, Marketa, and Alezandral suddenly felt too far away as the energy of the room shifted. My betrothed eased back in his chair. "Still no witnesses?"

"None."

"And you've assigned extra sentinels to the streets at night like we discussed?"

King Vilhelm hesitated, glancing at his queen. I could *feel* them talking to each other, and I sensed their fear.

"What is it?" I urged.

Marketa sighed. "The sentinels are disappearing now too. Anyone we place on night patrol is taken along with the elders. We're afraid to lose any more."

Alezandral looked at me again, his expression unreadable. *We can't bring soldiers here if the patrols are going missing.*

So how do we help? We need to do something, I replied.

"Is it only happening here, or are there other parts of your territory experiencing this?" he asked the king.

Vilhelm shook his head. "Only here, thank the Goddess."

There was the barest hint of relief in his voice, but I knew the entire territory had to be feeling this loss. The elders lived here, but their descendants were elsewhere. If it was starting here, who knew how long it would take before the disappearances spread inland?

It didn't escape my mind that this was the same as what happened in the human lands. People were taken close to the coast first.

The sutilus were behind this. There was no trace of doubt left in my mind.

I cleared my throat. "Is there a way to close the village in for a short time? With a shield, perhaps?"

"And keep our people contained to a handful of streets?" Marketa argued gently. "They would never agree to that."

Alezandral grimaced. "I don't see any other solution. Unless, of course, your village is willing to relocate entirely."

King Vilhelm's wings stiffened, a graveness settling over his features.

"No," he muttered. "We aren't going to do that."

Queen Valentina scoffed, pushing her plate away as stood from her seat. Near-blinding light twirled between her fingers. "Our people were already driven from our home a mere generation ago, and now you expect us to flee *again*?" Her eyes strayed to me, and I felt the weight of her judgment.

I felt my own rise to meet it.

My own father was cast out of his homeland too. After visiting these territories with Alezandral, I could see how much my family had lost in the war, especially those who had been there, who had fought, the ones who remembered what it was like to have a place of their own but could no longer touch it. How many times had I wished for a place of belonging while I was trapped in my father's city? While I was roaming the human lands?

I still longed for that now.

"You're right," I said, leaning forward to catch Valentina's eye. "We'll find another solution."

"You'd better," she ground out.

"Lee didn't mean it, Valentina," the king whispered. "He is a compassionate ally, like his mother was."

Valentina huffed a bitter laugh. "Yes and look at where that got her. Driven to madness and lost to their sea. This Halcyon is not equipped to care for a country. We shouldn't be letting him get involved in our problems when he has enough of his own."

Alezandral's wings drew up tight as he dropped his gaze to the table, his blue eyes stirring a small cyclone of frost above his plate.

King Vilhelm grunted in disapproval. "We can't do this alone anymore."

"We're all in this together, Val. Give him a little grace." Queen Marketa wrapped a hand around Valentina's wrist, right above where her illusionary hand began. It was an oddly familiar touch. They must have grown close in recent years if Marketa was brave enough to address her in that way.

The Sphinx queen bared her teeth at the consort and

wrenched her arm away with a threatening growl. Her magic flared brighter, flashing in my vision like a bulb—

And I thought of something.

"Photographs," I whispered.

Everyone at the table stopped, turning to look at me.

"We could rig cameras up around the village," I continued. "There must be a way to take photographs throughout the night, maybe through windows. That would at the very least give us a better understanding of what's going on here, right? Of who exactly is coming in and how? We can figure out how to safeguard the village from there."

Queen Valentina slowly dropped into her chair, staring at me with real interest.

King Vilhelm nodded. "Yes. That might work if we can figure out a way to automate the cameras."

"The Impundulu would know," Valentina interjected, rising again from her chair.

Queen Marketa stopped her with a warm smile. "After dinner, Val. You need to eat."

Valentina frowned but allowed the consort to placate her this time. King Vilhelm smiled at both of them before turning his attention to his own plate, and the energy of the room lightened. Business was finished for now.

Alezandral shot me an admiring look. *Brilliant, darling.*

Valentina is the brilliant one. I was only inspired, I replied, digging into the pile of food on my plate to hide the smile on my lips. *Unlike you.*

His silent laughter radiated like thunder through my head.

WHEN WE RETURNED to our little cabin, Alezandral grabbed a

change of clothes and absconded himself in the bathroom, leaving me alone in the bedroom for a few minutes.

This was our routine.

This time, though, I didn't take this opportunity to change. I just sat there on the bed, waiting for him. Now that I knew the streets weren't safe at night, I couldn't help but want him to stay here, *with me*.

When Alezandral emerged from the bathroom, his hair was damp, and he was dressed in loose, cotton-light clothing. He paused on the threshold as steam spilled out around him, seemingly disarmed by my perch on the end of the bed. "Is something wrong?"

"Where are you going?" I whispered.

"Excuse me?"

"Where do you go at night? Are you going somewhere… safe?"

Alezandral leaned against the edge of the door frame, a small smile playing on his lips. "Yes, darling. I am."

"Where?"

"What exactly do you want to hear?"

"The truth," I growled. "I don't care what it is, but I want to know. I *need* to know."

His eyes softened. "I've been sleeping in one of the libraries," he murmured. "The building next door."

"Oh," I exhaled, some of the tension bleeding from my body. "Okay."

He paused, as if waiting for me to elaborate on my question. When I didn't, he sighed through his nose and pushed himself upright. "I'll see you in the morning, Sia."

Alezandral crossed the room, and I didn't stop him. I let him leave.

If he was staying in one of the libraries, then at least I knew he would be safe. I didn't *need* to ask him to stay here.

That didn't stop me from wishing I had, though.

CHAPTER 23

I couldn't breathe.

The crackling of fire filled my ears. Smoke invaded my lungs, constricting them to the point of pain, and I lurched awake with a cough.

The room I'd fallen asleep in was gone.

I was no longer lying on a bed—in fact, it didn't look like I was in the Stymphalian territory at all. I'd woken up in a place far more insidious.

Honeycomb trees with black flames, the ground beneath me breathing, in and out, up and down; the scent of death crawled down my throat, and I coughed again, trying not to gag as I pushed myself up to my hands and knees.

How in the fuck had I gotten *here*?

The world burned around me, obsidian flames creeping towards me across the soft ground. If I stayed here, I would burn too, and who knew when the sutilis would find out that I was in their universe again? I needed to find the rift that sent me here.

I fumbled to my feet.

I scanned the trees, staggering between them, keeping far away from the flames that reached for me.

A slick sheen of sweat gathered on my skin, dampening my nightgown. Was this how the elders were disappearing? Were they being stolen away by a rift somewhere in their territory? I couldn't help but search for a sign of wings between the trees. I knew that if they had been transported here, they probably hadn't lived very long, but I wanted to know, just as the Stymphalian royals would want to know.

I didn't see any evidence they had ever been here, though. There was only ash and darkness.

A frenzy bubbled in my veins, and I couldn't stop the fear from sinking in. Where was the rift? *Where the fuck was it?*

Then, I heard a voice and froze.

"*Sabrina,*" it called again.

It was a voice I'd never heard before, and yet I recognized it. Down in my bones, I *knew.*

Twisting in place, I saw her standing between two burning trees in the distance. Her brown hair was a luminous halo framing her face. In that portrait in my father's throne room, she'd been pregnant and somber, but here she was. Alive. *Smiling.* My body leaned toward her even as my mind screamed that this couldn't be real.

Could it be real?

My mother didn't leave a grave behind. She'd faded to nothing, as all human consorts to the Winged Spirits faded, returning to stardust. What if she'd been sent *here*? What if she'd existed here, all these years? Logic told me that the chances were slim, but the evidence also stood before me now in all its impossible glory.

I took a step toward her. "Cinna?"

She smiled, her teeth glimmering through the darkness. "My daughter, come to me."

I wanted to. Goddess, I wanted to run to her with every

fiber of my being, but I hesitated. "How did I get here?" I whispered. "How do I leave?"

Her smile slipped. "You want to leave me already?"

Shaking my head, I dared another step toward her. "Come with me. We can leave this place together. We just need to find the rift."

Cinna's lower lip trembled. "You want to throw me away."

"No, *please*–"

She turned on her heel and ran.

I had no choice but to chase after her—every inch of my broken heart demanded it. She tore between the trees, her red velvet gown and brown hair bouncing behind her. How had she survived this place for so long? When Alezandral entered this world with me, he'd suffocated, and he was a seraph. My mother… she was only human. She was prey in this universe of creatures who should want nothing more than to tear her apart into functional pieces. It didn't make sense. Nothing about this made sense.

All I knew was that when I finally caught her, I was never going to let her go. She'd know just how much I loved her. She would know that I still needed her.

Despite her impressive speed, I was catching up. With every turn she took through the forest, I was getting closer, so close to touching her that I could almost feel her gown.

The trees thinned around us, and a large cliff slid into view. She was running out of ground.

Relief fizzled through my stomach when I saw a rift hovering just beyond the ledge. She'd led me here so we could go back home. A small voice in the back of my head whispered to me, pleading with me to stop, to *see*, but my way out was right there, within my reach, and so was my mother.

I couldn't stop now. Not for anything.

Cinna halted at the edge, keeping her back to me.

Chest heaving, I reached forward and grabbed her shoulder. It should have felt like velvet, but it didn't. It felt wet and cold and gummy. "I'm not leaving you behind," I gasped. "Come with me."

When I turned her around, I screamed and wrenched my hand away, but he caught it.

Him.

His face was a rotting mask of stitched together flesh, and I watched as the gown melted away to reveal a large, masculine body. This sutilis looked more human than the others, more put together, with fresh limbs and organs, aside from the face he bore that carried my father's strong, ancestral nose. The face he'd torn off my father's father to wear himself, as a trophy.

I was standing in front of the sutilis king.

"How easy you are to fool, little one," he rumbled. "That sensitive heart of yours is to blame. We shall replace *that* burden first."

I fought his grasp, horror crawling like spiders under my skin. "*Never,*" I roared.

He laughed, a smooth clicking that scraped across my bones. "You say that as if you have a choice. I know what is best for you. I will make you strong, little one. I will fix you." His fingers tightened on my arm, and he seized the other despite my struggle, pulling me toward the cliff behind him.

I screamed, summoning my flames.

Black sparks enveloped my arms and bit at his hands, and he growled. He wasn't letting go. Even as his skin bubbled and my flame devoured him, he held on, dragging me forward. I was going to fall over the edge with him into that black nothingness. The rift that had been there before was gone now, another illusion he'd dropped the instant I saw his face. I summoned more of my magic, as much of it as I could.

If he was going to take me, then I was going to make sure he burned as he did it. I'd rather we both be ash.

"*Sia!*"

Large hands latched onto my waist from behind.

An enraged roar filled my ears, and my vision blurred until I could no longer see the monster in front of me. I couldn't see anything but darkness as those hands around my waist tightened and wrenched me backwards, out of the sutilis king's grasp.

As I collided with hard ground, the breath was knocked from my lungs, and a cool shiver spread through my body.

As my eyes fluttered open, I saw stars before Alezandral's face slid into view, hovering above me. A choked cry shook my chest as I reached for him, and he gathered me into his arms, squeezing me so close that I couldn't get a full breath. I didn't care much for breathing at this moment, though.

Over Alezandral's shoulder, I could see that we were lying on a cliffside that bordered the Stymphalian territory.

The amber trees and black flames were gone, except for a small blaze that continued to lick at dead grass a few feet away, near the edge of the cliff. I had a feeling I was responsible for that one.

At least the sutilis king was nowhere to be seen.

Alezandral whispered my name against the crook of my neck, again and again like a chant, as if he was charming me to remain in his arms forever.

"How did I get here?" I whispered.

Alezandral reluctantly let me peel away from him but kept a firm grip on my waist as I searched his blue eyes. They looked as bewildered as I felt.

"Lee," I choked out, "what *happened?*"

A small muscle feathered in his jaw. "Psychic attacks. The sutilis are sending out psychic fucking attacks, and you nearly walked right off that cliff in your sleep. I can only assume something was waiting for you in the water."

"No, I," I started to argue, but then I realized that everything I'd just seen was a trick, a dream. I'd never been in the sutilis' world. I hadn't passed through a rift.

The sutilis king was right: I'd been so easy to fool.

"Oh, Goddess…" Another sob crackled out of me, and suddenly, I couldn't stop crying.

Alezandral's arms wrapped around me again, cradling me against his chest. "I've got you now. Just keep breathing, alright? I'm going to get you the fuck away from here, hold on."

He lifted me into his arms, and I buried my face in his chest. We didn't exchange another word as he stalked down the valley into the dark village. The door to our cabin was already open when we reached it, and he turned sideways to carry me in before kicking the door shut with his foot. As he headed for the bathroom, I realized that my nightgown was barely covering me anymore, a patchwork of burnt tatters clinging to my skin.

"I'll let you wash up, but I'm going to wait for you right on the other side of the door," Alezandral murmured as he set me on my feet next to the tub. His fingers pulsed against my waist, unwilling to let me go. "I'm going to sleep here with you tonight, alright?"

His eyes simmered with unvoiced worry.

Why aren't we talking about it? I whispered into his mind.

I wondered if he felt the same way I did. Talking out loud felt too dangerous right now, like one word might shatter reality and send me back to that awful place where monsters could lie to me and tear out my heart.

Alezandral ran a palm over my hair. *Because you've barely stopped crying. There will be time to discuss what happened later.*

He leaned over to turn on the faucet and then left the room. Thankfully, he left the bathroom door untouched, though I would have opened it myself if he tried to close it. I didn't like the idea of being alone right now.

I was scrubbing my blackened shoulders in the tub when he reappeared, a fresh nightgown in hand.

He walked two steps into the room and placed the bundle of fabric on the counter. His eyes roamed everywhere but directly at me. "Tomorrow, we'll begin training again. From here on out, though, we'll be focusing on the more psychic aspects of your magic. There are ways to guard against attacks like the one you just experienced. I'm going to teach you."

I paused at those words, my hands falling under the ash-clouded water.

So *that* was how he kept me out of his head when he wanted to. This was an actual *skill* he'd honed, one he chose not to share until now. With a scoff, I scrubbed my arms with renewed vigor. "You couldn't have decided to teach me that weeks ago?" I sniped.

Alezandral did look at me then, and his gaze wasn't gentle.

"My father brought an elven specialist into our country to train me in psychic shields when I was ten years old, Sia. I was tortured daily, within an inch of my sanity, until I showed the mental fortitude the shield requires. My father didn't care how badly it hurt. He forced me to learn because he believed I needed a defense. Against you. Against this bond. I didn't tell you I knew how to do this because I wish I fucking *didn't*."

I stared at him, rendered speechless.

"I'll share this knowledge with you now," he said. "And we'll teach the Stymphalian together. They need this defense too."

My eyes burned. "Alright."

As one hot tear slid free down my face, Alezandral crossed the room and brushed his knuckles across my cheek. "Please don't. Don't cry anymore, Sia. Not for me."

His fingertips grazed the length of my jaw, and I leaned in, following his touch.

As my body eased up out of the water, Alezandral inhaled sharply and stood. "I'm sorry."

Before I could ask him what he was sorry for, he fled the room.

Emerging from the bathroom, I found Alezandral settled into the couch next to the fireplace, staring blankly at the ceiling. He'd taken a pillow and one of the wool blankets from the bed.

I hesitated on the threshold, frowning.

A part of me had expected to find him in the bed. In fact, part of me *wanted* that.

I shuffled to the bed and slid under the blankets. My limbs bled into the mattress until I wasn't sure I knew where my body ended and the linen began, but sleep was still far away. I faced Alezandral, watching him watch the ceiling.

After a moment, he turned onto his side and met my stare.

We gazed at each other for a long minute before he said, "You know what this means, don't you?"

I shook my heavy head.

"It's not just your mind they can get into. Not just the Impundulu, either. They can get to *anyone*. What they said to you before—they could have lied. There's no reason to believe they are any more related to you than you are to your own family." And that was to say… not at all.

I wanted to believe that they had simply lied to me, but I couldn't.

Beneath King Craven's ominous words, there had been a glimmer of truth. I just didn't know what the truth was yet. "They used my mother's visage to lure me to the cliff. If you hadn't been there—"

"Stop," he whispered firmly. "We're not going to imagine what might have happened if I wasn't there. That won't do either of us any good."

The words wouldn't stop, though. I had to say them, all of them. "He told me he wanted to fix me. He wanted to take my heart," I rasped, my voice close to breaking.

Alezandral pushed himself up on one elbow, glaring across the room. "*He?*"

I nodded. "Their king. He had me before you showed up."

His blue eyes started glowing with rage—a deep, piercing blue. "He'll never have you, I promise. And if he ever gets close enough to try it, I'll tear him apart myself."

I closed my eyes to hide how much that promise affected me, how it seeped down my spine and swirled in my vision like hot honey. Another promise that bound us together, whether he realized it or not. When would he stop doing that? When would he stop making me feel like he wanted to keep me, and that I wanted to be kept?

"Not if I get my hands on him first," I muttered.

His low chuckle filled the room.

"What did King Vilhelm mean," I asked, "about your mother?"

Alezandral's laughter cut off cold, and I peeled my eyes open to find him lying on his back again, squinting at the ceiling. "You don't have to tell me," I reasoned. "I was just curious."

After a moment, Alezandral sighed in surrender. "She was a wonderful mother, and an even better queen. I think that's why it's so hard to talk about her, knowing what she did while loving us so deeply. But she had too many promises weighing her down. When she disappeared, my entire childhood went with her, but she walked into the ocean because she couldn't live that way anymore. How could I be angry with her for that?"

His eyes fluttered shut. "Living with my father made me want to die sometimes too."

I knew these were secrets being confessed. He thought I would understand. And I did. "What was her name?" I whispered.

His jaw feathered. "Elona."

My lips quirked to one side as I repeated her name in my head, committing it to memory. "That's a pretty name."

"She was."

"I'm sorry, Lee. I'm so sorry you lost her."

He opened his eyes into mine and smiled sadly. "I would have come looking for you, promise or not. You're worth it."

My eyes burned with tender surprise. I hadn't been prepared for such a confession, but Lee did seem to enjoy catching me off guard. His grin was unapologetic.

I smiled in return, my lips trembling, and granted him mercy. "So are you."

CHAPTER 24

Again, darling.

I groaned, twisting away from Alezandral's over-whelming presence. My consciousness was raised just enough to realize I was sleeping and that he was here, but not quite enough to surface. The scent of burning poppy seeds filled my senses, tinged with the faintest trace of mint.

Alezandral must be using his magic to keep me under. This wouldn't be the first time. We'd done this several times in the last month.

I don't want to. I'm exhausted. Go find another girl to psychi-cally invade.

Oh, but inside of you is my favorite place to be.

I felt his laughter rake across my thoughts. Why did he have to say it like that? *I'm going to roast you over a spit of flames.*

His presence intensified, bearing down on me like a winter storm, and I shuddered internally.

It was never pain he made me feel… only more of *him*, his ice and attention. I felt all of him entering my darkness, filling every empty space, and I let myself sink deeper. We found it was easier for me to focus here, in my sleep, where my body was separated from my mind.

Here, I could better sense the connections.

Little black streams poured out of me, out of my soul—that sphere of dark radiance vibrating in the nothingness. It was me, and more than me. Every person I'd ever touched, anyone I'd ever loved, they were all connected to me by rivulets, and I knew just from touching their stream who was at the end of each.

I recognized them. I fed into them constantly.

Search, Alezandral growled. *Find me.*

My incorporeal body didn't have fingers to flip him off with, so I settled for ignoring him a little while longer.

His frustration rumbled in retaliation. He funneled more of himself in around me until I was suffocating in his power, shivering in it. I summoned my flames, and as soon as I did, I felt his hoarfrost creep in to lick at the fire.

Very good. Now search *for me.*

My flames snapped at him, and his frost hungrily consumed it. My dark was full of him, uncomfortably full. His delight washed over me. He liked provoking me into action, overwhelming me until I finally took control and showed him just how capable I was.

I turned my attention to the streams, passing through them one-by-one.

The smaller streams belonged to those I knew, like the courtesans from my father's palace, those I'd helped in the gnashing forest. Then, there were larger streams: one for my father and my brother, one for Tova and Destin and Kori, and an especially plump rivulet for Erlene.

And then, I found the one that belonged to *him*. Alezandral.

The water in his stream pulsed like an artery, strong and insistent into my very core. It appeared larger to me every time we did this, and I couldn't figure out if it was because he was getting more aggressive with our lessons, or if it was simply because my thoughts of him never ended. He was always on my mind.

I centered myself in his stream, allowing memories of us to travel through me, allowing his presence to pierce me, to *become* me as I summoned more of my flame.

Burn, darling. Burn.

My flames sizzled through the transcendent water, breaking the flow. I didn't need it to dry up completely, didn't *want* it to. I had managed to dry up the stream the sutilus left behind during our first session, though, that morning after the sutilis king's psychic attack.

Right now, I only needed to evaporate this stream enough to push Alezandral out.

Any way to disrupt the connection would do, any way the magic in my veins could manage it. Lee had learned to freeze his streams; he was teaching me how to burn mine.

Slowly, his presence faded from my mind, lighter and lighter until I could no longer feel him.

With a gasp, I woke.

I was curled up in one corner of the carriage, the elegant cab shaking around us. It was dim, which told me we were still navigating the storm clouds on route to the Malforian territory.

Over the last couple months, we'd traveled to each settlement, met with each royal family aside from Alezandral's. His borders were still locked down. His father hadn't wanted to host us, and I took that as a small mercy from the Divine Mother. I wasn't sure I could handle being somewhere that abused humans for the sake of a treaty. At least in the other territories, the humans were ignored. They weren't held hostage and fed to serpents—if that was even the whole truth. I had no way of knowing, because Alezandral refused to speak about his territory with me, and always redirected the conversation when I brought it up.

I knew he was protecting them with his silence.

At least this would be our last stop on our tour. We would finally meet with the Wight, and then this would be over.

Alezandral traveled with me in my carriage now. Actually, there was rarely ever a moment when he wasn't by my side. He stayed in our room every night, sleeping on the couch or the floor. Every time I got up in the middle of the night to use the bathroom or to open a window for fresh air, he vigilantly watched me until I returned to bed.

I never saw him sleep.

Sometimes, I was tempted to invite him to sleep in the bed with me. That close proximity might grant him enough peace to really rest for a few hours. I just couldn't get the words to leave my mouth. I was afraid that if he started sleeping beside me, I'd get too used to it, to the sound of his breathing and the warmth of his body, and then I would grieve the loss of that when we went our separate ways.

I had a terrible suspicion I would be missing him well enough already.

Lee lounged on the opposite end of the bench, smirking at me. "You're getting better at that, even in your sleep."

"You're the worst," I said around a yawn.

"But just look at the results."

I glared at him. "I would have preferred to keep napping."

Alezandral glanced out the cloudy window. "We're getting close. I figured you'd rather wake up now, before the landing tosses you right out of your seat *again*."

I wiggled myself upright. "That only happened *once*."

"Yes," he said in a stern voice, "and it was adorable."

"You just like seeing me be thrown around," I said with a roll of my eyes.

A sharp, wicked smile spread across his face.

"You freak," I grumbled, biting back a smile.

Alezandral ran a gloved hand over his jaw, his golden scruff bristling the leather. "Oh, you have no idea."

I crawled across the bench to sit next to him. I probably settled in a little too close for his comfort, but I was feeling brave this morning. And he was too, I think, because he didn't react or pull away.

"You say things like that a lot," I teased, propping my head up on the cushion next to his shoulder. "Are you implying you're some kind of sexual deviant in the bedroom?"

He quirked a brow. "Suddenly interested in my sexual appetites, Sia?"

"Not interested," I said carefully. "Just curious."

A low hum radiated through his chest as he slid a hand over my leg, his leather-clad palm cupping my thigh. I glanced down at the casual touch. These touches felt like more when we were alone. A few weeks ago, I might have pushed him away, but I didn't want to today.

A playfulness swirled in his blue eyes, and I wanted to wiggle even closer. I wanted to see if he would let me into his head, to read the meaning of it in his thoughts.

"Curiosity won't be getting you those answers, darling," he murmured.

My stomach dipped, but I didn't let his rejection bring down my mood. Instead, I pouted. "You're no fun this morning. Wake up on the wrong side of the floor?"

He chuckled. "What about *you*, Sia? What do you like?"

I lifted my head off the cushion, blinking at him. "In bed?"

"If you want to know about my appetites, I think it's only fair you share some of your own first."

Shifting, I tried to get more comfortable. His hand remained on my leg, and I swear, I felt it tighten. He was right. I couldn't ask him about his sex life and not expect to reciprocate some information. I shrugged. "I don't know. I like all of it, I suppose."

"All of it?" he repeated, raising an eyebrow. "You *suppose*?"

When I nodded, he raised his other hand to my hair, running his gloved palm over the top of my skull until he was gently cupping the back of my head.

He liked playing with my hair lately. It had grown out a few inches since I cut it, now falling in mild waves around my shoulders. Sometimes, I caught him distractedly pinning a lock between his fingers, pulling the strands slightly as he caressed them to the ends. He didn't let himself get distracted this time, though.

Alezandral held my stare as he said, "You like *all* of it, darling? You like being the one in control and the one being controlled?" A dip of my chin, and a small smile tugged at the corners of his mouth. "You like being fucked, being worshipped?"

When my brow furrowed, he tilted his head in curiosity. Oh Goddess, he'd seen something in that response, hadn't he? "I like fucking," I breathe, trying to guide the conversation toward that.

"You like it rough?"

"Yes."

"But not gentle?" he pressed.

I shrugged again, fighting the urge to pull away. "I told you, I like all of it."

His eyes glittered. "Funny. You seemed to hesitate when I mentioned worship. Why? You're a female who *should* be worshiped. These thick thighs of yours demand it." He squeezed my leg, a little higher than I remember his hand landing earlier.

A small spark of pleasure slid up my spine and my legs parted. *On instinct,* I told myself. I hoped he couldn't tell through the layers of my dress, but as his smile spread, I knew those hopes were useless. He'd noticed. He was enjoying getting under my skin like this.

With a petulant sigh, I said, "No. I don't want to be worshiped."

"Why?"

"Because it's uncomfortable for me."

"So you don't like discomfort," he ventured, his gaze scrutinizing. "You don't like pain with your pleasure?"

"No, I–" I choked on the next words, trying to sift through them. This conversation had taken quite the turn. "To be completely honest, I haven't experienced much of that. Not physical pain, at least. I don't think I'd hate it. It's just the idea of someone worshiping me... it's–"

"Uncomfortable," he echoed, nodding.

Then in my mind, he whispered, *Vulnerability can be very uncomfortable for people like us, can't it?*

Was that the real reason I didn't like the idea of letting someone feast between my legs? Did the vulnerability make me uncomfortable? He might be right, but there was something else that kept me from spreading my legs for his mouth, a fear I'd carried for years before him.

"I get overwhelmed," I admitted. "And I can lose control."

He waited for me to explain, his eyes searching mine.

I took a deep breath. "I can barely have sex without burning the person I'm fucking. When I first started, I hurt someone badly, one of the courtesans from my father's palace. I had fisted their hair in my hands. They got between my legs, and I set them on fire. They nearly died that day because I started panicking, and the next thing I knew, the entire bed was burning. Since then, I've figured out what's safe and what's not. Someone feasting on me? Not safe."

Lee's eyes narrowed, his thoughts visibly churning.

There was nowhere to run or hide from him, not unless I chose to break away entirely and bring this whole conversation to an end, and I didn't want to do that. I still hadn't gotten anything from him yet, and I was so damn curious.

"Do *you* like pain?" I murmured.

He smiled. "Very much," he purred, his fingers flexing against the back of my head. "Both receiving it and giving it, but it's not so much about the pain for me as it is about testing my limits. The pain is an outlet. I like working past it to get to the pleasure."

"How much have you tested your limits?" I wondered aloud.

"Quite a bit."

I hummed, acknowledging his answer while I scrambled for a response. My mind was flooded with images of Alezandral like that—in control of another person's pleasure, doling out pain until it bled into ecstasy. I could almost see his smirk as he overpowered me, his look of adoration as I returned the favor. Red scratches bleeding down his sides, my nails the weapon.

I shouldn't be thinking of us together like that. He might see it in my head and interpret it to mean I'm actually interested. And maybe, just maybe, I was lying to us both when I told myself I wasn't.

Deciding this conversation was too dangerous to continue, I offered him a polite smile. "Good for you."

Then, I pulled away enough that he took the hint and dropped his hand from the back of my head. I stared at his hand on my thigh. "Why do you wear these gloves so much?"

"Because I don't like touching people."

My heart thundered in my ears. "You touch *me*, though," I whispered. He'd touched me without those gloves several times, both in the human lands and throughout this tour.

He gave me a shrug. "You're different."

"Because we're bonded?"

"Because you're *you*," he clarified.

He removed his hand from my thigh and tugged his glove off, dropping it into his lap before he brushed his bare knuckles across my cheek. It took an enormous amount of effort not to lean into his touch.

"Your flame has never scared me, darling."

The trajectory of the carriage shifted, and soft light filtered in as we broke free of the clouds. I saw the scar on his neck in all its confounding, grotesque glory.

He was touching me. Why shouldn't I touch him too?

I skimmed my fingertips over his mutilated flesh, and his eyes fluttered shut. He made no move to stop me, so I kept touching, exploring the raised skin.

His wings curled around us, forming a place just for us, for this moment.

"This scar. Where did it come from?"

When his eyes opened, a sad blue glow poured out from them. "From making a friend," he confessed. "And I would do it again."

His father had done that. The day of our heart bond. I couldn't remember the details, but I remembered the blood and my screaming, and that was enough. I'd sworn to protect him, and then I had to watch as he was hurt anyway.

Harsh, angry heat bubbled in my stomach.

I knew it was a foolish thought, but if I had the opportunity, I would annihilate Alezandral's father. I'd make him suffer for what he did to his son. To a *child.*

Lee had only been a child, afraid like me.

How could I have accused him of any malice that day?

The carriage touched down on solid ground, jostling us apart, and our bubble of intimacy was broken. I slid away, fussing with my dress and fastening my winter shawl over my shoulders. When I glanced across the cab, I saw Alezandral adjusting himself in his seat, so I knew our conversation had just as much of an effect on him as it had on me.

We'd been talking about sex, after all. It was only natural. I was thankful my arousal was easier to hide.

A small part of me did wonder if perhaps he felt more than general attraction. I noticed how much attention he gave me, because I loved every second of it. I loved the thoughtful compliments and affectionate touches. I loved that he gravitated toward me in every room, every day. I loved his fake kisses and whispered jokes, his winks and ruthless training.

He looked at me, and I felt seen.

As the carriage rolled to a stop, Alezandral turned to me and smiled, settling into his royal mask. "Ready to meet your destiny, darling?"

CHAPTER 25

I swiftly regretted wearing my winter cloak.

This was my first time visiting the Malforian terri-tory, and it was like stepping into a world of eternal spring. A glittering, honeycomb-shaped dome enclosed their capital city, shielding the land from the winter. It was a barrier created for the sole purpose of regulating the weather. Though it wasn't nearly as humid as my father's island, their proximity to the earth allowed a more mild ecosystem to form beneath the dome.

The grass was vibrant, and tiny, colorful wildflowers sprang up all around the carriage as we disembarked.

We had landed at the edge of their territory. There were no obvious roads to carry us forward, only a handful of foot-paths that led across a woody meadow towards some kind of epicenter. White smoke curled out of the forest in the distance. I could only assume that was where their homes were settled, in the secure embrace of the trees.

Alezandral took my hand and led me down one of the dirt paths, his eyes trained on the smoke as he navigated us through the meadow between the endless herb and flower gardens.

Flowers bloomed in their raised garden beds, plants that definitely *shouldn't* be blooming at this time of year. Peonies and hyacinths and... *tulips*.

Was this where Alezandral got the tulips for my birthday a few weeks ago?

I wanted to ask, but a handful of Malforian citizens were working around us, tending to the plants. They wore loose cotton clothing that suited the tepid air, barely acknowledging us as we walked past.

In my mother's flower journal, she had written once that plants responded to affection, that their spirits were as easily influenced as the human race was by kind words and loving touch. Seeing the attention and care the Malforian gave to this garden and how everything here was thriving, I sealed that little speck of advice as truth in my heart.

A female with four pink wings spotted us as we approached the dense forest, waving enthusiastically.

Bees flew in lazy circles around her head. She had been harvesting honey from a habitat the creatures formed in a tree hollow. Malforian possessed the power to influence the moods and emotions of those around them, so that gift must extend to even the smallest of the world's insects, because the female hadn't bothered to wear gloves while working with them. Setting her wooden bucket down beside the tree, she met with us where our path converged with the tree line. Her hair was a lovely shade of strawberry-blonde, falling straight and shiny around her petite shoulders.

"Highnesses." She curtsied with a light-footed bounce. "I'm happy to see you've arrived safely. Welcome. I'm Princess Maribel. My father has granted me the honor of preparing you for commencement tonight. Your cottage is ready for you, but I thought if you had the time, you might like to help me mix some honeyed liquor for the toasts later. I've just gathered some fresh—"

Alezandral interrupted her, "Tell your father that my betrothed and I wish to report directly to the Wight tonight. Commencement will wait until morning."

Her smile fell.

Alezandral and I had agreed on this course of action together. It just didn't make sense to endure another meaningless celebration if we could avoid it, but I felt a little bit guilty for spoiling the princess' plans.

"We're eager to get the Wight's approval for our union," I said, playing into my role. "So we can celebrate properly."

After a moment, Princess Maribel nodded. "I completely understand, Highness."

She turned her gaze to Alezandral. "My father will want to speak with you in person about this, though. I'm sure it won't be a problem, but he doesn't like being the last to know."

"I'll accompany you to tell him myself," Alezandral agreed.

Princess Maribel sighed in relief, and some of the sparkle returned to her eyes as she leaned toward me. "I'll show you to the cottage first. Our maidens are waiting for you."

"Maidens?" I echoed.

"Well, of course," she said with a laugh. "You didn't think we would let you get ready to meet our people without help, did you? Come along."

The princess turned around and led us up the path through the woods as I glanced at Alezandral. *Please tell me you understand what she meant by that.*

The maidens are like your maids back home, but... more involved. The Malforian are a preening sort. Prepare to be pampered within an inch of your life.

Wonderful.

He squeezed my hand. *Play nice, darling. It's just how they like to show their affection.*

Thinking back, I wondered if that was how Elena had become my favorite courtesan so easily, with all her gentleness and nurturing, handling my body and my thoughts with such tender love and care. I'd never realized it could merely be a product of her nature.

Then again, with the Malforian settled on the opposite side of the continent and my father never bringing me here, how could I have known?

The forest path opened to a wooded clearing, cottages of all sizes built between the trees. Smaller gardens sprawled in the yards, and the melody of songbirds echoed down around us. Malforian with wings of varying shades of pink and rosy cream wandered through the town.

Before we fully entered the glade, Princess Maribel veered to the side, crouching to rinse the honey off her hands in a small, burbling creek.

"I should warn you now that our only source of water stems from the hot springs up the hill. There's a river a mile or so to the east, but it's beyond the reach of our shield, so bathing in it at this time of year is not ideal. We have community bathing pools on the northern edge of the city. I know the other territories prefer to rely on more magical means for things like that, so I apologize in advance for any discomfort."

"We'll adapt," Alezandral chuckled. "I admire your self-efficiency."

I knew he was referring to the territory as a whole, but a thorny warmth bled up my spine anyway. I didn't like hearing him say that to her or seeing him smile at her back. My thoughts sifted frantically for the last time he'd complimented me while smiling like that.

If the memories were there, they refused to surface.

My nerves were balanced on a sharp edge. My skin, buzzing. Had his grip on my hand loosened, or was I imagining it?

I bit the inside of my lip, trying to steady myself. I wasn't feeling quite right.

Maribel straightened, turning to face us with a sly grin. "*But*, if either of you wish to bathe in more privacy, I can personally attest to the tranquility of taking a dip half-past midnight." Though the words were addressed to both of us, Maribel's eyes were trained on Alezandral... and her smile turned just a little bit too sweet.

I inched closer to Alezandral. "Thanks for the advice."

Her luminous green eyes slid to me, and the smile on her lips brittled. "Let's get you to the cottage so you can freshen up." She seemed so nice on the surface, but it was suddenly striking me as shallow, calculated.

Maybe I didn't know the full scope of Malforian nature at all.

As she turned again to lead us into the city, that razor-edge against my nerves receded, and my stomach dropped as my suspicions were confirmed.

The princess was toying with me.

Malforian could only manipulate feelings that were present. They could intensify and project them, which told me she had almost certainly taken an interest in Alezandral, and I was at least a little bit upset about it. But, honestly, fuck her for even thinking about it. As far as she knew, he was *mine*. I was all at once feeling apprehensive about our stay here, however long that ended up being.

Maribel led us through the city, her strawberry hair swinging like a pendulum down her back, the length grazing the round curve of her ass. Her cotton dress was thin and hugged her figure beautifully, and so my mood soured further.

Why should I care if Alezandral's eyes wandered?

If he felt even the slightest hint of desire for her, her influence would intensify that, but it was none of my business if he acted on it. If he wanted her, why shouldn't he have her? We'd spent months on the road now, and for most of it, we'd been sharing a bedroom. He had to be needing a little release, the same as me. One of us should be satisfying our needs. My sex was still hibernating in the total mortification I brought upon myself after the engagement party. The only touch it had received since then was my hand in the bath, and my fingers didn't even linger.

Just the thought of Alezandral being with her like that made my blood boil, though. She'd used her magic on me. I didn't want her to think she'd somehow bested me by getting what she wanted, that I somehow... hadn't been enough for him. These feelings were difficult to manage.

My head was a mess.

Maribel halted at a cottage with wooden siding and over-flowing flower boxes attached to the front windows. Gesturing at the door, she said, "Here we are. We've placed you close to the royal house—it's right up the road—and the bathing pools are about a five-minute walk beyond that. If you'll follow me, Alezandral, I'll show you the way."

I couldn't keep myself from glaring at her—not that she was paying any attention to me.

Alezandral's hand slid into place around my waist and guided me toward the door of the cottage. "In a moment. I want to say a proper goodbye to my bride." He smiled at me as we turned our backs to her, and a tiny flicker of delight spread like ivy over my sore belly.

Proper goodbye, huh? I teased him.

He seized my hips and pressed me up against the door. My body lit up like a thousand tiny fireflies had burrowed themselves into my skin, writhing, fluttering, glowing.

My heart leapt as his lips found mine.

He plunged his tongue into my mouth and consumed the kiss whole, claiming the very breath in my lungs. His fingers hooked around my waist and pulled me harder against him as he devoured me. Our mouths tangled messily, and I knew Princess Maribel had to be seeing every vulgar sweep of our tongues. Effervescent heat flooded my face and my neck, but it wasn't connected to any sort of shame or embarrassment; this was pleasure, and a small sliver of selfish satisfaction.

You see? He's mine.

Alezandral pulled away, his eyes sparkling around the edges like freshly-fallen snow. *There. Now try not to let the entire village feel your jealousy while I'm gone.*

My wings ruffled, and I was tempted to deny what I was feeling, but I knew I'd be making a fool of myself. Maribel had projected my emotions enough that he had felt it too.

Alezandral leaned around me to open the door to the cottage, and excited squeals erupted across the room as I reluctantly tore myself away from him to look at the pair of young Malforian females scurrying towards me.

"That's my cue to run," Alezandral said with a chuckle, letting me go. *Have fun,* he sang into my head as he rejoined Maribel on the path.

I certainly wasn't going to return that sentiment when he was walking away with *her.* With a roll of my eyes, I threw back a firm, *Drop dead.*

Alezandral laughed as he continued down the road.

The Malforian women pounced on me. They each took an arm and pulled me into the cottage, shutting the door behind us.

I was mildly annoyed that I couldn't see Alezandral anymore.

The maidens were both exceptionally beautiful, with a single set of wings each. The first was tall, with brown skin a shade or two darker than my own, her feathers tinted a light peachy-mauve. Her dark hair was intricately styled with braids and budding flowers. Her hand lifted to hover a couple inches above my shoulder. "Oh, your hair is absolutely *divine*. Can we play with you?"

I blinked. That question wasn't something I expected to fall from her plush lips, but I appreciated her asking. "Sure?"

She ran her fingers over the braid resting on my shoulder. *"Beautiful."*

"And your skin is the perfect canvas," the Malforian on my other side purred, tracing the curve of my cheek with her fingertips. Her skin was rather perfect as well. A light pink complexion that practically glowed from within. She had reddish hair, the shade of soft firelight.

I glanced between the two of them, scrutinizing their expressions for any hint of malice, but all I sensed from them was overwhelming *joy*.

"Thank you," I muttered, my face burning.

I wasn't unaware of my beauty by any means, but being fawned over like this was new. "One moment," I said as I took a small step back. "I'm sorry, I just feel like you have me at a slight disadvantage. I don't even know your names."

"My sincerest apologies, Highness," the flowery brunette replied. "My name is Tildy. I'll be assisting you with your hair for the duration of your stay."

"And my name is Emilia," the other female interjected. "But you can call me Em. I'll be assisting with your cosmetics and any facial serums you might require. I specialize in pigment alchemy. I'm the best."

"I have no doubt," I said with a smile. "It's nice to meet you both."

Tildy reached for my hand and drew me back toward them. The maidens led me to the full-length mirror on the other side of the room and nudged me down onto a pink velvet perch. "So what are you wanting for the commencement, Highness? Something regal, obviously. We can take the tamer route with your hair, since you'll be wearing a crown. That way, we can draw the focus to your sensational eyes."

"Yes," Em said with a nod. "That's what I was thinking."

I grimaced at them through the mirror. "About that... The commencement has actually been postponed until tomorrow. We'll be convening with the Wight tonight instead."

"Oh," Tildy breathed, her arms falling limp.

"I'm sorry. I don't imagine the Wight cares much for how I look." Even if I had no use for them, I wasn't ready to send them away yet. Their presence was like a thick blanket, safe and heavy and comforting.

Tildy frowned. "No, it doesn't, but I can lay out your sacred robe for you and apply oil to your hair before the meeting if you'd like?"

Oil? I wasn't quite sure why she would do that, but I nodded.

I also hadn't realized they required specific attire for the Wight. The Malforian were a ritualistic species, though, so I shouldn't have been surprised. Legends and folktales drove their belief system. They were protectors of the ancient world and everything that sprang from it. That was why they housed the Wight and why they had settled so close to the gnashing forest—they were comfortable with the extraordinary brushing against their doorsteps.

Em sighed, crossing her pale arms. "Yeah, well, I'm entirely useless here. Any pigment you wear would be washed away instantly."

I twisted to face Emilia. "Washed away?"

"In the springs surrounding the Wight's dwelling place."

When the confusion on my face remained, Emilia crouched in front of me, bracing her elbows on her thighs as she leaned in. "*Great divine.* Don't you know what you're walking into tonight, Princess?"

"Well…" I reached for some sense of certainty but failed. "No, not really."

"Hasn't anyone discussed the procedure with you?"

I shook my head, and Tildy's eyes bulged. She collapsed against the mirror, sliding down the length of it to sit on the floor next to my feet. "Goddess," she whispered. "How could your father send you in *blind*?"

"Why?" I asked. "You're starting to worry me."

"Please don't worry." Em reached over and squeezed my hand. "Don't let Tildy frighten you. She gets a little caught up in the lore of it all, but there's no reason to fear the Wight. Many have sought wisdom before you, and they all leave its springs unscathed."

Tildy shot Em a glare. "I'm not the only one caught up in the lore of that creature, Emmy. There's a reason it lives in a well on the outskirts of our territory. Even the king fears it."

"The king *respects* it," Em retorted, her eyes nervously flicking between Tildy and me.

She leaned even closer to me. "Anyone with any measure of sense would give that creature its space. Let's just put this discussion to rest."

I shook my head. "You have to explain it to me now, all of it. What kind of magic does this Wight carry?"

Em shook her head. "It's only legends, Your Highness. Silly stories."

"It's *history*," Tildy barked, sitting up straight. "History that most of our continent likes to falsify for their own comfort. Just because the stories are old doesn't make them untrue."

"Telling her this would not be prudent," Em growled.

"Whether *you* believe them or not, Sabrina has a right to know."

"What are they?" I demanded, interrupting their stare-off. "The stories. I want you to start from the beginning."

With a resigned huff, Em sat back on the floor and glared

at the ceiling. "Fine. Scare her if you wish, but if anyone asks, I had nothing to do with this."

Tildy's hazel eyes slid to me. "From the very beginning, Highness?"

"We have the time."

"The Wight became a pillar of our world the moment our Great Mother claimed this planet as Her own."

Oh. This traces back to our genesis...

"The elves occupied this world alone when She came, but when the Goddess stumbled upon this place, She fell in love with its magic. She decided to split the world into two parallel dimensions: one for the elven to remain in, untouched, and the other to fill with Her children. The magic of the world was finite, however. When She split the Earth, it split the magic that resided here too, and that made the elves *furious* with Her. They were used to having unfettered access to the Earth's energy. After the separation, some of that magic was transferred to *this* plane, for the humans and her wild spirits to wield for themselves. The elves did everything they could to claw their way through the veil separating our dimensions to reclaim that power, but when they realized the magic would never return to them—that it didn't *want* to return to them—they cursed the Goddess's children. The Wight is the embodiment of that curse. The first human to walk in death."

"Hold on," I gasped. "The Wight is *human?*"

"Used to be. It's something far different now, something *other*. Unlike the mortals who walk in death in this day and age, the Wight retained awareness of the world. It's speculated that the Goddess loved the human who died deeply, and so She blessed them with extraordinary powers to try and make up for what the elves had done. That's how the Wight we know was born."

My eyes roamed the room as I processed that information. A curse. *That* was why the humans walked in death? Why did they search for other souls in their walking, then? Was that part of the curse, or something more?

"I don't understand how that makes the Wight so dangerous," I admitted.

Em chuckled, picking at her nails across from us. "Because Tildy didn't tell you what the legends say it feeds on yet."

I turned to her expectantly. "And what is that?"

Tildy grimaced. "Fear, Your Highness."

A low ringing filled my ears as that word sank in. *Fear.* It fed on fear, like the elves did? "I thought it spoke to our destinies?" I whispered. "Why would it feed on fear?"

"It's not just your destiny it speaks to," Tildy muttered. "It sees into your soul and identifies your desires, your *secrets.* It brings all of that to the surface. It exposes your dreams and nightmares, and then it drinks in every ounce of fear holding you back from them. Why do you think every royal match is encouraged to meet with it? The Wight allows you to step into your highest self if it deems you worthy of that blessing."

My head shook of its own volition.

My father should have warned me. *Alezandral* should have warned me. "I thought the Wight was simply a masterful seer," I said, my voice weak.

Em sighed through her nose and glanced up at me. "In a lot of ways, it is precisely that. The Wight is willing to give you an answer to the question that burns brightest in your heart. Everyone is aware of *that* aspect of its power because it's appealing. Who wouldn't want a remedy for the unknown? But that knowledge comes at a price."

"So tread carefully in its presence," Tildy added ominously. "And *never, ever* lie."

CHAPTER 26

The Wight wanted us naked.

The sacred robe Tildy dressed me in was so thin, it barely veiled anything, but that wouldn't matter once we reached the springs. This was one of the *rules*.

We had to wade in with absolutely nothing separating us from the water. They said it was symbolic of the Wight's piercing knowledge and the openness we had to hold in our hearts for it and each other, but all I could think about right now was how irritated I was as I hiked up this steep hill against a fierce winter gale, holding the robe's flimsy hood down over my freshly-oiled hair.

The soft petals of a poppy brushed against my cheek; my arms were full of them as I marched up the dirt stairway, slowly closing in on the flames at the top of the hill.

Anger swirled in my chest. I was walking up here *alone*.

Alezandral had sent a note while I was getting ready, telling me he would meet me at the springs at twilight, since he was otherwise *occupied* with the royal family.

I'd torn the pink parchment into tiny pieces and thrown it into the blazing hearth in our cottage, ignoring the looks the maidens threw my way. Let them speculate if they wanted to. I didn't care. This ruse was almost over.

Alezandral had been too busy with Maribel to care if I responded anyway.

The Wight lived at the peak of the springs, from which all the streams for the city flowed. We would swim to the well in its center and hand over our offerings—which, for the Malforian, meant an armful of blooming flowers and a vial of honey with a lock of my hair wrapped around the cork. That was the extent of instruction I'd received before the maidens sent me on my way.

The weather shield fell away about halfway up the hike.

Snow fluttered around me now, building in small hills and draping blankets across the staircase. By the time I hit the top step, I saw the spring and the figure waiting up ahead. Alezandral's white wings were flared, shimmering flakes of snow dusting the hood of his robe, lit by torches lining the path.

He didn't turn to me as I approached, but I knew he could sense my presence when he inched to the side to make room for me at the pool's edge, an identical bundle of flowers and honey in his arms.

We stared at the dark water for a long moment, the steam curling lazily over the surface.

"Where have *you* been?" I finally murmured.

I watched him shrug from the corner of my eye. "The king was feeling talkative. They insisted I get ready for the Wight at the palace to save time. The sun was already starting to set by the time he let me leave his office."

My mouth dried up, and some of the irritation I'd carried up here started fading. "Oh."

"Where did you think I was? I sent you a note telling you I was at the palace. Didn't you receive it?"

"Yes, I got it. I just wasn't sure which member of the royal family was *occupying* you."

A pregnant silence stretched between us. Then, Alezandral chuckled to himself. "You're so cute when you're jealous."

My wings ruffled a bit. "Save it," I scoffed. "Jealousy would require that I actually *have* you, and I don't. After I leave, Princess Maribel will be free to swoop in and coddle your broken, kingly heart. Isn't that exciting?"

It was a prying question, but I couldn't help but ask. I couldn't help but prod.

He only shook his head, watching me from the corner of his eye. "I have no interest in letting that princess coddle any part of me."

A smile touched my lips. "That's probably for the best. I can't imagine her in a territory where flowers frost over."

"No. I can't imagine that either."

His body heat reached for me, caressing my shoulder, and I finally looked up at him. He gave me a grin, but it was the secretive sort, half-hidden. For a moment, it felt like we were children again, and he was the mysterious little boy I so desperately wanted to figure out.

"What are you smiling at?" I whispered.

He turned his grin to the stars. "I can imagine *you* there, in my city. I'd bet your flame could keep the entire territory warm in our darkest winter."

His words lit a candle in my belly, weak and flickering, but pleasant all the same. He could see me in his home, in his life. A small part of me wished I could see that future too. I'd refused to let myself imagine it so far.

"They're very particular creatures, aren't they?" I nodded at the bouquet in his arms. "The Malforian. These robes and the flowers. Did they put oil in your hair too?"

He shrugged. "Admit it: we're all particular creatures, in some way or other."

Alezandral crouched to place his bouquet on the ground before loosening the ties on his robe. I turned away to do the same, keeping my back to him as I undressed. My skin was raised by the cold, and my breasts were frozen in a permanent pucker. Luckily, Alezandral didn't turn around to look at me.

He'd seen me naked before, but somehow, it felt different tonight.

By the time I scooped my offering back up off the ground, Alezandral was stepping down into the spring. My eyes wandered over the rigid muscles of his back, the lean sculpting of his ass, the strength of his thighs.

I was following him into the water. Where else was I supposed to look?

As I descended the porous stairs, I let out a soft sigh. The water was hot. It didn't smell the best, but I knew that was only sulfur and all the other minerals that had seeped into the water. It felt like walking into liquid silk.

Alezandral led the way into the darkness, and as the light from the torches faded behind us, my eyes slowly adjusted. I saw the well take form in the distance, reflecting the moon's light. The water grew hotter as we neared it, teetering on the verge of scalding. The ground beneath our feet sloped until the water was lapping at my waist. I pressed the bouquet of flowers against my chest, and the combination of that and the water was almost enough to trick my battered nerves into believing I wasn't naked.

I understood why Tildy had insisted on oiling my hair now. Every inch of my skin tightened in the water. Without oil, the water might damage my hair.

When we reached the well, Alezandral walked around to the opposite side so he was facing me. The well stood between us, shielding us from the ribcage down. Bundles of dead and frosted blooms ringed the rough edge of stone.

My fingers flexed around the flowers. Slowly, I leaned in to peer into the dark plummet of the well. "I can't see anything."

"I don't think we're supposed to. Look at the walls. There's writing."

I shifted my focus to the outside of the well. There *was* ancient lettering, runes. I reached forward and grazed my fingertips across them. "'Pain, our Mother of Wisdom,'" I read out loud. My fingers trembled against the chiseled words.

Glancing up, I saw that Alezandral was staring intently at the letters carved on his side. "'Kneel, and She will come. Give, and She will return.'"

He raised his troubled gaze to mine. "It's telling us what to do."

We knelt together on either side of the well, the water rising to lap at the underside of my chin. He nodded, and we pushed our offerings over the stone ledge at the same time, letting them drop into the darkness.

At first, nothing happened.

I heard our offerings land in the bottom of the well, a crack of glass as the honey vials shattered, but otherwise, utter silence. The well didn't hold any water, apparently. Strange, considering where it was.

All at once, a vibration coursed through the water. It swept over my body as a cool sheen of sweat broke out across my forehead. Then, a brilliant ray of light erupted from the well, spearing into the night sky. A voice spoke, neither feminine or masculine, neither human nor beast, but something in between. "I have been waiting for you, young wings. Rise. Let me look upon you."

There was no room in my mind for shyness as I rose up out of the water.

Peering into the well this time was like staring into the sun. It burned, blinded. Spots pulsed in my vision, and yet, I could just see past it to a shadowy figure pacing at the bottom. I was fairly certain that the light was shining out of its eyes. It blinked at us, alternating one eye at a time, and as the figure paced, the white radiance moved too, illuminating the damp gray stone. I had no way of determining its size, but it *seemed* large.

The light shifted between Alezandral and me.

"*Yesssss*, this bond of yours is compelling," it crooned.

My eyes flashed to Alezandral, and I found he was already staring at me, reflecting my grimace with one of his own.

The Wight growled loud enough to shake the ground.

"Look at *me*," it demanded. Reluctantly, I returned my gaze to that brutal light. The tremors softened, and I heard a powerful hum echo between us. "What is this... *reticence* I feel?"

Alezandral cleared his throat, but his voice was weak as he confessed, "We haven't come for a blessing on our union."

"Then why have you come?" The question was sharp, displeased.

"Your wisdom," Lee answered. His face was drained of color, and the scar on his neck stood out in the Wight's blistering light.

"We have questions for you," I added, trying to redirect some of the Wight's focus to me. "We desire your guidance."

That light burned into me. "You want my guidance, but not my blessing?" The voice was dissonant. I couldn't determine whether the Wight was offended by that, or simply curious, but a shudder coursed through me. I could sense its immense power. This was a creature that could obliterate us if it wished to, and we were without weapons to defend ourselves.

Tread carefully, Tildy had warned.

So I would.

"We do not wish to ask for more than what we need," I said.

That light shifted away from me again to focus on Alezandral. "*Cold one,*" it seethed. "I wish to hear from you first."

A sliver of irritation razed up my spine. It *preferred* him. Of course it did. I was only a consort, after all, at least for one more night.

Alezandral gripped the edge of the well, peering in. "What do you wish to hear?"

"The question burning in your heart, *silly swan*."

That call back to the day Lee and I met startled both of us. Our gazes clashed, and something like laughter bounced off the walls of the well.

"*Well?* I am waiting, young wing."

Alezandral swallowed and leaned forward again, his voice dropping to a pained whisper. "Where in our world does Sia's Winged Spirit rest? Where can we find her origin?"

Another growl rumbled the ground, this one harsher and more volatile than the first.

"That is *not* the question in your heart. What trickery is this?" I could hear the creature's fury like a stroke of thunder. It threatened to knock me off my feet.

Alezandral collapsed against the well, his limbs trembling as something I couldn't see brought him to his knees. His face pinched, but I knew it wasn't in pain. If it was pain, I'd be able to feel it too. Anger pumped through my veins, hot and fierce. I didn't care if this creature could destroy us. I didn't care if it was imbued with magic straight from the Goddess herself. I wanted it stay the fuck away from him.

"*Stop*," I shrieked into the well. "This isn't a trick. He was asking that question for *me*."

"I am aware of what he did," the Wight roared. "Are you? You tried to take what was not yours, Daughter of Dark Embers. You were willing to steal comfort from your heart mate in order to make yourself whole, but that is not how wholeness is achieved. That is a lie, a perversion, and I will not help you."

The light was flickering, beginning to ebb. The Wight was going to leave us.

I threw myself more firmly against the well's edge. "Wait, *please*—"

"I offered my question up willingly," Alezandral protested as he pulled himself back to his feet. "You cannot punish her for that."

A dark, raspy chuckle rose to meet him. "Ah, but I can, cold one. I can punish you both if I so please. Do not assume you have escaped my ire with your selflessness. Giver, lover—that is what you are, but I know the reasons why. I see past your goodness to the sticky, black ooze in your heart. You gave her your question because you did not believe you deserved one. That is your transgression. But, lucky for you, that particular transgression… I am willing to forgive."

The skin bunched around Alezandral's eyes, his mouth thinning into a white slash. "I'll take her punishment," he rasped. "Just give her what she needs, I beg you."

"Alezandral, *no*," I objected.

Alezandral didn't acknowledge me. His gaze was trained on the Wight, whose light was intensifying again.

The Wight hummed. Alezandral had piqued its curiosity, and I knew neither of them would listen to me if I tried to argue further. I wasn't a part of this discussion anymore. "Very well, cold one," it said at last. "I will give your heart mate a choice, and if she makes the right one, I will consider showing her mercy."

That light swung to me. "You have one question. Choose wisely."

My body hummed in anticipation. I already knew my options. Either I asked for a way to break this bond between Alezandral and I, or I asked about my origin. There was a right answer. The Wight knew it, and so did I.

In my heart, I did not long to be separated from Alezandral. To the contrary, my stupid heart wanted nothing more than to hold onto him with all my might, to know him, to protect him. All I wanted—all I'd *ever* truly longed for—was an understanding of where I fit into this world, of where I belonged. All my fears concerning this heart bond with Alezandral didn't hold a torch to finding a place to call home.

I didn't want to drift anymore.

So I asked my question. "Where can I find my Winged Spirit?"

Alezandral's gaze snapped to my face in surprise, but I didn't return his stare.

The Wight's light flared, and I heard its low hum of approval. "A riddle, you have earned," it rumbled. "Well done."

My brow furrowed. "A riddle? How exactly is *that* supposed to help me?"

"It is a riddle only your heart mate can help you decipher. You must learn to rely on someone other than yourself, Dark Ember. That is crucial. If you wish to know your origin, it will be done with *him* at your side. This is your destiny."

I didn't appreciate the Wight's presuming nature, but who was I to argue? It could have decided to leave me without any answers whatsoever. In fact, it still could.

Tread carefully.

"Fine," I ground out.

The Wight's light flared again, a star in the darkness between us. I could no longer see Alezandral's face; all I saw was white, bright light. I squeezed my eyes shut against the burning as the Wight sang:

> *"As four winds blow and twelve tides turn,*
> *Ancient spirits lie in wait.*
> *Long ago, I traced each one,*
> *For a king with rosy wings that bait.*

A note of permanence resonated in the following silence, and the Wight's light dimmed.

I peeled my eyes open and found Alezandral searching my face, searching for answers, but I couldn't give him what he needed. I'd chosen to keep him, to keep this bond. After all this time I spent pushing him away, I'd given up my one chance to separate us.

He was confused, and so was I.

The ground rumbled, disrupting our wordless conversation. "Now, you, *cold one.* Come and have your truth."

Alezandral shook his head, drawing away from the edge of the well. "I have no question for you." Fear lanced his blue eyes.

A dissonant, wild laugh echoed from the well. "You may attempt to lie to yourself about your desires, but you cannot lie to me. I read the question in your eyes already. It weighs on you, night and day. There is no rest. There is no peace until you know. You understand what I speak of, Heir of the Halcyon Throne. Come, take it."

Alezandral exhaled heavily but approached the well's edge.

As he braced his hands on the stone and leaned into the light, something solid erupted from the stone. A pale hand wrapped around his wrist and wrenched him forward. The source of that brilliant light emerged from its enclosure to sneer up into Alezandral's face.

The Wight's scalp was hairless and smooth, with gray, wrinkled skin. Its eyes were indeed hollows that held sparkling orbs of light.

It had *climbed up the wall*, so silent and swift that we hadn't seen it coming.

I couldn't move, but every inch of my body screamed for me to run.

"You will not be the end," it rumbled. "The heir you bring forth shall be the beginning of a new world. She will be a uniter of realms, filled with grace and kindness and a wisdom much like my own. I can see her. In every future, I see her. The vision is certain. Her pain... *oh yesss*, she will have her share of pain, but it will not be more than she can bear. You will not be the source of her suffering, but rather, the balm. Rest assured, cold one, that the daughter you share with your heart mate will be a very happy child indeed. And Glorious Mother willing, I will gaze upon her soon."

My head spun as I deciphered the Wight's words.

It took a few sluggish heartbeats to realize it was *my* future too. The daughter he shared with his heart mate... but *I* was his heart mate. I was going to have a daughter?

The realization sickened me. I could see how much the Wight's words meant to Alezandral, though. It had the opposite effect. The fear fled from his eyes, replaced by a tenderness that tore my heart in two.

I fell back a few steps, distancing myself from both of them.

With a slow nod, the Wight released his wrist and retreated downward before it shoved off the stone entirely and vanished.

In the Wight's absence, the night seemed so dark, so empty.

Alezandral straightened, his chest rising and falling wildly as he lifted his eyes to me. When he saw the look on my face, the smile tugging at his lips evaporated. "Darling?" He stepped toward me, his hand outstretched, as if he expected me to take it and go to him, to melt into his arms and celebrate the news

I was going to have a child I didn't want. A child I never dreamed of. A future I didn't choose.

I thought tonight was the start of the rest of my life, but it wasn't. It was more of the same.

No choice. No hope. No answers.

"No," I rasped.

Before I could set us both on fire, I spun around and dove under the surface.

CHAPTER 27

My muscles quivered, but it wasn't from the steep hike coming down from the Wight's well. My feet stumbled over rocks and frozen clumps of grass, but I managed to keep my balance as I stalked down the hill.

I'd abandoned the path entirely.

The city lights were right there, within sight. Fuck going the long way. I was tempted to take to the sky, but my wings were drenched from the springs. My whole body was dripping. Having the winter wind whip at my skin didn't sound all that appealing right now.

Halfway down the hill, I heard Alezandral slam into the ground behind me.

His cold hand grabbed my arm and twisted me around. "Why did you take off like that, Sia? You can't keep running away at the first hint of conflict."

Anger exploded through me, and I reacted, raking a hand at his face, but Alezandral recoiled fast enough to dodge me. "You think I'm running because I'm *conflicted* about what happened back there? I'm running because I'm done, Alezandral."

I shoved his chest as hard as I could, surprise earning me a brief reprieve as he stumbled back. "I don't want to be around you anymore, and I don't want you touching me, so *fuck off.*"

Then, he was all over me, letting me punch him over and over until he finally managed to seize my other wrist. He held my arms to my chest as I lurched forward to snap at him.

We struggled for control. Me, trying to break free. Him, desperately holding on.

His expression shifted from bewilderment to frantic concern and then finally settled into an infuriated scowl as his fingers tightened on my arms. He wrenched me sideways, throwing me off guard as he twisted our bodies so he stood between me and the city. Only then did he release me.

I nearly tripped over my heels.

In my rush to escape the well, I'd forgotten to grab my slippers. The chill of the frost under my feet didn't bother me much, but now that I was standing still, I realized just how slick the ground was, thanks to my burning skin and the sparks flying off me in every direction. My feet slid, threatening to send me careening straight into Alezandral, but I dug my toes in and stood my ground.

Alezandral's body was outlined by twirling hoarfrost and the distant city lights glowing around his wings, a starry night sky spread out above us. Water had frozen in sparkling droplets all over his bare chest. He was shaking, from his flight through the sky or the anger written all over his face, I wasn't sure. "What the fuck is your problem?"

"My problem is that I am *not* having sex with you, Alezandral. *Ever!*"

His upper lip curled. "Yes, you've already said this. Many times. So many times, in fact, that you screaming it at me now is giving me a headache."

"Well, I think it bears repeating, considering what the Wight just told us about *our daughter.*" I spat the last two words at him, hoping he heard just how much I resented them.

No children. I'd made that decision for myself a long time ago, when I was still a child myself, left alone in my room for days at a time because I couldn't stop crying, because my flames wouldn't behave. Caring for a child was not the same as nurturing one, and I wasn't sure I had it in me. I wasn't sure my heart had enough blood for them.

Erlene was the only exception. A chance encounter. A blessing from the Goddess, even if it was only for a brief time.

I would always see her as a little bit mine after what we'd been through, and it had torn my heart to shreds to say good-bye, knowing I might never see her again, knowing she had a legacy of her own to carry. Children weren't meant to be pawns of legacy, and any child I had with Alezandral would bear that fate. They would bear my darkness too.

But I think what made me *really* angry was the fact that I *did* want to have sex with Alezandral.

I'd thought about it several times over the past few weeks. My resolve to keep him at a distance had been compromised... by *him.* By his sweetness and intimate touches. By his affectionate glances and warm smiles.

And now, the idea of *never* touching him, *never* being with him like that, for the sake of making sure he never got me pregnant—it made me near violent.

Alezandral sighed. "I don't know what to tell you, Sia. I don't understand why you're angry with me. *They* said it."

"But you're the one who's going to do it," I argued.

"Do *what?*"

"The one to get me pregnant!"

He groaned. "Oh, give me a fucking break, Sabrina. It's not as if I'm going to deny you contraceptive tonics if you want them. Fuck, I'll let you shove the tonics down my throat too if you want to be doubly sure. If we have a daughter in the future, it's going to be because *you* asked for it."

"I'm never going to ask for that," I hissed.

Alezandral gave me a slow, arrogant smirk. "I hate to break it to you, darling, but the Wight just confirmed to both of us that you will someday."

I crossed my arms over my chest.

"The only thing it confirmed tonight is that you're going to betray me. Someday, you're going to hurt me, because that's the only way we're having a child."

He recoiled, everything hard and mirthful seeping out of his expression. "What are you—are you suggesting I would *force* myself on you?"

"There's no other explanation, so yes."

The words erupted from me without my permission, and in the silence that followed, I knew I hadn't meant them. This was my deepest fear laid bare—that Alezandral would turn on me, just like everyone else in my life had. I was so angry at this moment, but I felt secure around him, and I really wished I didn't, because it was like my mouth had developed a mind of its own, regurgitating the darkness clinging to my heart.

Look at me, my fear pleaded with him, searching for both love and the validation of my worst thoughts in equal measure. *See how fucked up I am?*

Lee's pupils dilated as he took one slow step up the hill.

A deep, frozen emptiness opened up between us, gaping wider and wider as he drew closer. I had crossed into volatile territory without realizing it. I backed away up the hill, trying to keep my footing as he closed in.

Alezandral advanced too quickly, and the temperature dropped around us until my breath puffed in massive white clouds. There was intent burning behind his eyes, but it was veiled, and he wasn't letting me in.

Fuck, fuck, fuck, fuck.

My heel caught on the uneven ground, and I tripped backwards, landing hard on my tailbone. He kept coming. My stumble had done nothing to keep him at bay.

Before I could react, he was there, crouching over me with one knee pressed between my thighs. He grasped the underside of my jaw and brought my face mere inches from his. "The only females I *fuck*, Sia, are the ones who beg for it on their hands and knees. I require surrender before I take someone's body. And when I take it, I take until I've had my fill, until every bit of their pleasure belongs to me. I worship them and they worship me. Since you've made it clear you refuse to be that vulnerable with *anybody*, I think I can safely say you aren't my type. I have zero interest in fucking some closed-off brat who hates me."

My arms buckled.

His rejection rolled heavily in my stomach and spots bloomed at the edges of my vision until all I could see was Alezandral's intimidating snarl and the cold distance in his eyes. It made me want to dig myself a grave in this frozen ground.

Go ahead. Argue, brat, Alezandral goaded in my head. *Show me how right I am.*

I opened my mouth to respond, but I hesitated. I *wanted* to argue with him—no, I wanted to *scream* at him. *Not his type? How could he say that?*

He had to be lying out of spite, the stubborn asshole. I knew the way he looked at me, how his eyes followed me across the bedroom every night when I emerged from the bathroom in my nightgowns. He had to be attracted to me; otherwise, he'd have successfully fooled *me* with his orchestrated affection during this tour too, and how embarrassing would that be? How absolutely crushing?

All those whispered flirtations and sweet flattery. All the times he held me just a little tighter or longer than he needed to. The tour had been for show, but he made me feel wanted even when no one was in the room with us. There was no explanation for that.

Unless this wasn't about physical attraction to him.

He thought I hated him, but I didn't. I hated that he thought I did. I hated the way he was looking at me right now, like I had let him down, like I had disappointed him. And, most of all, I *hated* that he accused me of being invulnerable.

If he only knew the truth. If he only knew just how vulnerable I was all the fucking time. He just couldn't see it.

I hadn't let him see it.

The past, the present, and the future sat on my chest, taking turns beating my heart into a bloody pulp. I had kept myself isolated so long because I *knew* it would take so little for someone like him, someone so beautiful, to get past my defenses and carve a little piece of the bruised flesh away for themselves. Just like those little dark streams in my soul, I gave my heart away without meaning to. It was just too damaged to know better.

But fine. If he wanted to see it, I would show him. I would show him he was wrong. I was capable of anything, just like he said. I forced the anger out of me, pushing it away to make room for what was hidden beneath it.

I shook my head, letting the tension bleed from my face, looking up at him with tender affection as I grazed my finger-tips across his cheek.

His snarl faltered, and he blinked a few times as he pulled away. That dark, guarded gaze scoured my face as his hold on my jaw loosened, and then, just when I thought he might let me go and walk away, a small flicker of excitement sparkled in his eyes.

He let go of my jaw to thrust his hand into my hair.

I gasped as his cold fingers tightened into a fist and tugged my head back, tilting my face up as he towered over me. My chest tightened and my eyes watered, but the way he looked down at me made all the discomfort worth it.

There was still a bit of fire in his eyes, a low simmering of the anger from before, but with a cant of his head, he chuckled and brought his cool lips flush with my ear. "You're a naughty, manipulative little beast," he whispered, the words all teeth and sugary venom, "pretending to be a good girl just to win an argument?"

I couldn't breathe.

His nose trailed across the skin I'd offered him, his mouth hovering. When he reached the edge of the mark on my collarbone, he retreated up the length of my neck back to my ear. He was as worked up as I was. He could try to hide his feelings behind masterful smiles, but his body was like an extension of my own.

Our bond was stronger now. I could sense what he needed and, right now, that was me.

I lifted my hands to the front of his robe. The fabric was frozen, stiff. Grasping the material, I let the heat of my body extend to him, melting the crystalline droplets on his chest. I wanted to warm him. I wanted to do *anything* that would show him exactly how much I didn't hate him, anything that would keep him staring at me like this, like I was significant to him. Like he wanted to keep me. For whatever reason, I felt like I'd finally done something right, just this once, and his pleasure was my reward.

I tugged him closer, until our chests were touching.

As his lips brushed my ear again, he growled, "It's a pity I don't believe you."

An uneasy tingle spread up the back as his fingers slipped out of my hair. My heart stumbled, numbing to a heavy thrum in the back of my chest. "Maybe neither of us know me as well as we think we do," I choked out.

Alezandral paused, nodding. "Show me another glimmer, then. Let me see the rest."

My fingers twisted in his robe, and he allowed me to draw him so close that we were breathing the same air. His fingertips grazed the edge of the robe on my shoulder. I gasped, my body shuddering as he traced the silken hem towards my chest. He hooked a fingertip under the material, letting his nail scrape across the swell of my breast, and my eyes fluttered shut. "Yes," I breathed.

That should have been enough for him to continue, in my mind. I was telling him what I wanted. *Yes*, I wanted this. *Yes*, I could be vulnerable. *Yes, I am definitely your fucking type.*

Alezandral didn't seem to see it that way, though. He wasn't taking my thoughts.

He stood up, and I watched in disbelief as he turned around and sauntered down the hill, his robe dragging heavily behind him. I felt a thousand times colder without him, and that was such a confounding contradiction that I sat there and contemplated it for a long moment, letting the winter breeze lash at my bare skin.

Alezandral might have been collecting glimmers of me, but I was starting to realize I'd been searching for his too… and I think I finally caught one.

CHAPTER 28

When I returned to the cottage, Alezandral wasn't there.

I'd taken a long walk before returning to the city, processing everything that the Wight had said and my fight with Alezandral.

It had been terrible for me to accuse him of forcing me into a pregnancy. He'd done nothing to make me believe he would. In fact, from the moment he'd broken my father's shackles and handed me my freedom, I had a hard time believing he would force me to do *anything*.

Aside from dragging me into a pond to expose my true wings, I argued with myself.

Alright… so he wasn't perfect, but over and over, he'd proven his intentions were kind where I was involved. He fell into the pond *with* me. He never allowed me to suffer alone. In the moment, coming down from the Wight, that had been difficult to remember.

All I wanted to do now was find him and make things right, to explain why I had jumped to such an offensive conclusion. I wanted to apologize. But most of all, I wanted to make sure he never again looked at me the way he did when I accused him on that hillside. His disappointment was heavier than my father's, probably because, up to this point, it felt like Alezandral whole-heartedly believed in me. He believed the *best* in me.

Why did I have to show him my worst?

I stuffed a nightgown and towel into one of the wicker baskets the maidens left for me and abandoned the cottage. A long bath was precisely what I needed right now, and it was late enough that I could hope for some solitude.

Nothing illuminated the Malforian streets, no torches or faerie orbs. There was only the moon casting a silver glow over my path.

As I passed the palace, I admired its romantic blend of nature and white stone. Tall pillars crawled with ivy. Fragrant drooping blooms played along the edge of the bulbous roof and into the open archways lining the side of the palace facing the street. It looked like the pergola one might find in a garden, only magnified.

I tried not to wonder if Alezandral went there after our argument. I was certain there were plenty of females who would be willing to beg for him in there.

He might not be interested in the princess, but the Malforian were an amorous and affectionate people, and their courtesans were plentiful. *They* would get on their knees for him when I could not, even though a little voice in the back of my head wanted me to, or at least wanted to try.

It was a thrilling, dangerous thought, and I just couldn't stop indulging it.

By the time I reached the bath house, my thighs were chafed and stinging from the slickness between my legs. Sitting in that damp grass had soaked me through. I was eager to scrub away my unwelcome arousal and recoup a little control over my demented sex. The next time I faced Alezandral, whether back at the cottage tonight or when I went searching for him in the morning, my emotions would be firmly mastered.

We needed to talk about the future, seriously.

After I descended the mineral-washed staircase leading to the arbored pools, my heart and my feet tripped to a stop.

No need to search for him.

Alezandral was *here*, bathing.

The baths were a dozen or so individual pools crowded together, and Lee had settled into the one farthest from the entrance. He stood with his back to me, dragging a bar of soap across his shoulder and rinsing the suds away with his opposite hand. He'd put away his wings for the task. All I could see in the soft light of the torches was the magnificent slope of his torso, large and honed and narrowing dramatically towards his waist. The water lapped at his hips, not quite high enough to hide the powerful swell of his backside.

My feet seemed to move on their own, carrying me silently down the last few steps and toward one of the white pillars erected at the pools' edge.

Incense burned here, spilling smoke down from various charms hanging from the tree branches and those stone railings crisscrossed above the water. The charms hung like static spectators, gnarled wood and dried bundles of herb. It smelled like rain and earth, and a familiar warm musk that reminded me a little bit of powdered opium.

Maybe it *was* opium.

Considering the Malforian gifts, that wouldn't surprise me. Opium altered mood almost as well as their magic.

I couldn't explain to myself why I decided to hide behind the pillar. I just knew that I wanted to watch him a while longer, to watch him turn, rolling that bar of soap down over his chest and abdomen, to watch as his skin glistened in the firelight.

His scar…

He'd received that because of *me*. It was a memory of our shared rebellion, forever embedded in his skin.

As his hand dipped lower, I knew where it went, even though I couldn't see it. I held my breath, leaning into the pillar as my own hand wandered. *What am I doing?*

My hand slid over the silk of my robe, hesitating against my belly.

With a deep roll of his shoulders, Alezandral's wings erupted from his back, impeding my view of him. He looked down at himself, and it was like he was taunting me. *What I wouldn't give to see through his eyes right now...*

When his other hand joined the first, moving in an obvious languid pull as his head kicked back in pleasure, I forgot myself entirely.

My fingers slithered under the robe and toyed with the slick flesh between my legs. It wasn't a firm enough touch to relieve my aching, but it was enough to make my eyes flutter. It was enough to make me want to burn.

Who was he thinking about right now? Was he thinking about me? Could I dare hope?

I bit my lip as my forehead rolled against the stone pillar.

Alezandral's voice snapped me out of my madness. "Are you simply enjoying the view, darling, or are you debating whether or not to boil me alive?"

I wrenched my hand out of my robe before stepping around the pillar.

Alezandral was staring at me over his wings, his eyes guarded but lips curled to one side in an uneven smile.

I approached the nearest pool.

"I just got here," I whispered, delicately clearing my throat. I worried if I said anything more, my voice would splinter.

"I can leave if you want me to," he offered, inching toward the stairs.

"No," I said quickly. "It's okay. There's space enough for both of us." I needed time to work up the courage to apologize. He was far enough away that I felt like I could do it.

Alezandral nodded, turning away.

As I stripped, he set the soap down on the edge of the pool and submerged himself, and I took that opportunity to quickly slip into the pool.

There were bars of herbal soap and hair serums placed in small cubbies next to each pool. I grabbed soap first and lathered my chest with it, crouching so most of my body was engulfed. The minerals in the water were less potent here than they were in the Wight's spring, but it was enough to make my nipples hard, to pull my skin taut.

Now that the dread of meeting the Wight was gone, I could admit that I loved the feeling. It was a pulling sensation, like the water was drawing on my body, renewing it.

The water reminded me of what the maidens said about the Wight's powers.

Alezandral was back above the surface now, lounging against the edge of his pool. His handsome face was tilted upward, admiring the slivers of sky visible through the gnarled canopy.

"The Wight…" I started. Alezandral's jaw clenched, and he glared into the water straight in front of him, but I continued anyway, more than willing to face his anger head on. "When it answered your question, did it take away your fear?"

His face was overtaken at once with gentle surprise, and his gaze slid to mine. "What do you mean?"

I shrugged, returning the soap to the edge of my pool and grabbing a serum. "The maidens said that was one of its powers. It feeds on your fear and makes you braver, stronger." I glanced at him. "So, did it?"

Alezandral canted his head, thinking. "No," he replied slowly. "Though I understand why some people might think that. I felt it digging claws into my fear—but I don't think it took the fear away. I think it just showed me a way not to be afraid."

"How?" I asked.

"Well, it's…" He paused, shaking his head. "For example, I've always been afraid of having children. My country expects them from me, needs them, but for as long as I can remember, the thought of having my own terrified me. What if I hurt them? What if I ruined them? And it's not that I thought I would hurt them on purpose, but I worried that I *could*. I feared that I would get angry, like my father gets so angry, and it would just erupt from me. I feared I wouldn't be able to stop it."

"You could never do that," I murmured.

He scoffed. "Yes, well, try telling a bruised little boy that."

I didn't know how to respond to his bitterness in a way that wouldn't hurt him further, so I kept my mouth shut and rinsed my hair.

As I straightened, I saw that Alezandral was leaning his forearms on the edge of his pool, facing me. His sudden attention swept across my body, and I dipped lower in the water, hoping he wouldn't notice my body's reaction. Luckily, he was too distracted by his thoughts, his gaze distant.

He dragged his lower lip between his teeth. "I think what the Wight did was *move* my fear, just a little to the side, just enough that I could see past it. It let me see something else. The fear itself is still there, but once I saw more, it didn't seem so scary. It felt," he hesitated, searching for the right word, "*rectifiable*."

There was a light in his eyes that hadn't been there before, and I recognized what it was. *Hope*. Full, giddy, joyful hope.

The Wight hadn't done that for me, for my fear, and maybe that was my punishment. First, that made me jealous, but then my jealousy faded into something warm and tender, then into an inky ocean of guilt. I had nearly deprived him of this peace. He had been willing to live without his truth just so I could have mine.

The Wight was right. I had been selfish.

I smiled and willed myself to mean it. "I'm happy for you, Alezandral."

Confusion flashed across his features, a cold wariness.

"I mean it," I murmured. We didn't need to talk about how his future would affect me. Right now, that didn't really matter. *He* mattered. His happiness and his hope and his healing mattered. We could figure out the rest of it later. "I'm sorry for the way I reacted earlier, I was just—"

"Scared," he finished for me.

"Yes," I breathed. "And that had nothing to do with you. I know you would *never* hurt me like that. I should never have suggested it."

His smile quirked to one side, but I could tell he was still turning my words over in his head, trying to decide whether to believe them. "Thank you for saying that."

Then, Alezandral twisted away, allowing his eyes to slide closed as he held himself aloft by the backs of his arms.

I battled with myself. Should I leave? Should I push him for more? I turned around and set my gaze on the basket where I'd left my towel, tempted to leave this conversation for another time… but my curiosity won out, the way it often did around him.

"Alezandral?" I was still staring at the basket, telling myself that if he didn't respond, then I would leave.

He heard me, though, and responded with a hum.

"I think we need to talk," I muttered.

"About what?"

I seethed quietly. "*Everything*. The riddle." I waved a hand to nothing in particular. "Our engagement." I waved again. I squeezed my eyes shut, seeing stars as I braced myself. "Where do we go from here?"

Alezandral sighed, and I heard his body shift in the water.

When I glanced over my shoulder, I watched as sparkling black matter enveloped him. It disappeared then reappeared in the pool next to mine. The ether dust fell to the surface of the water, swirling as Alezandral emerged from the darkness and swam up to the ledge separating my pool from his new one. He folded his arms over the porous ledge and rested his chin on top of them.

"Well, let's start with the simplest problem to be solved."

I swam over to join him, propping my elbow up on the stone ledge a foot or so away, cradling the side of my jaw to stare at him. The incense in this place made the tension between us more bearable, made our proximity *exciting*. It was all too easy to forgive that, just an hour ago, he had his hand around my throat. I wondered if he would do it again. "And what is that?"

"The Wight's riddle. I already know the answer to it."

My eyebrows lifted. "You do?"

"Yes," he nodded. "The Wight alluded to a mystic map this territory safeguards. My father has mentioned it before. Back when the Malforian first offered to house the Wight, the Wight gave their king that map as a token of gratitude. Rumor is, that map tracks every Winged Spirit who roams through this plane. The Malforian won't give that up, nor will they even confirm it exists, but if we can find out where they keep it, we can search for the Spirits our territories haven't claimed —the ones that aren't accounted for."

"*If* we can find the map," I repeated. "The Wight said it's locked away."

Alezandral smiled. "When I was walking through the Malforian palace, I saw a room guarded against magical entry. I'm guessing it holds some pretty important items. *And* I'm betting the king keeps the keys to it in his office somewhere. All I need is an opportunity to search for them. We have plenty of time to do that if…" He trailed off, pursing his lips.

"If what?" I pressed.

His eyes slid to mine. "If we continue our tour, and that leads us to a more difficult conversation."

"More difficult than sneaking into the Malforian palace and stealing an ancient map?"

He ignored my teasing tone, his gaze hard and brimming with tension. "Are you really done with me, Sia? With this engagement? Do you want to leave? Because I'm not stopping you, and I sure as fuck won't allow anyone else to stop you."

His voice forewarned foul fates for anyone who stood in my way.

"I don't know," I rasped, scrambling for an explanation that made sense of the mess in my head. "I'm still here, aren't I? Do *you* want me to leave?"

His brow pinched. "Why do you think I would want that?"

"Because," I huffed, "I've been a pain in your ass. We argue all the time, and it's often my fault. I have no idea what I'm doing or what I am, or even what I want. I've hurt you."

"I've hurt you too." Alezandral's eyes burned into mine. "And trust me, you give me more than you realize."

"What?" I demanded. "What do I give you, other than the completion of this bond?"

He smiled faintly, his gaze dropping to the water beneath him. The incense smoke gathered on the back of his neck and his dark, golden hair. I wanted to reach out and feel all of it. The smoke. His hair and skin. This connection between us.

I wanted to know him.

"Well," he finally murmured, startling me out of my carnal thoughts, "for one, training with you has been the most exhilarating experience of my life. I think that, in particular, has nothing to do with the bond. You're very funny, too—I've laughed more in the past few months than I have in years. Your presence comforts me. You challenge me. You're clever and quick on your feet, and sometimes, I think I might get dizzy trying to keep up with your daring sense of direction." His eyes lifted back to mine, glimmering with blue light. "You are my match in so many ways, darling, but you are my friend in them all. I *like* your fire, even when it burns me."

My heart swelled. For a moment, all I could do was sit in those words. They made me feel so… *cherished.*

How did he speak to my deepest insecurities so easily? He made me want to face them—the shame in my heart, my fear and hopelessness. With only a few words, he made me believe that I could overcome them. I could dream something new for myself. I could be myself and he would accept me, always.

All I wanted was to get closer to him, but I held back, frightened of crossing that line between tentative allies and something more—friends and something more.

After what I'd accused him of earlier , how could I cross that line?

"I don't want to hurt you anymore," I confessed.

His eyes searched mine, considering me with a seriousness that made my skin tighten. Then, he raised a hand between us.

A small billow of black Materie shimmered to life in his palm, and as it fell away, I saw what it had left behind. *A ring.* The band was made of the same material my father had mined to use against me, and as Alezandral extended his hand toward me, the jet-black gem set into the band started glittering, shifting from one color to the next, amethyst and spring green, blues and yellows and the most luminous bursts of amber.

With a start, I realized it was black opal—a gem that was near-extinct on this continent. The witches of the forest found them useful in amplifying spells.

The sight of it tickled the underside of my heart, and I

could almost feel my mother whispering there in the darkness, in the emptiness, urging me to take it. Alezandral couldn't possibly know the truth about her, and yet, he was giving me a ring that felt so keenly like her.

A ring that felt like me too.

I looked into Alezandral's eyes, and they were more stunning than the jewel. "And where were you hiding that?" I said with a raise of my brow.

His lips twitched. "You don't want to know."

I smiled at his evasive words. He'd been carrying it around with him—but for how long? "What about the other ring?"

"I don't want you to wear my father's ring anymore," he said fiercely. "I want you to wear *mine*."

His.

Ours.

"You knew there would be no breaking our bond," I guessed. "Didn't you?"

"I suspected," he said carefully. "You were so adamant about asking the Wight, and I didn't want to take that away from you. I thought, 'I could be wrong, and if I am, that'll be the end of it.' I doubt you would have believed me if I tried to dissuade you in the first place. I had this ring forged for you… just in case you decided to stay."

Did I want to stay?

Could we be happy, especially after what he'd said on the hillside? *Not my type.*

What if I wasn't?

Or worse, what if I was, but I never stopped shielding myself long enough to let him see it?

He'd made it clear where his loyalties lay. With his country. With his crown. He'd made it clear that if he had to choose between me and them right now, he would choose them. Would staying really change that? What would become of me if it didn't?

Slowly, I asked, "What exactly does my staying mean to you?"

"It means you marry me, Sia." His eyes flicked back and forth between mine, intense and commanding. "It means you become my wife. I will become your most devoted friend, your closest advisor, and your kindest adversary. We can be together, always. If you can't handle that, then I will bear your decision to leave with grace. Tonight, you need to decide what to believe in. Do you still believe our bond was a mistake? Or do you believe *me* when I say it isn't? Do you believe we're better off without each other? Because I'm telling you right now, I don't." He hesitated, his expression pained. "I hope you stay. I hope you stay and that we never have to feel the pain of our bond again."

There was something more there, in his eyes, something he wasn't telling me.

I knew it was wrong—I knew it was deplorable of me to even *try*—but I anchored myself in his gaze and tentatively reached for his mind, letting the world blur to nothing around me.

"Go ahead, look," he whispered, and I realized he was already in my head. He'd offered himself up freely. "I have nothing to hide."

I'd spent so much time with Alezandral in my head. I knew his stream of consciousness, had memorized it. It was right there, flowing eagerly into my hands. How could I resist?

His thoughts rushed into me like a tidal wave, sweeping me along some never-ending stream of thought. *She didn't want to marry me before, so why would she now? She's been trying to figure a way out of this when there is none, just as I have. Fuck this goddess-damned bond.*

Those words rattled me to my core.

Pain slammed into my heart. I leaned into that river between us, overcome with bitterness as I fought against the current. If I was going to hurt myself with the truth, I might as well do it completely.

As I sank deeper into his mind, though, the tone of his thoughts changed. The connection grew darker, more volatile, churning with unexpected fear and resentment. I couldn't shake the worry that they were aimed at me, so I dug my heels in and *pushed*. The next barrage of his thoughts stunned me in their rawness.

I should have learned my lesson the first time, with my mother. I used up all her love until she was empty. I used up her sanity and drove her to oblivion. I shouldn't do this to Sia. She shouldn't have to deal with me for the rest of her life. It's a miserable duty.

I quickly pulled away from his mind, sick to my stomach.

That hadn't just been his thoughts. That had been more. I'd wandered into whatever pulsed beneath conscious awareness and heard things I was certain Lee had never said out loud before, thoughts he wouldn't have wanted me to hear.

He blamed himself for his mother's fate.

He was still searching for her, and for her forgiveness.

That little boy I'd bonded with in the birch trees was still here. He'd always been here, frightened of me in a way no one had ever been before, in a way I could understand. He would rather die than break my spirit. That was what our broken promise would do to him—he would surrender to oblivion so I could walk free.

Lee didn't seem to notice what I'd done, the lines I'd crossed to burrow into his mind. His face was as stoic as ever.

I wanted nothing more in that moment than to soothe the depths of his being, to reach into his chest and cradle his heart in my hands, to nourish and protect it so thoroughly that he never believed those terrible things about himself again. Because they weren't true. Even after the few months I'd spent by his side, I could say that with certainty.

There was only one way to banish his doubts.

"Yes, Lee. I'll marry you."

His eyes flashed to mine, surprise burning through his mask. "Are you sure?"

I chuckled. "Just give me the ring already. Or are you going to force me to put this one on myself, like you did the last one?"

Lee shook his head and took hold of my wrist, tugging me closer. Just our hands touched, but I felt him throughout my body as he slid that ring onto my finger. It was like he was wrapping himself around me, sewing himself inside me. Skin to skin, lung to lung. Then, his hand dropped mine, and my body emptied out again.

I lifted my hand between us and admired the black opal, watching as it winked at me even in the dim lighting. "The ring is beautiful, Lee. I love it."

"I'm glad." His eyes crinkled around the edges, and I knew he truly was glad. I loved seeing how pleased he was, how relieved and calm.

It made me want to rile him up a bit.

"Would you mind grabbing my towel for me?" I pouted. "The night air is cold."

Lee's eyes narrowed in steely suspicion. "Alright..." He swam to the opposite side of his pool and hefted himself out of the water.

By the time I met him near the ledge, he had my towel in his hands and his own wrapped around his hips, and he was looking at everything *but* me as I climbed the stairs out of the pool. He held the large piece of cotton towards me, but I only smiled and ran my fingers through my wet hair, gathering it up to rest on top of my head. "Do you mind?" I asked again.

His eyes met mine over the edge of the towel.

"Dry my wings?" I added innocently.

The back of my heels rested on the edge of the pool, so Lee had no choice but to wrap his arms around me, to lean over my shoulder as he dragged the towel down my spine. I shuddered, leaning into him as he dried each tier of my wings where I could not so easily reach. His touch slowed around the smallest pair, as if hesitating to pull away.

I nuzzled his bare skin over the scar we shared, and he stiffened.

A sliver of my arousal bled away as I wondered if that had made him uncomfortable. Just hours ago, I'd screamed at him, telling him I didn't want him or his children. Now, I was practically salivating on his chest. Perhaps that was too sudden of a change, even for me.

Lee pulled away, wrapping the towel under my largest set of wings so my smaller four were covered and warm.

I seized his arms before he could tuck the towel around my front. The open embrace left me exposed. "You can look at me, you know?" I whispered. "We're getting married. We're bound to see each other naked from time to time. You shouldn't get so flustered."

"I don't get *flustered*," he argued with a roll of his eyes.

I cocked my head, smiling. "Prove it."

My lungs caught as his eyes traveled with leisurely dominance down my neck and chest, lingering a moment before they dropped even lower. My waist tingled as he took in my curves, as his tongue slid out to taste the bow of his lips. I wanted to replace his tongue with my own, wanted to know the taste, but I held back.

He was looking at my naked body like I was the most fascinating creature in the world, and I reveled in the attention.

Before his gaze could reach the triangle of dark curls between my legs, he wrapped the towel around my chest, tucking a corner of the towel into the hollow between my breasts to secure it. Then, he took a step back and lifted my hand, kissing the ring on my finger.

"Don't worry yourself about a thing. I'll see to the wedding preparations after our tour is through. Our fathers will want this to happen sooner rather than later, but I think I can hold them off long enough to find your Spirit first, if that's what you need?"

Back to business. Back to distance. How incredibly disorienting.

Was this him blatantly rejecting my advances, or had my intentions not been obvious? Maybe I needed to say it, but I wasn't sure how. I couldn't mess this up, and I was convinced that if I opened my mouth right now, we would end up in another argument.

I nodded, feeling lost.

Without another glance, he turned to grab his robe from the other side of the room. He hadn't seen it—the change in me. What I felt for him was intensifying, evolving, but after all that I'd done to push him away, he couldn't trust I was staying because I wanted him. He believed I was staying because I *had* to, because of this bond. In reality, how could he believe anything else? When it came right down to it, how could *I*?

How did I know that what I felt was mine and not the fault of our bond—that unseeable connection forever tugging us toward one another?

Only, in my heart of hearts, I knew it was far more complicated than that.

CHAPTER 29

Our plan was simple.

Sneak out of the palace yard during this party. Gain access to the locked room. Find that map and get the fuck out of here without anyone catching us.

Lee had arranged for our luggage to be quietly moved into the carriage while we were occupied at the palace. That way, we had a quick escape if things went badly tonight. We could only hope we wouldn't need the carriages until morning.

Either way, this was the last evening we'd be spending in the Malforian territory.

They were sending us off with one last *flutter* in the palace's courtyard. There had been several "flutters" over the last week, as they called them, but in reality, it felt like I had returned to my life in the gnashing forest. The Malforian territory was large, and its proximity to the forest offered beautiful, wooded landscapes. We'd been taking hikes every day from one waterfall to the next. We spent hours in the wilderness, and then, as the sky darkened, the Malforian stripped, bathing together in the lakes and rivers.

Neither Lee nor I felt comfortable participating in the

nightly swims. That was how their sacrifices were made, after all. *Drownings*.

Drowning was exactly how it felt being surrounded by their people. The Malforians' emotions were intense, projected until I felt their blind joy as if it was my own. There was barely enough time for us to sleep and eat this week between the revelries, much less talk out loud without an audience. We slept every night on cots on either side of a blazing fire, the stars above us, lulled to sleep by the distant wildness of their people.

Our plan had been pieced together day by day, one whispering thought at a time.

In the courtyard, we watched the Malforian unfurl a white sheet at the edge. Two rosy-winged men hung the material between the elder trees and pinned it taut. Lee and I were led to a plush loveseat near the patio, but we didn't settle in yet. Apprehension vibrated between us, low and constant across our bond.

What if the Malforian sensed our nervousness?

Two other couches were arranged next to ours for the Malforian royals, all three seats upholstered with pale pink fabric. The staff buzzed all around us, lighting incense in brass lamps erected throughout the yard and setting food and drink on the tables. The scent of opium and poppy-laced lavender coalesced in my nostrils. It plummeted through my center, swirling and prickling under my skin. I curled my fingers into fists and pressed my thighs together, but still, the effects of the incense lingered.

Why did they need this smoke? What had the Malforian planned for us tonight?

Lee's glove grazed the edge of my wing as he reached for my waist, and I tore my gaze away from the bustling yard to look at him.

Our eyes met briefly before he looked to some place behind me, nodding once.

The Malforian king had arrived, his consort and all six of his daughters in tow. He returned Lee's nod before waving down a maid carrying mead.

We hadn't spent much time with the king during our visit, aside from the meals we shared. He was the opposite of his daughters. Where they seemed effervescent and eager to pull us into the community, he was reticent. His words were few and his emotions carefully guarded, which was rather impressive, considering the ways of his home.

Princess Maribel broke away from her family and approached us with a smile, a knit blanket rolled up in her arms. "Your Highnesses. You're early."

"We didn't want to be late," I replied, forcing a polite grin.

"Especially with our early departure tomorrow," Lee reminded her, squeezing my waist one finger at a time.

Since the proposal, he had taken to playing with my flesh like the keys of a piano, and it made me want to sing. Sparks of warmth skittered across my ribs and up into my lungs, and it was a struggle to swallow down my moan, but I managed, thank the Divine Mother.

"We weren't sure how long we'd be able to stay tonight," Lee continued. "We have a long flight ahead of us."

"Oh, don't tease, Your Highness." The flirtation in her voice made my smile curl into a sneer. "You two *have* to stay and watch this special treat. I assure you, you'll never experience something like this anywhere else. You must savor it."

Then, she had the gall to step forward and touch Lee's arm.

Lee brushed Maribel's hand away with a shrug. "I won't hesitate to leave when I wish to savor my bride instead," he said simply. "We've been without privacy long enough."

My skin tingled as his intimate words echoed in my head.

His arm tightened around my back to pull me closer. He pressed a kiss to my temple, and I could have *purred* at the affection. I loved his possessiveness, loved the way he soothed my jealousy, even if the affection itself was only for show.

The harsh words he spoke in the aftermath of the Wight still sat in my head, haunting me. *Since you've made it clear you refuse to be vulnerable with anybody, I think I can safely say you aren't my type.* I kept returning to that moment, to the hurt in his eyes. My stubbornness and silence. I couldn't find the courage to break that silence yet, so here we were, still just pretending.

Maribel's grin faded as she looked between us.

"I see." Her voice was cold, the words curt. "Well, I suppose I should tell the staff to get the show started right away." As she turned on her heel and stalked toward the sheet across the yard, my body unraveled.

I threw my arms around Lee's neck, knocking us both down into the loveseat.

His fingernails dug into my waist as I landed on his lap, but he chuckled softly as he shifted me into a more comfortable position. "Not that I'm complaining, but what's this for?" he murmured, his stubble bristling the soft flesh of my shoulder.

I smiled into his neck. "We're being watched, aren't we?"

"Are we?" he replied, nuzzling my cheek. "You're paying more attention than I am."

I clicked my tongue in mock disappointment and lowered my voice to a rasp. "That's a quick way to get us *both* caught."

"Stop distracting me, then," he growled.

I giggled and pushed myself upright to look at him. His eyes were pools of liquid winter right now, pale and soft. "I can't help it."

Lee leaned in until our noses touched. "I guess you'll have to pay attention for the both of us, my beautiful thief."

A current of heat surged up my spine as his hand slid down, curled around my hip, and squeezed. I brushed a lock of hair away from his forehead, but the golden strands instantly fell right back into disarray. Sighing, I shook my head. "What would you do without me?"

"Languish," he exhaled.

He said it without hesitation, without humor, and the truth in that one word struck me like a physical blow. It reminded me of the bond we shared, of how much of it I truly didn't understand.

The only information I had about bonds came from history books my father once allowed me to read and gossip. I'd yet to hear about any bonds that weren't cherished and celebrated, and that was perhaps the most persuading piece of evidence I had. Maybe the bond was undeniable. Did we have any real choice in this, beyond the one we made as children? Was this desire I felt for him *real*? Or was it the bond's desire?

With a weak smile, I slid off Lee's lap and grabbed a glass of mead from the side table, turning my eyes away from the handsome male who now grimaced at me.

The rest of the town started filtering into the yard, placing blankets on the ground to sit between us and that great white sheet. A bulky contraption was being set up several feet in front of the sheet, like a camera but larger.

A seraph, with wings streaked in layers of pink and sheer pastel yellow, fiddled with the bulb cone at the top of the machine. Their left hand glowed a faint, rosy hue—another hybrid. Malforian and Sphinx, with *four* wings. They were the product of a noble love match rather than an arranged marriage—a true rarity.

That was one thing I did admire about the Malforian: the way they honored love.

The seraph turned their glowing palm toward the cone, and the bulb lit up. The color ricocheted, flooding the white sheet with a warm, pink light. It took a moment for my eyes to adjust, but when they did, I saw there was a picture on the sheet, a still photograph of a male and female. She was swooning dramatically in his arms, and he looked down at her like he wanted to… well, do *something* with her.

The sheer magnificence of this gadgetry, the newness of it, made me smile and lean forward in my seat. "What is *this*?" I muttered, more to myself than in conversation.

"We call it a feature," a husky voice answered.

Lee and I twisted to face the Malforian king, who stood beside our loveseat with his six mauve wings flexing power-fully behind him. I hadn't bothered to remember his name. In truth, he was rather forgettable. I think he liked it that way.

His coppery blond hair was braided in two long sections, the tails resting on each of his shoulders, bright against the white linen of his shirt. He smiled at us, but the warmth didn't reach his pale green eyes.

My feet were being held captive on Lee's lap, his hands wrapped around my ankles and his fingertips tracing the hills and valleys with void tenderness. I hadn't even noticed he was doing that until the king's eyes caught on it. Our public displays had become familiar to us, even mindless at times.

I ignored the tingle of Lee's touch and returned my gaze to the king. "A feature, you said? What does that mean?"

"We found a way to make pictures *move*."

"Move?" I echoed, trying to comprehend that.

He gestured to the front of the yard, where the seraph at the camera was now turning a cylinder of amber film in front of the bulb. The picture on the white screen shifted. The female's eyes started fluttering, her gown wavering as if being disrupted by a breeze. The male on the sheet winked at us. Then, the movement stopped, and I watched everything happen again in reverse as the cylinder was twisted the oppo-site direction.

The king explained, "We have a camera that captures light signatures over a period of time, and we learned how to project those stills in such a way that they appear to be moving as our bodies move... or at least, very close to it."

Lee gaped at the sheet. "That's incredible."

"Quite," the king said proudly, and then his brow furrowed. "It's meant to be an *interactive* experience, but my daughter has informed me you might turn in early instead."

My heart pumped a little harder. "Oh," I gasped. "Well, we just figured that would be best, considering our morning—"

"It's not a problem, I assure you," he interrupted, lifting his hands. "We just happen to serve a sacred fruit close to the end of the feature and, if you two are indeed leaving the yard early, I'd like to offer it to you now instead." The king turned to a servant standing on the patio behind us and beckoned them forward.

The servant held a large silver platter filled with coin-sized berries. They were arranged in little clusters, and the skin reflected a rainbow of cool tones, each dipped in rich, almost-black chocolate.

Drool welled under my tongue just looking at them.

I reached for one. "That's very thoughtful, Your Majesty. Thank you."

Lee's hand shot forward and caught my wrist. "Hold on, Sia," he muttered, a hint of agitation in his voice. I glanced at him with a furrowed brow, but his eyes were still trained on the platter. "He's offering us passion fruit."

"So?"

He shifted beneath me. "It's faerie fruit, darling. An aphro-disiac, and a strong one at that. It'll drive you mad with want."

My stomach took a sharp dip.

The Malforian king threw his head back and laughed. "My, how dramatic you are. You'll only feel mad until you make it back to your room and indulge the urge, and that was your plan for the night anyway, was it not?"

Faerie fruit could only be grown and harvested in the elven realms. It didn't surprise me that the Malforian possessed such fruit—living this close to the gnashing forest, they were well-equipped for short jaunts to the elven realm. I *was* surprised that they wished to share it with us. Considering its origins, the fruit was priceless.

I turned my frown on the king. "Why would you offer this to us?"

"Why? It's tradition, Princess. Our people partake in passion fruit when we wish to celebrate love, and isn't that what this union of yours is all about?"

His smile was all wrong. This male was onto us. He knew something wasn't right about our engagement, or, at the very least, that we weren't being honest about it. What was he getting out of throwing us at each other, though?

Perhaps he could feel the confusion in my heart and the fear in Lee's. Perhaps he simply wanted to help. But I found myself doubting that.

Lee sighed. "Your Majesty—"

"Of course it is," I interjected with a laugh, placing a hand on Lee's chest to stop him. We needed to accept their gift, or risk suspicion. "I'm honored to partake in this tradition, and Alezandral is too. Aren't you?" I turned to him and fluttered my lashes.

His returning smile was strained. "Naturally."

What are you up to?

I plucked a berry from the platter. *Why do I need to be up to anything?*

He scoffed quietly enough that only I could hear it as he claimed a berry. *Because I know you. You're always up to something.*

I pinned the berry between my teeth and smiled wider,

silently daring him to do the same. *I guess you'll just have to play along and find out... unless you're scared. Has a little berry gotten the best of you, silly swan?*

He shoved the entire berry into his mouth and gnashed on it while glaring at me.

I finally bit into mine. The juice was sweet and slightly sour, and the instant it hit my tongue, my body reacted, tingling all over. I felt it in my mouth and my chest and my lower abdomen as I swallowed. Warmth followed quickly, as if I'd just downed a knuckle of liquor.

"Perfect," the Malforian king chortled.

My wings ruffled at the sound of his laughter. I'd forgotten he was there for a moment.

He simply nodded to each of us before returning to his seat, leaving us to the heat pooling low in our bellies.

I'D UNDERESTIMATED the passion fruit.

My skeleton practically vibrated against the loveseat. Every inch of my skin burned, and my legs were feeling weak. My attention was drawn to the arousal between them, the slick gathering against my will.

And I was *very* aware of Lee's hand resting on the cushion between us, of his every uneven breath and the agitated twitch of his wings as they brushed against mine.

He was feeling it too, and knowing that made it all so much worse.

I tried to keep my eyes on the feature, those pictures moving like illusionary enchantments across the white sheet, but even *that* distraction was short-lived. I had no idea what the people in the feature were doing or what the story was intended to be about.

A small group of musicians had taken up instruments on either side of the yard, and their symphonies did *not* help to keep my body under control.

I kept waiting for my arousal to ebb, to end, but it didn't.

Desire was a fire-breathing wretch underneath my skin, tearing and ripping at my sinews in a desperate struggle to break free. It was too much. She was a monster, and I had given life to her, so I had no choice but to face it.

I clenched my hands into fists, my fingers twisting in my purple velvet gown. For what felt like the hundredth time in so many seconds, I glanced at Lee from the corner of my eye. He was looking right back, staring at my white knuckles with a smirk. My pulse jumped, anger and frustration circling each other low in my belly. He was so much better at hiding his reaction to the fruit. He even seemed *amused*.

Are you ready to fuck off yet? I sniped.

Honestly, I wasn't sure how much more I could take before I attacked him right here, in front of everyone. Either with my mouth or my flames, it wasn't decided yet.

A soft, infuriating chuckle rumbled out of him. *Why? Are you suffering yet?*

I don't know what you're talking about. I turned back to the feature, trying to make sense of the pictures. *I'm fine.*

You're fine? The echoed words slithered through me.

Lee slid an arm behind my head. The instant his fingertips landed on my shoulder, I stiffened. My eyes closed as I clenched my gown tighter. He was toying with me and, to be fair, I probably deserved it.

I was the one who forced us to eat the fruit.

Lee leaned in and nuzzled my ear with his nose. *You know, I think you're right about that. You* are *fine. The finest female I've ever seen. Fine like a sweet, succulent wine.*

A soft moan bubbled in my throat, but I swallowed it down.

Lee gathered my hair into his hand, his fingers grazing my cheek. He hummed softly against my ear then nipped it with his teeth, and I was so surprised that my hand flew off my lap to grip his thigh. It was pure instinct. It was *need*.

Being touched by him felt like being touched for the first time, like I'd never been touched before him, and any touch I experienced after him would never measure up.

Gently, he turned my face toward his with one finger until our noses connected, his eyes glowing silvery-blue. "Do you think we're being watched right now?" He was so close. His sweet breath filled my nostrils, dragging me deeper into his magnetic pull.

I didn't know if we were being watched, but I knew why he had asked.

"Yes," I smiled roguishly.

He leaned in and kissed me.

A desperate noise shuddered out of my chest—an honest-to-Goddess *whimper*—as his tongue slipped between my pliant lips. His wandering hands were warm and fearless as they tugged me closer, as close as we could get without me climbing on top of him again.

Oh, I was tempted…

I just couldn't figure out if it was due to the Malforian influence pressing down on us, the fruit in our bellies, or the overwhelming and unreliable feelings I had for him. Whatever was to blame, I knew this wasn't the right time for it. We needed that map. I tried to pull away, but Lee stopped me with a hand on the back of my neck.

His lips clung to mine as he murmured, "Don't keep me waiting."

My face prickled with heat as I pressed my palms to his chest. *But isn't that what I do best?*

Lee released me with a chastising click of his tongue, fighting a smile as he stood. I kept an eye on him as he slipped away. Everyone was still absorbed in the feature, and those who might have been staring at us moments ago had respectfully averted their eyes when he kissed me. Darkness shrouded Lee's silhouette before he even reached the arbor out of the courtyard, and as he slipped through it, he disappeared in a cloud of glittering Materie.

Facing forward, I pretended to watch the feature.

I was supposed to wait here long enough to ensure no one would follow Lee into the palace. The door we needed to break into was charmed to deflect any kind of magical entry, Lee's Materie included, so Lee needed time to raid the King's study for the key. I was slightly irritated to be reduced to the role of a watch dog.

It was a good thing I did stay behind, though, because a mere minute after Lee left his seat, someone else stood up.

Maribel.

She turned to leave the yard, following the same path Lee had. Her gaze strayed to me once or twice, but I stared straight ahead, tracking her from the corner of my vision. The lust in my belly mutated, funneling into hot, red jealousy. She obviously had every intention of chasing after Lee. Who knew what exactly she planned to do once she found him, while he was *wanting*?

I waited for Maribel to disappear through the arbor before I left my seat, but I only made it halfway there before a hand latched onto my shoulder, uncomfortably close to my wing.

I spun on my heel, flames at the ready, but snuffed them when I saw it was the Malforian king who had stopped me. "You should return to your seat and finish watching the feature, *Princess*."

Panic and anger washed over me. The king didn't want me to follow Maribel, didn't want me to interrupt her. He and his daughter were in on some sort of plot together.

They were trying to sabotage this engagement.

Had someone put them up to it? Lee's father, perhaps? His Hand? Or perhaps they were doing it for their own selfishness. Affection stirred between his daughter and the Halcyon prince would offer extra protection for his people. Word of the disappearing seraphim had traveled far and wide since we discovered the source of them. Every territory was frightened, taking precautions, and this was a game our territories had been playing for centuries.

Extra-marital bonds were forged by desire and paid for in defense, and Maribel meant to take my male for herself. She would take advantage of him if given the chance.

That chance was now.

I ripped away from the king, staggering back as an amber film slid over my vision. "I suggest you return to your precious feature before I burn your treaties with the Fenix to ash." When my threat sank in and his eyes shuttered, I grinned. "That's right. My family won't be pleased to hear about your meddling, and soon, I'll have a hand in the Halcyon's treaties too. I may not be a queen yet, but I will be, and may the Goddess cast eternal darkness upon anyone who forgets that."

He looked me up and down, his eyes narrowing. He knew I wasn't bluffing. With a lift of his chin and an angry grin, he muttered. "We'll see about that."

Then, he turned around and stiffly ambled back to his seat.

CHAPTER 30

My footsteps clicked against the marble floor of the palace, echoing through the entryway.

I hadn't noticed before, because the few times we'd been in here before, it was surrounded by other people; their bodies and voices had filled the space, making it seem smaller and less menacing than it did now. Now, I could see exactly how intentional this design was. It was cavernous, amplifying even the smallest noises.

Walking down the hallway toward a split in wings, I scanned the faerie orb coves to either side of me. The lights had been covered with dark sheets.

Visitors were not welcome at the moment.

Lee said he would meet me in front of the locked room, so I pushed ahead, veering into the right wing, past the kitchens and library and a few formal entertaining spaces. I headed into an older part of the castle, the original fortress built by humans who eventually became the Malforian people.

When I reached the long corridor leading up to the charmed door, I still didn't see him.

A whisper of steps echoed behind me, and I spun around.

It was too dark to discern any kind of shape. Everything was a shadow.

I called out through our bond. *Lee, is that you?*

A flicker of cold covered my back. A hand slid into place on my waist, and suddenly, the corridor disappeared. My vision filled with a darkness deeper than anything I'd ever seen before. The atmosphere squeezed me, near-suffocating, and my stomach churned as I felt my body lift from the floor. There was a moment of weightlessness, of nothing, and then my feet slammed into hard ground. The blackness faded, revealing a small, dark room.

Luckily, my eyes already had time to adjust to the dim lighting of the palace.

I knew without seeing the finer details that it was Lee's arm hooked around my waist. His blue eyes glimmered over my shoulder as his hand quickly raised to cover my mouth, as if he was afraid I would scream. I wasn't afraid, though. It was hard to be afraid of anything when he stood so close.

The passion fruit simmering in my belly urged me to relax into his embrace, so I did.

A hungry hornet roams these halls, darling. We need to stay off them as much as we can. Lee's breathing was strained, his chest heaving against my back.

That was when I understood what had just happened.

Lee used his Materie to collect me from the hallway. We were now in a storage closet. Dusty crates and forgotten cleaning supplies were stacked on shelves lining three of the walls. I got the sense we hadn't traveled far, maybe a yard or two, into one of the rooms that lined the corridor. He told me before that he couldn't re-materialize very far on his own, so his gift must be twice as limited with me in tow.

Still, it was a rather useful trick.

We were hidden from the person passing by outside, their footsteps echoing through the door. I didn't have to ask who it was. Lee had successfully evaded Princess Maribel so far, thank the Goddess. I couldn't have guaranteed a peaceful exchange had I found her cornering him somewhere. Just the thought had the passion fruit twisting and writhing in the pit of my stomach, fueling both my arousal and my fury.

If her hands had touched him, I would have cut them off at the wrists. If she'd managed to *kiss* him, I would have burned this entire territory to ash. I would have unraveled in the smoldering cinders and sewn myself into the very fabric of Lee's soul, surrendering more than just my body to this thing between us.

It was a terrifying, delicious thought. I wondered absently if Lee might find the idea vulnerable enough to persuade him to touch me.

Did you find the key? I asked, trying to distract myself.

His voice touched my mind with an amused rumble. Flashes of memory accompanied his laughter. Glimpses of the music box the Malforian King had kept on his desk. The way Lee's frost crawled into the turnkey hole and froze the mechanism, stalling the trigger.

I smiled against the palm of his hand. *Good. Now remove your hand from my mouth before I bite it off.*

Lee lowered his hand to my waist. The effects of the passion fruit lingered between us; I could feel his arousal and need as completely as my own. In the dark, it was impossible to ignore.

We'll move through the adjacent rooms until we reach the door and hope the princess takes her search to another hallway before we get there.

I nodded, knowing he'd at least see an outline of the movement.

His hands tightened, and he took a deep breath before blackness swallowed us up once again. We rematerialized inside a small bedroom, old servant's quarters maybe.

As his Materie sloughed from our bodies, I realized that the scent of ether made me think of death. More specifically, of *grave dirt.* We were simply dust and star-fire given breath after all, however brief or long the life we lived. Eventually, we returned to it. Someday, my physical body would join the ether again, simple ashes to be absorbed into the earth and wielded by another.

From beginning to end, we were vessels for magic.

It was a morbid, but unexpectedly comforting thought.

Lee didn't warn me before de-materializing again. His arms held me tighter, pressing me flush against his chest as we moved from room to room. The expenditure of this magic weakened him. His heart raced against my cheek. Sweat gathered on his skin, the earthy musk filling my senses as I nestled my face in the crook of his neck.

His Materie shimmered and twirled like shooting stars, disorienting me.

The ether dust seemed to catch the light of thousands of other dimensions, reflecting them here. I could not tell which way was up. I could only hold onto Lee with all my strength and endure the ruthless crush of each de-materialization.

Somewhere in the darkness between one place and the next, I lost control.

My lips parted on an exhale, and I found myself tracing my open mouth across Lee's neck, exploring the raised scar there. His scent set fire to my nerves. I wished to consume it, to bite into his flesh and swallow a piece of him if that was the only way I could fill this emptiness.

You're distracting me again, he complained, but I sensed the lascivious desperation in those four words.

I couldn't help it. I *really* couldn't help it.

I needed just one taste.

Pressing myself even closer, I opened my mouth a little

wider and allowed my tongue to roll over his sweat-slick skin.

His resulting groan filled my ear. His salty sweetness permeated my senses. Would his arousal taste the same? Would it be better?

As our feet touched down the fifth time, we re-materialized in a room that wasn't as clean as the others.

Several worn, rusty, broken machinery parts had been thrown into piles all over the floor, and we landed right on top of one with a soft clatter. My feet slid out from under me, and Lee fell with me, holding my waist as his other hand shot out to stop us from colliding with the hard marble wall.

My surprise and worry echoed in his eyes as we both held our breath.

The footsteps out in the corridor paused, then loudened as they headed straight toward us.

Lee scrambled to regain his footing, his eyes flitting around the room. It was a small space, another closet. There was no place to hide here. As I summoned flames to circle around my body, Lee shook his head and brought a finger to his lips, warning me to keep quiet. He crouched beside one of the piles of junk and reached for a large gear. His next inhale sawed through the silence as Materie wrapped around the rusty metal. He closed his eyes, his brows furrowing in concentration as the gear disappeared.

A moment later, a loud clatter sounded from an adjacent hall. The footsteps changed course almost immediately, successfully redirected.

Lee jumped up and reached for my hand before he led the way out of the room and into the shadowy hallway. *Come on. We have to be quick. She'll return once she sees what that was, or worse, she'll call for the guards.*

We rushed to the door at the end of the hallway, which was swirling with pale tendrils of magic.

Lee withdrew a tarnished key from his tunic and slid it into the lock, the mechanism smoothly clicking free with a flick of his wrist. He shoved the door open and guided me through before closing us both inside.

Dusty faerie orbs stirred to attention immediately, illuminating the bowels of the room. Tall, wooden bookshelves stood all around us, some flush with the walls and others freestanding, arranged in a sphere around a stone platform.

Lee rushed forward. "That's a map table."

"It can't possibly be that simple," I muttered, following slowly. The stillness of this room struck something inside me. Perhaps I could sense the magic wafting off its shelves, or maybe it was because I *knew* the Malforian would never store the Wight's offering so carelessly, out in the open like this.

My suspicions were confirmed when we reached the platform.

Lee sighed, running a hand through his hair. "It's empty."

The circular stone was etched with elven script, an archaic version of the language that I'd only ever encountered in my studies and on a couple staircases in the very heart of the gnashing forest.

This slab of stone was older than my father's father, maybe older still. It was a miracle it had managed to stay in one piece for this long. Delicate stone pedestals spiraled out of the base, and each held a small orb of light at the tip, four in total. They looked nothing like the faerie orbs illuminating the rest of the room. They were clouded, and a single dark dot flitted in the center of them, like *eyes*.

I hoped they weren't watching us.

I spun on my heel, scanning the room. "The map must be stored on one of these shelves. One of the scrolls, perhaps. It'll take hours to sort through them all."

Lee pursed his lips. "Maybe," he said. "Or maybe not. Your mother was a witch, wasn't she?"

I turned to him, more than a little surprised. I hadn't told him that. I didn't bother denying it, though. We were long past hiding things from each other, and he'd shared plenty about his own mother recently. "How did you know?"

"It was a calculated guess. Thank you for confirming it, though," he said with a smirk. I glared at him, and he shrugged. "I suspected as much when you told me about your mother's garden in the gnashing forest. Only witches feel protected enough by the land to do that. And when you tracked down my camp a few months ago—the night you tried to assassinate me—I thought I sensed the imprint of the arcane on you."

"Yes, well…" I turned back to the shelves. "I don't see how my mother's magic can help us here."

"A detection spell," he replied, drawing so close to me that his wings caressed mine. "If the Wight blessed this map, then it would be imbued with powerful energy, perhaps the strongest on our continent. A sprite spell should lead us straight to it."

I blinked a few times, rifling through my memory for what a spell like that would require.

Usually, it was done with a candle or smoldering coal to allow the flame or the smoke to lead the way. I supposed my own flame could serve the same purpose.

"Hmm, that's clever," I admitted.

He gave me a playful wink. "Why, thank you. Flattery will get you *everywhere*, darling."

"I'm not sure you should feel flattered by that. I only mean you spend just as much time scheming as I do."

"This still sounds like a compliment to me," he argued.

I shook my head and summoned a black flame into my palm. It took a few moments to unearth the right words from my memory, but then the incantation flowed out of me, my voice filling the room with the elven tongue.

"Fire Sprites, warm and true,
Guide me to the prize I seek.
Take possession of this flame,
Stoke the fire, lead the way."

My black flame flickered, spitting sparks as it doubled in size. I held it away from me, sensing the dangerous hold of the spell. I'd invited fire sprites to tamper with my magic. They were hungry little creatures, wild and fierce. This flame wasn't only mine anymore, and it wouldn't be again until I snuffed it.

I ignored the unwelcome sensation and studied the sprite appearing within my fire.

It was wrapped in my black flame, humanoid in the barest sense, a faceless shadow. It twisted and stretched in several directions, considering our surroundings, searching the room for the strongest current of energy.

It was eager to consume.

A large spark crackled out of the flame, spitting toward a section of shelves to our right. I followed its bidding, ambling past several shelves until the spark spat again at one aisle in particular. As I walked up to it, the flame lost all semblance of control—it ballooned and split into several licks, roaring and snapping like a beast in my hand. Before it could catch any of the old volumes on fire, I curled my hand into a fist and banished the sprite.

My magic retreated, cowering in the pit of my stomach, relieved to belong to itself once again.

"It's somewhere over here." I stepped forward and started sifting through the scrolls on the shelf. There were so many that they were stacked in tall heaps, filling the shelf, so I removed them one by one. Some were labeled, others I had to unroll a few inches to see what they were. Anything that didn't have a map, I discarded on the dusty floor.

Alezandral helped me clear the shelves as quickly as possible, top to bottom.

By the time we were finished, I was sweaty, shaking with irritation as I glared at the mountain of scrolls beside us. Nothing. Not a single map on any of them. I curled my hands into fists, holding onto the heat bubbling just beneath the surface of my skin.

I didn't understand. The sprite led me to *this* shelf.

"Now what?" Lee muttered. "We're running out of time. I don't know how long those features last, but if we don't return the key and leave before it's over, someone will realize what we've done."

The feature was still playing for now. I could hear its music in the distance.

I returned my gaze to the shelf in front of us.

Without really knowing what I would do, I reached out and touched the closest shelf with my fingertips. A thick layer of dust coated the wooden panel from decades of neglect. Even underneath the scrolls, a collection of dust had gathered, suggesting that the shelves had been here longer than the scrolls, which I found… odd.

In the area my fingertips grazed, some of the dust was displaced, and I saw something painted there, lines of green and white and blue that were—were they *glowing*?

I twisted toward Lee, a smile breaking free over my lips. "It's not anything on the shelves. It's the shelves themselves."

He leapt to my side, sliding a hand across the surface, displacing more of the dust.

"Goddess beside us, they broke the map into pieces." He turned to me with luminous eyes and cupped the back of my neck, pulling me in to press a kiss to my temple. "You are brilliant, my darling."

For a moment, all I could think about was turning my head enough to really kiss him, lying down on this floor and letting him claim my body for his own as the dust of our world's past twirled around us.

My sex pounded at the idea, begging.

Alezandral leapt off the floor before I could appease her, flying to the top of the bookshelf and lifting the first wooden shelf away from its pegs.

I pushed my arousal away and joined him, grabbing the next shelf down, and we carried them to the platform in the center of the room. We continued until every shelf was on the map table, each panel fitting together to reveal the expanse of our continent.

When we pushed the last panel into place, the orbs surrounding them swiveled and lit with a dark blue light. A stream of magic shot out of each one, aimed at the map. The ground hummed beneath our feet, blue light skittering over the surface of the panels, and as if at the mercy of some supernatural breeze, the dust lifted away from the paint, scattering like blue-tinted mist above the map. We could see it all, the entire continent and the ocean surrounding us.

The blue-lit dust seemed to clump together, forming brilliant little orbs over each of the seraphic settlements.

Then I realized… it wasn't showing us the placement of the settlements. It was showing us where each *temple* was, where each Winged Spirit rested.

Unsurprisingly, the ocean to the southwest of the mainland was barren—the Fenix was no longer on my father's island. We cataloged each light attached to the territories, and after we'd counted those, we were left with only two others— two unknown lights: one to the northwest of the continent, suspended in the middle of the ocean, the other to the southeast, on the cusp of a neighboring continent.

Lee pointed at the one to the northwest. "This is the one. It must be. It's right off the coast of your father's city, and from what I've read, the Spirits don't like migrating long distances after breeding."

"It's in the middle of the ocean."

"Probably not, actually. This is an old map, and it doesn't even bear the paint of your ancestor's islands. I'm guessing that the Spirit settled on another island that isn't recorded here. Once we get back to our room, we'll look."

"What do you think the other one is?" I wondered, nodding at the second stray light to the east.

"There's no way of knowing," Lee replied quietly. "Whatever Spirit it is, it must have fled our continent. Or perhaps it never belonged to us, and it's something else entirely. Either way, we don't share its magic. We should leave it alone."

Curiosity simmered in my belly, but I knew he was right. We were looking for *my* origin. That was it.

After returning the shelves and cleaning up the scrolls, Lee and I emerged from the room, locking the door behind us.

Lee took my hand. "Deep breath," he whispered. Then, the atmosphere squeezed my body as we re-materialized in an adjacent wing of the palace—the one that held the Malforian king's office. Lee doubled over the instant our feet landed on the ground, clutching his head.

I crouched beside him, reaching for his face. "You shouldn't have done that. You're already beyond your limit."

He'd exhausted his Materie getting us *to* the records room, and this had been at least triple the length of those jumps. With a hissing breath, he forced himself upright, his eyes glassy and his hand gripping my wrist tightly. I knew he was using my body to balance himself. "We didn't have time to spare walking."

We could both hear the bustle of the yard, mostly muffled by the walls of the palace. The feature had finally come to an end, and the king's family would return to the palace soon.

I let Lee lead me to the door of the office, frowning as he

let go of my hand. I watched him dematerialize once more and waited for him outside the door, listening to his distant heaving breaths as he returned the key. I didn't like seeing him like this. How far was he willing to go to give me what I need? How much would he risk?

Lee was a better male than I ever imagined, the best I'd ever known.

The click of footsteps sliced through my tumbling thoughts, and I faced the sound. Someone was approaching this wing of the palace. Faerie orbs were slowly being uncovered beyond the threshold of the archway, their combined light creeping toward me.

I twisted, whispering into the seam of the door, "Lee, we have company."

A small crash sounded from inside the room, but then Lee appeared, materializing in the space beside me. His hair was damp with sweat, and dark circles had settled into the skin beneath his eyes. He licked his lips and grabbed my forearms, his eyes flicking over to mark the footsteps. "I might be able to manage one last Materie, but I'm not sure how far we'll get. If we're caught, I'll distract them while you make a run for the carriage. I'll catch up with you after."

The way he said *after* made my stomach turn.

What was his intention—to *fight* his way out? That was an awful idea.

On the other hand, what else could we do? We were moments away from being found here, alone in this dim hallway in front of the king's office. They would have our hands for stealing from their king. Or worse, our wings. We were in their territory now and would face their wrath.

But then, a glimmer of memory hit me.

It sent me back to another hallway, another life, another man kissing me like his life depended on it. I understood now why Destin kissed me, why it was the only solution he could think of in the moment. I was in the same position he had been in: trapped and lust-addled, though the situation here was even more dire and the effects of the passion fruit roiled heavily in my center. All I could think about was the male in front of me, getting closer to him, feeling him.

Using this opportunity as a cover was simply… *convenient*.

I could touch him without any worry of what it would mean tomorrow, whether he would want me or push me aside. I wouldn't have to wake in the morning feeling like a monster for allowing this, for encouraging him to care for me or I for him. We could simply *be*.

I spread my hands over his chest, felt his heart thundering away beneath my palm. "I have a better idea. Trust me?"

Lee's eyes pinched with worry. "Completely."

The trust in his voice brought a smile to my lips as I slid my hands down to the drawstrings on his pants and started untying them.

CHAPTER 31

I loosened the knot of Lee's pants with nimble fingers and, thank the Goddess, he didn't stop me. I think he was too shocked to do anything but gape at me with those big, blue eyes.

Until, finally, he managed a soft, "Sia, what's happening?"

The laces pulled apart, and his pants slid down his thighs. I forced my gaze up to meet his and smiled, feeling all too exhilarated as I tugged him closer by his tunic.

"We were simply looking for the nearest dark corner to rut in," I explained breathlessly, wrapping my arms around his neck. His hands found my waist, trembling slightly. "Lift my skirt and pin me to the wall. Make it look real." Then, I gave him a challenging smile.

Don't keep me waiting.

Surprise and curiosity and fear all flooded his eyes in the span of a heartbeat, but his arousal prodded my belly, driving me further into madness. The footsteps drew closer, louder. So much light was spilling into the hallway, I could see his scar glistening with sweat.

He spared another precious second to say, "Are you sure you're okay with this?"

I leaned into him until there was only a breath between our lips. "Just kiss me already, silly swan."

His hands slid down over my hips, squeezing roughly.

"*Fuck.*"

Lee kissed me hard and lifted me off the floor, his hands hooking under my thighs. His hips pushed between my legs as my back and wings collided with the wall. Time ceased to exist as he shoved my skirt out of the way and pressed his erection against my center, as he did *exactly* as I asked. He made it look convincing. A thin layer of silk remained between us, but no one would see that from a distance.

It felt close enough to the real thing for me.

I moaned into his mouth as his hips ground against me. My nails tore into the skin of his neck, my body rocking in tandem with his.

"Dig your nails in deeper than that," he growled.

He once told me that he liked pain with his pleasure, and I wanted to give him everything he desired. I wanted to be everything he needed. In this moment, I dared to believe I already was.

I tugged him closer, our teeth clashing as I bit into his lower lip.

He bucked between my legs, and my veins sizzled. I was sensitive there. The passion fruit had slithered its way down through my center, and my clitoris was *swollen*. It was all I could focus on—the raw ache and my primal need. Every push of his hips raked across my nerves.

I was only vaguely aware of the light intensifying beyond my closed eyes. If we'd been caught, no one was stopping us. That should have been enough to make me want to end this, to see if we were still alone.

I didn't, though.

Instead, I reveled in his touch and kisses, and when his mouth moved to my neck, I tilted my face to the ceiling, silently begging him to brand every inch of skin laid before him. Tilting my hips, I met his thrusts with eagerness. It would be so easy to reach down and slide the lace out of his way, to let him claim completely.

Somehow, I kept my hands from doing just that.

It wouldn't be right. He didn't agree to the real thing, and if we ever got there, I wouldn't want it to be like this. I would want it to be... *special.*

Lee had me all kinds of fucked up in the sex department. I barely recognized myself.

Just the thought of being with him like that tossed me into oblivion. Heat spider-webbed into my neck and cheeks. My head emptied out as his erection pushed between my thighs again, and pleasure exploded through every inch of my body. A cry erupted from my lips. My body went limp in his arms, and I whimpered as waves of lust continued to crash over me.

Lee's hips stilled.

I wished he wouldn't have stopped. He hadn't reaped nearly as much pleasure as I had, and now that I'd had a taste of him, I wanted so much more.

Slowly, that desire faded, and I came to my senses.

The faerie fruit had been satisfied.

I realized what had happened, what he'd done to me, how he'd *heard* it. When I opened my eyes, I discovered that Lee hadn't just heard it. He'd *watched* it happen. His pointer finger burned against my cheek.

He had turned my face toward his when I came.

A wicked smile spread over his face as his voice entered my mind. *Did you just—?*

I squeezed his shoulders hard enough to break a nail. *Shut up, right now.*

But I haven't even told you how beautiful you looked yet.

I couldn't keep the smile from my lips. *Shut. Up.*

"As *delightful* as that little display was, I don't believe you two have permission to be in here." We both turned our attention to Princess Maribel, who was propped up against a column down the hallway. Her eyes glistened with suspicion and the faintest thread of desire.

She straightened and took a few steps toward us. "Kindly get the fuck out."

Lee grappled with his pants, retying the laces as I smiled over his shoulder. "Of course," I said sweetly. "Our apologies."

I didn't feel sorry at all.

Lee wrapped his arm around my back and guided me past her, nodding politely. "Good night, Maribel." Then, we ducked through the archway into the bowels of the palace.

When we finally stepped out onto the dirt road leading back to our cottage, far from any prying eyes or ears, Lee hurried his steps, leading us past our temporary housing. Apparently, we weren't staying here another night.

Echoing the turn of my thoughts, he said, "We should make use of our carriage tonight, in case our plot has yet to be found out. I may have shattered a glass goblet in my rush to leave the king's office."

I nodded, though I would have preferred to return to our room to finish what we'd started in the corridor.

But that was just pretend to him, wasn't it? He'd indulged my devious machinations, but this was as far as this went. I thought that was what I wanted. I thought that would be easier. It was tormenting to realize I'd been lying to myself again.

I should say something, anything.

I squinted at the back of Lee's head as we marched onward. I wasn't sure how to voice these confusing feelings, but I knew I couldn't keep them locked up inside anymore. He'd told me to be forthcoming with him. Even if he didn't feel the same, he had a right to know that I didn't want to pretend. He should know that I wanted to *try*.

As I opened my mouth, I collided with what felt like a wall on the dirt road.

Lee was thrown sideways by an invisible force.

I staggered backwards, reeling away from the tall, hooded figure blocking our path. My gaze flashed to where Lee had been thrown.

He groaned, holding his side as he kneeled on the ground.

I took two long strides toward him, but the ground beneath my feet split open, and three walls of solid stone erupted from the road, enclosing Lee in a triangle of coarse rock. As my hands collided with the stone, my eyes bulged.

They were solid, and shimmering with a pale charm. Lee wouldn't be able to use his Materie to get out.

His muffled voice called my name.

"Hello, Sabrina," the figure behind me crooned. The voice was familiar, yet totally foreign in the way they spoke. Like a song. A deadly, deceptive song.

I turned to face them.

The stranger's silhouette was slender and masculine, without wings. Long, red hair peeked out from beneath their emerald cloak. They held their hands behind their back in a reserved manner, and in the shadows of their hood, I could just make out the sharp angles of their face: an elegant jaw and high cheekbones, and a pair of vibrant green eyes.

These green eyes seemed out of place here, too severe for the Malforian territory.

My hands curled into fists, sparks biting into my palms as I held my flame at bay. I shouldn't attack. This creature might readily retaliate. They carried power; I could sense it in the air. The scent of wild violets filled my nostrils, and an invisible current of electricity caressed my skin.

"Let him go," I demanded.

"I will once we've spoken."

"And who are you?"

Lifting a hand to their hood, they pushed it back, revealing a set of elegant, pointed ears and a circlet of gold sitting across their brow.

An *elf*. A full-blooded elf, in the flesh.

And they knew my name.

CHAPTER 32

"I'm either foe or friend," the elf purred. "It depends on how you respond to my questions."

It was a not-so-subtle reminder to be very careful about the way I spoke.

Give only kindness, accept only smiles. That was the highest code of conduct when it came to elves. They could hold grudges for centuries, longer than I would be alive, and any ire I earned would trickle down to the rest of my family. My father. My brother, and any children he had. Lee.

"You have questions," I repeated, a statement rather than a question. No questions, not unless I wanted to owe this creature.

No, wait—oh Goddess, I'd already asked him a question. *And who are you?* I already owed it.

The elf smiled. "Do not fear me, Sabrina. Not *yet.*"

"I won't fear you," I echoed.

I'd learned during my time in the gnashing forest that mirroring them was the easiest way to appease their curiosity, and the quickest way to bore them. A witch once told me it was better to repeat them than say something that could land you in a world of trouble. *Their* world of trouble.

I was pretty sure this elf wanted something from me, though. This wasn't just a passing fancy.

A soft fluttering drew my attention to movement on the triangle of stone beside me. I stumbled back in surprise when I saw another figure clinging to the rock above my head.

A seraph.

Its laughter echoed down around me as the seraph pushed away from the triangle. Six black wings. Black hair and onyx eyes. A *Great Raven*.

This Raven had the loveliest curves and was clothed in a green dress and brown leather leggings, silvery blades strapped to her every limb. She settled into place next to the elf, continuing to hover above the ground, her eyes sparkling as she rested a hand on their shoulder.

They were here *together*.

What was a Great Raven doing with an elf?

"This is Mionmïr," the Raven said, patting the elf's shoulder. "And I am Niaras."

My eyes flicked between the two of them, trying to reorient myself. It was interesting that an elf would make a companion of our kind. Elves were raised to despise our world and everything in it, everything save for the magic that had once been theirs. Seeing the two of them at peace with one another soothed some of my worry, but not much.

"It's very... nice, to meet you," I said carefully. It was a vague enough statement that it didn't feel like a lie. I knew better than to lie.

Niaras giggled. "Oh, you are *so* polite. We didn't expect you to be polite. I think she *is* scared, Mio. We've frightened the spark right out of her." Her giggling intensified, and I could have sworn the laughter echoed out of the forest all around us too.

"Hush." Mionmïr's command was a whisper, but it silenced Niaras instantly.

The sky seemed to lean in around us, the elf's attention a rope drawing me forward even while my feet remained rooted to the same spot. Unease bled up my back, tingling across my neck like a thousand needles.

"It has been brought to my attention that you were the last person to see my son," they said.

My heart dropped.

Those eyes. That voice. I understood why they seemed so familiar now. "Ehlark," I gasped.

I hadn't meant to say his name out loud, but too late.

"Yes," the elf snarled, their face twisting with an emotion that was vulnerable, primal, dark. A father's vengeance. A mother's protective arms. "*Ehlark*, my son. Where is he?"

I swallowed hard. "He was alive the last time I saw him."

Mionmïr's eyes flashed with irritation. "I know he is *alive*," they seethed. "Trust me, I would have felt it if he wasn't. *You* would not be alive if he wasn't. That was not my question. I want to know *where he is*. I want to know why his home is overrun by monstrous creatures and he is nowhere to be found. I want to know what *you* know. Now."

Looking between the Raven and the elf, I could barely keep myself upright as my pulse hammered in my ears. I had to say something, but I couldn't tell the truth.

"I don't know anything." The words shredded my vocal cords on the way out.

The elf's entire countenance shifted, warping like an animal was shifting beneath their skin as their eyes turned black. As I backed away, my back hit the triangle of stone. I was trapped. "You're *lying*," they snapped.

Niaras remained in the air, her wings beating hard to lift her a few more inches, until she was towering over me. "*Liar.*" The word repeated all around me, echoing out of the stone and trees and pummeling my senses from every direction. They overlapped in a dissonant whisper. *Liar. Liiiiiar. LIARRRR.*

"You left a bloodied feather behind in my son's woods," Mionmïr continued through gritted teeth. "I tracked you here, and I will track you down again, wherever you go. You cannot run. You cannot hide. Tell me the truth while I am still feeling civilized."

I was done with the running and hiding anyway.

"I have my suspicions about where Ehlark is, but I don't know how to reach him. I don't know if I *can* reach him." That was as honest as I could be.

It seemed to soothe a drop or two of Mionmïr's fury.

They fell back a step, tilting their head. Niaras lowered herself to the ground, wrapping a hand around the inside of her elf companion's thigh. She was glaring at me like she wanted to collapse the sky in over my head, though.

Mionmïr clicked their tongue. "I advise that you find my son quickly, Sabrina. Because if I do it first, and I discover him in any state of pain or suffering, I will ensure that you pay dearly. Twice whatever he endured." It was a threat but also an agreement. It was mercy.

"I will find him," I agreed.

"Then the matter is settled. Until we meet again." Their viridian eyes drilled into mine. "Daughter of Dark Embers."

Before I could fully process the elf's farewell, they withdrew a gnarled wand from the inside of their cloak. They raised a hand to their chest and clutched a pendant hanging on a chain around their neck—a sharp, emerald-like stone. They touched the tip of their wand to it, and a stream of green light poured out. The elf drew it around the crown of their head, and the mist followed in a long, weeping gash, like they were drawing curtains closed around their body. It enveloped them and their companion in a flash of wind and light.

I recoiled, closing my eyes as the scent of lilacs assailed me. When I looked again, they were gone.

Only a circle of purple petals remained on the ground, fluttering in the night breeze. *I'm so fucked, and not even in the way I was hoping for tonight.*

The stone walls around Lee fell, crashing into the road.

I ran to him and threw my arms around his shoulders, drawing him close. I knew he must have heard everything, but if he was upset with me for roping him into this mess, I didn't feel it. His arms returned my embrace, his fingertips gently petting my back.

It was only later, as we climbed into the carriage and set off into the sky, that I recalled what the elf said in farewell.

Daughter of Dark Embers.

They had been there, at the springs. They had watched Lee and I commune with the Wight.

If I didn't bring Ehlark home soon, there was no way of knowing where else that elf would follow us, or how they would wreak havoc upon our lives.

CHAPTER 33

Mist clung desperately to the ocean, caressing every inch of the ship, twirling along old wooden beams and rusted iron fastenings. A vicious chill accompanied it, slithering beneath my wool clothing and turning my bone marrow to solid ice.

My mouth salivated with each inhale; I could taste the ocean. That brine had pervaded all my senses for days now. Three, to be exact. That was how long we'd been treading dangerous waters, enroute to find the source of my power, my origin. We were nearly there now.

I stood at the front of the ship, my eyes scouring the mist for the first sign of land.

When the warmth of a body settled in beside me, I knew it was Lee. His wing curled around mine, familiar and protective. After our visit from that elf, Mionmïr, Lee had thrown himself into action, eager to get some answers for both of us. If anyone understood why my blood had done that to his son, if anything could help us set it right, it was my Winged Spirit —that was, long as we could find it, and quickly. We'd hardly arrived back at my father's island before Lee and I set off again. We borrowed a ship and hired a crew from the Impundulu territory and sailed toward an abandoned island off the northern coast, approximately in the same location of where we'd marked the unknown Spirit on our map.

Consequently, that meant I'd seen little of Lee since that night in the Malforian palace.

We hadn't discussed what happened there, and I was starting to doubt that we ever would. If he had thought anything of it, or wanted something like that to happen again, surely, he should have brought it up by now.

I should have brought it up by now.

I didn't know when it had happened, when I had grown so... *fond* of him. It was terrifying to realize I desired nothing and no one else more sincerely.

I had no idea what he truly felt for me, and that was what scared me the most.

I had to work up the courage to find out eventually, but this wasn't the time. I could only deal with one life-altering dread at a time.

Soon, I would know what filled my mortal mother's womb and gave me breath. Would it be as terrible as the sutilus, my supposed kin, or would it be something else? Would it be worse? I didn't dare hope that it would be better.

There was a reason humans once considered these Spirits to be gods. They were magnificent creatures, as fickle and dangerous as elves, but without the restrictions this plane of existence so often lends to strange magic. Winged Spirits were capable of extraordinary things—my life was evidence of that.

We'd be lucky if such a being didn't annihilate us on sight.

"We'll have answers come twilight," Lee murmured, his hand grazing my lower back before falling away. "How do you feel?"

"Like I might vomit," I replied.

Lee stepped even closer, and a calming chill fluttered over me, loosening my muscles and massaging my aching chest, bringing me... *peace*, as brief and false as it was. He was offering me what little rest he could. His magic. His ear. His gaze. He stared at me intently, expectantly, and I felt absorbed by his eyes. I relaxed in that blue embrace for a long moment, but then I shook my head and pulled away, frowning.

"I need to stay alert, and so do you."

Lee's influence receded instantly, and I felt both warmer and lonelier for it. "You're right. We aren't on solid ground yet." His eyes shifted to the ocean spread out before us.

He'd been on edge since we boarded, but even more so now that the mist had set in. It was as if Lee *knew* something in these waves that I didn't, as if something was making itself known to him, speaking in whispers that no one else could hear. More than once, I'd seen his head snap up and away during conversation, towards the edge of the ship.

What was calling to him, and why?

He had refused to give me a definitive answer when I asked about it. *It's just my nature calling to another,* he'd said, whatever that meant.

Shouting drew our attention to where the crew was now scrambling about the deck. They were dropping the anchor, and confusion spread through me as Lee left my side, his gaze trained on the captain.

"What's going on?" he demanded. "Why are we stopping?"

The captain's auburn hair was streaked with silver, conveying his age and the humanness of his blood. This seraph carried only one set of ash-brown wings on his back. Impundulu, but only barely. His long, gray beard shivered as he spoke. "We sail no further, not even for you, Frost Prince. We'll drop the boat, and you two can continue on without us."

"The *row*boat?" I gasped. "In the middle of the ocean? Are you mad?"

The captain smiled, revealing yellow and gnarled teeth. "All the best sailors are, Princess. But as you'll soon find out, it's not without reason."

"You swore to deliver us to the island," Lee growled.

"And I have," the captain replied, waving toward the bow of the ship. "Look for yourself."

I spun on my heel, squinting through the mist. To my surprise, I saw that he was right—the faintest speck of darkness loomed up ahead, an outline of land that shifted in and out of focus as the fog swirled around it. If I hadn't been made aware of its existence, I wouldn't have seen it at all. The mist made it look like an illusion.

"Why aren't you dropping us closer to shore?" I asked.

The captain's jaw clenched. "I have no desire to drown with my crew today."

My brow furrowed.

We were nowhere near wrecking distance of the shore, yet the captain's ominous words weighed on my chest as he turned his back on us. Lee seethed quietly at my side. I felt his anxiety spill towards me, radiating off him in bursts of icy air. I was feeling a little annoyed by this turn of events, but Lee was beyond that. He seemed *furious*, and perhaps more than a little frightened. He glared at the crew as they prepared the rowboat for us, his hands curled into bone-white fists and his breath billowing in front of his face.

"Lee," I whispered, "what did he mean by that?"

"He's a paranoid old cod," he replied gruffly. "We'd be fine if we remained on the ship. They can't—" He shut his eyes, breathing deep, as if to steady himself. When he turned to look at me, his gaze scorched my face. "You need to do precisely as I say once we descend. Promise me."

My stomach clenched. "Why? What's out there?"

"I-I don't know. Not exactly. If it's anything like the ocean bordering my country, though, we'll need to be careful. Now, promise me, Sia. Promise you'll obey my every order down there, that you won't let your curiosity get the best of you."

The hair on the nape of my neck rose, and my scalp prickled in discomfort.

"Fine, I promise, but only until we reach the shore," I clarified. I couldn't afford to let a promise like that overstay its welcome. I cared for Lee deeply, but I didn't like the idea of him having the power to control me. Every time someone held that kind of power over me, they abused it.

Lee nodded once in agreement before taking my hand.

We took our seats in the rowboat, and the crew lowered us to the waves. The mist enveloped us instantly, thicker down here on the surface of the water. Waves slammed into our small watercraft as Lee went to work unhitching it from the ship's ropes. A singular faerie orb swung precariously on the front of the rowboat, our only light.

I grabbed the oars and did my best to keep us steady.

The captain shouted at us over the edge of the ship, his voice tinged with amusement. "We'll wait here for a while, but I'm warning you now: you best be quick. If you haven't returned by first light, I'll accept you've both been lost and take the news back to port."

He'd been wise to wait until we were down here, balancing in the boat, to say that. Lee snarled up at his shrouded visage like he was seconds away from flying up there and rending it in half.

I took hold of Lee's shoulder and pulled him into his seat. "Don't mind that washed-up gargoyle. Let's just go."

Honestly, we should have anticipated the captain turning on us the moment he saw fit to. These were sailors, masters of intercontinental trade. The ocean was their only home, and they owed no allegiance to any king or queen. Even the heavy sack of gold Lee had offered them at the docks would not sway them into danger for us.

They'd just better not expect the second half of their payment after this. Lee may bludgeon them with it.

Still snarling, Lee took the oars from me and started rowing us away from the ship, towards the shadow of an island on the horizon. I had to twist in my seat to see our destination, but my neck quickly grew tired, so I faced forward to study Lee instead. His eyes vigilantly scanned the ocean as the mist closed in. His hands gripped the oars so tightly, the veins beneath his skin bulged in response. He wasn't wearing his gloves.

I'd noticed how the cold didn't seem to affect Lee the same way it did me.

The frost in his veins provided him with a certain resistance to freezing temperatures. In fact, I was fairly certain he preferred them. He removed his gloves more frequently since the heart of winter had fallen, and he had a habit of absently running his fingertips along every manner of icy surface, like the frosted windows of our carriage when we flew or the outer walls of buildings as we walked by them.

I understood that—his instinct.

The more comfortable I became using my powers, the more I wanted to be around flames. Hearths and braziers, torches and bonfires. It was an elemental kinship, one I hadn't allowed myself to indulge in before Lee. There was none of that kinship to be felt out here, though, and I found myself missing it.

The island's shadow grew larger, and the mist thickened, clinging to my face and invading my mouth with a musty, salt-tainted film.

Despite the luminous white orb hanging on the front of the boat, our surroundings suddenly appeared darker.

A splash sounded to our right, alarmingly close, and a soft hiss caressed my ears, undulating in and out of clarity as dread trickled down my spine.

I turned to squint through the mist, trying to ascertain the source of that noise, but I saw nothing. Another hiss and splash came from the opposite side of the boat, and my head snapped toward it, my breath quickening as I caught a glimmer of dark flesh disappearing beneath the surface. "Lee? Did you see that?" I said uneasily.

He had.

Lee quickly tore his gaze away from the water and looked at me, his jaw feathering before he whispered, "Release the faerie orb from the boat—let it fall under the surface. If you see anything move in the water, close your eyes. Whatever it might say or do, don't look."

"What?" I squeaked, my heart thundering. "That's our only light." There could be any number of obstacles between here and the shore. Reefs, rocks.

One collision and this boat would sink.

Lee's eyes flashed with anger. "Better we be blind than dead. Do as I say, Sia. *Now.*"

The promise I made to him seized my mind, twisting my nerves into knots, and as I attempted to resist long enough to continue arguing, I shuddered under the crushing force of his control. There would be no arguing, not about this.

Lee had already shifted his attention to the boat, maneuvering the oars through the water with frantic energy.

Quietly fuming, I turned around and clambered to the curved peak the orb dangled from. The mist swirled viscously around my head, assailing my skin. Hissing radiated out of the water in front of the boat as I grappled with the miniature net holding the light, and my irritation fell away. Terror filled my mind as the hissing transformed, as it turned into *clicking*—the same clicking that haunted my nightmares. A black mass shifted beneath the surface of the water.

The sutilis king was here.

He had found us.

I withdrew from the edge of the bow, trembling. My promise to Lee and my fear warred. "Lee, they're in the water," I cried. "The sutilus."

"*The orb*," he roared. "*Get rid of the orb.*"

His command took root in my spirit, and I allowed it to drive me back to the edge. Tears streaming down my cheeks, I took hold of the netting and ripped it open then fell backwards into the belly of the boat as the orb dropped into the ocean.

We were plunged into darkness.

A mass of ebony flesh erupted from the water. I could see its silhouette through the gray mist. The rotting body was turned away from me, but it was the same one I'd seen in my nightmare, with the same crown of bones.

But it was larger now, impossibly so.

Before the figure could turn, I summoned a sphere of obsidian flames into my palm and launched it. To my horror, the flames passed right through his back, finding no substance to latch onto. I launched another, but the king's body remained whole, impenetrable. The clicking wavered, lightening to a bubbling hiss as he slowly turned to look at me.

We were doomed—all of us, the entire fucking continent.

"Close your eyes, Sia," Lee screamed. "Don't look at it."

Fighting the promise I'd made to him, I summoned another ball of heat into my hand. I forced it to spread into a flickering shield. I'd go down fighting. I wouldn't close my eyes and let death take us both. "I won't let him take you," I shouted. "I won't."

"*Sia, look at me.*" The commandment was iron-clad.

I craned my neck to look at Lee. He was still rowing, but he slowed as our eyes met. Damp blond hair clung to his forehead as his panicked blue eyes seared into me.

He nodded, smiling weakly. "That's it. Eyes on me, darling. We're going to be okay."

"But the sutilus," I whispered.

Lee pulled the oars in to rest across his lap before extending a hand to me. "Come here."

I didn't blink as I turned over and made my way to him, holding a palm behind me to maintain the flame shield.

He grabbed my free hand and drew me forward into the space between the benches. His wings curled around me, closing us in together. It was so dark in this embrace, but his eyes shone bright enough to illuminate the sharpest features of his face in a blue hue. My arm started aching behind me, but I didn't let it fall. I could still hear the clicking.

The king was on the other side of that shield, but he wasn't attacking. Why wasn't he attacking?

Lee kissed the inside of my wrist, over the burns embedded in my flesh, then cradled my face in his palms. "The sutilus aren't here, but something else is, something that can reflect your deepest fears. Something that can take you from me the moment you look into its eyes. So don't look, don't listen. Just keep your eyes on me."

My voice shook as I asked, "He isn't really here?"

"No. You're safe as long as you don't let your gaze leave mine. I promise you."

I exhaled, letting my terror melt away.

"We're safe," he repeated.

The clicking faded, and I suddenly heard the illusion in it. It was actually *hissing*—but the sound had warped in my ears. Lee knew what it was, what it was capable of, and I knew I could trust him with my life. I could trust him with everything.

He nodded. "That's right. You can let go now, darling. It can't take you without your permission. I've got you."

Reluctantly, I released my hold on the shield at my back, and aside from the hissing growing louder, nothing else happened. Lee leaned back, his wings parting, and dropped his hands from my face. He picked up the oars and resumed rowing without dropping my gaze, and we continued forward like that. His wings tried to shield me as best they could from the ocean, but I still sensed the creature threading through the water around us, taunting me, doing its best to draw my attention to it.

Lee was my anchor, and I didn't let go of him.

"I've got you," he whispered again, as if afraid I would forget it.

Before I knew it, the bow of our boat collided with the shore. The hissing was so far away now, it could be mistaken for the crashing waves.

When Lee tore his gaze from mine and leapt out of the boat to pull us further up the shoreline, it felt like the air in my lungs flew away with him. I braced my palms against the bench he'd emptied and bowed my head, forcing myself to breathe deeply. Whatever that thing was that attacked us, it had been a convincing mimic. Even now, my heart squeezed at the memory of the sutilis king rising out of the ocean, his massive, desiccating body towering over me. A crown made of my father's father's bones…

"It was a baezilisk."

I looked up and found Lee watching me from beyond the bow of the boat, concern swirling in his eyes.

"A what?" I gasped.

"They're primordial beasts," he explained. "As old as the world itself. They're guardians of forgotten realms, forgotten magic. One look is powerful enough to kill you. I'm not surprised one of them found their way to this place. It was abandoned long ago."

"And what is this place exactly?" I demanded, rising on shaky legs to leap out of the boat beside him. "You never said."

"This island once belonged to the Great Ravens, before their Spirit was destroyed and their people scattered. The ruins of their temple are here." He turned, and I followed his gaze to the heart of the island.

Snowy mountain crags pierced the sky and a dense forest speckled the rocky terrain. Halfway up the peak, the rock had been hollowed out, and I could see a glimpse of those ruins.

Their temple had been carved into the mountain.

A strange sensation writhed beneath my skin. Recognition. *Certainty.* My Winged Spirit was in there somewhere. "I feel it," I murmured. "We're close now."

Lee nodded. "I feel its presence too. The pull isn't as strong as I thought it would be, not the same way other temples on our continent are. It's as if the Spirit inside is sleeping."

"Well then, we'll just have to wake it up," I said.

Lee chuckled. "So we will. Let me anchor the boat."

As he left my side to retrieve a rope from the boat, I turned to scan the ocean behind us. In the distance, a serpentine body weaved in and out of the water—the baezilisk, forever guarding this place our world forgot.

CHAPTER 34

The flight up to the ruins was brief but bitterly cold. My clothes barely shielded me from the brunt of it. My sinuses tingled. Beneath my gloves, my fingers were starting to lose feeling.

As I landed in the cavern, I paused at the entrance, considering our surroundings. The temple was mostly intact. Some of the ceiling had collapsed at the edges of the room, leaving behind avalanches of rock and precious stone, but the entry chamber still stretched back to an elegantly hewn archway without obstacle, leading farther into the mountain.

The Great Ravens' affinity for stone was celebrated here.

Every inch of the temple was decorated with elaborate runes and poetry had been chiseled into the walls in an ancient tongue that I could barely read.

Veins of emerald and luminous diamond glittered throughout the stone.

Lee landed on the rock platform beside me and took my hand, leading us forward without hesitation. "Stay alert, darling. The temple might be abandoned, but the Great

Ravens wouldn't have left it defenseless. Even the death of magic can leave phantoms behind."

We passed under the archway and descended a long stone staircase. I took the lead before we reached the foot of it, following the strangely familiar pull in my chest.

There used to be a set of arbor doors here, but they'd been destroyed. Old burn marks covered the threshold.

I knew what had happened to the Great Ravens the day they lost their Winged Spirit—the day of all this destruction. For as long as I lived, I'd never be able to forget it. The story was often used by elitist seraphim like my father, as a warning against our kind fraternizing with humans.

Several decades ago, the Great Ravens offered sanctuary to a group of shipwrecked humans.

They didn't know that the humans had come here with a very specific purpose, and they were sent by the human queen. They stayed for months here, formed friendships with the Ravens, slowly earned their trust. And when they were finally granted entrance to their temple, they entered with an arsenal of firebombs and tore their way to the Great Ravens' Winged Spirit.

They murdered a god that day.

The Ravens who survived that initial attack told stories of how the Winged Spirit had erupted beneath the mountain when it died, how the most intimate chambers collapsed as the Spirit's death consumed the intruders in one final act of glory, one final act of love for those it had created.

That was what the Ravens' believed, anyway.

I climbed over the wreckage of lumber and rock, staggering into a large hall with overturned and dusty furniture. Half of the ceiling had collapsed entirely, and snow swept across the far end. This was the preparation room for sacrifices. The tables and chairs were broken in the attack, but a few iron racks on the right side of the room were still intact, holding stacks of fine robes and jewelry tarnished by age.

"Goddess… look at this place," Lee breathed.

Before the Great Ravens were scattered, they had been a powerful people, performing sacrifices almost daily. They handled the process of divine conception like a scientific experiment, though I was certain they would argue it was an art. It wasn't only reserved for royalty. *Any* human woman who approached their settlement looking to be a mother of magic was welcomed. They were lavished with a short life of unparalleled pleasure, and then they surrendered themselves to the Winged Spirit. Many took that offer, rich and poor, old and young.

It was rumored that even the human queen's sister submitted her body to the Ravens, and that was why the soldiers were sent here.

The Ravens made many enemies in that time, specifically the families and friends of those women they sacrificed. It didn't help that not every sacrifice resulted in conception. There were hundreds of meaningless fatalities, women who fell to their deaths and were never seen again. When a Spirit had their pick of souls, they could be selective about which ones they accepted. I was thankful the other seraphic territories didn't allow such recklessness.

"We should be glad we aren't witnessing it in its prime," I muttered, mostly to myself.

Lee said nothing, but I saw the compassion on his face. He agreed. We were both glad that this temple had come to ruin, but we didn't dare speak that truth out loud.

It was such a terrible feeling—to come from this pain, this death, to be alive because of it but to wish you weren't in the same heartbeat. How did we balance our lives with the ones that were lost? Maybe we never would. Maybe we would always regret the means of our existence. But it was better to regret these horrors rather than feel nothing at all. It was better to feel than to forget.

"Let's keep going," I whispered.

Another broken passage led into a cool, dark cave. The pull in my chest intensified as I ducked through the half-obstructed archway. We were closing in on my Spirit—my body was tingling all over, brighter with every step. I tripped to a stop just beyond the passage, when I saw that the ground dropped into a steep chasm.

Massive, wicked-looking stalagmites stretched up out of the darkness toward us.

This would have been the last thing those women saw—the vicious dark and these sharp points prepared to skewer them. My stomach churned, but I swallowed my disgust and turned to Lee with a grimace. "I guess the only way forward is down. The pull is stronger here."

I glanced at the chasm over my shoulder, trying to ignore the dread burrowing itself beneath my skin. Something else could be down there, too. I was almost certain there was. In this place of death and sacrifice, there had to be.

Lee took my hand. "I'm with you," he said. "No matter what."

I squeezed his fingers before turning to face the chasm. Spreading my wings, I gathered my courage and leapt into the void.

A HEAVY GREEN mist danced between the stalagmites, thickening the lower we flew into this stone forest. By the time we reached the base of the chasm, the air was as shrouded as it had been on the ocean.

The ground was wet, and every breath filled my nostrils

with putrid iron. This was a graveyard. Some of the stalagmites were stained still, with brown veins running down the stone that could only be old blood. No skeletons, though, which I found peculiar. If some of those women died when they fell, their bones should be here, impaled by the stone pillars or crushed upon the floor.

Even with all the rubble scattered around the stalagmites, we should be seeing at least *some* of their corpses.

I didn't pause to investigate further.

Now that we were this close, I was eager to see our mission through. I followed the pull of my spirit, allowing it to lead me between the stone pillars toward the center of the chasm. Lee followed closely, his footsteps echoing in tandem with mine as I weaved onward.

We were so close, I could almost taste it: the sweet satisfaction of knowing the truth at last, an answer to the question I had asked myself every day for the past twenty-five years.

What was I made of?

What was I made for?

I heard Lee trip behind me. "Sia, wait. I think something is following us."

But I didn't wait.

Surely, he was just hearing the echo of our footsteps. They rebounded off the stone all around us.

The path I burned between the stalagmites eventually opened up to a clearing with a massive nest in the center. That was the best word for it. It was actually a pile of rubble, but the rock was displaced atop it, as if something heavy had been lying there for a long time, though it wasn't there anymore.

Whatever it had been was at least a hundred times my size. And I could see where all those dead bodies had gone now.

Dozens of corpses littered the ground, but they were perfectly preserved. They didn't look like they were dead.

They could have been sleeping for how peaceful they appeared. Not an ounce of rot had touched their bodies, and every detail—every wrinkle and freckle—remained. Either the frigid temperatures of this cave had protected them in death, or there was frightful magic at work.

Lee screamed my name from somewhere behind me, and I heard the familiar sound of his sword being unsheathed.

My attention was drawn back to the nest, because those corpses in front of it had started *moving*. Their limbs peeled away from the ground, the audible crackling of their liberation filling the cavern. Magic—this was definitely magic.

I had run straight into a trap.

Unsheathing my blades, I started backing away as the corpses turned to face me. Their eyelids creaked open, revealing clouded irises. They each carried the evidence of their death, preserved in horrifying detail: shattered skulls with bone shards and brain matter clinging to frozen hair, gaping abdomens with intestines spilling out like coils of rope. They weren't like the walking dead humans normally became. There was no presence of soul.

This was a darker summoning; these bodies were only vessels.

The corpses ambled toward me, their movements jerky at first, but growing more fluid with each step. They were still waking up. I had to find Lee, *now*.

I twisted around to retreat but came face-to-face with a corpse. It took a swipe at me, and I ducked just in time to dodge the attack. The creature's pale hand was covered in a pale green mist. As it collided with the stalagmite to my right, thick ice erupted across the surface, veined with wriggling green worms.

Necrotic magic.

These bodies had been tasked with killing anything that

came close to the nest. One slice into my skin, and I'd be paralyzed, or worse.

As if the ice wasn't bad enough.

I weaved back and kicked the corpse in the stomach, pushing it back. Then, I summoned flames to encapsulate my blades and slashed at the creature.

My fire was weaker than it should have been. The cold temperature in this cavern was inhibiting my magic, but the corpse shrieked as I left a scorching slice across its chest. My black flames licked at its flesh, and that little slice grew, sizzling like wildfire into the rest of its body, crumbling it to fine ash right before my eyes.

I exhaled shakily, glancing over my shoulder long enough to see the corpses from the nest running at me. My fire seemed to do quite nicely at dealing with them.

Thank fuck for that.

I leapt over the pile of ash in front of me and sprinted between the stalagmites, shouting Lee's name. Within a few heartbeats, I heard the whisper of steel to my left and veered toward it.

Lee was being overwhelmed by corpses.

They surrounded him, his sword barely making a dent in the onslaught. He wielded his steel in one hand and his frost in the other. His frost, at least, seemed to effectively freeze the corpses in place.

That wasn't enough to make this a fair fight, though.

I ran to him, sheathing one of my blades. My gloves had been burned away already, so the chill of the cavern bit at my fingertips, but I fought the cold and summoned a ball of obsidian into my hand. I flung it to the left of Lee, striking a corpse that had been inches from raking a claw across his wing. Turning my second blade over in my palm, I leapt onto the closest creature, plunging my flame-shrouded dagger into its shoulder. Its body crumbled under my hands. I raised my free hand over my head, drawing a line of shimmering black fire through the air, letting my magic lengthen into a narrow whip. I seized the end of that whip before the flame could fade and snapped it forward. It slashed across three of the corpses on Lee's other side, burning them to ash.

Lee was made aware of my arrival then, and his eyes greedily drank me in before he turned back to the corpses closing in. The ones from the nest were here now.

Magnificent as ever, darling, he praised me mind-to-mind.

If I had a moment to spare, I would have smiled. *I've been learning from the best.*

Wordless pride and joy swept through our connection, and I let it fill my chest with warmth as I summoned another flame. The first dozen corpses were easy enough to fell, but more and more of them slunk out from behind the stalagmites. Every woman who died down here, who was rejected by the Ravens' Winged Spirit, was attacking us. There must have been hundreds.

It was a mistake to come here. We wouldn't survive this.

The instant I formulated that thought, I felt Lee's mind resonate in agreement.

We had to leave.

If my Winged Spirit was here, they hadn't made themselves known. Perhaps they weren't here after all. Perhaps the pull I felt was toward these creatures, toward this magic.

Towards death.

I'll create a shield and hold them back long enough for us to take to the sky, I told Lee. *Ready?*

As ever.

Black flames erupted from my palm, and I spread them into a shimmering wall, forcing the corpses back in a flurry of sparks and ash. My flames flickered, weakened by the cold but strong enough to serve its purpose. I sheathed my other dagger and brought my second hand up to join the first.

Stretching the shield, I managed to wrap it around us in a blazing crescent.

Lee was still partially exposed, but if I spread it any further, my flames would buckle. I backed up until my wings were flush with his, offering him as much cover as I could.

A thunderous roar shook the cavern, accompanied by the distinct flap of wings. I glanced skyward quick enough to catch a glimpse of ebony circling high above us. My heart leapt with surprise, my blood fizzling. I felt my spirit reach for those wings, urging me into the air, urging me to follow it.

It was here. My origin.

CHAPTER 35

"Now," I yelled.

Lee and I pushed off the floor in the same heartbeat. I knew he'd seen the Spirit too or, at the very least, heard my thoughts about it. The channel between our minds was wide open, overflowing with his fear and my desperation, all the words we did not have the time to say. Which was how I knew the moment a set of claws latched onto his leg, could *feel* the jagged nails and cold, necrotic magic sinking into his flesh.

Gritting my teeth against the phantom touch, I spun around.

Lee's wings battled gravity. A corpse was clinging to his leg, trying to drag him back down into the swarm. They were crawling on top of each other now, reaching for him as they coalesced into one writhing body of death. Lee's strength was no match for their combined weight.

There was only one solution, and I hated myself for it already.

I dove for him, grabbing him under the arm as I extended my other hand toward his leg. A torrent of black flames spewed from my palm, engulfing his ankle and the corpse's body. Lee cried out in agony, and my heart clenched with regret, but it worked. The corpse holding onto him crumbled, and I was able to pull him up, away from the grasping hands.

As Lee recovered, his wings spread and started beating again, helping our ascent.

A sheet of sweat glistened on his forehead, and I could smell the burn from here. I glanced down. Half of his trouser leg had melted away, and the rim of his boot was fused into his flesh. That was all I made out before I forced myself to look away. Bile tickled the base of my throat. I hurt him badly. He had to be in an incredible amount of pain, and I couldn't even feel it with him the way I deserved, because I'd been the one to do it to him.

"I'm sorry, Lee." The words were strangled, because I wanted to cry. "I'm so sorry."

He lifted his gaze to mine, the depths surprisingly soft. With a shake of his head, he thought, *You never have to apologize for saving my life. We have to keep going. We've come too far to lose sight of your Spirit now.*

I could tell by the look in his eyes that he wasn't going to be much help with that. He couldn't even muster the strength to talk aloud.

Lee had been touched by necrotic rot. I'd seen the nails break his skin. We needed to get to a healer quickly, before the magic spread to his organs and paralyzed him entirely. I could only carry him so far on my own, and we were alone on this island, miles away from the nearest ship.

What if I lost him? After all we'd been through, what if he died here? I wasn't sure I could endure that.

We were in need of a miracle. Luckily, a living miracle was precisely what we were already searching for. I lifted my head, scanning the cavern above us.

A rough stone ceiling hung over our heads, dappled with

stalactites and shadows. There, in a large crevice near the top of the cavern, I caught a glimpse of movement, the edge of a retreating black wing, barely visible. The wing was transparent, pure shadowy spirit. Spirits took form in whichever element they desired, like frost or mist or flame.

It seemed mine preferred the darkness.

Keeping a tight grip on Lee's arm, I flew higher, my eyes fixed on that gap in the stone.

As we finally cleared the ledge, I hesitated, letting my gaze absorb the enormous beast pacing in front of me. It walked on four legs with clawed feet not dissimilar to a canine, though the rest of its body resembled something more reptilian. A tail dragged behind it, tapering like a serpent's until it flared at the very end in a three-pointed spike. Wings as large as the ship we'd left behind twitched against its back, gossamer as a silken web.

The Spirit turned to look at me head-on, a sharp huff vibrating his hooded nostrils.

It had a long muzzle, like a horse. The flesh all over it was textured, with ridges and a reflective sheen. Then, its massive jaw opened, revealing a mouth full of fangs the size of my arm as it said, "I suppose it was too much to hope you would not seek me out, despite the distance and peril I have placed between us. It was foolish of you to follow a ghost into a dead god's lair. You may approach, child. Let your companion rest while we talk." The voice rattled through my head with a voracity I had never felt before, so deep, it could have been an echo of the dark, but as lilting as a songbird.

Lee released a shuddering gasp, and I helped him sit on top of the stone ledge. His wings trembled as he shifted his weight away from his injured leg. I knelt beside him and brushed my fingertips against the melted material.

"How are you feeling?" I glanced up at him.

"Aside from some maimed and charred flesh, I'm... I think

I'm alright," he said through gritted teeth. His eyes flicked to the Spirit. "Go, ask your questions. Don't worry about me." He pressed a knuckle under my chin, trying to draw my attention away from the burn.

I scoffed, pushing his hand away in frustration.

"Don't worry about you?" I hissed. "Remind me to punch you in your smug, aspiring martyr, knight-in-shining-armor face when we get home. You are *not* dying for me."

His eyes flashed with humble surprise.

With careful fingers, I tore the material above and beneath the wound, trying to get a better look at the damage. His leg was a mixture of blackened, melted fabric and shiny, raw flesh. I couldn't see the necrotic worms, though. The burn must be masking them. I wouldn't be able to pluck them out myself, even if I found them.

I turned to my Spirit, swallowing my fear as I approached its magnanimous form. "Please," I pleaded. "Help him."

The Spirit surveyed me with cunning, amber eyes. Its broad face tilted as that fearsome jaw unhinged again. "Do not fear," it said in a dark, rumbling voice. "Your companion will survive. Your flame has consumed the necromancy in his skin. You did well to take care of that quickly. He'd already be dead otherwise."

Relief swept through my body, but I could barely feel it. That left me with more questions still. "I didn't know—how is that *possible*?"

"What's going on?" Lee rasped. "What is it saying?"

I twisted to look at my betrothed. Lee's eyes were flicking between the Spirit and me, his hands wrapped around his calf, just below his knee, gently applying pressure.

"Can't you hear it?" I asked.

"I can hear it," he replied slowly. "But I don't *understand* it. Only you can. An advantage of being bound to it by spirit. What did it say?"

"It said my flame consumed the necrotic magic in your wound. You'll be fine."

Lee's shoulders slackened on a great exhale. "Well, that's a fortunate discovery." His gaze dropped to the wound on his leg, considering it more calmly. He might not be on the brink of death, but he was still gravely injured. We needed something clean to dress the wound.

I'd left another mark on his body, another scar.

I didn't want to be the source of his scars. I wanted to be the one to soothe them, to *mend* them.

The Spirit took a step forward, demanding my attention. "Come, child. Let us speak before I take flight."

I walked toward the creature, pausing a few yards away. "You're fleeing? Where are you going?"

"Away from this place. You woke the slumbering guardians, and it's no longer safe here, even for me." Tendrils of shadow curled lazily around the Spirit's form, twisting toward me in recognition.

Its skin was mostly black, with patches of dark blue shimmering amidst the shadows.

Like my wings.

The resemblance was striking.

"I have..." I tried to find the right words, but they were eluding me.

"Questions?" It prompted gently. "Yes, as would I. Ask them if you must, but do it quickly."

"I—" It was more intimidating than I thought it would be, to look upon my Spirit. Here it was, and I wasn't sure where to begin.

The Spirit drew closer and lowered its head to meet my gaze more intimately. Its neck was long and lined on either side by sharp spikes. "Your spirit twists and simmers. What troubles you? Why are you so afraid?"

Out with it, I urged myself.

"A sutilis told me that we share the same blood, the same creator, which would be *you*. They told me they're my kin. Is this true?"

The Spirit rumbled thoughtfully. "I do not know this word: *sutilis*. I can only assume that the creature you speak of was the spawn I gave to another world—an old, dying world. It is true that you aren't my first creation, child, though you are my last."

My heart plummeted. "So they *are* my kin."

I'd expected it to be confirmed, but the truth still slammed into me with the full force of my disappointment.

"I suppose you could view them as such," the Spirit said, but it shook its head at the idea. "They are related to you, not by blood but by spirit, as many unwilling bonds are, though I would caution you against sympathizing too deeply with them. You are different. The creatures who bore my spawn in the previous realm were wicked things, twisted and desperate in a way that only the dead and dying can be. We had hoped our spirits could change them. We had hoped we could save them and their world, but we were *wrong*."

My focus narrowed in on one word. "*We?*"

The Spirit drew back, straightening until the crest of its face nearly touched the ceiling. "Yes. I was not always alone."

"There was another like you?"

"I do not wish to speak of them," they growled, "My Greatest Sorrow. I lost much in that world. There is much I… desire to forget."

"You speak as if that realm wasn't your home."

"It was not. I was cast out of my true home long ago, *banished* by those I called family," the creature bristled, shifting on its front claws. "Though surely, you do not wish to learn of *my* history, which is as ancient as the rock you stand on. You would like to learn of what *is* rather than what has been." Its tone was forceful, borderline threatening.

If I wasn't careful, my Spirit would take off before I got any answers.

"What am I meant to be?" I held my hands out in front of me as black flames curled around them. "What are you? What is this magic I carry?"

The Spirit took another step toward me, and I did not balk. I was enraptured by the creature. Its eyes were enchanting pools of amber fire, swirling with intelligence and a certain softness I didn't anticipate. "There is no word for what we are in this world, but in others, we are called Draconia or Draken. As for your magic, you carry the full depth and weight of my Spirit. Everything I was, I have given to you. I see you are already familiar with the flame of my heart, but that is only the beginning. If I was to explain it all, I fear we would be here for many days, and I do not have that time. You'll need to be more specific."

I raked in a steadying breath, organizing my thoughts in order of importance.

"An alchemist disappeared while experimenting with my blood. Now there's an open rift sitting in his home on the elven plane. He's still missing. Do you know what happened to him? I need to find him as soon as possible."

The Spirit inclined its head. "If this alchemist opened a rift with your blood, he could be anywhere. Did you see which world this rift leads to?"

"Considering the sutilus that fell upon us the moment we entered it, I assume it was theirs."

The Draken huffed, rearing back. "Then he has likely already been lost to their bloodlust. You should be more concerned about the rift. It is imperative you close this gateway at once, before the spawn overrun that realm and find a way to spill into this one. They will not stop until they are victorious. They will do anything for eternal life, for power beyond what is natural."

Mionmïr wouldn't be pleased with this development, but my Spirit was right. Our world wouldn't survive a second flood of sutilus while we were already living in fear of the first.

I nodded, accepting the task. "Alright. Just tell me how."

The Draken's amber eyes flared, and a rough laugh echoed through the cavern. "Tell you *how?* My child, you already possess this knowledge. I, myself, felt your magic cross the ocean to me only months ago. You tore through the atmosphere into another world then stitched it back together in the same breath. I caught but a glimpse. A rift opened in water, black shackles circling your wrists. I witnessed your power. I heard your distress."

"The river," I muttered, my mind reeling. When I was bathing in the river down in the human lands, trying to remove my father's shackles, I'd opened that rift. Then I'd closed it… with my flame.

"You saw that?"

"I see many things where you are concerned."

"I can open and close rifts," I whispered, trying to come to terms with this information. "Why is that?"

"Because the world I come from has a natural affinity for such magic," the Draken explained. "We watch the space between worlds. At the best of times, we ensure everything is kept in its proper order. At the worst of times, in *these* times, my people are little more than stars twinkling in the darkness. They are too few. The chaos is too great."

My brow furrowed. "But if I can create rifts, doesn't that mean the sutilus can too? They could simply open more."

"No. They are incapable."

"I… don't understand," I admitted, heart thumping.

"I did not give them that power. The only reason they are in this world is because they exploited the rift I opened for myself to escape *their* world. In reality, I gave them very little of my power. My," the Draken hesitated, then continued on in a steely voice, "my mate surrendered much more. We blessed those spawn together. The only part of *me* they carry is their divine aptitude for medicine. I was a healer in a previous life."

So *that* was where the sutilus learned their skills with a blade. Not as warriors, but as healers.

As I ruminated on this, the Draken stood, stretching its wings wide behind it. "It is time for us to part ways, child. I have given you all that you need."

Fire bristled under my skin.

I shook my head and stepped closer, spreading my own wings in protest. "That's not even close to enough. You can't just leave us to fend for ourselves after what you've done. *You* brought those foul creatures with you. *You* need to help us get rid of them."

The Draken bared its fangs. "I don't *need* to do anything," it roared, loud enough to send me staggering backwards. The words were vicious, but I heard desperation in them. I heard *fear*. "Do you not understand? I am *dying*. My magic is spent. All that I had left after I entered this world, I gave to you. That is why you can open rifts. That is why you have my breath and the flame of my heart. You are everything I once was. If you want this world to be cleansed of your *kin*, do it yourself."

There was a great deal about these Spirits I still had to learn, but if the Draken was implying what I *thought* he was, then it hadn't just blessed me. It had *transferred* all their magic to me, every ounce of it. They'd given it all away, and in the same breath, had surrendered any and all responsibility for the mess they'd made. They had put everything on *my* shoulders when I was no more than a babe in a human mother's womb. It was a callous and cruel destiny they'd given me.

"You're a fucking monster," I hissed.

The Draken blinked once, slowly, with an air of unspeakable exhaustion. "I am what I am, and soon enough, I will be nothing. I will not kill, not again. Loss is no more than a swelling tide, child. It rises to its own satisfaction and will sweep everything away with it if you allow. It would take everything you are. It's too late for me. The only thing left for me to do is take to the skies one last time and ensure you do not follow. Now, brace yourselves." It took two languid steps forward, and I retreated a fair few more until my leg brushed against Lee's shoulder.

Lee lifted a hand to wrap around my thigh, squeezing gently in support. He made no move to stand and intervene; he only kept his hand there, comforting me as the Draken closed in until it towered over us.

"Brace ourselves?" I echoed shakily. "For what?"

Its jaw parted in something like a smile. *"Banishment."* The word descended like an executioner's sword, chilling me to the bone. Then, a torrent of ethereal black flames erupted from the Draken's mouth, enveloping us as the ground evaporated beneath our feet.

I fell and kept falling.

The phantom flames evaporated, revealing a wide expanse of air and sky. We weren't in the temple anymore. There was a sunset spilling color through the clouds, and as I tumbled through the atmosphere, I saw a glimpse of water below me. I was falling towards an ocean, but there was no mist here.

There was no time for my wings to catch me.

The water enveloped me, glacial and jarring. My lungs screamed as I fought the tide. My head broke the surface, and I managed to suck in a stuttered breath before the next wave crashed over my head. I scrambled for the surface again, my eyes stinging in the salty water. When I breached the surface, I heard the thunderous roar.

I'd fallen from the sky, and above me, my Winged Spirit circled a glimmering portal.

The Draken must have torn through the atmosphere to transport all three of us away from the Raven's temple. I wondered if that was the extent of its lingering magic, portals where there had once been rifts, phantoms where there had once been life. It opened its jaws, and the sky filled with sheer black flames, and I watched my Winged Spirit's fire burn the portal away.

The cold water swallowed me again.

I fought against the crashing wave, and when I resurfaced, I saw the Draken breathing fire again. The colossal shadow ripped a second portal open and flew into it, disappearing in a blink.

By the time the next wave finished crashing over me, the second portal was gone too, nothing left in the sky but the sunset.

I quickly scanned the surface of the water, my chest swelling with relief when I saw a sliver of land in the distance. I swam toward it, searching for Lee between each wave. As I closed in on the shore, I finally spotted him crawling up onto the rocky beach. When he staggered to his feet, he turned around to face the ocean, his eyes frantically scouring the waves, looking for me. He found me with ease and waded back into the ocean to meet me.

My boots caught on the rocky shallows, and I exhaled in relief, but then something latched onto my ankle, sweeping my foot back out from under me.

The salty ocean enveloped me.

I twisted underwater, squinting through the wave even though it stung my eyes.

It was a *serpent*.

The creature's brown skin glimmered with an ethereal silver sheen. Its golden eyes were narrowed to slits, sharp teeth bared in a hungry smile. I kicked at its face, and the serpent tried to seize hold of my free leg, but I kept moving, twisting and writhing under the waves until my boot finally connected with its jaw. My leg broke free of its grasp, and I wasted no time grabbing hold of the rocky ocean floor, using it to propel myself to shallower waters.

My head broke the surface, gasping and coughing, and I saw Lee up ahead, running through the water towards me.

The serpent grabbed me again by my calf. It pulled me back, and suddenly, its body was covering mine, holding me underwater. I felt its sharp claws dig into the hinge of my upper wing, and I screamed. Then, I was rising, emerging from the water with those claws still embedded in my skin, my throat and lungs burning.

Blinking away the excess water from my eyes, I saw that Lee had lifted the serpent up by its hair, holding his sword to its throat. His face was twisted in a formidable snarl.

The serpent loosened its grip on my wing, its eyes bulging and smile lost.

"Release her," he commanded, "by order of the Halcyon crown."

The creature let go of me without hesitation, and I scrambled to get my feet beneath me. I stood, swaying in the hip-deep water.

Lee didn't let go of the serpent, though. He seemed to be debating whether or not to slice its throat anyway.

The serpent sensed this too and raised its hands in surrender. "Your *Highness*," it hissed. "We didn't realize you had returned home. Your General told us you'd be away for at least another ten-day—"

"Well, I'm back." Lee's eyes glittered with violence, but he reluctantly released his hold on the serpent, keeping his sword raised to it as he added, "Return to the depths and warn your brethren before I decide to make an example of you. I don't want to see any of you within a mile of shore."

The serpent's eyes slid over to consider me, half-shielded by Lee's wings, and it smiled just before flipping backwards into the waves.

I shuddered, the temperature of the water registering fully now that we were alone. My legs were numb, and the rest of my body trembled, every caress of the wind leaving snowflakes on my eyelashes. "I'm so sick of these Goddess-damned oceans," I breathed. I staggered toward the shore, nearly toppling as my knees buckled.

Lee's body heat crowded my back as he reached for me. "Me too, darling. Come here." He slid an arm around my back and crouched to sweep my legs out from under me. His body was a welcome warmth.

But then I remembered his injury and pushed him away. "Wait! Your leg."

Lee shook his head, smiling faintly. "I felt it mend in your Spirit's breath. I suppose we can take them at their word about their penchant for healing."

I exhaled in relief and wrapped my arms around Lee's neck, allowing him to pick me up. He waded to the shore, and my body shook harder as we emerged from the water. The rocky beach didn't slow our ascent; Lee seemed accustomed to this terrain, his every step steady as we left the turf behind. The beach led up onto a snowy valley dappled with pine trees and a mountain range standing tall in the distance.

"At least my Spirit made itself useful in one way," I murmured, my teeth chattering.

Lee shrugged. "And it saved us from making the boat ride back to the ship. We're back on the mainland."

"We are?"

He set me back on my feet but kept a hand on my waist as he scanned our surroundings. "We're in my territory, in fact. I recognize this coast. We're near the southernmost key, miles away from the closest town, unfortunately, but at least I know which direction to go." He pointed northward. "There's a pass that way, about a two-day walk to the closest farmsteads. We can find some transportation to the capital there."

I shook my head. "We need to find a staircase first. The

portal in Ehlark's home needs to be dealt with immediately. The Draken is worried the sutilus will find a way through."

Lee frowned, scrutinizing me as I trembled in the knee-deep snow.

Sighing, he relented. "Then we'll head to the forest first. There's a reserve not too far west of here, but we should find a place to rest first. We can't travel like this." He gestured to our wet clothes. I nodded, and he took my hand, leading the way across the valley.

"A Draken, you said," he mused after a minute. "Is that what you are?"

"Apparently."

He threw a smile over his shoulder. "That's tremendous, Sia."

"It doesn't feel that way," I whispered. "The sutilis was telling the truth—they came from the same Spirit, from the Draken and... another. We're all connected."

After a moment, he whispered, "Their history doesn't damn you, darling. You're different."

"The Draken said that too."

Lee must have heard the dejection in my voice, because he paused, hooked a knuckle under my chin, and leaned toward me, demanding my gaze. "Because it's true. You're still part human, half-belonging to *this* world, thanks to your mother. You'll do yourself a grave disservice to forget that. You still have your heart, and you can keep on using it."

I latched onto his arm with both hands. I felt so vulnerable in that moment, looking into his eyes. Dizzy, almost. It took me longer than it probably should have to realize that my weakness was more physical than emotional. I shivered in the next breeze, and as I reached for the warmth in my belly to protect me, I found nothing.

My flame was silent.

Only elusive, dwindling embers.

"Lee?" My voice was little more than a murmur. It was all my panic allowed.

He was looking intently at my mouth. When I said his name and his gaze lifted to search mine, I saw a glint of reluctance there, as if he'd been having a silent argument with my mouth and I had interrupted them. "Yes?"

"Something's wrong," I gasped.

Lee's smirk fell as he realized my state.

"My flame—it's not listening to me. I don't feel well." I took a step forward, drawn to his body heat, and my knees buckled.

Lee caught me, cursing. "You're too cold," he seethed. "We need some cover to get warm and dry our clothes."

I felt him twist from side-to-side, but I was too tired to keep my eyes open. My body felt so hollow, drained of the delicious heat that usually filled my every limb, the spark that kept me going. I nuzzled Lee's chest, desperate for the skin beneath, needing it to drive away this cold. I couldn't stop.

He cursed again, a deliciously colorful word that would normally have me grinning at him. "I'm sorry, darling. You need to wait here while I search for a safe place. Keep reaching for your flame. We're going to need it."

He leaned me against a nearby pine.

My wings pressed against the trunk, catching on half-frozen sap. I forced my eyes open, watching Lee's retreating form as he disappeared into a copse of trees.

The ground was cast in a periwinkle hue from the setting sun. It was… rather beautiful.

I slid down the length of the trunk until I was sitting in the snow. I realized too late that that had been a mistake. The icy powder sank through my trousers, stinging the skin below and stealing the breath from my lungs.

I was too tired to get back up.

I knew, in that moment, that I was freezing to death.

Gritting my teeth, I turned inward, searching for even the faintest flicker of heat—that all-encompassing embrace of my flame. It was still inside me somewhere, I knew, because when I called to it, I felt a writhing in the pit of my stomach.

It just refused to surface.

It was *afraid*.

Never in my life had my flame failed me. On the contrary, it had a habit of surfacing even when I didn't want it to.

There was something about the Halcyon territory it didn't trust.

I wondered briefly if, like the Malforian and the Fenix, the Halcyon had charmed their territory with weathervanes that caused a surplus of frost and snow year-round. Or perhaps the land itself had been touched by their Spirit's frost. If the Halcyon Spirit lived in the ocean bordering this coast, every wave crashing into the shore was fraught with that magic. And I, a Draken, was thoroughly unprepared to weather such elements.

"Lee," I whimpered to the empty valley.

Tears pricked my eyes, freezing on my cheeks as they spilled over, the last of my consciousness slipping through my fingertips.

WHAT COULD HAVE BEEN seconds or centuries later, I was jostled awake by a pair of arms scooping me up off the ground.

"Hold on just a little longer, Sia. Open your eyes for me."

With considerable effort, I managed to squint through my exhaustion.

Lee was running through the trees, his eyes flickering between me and our surroundings. When his gaze caught mine, he gave me a tight smile and squeezed my body closer. "There's my clever girl. Stay with me, alright? I found an abandoned military outpost; we'll be there in no time."

Then, the world darkened, and I lost sight of him. We were dematerializing.

When his Materie fell away, the canopy of pine needles had been replaced by a stone ceiling braced with wooden beams. As he kneeled to place me down, I realized we were in a cave no larger than my quarters back in Father's city. A deep bevel had been carved into the floor at my feet. At one time, it might have been used to hold a fire. There was no evidence of that anymore, though, not even a pile of ash. Simple, decrepit furniture had been pushed up against the walls, rusty weapons scattered across the floor.

The mouth of the cave shielded us from the wind, but it was still freezing. Snow piled up in drifts around the entrance, and particles of ice swirled through the air beyond.

Lee left my side to rifle through the supplies left behind. He cursed under his breath, and I knew without his needing to say it that any items of use had probably been raided a long time ago. Accepting this fact, he returned to me and started stripping the wet clothes from his body.

If I was feeling better, I might have exercised some restraint and looked away. But as it was, I couldn't tear my gaze away as he revealed inch after inch of his perfect body to me, every limb flexing with power, his scar bared in the most breathtaking way.

After dropping his clothes around one side of the fire pit, he turned to me.

I didn't argue. I only lifted trembling hands to him, both consent and acceptance. Without a word, he knelt and removed my clothes for me, peeling my tunic away first.

As the open air hit my bare chest, I shuddered, hissing as my breasts responded with a painful pucker.

Lee moved to my pants, helping me wiggle them down my legs and tossing them to the other side of the pit before gathering me in his arms. He pulled my back flush to his chest, and I realized with a start that my wings weren't getting in the way. He must have tucked them away.

Good. It was better that they were hidden in my back rather than suffering with the rest of me out here.

As Lee wrapped his arms around me, his body heat bled into my back. My back vibrated, reveling in his warmth. Nearly every other part of me was still screaming in pain, but at least I had this, just this one sliver of heat to comfort me.

"Thank you," I whispered. *"Thank you."*

He squeezed me in response.

After a long minute, he started shivering too. Even his resistance to cold couldn't protect him from these temperatures. His hot breath grazed my ear as he said, "We won't survive like this, Sia. You need to summon a fire."

A lump formed in my throat. "I don't think I can."

He sighed, and I arched my neck to feel more of his hot breath on my skin. At the same time, he splayed a hand over my stomach, low enough that my attention was drawn to its proximity to the band of my satin undergarments as he whispered, "Your flame doesn't reside within you, darling. It *is* you. Every breath. Every heartbeat." His other hand slid up between my breasts to cover the scar over my heart. "This is who you are. Seize hold of it, and don't let go. You can do this. You can do anything you put your brilliant mind to."

A fire wasn't where my mind was at.

His touch was pillaging my thoughts, distracting me, and yet that dying ember in the pit of my stomach threw a spark. Just one. I grappled internally with it, but my flame was still too weak to command.

So, I focused instead on Lee's broad hands, burning against my chest and stomach.

I glanced down, admiring the sight of his flesh against mine. His hands were riddled with bulging veins, and my body looked so soft beneath them. A few more sparks sputtered to life, wriggling wildly beneath my skin. My flame was more at ease in his arms, and I could understand why.

He made me feel safe, always had.

Lee noticed my distraction and moved his hands, but I caught him by the wrist before he could pull away.

"Wait," I murmured. "That was helping me."

He returned his palm to my belly, his fingertips grazing lower than they had before. "This?"

I nodded, staring ahead at the fire pit. To my delight, a small black spark licked at the air before quickly fizzling out. Now knowing what I needed, I leaned against Lee's shoulder and arched my chest toward the ceiling. "Give me more."

Lee's breath caught, and I craned my neck to see the expression on his face.

His eyes were fixed on my bare chest. He exhaled heavily, his eyebrows furrowing in confusion and *desire*. He wanted to touch me, but still, he hesitated.

"You can touch me as much as you want," I reassured him. "I'm going to be your wife soon."

His fingertips twitched against my belly, and I found myself wanting to ride them. "You keep saying that like it means something," he murmured.

"Let's find out," I whispered.

Lee bit his lip, his gaze searching mine for a long moment. Then, his fingertips trailed down my belly. His other hand shifted over my chest, his thumb grazing the underside of my breast. I wiggled between his legs, trying to guide his hands where I wanted them, but his arms tightened, holding me still as he caressed the flesh between my breasts and the swell of my lower belly with excruciating control. He took his time teasing me.

He was watching the journey his hands were taking across my skin, his broad chest rumbling with pleasure.

I reached down and slid my hands over his, but before I could move them even an inch, he seized my wrists and ripped them away. He met my gaze, his blue eyes piercing. "If you want me to touch you, keep your hands out of my way," he ordered. "This body is *mine* until I tell you otherwise."

My breath caught, but I nodded.

When he let go of my wrists, I reached over my shoulder to wrap a hand around his neck, urging him on without a word. He returned his hands to my breasts, first kneading the soft skin, then circling my puckered nipples.

My hips rolled against his lap, where I felt him hard and pulsing against my lower back. It wasn't enough to persuade him into action. Only my obedience would do that.

I moaned instead of writhing and forced myself to relax, surrendering to his desire.

He rewarded me by pinching my nipples.

I cried out, turning my face into the crook of his neck, my lips brushing against the twisted flesh of his scar—the scar he'd received the day he chose me, chose *us*.

"I always dreamed you'd be this responsive. The way you move is delicious." His voice was rough, thick with arousal and admiration. "Next time, I want to tie you down and see how frustrated you can get. I'm going to find your breaking point, darling."

His fingertips sifted through the curls between my thighs.

I gasped helplessly against his neck then closed my mouth over the side of his neck, sucking his skin between my teeth and stroking his scar with my tongue. His throat bobbed against my chin, and I bit down on his scar, urging him to react, to respond.

His groan filled my ear.

Lee's hips thrusted against my lower back as he pinched my nipples again, harder now.

A fresh shock of arousal bled down my spine, pooling in my center as Lee growled in frustration. His fingertips stilled in my curls, denying me. "Vicious, darling," he whispered. "Feeling desperate?"

I licked the length of his scar then pressed a gentle kiss to it. That was the only response I could manage.

Lee seemed to understand that, because his fingertips shifted lower, diving between my folds. He grazed the bundle of pulsing nerves at the peak, bypassing it to investigate the rest of my slick flesh. Slowly, purposefully.

A chuckle radiated through my back.

"Your pussy is soaked, Sia." He stroked even lower, finding my entrance, and I tilted my hips up to urge him to enter me, but he retreated to the bundle of nerves above it, drawing a wide circle around my clit.

He clicked his tongue in admonishment. "My body, Sia, remember?"

So what are you going to do with it? I urged.

Lee smiled against my cheek. "What do you think? I'm going to take my sweet time savoring this pussy, playing with you as I like. You've built a pretty little fire for us, and I'd hate to see it snuffed out so quickly." Somehow, him saying those words out loud instead of in my head made them that much more arousing.

I wasn't paying any attention to the fire, but I could feel it. The entire cave was heating up.

"*Lee,*" I whimpered.

He pressed his lips to my ear, circling his fingertips tighter and tighter until they were fluttering over the bundle of nerves, just firm enough to drive me crazy with need. He pinched and rolled my nipples, aggravating the already unbearable ache.

I writhed in his arms, losing control.

"What are you waiting for, darling?" he urged in a heated whisper. "Go ahead. *Beg for it.*"

My mind emptied out as I grappled with his command.

In my silence, he explained, "I need you to tell me how much you want this, Sia. With your words. I'm not going to assume it. I'm not going to accept silence and hope the necessary enthusiasm is here, even if I can feel how desperately wet you are. Come on, it's just three little words."

My breath caught, and I waited for him to continue speaking with sparkling nerves. *Three little words.* To give him my enthusiastic consent was one thing, but voicing those three words was something else entirely.

They weren't little.

They were enormous, as vast as the skies and oceans and the galaxies far beyond our reach. Larger still, because they were the truth.

"You can say it. I know you're already thinking it." He lowered his lips to my ear, and my heart felt like it was trying to tear a hole through my chest. He heard it. He *knew.* But then he ripped the ground out from beneath me by telling me exactly what he wanted to hear. "*Please. Fuck. Me.* You could even use my name, if you're feeling particularly polite."

A moment of breathless relief crashed over me, but that soon fell away, and I plummeted into bereft silence.

Because I'd been thinking, *I love you.*

I stiffened in his arms, my heart crackling as I realized that he was toying with me. He wanted me to beg for this, for him, the way he said other women begged him. My blood rushed in my ears. My pride crawled up out of the pit of my stomach, numbing my desire.

Why should I have to beg for something we clearly both want?

Was this just sex to him, just dominance? Was he just trying to prove a point?

I thought this was more.

How could it be more, though, when I couldn't even muster the courage to tell him how I truly felt? I certainly couldn't do that *now*, when his fingers were on my cunt and his lips were demanding my submission, when I was feeling more vulnerable than ever.

If I did what he demanded, would he see me? Or would he only see another female begging on her hands and knees for him?

I twisted to meet his gaze and nearly lost my nerve. His mouth was so close to mine, those blue eyes damn near mesmerizing. I steeled myself and said, "Don't let my arousal go to your head, silly swan. I'm starving for affection. It's been months since someone touched me like this."

A thread of disappointment weaved through Lee's eyes.

He removed his hands from my body. "I think our clothes are dry enough now. Just keep your flame close to the surface, and you'll be fine." Lee pushed me away from his chest and stood up, walking briskly to his clothes.

My black flames blazed in the fire pit, large and wild. It emanated delicious, full-bodied heat, but I shivered as I watched Lee dress.

I shouldn't have said it like that, like *anyone's* touch would have sufficed.

"Lee, hold on."

He shot a chilling look over his shoulder, silencing me. "It's fine. That was a mistake. Let's just focus on getting to a stair-case before daybreak, alright?" He turned his back on me and retrieved the rest of his clothes from the floor, effectively ending the conversation.

A sticky gray emotion swept through me, tightening my

chest. Disappointment, but something else too—something infinitely more painful.

CHAPTER 37

"We don't have any Fluxroot," I whispered at the foot of the staircase.

This staircase spiraled tightly as it speared into the sky, the steps piled with snow and its stone railing worn by decades of harsh weather.

"We'll just have to be prepared for a difficult passing," Lee replied, circling the base of the staircase, examining the runes carved into the stone. "If we walk through together, the elven spirits might be less tempted to mess with us. I've dealt with them plenty on my own anyway." He came to a stop at my side, grimacing. "We'll hold onto each other."

"You dealt with them that day in the human lands," I recalled. "How *did* you manage that? How did you know I needed help?"

"I was watching you, nearby." Lee glanced at me from the corner of his eye. "I couldn't sense your thoughts while you were in the elven realm, but once you returned to the portal, even though you were stuck between realms, I sensed you again. The portal started flickering, changing color, and when other voices echoed out of it, speaking in the elven tongue, I figured it out. They knocked you unconscious when they caught you, preparing to deliver you to the elf court. They thought it was quite the coup, capturing a seraphic princess. Naturally, I eviscerated them and dragged you out." He said it as if he was telling me the time, his voice void of emotion. He'd been giving me the cold shoulder since we left the cave.

"I had a dream when they knocked me out," I said.

"They like to torture their victims in the subthereal plane," he tapped a finger to his temple, "in the mind. You should be thankful you weren't stuck there forever."

"I dreamt of *you*."

He huffed a bitter laugh. "Me? Well, I suppose I *shouldn't* be surprised that you consider me your worst nightmare."

"It wasn't a nightmare at all," I argued, closing in on him. "It was a memory. I dreamt of the day we met, the games we played together." I didn't know why I was telling him this. Maybe I hoped it would breach the distance between us, would get him to look at me again. "That's actually…the only part of that day I *can* remember."

"Lucky you," he muttered, still refusing to face me.

I sighed. "Lee, don't do this. I know you're angry with me, but I didn't mean—"

He cut me off before I could finish my sentence, turning the full force of his glare on me. "I'm not angry, Sia. I'm *tired*. It's been a long fucking day, and we need to focus our remaining energy on closing this rift and returning to my father's palace before we send both of our families into a panic. Save the reminiscing for later."

He had a point.

We only had until daybreak before that ship would return to the Impundulu harbor, and word would spread that we'd been lost on the island, but I couldn't stop thinking about what we'd done in that cave.

"Can you just answer one question for me, please?" I asked.

I was starting to believe that *please* was the magic word when it came to Lee, because the instant he heard it, he stopped and really looked at me. His stormy gaze cleared enough to see the sad, blue-eyed boy I used to know.

"Do I have to?" he said flatly.

"If you want me to drop the argument, then yes."

He crossed his arms. "I didn't realize we were arguing, but fine." He stared at me with an unimpressed look, waiting for me to talk.

I forced the question out before I could change my mind. "Why did you want me to beg?"

Was it simply a desire to exercise control over me? I had to know. If he admitted that his own ego was to blame, then I could start to accept that we weren't suited for each other. Our relationship would never go there again. Somehow, I'd learn to stop loving him so deeply, and we could continue with our engagement and marriage as strictly friends.

But instead of confirming my fears, Lee's response stunned me.

"Because I don't think you've ever admitted you need someone before, and I think you should. Isn't keeping everyone at a distance all the time exhausting? Aren't you tired of being alone?" His hands gestured between the two of us then clutched at his heart. "No matter what I do, I can't keep my promise to you. I can't stop breaking it. Because you're still lonely, even when you're surrounded, even when I'm standing in front of you, asking you to open the door. I don't want to feel like I'm forcing this, like I'm wearing you down just to steal what I need."

It wasn't his ego in the way. It was *mine*.

Lee hadn't been trying to belittle or punish me. The begging had nothing to do with the desire to overpower me.

He'd wanted my *vulnerability*.

I battled my anger over his retaliatory questions because I

truly wanted to understand what he meant by them. He was obviously worried about me. He was worried that I was lonely, that he wasn't holding up his end of our bargain. It didn't need to be true for him to believe it. And if he believed it, then he was likely hurting himself with it.

My eyes drifted to his chest. "Has your scar been bothering you again?"

The shame that immediately flickered in Lee's eyes told me the answer was *yes*, but out loud, he only said, "You asked your question. It's time to go."

Lee took my hand and led me up the staircase. Under his breath, he recited the ancient spell to activate the portal. He had it memorized, of course. I expected nothing less. I was certain there were thousands of books worth of arcane knowledge carefully cataloged in that remarkable head of his.

The railing to either side of us lit up with a faint blue glow, each rune pulsing.

By the time we reached the final turn at the top of the staircase, the portal flickered to life, its mirrored face rippling like water. There was no light emanating from it, not the way there had been when I first summoned a portal to Ehlark's home. It was dark on the other side.

Lee charged ahead, tugging me through the portal alongside him.

The barrier swallowed me, and there were no fearsome beasts waiting within. There was no resistance to our passing.

We emerged.

It was drizzling in Ehlark's realm, and the sky was a deep, charcoal gray. The trees were pale and lifeless, their leaves scattering the ground between the dim mushrooms. If the earth sprites were still here, I could no longer feel them.

I wasn't sure what I expected, but it wasn't this.

Nothing walked amidst the trees except for the wind. There was no clicking.

"Am I the only one who thinks that was a little too easy?" I mumble.

He nodded, keeping his gaze glued to the barren trees. "Maybe the elves are keeping away from this particular plane. If Mionmïr knows what's here, he likely warned the others. Maybe we should consider ourselves lucky."

I shake my head, glancing back at the portal and the world just beyond it. "The sutilus. We should be getting swarmed right now. Something's off."

Lee took a few venturing steps forward, then stiffened. "Look at the ground."

I surveyed the forest floor. At first, it looked like dirt and dying grass, but then I saw the deep trenches dug out of the earth every few yards. The masked pits. Trip wires glistening between trunks. "Someone's securing the outer forest."

Lee smiled. "And I think we both know it isn't the sutilus."

"Ehlark's alive. He's here," I whisper.

I spin in place, reconsidering the forest.

Behind the portal, more traps had been rigged. Some of them had already been triggered, and evidence of fire and makeshift shrapnel bombs mutilated the trees. No sign of corpses, but there were splatters of black blood on the pale trunks. Ehlark must have gotten away from the sutilus and escaped back into this realm after we aggravated the rift.

Perhaps he secured some kind of safety away from the rift before moving in to reclaim his home.

That was what I would have done.

Relief swelled in my chest, and I couldn't stop myself from returning Lee's smile. The world around me grew quieter the instant our eyes met. One smile, and my heart was mending.

Then, seeming to remember himself, Lee let his grin fall and looked away.

I pushed away the sinking feeling in my stomach and

started following the trail of traps behind us. It had to lead to Ehlark, or at least close enough to his base to alert him.

Lee and I barely got a few feet in before he tripped a wire.

We dodged a log that swung free from the adjacent trees. As we scrambled away from it, keeping close to the ground as the sharpened log made its second journey over us, I heard something slam into the ground. Then, I heard a whistling screech, and Lee gasped.

I glanced over at him, my heart in my throat, and saw that a sutilis blade had caught the edge of his torn pant leg, pinning him to a tree. I whipped around, pulling my blades.

Ehlark stood across from us, staring at me with a confounded but equally furious expression on his face.

He was scraped up and covered in so much mud that his silver hair looked brown. Survival. That had been his life for the last several months while I'd been living in luxury, hoping he was dead since the alternative was too horrible to believe. The first words out of his mouth solidified my guilt. "You dare show your face here?"

The log was still swinging back and forth above my head, but I waited, because I wasn't about to abandon Lee.

He wrenched on the hilt of the blade with all his might. Ehlark must have thrown it hard, embedded it deep into the tree trunk, because it wasn't budging.

All I could think to say was, "I can close the rift."

The snarl fell from Ehlark's face. His green eyes flicked between me and Lee then narrowed in on the log above us. He swept a hand through the air, and the log burst apart into a thousand fluttering, purple petals.

Lee finally managed to free the sutilis blade from the tree, tossing it aside with a grimace as he straightened.

"How?" Ehlark demanded, stepping over a trip wire.

"We need to get close enough to the rift that my flame can touch it," I told him.

Ehlark considered that for a moment, then shook his head. "That's never going to happen." He turned and walked away from us.

"Where are you going?" I shouted, chasing after him between covered pits and razor-sharp clamps hidden beneath fallen leaves. I took note of every step he took, mirroring them to avoid his traps. "Don't you want your home back? This is the only way."

I heard a shuffle and grunt behind me, then cursing as Lee fought the sappy bark of a tree—a clever charm to snare any pursuing enemies. I inched away from the tree closest to me.

Poor Lee. Maybe it was for the best if he was immobilized for a while, considering his luck today.

"The enemy lines around my home are impenetrable. You'll be killed before you can even *see* the rift, much less touch it," Ehlark tossed over his shoulder. "Just leave. I'll kill those fuckers on my own."

"I'm the only one who can seal the rift," I said. "Any progress you make will be futile, because more will come through. Let's work together."

He turned on his heel, crossing his arms over his chest as he nailed me with a skeptical look. "And how do you suggest we go about doing that, Princess?"

Lee cleared his throat where he was still half-stuck to the tree. "A little help here?"

Ehlark reluctantly slid his gaze to my betrothed and flicked a hand in his direction. The tree lit up with a purple film and broke into pieces, creating a hollow around Lee's back. Lee stumbled forward a couple steps, stringy sap still clinging to his leathers. He stared down at the mess, making a small noise of disgust.

The tree reassembled itself behind him, swallowing up the sheet of sap.

As I watched the tree fall still, my thoughts twirled.

A small smile crawled across my lips. "I have an idea."

Rain pelted my back and wings as we flew above the forest canopy.

Lee carried Ehlark in his arms, cradled like a child, as we coasted toward the massive elder tree. The clouds were darker above it, brewing a storm. That tall, spindly creature that had first torn through the rift was still here, patrolling the forest nearby. Its narrow head stood a few yards above the forest, so we flew in a wide arc to evade its notice.

I caught glimpses of the enemy below.

They scurried like rodents between the trees, crazed and ravenous. The rift rumbled in the distance, drowning out the flap of our wings and every measure of clicking from the creatures below. Swallowing hard, I flew nearer to Lee as we closed in on the elder tree, close enough to exchange words.

"Ready?" I shouted.

Both males nodded, but then Ehlark added, "If I die today, I'll rip my way out of The Veil to punish you both. Remember that."

"The elf Mionmïr has already announced their plans to avenge you should we fail," Lee countered cheerily.

Ehlark's eyes bulged.

"You've spoken to my *father*?" That last word was screamed as Lee dropped him above the elder tree.

Before Ehlark collided with the upper boughs, the weeping limbs of the tree slithered up to meet him, wrapping around his limbs and slowing his descent. Then, the center of the tree opened, allowing him passage to the room beneath like a chimney flue.

I pitched myself into the tree after him, and Lee followed.

Ehlark had displaced the heartwood, making a hollow large enough for all three of us to slide through with ease.

As I staggered out of the base of the hollow, I saw that Ehlark had thrown up a rather impressive defense. Over a dozen sutilis were impaled on a jagged stone wall he'd summoned out of the floor, and the rest were occupied by the weeping limbs wriggling throughout the room, thin earthen cords wrapped around their slimy throats and ripping their legs out from under them.

Ehlark collected bottles from a nearby shelf and threw them. They exploded on impact, spitting sparks in shades of blue and red and green.

I leapt past him, fixing my gaze on the rift humming on the other side of the room.

A sutilis beyond Ehlark's reach surged toward me, blades brandished, but then Lee was there, pushing them back with a powerful gust of wind. Ice bit at my back as I raised my hands to the rift. There was nothing coming through at this present moment, but that could change in a heartbeat. Every second mattered.

A torrent of flame erupted from my palms, and I aimed it at that vibrating chasm.

The rift sucked me in greedily. Inch by meager inch, the ends started sealing. I leaned into my flame. I poured all that I had into it. Rings of amber and gold flickered to life, spinning wildly around my head.

I squinted through the light.

Lee moved like a phantom, his ice drifting over my back in waves as I heard his sword collide with flesh and metal. Ehlark moved in behind me too. I smelled his magic whipping to either side of me—the faintest scent of lilac and rain-drenched earth.

The ground shook hard beneath my feet, and then it

happened again, a second and third time. I realized what it was at the same moment Ehlark bellowed, *"From above."*

A massive rod of black bone crashed through the boughs of the elder tree. It collided with the stone floor to my right, nearly piercing my wing. I staggered away, my flame buckling. It was the giant, spindly monster that had initially followed us through the rift—the one that was no longer patrolling the forest. It must be connected to the hive mind too. The other sutilus had alerted it to our presence.

Thank the Goddess for Lee's mental training, otherwise they probably would have sensed us coming the moment I had this idea. Their psychic connection to me was still barren, burned dry, but I felt a stirring there in the back of my mind.

Could they attempt to drag me back into the hive mind if they wanted to? If they tried?

The thought was frightening.

Lee ducked out of the way as that blade-like limb wrenched free from the floor, preparing to strike again. Before it could, roots sprouted from the ground beyond the walls of the house, wrapping tightly around the creature and its limbs, stalling it.

I wasn't sure how long Ehlark's defense would last. Already, I could hear the wood straining, snapping.

I returned my attention to the rift, forcing myself to expend my flame faster. I was rapidly closing in on the ceiling of my power, and the rift was only halfway healed.

"Sia, *move!*"

Lee's command registered in my body before my mind. I acted on instinct, taking to the sky as one of the creature's limbs broke free and hurtled across the room toward me. It collided with the surface of the rift, and my flame latched onto it.

The creature screeched. It writhed, fighting my flame, which seemed to have... *captured* it somehow.

The sutilis beast couldn't pull free.

Bewildered but curious, I stretched my flame up the creature's limb, enveloping more of it. The rift reacted like an extension of my power, sucking the limb deeper, every inch it swallowed becoming another inch of the rift sealed. With the intervention of my magic, it was as if the creature's flesh was acting as an accelerant. *Fuel.* I funneled more of my magic toward the creature, letting the rift's hunger do most of the heavy lifting.

A terrified roar rumbled through the house. The creature was still restrained outside of it. Another foot, and the rift might tear its arm clean off.

We could do better than that.

"Let it go," I screamed.

Ehlark twisted to glare at me. "Do you want to *die?*"

"Trust me!"

He grumbled something under his breath but did as I asked, sending his roots back into the soil.

The creature lurched forward, at the mercy of the rift's pull. Lee and Ehlark dove out of the way of its body, and I flew as close to the ceiling as I could manage as I spilled the rest of my energy into the rift.

I only had one chance to get this right.

If the rift closed too soon, we'd be stuck with pieces of this monster right on top of us. But my magic also had an end, and I was quickly closing in on it. I was careening straight past my limit at this point, my flames taking on a mind of their own. They were hungry, like the rift, consuming everything in their path, licking across the creature's torso until everything but its head was swallowed by the gateway between worlds.

Its head was oblong, black and fossilized, but its black eyes were alive, drilling into me.

An iron tang soured my mouth as my head ballooned and

my wings shuddered in rebellion. I fell to the floor of the house, catching myself on my hands and knees.

In my distraction, the creature fought back, attempting to wedge its limbs back through the rift to our side. The rift split an inch before I could muster the strength to summon my flames again. I siphoned all of myself toward the gateway, willing it to seal completely, even though every heartbeat thundered too loudly in my ears, my lungs tightening as every vessel in my body felt like it was *burning*.

The creature shrieked as the rift dug into the sinews of its neck, and my vision wavered.

I could no longer see it.

I couldn't see anything.

CHAPTER 38

I woke to the rhythmic tremble of a carriage beneath my back. The wheels creaked loudly, giving away the age and condition of the vehicle we were in, so I knew it wasn't a royal carriage. There was also a faint clip-clopping of hooves; we were traveling on the ground, on a road.

When I fluttered my eyes, they flooded with sunlight. I saw only a glimpse of my surroundings. I was lying in the back of a wooden storage cart, one with a patched canvas cover and curtain flaps. "Oh," I moaned. "My *head*."

I covered my eyes with my hands, massaging the ache.

Warm hands slid under my back. "I know, darling." Lee's arms wrapped around me, and his wings blocked out some of the sun filtering through the front and back curtains.

I dropped my hands a few inches and peered through my fingertips.

His lapis lazuli eyes searched mine, as if looking for some kind of wound. I didn't think I was wounded, though. I was achy and weak, but not in agony. I tried to remember *why* I was so achy. My head was all fuzzy and disconnected.

It smelled like rain and manure in here.

Tearing my gaze from Lee's, I glanced around at the inside of the cart. It was a farmer's carriage. A few empty produce bags were stacked in the far corner, and a few shriveled potatoes were scattered across the floorboards.

"Let me take a look at that bump on your head." Lee framed my jaw in his hands, tilting my head toward the light.

I let my eyes slide shut, resting in his touch.

His thumbs traced a sore spot above my right temple, and I winced. He instantly shied away from the bump, drifting his fingertips down to my jaw, holding it lightly.

"Is it bad?" I asked.

At first, he didn't respond, so I cracked an eye open to watch him. He was studying my face. When our eyes met, he leaned in and pressed a healing kiss to the bruise. "No," he whispered. "Nothing about you could ever be bad."

My heart pumped a little harder. I leaned in until I was nearly kissing his lips. "You're very sweet when you want to be, you know that?"

"You think *I'm* sweet? You must have hit your head very hard," he laughed, pushing me back.

I frowned at the distance between us.

"Where are we?" I mumbled.

Lee ran a palm over my hair, brushing the flyaways out of my face. "Getting close to the capital now. You've been sleeping for a few hours."

I jolted upright. "Wait—the rift."

I suddenly remembered the gateway beheading that giant sutilis, but I'd blacked out before the beast's head even hit the ground. "Did I—"

"You closed it," he interrupted. "It took just about all you had, though. We'll need to start testing your limits when it comes to the rifts. I'll add that to our training."

I blinked at him. "You want me to open *more* rifts?"

"How else would you get better at closing them?" he countered. "Don't worry, we'll set up the necessary safety measures beforehand."

"And Ehlark? Is he—"

"Livid, but fine. We dealt with the sutilus around his home, and I have a feeling he'll be tracking down the stragglers for a while. At least the perimeter of him realm is rigged to keep them contained."

I pursed my lips. "Maybe we should have stayed. It's my fault they're on his plane."

Lee chuckled. "Oh, no. Ehlark was adamant about us leaving. He was practically shoving us back through the portal the moment his house was secured, told me to let you know he decided on the favor you owe him."

When I raised my eyebrows in curiosity, Lee could barely contain his laughter. "He never wants you to set foot on his property again."

I melted in relief, rubbing a palm over my forehead. "Alright. That's fair."

"It certainly could have been worse. I can't believe you swore an open-ended favor to an *elf*. You put yourself in an extremely dangerous position, trusting him."

"He's only half-elf," I muttered petulantly.

Lee gave me a scathing look. "That's elf enough to cause problems for you if he so desires."

"Yes, but he won't," I argued. "And I'm perfectly capable of causing problems for myself, thank you very much."

Lee paused, a slow smile spreading across his lips.

A laugh rasped out of him. "That's true." Then, he laughed harder.

I fought the mirth in my chest the best I could, trying not to let it bubble free, but when he threw his head back and cackled at the ceiling, I lost my cool. "Stop laughing at me," I said through a giggle.

"It's not at *you*," he gasped. "It's at the absurd way in which you tell the truth sometimes." He pulled me against his chest, and I knew it was his way of comforting me, his way of telling me he really *wasn't* trying to insult me.

I surrendered to his embrace. "So," I sighed against his collar. "How did we end up in a vegetable cart?"

Lee reached behind him to sweep the front curtain open. "Say good morning to Mr. Finley."

A man sat on the spring seat of the wagon. His salt-and-pepper hair glistened in the dappled light of the forest as he smiled over his shoulder at us. "Happy to see you awake and well, Princess. You gave His Majesty quite the scare, I think. He's been muttering under his breath all morning. I'm afraid not much of it was gentlemanly."

"Is that so?" I said with a laugh.

Lee's eyes flicked back to me, his mouth tightening. "I wasn't *scared*."

Mr. Finley chuckled to himself, and I found it so wonderfully refreshing to be in the presence of a human again, and to know that he wasn't afraid of us. He should be afraid, after all. Our wings were visible, and we were obviously still in the Halcyon territory. He'd called me Princess. He'd called Lee His Majesty.

Hold on.

Not His Highness. *His Majesty.* That was the King's title.

Lee's father wasn't dead, though.

I tried to convey my confusion to Lee by thought, but he simply shook his head. *I'll explain later.* Then, he returned his attention to the farmer. "Are we closing in on the gate yet, Mr. Finley?"

"Soon, Your Majesty. Are you sure you don't want to make your presence known?"

"No. I'd like my bride to see the city first," Lee replied, squeezing my waist as his voice dropped to a whisper. "You carry a few misconceptions about my territory that I'd like to set right."

"Please present proof of residency or your trading permit."

Lee and I peered through a tear in the front curtain, watching as Mr. Finley withdrew a scroll from his jacket and handed it to the seraphim at the front gate, a pair of white-winged males in silver armor. I could see only a small sliver of the towering stone walls barring us from entry and the solid iron gates waiting straight ahead.

The armored guard on the right stepped forward and took the scroll. He unraveled it, his eyes scanning the permit before returning it to Mr. Finley and waving at someone high up on the wall, out of our line of sight. "Raise the gates."

Lee and I ducked down, pressing ourselves flat against the floor of the cart as we rolled under the gateway.

The sounds of the city quickly filtered in through the curtains as we left the gates behind. Other creaking wagons joined ours, and voices rumbled to either side of the road. Bells rang out from nearby shops. Children squealed some-where in the distance.

This city didn't sound empty in the slightest.

I pushed myself up to my knees, staring at the sliver of life I could see through the flaps at the front of the cart.

Lee urged me forward with a nodding smirk. "Go ahead. Take a look at our city, darling."

I crawled to the curtain and lifted the panels to get a full view of the street. The smell of fresh-baked bread and roasted meat tickled my nose as busy shop fronts slid in view. The sidewalks were crowded with bodies. So many, in fact, that it took me a long moment to realize some of them didn't have wings.

I could tell by their ordinary eyes—they were human.

When I caught sight of a seraph kissing one of those humans, right there in plain view, I stopped breathing. Any seraph in my father's city or any of the other settlements wouldn't dare be caught doing such a thing. And that wasn't the only one here. Several seraphim were mingling with the humans. They smiled at each other. They *laughed*.

I hadn't yet caught my breath by the time the shops fell away and we passed a large, snowy courtyard. Children were playing there, bundled up in thick coats and knit mittens. Children who were most certainly *not* Halcyon or magical in any way.

"What?" I gasped, my eyes watering. "Are those—"

Lee shuffled up to the curtain beside me, nodding as he ran a hand down the center of my back. Maybe he thought I was going to cry, and damn it, I might. "Human children playing with our kind? Yes."

"How?"

He cleared his throat and said, "They live here."

They live here...

All of them. Together. They were *citizens*.

I turned to Lee, my mouth gaping because I was suddenly at a loss for words. "How long has this been going on?" I finally managed.

"Officially? Just over two years now."

I shook my head. "I can't believe this."

In the silence that followed, Lee said, "Permits were the only way I could get all the nobles to agree to opening the gates, but I made sure it wasn't too difficult to procure one. I oversee the applications myself."

A city sprawling with seraphim *and* humans, and no sign of bloodshed in the streets? It was unheard of. No wonder the

Halcyon had locked their territory down. Not because they were feeding humans to the ocean, but because they were entertaining what had to be the greatest experiment in recent history. If the other territories heard about this, the backlash would be formidable. No—*insurmountable.*

Lee was no doubt keeping this quiet until he could prove it would work, until the city had a fair few years under its belt.

How had they done it? How had they kept this a secret from the rest of us?

"With painstaking diligence," Lee whispered, answering my unvoiced question. "Vows of silence for all winged citizens and extensive tongue-binding spells on every human who steps foot within the gates."

My eyebrows lifted. Every human in this city was spelled? Witches must live here too, then.

"They are all here willingly, I assure you," he said quickly. "The witches and humans who live here want to see this city succeed. I've made sure they're well taken care of."

I looked again at the citizens strolling to either side of the road. "Lee, this is incredible."

He smiled at me, sheepishly dropping his gaze to the floor of the cart.

I slid my hand over his. "You should be so proud of what you've done. I'm absolutely stunned, but in the best way. How has it been working? Are people happy?"

"Mostly," he said, though I felt a world of complications behind that one word.

It would be foolish to assume the adjustment for either group was *easy,* but it was happening. That was enough for now. "I want to hear all about this later," I told him, squeezing his hand. "Every detail."

He smirked, threading our fingers together. "You have yourself a date, darling."

CHAPTER 39

On the far end of the city, another set of gates cut the road off from the rest of the city.

The road beyond it was long and winding, completely barren. The closest houses on the other side of these gates were run-down and abandoned.

Mr. Finley turned the cart around and climbed down from his seat to open the back curtain for us. When he offered me his wrinkly hand, I indulged his kindness, even though I could have easily fluttered off the back of the cart myself.

Lee jumped down on his own and turned to address the old farmer with a smile. He shook Mr. Finley's hand, resting his other hand on the man's shoulder. "Thank you for your help. If you don't mind sticking around the city a while longer, I'll send a palace page out to repay you for your generosity."

"That's not necessary, Your Majesty. I was glad to do it."

"I *insist*. I'd also like to fund your next year of crops, so long as you promise to bring the best of your harvest to the Summer Equinox Festival. I'd love to see you there."

Mr. Finley's eyes lit up, and he started shaking Lee's hand with more vigor. "It's a deal. Thank you, Your Majesty."

Lee and I backed away from the cart.

"That was generous of you," I muttered as Mr. Finley climbed back into his seat.

He shrugged. "It was calculated. Mr. Finley owns some of the best soil this side of the territory, and we could always use more human vendors during the festival—the farmers are still somewhat hesitant to participate. It can get a bit rowdy in the streets."

As the cart rolled away, Lee and I turned to face the gates. They were rusted shut, which told me everything I needed to know. Humans didn't travel down this road. The only travelers welcome here were those who had no need for the street, those who could fly above it. The Halcyon palace lay somewhere up ahead.

Lee's father was there.

"Why was Mr. Finley calling you that?" I couldn't keep myself from asking any longer. "Your father is still alive."

Lee glared ahead, hands fisting at his sides. "My father has been mostly dead for most of my life, Sia." I inched to his side, looping my hand around the inside of his elbow.

He slowly slid his gaze to me.

"I'm with you," I said gently.

He nodded once.

Then, we took to the sky together, soaring above the gates and into the gray sky beyond. Within a few minutes, we crested a steep incline, and the fortress came into view. It was a glassy, white fortress. Not made of glass, of course. The walls were constructed from translucent crystal and pale, marbled stone. It spanned the entirety of a valley leading down towards the coast, bordered to the north by a forest of birch trees and armed guards.

As we neared the front entrance, a few sentinels raised their weapons and called to us, demanding we land.

They lowered their weapons once they saw Lee, and one of the guards standing at the door broke into a smile as he descended the staircase to meet us. "Prince Alezandral! Goddess Divine, am I glad to see you. The courts have been up in a flap all morning, Abaddon especially. He's spitting mad."

Lee shook the guard's hand in greeting. "I'm sorry I wasn't here to head off his unpleasantness earlier. My bride and I had some affairs to settle. Is my father awake?"

"Servants have been scurrying in and out of his room all morning."

"Inform the court of my arrival, would you?"

"It's done, Your Highness." Then, the guard's gaze slid to me. "And here she is, our future queen. Pleasure to meet you."

A warmer welcome than I was expecting. I smiled. "The pleasure is mine, Mister...?"

"Clayfield, Your Highness."

Lee's hand slid into place on the small of my back. "Clayfield is a recent recruit of mine. We'll have plenty of time for proper introductions later; right now, we require an audience with the king."

Clayfield smirked, nodding towards the entrance. "He's already expecting you."

We were led into a private wing of the palace, as bland and cavernous as I remembered. Nothing on the walls. Dusty floors. Massive skylights flooded the corridors with gray sunlight, and a musty smell filled the air. This castle was *not* cleaned regularly.

As we turned into a long hallway without windows, silvery faerie orbs flickered to attention on either side. Only a single door sat in this corridor, and we were marching straight toward it. Before we could reach it, though, two figures rounded the corner at the end: Gus and Lana. They rushed up the hallway to meet us, and Gus grabbed Lee's shoulder to pull him into a tight embrace. I immediately noticed the red swelling around his eyes.

Lee returned the hug for only a moment before peeling his General away from him. "Relax, Gus. I'm fine."

Lana crossed her arms in a huff. "We've been worried sick about you, you fucking asshole."

Gus turned and pulled me into his arms next, and I was so shocked, I couldn't return the hug before he pulled away. He smiled down at me, squeezing my upper arms. "We were worried about both of you."

"Speak for yourself," Lana muttered under her breath.

She was definitely still pissed at me for what she'd seen at the engagement party, and I couldn't blame her. I should make a point to speak with her, and soon. Now that Lee and I were actually getting married, I should try to mend that bridge.

"Let's get this over with." Lee waved at the sentinels guarding the door.

The doors opened, revealing an extravagant room without windows, illuminated only by a handful of candles and a fire crackling in the hearth to our left. Embroidered white rugs stretched beneath our feet, and banners hung from the ceiling featuring the silver crest of the Halcyon.

A putrid scent curled in my nostrils as we filed in—rotting flesh masked by a blend of fragrant herbs and strong liquor.

Every piece of furniture gleamed in the firelight, impeccably polished and free of clutter. Dark walls absorbed the meager light, shrouding the figure in pale blue robes who sat alone at the table. A feast had been prepared before him, but it didn't look like he was eating it.

The Halcyon king, Godfrey, stared down the length of the table at the flames snapping in the hearth. His thin, white hair was patchy, his cheeks gaunt.

Lee was telling the truth earlier. The male before us was mostly dead.

"About time you got here. We've received several letters in the last hour telling me you were lost, but I told Abaddon—I told him you'd show up with your wings tucked between your legs." Godfrey finally glanced in our direction and frowned.

"And you brought your little bitch back with you," he spat. "A pity, that."

Godfrey moved a hand to the armrest of his chair, and when a faint metallic clicking filled the room and he started gliding backwards, I realized it wasn't a chair at all.

He could no longer walk.

I'd seen marvelous inventions like that before, in my travel throughout the human lands. It was a brilliant bit of human engineering that served to make life easier for those who had lost their legs to illness or injury, so long as they possessed the means to pay for it.

This was different, though.

It was a broken promise that had put the king in that chair, and it would keep taking from his body until he finally surrendered to oblivion.

Lee's hands clenched, his right wing spreading protectively in front of me as his father rolled across the room toward us. "*Sia* is a princess of the Fenix crown," he said in a dangerously soft voice, "and a queen in her own right. In a matter of days, she'll be my wife and the future queen of *your* people. Be careful how you speak to her."

King Godfrey offered him a yellow smile. "I'll speak to her any way I desire, boy. You seem to forget who the King is in this room."

Lee bristled at that, shifting on his feet.

But I saw no King as I looked upon Godfrey. I saw only a father who had tortured his son to the point where he flinched from physical touch. I saw only the scars on Lee's neck.

Godfrey leaned back in his chair, his wings shuddering from the shift in position. There were barely any feathers left on the leathery white skin, and several open sores oozed pus all over his wings and neck.

"Bring her to me," he commanded. "Let me see this *queen*."

Lee made no move to obey his father's wishes, and I watched Godfrey's expression darken. I stepped forward, submitting to the king's scrutiny to spare Lee any trouble.

Godfrey rolled forward, his eyes burning into every inch of my body as he circled me slowly. He halted in front of me, closer than I would have liked. His rancid smell washed over me again, and I had to forcibly swallow the bile tickling its way up my throat.

"A poor countenance and venomous eyes," Godfrey growled. "You carry none of your family's tolerable breeding —Fenix you are not. Declare yourself to me. My son says you are a queen? Queen of *what*, exactly?"

Lee inched toward us. "Let her be."

I twisted toward him before he could reach us, stilling him with a firm look. *It's okay, Lee.* Then, I looked at Godfrey and said, "I'm a Draken, and I'm the first and last of my kind."

Godfrey obviously wasn't expecting a real answer to his question, and I took great delight in the surprise threading through his pale blue eyes.

"Well," he muttered. "That's very convenient, isn't it?"

I scoffed. "It has never been convenient to me."

"Nor I. You've made yourself a problem for my people, for my *son*. You just couldn't stay away, could you? Queen of the Draken? Ha! You are the Queen of Nothing. You *are* nothing, and you always will be."

His insults shouldn't have bothered me, but they did.

Lee walked up and grabbed my hand, positioning himself

between me and his father again. "Sia and I are leaving in the morning to prepare for our nuptials back in the Fenix territory. After that, Sumner House will be ready for us. By the time we return, we'll have no need to impose on you again. We'll take our leave of you for the last time."

Godfrey bared his teeth. "You're a foolish boy to follow through on this bond. I raised you to know better. She makes you *weak*."

Lee didn't show his wince, but I felt it—his wing twitched stiffly where it was tucked around mine. It stirred up a vicious urge within me to protect him. I wanted him to know that his father was wrong. He hadn't grown up learning how to push love away. He'd learned how to cherish it.

I gripped Lee's arm and leaned around him to sneer, "Our bond was made a long time ago, and it had nothing to do with you. *He* has nothing to do with the likes of you."

Godfrey turned his glare on me. "Do not speak out of turn, female. I will not have patience for your tongue today."

"My bride will speak to you as she likes," Lee snapped back, shocking both of us.

The king took a deep breath. "Is that so? Perhaps I should remind you—" His gaze caught on the hand I had resting on Lee's forearm, and he paused. "What is *that* gaudy thing?"

I glanced down and realized he was referring to the ring on my finger.

Godfrey leaned forward in his seat, his body trembling. "I told you to use the ring *I* gave you."

Lee smirked, sliding a hand over mine, as if he was trying to shield the ring—one of the few things that was truly ours. "If you wanted that ring to be used, perhaps you shouldn't have driven the wife it belonged to into the sea. Not to worry, though. I made sure the ocean received it on your behalf."

King Godfrey's eyes flashed, wide and wild.

Without uttering another word, he slashed a hand through

the air, and a shard of ice took form in mid-air before tearing across the room.

I watched in disbelief as it sliced into Lee's cheek, so fast I almost didn't see it. I *felt* it, though. My promise to Lee left a mirrored sting across my face, and I cried out, staggering back a step as I raised a hand to the deceptively smooth skin of my cheek.

Fury swam in Lee's eyes as he turned to face me, but I knew he was only upset because I had felt it, not because his father had just *attacked* him.

He stepped forward, reaching for me, but my eyes were locked on his father.

Godfrey was smiling. He'd gotten what he wanted. He not only hurt Lee, but he'd hurt me too to punish Lee for his insolence.

He was trying to prove a point—that I was Lee's weakness.

The pain in my cheek fell away. I could barely feel my own feet as I dodged Lee's arm and lurched toward the dining table. I saw nothing but red where I wished to spill the bastard's blood. I made it all of one step before Lee's hands were on my waist, his wings enveloping me in a dark, ivory cocoon. I tried to shrug him off, but his grip was unyielding.

He grasped the underside of my jaw and forced my gaze up to meet his. *Don't. You'll only make things worse. These guards have promised to serve and protect him, regardless of what he does. They will not hesitate to kill you.*

Not if I kill him first, I bit out.

Lee grimaced. *Trust me, he isn't worth the trouble. He'll be dead soon enough without our help.* There was a sense of desperation to that thought. I could sense the war waging in his mind, the hatred he felt for his father and the sense of family associated with him.

I stilled, my body softening as I realized how confusing this must be for Lee, how painful. This was his father, and he felt compassion for him, even if he received none in return. It wasn't right, wasn't fair, but Lee didn't seem to care.

Somehow, that made me love him all the more.

You are worth the trouble, I told him, hoping he believed it.

Lee's eyes were pools of luminous blue burning through the darkness. *The only thing I need, darling, is for you to outlive him. Live beyond him with me.*

He needed more than that. A hug, to begin with. Better treatment in this country he loved so deeply, definitely. But mostly, I knew he was in dire need of a bath and some real sleep, because it had been a long night.

He hadn't slept much on the ship.

I wouldn't let Lee sleep on the floor tonight. I wouldn't let him feel alone. In fact, I already had plans to nuzzle the shit out of him once we were alone, by any means necessary.

Choking on my rage, I allowed Lee to guide me away from his father.

Lee steered us toward the open doors leading into the corridor. I held on to his arm, watching the gash bleed along the slope of his cheekbone, letting the sight torture me.

Godfrey's voice followed us out, and what he said was almost enough to make me turn me around and end his existence right there.

"She will never take your mother's place, boy. *Never.*"

CHAPTER 40

The walk to Lee's corner of the castle was short.

Lana and Gus fell into place at our sides, flanking us as we hurried along the corridors until we slipped inside a pair of white doors in the southern wing.

"I'll monitor," Lana muttered, remaining in the hall as Gus followed us inside the room. As Gus closed the doors behind us, I looked around.

There was *stuff* everywhere.

It wasn't dirty or disheveled exactly, just full. There were several chairs and fluffy cushions arranged around the front chamber, a few tables cluttered with books. A miniature model of the city was set up on the far side of the room. Warm, colorful art was scattered across the walls.

It reflected the depth and fullness of Lee's mind. Always thinking. Always collecting and sorting, retaining every shred of valuable knowledge.

Lee strode purposefully to a desk tucked into one corner.

Tugging open a drawer, he withdrew a small coin pouch, pocketed it, then pulled out a sheet of paper. As he bent over the edge of the desk to write on the paper, I saw his wings shudder. Our brisk walk through the palace hadn't done much to ease his tension.

I approached slowly, trying to find the words he needed. "Lee?"

He straightened, turning on his heel as he folded the paper in half. "Not right now, Sia. I have to take care of Mr. Finley."

Lee started walking toward the door, but I blocked his path. "Wait. Lee, we need to talk about what just happened."

He stepped away as I reached for him, his eyes wide. I realized suddenly he was gasping for air under his breath. He couldn't hide how unsettled he was. I tentatively reached for that connection between us, and as I breached his mind, I heard his thoughts *screaming.*

I can't. Please don't make me do this now.

My chest tightened, and I reached for him again.

But Lee shook his head, holding his hands between us to keep me away. "I have responsibilities to tend to. I'll be back later. Gus will keep you company for a while?" He flicked a glance in the General's direction.

Gus nodded in agreement, his expression tense but dutiful.

I spun around to argue with Lee, to get him to just pause for one second, the way *he* always told *me* to, but he was gone.

All I could do was stand there, staring at the door as it slammed shut on my heart. Lee hadn't been ready for me to see all that, to see *him* like that. I was getting a taste of my own medicine right now, watching him run away when all I wanted to do was comfort him. I didn't like it.

I started pacing the room.

Gus watched me, but didn't say anything as I buried fingers in my knotted hair, trying to ground myself.

Finally, I turned to where Gus was standing on the edge of the room. His expression had softened, sorrow swimming in his brown eyes. This wasn't the first time he'd witnessed Godfrey's violence. He was used to this.

"How often does the king hurt him like that?" I demanded.

"Too often."

Fury bubbled in my skin, and I ground my teeth together to keep from screaming at him. "How can everyone just watch that happen? Why isn't anyone doing anything about it? Why isn't *he* doing anything?"

Gus sighed, closing his eyes briefly, as if he was ashamed. Maybe he'd asked himself this question several times before and was still searching for an answer.

"Lee told us not to," he confessed. "The king is fading, more and more every day, and Lee believes it's better to let the end of his life play out naturally. If the king was to die suspiciously, there are laws in place that would demand investigation by his father's court. That court already disapproves of Lee. We can't afford to lose his succession."

I shook my head, unsatisfied with that explanation. There was no world in which such senseless violence could be excused. "I can't watch that happen again. If he lays another finger on Lee, I'm not going to be able to help it—I'll rip the wings from his back myself."

Gus smiled, but there was no joy in his expression. "If it ever comes to that, Your Highness, know that my blade will accompany you to the end."

I couldn't muster the compassion to be grateful for his sword. Lee's father should be dead already, and I wished I had finished it years ago, back between the birch trees. I could have saved Lee years of torment.

I twisted, reassessing the room, and swiftly stalked to the liquor cabinet. It was fully stocked, thank the Goddess. My hands shook as I retrieved a glass and the bottle of mead. I swallowed a few ounces before turning back around. Gus had settled into a chair in the center of the room, but he was watching me with thoughtful eyes.

"I have to tell you, Sia—I'm relieved."

Oh no. I had a feeling I wasn't inebriated enough for this conversation. Even so, I asked, "Why?"

"You care for Lee so deeply," he said. "I was concerned."

"Concerned?" I repeated, unable to keep the bitterness from my voice.

"Yes. I hope that doesn't offend you," he rushed to add. "You have to realize, you were an enigma to us all for such a long time, to me and Lana and Lenz. Would you be the girl Lee remembered, or would you have changed? We prepared ourselves for the worst... even me."

He paused, his brow furrowing. "*Especially* me. I know you're aware of our history, Lee's and mine, but I would like to tell you more, if you're willing to hear it."

I slowly turned to face him. "I was under the impression that it was over."

"Oh, yes, quite," he insisted, his eyes open and honest and not in the least bit unkind. "I just know something that might prove interesting to you, something I'm not sure Lee himself is even aware of. As his wife, I think you deserve to know what happened to us, why I ended it."

Gus had been the one to end things?

The mead was finally swirling through my head, so I ambled to the chair next to Gus and sat down. "By all means."

Gus rubbed a palm over the dark, shaved hair on the side of his scalp then leaned forward and clasped his hands together between his knees. His strong jaw fluttered as he chewed on his words. "I won't pretend to understand what it's like, but I watched Lee wrestle with your shared bond his whole life. We met down in the city when we were children. It was like the Goddess had destined it. I was so bitter, and he was so full of hope for his country, so hungry for change. He took me under his wing—a scruffy kid with ordinary parents and barely enough magic in my veins to muster a breeze—and he gave me a job in this palace, a place in his *family*. You don't understand what his life was like here. He kept himself busy all the time, sneaking around under his father's nose, trying to help those suffering under his father's rule and constantly enduring the consequences of it."

"I know that he suffered," I said softly.

He grimaced. "I know you do. I'm not trying to say any of it is your fault. It wasn't. He would have suffered at his father's hands whether he had bonded to you or not. I just want you to realize what kept him from searching for you for so long."

Gus paused, assessing my reaction, and I nodded to let him know I wanted to hear more.

"The moment Lee's father was prescribed bed rest, he convinced the nobles in this city to consider co-existence with the nearby human cities, winning them over one-by-one. He did the impossible, Sia. He dreamed a dream so powerful, it was as if he had ripped it down from the stars with his bare hands. He worked himself to madness every day for a decade, and everyone around him could *feel* it, even the nobles who were hesitant to open the gates. He believed in this dream so much that they knew nothing would stop him from making it a reality. I watched him change our territory for the better, even when he bled for it."

He hesitated, his eyes glazing over a bit. "And then, somewhere along the way, the relationship I had with him changed too. We started sharing more than our dreams, more than friendship. At first, it was only a casual intimacy, but over time, it became more serious... for me." He swallowed hard, then added, "The details aren't important."

Gus met my gaze, his eyes swimming with sadness. "Then the pain came for him, shortly before we opened the gates."

The pain. I had assumed the heart bond hit him earlier than it had me, since he came of age first.

"He tried to ignore it," Gus muttered, "tried to keep it from me, but I could see it building within him. He was losing himself in the work, sacrificing sleep and training and all the other things that had once given him a reprieve from his duty, because if he could just keep busy enough, he stopped thinking of you. If he kept busy, his father left him alone. We were given the freedom to shape this city into a place he felt was worthy of the Halcyon name, worthy of his mother's sacrifice. He never truly forgot about you, though, Sia. He pretended to for a while, but the deeper he buried your bond, the more obvious it became to us both that he would need to find you. I saw the signs."

He scrubbed his palm over one side of his head as he let out a broken laugh. "At night, he would say your name. He'd be tossing and turning, and I would wake up in bed beside him. I would lay there and listen to him call your name. Just your name. At that point, I knew something had to give. We had to stop. I was falling in love with him, but he needed *you*."

A flutter sparked low in my belly.

I knew it had to be hurting Gus to tell me all of this. Regardless of whose decision it was, he'd fallen in love, and it didn't work out—because of me.

"I'm sorry." The words escaped me in a broken rasp.

Gus stunned me by placing his hand on my knee. "There's no need to apologize to me, Sia. You did nothing wrong. No one did anything wrong. When I told Lee I wanted to end things between us, he didn't even hesitate. He agreed. The thing is, I don't think he ever loved me in the way I'd hoped he would, and in hindsight, I think my love for him was born out of desperation. I saw the way he was suffering. I cared for him. He was my prince, our country's future, and I wanted to be something for him that I had no right being. I just wanted to be *needed* by someone, and he wasn't the right man."

I nodded. "I can understand that more than most."

Gus squeezed my knee with a kind smile. "When I pulled away from Lee, his condition worsened, I think because I was no longer distracting him. I was no longer a barrier to your bond. A few months later, he made the decision to go looking for you. His father wasn't happy and tried to keep him here, but Lee left anyway. He said he needed to find you, and I see why now. He found his perfect match."

Doubt assailed my mind instantly, trying to pummel my heart back into submission.

Did a *perfect* match exist for any of us? How could something like that ever be quantified? For all we knew, a heart bond was nothing more than blood and gene compatibility.

I couldn't quite convince myself of that, though.

"Anyway, I just wanted you to know," Gus murmured. "I'm happy you have each other. He needed someone like you, someone who sees past his duty, who's unafraid of his father and the politics of our country, someone who will need him as honestly as he needs them. I've never seen him stand up to his father like that, not for himself. I think you help him believe in himself as much as he believes in the dreams of his people. Does he do the same for you?"

My chest tightened.

Yes, he did do that for me, and that was the most frightening knowledge I'd ever been given, because it meant I couldn't keep myself from him anymore.

"I'm scared to let myself need him like that," I admitted, wringing my fingers in my lap.

Gus's brow furrowed. "Why?"

"Because I could lose him," I said honestly.

He squeezed my knee again, chuckling under his breath.

"Yes," he replied with conviction, "you *could*. But that's better than never loving him at all."

I looked away, blinking back tears.

After a long minute, Gus stood, his large hand finding my shoulder. He waited for me to look up at him, and when I did, his brown eyes seared into me.

They were warm, comforting.

"It's okay to need somebody, Sia. Sometimes, simply wanting them isn't enough."

CHAPTER 41

Lee returned to our room long after the sun had set, and I nodded off more than once while waiting up for him. When the door finally opened and he walked in, I crawled out from under the covers, shuffling forward to kneel at the edge of the mattress.

"You came back. I was starting to worry you wouldn't."

"I said I would," he muttered. The words were terse, sharp. Something had him riled up; every muscle in his body was tense.

Lee turned without glancing at me, so I could only see his back as he went to work unbuttoning his tunic. He dispensed with his torn pants, tossing them into the trash bin beneath the calling rope beside the door, and his bare ass stared me down from across the room.

If he cared that I was staring at it, he didn't say anything.

Lee simply shook out the bundle of fabric in his hand—a pair of light, loose trousers—and donned them before turning back around. The maids must have tracked him down after dropping off a nightgown here with me.

He ambled to his desk, detaching the pocket watch from the inside of his tunic, and I felt my heart shrivel a bit.

Why wasn't he looking at me?

I sat back on my heels, rubbing the silk of my new nightgown between my fingertips as I tried to wait patiently. It was difficult, considering I'd been craving his attention all day, especially after my conversation with Gus. I'd been obsessing over what he shared with me. Did Lee still dream of me, or had the last few months disillusioned him of such fantasies?

"You said you would," I mumbled, "but it's been hours."

"Yes, well, Abaddon cornered me," he sighed.

I imagined Godfrey's Hand had several questions for him. I was curious to know what Lee had told him and what he chose to withhold, if anything.

"I told him nothing about your origin," he answered before I could ask. "The details are yours to keep or share. I won't force your hand either way. Trust me, I learned my lesson the first time." He finally lifted his eyes to my perch on the bed and stiffened, his hands dropping heavily.

"Sia?" He said my name like he didn't quite recognize me.

His eyes scanned the length of my torso, a muscle feathering in his jaw.

"What?" I ventured uneasily. "What's wrong?"

He swallowed hard, forcing himself to look me in the eye as he nodded in my direction. "That nightgown. It was my mother's."

"Oh." I glanced down at where the dark blue satin pooled around my knees. It was a beautiful gown. The underdress was a deep jewel tone, and the accompanying robe was a few shades lighter, sheer, and fastened around my waist at a flattering angle. I was freshly bathed, and my skin glistened with fragrant oil. I thought I'd looked pretty. Tempting, even.

I saw the look on his face, though. This made him uncomfortable.

"Would you like me to take it off?" I asked, smirking mischievously. "I actually prefer to sleep naked."

Lee laughed. Then he clicked his tongue, shaking a finger at me as he approached the bed. "Oh no, you don't, you little nymph. Keep the gown. It looks lovely on you." His compliment fluttered over me like sunlight, warming my skin and calming my nerves.

"Alright," I whispered. "I sort of love it anyway."

Lee smiled and reached for the pillow next to mine, so I pitched myself sideways to land on it. He looked between me and the cushion under my arm. "What? Is this pillow special to you?"

"Sleep with me."

His head rocked back in surprise. "*What?*"

"No, I mean *in* the bed, not like—" I scrambled for words, panicking. "I wasn't saying sleep with me, like *sex*. I just meant sleep *with* me. We should share the bed. You've been sleeping on the floor and uncomfortable sitting furniture for months now, and it's not fair. Equals, remember?"

Lee's gaze scanned me from crown to hip. "I don't think that's a good idea."

"Why not?"

"Because you're barely clothed."

"This dress has two layers," I argued.

He leaned in, his warm exhale caressing my cheek as he whispered, "And yet I can see the outline of your pretty nipples through them both."

Our gazes met, and an electric current ricocheted between us, vibrating through our bond.

A faint smile tugged at his lips.

He wouldn't be sleeping anywhere but at my side after saying something like that.

I wiggled down into the mattress while holding his gaze

captive, smiling seductively. It was very nymph-like. "It's just a bed, silly swan. We don't *have* to do anything in it."

Even though I really, *really* wanted to.

He rolled his eyes before tugging the pillow out from under my head. "Right."

"I mean it," I insisted, catching the other side of the pillow as I knelt up on the mattress again, closing the space between us with an effervescent laugh. "We can do *other* fun things in this bed that have nothing to do with sex."

He chuckled at my behavior, which, I had to admit, must have seemed a little strange. Usually, I didn't laugh so easily. I didn't hoard pillows. I didn't beg him to sleep in our bed.

The feeling in my chest was foreign to me too.

I'd never felt anything quite like it—even poppy highs didn't measure up. His smile was intoxicating me. His playful looks. His scent. I felt my smile falter as I realized… this must be happiness. And, more surprising still, I could sense no dark cloud rolling in, no regret or guilt looming along the edges of my mind. Only this moment existed. Only warmth.

Hope had filled this moment with an entire future, and I was no longer afraid to look ahead.

Lee eyed me skeptically. "Like what?"

I scoured my mind for an answer. What *could* we do on this bed that had nothing to do with his hand between my legs or my mouth on his skin? Nothing to do with the softness of his lips or this tenderness growing in my heart for him?

A flash of his father's violent outburst razed across my memory, and my stomach turned.

I was in complete awe of Lee—not for what he'd survived, but for who he was in spite of it, who he was with *me*. Lee never hesitated to stand up to me. He argued and trained with me until we were both sore and bruised. When it came to us, he never flinched. He was never afraid.

I had become *his* safe place, just as he had become mine.

Smiling deviously, I ripped the pillow out of his grasp and smacked him with it.

As the cushion fell to the mattress between us, Lee stared at me in bewilderment. Then his eyes narrowed in a maelstrom of irritation and amusement as he prowled forward on his hands and knees, crawling up over my legs.

I giggled under my breath, scooting backwards across the mattress.

The pillow I'd hit him with was forgotten somewhere to his side. He wasn't quite smiling, and I wondered if perhaps he was still fighting his way out of a cloudy mood. Perhaps he needed to work off a little bit of that steam, and I was more than happy to assist.

"Sia," Lee said in a warning tone.

I smiled sweetly. "Lee."

"You're asking for it, darling."

"Am I?" I fluttered my lashes at him. Then, I grabbed the pillow behind my back and whacked the other side of his face with it.

He wrenched that pillow out of my hands and reared up. "Oh, ho," he laughed. "Now you've done it." The pillow came down on me, and I barely got my hands up in time to block it.

Lee continued raining feather-light blows all over my arms and shoulders. I bucked my hips to knock him off balance, shoving him to the side before leaping off the bed. By the time I turned to face him, he was already up and jumping after me. I scrambled to grab the pillow that had fallen off the bed and veered to the side as he narrowly missed nailing me in the back. With a squeal, I took to the sky and flew to the other side of the room.

Lee was right on my heels. "You'll be sorry when I catch you," he warned in a low, rumbling voice that made me squeal again. "I'm going to make you cry."

The two of us bounced from one corner of the room to the

next, like a game of tag. We toppled a night table and scattered a stack of books across the floor.

A cold tingle spread across my back as his fingertips grazed my wing, and I fell out of the air as my wings dematerialized. In the same heartbeat, he launched himself at me, his pillow slamming into the shoulder.

I turned around, gaping at him. "That's cheating!"

He rolled his shoulders back, and his wings disappeared. "There. Now we're even."

I whipped my pillow at him before he could step away, giggling to myself when it successfully hit him in the face again, right in the eye.

Lee groaned, holding his eye as he reached for me.

Dodging his arms, I crawled up onto the bed and braced my fists on my hips. Then, I cleared my throat and said in an authoritative voice, "'Tis I, Captain Sia, adventurer of the eleven seas, conqueror of basilisks and serpents alike. Step forward and pledge your allegiance, welp, and I *might* be obliged to spare you."

Lee approached the edge of the bed slowly, biting back a smile as he bowed at the waist. He kept holding that hand over his battered eye like it was an eyepatch. "Of course, your grand Captain-ness. You have my most humble gratitude. After all, it is not every day one is shown mercy by such a beautiful and formidable lady of the sea."

"You think I'm beautiful?" I smiled down at him.

"Oh, yes." He nodded enthusiastically, but he hadn't dropped his pillow yet, so neither did I.

"Mmm, I *am* rather impressive, aren't I?" I shot him a tempting look. "We could be great together, you know. If only you'd join me."

Lee tilted his head, pretending to consider my offer. "We *could* be great. It would be a pity if I was to... *challenge you to a duel instead."* His eyepatch hand snaked out and swept my legs out from under me.

I fell into a fit of giggles as my back hit the mattress, and then Lee was crawling up onto the bed next to me. I pushed myself up onto my knees, and we slammed our pillows into each other until downy feathers exploded from their seams, fluttering thickly around us.

When the pillows were spent, Lee's hands found my waist and started *tickling* me.

A screech tore out of me as I tried to fend him off, but it was no use. I crumbled at the tips of his vicious fingers. He pinned me to the mattress, straddling my thighs as his hands squeezed and prodded every soft angle of my body. I gasped for air between giggles, my head swelling from lack of oxygen. My body writhed helplessly as an ache filled in my belly. I tried begging him to stop, but my voice was too overcome with laughter for him to hear it.

My eyes started stinging, my vision flooding with a black film. I was going to pass out.

But then, Lee's hands slid up and grasped my wrists, pinning them up above my head. His thumbs gently caressed my old burns, and as my eyes fluttered open, I saw he was gazing down at me with a look of warm admiration. "There they are," he exhaled. "Prettiest tears I ever did see."

He'd made me cry, just like he said.

I didn't mind these methods.

Lee rolled off me, sinking into the mattress on his side. He plucked a feather off the bed and blew it into the air, shaking his head in disbelief. "We ruined all our pillows."

I turned on my side to face him. "It was worth it."

His gaze slid to mine, and for a few minutes, we just watched each other as our breathing returned to normal.

"Where did you go today?" I finally ventured.

His mouth twisted to one side. "Honestly?" he replied. "I went to the stables."

"Stables?"

"I've had a hand in establishing a few stables in the city that are open to the public. They take in pegasi most breeders toss aside, and they train them for use around the city. For public transportation, mostly. That's where I stumbled across Legend a couple years ago."

There was something very endearing about his love for the gentle beasts. "What did you do there today?" I asked.

"I spent some time riding," he said with a shrug. "Legend's mare is pregnant with their fledgling, so I was checking on her. She's been antsy the last few months. It's like she can sense he's not coming back."

I frowned. "That's so sad."

"I hope she'll find some peace once the foal comes. It should be soon—any day now." Silence stretched between us again, but it was comfortable now, hopeful.

I rested my hands on the bed beside him, as near to his body as I allowed myself. The black opal of my ring glimmered blue and amber, reflecting my desire to become one with him. "Did you really throw your father's ring into the ocean?"

Lee closed his eyes briefly. "Yeah, I did. Back on the ship, when we were sailing to meet your Spirit."

So *that* was why he'd been so broody that day.

He shook his head. "I couldn't carry it around anymore, the reminder of how my father treated her, how he expected me to treat you. Watching you wear it every day on our tour nearly killed me. Every time I looked at it, I felt like I was betraying you both."

My heart swelled.

I reached forward and cupped Lee's cheek, and his eyes opened into mine. "I'm so proud of you, Lee."

He covered my hand with his own.

"Thank you," he rasped.

I slid my hand down over his jaw until my fingers found his scar. His breath caught, and my stomach plummeted as he started pulling away, rolling toward the far end of the bed.

I quickly grabbed his hand, tugging him to a stop.

"Just sleep in the bed beside me," I whispered. "I'll keep my hands to myself for the rest of the night, I promise."

The promise took root immediately, and I gently pulled my hand out of his.

His eyebrows lifted, a small smile forming on his lips.

I wondered if he caught my deliberate choice of words. Just for tonight. Because as soon as the opportunity presented itself to get our hands on each other again, I would take it.

"You shouldn't look at me like that," he murmured.

"Like what?"

"Like you want me."

I stared up at him, a coldness washing over me. Would me wanting him be so awful?

I did want him. I was torn between telling him that plainly and wanting to know what he was thinking first. I didn't allow myself to pry through our bond. I was still feeling guilty that I had trespassed too far that evening after the Wight.

And besides, I wanted him to share his feelings freely, the way he wanted me to.

"Why not?" I made myself ask.

He stared at me warily, his silence taunting. "Because one of these days," he said eventually, "I'm going to forget that you're a brat."

I smirked at him, loving that plan.

"Please?" I pressed, pushing my lower lip forward in a pout. "Just sleep here with me."

Lee hesitated only one more moment before he rolled back towards me.

I wiggled my body as close to him as possible while keeping my hands from touching any part of him. My promise didn't stop me from nestling my face against the mutilated skin of his neck and nuzzling it. My nose and lips were not my hands. After a long minute, Lee sighed and drew me closer with his strong arms, burying his nose in my hair as we settled our bodies together. I had to tuck my hands under my arms to keep my promise, but at least he was holding me now. I felt wanted.

So, I decided to tell him. "You're keeping your promise, Lee. I never feel alone when I'm with you. You make me feel seen and wanted—most of the time."

His cheeks creased with a genuine smile. "You *are* wanted, *all* of the time."

I soaked up his words, letting them fill me up and soothe my nerves. "Then why were you late for our date?" I whispered, exhaustion clinging to my voice.

Lee's arms squeezed me. "I'm sorry. Do you really want to listen to all those city politics right now? We don't have to."

I nuzzled closer. "Shut up. Of course we do. Tell me everything."

He chuckled and pulled me impossibly closer. As I drifted to sleep, his fingertips drew blazing trails up and down my back and his voice whispered to me about the beautiful city beyond this terrible palace.

CHAPTER 42

My wedding dress was perfect.

Kori had done a beautiful job; I couldn't stop staring down the length of my body to admire it. The gown was broken into two pieces. Light panels of deep purple satin hung from my hips beneath the bodice. The bodice was sheer and the loveliest shade of pale purple, falling like a rippling curtain to the front and back of me before the hem curled and fluttered around my ankles.

Long slits in the fabric left my legs exposed, and several thin, golden chains were wrapped around my waist and hips, highlighting my curves. A strapless, solid-gold bustier had been molded to the shape of my breasts. It peaked at the edges and was delicately engraved to look like a pair of wings.

Kori had asked for permission to make the wings golden. She said it would be a thoughtful way to honor my childhood with the Fenix, and I agreed. It didn't matter if things were complicated with my family; my real wings were known now, and everyone would see them.

Running my fingertips over the golden chain on my waist, I caressed the tiny beads pebbling into my skin.

My heart was hammering, my stomach all twisted up. I hadn't been able to eat breakfast this morning because I was liable to throw it up.

Soon, I would walk through the door in front of me, and my heart bond with Lee would be confirmed in front of hundreds of witnesses.

The antechamber I was waiting in was small but luxurious. Deep red curtains swept down from the ceiling and clung to the walls. A single red chair sat in front of the door, but I was too restless to use it. I ignored the cart of liquor parked nearby too. Alcohol would not be a good idea right now.

I found myself missing Lee as I waited for the ceremony to start. The last time Lee and I shared any significant time together was the night we spent in the Halcyon territory… a handful of days ago.

We'd woken up the next morning tangled together on top of his sheets, my hands cradled against my chest and Lee's body wrapped around me from behind. I woke before him and simply laid there in his arms for a while, listening to the cadence of his breathing, his every exhale caressing my neck. After a few minutes, I felt him stir behind me, and I hadn't been able to help myself. I'd pushed my ass against his lap and found him hard, but that was the end of it. He'd woken with a sharp inhale, his body stiffening before he gently disentangled himself from me. I let him think I was still asleep as he rolled out of bed and disappeared into the bathroom.

Much too soon, it was time to depart from his territory, and Abaddon enforced the "separate carriage" etiquette by traveling with Lee.

I could only imagine the torture he'd endured traveling with that asshole.

By the time we got back to my father's palace, Lee was dragging his feet. He retreated to his own room that evening and slept in late the next day. Abaddon came back around that afternoon and stole him away once again, and then the wedding madness ensued in earnest. We'd barely been in the same room together for more than a minute.

At least I would have him all to myself tonight.

I wondered what Lee was doing in this moment. Was he nervous? Were his feet wearing a hole through the crimson carpet too?

Beyond the door, I heard the drums kick to life, beating in a slow, even rhythm. Then, the cadence slowly changed, and the drums started speaking to each other. This was a traditional song played at every royal bonding ceremony. It was more than just a song: it was a story. The music was symbolic of two hearts beating to a similar rhythm, then stumbling upon each other, eventually learning to beat again in a way that fit together more harmoniously. It was a lovely melody, but it was also agonizingly long.

The door behind me—the one leading out to the corridor—started jiggling.

I spun around to face it, a slow smile crawling across my face. What was Lee thinking, coming to see me now? The doors to the ballroom would swing open any minute. Perhaps he was missing me just as badly as I missed him. I rushed across the room and unlocked the door.

When I swung it open, my smile fell.

All sound muffled in my ears as my eyes landed on the man in front of me. Disheveled brown hair. Strange, stiff wings. Stormy gray eyes.

Destin surged forward and embraced me. "Sia, thank the Goddess."

I couldn't react for a moment, I was so shocked. My hands landed on the wings attached to his back, and I saw that they were made of animal feathers, a few different types from the look of it.

Regaining some of my sense, I pushed Destin off me. "Destin, what are you doing here? What are you *wearing?*"

"I came for you," he cried. "I'm sorry. I never should have let you leave like that."

My stomach simmered with disgust. How dare he? *He* was the one who called me a nightmare and wouldn't allow me to hug Erlene goodbye. He had no right to be here. He should be home with his daughter. "You didn't *let* me do anything. I left. I'm exactly where I need to be, and you need to get out of here, now. One wrong step, one look too long, and someone will see right through this. You'll be killed on the spot."

"I need you to come with me," Destin begged. "Everything got so fucked up so fast, and I can't make it right without you. *Please.*"

The drums came to an abrupt stop, and my head swiveled to stare at the door on the other side of the room. Our guests in the ballroom started stomping their feet, quickly working themselves into a frenzy.

Two hearts, two families, joining together as one.

And here I was, standing halfway out the door with an ex-lover.

Before the ballroom door could open and reveal us, I pushed Destin out into the corridor and followed him, closing the door behind me. Faintly, I heard the crowd continuing to stomp through the walls. I didn't have much time.

I looked Destin in the eye and said, "I *am* home. I'm not coming back. Ever."

The stomping stopped abruptly, and there was a moment of total silence as my words sank in for Destin.

I cringed as a commotion broke out in the ballroom, the guests were probably wondering where I was. They would come looking for me soon, so I pushed Destin down the corridor, hiding the two of us behind a red curtain in an alcove.

Destin shook his head in denial, his hands latching onto my waist, trying to pull me close. "You have to come with me. I can't leave here without you." He was frantic, desperate, and I didn't like the way his hands felt on me. All that desire from before—it was gone, and I knew why.

I tried to pull away, but he followed out of the curtain. He wasn't letting me go.

"*Let go of me.*" I shoved at his chest, but his grip only tightened. Any rougher, and he would tear my dress—and I loved this dress.

I grabbed his hand on my waist and tried to pry it away one finger at a time, but that only gave him the opportunity to draw me closer. He trapped me in the circle of his arms.

"No," he cried. "Just listen to me for a minute. I need you to listen."

"Listen to you?" I whisper-yelled. "I should burn you alive for leaving Erlene all alone to come here. What the fuck were you thinking?"

He shook his head, smiling like a maniac as tears brimmed over and trickled down his cheeks. "You don't understand. That's what I'm trying to *tell you*—"

The door to my private antechamber flew open, and my heart rattled in surprise as my eyes met Lee's. He saw the two of us down the hall and paused on the threshold of the antechamber. Pure shock rattled across our mental bond.

Fuck.

Lee's gaze narrowed in on the arms Destin had around me and he burst into motion, stalking toward us with a cold, murderous kind of determination.

Destin, suddenly realizing the danger he was in, let me go.

I staggered back a step and nearly fell, but I caught myself in time to rush between Lee and Destin. That look in Lee's eyes told me he had some violence in mind, and I couldn't let it come to fruition.

Destin was in the wrong here, and sure, he was an idiot, but I didn't want him to get hurt.

Erlene still needed her father.

"Don't," I whispered.

Lee stopped short as I raised my hands between us. His anger evaporated. Hurt swam across his features instead, and my chest suddenly felt like it was caving in. I might as well have slapped him across the face. He probably would have taken that better.

Lana and Gus exited the antechamber behind Lee, their eyes drinking in the situation.

I walked up the corridor toward them, shaking my head. "Lee, this isn't what it looks like."

Lee ignored me, watching Destin as he followed close behind me.

"Really?" Lana said in a mocking lilt. "So you *aren't* fucking around behind Lee's back again? On your wedding day, no less? You're a cruel, shameless bitch."

Unbridled fury swept through me, and I bared my teeth at her. "I didn't *ask* for your opinion, and I didn't ask for this. The only thing I'm trying to do is get this idiot out of here before he kills himself. He's human."

Lana's eyes bulged.

"Holy fuck," Gus whispered before turning to shut the unlatched door.

Destin stepped forward. "Sia, no. I need you, please."

"Lana, please escort Destin back to the forest," Lee commanded, ignoring the pleading look I threw at him. "Make sure no one else sees him."

My heart skipped a beat as Destin pulled a pistol from behind his back and aimed it at Lana. She'd taken a few steps toward him, but the sight of that barrel stalled her. Her silvery-blue eyes brimmed with violence.

Destin wasn't in his right mind, I could see that plainly. He was panicked and desperate. His eyes flicked from one set of wings to the next, his upper lip curling in disgust. "You savages stay the fuck away from me. The only way I'm leaving here is with Sia at my side." His gun shifted slightly, aiming at Lee, and my stomach bubbled with horrified revulsion.

I stepped in front of the gun, shielding the others as I grasped the iron barrel and held it captive against my chest.

Destin's eyes widened, his resolve crumbling.

Before he could make another life-altering decision for the both of us, I summoned my flames and melted the muzzle of his gun. I was careful not to force my heat in too deep. I didn't want the gun to blow up in his hands, but I wouldn't allow him to threaten Lee or his family.

Within a few seconds, the iron barrel collapsed, leaving behind only the mangled hub and a pool of silvery-gray metal on the floor.

"I'm not coming with you. Go home, Destin," I snapped, backing out of his reach as that iron hardened on the ground between us, reflecting our calcified relationship.

Destin fell to his knees, a primal cry ripping from his chest as he threw the gun across the hall and buried his hands in his hair. His eyes flooded with tears. "You don't understand. *I. Fucking. Can't.* They took Erlene. They fucking took her."

My heart stopped.

The world moved a little slower.

"What?" I whispered, not quite believing the words he spoke. "What are you talking about? *Who* took her?"

"The queen's men," he choked out. "Felicity saw the photo in the papers announcing your engagement, and she reported our family to the crown. She told them I'd housed a seraphic princess at Gwaith House. They came in the night and raided the house. They took Erlene, and now they're holding her hostage in one of the warehouses down in the city."

Lee cursed under his breath then took a step forward to

stand between Destin and me. "You piece of shit," he growled at Destin.

"Lee," I gasped. "Please, he's asking for our help."

His blue eyes flashed to me, burning with anger. "Don't you fucking get it, Sia? This is a trap. He came here to retrieve you by order of the human crown. I'd bet there's a troop of heavily armed soldiers waiting for you just below the city. You go with him, you die. And who knows what they plan to do with you before they kill you?"

My ears started ringing, and I shook my head, because surely, he hadn't just said that. It couldn't be true.

"No, he wouldn't do something like that." I looked to Destin, but he had dropped his chin, now staring intently at the ground. "Destin, tell him he's wrong."

"I had no choice, angel," he said in a crackling voice. "They have my daughter, and you were the price."

My stomach churned.

He'd been trying to *abduct* me?

The betrayal burrowed under my skin, striking far deeper than I was comfortable with. We weren't in love, Destin and I, but I thought I'd meant more to him than this, more to Erlene. What I'd found with them was special. In my fucked-up head, I'd started to think of them as... *family*.

Tears started streaming down my cheeks.

I couldn't help it.

"Don't you call me that," I whispered viciously, fighting the sobs threatening to overtake my chest. "I'm not your angel anymore, and you certainly aren't anyone *I* recognize."

Destin didn't say a word in response.

"What would you have said after it was finished, huh?" I shouted. "How would you have explained that to Erlene?"

Nothing.

I knew why he had nothing to say.

He would have lied to her. Or worse, he would have never

mentioned me again. Erlene would have lived the rest of her life forgetting me.

Lee glanced between Destin and me, contemplating. His body leaned toward mine, as if he *wanted* to step forward and pull me into his arms. He didn't, though. I stood alone, coming to terms with the fact that the child I'd worked so hard to protect was in peril again, more now than ever, and her father would have made me suffer for it. He would have had her forget me.

All that love I'd given them—it meant nothing to him.

I bit the inside of my cheek hard enough to draw blood and raised my chin, shoving all those twisted feelings down, down, down.

Turning to Lee, I muttered, "I have to find her, Lee. She's mine."

It was a bold declaration, but it was the truth. In all the ways that mattered, Erlene was mine—her soul irrevocably woven into my heart. This had nothing to do with Destin, not anymore. If something happened to Erlene, if she stopped existing, I wouldn't be able to live with myself.

I held Lee's searching gaze, letting him read every thought in my head.

His jaw feathered, but after a long moment, he nodded and turned to Lana. "We rescue the child today. In and out, kill them all if you must, just bring the child back safe. There's no time to come up with a more sophisticated plan."

Lana was seething, her nostrils flared and her wings trembling as she glared at Destin and me. She didn't argue, though. "We'll need to wait until after the binding dance at the reception to leave," she said tightly. "It'll raise too much suspicion if we miss that, and we can't risk having Abaddon's men track us down. If they see what we're doing, they could interfere and jeopardize everything."

Gus stepped forward. "The moment the dance is over,

Lana and I will find her." His eyes caught mine, and I wanted to shrivel up and die on the spot.

"I want to come with you," I asserted.

Lee rolled his eyes and faced me. "Think this through, Sia. All eyes are on us today. There's no way either of us would be able to sneak out of this city without sending the entire palace on high alert, and that's too dangerous. A small rescue party is Erlene's best chance of making it out of this unscathed."

I closed my eyes, battling the voice inside me that yearned to fly down there and save her myself, to take my vengeance out on all who had touched her. "You're right. I know you're right."

Destin scoffed, and I opened my eyes to see his face reddening, that familiar little vein pulsing in his temple. He scrutinized the seraphim between us, and I could tell by the set of his jaw that he wasn't impressed with our plan. His eyes fell on me as he whispered, "You can't really be entrusting Erlene to these strangers."

"They aren't strangers," I said. "This is Lee's family, and I *do* trust them. It seems I can trust them a hell of a lot more than I can trust you."

His gaze softened, shame threading through his features. "Sia…."

He reached for me again, and I recoiled hard, black flames wreathing my fingers. "Touch me again, and find out what happens to you," I hissed.

Destin fell back a step, breathing hard.

Lee spun away from us. "Lana, please escort him to my rooms, *carefully*. Keep him out of sight. Get as much information as you can."

"My pleasure," she purred.

Destin blanched, looking at me as if he expected me to step in and protect him. I simply glared at him; Lana could eat him alive for all I cared.

Lana gripped the back of his collar and pulled him uptight then shoved him forward. He was sent stumbling down the corridor. After he caught himself, he turned to say something to her, but he must have seen something intimidating in her face, because he clamped his mouth shut and spun back around, stiffly marching around the corner with her.

As they slipped out of view, I turned back to Lee and Gus, who were now staring at each other intently, having an entire conversation with just their eyes.

An oily ache swirled in my belly.

Lee looked away first, and Gus cleared his throat before he said, "I'm going back to the ballroom. I'll see you two in there." He turned on his heel and retreated through my private entrance.

They would be preparing the room for our return. We couldn't linger.

But Lee still refused to look at me, and my stomach wouldn't settle. He was upset with me. Not angry, exactly, but I would have felt better if it *had* been anger. His eyes were clouded, and he felt too far away. I felt the distance between us grow until I was drowning in it.

"Lee, say something."

"Let's go," he said in an emotionless voice. "The sooner we get this ceremony out of the way, the sooner we can secure the girl's safety."

CHAPTER 43

My pulse raced quicker than the feet stomping on the other side of the door.

Thump, thump, thump, thump.

I felt their anxiety pounding in tandem with my own.

Erlene. My sweet girl was in danger again, and if I wanted to save her, I had to endure the vigilant watch of our wedding guests for the next hour. I had to stay even while my entire body pleaded with me to go. My heart twisted and screamed against my ribs, calling out like a prisoner—which it was, in a way. I was prisoner to my duty now, in a way I never wanted to be, but this had to be done.

I *wanted* this to be done. I wanted our bond witnessed and recommitted, but I hadn't expected it to happen like this, with Lee jealous and upset and me battling fear and worry with every breath.

I considered it a miracle I was still standing steady.

All too soon, silence fell, and my heart tumbled in my chest as the door in front of me opened. Several golden eyes met mine—the Fenix witnesses sitting on benches arranged throughout my side of the grand hall. I had a clear view of the door standing open on the opposite side of the ballroom and the male staring at me from its doorway.

Lee's bright blue eyes drilled into me.

There was no trace of the last few minutes on his face. There wasn't any emotion conveyed whatsoever, just a dark, foreboding intensity that twisted my stomach into knots.

One resounding drum pummel sounded through the room. We stepped forward as one.

Another drum beat, and we followed the call of it. We emerged from the antechambers, walking along the narrow, red and golden rugs that led to the raised platform at the front of the ballroom. *Thump, thump, thump.* We climbed the stairs, walking parallel with each other without breaking eye contact. I could feel the witnesses' gazes on us, could sense the presence of someone else standing up on the platform—the priestess, I assumed—but I saw nothing but him, because he was my anchor, the one thing I could hold onto right now. My one speck of goodness in the madness.

Thump, thump. Thump, thump.

Everything I was, I poured into his eyes, leaving my mind open to him, wanting to feel the familiar comfort of our bond.

Lee didn't breach the gap between us. I had so much to say, but he wasn't listening.

Our paths met on either side of a pedestal erected in the center of the platform. The drums stopped thumping as we came to a halt, and I searched his eyes, finding no cracks in his façade, no sign of anger or mercy in his eyes—I would have been satisfied with either. The nothingness was driving me crazy.

Lee looked away first, dropping his gaze to the bowl between us.

The bowl was small, the size of my hands cupped together, filled with a viscous, amber-colored liquid. Holy oil. The priestesses brewed it in golden barrels for months, steeping it with herbs and arcane magic. It was a powerful elixir—and a popular contraband amongst the nobles, seeing as it amplified the full spectrum of emotion.

Its official uses ranged from high-level interrogations to ceremonies like this, because it was a truth-urger. I'd only used it once, in conjunction with poppy seed one night several years ago—it messed me up so bad, I never touched it again. How fitting that I would now return to it with Lee at my side.

Lee was my truth-urger too.

The priestess standing on the stage walked up to the pedestal and sang a short hymn over the bowl. Her robes were silken white, and she wore a veil over her hair and face, beautifully gossamer, glistening under the faerie orbs. When her hymn was finished, she gestured for the two of us to step forward and partake.

Lee's eyes locked with mine again as we inched closer together, our faces hovering above the bowl. He reached down and swiped his thumb through the oil then brought his hand up. His thumb anointed my forehead, the holy oil seeping down towards my eyebrows as I felt its magic crawl under my skin.

Warmth flushed my cheeks before a wave of peace crashed over me, all-consuming and, actually, rather lovely. That was what I always felt around Lee. *Safety.*

The oil in the basin shifted and bulged towards me, drawing my attention.

Amber-colored wings took form first, then the long, sturdy body of my Winged Spirit rose from the oil, lazily circling the circumference of the bowl.

The basin had been charmed.

The oil on my forehead was connecting me to the magic in my veins, pulling memories from me that weren't my own. I saw the shadow of a second Spirit, trapped in the bottom of the bowl—and for a brief moment, I wondered if that was my Winged Spirit's lost mate, their Greatest Sorrow. I wondered if it might be possible to reach in and touch them, to bring them back from the depths, but in my heart, I knew it wouldn't work.

The oil crawled up the side of the bowl towards me, begging for reciprocation.

I dipped two fingers into the bowl and reached up to swipe them across Lee's brow as he watched me, unblinking. If he felt the same serenity, I couldn't tell. I hoped he felt *something* good. The oil was amplifying whatever we felt for each other.

I tried sneaking a glimpse of his thoughts, but my projected intrusion hit a blockade. He was shutting me out.

My fingertips lingered on his face. *Talk to me.*

As I slid my touch down his cheek and over his jaw, his lashes swept low. He took a shaky breath as I found the beginnings of his scar. His lips pressed into a hard line, and as he met my gaze again, he narrowed his eyes. He wanted me to stop touching him.

So I did.

I let my hand fall away from his face, and the priestess stepped forward, delicately grabbing both of our arms. Lee stiffened, and I was tempted to shove her hand away from him. *Don't touch him.*

This was part of the ceremony, though.

I glanced down at the basin, watching in awe as Lee's Winged Spirit danced with mine—two definitive forms writhing together in the golden pool.

The priestess' sweet voice echoed through the ballroom. "Prince Alezandral, do you take Sabrina to be your life partner? Do you swear to love and cherish her, protect and worship her, to give and seek her trust, as long as you both shall live?"

Lee's eyes searched mine, swimming with uncertainty.

Love. Worship. Trust. They were all things I craved from him but didn't deserve. On the other hand, these weren't promises. He didn't have to mean them. I thought it was a terrible tradition, to omit promises in a ceremony like this, because it was intentional. Marriages so rarely were made in love.

He cleared his throat and said, "I solemnly swear it."

Tears stung the back of my eyes, but I quickly blinked them away. Fuck… I was crying so often these days, and the holy oil was making it worse. Erlene haunted my thoughts. Her smile. Her unconditional love. I wasn't sure what I would do if she was taken from this world; I only knew I would burn hot enough to bring my entire life to cinders.

My mouth was bone dry as I swallowed my flames back.

I wanted to walk around this pedestal and hold Lee, to take comfort from him as well as give him some in return, but that wouldn't be proper. He was already on edge, anyway. More touch wasn't what he needed.

The priestess squeezed my arm, and I startled, turning to gaze up at her.

"Princess Sabrina, do you take Alezandral to be your life partner? Do you swear to love and cherish him, protect and worship him, to give and seek his trust, as long as you both shall live?"

"I solemnly swear it," I replied without hesitation, and I meant every word.

If this was an ordinary wedding, the ceremony would have ended here, but this was more. *We* were more.

The drums started up again. *Thump, thump, thump.*

We circled the pedestal in slow, even steps as Lee and I turned to face a veil that had been hung from the rafters behind the bowl of holy oil. The veil would give us some semblance of privacy, an intimate space that still allowed the witnesses to watch our bond be recommitted. Lee and I passed through either end of veil and met back in the center.

A small table was set up here, holding a velvet cushion with a blade nestled upon it.

The drums kept pounding, every thump echoing in my veins. Lee turned his head to stare at the knife, his apprehension palpable, the chasm between us growing wider, and I just couldn't take it anymore.

"Lee," I murmured.

His gaze flashed up to meet mine, his eyes swirling with surprise.

I didn't care that we weren't supposed to talk. I didn't care that people were watching us through the veil. I doubted anyone would be able to hear us past the drums anyway. He was being stubborn and distant, and I hated this feeling.

I needed him right now, when the rest of my life felt like it was falling apart.

"I know—" I licked my lips, searching for a way to verbalize my feelings without upsetting him further. *I think I might love you* would definitely do it. Who would want to hear that after catching their betrothed in the hands of an ex-lover? Certainly not me. I knew the irrational jealousy he was feeling. I understood it. *But I didn't do anything wrong*, I reminded myself. I'd been ambushed too. "I know you aren't happy with me but... could we pretend again, just for today?"

He narrowed his eyes in confusion.

"To love each other," I added shakily, dropping my gaze to the front of his tunic. It was unbuttoned, hanging loose in preparation for the binding. "I know it's just me and you back here. I know we have no one to perform for, but I—I don't want it to feel like this. I don't want you to look at me like this."

"Like what?" His sharp tone almost made me say "never mind," but I wouldn't run scared from him, not anymore.

"Like you'd rather be anywhere else," I said quietly. "Please, can't you just pretend a little while longer, behind the curtains, for me? You can continue hating me tomorrow, and I won't begrudge you for it, I promise."

"Sia…"

"I know. This wasn't the deal, but—"

"*Sia.*" Lee hooked a knuckle under my chin, urging my gaze back to his face. He was watching me with unexpected tenderness, and I practically melted in relief, bracing my hands against his broad chest to keep myself from collapsing.

He gave a slight shake of his head. "I could never hate you, Sia."

The words filled my chest with light, and the tension in my shoulders lifted away. We were barely touching, and yet I felt him all over me, his nearness and affection. While it didn't feel completely solid—the connection between us—I could feel the effort he was making, and that brought me worlds of peace.

Amidst the horrors this day held, at least I had this. I had *him*.

He dropped his hand from my chin and reached for the knife on the table. With deliberate movements, he tugged his tunic away from his chest and made a long slice over his heart, over the healed scar. Then, he sliced into the palm of his right hand and offered the knife to me.

"Your turn," he whispered.

Lee had said those exact words to me when we were children. The memory razed across my memory, and for a moment, I saw that small boy's face as I looked into his eyes.

I'd told him we were just pretending, but that wasn't how I felt. This was real to me.

I took the knife from his hand and brought the knife to my own chest. I hissed out a breath as the blade bit into my flesh.

My scar was incredibly tender, and dragging the knife across my palm was no less painful.

As I returned the blade to the table, Lee stepped closer.

Our gazes locked as he placed his bleeding palm over my breast. His fingers were deliciously bare and warm as his wound bled into mine, and a fuzzy mist filled my head. I felt like I was floating above my body, watching this moment unfold.

I raised my right hand and slipped it beneath his tunic, aligning our cuts.

Lee inhaled sharply, his body leaning into mine. He was feeling that little tingle too, the bond pulled taut between us. He covered my hand on his chest with his other palm and lowered his brow to mine. Out of the corner of my eye, I watched as our magic spun to life all around us, enclosing our bodies in a cyclone of snow and hungry black flames.

"I'll never let you be alone," he murmured.

I nudged his nose with the tip of mine. "And I'll never let anyone hurt you again."

It didn't need to be promised in so many words—the promises were already here. Simply acknowledging them brought all those old feelings to the surface. Our shared lone-liness. The comfort we'd found within that copse of birch trees. *Hope*. A dream we'd built upon years of helplessness.

A dream for just the two of us.

As our magic faded, Lee leaned in and pressed a gentle kiss to my lips. I couldn't tell whether he'd done it because he wanted to, or because those on the other side of the veil would want to see it, but I didn't care. Because he was kissing me.

When he pulled back, the drums slammed around us in a victorious beat. The ground vibrated beneath our feet as the crowd stomped in accordance to the rhythm. Whistles tore through the air and wild calls echoed through the hall.

Lee took my hand and led us back around the veil, and I followed him.

This male had found me seventeen years ago and never let me go. He was my heart mate, my equal, and now... he was my king.

THE RECEPTION HALL was already bustling with bodies when we arrived. The witnesses from the ballroom filed in around us, mingling with the rest of the guests. Nobles from every settlement had been invited to the reception to celebrate with us, to drink and feast and dance.

The ceremonial dance symbolized the merging of our two territories, our two families. Court members and relatives were expected to participate, to display their approval of the union, and that was why Gus and Lana had to be present for it.

As we crossed the threshold into the reception hall, we were swarmed with warm congratulations. There was barely enough room to breathe, much less walk.

Why were people so *touchy* at weddings?

The evidence of Lee's discomfort was subtle, but I noticed it. The clench of his jaw. The forced kindness in his eyes. He was wearing his gloves again. Honestly, that was probably for the best—he'd be touching a lot of people here in a moment.

We worked our way through the crowd, aiming for the center of the room, where the dance floor had been cleared for us. My stomach flipped when we stepped out onto the polished wooden panels.

Lee took my upper arms in his hands and drew me in until our chests brushed. "You wait here now. No running off," he warned with a smirk.

I smiled. "I think that'll depend on how well you dance. No promises."

Lee pressed a feather-light kiss to my temple then strode toward the opposite edge of the floor. He dispensed with his tunic, tossing it across the back of a chair before turning to face me again in his thin linen undershirt and a pair of tight leather pants that made me want to kneel at his feet.

The crowd leaned in around us, watching, waiting.

He waved a hand toward the orchestra, and the drums struck up a driving rhythm. I had no hand in the music this time. Lee had been serious about taking care of every detail of the wedding for me, and it seemed he would not disappoint me, even in this. Flutes fluttered in alongside the drums before a variety of strings joined, raising the song up, up, up. The melody was full and warm, deeply joyful. Cymbals crashed at the end of the next stanza, and a smile spread across my lips—it was beautiful.

Even if it was at odds with the dread pumping through my veins.

Erlene was being held hostage right now. She had to be so frightened, surrounded by strangers who only viewed her as a weapon, a child of value, but not because of who she was. It was because of who I was. I'd put her in danger just by loving her.

We're going to save you, sweetheart. Hold on.

Lee's eyes met mine as he walked out onto the empty dance floor, rolling his sleeves up his forearms. He halted in the center of the floor and bowed at the waist.

When he looked up at me, he was smiling broadly in invitation, and I rushed forward, practically running across the floor to meet him in the center. I bowed low until we were cheek-to-cheek.

"Ready, darling?"

"As ever," I breathed.

Lee stepped to the right, and I mirrored the movement, our steps in tune with the melody. With light feet, we leapt forward, letting our wings lightly brush before retreating to our previous positions. It was impossible not to smile as the song overwhelmed my senses. The melody demanded my joy, and that was how true fear survived anyway, in partnership with joy and hope. Neither could exist without its adversary.

Lee wiggled his eyebrows, attempting to alleviate the dark shadow following me, and I laughed, unable to help it.

I threw myself into the music, letting my body drop every ounce of tension. We kept our hands to ourselves—for now. Only one look, and I could read his next step, his every desire. We whirled around each other, traveling across the floor as we took turns leading the dance.

Then, others joined us on the dance floor.

For a while, I paid no attention to them. My eyes were on Lee. I wished we could stay in this moment forever, where music filled our spirits and moved our bodies, the complications of our bond far away.

Our families weaved together in a wide sphere on the outskirts of the floor, creating a barrier between us and the rest of our guests. They danced with one another, waiting for us to join their binding ring. The air above our heads was charged with magic. Flurries of snow twisted, and orange flames darted around like shooting stars. Some of the snow melted as it fell, sprinkling the dance floor and everyone on it with a light mist.

Lee grabbed my hand, twirling me toward the bodies circling us.

I spun straight into my brother's arms. Kahem gave me a breathtaking smile and continued to spin me, prying another wave of laughter from deep within my belly. We easily fell into step with each other. This was one thing my brother and I had in common—we loved music. Spinning around with him during parties was perhaps one of the most cherished memories of my youth. He was the only one I was *allowed* to dance with, since he was the only one who knew about the paint on my wings and how to avoid ruining it.

Those memories passed back and forth between us as we stared at each other, and then he was passing me to the next person in line.

My father caught me, his eyes glistening with golden tears. I wasn't expecting such a blatant show of affection. It tugged at the thread of love I still held for him.

"Little love," he murmured. He swept me up into his arms, leading us in a sharp, prancing quickstep that made my head spin.

Too soon, he passed me over.

I moved through the rest of my father's court at a frantic pace. The song lifted me higher, until I was wild and free. I wasn't sure when the tears started flowing, only that my cheeks were wet and my throat ached.

The first member of Lee's court who caught up to me was Gus. He twirled me in his arms, his hands nimble and strong. A gentle breeze tickled across my back before he let me go, and my face prickled with heat as I stumbled into Lana.

We both hesitated.

Her eyes were alight with gentle rapture over the music. Before she could refuse me, I took her hand and swung her under my arm, letting her spin around me until we were both dizzy. She pursed her lips, and I could tell that she was trying to hide a smile.

The rest of Lee's court was a blur. The only other person I recognized was Abaddon, who gave me a slimy smile as he slid his hands over my waist and over my bare arms. I couldn't be rid of him fast enough.

By the time I had broken free from the circle and re-entered the center of the dance floor, the song had slowed.

Lee stumbled out of a dance with my brother on the other side of the room, smiling so wide that his cheeks were beautifully creased. His eyes locked onto me, and he stalked toward me. I drifted to him, deaf to everything beyond the pulse in my ears.

He reached for my waist, and I threw my arms around his neck.

We moved in the same way we had at the beginning, only now, we were closer. Our hips led the way, and we took smaller steps, our bodies grazing each other. He nuzzled the side of my face as my fingers slid into his hair, scratching his scalp, relishing in his nearness.

The song dropped to a low, intimate rumble, and our courts stopped dancing around us.

As the melody surged for one last stanza, Lee took my hips between his hands and lifted me into his arms. I smiled down at him as the strings drew the final note of the song out.

Lee let my body slowly slide down his torso until my toes touched the floor.

Our noses were nestled together, and when our lips brushed in the beginnings of a kiss, a sharp pain hit me in the gut.

I gasped and swayed on my feet, feeling dizzy.

Lee leaned back an inch, scanning my face, his brow furrowed. His face blurred in my vision, and I staggered back a step, away from his lips. My mouth was watering. Something tasted bad… *really bad*. Not him, but something in the air maybe, or something inside me. My stomach churned, and bile started creeping up my throat as my knees gave way. I collapsed, but Lee caught me before I hit the floor.

What the fuck was happening to me? I clutched the front of Lee's shirt, squinting at him through blurry eyes, hoping he heard my thoughts since I suddenly found myself unable to speak.

His hand lifted to my forehead, and he cursed under his breath. "You're burning up."

Help, I pleaded.

"We need a healer," he screamed as I slumped against him.

My flesh broke into gooseflesh, a tremble radiating through my bones. I fought with all my might to stay awake, only vaguely aware of the bodies that ran in to crowd us. My vision wasn't offering me much clarity as foreign hands ran over the length of my body, two or three pairs of them. They were inspecting me for injury. I hadn't been hurt, though. I would have felt that happen.

Someone grabbed my hands and turned them over. "Goddess... I think—"

"What?" Lee snapped, his tone murderous.

"I think she's been poisoned, Highness. There are dried markings on her skin, on her arms and palms."

Poison? Fuck, the healer might be right. Now that it was brought to my attention, I could feel a dark, oily substance pumping through my veins, sapping the strength from my blood.

"Fix her," Lee growled. "Right now."

The healer spluttered, "I have no idea what kind of poison this is, Your Highness. Luckily, her body seems to be fighting whatever it is. We should take her to the infirmary. I have more at our disposal there."

"This was an act of treason. Shut the doors. No one leaves this fucking room," Lee shouted. Then, his face drew close enough to mine that I felt his breath puff against my cheek. "You can burn it out, darling. Remember? *Burn for me.*" His hand slid to my chest, pressing firmly against my sternum.

The bond surged with his thoughts. Lee believed my magic would cure me, the same way it had cured the necrotic wound on his leg. Gritting my teeth against the exhaustion, I lifted my hands and placed them over the palm he held to my chest.

I focused on the sensation of his fingers spreading ice between my breasts.

He was trying to anchor me, and it worked.

I pulled my flame up out of my belly, urged it to fill my veins. My limbs filled with heat as black flames sparked to life across the surface of my skin.

"That's it, darling. Well done." Lee's hand pressed harder against the center of my chest.

His hoarfrost followed the lead of my flames, skittering between my skin and the material of my dress, keeping it from turning into ash.

My fire devoured the poison in my veins, just like he thought it would, my power strengthening as it swept through my blood.

The effects of the poison faded, and my trembling slowly eased. My vision cleared, and I blinked up into Lee's eyes.

His gaze consumed me, dark and menacing. I wasn't sure I'd ever seen him this angry. Before I could say a word, he lifted me off the ground, cradling me against his chest before he turned to my father. "I want every single person in this room examined. No one else leaves until they've been inspected for evidence."

My father nodded sharply, his jaw set. "You have my word." He gave me a lingering look before turning away, waving his sentinels forward.

"Augustus and Lana, with me." Lee stalked across the room, glaring at the guards as they opened the doors for the four of us. As we emerged from the reception hall, I heard my father barking orders, his voice carrying evidence of his worry and pain.

Perhaps he'd been right all along.

Father feared I would become a target if the settlements knew what I truly was, and now, it was confirmed. I was one.

CHAPTER 44

So much for getting some alone time with Lee.

Lee set me down on the couch in my sitting room as Lana and Gus followed us inside. Gus collapsed in the chair next to me, watching us with concern, while my husband straightened, his eyes flicking between the empty seat at my side and his cousin.

Lana was pacing back and forth in front of my balcony doors. "This doesn't bode well for the situation back home," she grumbled. "The nobles will want to know who poisoned her. If it was one of her father's people…"

"I know," Lee muttered. "Our people will riot."

I propped myself up in the crook of the couch. "Why?"

Lee's eyes strayed to me and lingered. "They'll wonder how your home settlement could turn on you so quickly, if there's more to the story we're not telling them."

Lana scoffed. "There always is more to the story, isn't there? They aren't wrong."

"They'll think you're a danger to our territory, Sia. We need to head this off before the situation spirals out of control."

Suddenly, a sharp knocking came from the magical door leading to Lee's room.

"I can hear you assholes talking in there," Destin shouted. "Let me *out*."

Lana's head whipped toward him so fast, I was surprised her neck didn't break. She took two brisk steps toward the door and yelled, "Shut the fuck up, you little rat! I'll come in there and rip your tongue out myself if I have to."

A muffled grunt sounded through the door, but Destin's footsteps padded away. Lana had made quite the first impression on him, hadn't she?

"What about Erlene?" I asked, my nerves returning now that we were alone.

My girl. My sweet girl.

Lee slowly sat down on the cushion next to me, placing a hand on my thigh and gently squeezing it. He didn't acknowledge Destin's interruption. "Now is the best chance for you two to slip away unnoticed, while Abaddon and his men are preoccupied in the reception hall. Did you figure out which warehouse the girl is being held at?"

Lana nodded. "The human was surprisingly forthcoming, but we can't be sure about the legitimacy of his story, Lee. What if he's laying another trap? We'll be outnumbered down there. Perhaps we should gather some reinforcements first—I can have a letter sent out immediately."

I shook my head. "Destin isn't a fool. He would have told us the truth."

"I disagree," Lana bit out, barely glancing my way. "We can't trust him."

"He would never endanger Erlene like that." I stood from my seat, forcing her to meet my gaze. "Time is precious. Once the soldiers realize he's not coming down with me, who knows what they'll do to her. Now that we're helping him, now that we know the truth, he won't double-cross us. Trust *me*. I know him—or *knew* him. Erlene is his whole world; he'd do anything to protect her."

Lana's eyes held mine, cold and calculating. "The only person I trust is my king."

"Ouch," Gus said, thumping a fist over his heart, though his attempt to break the tension went thoroughly ignored.

Lee sighed. "*Your king* is telling you to believe the human, Lana. Sia's right. He only did their bidding because he felt he had no other choice. We'll give him the benefit of the doubt for now. Go." He waved them toward the door.

Lana rolled her eyes before sweeping out into the corridor.

Gus started following her but paused next to me, reaching up to squeeze my shoulder. "I'm glad you're alright, Sia. Don't be scared. We'll be back with the child soon."

I tried to smile and failed.

The General nodded at Lee and left the room, closing the door gently behind him.

Lee stood and turned the lock on the door before walking back to me, his eyes studying the floor. His elegant brows were drawn together, and he chewed on his lower lip. The events of the day were clearly weighing on him. He ran a hand through his blond hair and lifted his gaze to the wall next to us.

In his silence, I said, "Tell me what you're thinking."

Breathing deep, he turned to me and grabbed my hands, holding them up between us. "Promise me something, Sia."

"Anything," I exhaled.

He looked into my eyes then said in a velvety whisper, "If we bring that man and his daughter back to the Halcyon territory, promise me you'll be discreet about your relationship."

My jaw slackened. "You'd allow them to come with us? Truly?"

I couldn't believe it. Why would he do that for them?

"How could I not?" He peered at me with tired eyes. "She's yours."

A smile tugged at the corners of my mouth.

The warm feeling in my chest was annihilated when he said, "I never want you to feel trapped by this marriage, Sia. When I promised to never let you feel alone, I meant it, no matter what. If you wish to have them both, if they will quench your loneliness, I won't deny you that happiness. Just don't let me see it. Don't let me hear about it. Please." His face twisted, tormented. "I'm begging you."

I took Lee's face in my hands, my thumb grazing across his stubble to the corner of his mouth. I shook my head, my eyes stinging. "I don't think you understand—"

A fist pounded on the door to my room, startling us apart.

"Alezandral, a *word,* if you please." Abaddon had already slithered his way out of the reception hall, and he was obviously furious about being detained. He banged on the door again, hard enough to shake the hinges. "*I know you're in there.*"

Lee hung his head and backed away. "I have to go with him."

I nodded, knowing I couldn't convince him to stay. He had to make sure his father's Hand didn't turn the entire palace against us. And besides, there was a human in the next room I had to deal with.

"See you later tonight?"

He grimaced. "I don't know. I'll be back by morning for certain. I'll try not to wake you up when I come in."

"I doubt I'll be getting any sleep."

Lee glanced at the door leading to his room while Abaddon pounded on the other. Before I could assure Lee that Destin would have nothing to do with my sleeping troubles, he retreated across the room.

He opened the door just wide enough so his body could slip into the hall, but that didn't stop me from catching a glimpse of Abaddon, and him of me. His eyes narrowed in a glower sinister enough to raise the hair on the nape of my neck.

Then, the door snapped shut, and I was alone.

I stood there for a few long minutes, forcing myself to breathe. My body was heavy and cold. I had to snap myself out of this. Lee was dealing with his responsibilities, and I needed to do the same.

With dragging steps, I pulled myself out onto the balcony and splashed my face with water from my moon basin. The icy water rolled down my neck and chest, centering my mind.

There was no use in putting this off.

I flicked away the excess water and returned to my sitting room, walking over to the charmed door. My side was the one locked. I turned the tumbler free and twisted the knob, and the door swung wide open.

Lee's room was a wreck.

The furniture was displaced, his books were strewn about the floor. Destin looked up from where he sat in the center of the room. There were plenty of chairs and that long dining table behind him, but apparently, he'd rather sit on the floor. The anger on his face faded to regret as I entered the room.

I frowned at the mess but continued toward him. As his eyes dropped to my dress, I folded my hands in front of my stomach, trying to shield myself from that hungry look.

I broke the silence first. "What were you thinking, Destin? Do you have any brain at all, or is it just a pint of liquor sloshing from one bad idea to the next up there?"

His upper lip curled. "Don't patronize me, Sia. I haven't touched a bottle in months."

I felt my brows lift in surprise. "Well," I murmured, lowering myself to the floor across from him, "that's good to hear. It's a pity you nearly wound up dead on my doorstep anyway."

"I didn't want to show up like this." His voice fractured. "I didn't want to betray you. I love you."

My skin prickled, and I shifted uncomfortably on the hard floor.

"You don't love me," I whispered sadly. "You loved that I made you *feel* something. Any feeling would've suited. Remember the way you despised me at first? It's no surprise what we became."

His face screwed up in irritation. "Don't tell me how I'm supposed to feel."

"Fine, then I'll tell you how *I* feel. I am not in love with you, Destin." I held his gaze, even as his face pinched in despair. "I enjoyed your company, lusted after you, but what we had—what we have now—it isn't love. We were there for each other in a very dark period of our lives. We grieved over the same woman. That brought us together in a special way, and I'm glad it did, but we had to end. I always knew that we would end."

His breathing hitched as he glared at me. "So you don't even want to *try*?"

I shook my head then reached forward to place a hand over his. "I don't dream of you, Destin. I don't fall asleep envisioning your face. I've even forgotten the details of your touch." Then, I finally admitted it. "My heart is elsewhere."

Destin's gray eyes flashed to mine, his face paling as my words sank in. Surprise flickered, then understanding. "You love *him*."

I didn't respond to that. Couldn't.

Destin wouldn't know before Lee did.

He saw the truth in my eyes anyway and ripped his hand away from mine. His palms bracketed his thighs, and he rubbed them up and down, rocking slightly. "I guess I get it. He's a fucking prince. He has magic and wings, everything I'm not."

"He's my best friend," I said, "and I choose *him*. You deserve someone who chooses you too."

Destin shook his head. "I already had her, and she died."

"Destin…"

"You better hope your *husband* made the right decision sending those two to rescue Erlene. I want her back in one piece."

"They're good people, Destin. They'll bring her home."

Home. With him. With me.

That fleeting dream crashed from the sky as he growled, "We're leaving this Goddess-forsaken coast as soon as I have her back, and we're moving far away, somewhere the queen's men won't be able to find us."

I straightened my back, bracing myself for a fight. "You should, and I'm going to help."

He squinted at me. "What do you mean?"

"I'm bringing you and Erlene to Lee's territory—*my* territory," I corrected myself. "It will be safe for you there."

Destin scoffed. "I hardly think traveling to another angelic settlement is what's best for my daughter."

"There are humans there, Destin. They cohabitate with the seraphim as equals."

His face paled. "What? How?"

I shrugged, fighting a smile. "Lee."

Destin rolled his eyes, the vein in his temple pulsing.

"Listen," I sighed. "You'll be safe there. I can keep an eye on you and Erlene. I can be a part of your lives again, and we can be… *friends.*"

"Friends," he echoed, chuckling bitterly as his gaze dropped to the floor.

"You have nowhere else to go, Destin. If you set out on your own, you'll be putting Erlene and yourself in unspeakable danger. The queen's men will track you down wherever you flee to. At least if you come with me, they'll hesitate to follow—they might even give up on you altogether."

Miraculously, he didn't argue with me. His gaze traced every swirl in the marble flooring, seeming a thousand miles away.

I smirked. "You're thinking about it."

"I'm not saying yes."

"But you're not saying no," I retorted.

"Once Erlene is here, we'll discuss it more. I can't think straight right now."

I pushed myself up onto my knees. "Come on, get up. We should clean up before they get back—you don't want Erlene seeing you like this."

As Destin and I straightened up the room, an all-consuming silence fell over us, and it remained long after we were done.

I retreated to my room but left the door open, wanting to know the very instant everyone returned. They'd take Erlene there first, to her father. I paced my sitting room and chewed my nail beds raw.

It was just before dawn when I heard commotion in the corridor.

I'd barely passed the threshold of Lee's quarters when the atmosphere displaced on the other side of the room, and Lee stepped out of a spinning cloud of Materie. He carried a small bundle in his arms.

Erlene.

Her little arms were wrapped tightly around Lee's neck, and a brown wool blanket was tucked in around her body as she keened quietly into the crook of his shoulder.

Destin rushed forward to lift her out of Lee's arms.

They didn't look at each other as they made the exchange, not a single glare or curling lip. I watched, my feet frozen to the floor, as Erlene fought her father's arms, burrowing herself harder against Lee's neck.

"*No, no, no,*" she cried.

Hurt flashed across Destin's expression as he whispered, "It's me, baby girl."

Erlene's beautiful, plump face popped upright, flush with silvery tears. She saw her father and threw herself toward him, latching onto him with all her limbs. Destin's eyes fluttered in relief as he squeezed her close.

Lee stepped back with a wince, rubbing his shoulder. That was when I saw the mark on his neck, a dark purpling spread across the scar tissue at the juncture of his shoulder.

"What happened to you?" I gasped, reaching for him.

Lee quickly stumbled away, flinching from my touch. "Please, don't touch me right now."

What the fuck does that mean?

Out in the corridor, the shouting grew louder, and I immediately recognized Abaddon's voice. "Get out of my way, you worthless, half-wing bastard."

Gus must have been tasked with stalling him, then. At least he'd succeeded long enough for Lee to get Erlene through the palace.

A feminine voice responded to Abaddon. "Watch your mouth, you old pigeon."

Lana. I wanted to smile at her nerve, but I was too frightened for her to indulge the instinct. She'd just insulted Godfrey's Hand.

Abaddon's growl echoed my fears. "Don't think your noble blood will spare you, little girl. I'll have you both imprisoned for obstruction of justice if you don't *remove yourselves.* I'll bring your entire prince's court to its fucking knees."

Lee turned to glare at the door as Abaddon started jiggling the doorknob.

I lurched over to where Destin was standing, intending to grab his collar and drag them into the other room, but it was too late.

A high-pitched squealing sound filled the room, followed by a clap of exploding metal.

I stepped in front of Destin and Erlene, shielding them from the flying shards of ice and wood as the door was blasted to bits. My back was to Erlene, so I only heard her small gasp as she finally saw me. "Sees?"

Her little hand grazed across my upper wing, and I jolted, quickly walking forward. I couldn't bear to have her touch me in this moment. *No distractions.*

Abaddon stalked in, his eyes skipping over us to scan the room. When his gaze finally landed on Destin, he stiffened and took a menacing step forward. "You brought humans here. Why? Who is this?"

Lana and Gus slipped into the room to either side of him. They'd been roughed up, their skin smeared with dried blood and their leathers scuffed all over. I tried not to think of how many bodies fell on their blades last night. I only hoped Erlene hadn't seen too much of it. My eyes flicked over to catch on Lee's, but he averted his gaze back to Abaddon before I could wiggle my way into his thoughts.

"He's a spy," Lee announced.

All eyes snapped to him.

What the fuck are you doing? I demanded.

"*My* spy," he clarified with a smile. "Destin here has been running an intelligence mission against the human royals over the last several weeks. This is *after* he dismantled a nearby baron's estate and wiped out a legion of foot soldiers. Unfortunately, his cover was compromised yesterday, so we had to pull him out. His daughter too. They'll be traveling home with us."

You brilliant swan.

Abaddon shook his head, squinting at all four of us. "They don't belong in our territory, Alezandral."

"They do now."

"Your father will be hearing about this." Abaddon turned away and swept back through the doorway into the corridor. The door was shattered, hanging in icy pieces from the hinges, but I imagined he would have slammed it behind him if he could have.

I couldn't believe it. We had won, at least for now, and it was a sweet, sweet victory.

"Sia!" Erlene shouted.

I huffed a breathless laugh and turned to face the impatient little girl at my back. Hearing her say my name made a warm and fuzzy sensation bubble in my chest. All I wanted to do was take her into my arms and never let go. "Hello, sweetheart."

"Sees," she whimpered, reaching for me while clinging to Destin's neck, her little hand grasping at the empty air between us.

A knot caught in my throat, and I tried desperately to swallow it down, but it *wasn't going.* In my hesitation, I watched her eyes well with dejected tears as Destin glanced between the two of us. He saw his daughter's sorrow, and his eyes softened. He removed one of his hands from around Erlene and extended it to me, inviting me to join their embrace.

How could I refuse her?

I walked over to Erlene and held her the best I could without taking her from her father, ignoring Destin's arm as it curled around my back. The little girl's face nestled into my hair, and I felt the wetness of her cheeks. Her hands found my face as she gently patted me, the way I used to pat her back to help her sleep in the middle of the night.

"Don't go away ever again," she commanded.

My face twisted with tears as her voice filled my ears. "It's okay," I rasped. "You get to come with me from here on out."

Erlene melted in relief, and I squeezed her a little tighter before finally pulling away. I smiled up into her gray-blue eyes and wiped away her tears.

A clearing throat drew my attention away from her, to Lee, and I stepped away from Destin when I saw Lee glaring at his arm still around me. I nervously glanced around at the rest of the room.

Gus was looking between me and the child, shocked by our behavior.

Lana was staring daggers at Destin.

Lee busied himself with the buttons on his tunic. "We'll leave this territory once I've taken a shower." His voice was steely. "Clear out of my room, please."

Without glancing at me, he stepped toward his bedroom.

I followed him, skirting the dining table to catch up. "Lee, wait. I need to talk to you."

He turned on his heel to face me, and I nearly collided with his chest.

I instantly staggered back from the fierce look in his eyes, and he caught my wrists to steady me. His jaw feathered as he glanced over my shoulder, and as his blue eyes slid back to me, he slowly shook his head.

It was obvious Lee didn't want to talk right now, not with Destin listening in, but I needed to know where that bruise on his neck came from.

"What happened to you last night?" I demanded in a whisper. "Why are you hurt?"

He sighed and responded in my head. *My father has ways of*

punishing me from a distance. Abaddon is his Hand, and he serves his purpose well.

"No," I croaked. "Don't tell me you let him do that."

Lee's brilliant blue eyes narrowed. "Fine, I won't. Just go," he muttered. "I don't have the energy to fight."

Well, that's too damn bad, I argued.

I forced myself into his head, diving into his memories despite his weak attempts to shut me out. His mental barriers were weakened. He was truly exhausted. I could feel the weight of his bones, the ache in his neck. I pushed a little deeper, and the events of his night swarmed me. I saw Abaddon's men holding him in place. I saw a device with bottled lightning, the prongs that had burrowed into the flesh of his neck, felt the phantom of their electric sting.

I pulled away with a hiss of pain and clutched my neck where I felt the echo.

Lee stumbled back into the shadows of his bedroom as bitterness twisted his features, his body trembling. "Fuck, Sia," he said in a strangled voice. "I didn't want you to see that."

My heart clenched with compassion for him. He wanted to face his pain alone, but I was right here, and I wanted to help him.

I stepped forward. "Lee, it's really alright."

He scoffed, shaking his head. "No, it's really not," he said quietly, only loud enough for me to hear. "I didn't give that memory to you—you took it. I don't appreciate feeling like my thoughts aren't sacred to you."

"They are sacred to me," I murmured, my stomach sinking. "I was worried about you."

My feet refused to lift from the floor. I needed him. Emotionally. Physically. In every way, I needed some part of him right now. He had to feel that. He had to *know.*

"I think it's best if you go," he said evenly. "Please. Erlene missed you."

Hearing her name, Erlene piped up again. "Sees?"

I glanced over my shoulder and saw she was reaching for me from the threshold of my sitting room. She was really here. She was safe.

She remembered me.

Doors snapped shut beside me, and I faced forward to find that Lee had shut me out of his bedroom. My insistence on being there for him had only served to unsettle him, and after the night he had, I felt sick over being another source of discomfort.

I didn't know what else I could do.

He'd refused me.

I retreated across the room and took Erlene's hand, letting her hold my fingers as we left the room together.

Half of my heart remained in the room I left behind, though. It broke, over and over. It broke from sorrow, from anger, from Lee's cold rejection. I cared about him so much, though, that I didn't mind the pain, and he didn't see that.

Or at least, I hoped he didn't see it, because otherwise, his behavior suggested he didn't want my love, my comfort, and I refused to believe that.

Deep down, I knew he was pushing me away because he didn't want me to feel his pain. Lee didn't like showing his scars, didn't like people seeing his suffering. He was used to dealing with it alone, and it was even more dangerous for him to share it all with me. We had no way of knowing how it would affect me.

Luckily, seeing the pain in his memories just now hadn't affected me nearly as much as seeing him harmed in real time, but even if I didn't feel the full weight of his pain, I certainly still carried it with me, and I was determined to make it right.

Both Godfrey and Abaddon were going to die for their treachery. *Soon.*

CHAPTER 45

Destin carried Erlene to the couch in my sitting room and sat down with her, not letting her go for a second. She looked frailer than I remembered. They both did. Destin tried his best to remain alert, watching Gus and Lana as they lingered on the edge of the room—but his blinks were languid, and I could see that he desperately needed some sleep.

I stalked to the summoning rope next to the door, but before I could ring for a maid, a large hand wrapped around my elbow and brought me to a halt.

My gaze flashed down to it.

The hand was streaked with blood and the knuckles were bruised, but it held me gingerly, with respect. "What do you need?" Gus asked, his brown eyes swimming with compassion. "I'll get it for you."

I heard what he didn't say—we probably shouldn't let anyone else in the palace see our human guests.

We were still in my father's city.

"We should feed them," I whispered.

Gus nodded. "I can take care of that. I'll bring something in for you too, you didn't have time to eat at the reception."

"That's not necessary."

"Yes, it is," he insisted. "You are my queen now, Sia, and it's my job to take care of you. Please let me."

My heart clenched. "Alright."

I expected him to let go of my elbow then, but he didn't.

From the corner of my eye, I watched as Lana crossed the room and sat in the chair next to Destin. He leaned away from her, but his gaze was trained on her as she studied him and the child in his arms.

His leg bounced restlessly in front of him.

The hand around my elbow squeezed, and I turned my attention back to Gus. His brow was furrowed, his chiseled jaw clenched.

There was something more, something they hadn't told me yet. "What is it?" I urged.

"There was an old woman in the warehouse with Erlene."

A tingle spread over the nape of my neck. No. They wouldn't have taken Erlene's governess. But then, who else could it have been? Who else would have followed Erlene into that place?

"Lila," I breathed, and Gus nodded. "Where is she?"

"She died, Sia."

My heart grew sluggish and heavy, and it took a moment for those words to fully sink in. When they did, my knees buckled, but Gus caught me before I could collapse.

I backed away a step, needing space to breathe and process.

The initial, deceptive nothingness of loss swirled through my body—the feeling of all that life and love losing its place inside me. Then, the ache set in.

Silent tears filled my eyes.

I should have been used to it by now—*death*—but the course of my life had proven that death really wasn't something I got used to. It was devastating, always. The only time I didn't feel the impact of it was if I silenced my own heart to make it hurt less.

"When we broke through the doors of the warehouse, a few of the rebels seized Lila and Erlene," Gus continued in my silence, giving me the only thing he could—an explanation. "They tried to slip into an underground tunnel as the rest of the warehouse dealt with us. Lila fought back, snatched a blade off one of the rebels and freed Erlene, then told the little girl to run and hide between the shipping crates. By the time we reached them, Lila had been shot. We were too late. I'm so sorry."

I glanced over my shoulder again. Destin was starting to doze, despite himself, and Erlene was already snoring.

"Where is she?" I asked quietly. "Did you leave her there?"

I was afraid to hear the answer.

Gus reached for my arm again, squeezing it with a comforting pressure. "No, we stole a carriage for her and hid it in the forest below us, somewhere the other rebels won't stumble upon her body."

"Good," I sighed.

"Is there someone you want us to contact? Her family?"

I shook my head, cold tingles stretching down into my abdomen. "Gwaith House was her family."

And now, Gwaith House was nothing, and the future of the Gwaith bloodline had been placed under the protection of the Halcyon crown.

I looked up at Gus with a coal of hope smoldering in my chest. "I want to bring her body with us. I want to bury her somewhere Erlene can see it. Can you take care of that?"

Gus gave me a small, reassuring smile and let go of my

elbow. "I can, my Queen. Consider it done." He twisted away, opening the door to the corridor.

Before he could disappear down the hall, though, I caught his hand and gripped the edge of the door, keeping it open between us. "And Gus?"

He glanced down at my hand in his then met my searching gaze. "Yes, Sia?"

"Thank you."

Gus shrugged, smiling faintly. "This is what family does for one another."

I allowed the warmth of his words to wrap around me. Family. Would I be able to keep this one? Would I be able to keep Erlene? Or was it all an illusion?

I wanted to hold onto it, all of them.

Dropping Gus' hand, I stepped back from the door, letting it swing closed.

As I turned to face the room, I saw that Destin had shaken off his drowsiness. He'd watched me take Gus' hand, watched our conversation. I could see the thoughts turning behind his eyes, could sense the jealousy and anger brewing there. He opened his mouth to say something—and then a small bundle of fabric collided with the side of his face.

Lana chuckled, lounging back in her chair as her bare arms stretched to either side of her. "Oops," she murmured with a flash of her eyes.

She'd taken off her outer tunic to throw it at him.

Whatever Destin had been about to say, she'd saved us both from it, Goddess bless her.

Destin's eyes dropped to survey the length of her body. She wore a black corset cinched loosely around her torso, only partially concealing her slender curves. It must have been the corset she wore underneath her dress for the wedding. The contrast between the dark clothing and her silver hair, blood-flecked skin, and those white wings splayed behind her was a stunning sight, a work of passionate violence. She stared him with an intense look in her eyes, practically *daring* him to yell at her.

But Destin only flicked her tunic away from his body with a frown, refusing to say a thing.

LEE DIDN'T TALK to me the whole journey home, and it wasn't just because we were trapped in separate carriages again.

He kept to himself and his court, even during the brief breaks we took on land. I sent him notes with my enchanted quill that he didn't respond to. He was actively *ignoring* me.

I guess I made it easy enough for him to do that.

I was preoccupied with Erlene and Destin, who were sharing my carriage, and I didn't feel comfortable leaving them alone surrounded by Abaddon's men. Gus came around a few times, sneaking sweets to Erlene and keeping me updated on the ongoing battle of wills in Lee's carriage. Abaddon, Gus, *and* Lana were sharing a cab with him. Unsurprisingly, Abaddon was trying to persuade him against allowing Erlene and Destin citizenship. Lee, also unsurprisingly, was hearing absolutely none of it. Lana, of course, was taking every opportunity to piss Abaddon off, which Gus and Lee took turns dealing with.

For two days, I was hand fed every ounce of information, and it wasn't even the hand I wanted. Exactly how long was Lee going to ice me out?

My every nerve was on edge, and an irritating little tickle teased the edges of my scar.

The pain had started like that before. Just a tickle, then a twinge, then debilitating waves of pain. The amount of time Lee and I spent apart must play a part in that. It was escalating quicker now, as if the recommitting of our bond had intensified our need for each other.

When we finally arrived at the Halcyon territory, we flew straight over the barricade guarding the border, and it was only another twenty minute descent towards the capital. We could have flown into the city, but we were stopping here instead, in front of the gates.

I opened the door when we rolled to a stop, scanning the procession up ahead. We were guarded on all sides by sentinels, but they were reorganizing now. All of Abaddon's men were moving up to frame the first carriage—the one Lee was traveling in.

Before I could flag down a nearby sentinel to ask what was going on, the door to Lee's carriage flew open, and he emerged from it, Gus on his heels. He turned and started toward my carriage, and our gazes met for the first time since he kicked me out of his room at my father's palace.

I stepped out of the cab, taking a tentative step toward him.

Lee's expression didn't change as he approached. With swift, fluid steps, he closed the distance between us and brushed straight past me to enter my carriage.

I blinked, pulling my hands back that had been instinctually reaching for him.

My scar twinged with a startling stab of pain, and I rubbed at my chest as I turned to the other male in front of me. Gus grimaced, squeezing my shoulder as he slid by. The flutter in my stomach twisted, shifting from excitement to sadness to anger, all in the span of a heartbeat.

I was one delicate breeze away from toppling over the edge. Into what sort of abyss, I wasn't sure. All I knew was that Lee would be on the receiving end of the consequences.

He couldn't do this. He couldn't make me fall in love with him and then push me away.

What happened to communication? He was all about that when *I* was the one brooding in silence. Our roles were now reversed, him pulling back and me leaning in, and I had no idea how to deal with it.

At first, I had been shocked by his reaction. As soon as Destin showed up, Lee showed me just how scared he was. Scared of my past. Scared of our future. I gave him space and time, the way he'd asked, but clearly, that wasn't helping matters. I thought we'd have more chances to speak alone. I thought he simply needed a chance to think.

I was wrong.

Retreating into the carriage, I found Destin holding Erlene on his lap, staring warily at Lee, who had settled into the seat across from him. Gus was sitting on the same bench as Lee, but I ignored both him and Destin's pleading gaze as I stalked across the cab and sat as close to Lee as I could get. I grabbed his hand and lifted it to my chest.

Lee stiffened slightly, and I closed my eyes. I didn't want to see him react like that to me.

It was just the back of his hand, and he was wearing his gloves, but this was enough to calm my aching scar. This was what I needed. Closeness. I was still furious. I wanted to scream at him for ignoring me, but my need for this overcame that, just for a moment.

After a few deep breaths, when my body had finally stabilized, I let go of his hand and slid back on the bench until my wings were flat against the cushioned wall of the cab.

Lee's hand didn't move for a moment. It just hovered in front of me—the sincerest form of torture—until he slowly lowered it back to his lap. I didn't have the nerve to look at the expression on his face, or on anyone's face, for that matter.

Instead, I focused on smoothing the material of my dress

as I said, "Why the sudden carriage change?" *And why didn't you make that change two days ago?*

Lee shifted in his seat, moving neither closer nor farther away from me, and cleared his throat. When he answered my question, his voice was gentle. "We have the burial of a brave old woman to take care of."

We buried Lila on a hill overlooking the ocean, halfway between the bustling city and the coast. It was only the five of us: Destin, Erlene, Gus, Lee, and me. We took turns digging her grave with shovels, my flame licking at the ground to soften the frozen earth.

From mid-day to dusk, we dug.

One person was always up on higher ground with Erlene, sitting next to the fire I kept burning for her, trying to distract her as silent tears streamed down her face.

Lee was the only one who didn't take any breaks. He just kept hacking into the ground like he held a grudge against it. By the time the grave hit seven feet deep, a thick sheen of sweat was glistening across his skin. I could smell his musk, intoxicatingly sweet.

Unfortunately, this wasn't the time to lean forward and taste it.

I shook away his scent and leapt out of the grave behind him. The orange sunset curled around Lee's shoulders like a cloak. As he crouched next to the body, his eyes met mine, and I swore, I had never seen a color so blue or a gaze so tender. Whatever issues we had to work through, they weren't present in this moment. Grief took up all the space between us, his and my own and that of the little girl with us.

Losing someone was eternal like that. It would never go away—not really. Every time death came around, it reminded us of all the ones who left before.

Life took no prisoners. There was rarely a choice or reason in death when it came for the ones we loved, and remembering them was the same. We would always remember, regret, hurt. I could still choose to live, though. I could still love beyond the pain.

I grasped one end of the linen-wrapped body and Lee lifted the other, and we carefully lowered Lila into her final resting place. Then, I set fire to her body, and we watched it burn.

Lee took my hand as I cried, squeezed my fingers gently as I thanked her and said goodbye.

Then, darkness fell across the territory, thick and cold. When we left the freshly piled grave behind, Erlene was already sleeping on Destin's shoulder. We filed into the carriage in silence, and that silence thickened as we traveled back into the streets of the city.

A few citizens were strolling the sidewalks, their paths lit by blazing streetlamps.

Destin's eyes clung to them—the humans and seraphim walking together. His gaze was softer now than it had been upon our arrival. Perhaps he was too tired to be cynical, or maybe he was starting to see just how special this city was, all the potential it carried.

You could be happy here, I wanted to say.

But I didn't.

The silence in this carriage was sacred, and I wouldn't be the one to desecrate it.

We rolled to a stop in front of a large estate. Under the

measly light of the crescent moon, it was difficult to see much. I did see that it was built from stone instead of crystal, though, and that comforted me. I didn't want to live in a palace of ice.

As we emerged from the carriage, I craned my neck to take in the tall, romantic towers. The washed stone steps. The hibernating vines sprawling all over the front wall.

Sumner House.

Lee brushed past me and led the way up the front stairs, and I stopped ogling long enough to follow him through the front door. Instead of a foyer, the door led straight into a curving hallway with a low, bulbous ceiling. I trailed after Lee as he rounded the corner, gawking at the gray stonework that encompassed us.

When we emerged from the passageway and I tripped to a stop, because this was a living chamber. Not an extravagant receiving hall. Not a cold, empty sitting room. A living chamber.

This room was small and full of *life.*

The stonework covered the floor and walls and arched ceiling, but it felt warmer in here than a stone room should. I attributed that to the round fireplace crackling on the left side of the room and the greenery clinging to every flat surface, dangling moss and leafy shrubs. A large conglomeration of patchwork windows spanned the southern wall. Two couches and one chair were arranged in front of the fireplace, all emerald velvet.

A wave of serenity crashed over me as I ambled farther into the room. I could easily curl up with a book on one of those couches and read here for hours.

Lee paused at the mouth of a corridor on our right, watching the others enter behind me.

Gus walked straight past us, nodding at me and Lee before disappearing through an identical corridor next to the wall of windows. Destin paused on the threshold, scanning the room with a glimmer of awe in his eyes.

"Guest rooms are on that side of the house." Lee gestured to the corridor Gus had taken. It was clear he was talking to Destin, though he wasn't looking at him. He was looking at me. "Kitchen, too. It could take a while to find a suitable house for you down in the city, so just make yourself at home. Take what you need."

Destin nodded, carrying a groggy Erlene toward the empty archway.

She saw me, and her little hand reached out.

I knew what she wanted—a bedtime story.

"The same goes for you," Lee muttered, and I turned to face him. He was walking backwards into the dark. "Take whatever room you want."

My brow furrowed. What was he saying?

The answer struck me as he slipped away down the hall.

He thought I would want my own room—or worse, that I wanted to share a room with Destin. These assumptions of his were getting out of hand. We were *married*. He was the one ignoring *me,* and now he wanted to sleep in separate rooms?

That wasn't happening.

"Sees?" Erlene's little voice called to me, ringing through the corridor at my back.

Destin had paused just inside the hallway, because Erlene was wide awake now and fisting the air.

I sighed. *Alright.*

I'd help get Erlene to bed first, and then I would track down my delusional husband.

LEE HAD LEFT the door cracked to our bedroom, as if secretly hoping I would come searching for him. It was a small gesture, but it gave me hope. Perhaps he *did* feel the love I had for him, even if he couldn't quite believe it yet.

The warm room was a symphony of white and gray. A fire crackled in an ornate hearth in one corner, the stone painted ivory. Straight ahead, another patchwork of windows filled the far wall. It was pitch black outside, so there was no way to see what the windows looked out over, but I had a sneaking suspicion it was the ocean. I could hear the muffled crash of waves from here.

A few watercolor paintings decorated the walls, sparks of vibrance against the gray. The furniture was sparse. Only one couch sat in front of the fireplace, and a massive four-poster bed was pushed up against the wall to my right.

Lee was in the bed, though he didn't move an inch to acknowledge me, and all I could see from here were his bare back and wings.

The air swirled with humidity.

He must have taken a shower while I put Erlene in bed, to wash away the grave dirt and sweat. That was a good idea, actually.

I headed towards the bathroom, undressing as I went. I didn't bother checking to see if he was really asleep. If he was awake, then he knew I was here and was ignoring me. If he was asleep, he'd find out I was sleeping beside him soon enough. I didn't want to get the sheets dirty.

Silvery faerie orbs shimmered on the ceiling of the bathroom, offering just enough light to see by. A large glass shower spanned the right wall, and a massive quartz crystal tub sat on the far end of the room, beneath a round window. Most of this house seemed to rely solely on natural light, with the orbs installed only where the sun could not reach or where sight was required at night.

I stepped into the shower and bathed quickly, using the oils that sat in the crevices of the marble. They smelled like him, pine and mint.

As much as I was tempted to linger under the warm water, I decided against it.

After drying off and brushing my teeth and hair, I emerged from the bathroom. I saw that Lee had rolled over in his sleep, his stomach flat against the mattress, his hand reaching toward the other side of the bed. *My* side of the bed.

I ambled forward, naked and shivering, and stood at the foot of the ivory bed frame.

I hadn't been given many chances to watch Lee sleep. Usually, he did the watching. After dealing with Abaddon for three days straight and digging a seven-foot grave into frozen ground, I knew it couldn't be helped. He deserved some rest. He deserved to be the one cared for, the one cherished. I wouldn't wake him up right now just to fight with him.

We could fight in the morning.

Leaning over the edge of the bed, I brushed my fingertips against his brow. There was the faintest crease in his skin, identifiable only by touch—a worry line. My body could feel his yearning. The last few days had been just as difficult for him as they were for me, despite his silence and distance.

I carefully crawled up onto the bed and lowered myself to my forearms right next to him.

He didn't stir, so I inched a bit closer, propping my head up on one fist as I studied his face. I soaked up his peace and quiet; his hard angles were softer when he slept.

He was perfect.

Unable to help myself, I pinched a lock of his hair between two fingers, admiring its golden sheen as I rubbed the strands apart. My hand trembled with the desire to touch more of him.

I leaned in close and whispered, "I don't want him, silly swan."

Other than drawing a deeper breath on his next inhale, Lee didn't react. So, I pressed a featherlight kiss to the crook of his shoulder, where the scar from his father stretched down his back. He made a small noise but didn't wake.

I felt the sheet move next to me and glanced over to find his hand fisting the ivory material. Careful not to jostle the bed too much, I pushed myself up to scan the room again. I wasn't tired yet, and I shouldn't sleep naked, although that was a wickedly tempting idea.

Lee and I had to talk in the morning, and I didn't want to push his ire any further.

There were two more doors leading out of his bedroom, apart from the bathroom and hallway. I explored the one closest to the bathroom first. It was a walk-in closet, already flush with clothing for both of us. I ambled inside, running my hand along the curtain of clothing on my side. I rifled through the drawers until I found a white nightgown with pretty lace detailing and a floor-length skirt.

After dressing, I walked across the bedroom to the second mystery door.

It opened to another curved stone passageway. As I turned the corner, a small private library slid into view. Everything was covered in a thin layer of dust, as if it had been cleaned recently, but not within the last few months.

The room was painted dark blue. Faerie orbs hanging from the ceiling flickered to attention, swirling lazily in what almost looked like a constellation of stars. Midnight blue couches were arranged around a matching ottoman in the center of the room, and beyond that, an inlet was carved out of the stone wall—an alcove to sit and read, upholstered with pale blue cushions.

Instead of a window, a large painting sat on the wall within it.

A woman with light brown hair stared back at me, ice-blue eyes captured on canvas. Her face was pale and solemn, and she held a small child in her arms. I knew right away it was Lee, so that woman… It must have been his mother.

This was *her* house, *her* bedroom, *her* library.

A small smile tugged at my lips as I skirted the edge of the room. The bookshelves were built from red mahogany, and the book spines were worn, all leather and parchment and frayed cloth. I perched on the seat of the inlet, dragging my bare feet up so my thighs were pressed against my chest.

Lee's mother was gorgeous, plush curves and a heart-shaped face, and though she wasn't smiling, I sensed kindness in her eyes. Sadness, too. I raised a hand to the canvas, letting my fingers graze across the hardened paint, the same way I used to touch the painting of my mother back in my father's palace.

I touched her face, the eyes she'd given to Lee, then trailed my fingertips down her torso to the bundle of fabric in her arms. And I felt the canvas give.

My brow furrowed.

There was a ledge in the wall, deeper than the divots between bricks. *Huh.*

I kneeled up on the seat and dropped my hands to the edge of the painting, gently lifting it away from the wall. I peered under to find a hole in the wall, a shelf, and one leather-bound book in the dark recesses of it.

I snaked my hand under the canvas and pulled the book out.

It was dustier than the rest of the room, so I brushed a palm over the brown leather to clean it. The pages of the book were bound by hand, with varying sheet sizes so the edges were rough and uneven.

I knew whose book it was before I even opened the top cover. There was her name, written in an elegant flowing script on the front page. *Elona.* I flipped through the journal, splaying it open on the last inked page. It was an entry dated seventeen years ago, and there were only two sentences impressed upon the yellowed parchment.

I don't think I can resist it anymore. I have to return to him.

CHAPTER 47

*T*hunk. *Thunk. Thunk.*

I stirred awake, my neck stiff and achy. I had fallen asleep in Elona's library. Her old journal proved difficult to put down last night, and I had lost track of the time. Flashes of her past returned to me as I rubbed the sleep from my eyes. They felt like memories of my own, like the threads of a dream slipping away.

A glacial ocean.

One sacrifice, drifting on a thick sheet of ice, on and on, with no end in sight.

The Winged Spirit wasn't coming.

Death had come to claim her instead, but then, *he* surfaced.

The journal's words faded, and I blinked up at the silvery orbs hanging from the ceiling, letting them anchor me in the present again.

Thunk. Thunk. Thunk. My head whipped toward the noise, and I winced as my neck tightened in protest.

Lana was leaning against the corridor leading into this room. She flipped a large volume between her hands as she stared me down. That must have been what made the hollow thumping sound—she'd smacked the book against the stone to wake me up.

Elona's journal was lying open against my chest, pages down.

I was grateful for that, because it meant Lana hadn't seen what I was reading. I didn't want her to tell Lee about what I'd found before I could. Quickly closing the journal, I set it down next to me and nudged it beneath a pillow before twisting toward her.

As our eyes met, Lana smiled and tossed her book onto the ottoman between us. "Rise and shine, Princess. It's time for training."

I slid my feet off the seat, rolling my head to loosen the tension in my neck. "Why are you in our bedroom?" I tried not to sound too irritated, but she was the last person I wanted to deal with this morning.

Animosity brimmed in her every word. "Lee left the capital early this morning and asked me to keep you company for the day," she sighed, conveying the full weight of her frustration, though my own immediately rose to rival hers.

I met Lana's gaze with a pinched brow.

Lee *left*? He wasn't here?

"Since I'm sworn to protect and obey my king," she continued in a tired voice, "I had no choice but to acquiesce. Apparently, he can't leave you alone, so I get to be the royal babysitter. Isn't that fun?"

"Where did he go?"

"He had some business with a few townships on the southern key," she said airily. "Nothing for you to worry about." She smiled briefly, but there was a brittleness to the curve of her lips, an emptiness in her eyes.

"Why would I worry?" I wondered aloud.

Her lips flattened, her white wings flaring so wide that I could see a glimpse of silvery-metal feathers near the hinge for her pinions. "Come on," she muttered. "I let you sleep in long enough. I'll wait out in the hallway while you get changed, but if you fall back asleep, I'm returning with a bucket of snow."

As I donned a new set of black leathers in the closet, Elona's journal entries circled through my head. I couldn't shut them out. They had spun a tale I wouldn't have imagined even in my cruelest dreams.

The Halcyon's treaty with the serpents had nothing to do with the territory, or the humans within it, for that matter.

Lee's mother made a promise to the serpent king in exchange for his help surviving the brutal conditions of the ocean on the day of her sacrifice. She should have died, but he kept her alive long enough for the Spirit to take notice and rise to meet her. From that point on, Elona had been indebted to another king. Elona had promised to return to the serpents, to the ocean, as soon as her child was born. The journal never stated why. Perhaps she was afraid to admit what that truly meant—that she'd traded both her life *and* her territory's resources to that monstrous creature.

She'd been sent out as a sacrifice with only one purpose: come back with a child of spirit by any means necessary.

Elona was an experiment.

Godfrey had no idea whether she would survive the conception or not, and as the first seraph to submit to such a harrowing experience, she'd negotiated equal rulership in exchange for her sacrifice. Because of that, she'd been able to make a promise to the serpent king.

The serpents were free to hunt along this coast, taking any and all lives they desired, but only for as long as King Godfrey reigned alone over this territory.

Which explained why the serpent that attacked me when we first arrived here had been quick to release me on Lee's orders. This was a time of transition for the Halcyon territory, teetering between one king and the next. I could only assume while Lee was here, while he was actively running the country in his father's stead, that the coast was safe.

That was also why Elona had stayed despite her deteriorating health—she'd been trying to protect her son and her people from the terrible promise she made. She fought it as long as she could. Six years, she fought to stay here with her son.

The battle had slowly driven her to madness.

The first hundred or so pages were written by a woman with a great deal of compassion and courage, a woman who loved her son and her territory, whose thoughts were all carefully laid out on the parchment. It felt like I was meeting her for the first time, reading her thoughts. And just as I suspected, I fell in love with her as completely as her son had.

As I read on, though, her clarity of mind dissipated.

She made less and less sense with each new day. Her entries were cut short. Sentences soon became a jumble of indiscernible words. At one point, she admitted to loving the serpent king, and then the next page was filled with her denial and shame. Even her handwriting grew reckless and nonsensical, deep scratches and shaky lines; I had to tilt the journal in several directions sometimes to read them correctly.

Until finally, on that last page, she made the decision to return to *him*.

There was one thing in particular she said that clung to my thoughts, forming a sticky sap. I kept turning it over in my head, wrapping it around me, tangling myself in its honeyed strings.

She admitted that the heart bond she shared with Lee's father was only a promise soaked in blood and duty. Stronger, yes, but essentially the same. She admitted that she didn't love him. She stayed for Lee, which meant the feelings *I* had for Lee hadn't been born from the bond we shared.

What I felt was entirely my own.

I wanted to talk to Lee about it, about everything I'd read in his mother's journal, but now, he was gone. He'd fled Sumner House and left me behind. I wanted to be understanding—he was a king with responsibilities, and I had no idea what had pulled him away—but I was disappointed. He could have at least said goodbye.

My body felt both heavy and empty at once as I exited the closet, a confusing combination. Before I could make the mistake of crawling back into bed, I emerged from the bedroom and found Lana waiting for me in the hall.

She turned as soon as she saw me and led us down the corridor, through the cozy living area to the hallway on the other side. We passed a few closed doors, then an open archway appeared on our right. The kitchen.

Voices echoing from inside made me pause. Destin and Erlene were eating breakfast at a tall wooden counter. Well, Erlene was eating. Destin was still filling his plate.

Lana's gaze latched onto the pair at the same time mine did, and she brazenly entered the room. I trailed after her, glancing at the iron stove, steel refrigerator box, and the polished lumber countertops stretched around the perimeter of the room. Erlene was sitting on a stool at the island in the center. A blue-tinted window was set into the wall on the right side of the room, with beautiful arched panels and a small planter sitting on the ledge beneath.

As I entered, I could *smell* it. Sweet mint.

My eyes landed on the teapot steaming gently on the stove; apparently, Destin made tea with mint from the planter. He'd also cooked up some eggs and root vegetables, along with something else that rolled around on his plate that spewed steam from charred, burst seams.

Lana strolled right up to him and swiped one of those small rolling logs from his plate. "It's about time we had someone in the house who can cook for us." She took a bite and smiled.

"Do you mind?" Destin grumbled.

Lana shrugged, taking another bite. "Not at all. It tastes fine."

"Are those sausages?" I squeaked, leaning over the counter to snatch one up for myself.

I bit into the meat and moaned softly as its juice flooded my mouth. After three days eating Halcyon travel rations, I'd nearly forgotten how good a hot meal could taste. I swiped another sausage for the walk to the training room, and Lana did the same.

Destin threw his hands up in frustration, his eyes flicking between us and his now half-empty plate. "Really, ladies?"

"*Ladies*," Lana mused with a sharp smile. "So, the rat has manners?"

"Would you quit calling me that?" he growled, narrowing his eyes at her.

She chuckled. "I'd be happy to. Once you quit looking like one." Her free hand raised to ruffle his overgrown hair, and his face paled in surprise—a glimmer of curiosity and confusion, but those emotions were quickly overcome by seething irritation.

Destin batted her away, but Lana easily sidestepped his arm, retreating around the counter towards me.

"Aren't you supposed to have someone here who's paid to cook for you all anyway?" he demanded. "I thought the one with white wings was supposed to be a prince."

"Lee's our *king*," Lana corrected him, her gaze traveling to Erlene as the little girl stuffed her mouth full. "And there really isn't much of a point to keeping a cook on hand for Sumner House. It's easier to stock the pantry and graze. Lee prefers to eat down in the city for dinner anyway, so he can keep a close eye on the market, make sure they're treating the humans right."

Destin paused, considering that, and his irritation softened. He simply replied with, "I'm not going to be your cook."

"Sure about that?" she muttered. "What else are you good for? You don't look like much of a soldier." Her eyes surveyed him with thinly-veiled disgust, and he bristled.

Straightening his spine, he replied, "I'm a good shot with a pistol."

"Hmm." Lana's eyebrows raised, unimpressed.

Destin rolled his eyes and returned his attention to his plate, scarfing down the rest of the sausages before we could swoop in and steal them.

Lana sauntered out of the kitchen, and I hesitated long enough to kiss Erlene on the brow and tickle a giggle out of her before I followed my royal babysitter out and up the hall, leaping forward with a flutter of my wings to catch up to her. When we reached the end of the corridor, she opened a door there, and a frigid wind swept in around us. She pushed through the heavy wood and iron, leading us out onto the veranda of a courtyard.

A few feet past the back door, a huge box of solid crystal sat on top of the stone patio.

As Lana and I mounted the two steps leading up into it, I saw that it was a *room*. This was where we would be training. Inside, a brazier burned in each corner of the room, but nothing else, just an endless expanse of cold, white crystal. Every collision with the floor in this room would hurt... *a lot*.

A low groan had me spinning on my toes.

The doorway into the room was closing. A thick panel of crystal descended over it, and when it aligned with the opening, the rectangle slid backwards into place and the seams glossed over. I looked around in bewilderment and saw Lana dropping her arms, a smirk on her full lips as silvery threads of magic faded beneath her palms.

"How did you do that?" I breathed.

"Didn't Lee explain I was part Stymphalian?"

"Well, yes, he did," I replied slowly, following her into the center of the room. My neck craned to observe the ceiling. There were a few slats made in the crystal for air flow. "I just didn't realize the Stymphalian could manipulate crystal. I thought their affinity was with metal."

Lana gave me a sly smile. "All metals are crystals, Princess, millions and millions of tiny crystalline atoms. Our affinity is for a very specific subset of atomic structures. Metal and crystal just happen to fall under that."

"I had no idea."

"The Stymphalian keep their share of secrets. Every territory does, but I'm sure you've figured that out by now."

"Unfortunately," I muttered under my breath.

Lana ambled toward the edge of the room. "Let's begin."

I turned to face her, palming the daggers on my hips, but Lana shook her head. "You won't need those. We're not training with blades today. I've been tasked to begin your training with rifts."

I staggered back a step, glancing over my shoulder at where the door used to be and beyond it, to where Destin and his daughter were currently eating their breakfast, blissfully oblivious.

"I can't do that here. Erlene—"

"This crystal is five feet thick and totally impenetrable," Lana snapped, rolling her shoulders as an entirely different side of her surfaced. Her smile fell away as her silvery-blue eyes pierced mine, hard determination filling their depths. "There's no safer place to do this, nor a more essential time. This room was built for you, for this precise purpose, and I'm here to protect you and the rest of our territory should your practice go awry. If you *do* manage to create a rift, I'll surround it in a case of crystal until you can properly close it again."

"You don't understand," I argued. "Anything could happen. I don't know what might try to slip through."

Lana smiled wryly. "I'm a big girl, Princess. I can defend myself."

"Call me princess again, and the only thing you'll have to defend yourself from is *me*," I grumbled before turning away, ignoring her retaliatory laughter.

Out of the corner of my eye, I watch her gesture towards the belly of the room, urging me into action. *Right,* I told myself. *Just open a rift. It should be simple. I've done this once before, down in that river—without knowing what the fuck I was doing, but it still counts. If I can do it without thinking, I can do it again now.*

As I stared across the room, though, my body locked up.

How?

I raised my hands in front of me, palms burning. My vision blurred as my flames poured into the air like billowing smoke. I willed my fire to break through the atmosphere, and my flames licked and spat wildly, trying to obey my wishes but not quite succeeding. I leaned into the flames until sweat gathered on my skin. Still, the atmosphere remained in one piece.

With a growl of frustration, I dropped my arms, and my fire evaporated.

I wiped away the sweat on my brow and paced towards the nearest wall. The crystal was ice cold, and I sighed in relief as its chill crept towards me, soothing my overheated skin.

Lana leaned against the opposite wall. "I thought you had done this before?"

I spun on her. "Not on purpose, and your commentary isn't helping me."

"It helps *me*." She crossed her arms with a vicious grin. "What—would you rather I judge you silently? Like some kind of coward?"

No, I'd rather have Lee in this room with me, but that's not an option.

"Yes," I bit out. "In fact, I'd like you to turn around."

She piqued a brow. "What?"

I glared at her and circled a finger in the air.

Lana's eyes flicked towards the ceiling, but she slowly turned so she was facing the wall. Her boot impatiently tapped the floor.

As I returned to my position in the middle of the room, I took a deep breath and let my eyes flutter shut. I could do this. I just had to get out of my own head long enough to make it happen. Lee's words drifted through my mind. *It's not just within you. It is you.*

The unknowable depths of my power swirled in my veins, a thick, inky blood. That piece of darkness was always present, always lurking and watching, waiting for me to tug it into the light so that it might finally see me and I would see it.

Come to me, I said to it. *Cut your way out and bleed from me if you must.*

When I tore that rift open down in the river, I had felt trapped. I'd needed an escape. So I tapped into that moment again and held onto it, that feeling of desperation and scorn, of *loneliness.*

That ball of anger surfaced again, and I let it erupt.

More than flame ripped its way out of my body. The magic snapped a little piece of me with it, and I screamed in agony. The pain was everywhere, like burning pokers impaling me from the inside out. I forced my eyes open, though, because I had to know.

There, in front of my outstretched hands, a rift the length of my forearm rippled into existence.

I heard Lana gasp behind me. "Mother Divine." I saw her ambling toward the rift, her eyes wide and her delicate jaw slack. She studied it without blinking, stretching a hand toward it.

I lurched forward, seizing her arm to drag her away. "You touch that, and you'll suffocate to death in another world."

Lana looked at me, the pink flush draining from her cheeks.

Before she could say a word in reply, the rift shuddered, and a horrific moan filled the room as a black mass crawled through the lips of the world toward us.

Lana stumbled back but wasted no time summoning panes of crystal up out of the floor and the walls, trapping the sutilis in a heartbeat. Luckily, the rift I'd created was small. Most of the creature's body was still stuck on the other side. I could see the dark outline of it moving on the other side of the crystal, though, as its head jerked from side to side.

Muffled clicking echoed through the room around us.

An inaudible screech radiated through my head, and my knees buckled. I collapsed, clutching my scalp as a thousand overlapping voices filled my mind. I grappled with my defenses, sifting through water after spiritual water. I needed to break their connection to my mind, but I heard *his* voice before I could find their stream.

We're coming for you, little one. So close now, we can practically taste your flesh. Your little pet cannot hide you. An ice spirit and its spawn is no obstacle for us.

They knew where I was. It couldn't come here, where everyone I cared about would be. I staggered back to my feet and lifted my palms in front of me. "Let it out," I shouted.

Lana looked between me and the rift, suspicion tainting her stare. "It was in your head just now, wasn't it? Is it there still?"

My angry eyes flashed to hers, and she fell back a step. "As your queen, I'm ordering you to drop the fucking crystal," I growled, my hands encapsulated in ebony fire. *"Do it."*

Her brow slanted in fear, but the crystal obediently slid away.

I slammed the full strength of my flame into the rift, allowing the gateway to seal around the sutilis' rotting abdomen. Black blood erupted from its stomach as it was quickly sliced in two. The voices in the back of my mind faded as the atmosphere sealed, and the sutilis' upper body fell in an oozing heap on the crystal floor.

My mind went eerily silent.

"There," I choked out. "Now let me out of this goddess-damned cage."

I stalked toward the designated wall, but the exit panel didn't move. When I twisted to look at Lana over my shoulder, she was glaring at me, her arms folded over her chest. Fear and defiance waged war in her eyes.

"You will never be my queen, Sia."

I was too surprised to be angry, but I was alive enough to be hurt. "I get it, Lana. You hate me. I'm not particularly fond of you either right at this moment, so if you intend to be a pain in my ass the entire day, then you can leave me alone. I'll ask Gus to keep me company instead."

Something dark and unfamiliar flashed across her face.

Then, she composed herself with a wicked smile. "Oh, dear," she crooned. "Did I forget to mention that Gus accompanied Lee this morning?"

My entire body recoiled. "What?"

"You're stuck with me," she said emphatically. "Lee and Gus are preoccupied with each other."

She was taunting me, but I didn't indulge her cruelty. I was more concerned with the details of this little trip.

"Why would he ask Gus to accompany him on a township

visit?" I pressed. "You're his Hand. Aren't *you* the one who should parlay with the nobles on his behalf?"

Lana waved a hand in dismissal, but I caught the look in her eyes, that briefest flash of panic. She could sense that I was on to her. "Those two have always run around the territory together. If we're lucky, they'll only be gone for a night. Considering the circumstances, though, it could be a few days. Lee looked like he had some steam to burn off." She had done her best to make her insinuation convincing, but there was no reason to doubt my husband's relationship with Gus. After what Gus confessed to me, I trusted him. I trusted both of them.

"Stop baiting me," I said, crossing the room to her.

"Why?" She folded her arms over her chest, smirking, believing she'd gotten under my skin. The truth was, she had, just not for the reason she'd intended. "Don't tell me you're *jealous*, Sia. We both know you have no qualms with sharing your marital bed."

"What aren't you telling me?" I demanded. I kept advancing on her until I was a mere breath away.

She leaned back, squinting at me. "I have no idea what you mean."

"Yes, you do."

Lana huffed a sharp laugh and marched toward the wall, waving a hand to part the crystal doorway.

As she passed by me, I grabbed her arm. "You're lying, and I want to know why. What's going on? Where is my husband?"

"Husband?" She scoffed, wrenching her elbow out of my grip. "That's bold of you."

"That's what he is to me," I snarled, stepping into her. "He's more than that, actually, and I won't allow the bond we share to be disrespected by *anyone*. You may be his family, but he is my heart. He belongs to me. So either you tell me where my husband is now, or I'll tear through this city looking for someone who will, and I can promise you, I won't be gentle about it."

Lana's throat bobbed as her expression lost its humor. She knew that I'd caught her, and I wouldn't let go until she told me the truth. "He didn't want me to tell you, Sia, just in case they…"

"In case they what?" I growled.

She hesitated, her eyes shining, but then she exhaled shakily and confessed, "In case they lost the coast to the sutilus."

CHAPTER 48

The sutilus were invading the southern coast of the Halcyon territory, and Lee chose *not* to tell me. He chose to fly down there with Gus and a hundred soldiers while I slept alone in his mother's library. And to top it all off, he'd told Lana to *lie to me*.

If he didn't get injured on the battlefield, I was going to maim him myself.

The last update from the field informed us that the battle wasn't going well. We'd experienced a handful of deaths and over two dozen wounded. So, here I was, arriving with a hundred more troops and the thirst for vengeance.

Lana helped me gather the soldiers after I told her I'd be coming here, either with the needed reinforcements or not. She was quiet at my side, observant. She didn't voice any antagonizing comments on our flight here, surprisingly.

Lee's recruit, Clayfield, accompanied us as well.

He was agreeable company, mostly silent, and I was glad for that. It gave me time to think of the thousand different things I might say to Lee once I found him.

I could handle his bad moods.

I could handle his silence. What I couldn't handle was feeling excluded from his court, excluded from his territory. This wasn't what he'd promised me.

The outpost camp in the southern key was teeming with nervous bodies. Several citizens, mostly seraphim, ran from tent to tent to assist with the dying and injured soldiers. The troops didn't have enough hands to spare. I directed a handful of our men to the medic tents and continued toward the battlefield.

Blood stained the snow underfoot and the canvas tents to either side of us.

The battlefield was just beyond the outpost camp, down a steep hill, forming a writhing sea of black mold and white wings as the terrain shifted from earth to sand. Farther down, where the sand darkened, a thick barrier of ice had been erected, holding back the ocean's waves. Several seraphim were flying above the barrier, building it while fighting back the troops of sutilus who were trying to climb over or shatter their way through the ice.

The barrier stretched down the coast. Lee would be at the very front, working to secure the coastline. I'd have to fight my way to him.

I turned to Lana, Clayfield, and our troops. "Move in slowly," I ordered. "Clear the ground as you go. Strike the head or heart. Anything less will only aggravate them, and they might try to swarm you, so stay in groups. Don't let them get you alone."

Clayfield pounded a fist over his heart as he bowed. "As you command, my Queen."

Queen.

I wasn't used to hearing that, but those loyal to Lee had been addressing me as such all afternoon, just like Lee was their King. In their eyes, Godfrey was already dead—and he would be soon enough.

"I'm coming with you," Lana interjected, stepping towards me.

I studied her carefully. There was no hint of friction between us right now. Her eyes were wide and honest, and though she hadn't asked for permission, I saw she was looking for it. Whether she'd promised Lee she wouldn't leave me alone or not, I could tell she was making this decision for herself. She *wanted* to stay with me.

Nodding, I turned back to the battlefield.

We took to the sky together, flying high to see more of the field. Ice barricades dappled the snowy hillside to protect higher ground. A handful of archers took cover in the pines, flying from bough to bough, taking out sutilus that dared make a run past our troops for the hill. So far, it looked like none of them had gotten closer than a foot up the steep slope.

We left behind the forest canopy, gliding down the hillside, coasting close enough to the ground to smell the blood and iron as the sounds of battle consumed us.

Grunts of pain and clashing metal and that *clicking*. Their *laughing*.

The sutilus outnumbered us, but Lee's troops were holding the line. As we neared the coast, the sky got more crowded. Several archers were darting above the field, shooting arrows that glittered with a silvery sheen. A brief moment of observation revealed that the arrows were charmed; they bucked and weaved between bodies to hit the intended targets.

One arrow hit a giant, lumbering sutilis—a beast similar to the one Lee and I had faced in the human city on the other side of the country, with several limbs and weeping pustules of bloody ooze. Magic flashed as the sharp head of the arrow sank into the creature's neck. Frost spread outward from the wound, ice solidifying in its veins and seizing its limbs. It went down hard in the snow, screeching, and a handful of seraphim raced in to finish it off.

I could see another beast just like it pounding through the ice barrier out in the ocean, and three others wrought destruction farther ahead on the battlefield.

The sutilus had been strategic with their attack. A storm was brewing on the horizon, and the sun couldn't break through the clouds; this weather was the perfect cover. I could only assume that the Halcyon's gift for manipulating snowstorms didn't work so well at driving them away, at least not here. The ocean was cold too, and the sutilus thrived in that.

Every sutilis soldier crawling out of the waves was partially frozen already.

I glanced over at Lana, catching her eye before motioning toward the battlefield, where the three giant sutilus were working together to push their way through our troops. A handful of Halcyon already lay dead around them.

We dove into the field together, pulling our blades before we threw ourselves into the fray.

Lana joined the soldiers teaming up against the giant sutilis on our left, and I surged for the one in the middle. This beast didn't have near as many soldiers crowding it. Its position in the center provided it enough cover to act as a battering ram, sweeping at soldier after soldier with multiple arms.

I set my blades ablaze and launched at it.

Unfortunately, the lack of crowding also allowed it to see me coming. Two of its swollen, oozing hands swiped at me. I dodged the first, but the second hit my shoulder. Pain erupted through my back and arm. It latched a hand onto my hip and tried to wrench me to the side, to throw me off balance and trample me like it had so many others, but I twisted in its grip and brought my blade down on the thick, mold-speckled fingers.

Stitches ripped and flesh split, and I was sprayed with

putrid black blood as its fingers fell to the ocean of corpses underfoot.

I sensed more than saw its shift in balance, warning me of its intention.

Its four arms wrapped around me in an attempt to pin my body, to crush me, but I leapt into the sky, and it grasped at empty air instead as I buried both of my blades into its blood-shot eyes. The creature screeched, its arms lifting to bat at me. It was blind now, though, and I dodged its wild swinging easily.

I pushed my blades deeper until, finally, I hit something vital, and it dropped with a whining click.

As I wrenched my blades free from the giant's deformed skull, something akin to a memory flashed across my mind.

I saw Lana's face.

The powerful swing of her sword.

A massive hand wrapping around her face and crushing her head.

Spinning on my heel, I found Lana bearing down on the giant sutilis to my right. She was still alive, attacking the beast before her with reckless abandon, diving in as the other soldiers drew back, braving each wild swing of the monster's limbs.

I knew what the sutilis planned on doing to her, how it would trap and kill her. Impossibly, *I knew.*

I managed to rip one of my blades free before I lurched toward them, catching the arm careening for her face with my dagger. Blood gushed in her face, but at least her life was spared.

Having taken the giant by surprise, I drove my blazing blade into its chest and saw another flash of memory, the blur of fading vision. *Goddess Beside Me.* I was reading the monster's mind. That was how I had seen what it wanted to do to Lana. I was still connected to the hive mind; I hadn't fully severed my connection to them back at Sumner House.

My head spun with surprise and panic, but I quieted those thoughts long enough to force my flame into the giant's body as the soldiers around me kept its arms away from me. I spread my heat into its heart, and it fell with another blood-curdling screech.

I ignored Lana, who watched with bewildered eyes as I removed my blade from the smoking, burnt chest and returned to the first giant to retrieve my other dagger.

The third giant was already being overwhelmed by the dozen or so soldiers. When it fell, they took great pleasure in tearing it apart, like wolves to a meal, taking vengeance for their fallen brothers the only way they could.

I couldn't quite believe it.

I tapped into the hive mind, and they didn't seem to notice. Maybe the sutilus assumed I would have cut off our connection already. If they were truly clueless, then that gave us an advantage, at least until they noticed. I would have to trespass as delicately as possible.

My gaze caught on piles of flesh as I moved forward to step over them, but I paused when I saw the corpses shifting.

There was something still alive down there, and it wasn't the monsters that just fell. I crouched to look closer. I saw armor, a bloody white wing flexing weakly. I lifted my head and scanned the field, my stomach dropping when I saw the troops moving on without us, drawn to the fighting a few yards ahead.

"*Stop!*" I shouted, making the soldiers closest to us pause and turn.

I stowed my blades and started digging through the mass of blood and soft, rotting skin. "I need two soldiers over here *now*," I commanded.

Two large bodies crowded in next to me and helped me

displace the body parts. Slowly, an injured seraph was revealed to us—a broken arm, dented chest plate, and a deep gash weeping on the back of his neck.

I reached for him, firmly grasping the soldier's broad white wings to keep them stable, helping him wiggle his way out. He had barely freed his upper body when he collapsed again, his eyes sliding closed.

"Thank the Goddess, his wings are intact." I looked at the soldiers across from me, grappling with that sly connection in my mind. The sutilus were losing their hold on the shore. The ice barrier was working. They weren't sure what to do next. "I want you two to fly your brother-in-arms back to camp. On your way back, find the additional troops we brought with us—they're moving slowly up the field. I want you to guide them towards the front lines. We need to move in before we lose the advantage."

They agreed without argument and pulled their fellow soldier into their arms. Together, they lifted him into the sky.

"Thank you for saving me back there," Lana gasped out once the injured seraph was well on his way back to camp. I kept watch to make sure the three of them would make it, Lana still trembling with adrenaline.

"Don't mention it," I murmured. "You would have done the same for me, right?"

A flash of guilt darkened Lana's features as she met my gaze. I let her see that I truly believed that. I knew she didn't trust me yet, but she did care for her cousin, and that care extended to me now, because Lee was mine and I was his.

"Yes," she whispered.

Even if it would have been a half-hearted admission before today, it wasn't at this moment. She looked around at the pools of sludge and black guts around us, at a loss for further words. Then, her gaze caught on some of the fighting up ahead.

I stretched my wings, beating them to slowly lift off the ground. "You coming?"

Shaking her head, she gripped her sword a little tighter and turned to face me. "I think I'm going to assist the troops down here. Find Lee. Show him exactly how wrong he was to keep you from this."

I smirked. "That was the plan."

Before I could take off, Lana staggered forward. "And Sia?" When I met her stare, she smiled faintly. "I was wrong too. I think you'll make a wonderful queen."

I nodded, swallowing the emotion that rose to choke me. "I hope so."

Then, I lifted away from the battlefield before she could say anything else. Lana had softened considerably toward me over the last few hours, but it was a profound shock to hear her offer that crumb of acceptance.

I ascended a couple hundred feet and surveyed the ice wall. They were nearly finished with it. As I drifted toward the ocean, I caught my first glimpse of a sutilis in the air.

In. The. Air.

It was flying with stolen Stymphalian wings, the metal feathers glinting through the gloomy sky as it dove toward the field, glowing daggers brandished. The monster was intercepted immediately by a burly, dark-haired male with gray wings.

As the seraph plunged his sword through the sutilis' stomach, brown eyes met mine over the creature's stitched-together wing.

Gus.

Surprise registered on his face before he wrenched the sutilis up and flipped it around using the hilt of his sword. Then, Gus' gloved hands grasped the peaks of the Stymphalian wings and his foot landed in the center of the creature's back. He tore open the stitches holding the two together.

Gus moved the twitching wings into one hand and leaned around the sutilis' body to pull his sword free. He swept his blade between the sutilis and the wings, severing the rest of the stitches, and the creature plummeted to the ground.

I scanned the rest of the sky, palming my blades.

There were only a handful of other sutilus with stolen wings, but they were *meteoric*, too quick to track for more than a few seconds at a time.

"Sia!" Gus gingerly grabbed my elbow and turned me toward him.

His wings were beating hard behind him, forcing an uncomfortably cool breeze to swirl around us. He was still clutching the Stymphalian wings—he probably wanted to dispense with them properly. He didn't want to drop them where they could be taken again.

"As good as it is to see you, my Queen, I don't think Lee is going to like that you're here."

"Good," I snapped. "I'll have the advantage over him, then."

"Don't kill him right now, Sia." His tone was teasing, but the words were laced with fear. He knew what Lee had done. He knew his king deserved my ire. "Wait until tomorrow, I'm begging you. Or at least another few hours, until reinforcements get here."

I pulled away with a sigh. "I'm angry, not utterly raving mad."

"And Goddess knows we're thankful for that."

"*Yet,*" I added under my breath, ignoring Gus' amused smile as I glared into the sky behind him. "Where is he?"

Gus pointed to the west side of the beach. "Attempting to secure Marming Cliffs. Once the ice blockade extends to the bluff, we'll have the entire southern edge of the coast under control. The sutilus are fighting harder down there, though. It's not pretty."

"And here I was, hoping for a pretty battlefield," I replied dryly. "You said reinforcements are coming? Beyond our own army, I hope? Abaddon barely permitted the troops I brought here."

"Yes. The Quintessentials have agreed to run a few Stymphalian over here. They're going to help us raise a more permanent barrier along this coast, and then we'll continue north if we must. Who knows where they'll attack next."

"Knowing our luck, it'll be the capital."

He shook his head as he brushed past me, eyes on the outpost. "Don't worry. We're prepared for that. Go on. They could use your flame down at the bluff. Better hurry, though, before the word of your arrival spreads and you lose the element of surprise against your heart-mate."

Heart-mate.

And yet, he'd betrayed my heart today.

I kept to the shore side of the wall, watching ice stretch to my left and the battle rage below me. When I saw an opportunity to assist down in the field, I took it. With a sweep of my hand, I set fire to several sutilus, my black flames licking at their skin, but they were too wet and cold for my fire to effectively devour them, nothing substantial for my heat to cling to. Snow fell from the sky, surrounding me, chilling me to the bone.

That weakness I'd felt before on my first day in this territory returned, tickling menacingly across my back.

So I summoned more heat into my veins, letting it crest and crash through my limbs. I pulled my blades out, reserving my magic for the internal hearth I had blazing while slicing a path through the wet sand bank. Lee's soldiers saw me, shouting my name, both in shock and in greeting, but I didn't linger long enough to acknowledge any of them in return. I was lost to the violence, to my search.

When I finally laid eyes on Lee, I was rising out of the fray.

Lee flew back and forth between the cliffside and the ice barrier, wielding his magic in a frenzy. He threw waves of snow down the craggy bluff, lulling the sutilus climbing it into a dead sleep before they fell to the jagged shallows below. At the same time, he ripped hail from the clouds—fist-sized balls of ice, pelting the battlefield below him.

Then, I saw a winged sutilis creep up behind him, but Lee was too distracted to notice.

"TURN AROUND," I screamed.

There was no way he could have heard me. I was too far away, and there was too much between us, but Lee turned around anyway, as if he had heard me scream.

He caught the sutilis' blade with his own. The creature lashed out again, and its fist collided with the side of Lee's face. I felt the sharp blow to my cheek, but I didn't react. I didn't flinch or blink or *breathe*. The pain was distant, barely more than a flickering thought. I beat my wings faster, eager to reach him, but a wind smelling of pine and mint slammed into me.

My body dropped a few feet as I wrestled with a sudden wave of weakness.

He was projecting his magic out in some kind of energy shield. Everything that crossed into it had to fight back crippling exhaustion or fall to the field. The sutilis that just hit Lee was plummeting now, its coppery wings freshly severed from its body.

"Reel it in!" I seethed through my teeth, hesitating mid-air as my head started throbbing.

Almost instantly, the weakness in my body receded.

As I launched forward again, I saw Lee diving for the shore. He threw a large sheet of sharp ice formations across the shallows, slowing the next wave of ocean and sutilus as the water formed spikes and impaled them. He tossed a blanket of slumber on top so they were swept back out with the tide.

Then, he worked his way inland, taking on the next sutilus troops alone.

Curling my lip in annoyance, I plowed through a dozen of the sutilus in front of him with a ribbon of obsidian flames.

Lee twisted around then, his jaw slackening as he saw me flying toward him, diving down on his other side and raining fire down on the sutilus pouring in through the break in the ice barrier. My heart-mate immediately fell into place beside me, and we turned our attention to the gap slowly closing in toward the cliffs.

Even more sutilus were pouring through now. They could see their window of opportunity closing, fighting with reckless desperation. They left themselves vulnerable as they overran the shoreline, but there were so many of them, it was like our soldiers were barely making any difference at all.

I wasn't doing much better.

My flame wasn't as effective here, not on this coast, and the sutilus were resistant enough to the cold that the Halcyon had to kill them with their blades.

This wasn't working. We needed a weapon with greater reach, something that would drive them back into the ocean long enough for reinforcements to arrive.

If only the clouds weren't blocking the sun. It hadn't set yet, if the internal clock I'd developed in the gnashing forest could still be trusted.

Wait...

I gasped for a breath, startled by the sudden idea.

The clouds.

Halcyon magic couldn't drive the storm away, but the

clouds could be evaporated by heat. Thinned, at the very least.

I flew up into the dark clouds before I could talk myself out of it. Lee called after me, his wings beating the air behind me. Swirling dark mist enveloped me, and the cold humidity hurtled down my throat. It was as dark and hollow as the Halcyon palace in this cloud. I paused in the center and extended my palms to either side of my body, dragging the hearth under my skin up to the surface.

I pushed my magic out, subjecting my body to the brutal conditions.

Pillars of ebony fire erupted from my hands, devouring the wet air, yard after yard of darkness. Every place my flame touched, the cloud matter released its weight, and as rain fell from the sky, the mist lightened.

Lee gasped behind me, but I didn't turn away from my task.

As the cloud unraveled, I felt the sun prickle against my back and wings. Below, a mile of battlefield was illuminated. I shuddered in relief then redirected my flames to an expanse of cloud behind me, trying to blast away the expanse shielding the gap. With all the Halcyon present, the sunlight wouldn't be enough to wreck the ice barrier, but it would weaken the sutilus.

I flew higher so more of the sun's heat was soaking into my skin. It seemed to energize my flame like a power source, its heat becoming my own.

Lee cursed beside me, and I glanced over quick enough to follow his line of sight.

A handful of winged sutilus were flying toward us, their lips peeled back in permanent smiles.

Lee unsheathed his sword. "Just keep blazing, darling. Don't watch."

Then, he dove beneath the mist.

Fear slithered down my spine. *Don't watch?* He didn't want me to watch in case he got hurt and I felt it. Five sutilis. He could deal with five sutilis; I'd seen him do it before. Why didn't he want me to watch?

Fuck him, I'll watch if I want to.

As I glanced down, I was reminded of how fast the sutilis with wings were as Lee collided with one of them. The creature broke free of Lee's attack and darted behind him to attempt to get its blade on his throat, but Lee dematerialized, appearing at its back and beheading the sutilis in one, smooth slice. He flipped backwards without a moment to spare, engaging the next sutilis as it arrived.

Panic seized my chest.

Lee had been fighting too long now, even his strongest gifts had to be running weak.

Another two sutilis were flying up behind him, so I removed a palm from the cloud and swept the living pillar of fire down on them. The winged sutilus weren't as wet as their kin below, so my flames caught on their stolen wings and they *burned.*

They fell from the sky, screeching.

Lee glared up at me as he split the sutilis in front of him in half then turned to the last creature hovering below him.

Don't tell me what to fucking do, I said into his mind.

I returned both my hands to the sky, watching as the sun's light crept toward the ice barrier. The gap was nearly closed now. All the soldiers farther up on the shore were running in to assist—the sutilis there had been weakened by the sun, quickly eliminated.

My plan was working. *It was fucking working.*

I leaned into my reserves of power, draining myself entirely. Circlets of amber flickered faintly around the crown of my head. My halo was weakened by these temperatures, but near-blinding all the same.

The sun alone kept me warm enough to keep burning.

As the last few inches of cloud evaporated, the ice barrier below was plunged into sunlight.

I swayed in midair, my wings barely keeping me upright, my head swimming with lightheadedness as I watched the gap in the ice close. It finally crawled onto the side of the cliff, and the orders sweeping through the sutilus' hive mind warmed my whole body.

"They're retreating," I whispered. "They're admitting defeat."

Lee's hand appeared around my upper arm, and I was too dizzy to fight him as he guided me back to the ground.

CHAPTER 49

As we landed, the soldiers who weren't maintaining the ice barrier rushed in to meet us. They greeted us with low bows and victorious smiles, speaking our names with reverence.

Unable to help myself, I reached out and touched them as we marched through, brief, comforting squeezes on their arms and hands. They clearly weren't used to such affection, especially from royalty, because their eyes widened and only a few of them recovered in time to return my touches before I was moving on.

I told them how well they did. I told them that I was proud of them, because it was true.

Lee glanced at me from the corner of his eye, watching me interact with his men, his hand holding my elbow as we traversed the battlefield.

When we finally reached the hill, he let go of me, and we flew to the peak, where many of the injured soldiers were already gathered—they'd been watching the battle. Other soldiers were following us back to the outpost, but they gave us space as we headed toward the gates, enough space for Lee to whisper, "You shouldn't have come here, Sia."

I scoffed, looking over at him in disbelief. I couldn't believe he was still of the opinion that he didn't need me here. He clearly *had* needed me. "No. *You* shouldn't have left me in the dark."

His jaw feathered, his every step stiff. "I have responsibilities, wife."

The way he said that made my toes curl. *Damn him.*

"*We* have responsibilities," I corrected him. I matched my stride with his, jogging to keep up with his brisk pace.

"I didn't want to be distracted by you," he growled. My skin started crawling. *How could he say that?* "Now, I'm going to accompany you back home, because, apparently, I can't trust my Hand to watch over you."

He refused to meet my gaze, even though I was tailing him close enough that our wings brushed.

"I don't need to be watched over. I need to be *included*," I argued. "You had no right to lie to me, and you certainly can't force me to leave now. Just try it. I'll burn the carriage to ash before we even leave the ground."

"The barrier is complete," Lee murmured. "There's no reason to stay here, but fine, go and frolic in that goddess-damned graveyard if you want. I'm heading back home."

I tripped to a halt and wrenched my arm away from him, trembling with rage. Why was he acting like this? This wasn't like him. I was ending this newest mood swing right now, before my head exploded.

"*Look at me*," I screamed.

Lee turned to face me, his blue eyes wide and pulsing with a faint glow. His gaze slid to the soldiers around us who had stopped to stare at me, at *us*. "This is hardly the place, Sia. Come along. We'll talk at home."

Panic wrapped around my spine, spurring an icy shock up the nape of my neck.

I knew those words. I knew that look in his eyes. It was the same look my father used to give me when he silenced me with lies and shame. I wouldn't go back to that place, and I sure as fuck wouldn't let Lee be the one to put me there.

We were different. He was fucking *different*.

Before I even realized what I was doing, my daggers were unsheathed, and I was advancing on him. *If I have to force you to listen, so be it.*

Lee gave a subtle shake of his head, but my fury was beyond pacifying.

When he realized I wasn't going to stop, he drew his sword, continuing to backpedal slowly as he whispered my name.

"I warned you," I growled. "I *told* you it would come to blows between us."

I launched myself at him, swiping with my left hand first. He leaned back to dodge my dagger, using his sword to knock the blade down, but I parried forward again, slashing with my right before he could balance himself, and his free hand caught my wrist, just like I knew he would.

Whipping around so my back was flush with his side, I jabbed my unrestrained elbow into a soft spot underneath his ribs.

A soft grunt hit my ears as he bowed at the waist, and his grip on my wrist loosened enough to rip free. Without hesitation, I flipped back around and kicked him in the stomach, knocking him flat on his ass in the snow.

I was still seething, but I backed away a couple steps.

"Get up," I snarled.

It was at that moment I realized a few soldiers had drawn their blades. They were crowding in on me, preparing to seize me.

Lee waved them away. "No. Leave her to me," he rasped.

"You sure about that?" I sneered. "You had no problem pawning me off this morning. You lied to me. You kept me in the dark *again*. I thought you were done doing that."

He pushed himself back to his feet and raised his sword, his arm trembling. "I was only trying to protect you, Sia. You know that."

"I don't know *anything*," I cried. "That's the problem. You told me we were equals, but do you actually believe that? Because the male who left me behind today isn't doing a great job of proving it. I don't feel like an equal right now. I feel like nothing. You made me feel like nothing."

His jaw clenched in frustration, even as a note of inky guilt vibrated across our heart bond.

"Was any of it real?" I whispered, softly enough that only he could hear it.

Lee's eyes shuttered, but he didn't respond.

The silence was too great, too deafening, so I surged forward and crashed my blades against his, forcing him to retreat as I poured every last ounce of strength into the assault.

I was half out of my mind.

My vision blurred, funneling, and I wasn't entirely in control of my decisions. My instincts had taken over. Every clash of our blades was muffled. My limbs were numb. It felt like my mind was submerged under water, suspended in place as my body shimmered like sunlight above the surface, elusive and distant.

It gave me an edge I'd never had before.

Lee was unsettled by it—my wild anger. By the time my mind broke the surface, Lee's sword was flying out of his hand. It landed in the snow in the same moment my daggers wrapped around his neck, one on his throat and the other at the nape of his neck. He was trapped. The position pressed me right up against his chest, which was heaving with sharp, ragged breaths.

I heard the crunching of snow behind us, and my heart kicked against my ribs. The soldiers were moving in again.

Lee lifted his hands in surrender before his gaze flicked to the men behind me, and he shook his head. "Don't touch her." Despite the blade against his throat, a glimmer of pride sparkled in his eyes.

Then he turned that glittering gaze on me. "It was real," he whispered. "All of it."

I ignored the urge to lean in and lick his lips, the urge to press my blade harder against his skin until he bled. It was disorienting, my warring desires—love and violence, passion and fear. "How could you leave and not tell me the truth about where you were going, what you were doing?" I demanded breathlessly. "You could have *died* today. Why didn't you ask me to fight beside you?"

His lips pressed together. "Because," he murmured, "you have a family to comfort you should I die, Sia." His words swirled between us, his hot breath caressing my lips. "I didn't want you to see my pain. I didn't want you to feel it."

"You don't get to make that choice for me," I whispered angrily. "I have just as much right to protect you as you do for me. *You* are my family, and I would take all your pain if it meant you would stop pushing me away."

Lee's eyes softened slightly.

"You don't understand," he pleaded, voice low and urgent. "What I did today was abhorrent. I knew it was wrong. I knew you could have helped us. Fuck, if you had been here, this battle would have been over hours ago."

My body buzzed in anticipation of what he didn't say. "You're right," I rasped. "I don't understand."

He grimaced, his eyes pinching with remorse as he leaned even closer, as his neck started bleeding and his voice dropped to a breathless rumble. "From the instant you decided to stay, you became the most important thing in my life, more important than my court and my country, and —*Goddess, spare me*—my men. I wish I could feel guilt over that, but I don't. I would sacrifice all of it for you."

My eyes started stinging. "Lee, that was never a decision you had to make. If this country is ours, then I belong to it too. This is a burden we share, always."

As my mind unfurled into his, he opened to receive me.

Lee allowed me in, allowed me to pour memories into that stream connecting us. The fear I felt on our wedding day when he pushed me away. My desperation for him on our flight home—the way I watched for him, waited for him, but was disappointed time and again. The moment I told Destin I didn't love him. *I don't want him, silly swan.* Then, my panic this morning when I realized Lee had left me behind and the angry tears I shed in the carriage on the way here. The moment on the battlefield when I'd watched him take a blow to the head, but I barely felt it. He was more important than the promise.

Because the pain I would feel because of you is nothing compared to what I feel without you, I told him.

Lee's eyes started glowing, burning with anguish. The hands he had raised drifted forward, closing in to frame my shoulders with heart-breaking gentleness. When he finally spoke, the words were barely audible, choked with emotion. "I'm sorry, Sia. I'm so sorry."

His mind opened in return.

I saw myself through his eyes, disheveled and filthy, rotten blood soaking into my leathers, but I heard his voice, too. *Beautiful,* he thought. *So beautiful.* Something in that connection between us broke, and suddenly, I was drowning in him. He was letting me in.

It wasn't memories he gave me as much as feelings.

A warmth, like whiskey burning down my throat and swirling in my belly. Filling, swelling, bursting. It overwhelmed my senses—the wholeness of that feeling. Sunlight and melted chocolate, soft flesh and the burning edge of ecstasy.

Tender, like a bruise. Like a kiss.

"I'm so sorry, darling," he repeated, his gaze dropping to my lips.

Longing swirled in his pale blue eyes, and I felt it everywhere. I wasn't sure who moved first, but suddenly, the daggers were slipping out of my hands. I let them fall to the snow as I threw my arms around Lee's neck, my lips colliding with his.

He met my kiss eagerly, our teeth crashing.

His warm tongue licked its way into my mouth, forcing my lips open with strong, deep sweeps. He grasped my hips and jerked me forward roughly, and as he pressed me up against him, he bit my lower lip.

I felt his excitement when I gasped into his mouth. Even his hard leathers couldn't hide his arousal.

He smiled against my lips, and the rest of the world fell away. This was the first kiss we'd ever chosen because of each other and not for the people around us. All my hesitation was gone. The lies I'd told myself were shattered.

I'd never felt a connection like this before, an attraction this powerful.

We were drawn together by a force greater than mere words or promises. This was magnetic, catastrophic, beyond spirits or gods, a design of the dark cosmos itself. And yet, we'd chosen each other too.

Lee's strong hands hooked under my thighs, lifting me to wrap my legs around his waist.

A shock of electricity raced up my spine as his lips slid

against mine. My stomach fluttered, alive and swarming with wild, feathery insects.

Then, I heard real wings rustling nearby, and I reluctantly peeled back.

Some of the soldiers were staring at us with wide eyes while others had turned away in respect or left us behind in this copse of trees entirely. I smiled nervously, pushing at Lee's chest so he would let me down. He did, but his arms lingered around me.

His fingers dug into my waist with a hint of possessive force.

When I peered up at him, my heart thumped a little harder, warmth swelling through my chest. His gaze was trained on my face, his eyes soft and strong jaw clenched.

I was his sky again, his prayer.

And this time, I wanted to stay there.

CHAPTER 50

I stood on a sheet of thick ice, drifting across the ocean, on and on for what felt like forever.

The water was dark blue, but luminous green foam danced across the surface, and the waves glittered a little too brightly. This was a place touched with magic, and… I had no idea how I got here. The ocean stretched before me, hazy around the edges of my vision.

I tried to take to the sky, but I realized too late that my wings were gone. I couldn't feel them folded into my back—they were just *missing*.

A soft sniffle had me spinning around, and when I saw him, I fell to my knees. Lee was sitting on the ice beside me, his face pressed into his knees. His shoulders and wings were trembling with deep sobs.

"What's wrong?" I asked, my hands sliding up his arms to the sides of his face.

He was so cold. His luminous blue eyes peered up from the cradle of his arms, paralyzing me. "I got lost. Really lost."

I shook my head, stroking his cheek with my thumb. "You're not lost. I see you."

"I'm going to disappear," he whispered. "I have to."

"You can't," I cried.

Lee dropped his eyes. "There's no stopping this."

A silvery arm erupted from the ocean and seized Lee's upper wing. He was ripped away from me in an instant, dragged down into the dark water.

"*No*," I screamed, and without thinking, I dove in after him.

As the water enveloped me, I caught a flutter of white deep below, in the darkness. I swam after it, and when I caught up with it, I saw that it was a single feather, then another, until suddenly, a dozen feathers were suspended around me, twisting through the water as I swam past them.

I had to keep going, deeper into the darkness.

A glimmer of white remained in the distance, taunting me. A slimy arm wrapped around my neck, and I knew I would never reach him.

I kicked and shoved at the body pressing into my back, but it was useless—I knew who this was, and that its imprisonment was beyond the physical. "Your world will consume him," the sutilis king warbled into my ear.

I shook my head. The water slowed my every movement, and it felt like I was suffocating—my mind seemed to believe it was underwater.

But I was dreaming. I knew that now.

The sutilis king had launched another psychic attack and stole this nightmare as the setting for it. He'd stolen my fears. How much access did he have to my mind when this happened? Could he hear my thoughts? Could he know what I know?

I needed to push him out. Now.

That stream connecting us was a glaring red mark in my mind. It emanated wrongness. I forced my flames up and out, frantically working to evaporate our connection.

Before I could sever his attachment, I heard the king's

clicking laugh. "You can push me out, but you can't escape the truth. Your little swan is going to die someday, perhaps soon. Come to me, little one, and I will teach you how to save him. I'll teach you about the gift we share."

My upper lip curled. "Not a fucking *chance*," I replied.

I ripped through our connection with the force of a volcanic explosion, my body flooding with lava and fierce black heat.

I startled awake, breathing hard as silent tears continued to stream across my temples.

We weren't in the ocean, but I could hear its waves crashing nearby—we were back at Sumner House, in bed.

Dread was a looming darkness hovering above me.

I had only a faint recollection of Lee carrying me into the house and removing the blood-soaked leathers from my body, holding me up in the shower and scrubbing the ichor from my skin. We'd both been too tired for it to feel sexual. It had been intimate, though, more intimate than any other time I'd been naked with another person. I felt safe, cared for. He carried me to bed like that, naked and damp, and then pulled me close underneath the blankets, more than comfortable with the sensation of my bare skin sliding against his.

I fell asleep nuzzling his chest.

My cheek was still pressed against his hard chest now, my hand splayed across his stomach, rising and falling with each of his breaths.

Lee was here. He was alive.

I curled my hand on top of his stomach, letting my fingernails gently scrape over his skin. His abdomen clenched and his breath stuttered, but he continued slumbering. I craned my neck to look at his face, willing his eyes to open. I didn't have the strength to wait until morning. I needed to hear his voice, feel his touch—it was the only thing that would make me feel safe again.

I knew it was selfish to wake Lee up after the day we'd had, but I could make it worthwhile for him. *With my worship.*

My fingertips glided up his abdomen, tracing the small scars peppering his skin—scars I had every intention of asking him about. I would keep track of them now, every pain he'd suffered at his father's hand.

I leaned in and pressed an open-mouthed kiss to every scar, following the path of my fingertips. When they reached the healing seam of skin over his heart, I licked it, closing my eyes to savor every detail. His minty soap. The tenderness of his flesh, the wound still pink.

His heartbeat pounded against my tongue.

Lee stirred, his brow furrowing.

Sliding my lips down his chest, I swirled my tongue around his nipple, biting it gently until his hips lifted off the bed. I kissed my way down his abdomen, which hardened as he shifted on the mattress above me. His breath was coming in shaky gasps. He was awake.

And he was watching me.

I ignored his stare a while longer and wiggled my way underneath the blanket, stroking every inch of his skin with my hands, worshiping him with soft kisses. One for every scar. One for every hurt ever given to him.

"Sia." His voice was thick with sleep. "Are you awake right now?"

"Do you want me to stop?" was all I whispered in return. *Please don't stop this,* I pleaded. *I need you more than I need air.*

I lowered my lips back to his skin, kissing his hip as I peered up through the part in the blanket. Lee's eyes shuttered, his chest expanding in great gasps.

"I want you to keep going," he admitted.

A small, relieved sigh escaped my lips, and I lowered my face to nuzzle the soft flesh between his hips, kissing down the trail of hair beneath his navel. His erection twitched against my breast, and I peeled myself away from his body, letting his cock spring free and tall.

I brushed my fingertips down his length. He was velvety-soft, large and warm in my hand. As I tightened my fingers around the base of his cock, he groaned.

"You're perfect," I told him, stroking him slowly.

Lee buried a hand in my hair and tilted my head back so he could see my face. His eyes were black, his cheeks flushed. "Open your mouth," he ordered. "Stick out your tongue."

I obeyed immediately, and he slid two long fingers down my throat until I gagged.

Lee chuckled darkly. "Are you sure you can handle my cock, darling? You're choking on just my fingers."

Would you rather I bite them off? I threw back.

He smiled at me.

I sucked on his digits, forcing my throat to relax as I swallowed, then pulled back to swirl my tongue around his fingertips. I showed him exactly how well I could *handle* him. All the while, he grinned down the length of his body at me, between the blanket and his hard abdomen.

When he opened his mouth, his voice was silk. "I love it when you act like my good girl, when you force yourself to surrender. You look so pretty sucking on my fingers."

My core clenched, the emptiness throbbing painfully.

I stroked his cock, hard and slow, twisting my palm around the head. Lee's hips twitched as he gave a guttural groan. Another stroke, and he was tugging on my hair again.

"*Open*," he growled, and I parted my lips. He withdrew his fingers, then tapped the side of my cheek, and I opened my mouth wider, sticking out my tongue and flattening it against my chin. He nodded in approval. "Now, you don't move a muscle until I tell you to, understand? You keep your mouth open, just like this."

I listened to him, and he moved my hands to his thighs.

Then, he threw the blanket off our bodies. He wrapped a hand around his erection and gave himself a few hard strokes as I watched, unblinking, in rapt awareness of the moisture beading at the tip. My mouth salivated, and because I couldn't close my mouth and swallow, spit started sliding down my chin and neck. It was slightly uncomfortable, my body thrumming in anticipation and my tongue tingling with desire, but arousal pooled heavily in my core—irrefutable evidence that whatever this was, I loved it, discomfort and all.

Lee dragged my mouth closer by the hand in my hair.

He rubbed the head of his cock over my flat tongue and groaned, his head kicking back. I huffed a quiet moan of my own as his arousal filled my senses. Salt and water, as potent as the ocean. "You have no idea how many times I've imagined coming all over this venomous tongue of yours, to make you taste what you do to me. Do you like torturing me?"

I blinked up at him, the truth radiating out of my eyes.

"I know you do," he smirked. "Go ahead. Show me how much you like it."

Wrapping my lips around the head of his cock, I sucked him hard before rolling my tongue over the tip, savoring his sap. I licked at the veined underside, massaging him with my tongue, and his head kicked against the pillow again.

"*Fucking torture,*" he moaned. "I've wanted you like this since the moment you threatened to shove tulips down my throat."

His hand tightened in my hair, pulling my head down at the same time he leaned up to watch his cock slide deep into my mouth. He was so thick that my lips burned as they stretched around him. I fought the urge to gag as he bumped the back of my throat. My eyes watered, both spit and tears dampening my cheeks as he slid out and back in, his hand guiding me into a rhythm he liked. Slow and steady, but with just enough force to convey the seriousness behind his every thrust.

There was no coming back from tonight. This would change everything, and I had known that going in. This was what I wanted. I wanted *him*.

Lee must have heard those thoughts, because his spoken reply echoed them. "Our charming little back and forth is finally coming to an end, isn't it, darling?"

I hummed around his cock, and he seethed a deep breath.

"Is your gorgeous pussy soaked for me? I want to see."

He choked me with his next thrust, his length sliding into my throat. My throat tightened around him, and he quickly pulled me off him, close to coming. He held me near enough that his cock continued to twitch against my lips.

Hungry, I stroked his swollen head with my tongue.

"Slide a hand between your legs," he commanded, his voice a rough rasp. "Fuck your fingers as I fuck your mouth. I want to feel you come."

My core clenched again, a wave of arousal heating my center, but this wasn't about my pleasure. It was about him. I was hoping it might convince him to stay, to fight, just in case that ocean tried to sink its claws into him too. Just in case what I saw hadn't been a dream.

I ignored his last demand and leaned forward to take him back into my mouth, but he stopped me with a tug on my hair. His gaze was vicious as he said, "The only way I'm coming down your throat is if you come while swallowing me down."

Pleasure swept through my body, tingling through my fingers and toes, and I felt my back arch in desperation as I whispered his name. His gaze didn't falter, though; he just stared at me with that dark need flooding his eyes, waiting for me to obey his instruction. I heard what he didn't say. Either I did what he asked, or it ended here.

I slid my hand off his thigh and down the soft curves of my body, letting my fingertips explore the wet flesh between my legs.

As my fingernails grazed the bundle of nerves there, I cried out.

I was already close to my own release, just from having him in my mouth.

Lee guided me back down over his cock, thrusting deep and slow, groaning every time he nudged the back of my throat. My core fluttered like mad. I needed something there, *lower*. Nothing would compare to the beast in my mouth, so I had to settle for a couple of my fingers, as much as I could take. I plunged deep, mirroring his thrusts as my arousal dripped down my fingers into my palm.

"Mmm," he hummed. "I can smell your arousal. So fucking sweet. Look at you, pretending to be such a good, sweet girl for me. You're a pretty liar." His hand loosened in my hair enough to grant me a response.

I pulled back far enough to whisper, "Only for you."

Lee's eyes lit up like the night sky. "Say that again."

"I'm good for you. Only you."

He nodded, his abdomen rippling with sweat-slick muscle. "Touch yourself quicker than that, Sia. I want to see you come now."

As my fingertips circled in just the right spot, Lee caught the shift in my body and picked up the pace of his thrusts. Sharper, deeper. I smiled, swallowing greedily, allowing my teeth to graze his length.

Lee seemed to like that, because his voice dropped to a honeyed growl. "*You* are perfect."

Lightning skittered across my back. Pleasure swelled outward, and my cunt clenched, milking emptiness as a cataclysmic orgasm swept through my body. The burst of pleasure blocked out Lee's release filling the back of my mouth, but I heard his roar aimed at the ceiling. I felt his magic flutter down over me.

I swallowed quickly, a triumphant smile spreading across my swollen lips as I sat up.

The entire room was dusted with a thin layer of frost. The walls. The furniture. The sheets. *Everything.* Even his skin shimmered softly.

I was the only thing left untouched by his hoarfrost, and that was only because my skin was simmering with heat.

My smile slipped when Lee's eyes opened into mine.

A wolfish smile creased his cheeks. His gaze was dominating, all-consuming. As his eyes flicked down to the mess I'd made on the sheet, my damp thighs, I knew what he wanted. He lurched forward, grabbing my ankles to yank me closer as he kneeled on the mattress.

Fear lanced through me. I'd never let anyone do this before, and he was moving too fast for my mind to process whether I wanted him to or not.

I kicked my legs out of his grip and scrambled back on the mattress, my chest caving in when I saw the confusion twist across his face. *Shit.* Dread pumped through my veins, quickening the beat of my heart. There was no meaning for it. The problem wasn't that I didn't want Lee to taste me; it was that I didn't know what to expect. This was the one part of myself I didn't share.

What if I didn't like it?

What if *he* didn't like *me?*

What if he saw all of me, down to my most hidden parts, and he finally found them lacking? I was waiting for that still, apparently. I still didn't understand how he could believe in me so deeply. Lee saw so much good in me, even when I wasn't sure I possessed it myself.

My fears were powerful enough to make me hesitate.

For the first time in my life, I didn't want to have sex just to hide from what I was really feeling. I wanted to know what I needed, what it meant. "Don't," I breathed, wrapping my arms around my knees.

Lee crawled forward, moving with diligence to show me he wasn't about to pounce.

The moonlight softened the angles of his face. His eyes held mine, the blues glittering and his pupils dilated. He gave me a tender smile as his hand wrapped around my calf. His fingers slid down and circled the inside of my ankle, soothing me.

"I only want to return this pleasure to you," he said, his tone soft and reconciliatory. "We can slow down. I'll show you how to enjoy it." Then, he leaned down and kissed the top of my foot.

He ran his nose up the inside of my leg and blew a cold torrent of air against my wet, heated skin. Fresh arousal swirled between my thighs, and my stomach flipped. I gasped for air, but my lungs were shrinking. The air refused to come.

Shuddering, I reached down and gripped Lee's shoulder, pushing him back. "I'm not ready for that. It's just… I feel like I can't breathe again. I'm sorry."

He immediately sat up, concern etching itself into his brow. As he shuffled closer, his hands framed my shoulders, squeezing gently. "Don't be sorry, Sia. It's alright. Just keep breathing, that's all I need. Can I hold you instead?"

All I could do was nod as I fell into him, my eyes prickling and throat swelling.

Lee's arms wrapped around me, spinning me so we were spooning at the wrong end of the bed. I squeezed the arm he had banded across my chest, letting my confused tears brim over. "What are you crying for?" he whispered against my temple.

I swallowed around the thick ache in my throat, slowly coaxing the words out. "They tried to take you from me, in my dream," I told him. "They drowned you and took your wings, and I couldn't save you. You left me."

He held me tighter. "I'm right here. I'm not going anywhere, my darling."

"I love it when you call me that," I murmured, nestling down.

Lee ran a hand down the length of my body, his knuckles caressing my curves, up and back down. His touch mollified me. "Good, because I love calling you that."

A mixture of mint and pine filled my senses, and my muscles finally unraveled.

CHAPTER 51

Getting a private audience with King Godfrey was surprisingly easy.

Once I figured out he had a Cockatriz healer tending to him in the castle, the pieces of my plan fell perfectly into place. The Cockatriz herself wasn't much of a barrier; she took the day off from the king's service with a smile on her face and a spring in her step.

If she realized I was lying to her, she didn't care. Even when I asked for one of her spare veils and made her swear her discretion, she didn't bat an eye.

Not that I could *see* her eyes.

Cockatriz devoured energy through their eyes. One glance, and they could suck the life out of their prey. They could devour *souls*—that was the rumor, anyway.

Needless to say, there were strict regulations concerning what Cockatriz had to wear outside of their territory and whenever they had visitors. The black veils were an essential part of that.

Now that I knew a few of the other territories' secrets,

though, I had to wonder if what I'd been told about the Cock-atriz was entirely true. Were their eyes really that dangerous? Or were the veils covering up something else altogether?

The king was undergoing frequent acupuncture, three times a week. When I saw the Cockatriz carriage flying over the city that first time, I turned to Lana for answers. With a little leading, I got her to a rant about the king's extensive servicing, down to the daily bleeds and hourly salving. They were accustomed to working around it.

For the last six days, I'd been preparing for this.

Since the invasion attempt, Lee had been pulled in for daily meetings at the palace with various nobles and officers from nearby townships, and I accompanied him. I studied the movement of the sentinels, the staff, and strategically stum-bled upon the healer's wing of the castle while they were preparing for one of the king's treatments.

Every evening, Lee and I walked down into the city for dinner, sharing a table at one of the restaurants with our court, then came home and tumbled into bed together, too worn out to do anything more than hold each other close. Every morning, though, as dawn broke on the horizon, he woke me up by playing with me. My nipples. My curves. The tender juncture of my wings. It always ended the same way— with his hand between my legs and me whispering his name as I came. Then, he would kiss my shoulder and roll out of bed before I could peel my eyes all the way open, licking my arousal off his fingers as he disappeared into the bathroom to get ready for the day. The bastard knew I was too slow at waking and too sated with pleasure to stop him.

Generous, busy bastard.

I shook my head to clear Lee from my thoughts. It was time to focus.

I quickly wiggled into the Cockatriz's robes and donned

their spare veil, moving slowly to keep the fresh green paint on my wings intact. Then, I pushed the brass cart filled with pins and salves into the king's room.

Godfrey had been stripped down and moved to a chair that held him upright by a cushion against his chest; that way, he could watch the room through the mirror across from him. His chin was propped up on a crescent rest, and his arms were stretched out above his knees. He looked more fragile without clothing.

All the skin on his body was loose, clinging to his skeleton. Open sores covered most of his back and sides, and it took all my willpower not to gag as the smell hit me, uninhibited by bandages.

"You're late," he barked when he saw me, his weak body trembling with the force of his voice.

I hummed in a sweet, complacent way as I approached with the brass cart.

I parked behind him and turned my back to him to organize my workspace. He wouldn't be able to watch me prep the needles from this angle, and with his deteriorating vision, he probably wouldn't be able to tell that I was slightly taller and curvier than his Cockatriz healer.

After opening a few salves exuding strong, medicinal odors, I started dipping the needles and diligently punctured Godfrey's back in the proper arrangement.

I'd memorized a heavy handful of acupuncture points for today's purpose.

As I worked my way to his right side, I leaned over his upper wing to riddle his shoulder with pins, and I felt a hand grasp my leg. I jumped and looked down at the bulge beneath my skirt.

"My right side needs extra attention this week," Godfrey said softly. That hand squeezed me, and I realized Godfrey had reached back under his wings to grab me. "I haven't been able to move my lower right wing since yesterday, and I need you to fix it, the way you did before."

He gathered my dark robes in his palm as his fingers ventured upward. *Oh, goddess, no.*

I smoothly slid out of his reach, biting down on a shudder.

His right wing was fading? I couldn't believe my luck. This would be easier to cover up than I'd anticipated.

The guards assigned to the doors of his room kept watch, but their eyes were distant, bored. Obviously, this wasn't the first time Godfrey had admitted to losing feeling in his wings.

I returned to work, plunging a few more needles into the flesh around the base of his wings. The exact points for each wing were fuzzy in my memory. After experimenting for a few minutes, I stepped back, gesturing for him to move.

Godfrey stared at himself in the mirror and rolled his shoulders, his brow furrowing as his stare turned into a glare. "That didn't work," he muttered. "Why isn't it working?"

I simply shook my head and stepped forward with another pin, its tip coated with an inky blue serum. With nimble fingers, I pierced the flesh directly beneath one of the purple pustules on his back, letting the inflamed skin act as a cover for the injection spot. This poison left behind a faint greenish residue under the skin, but no one would see the evidence beneath his sores.

I flicked a pin on the other side of his back to distract him from the pain, forcing his right wing to twitch ever so slightly.

"Ah! There," he gasped. "That's it. Try that again."

I watched the seconds tick by in the clock across the room, counting under my breath as I tweaked the pins in his shoulder.

After a minute and a half had passed, I backed away and grabbed the handle of the cart, walking it in front of Godfrey. I watched his eyes flick wildly over my figure. He could see that I wasn't his healer now—not that it mattered anymore.

I picked up a few more needles and bent forward, running my fingertips across his frail cheekbones under the guise of measuring his face.

"By now, you've probably realized you can no longer feel your limbs," I told him. "You cannot move. You cannot speak. There's a reason for that, but before you lose the ability to listen, I'm going to satisfy your next question. *No*, there's no way out of this. You won't be getting any better. You will never raise your hand against my husband again."

Recognition flashed in his eyes before they dilated in fear as I brought one of the needles to his face.

"I've got your attention now, don't I?" I chuckled softly, sliding the sharp tip into his forehead. "Naverum Root is a carefully guarded secret among witches, an undetectable poison. The only reason I know about the root is thanks to my mother's old flower press. She recorded several plants like that. Poisons. Psychedelics. Anything that flowered. When the tubercles of the Naverum Root mature, they bloom in clusters of delicate white flowers on a thick stalk, in case you were wondering."

His eyes were practically vibrating with terror now.

"They can be found in tree hollows," I continue airily, "if the tree is still standing. The conditions have to be just right, though. Cold and damp, with thick walls to prevent a total freeze. Hollows like that are often occupied by witches in the gnashing forest. They like to grind the Naverum Root into a paste. One drop of its poison, and they can paralyze any enemy for days."

I leaned forward to whisper my next words into his ear. "And the best part is, this *particular* poultice causes permanent damage, so even if you *were* given the chance to fully recover, you'd probably never be the same."

Straightening to my full height, I retreated around to his back and forced a few more needles into his flesh, flicking elsewhere so it would look like his body was reacting to the pins. He would continue to move until it was time for me to go, and then I would make it seem like he fell asleep during the acupuncture. For all the guards knew, I was whispering sweet nothings to him. Considering the way he felt me up when he thought I was his usual healer, that didn't seem like such an outlandish possibility, though it made my stomach turn to think about.

Godfrey must have been paying her an astronomical amount to return every week.

I stuck another poisoned needle into a boil next to the hinge of his wing, reveling in the faint hitch of his breathing—the only outward sign of his distress.

"I only have you to thank for this marvelous idea, of course. If you hadn't set me up to be poisoned at the wedding reception, I would have never thought to visit the forest reserve within your territory's boundaries. You know that patch of woods where you've forbidden all occupancy? I think that was a good move on your part. There are some *terrifying* things buried out there, your Majesty. But don't you worry." I pressed the needle in even deeper, twisting to grind his meat under my thumb. Warm satisfaction curled through my chest, and the amusement was thick in my voice as I said, "I dug them all up for you."

He was unable to move, but he could still feel the pain. He would have to suffer in silence, the way Lee had. I tore into several more boils, forcing more of the paralytic into his bloodstream as thick, green pus weeped down his back.

A needle for every scar on Lee's body, pushed deep enough to scrape bone.

Once I was finished, I sashayed back around to his front. His eyes were glassy, blinks slow, the poison finally lulling him towards sleep. I leaned down, tapping each pin in his face. "It's time to give up the spirit, Godfrey," I said darkly, so close to him that my veil brushed his cheek. "Because otherwise, you'll be living in this nightmare for the rest of your miserable existence. I will never, *ever* let you wake up."

I manipulated three of the needles protruding from his face, and King Godfrey's eyes slid shut for the final time.

After my time with Godfrey at the palace, I returned to Sumner House and bathed, scrubbing the skin of my hands and arms until they were red.

I didn't feel guilty for what I'd done to Godfrey.

I did, however, feel the stain of his continued existence lingering upon my skin.

The Nevarum Root wouldn't kill him outright. I hadn't used enough for his lungs to stop working. Whether I would achieve what I actually wanted—his surrender to The Veil— would be known in time. It had been cruel of me, inhumane, and that was precisely what he deserved. Now he would be trapped in his own head, with no sight, no feeling except for pain, only an endless void and a well of wronged phantoms to keep him company.

It might take a few days, but once he realized I was serious about never letting him wake up, he would give up the spirit. No one could survive that kind of loneliness.

After donning a lavender silk gown, I joined Erlene, Destin, and Lana in the living chamber at the heart of the house. Lana was lying upside down on the couch, her ankles crossed and resting upon the back cushion, her head hanging off the seat. She held a small string instrument, and as her fingers caressed the strings, silvery ribbons of magic twisted around them, tuning the chords. She tested the strings with a sweep of her fingertips, and a beautiful, harmonic ring echoed through the room. Her wings were splayed out underneath her, taking up most of the couch, Erlene and Destin on either side of her.

Destin jerked his hand away from the cushion next to him when he saw me enter the room, as if he had been close to—if not already—touching the edge of her wing.

That's curious.

Lana didn't seem to notice his reaction, her attention wholly absorbed by the instrument.

Erlene was beyond acting shy around Lana. The little girl wiggled around restlessly, ducking her head under and over the Halcyon's lower right wing in a fit of sheer boredom. When she saw me, she jumped out of her seat and ran to me with a big smile. "Sees!"

I swung the child up into my arms then collapsed in the chair across from Lana and Destin. For a moment, I simply savored the feel of her small body safe in my arms. She was alive. She was here. She was tracing the silver filigree sewn into my sleeve.

"It's so good to see you," I told her, holding her closer. "What have you done with your day, sweetheart?"

"Oh, lots! Daddy and I took a walk this morning while the sun was rising, and it was the most beautiful sky I'd seen yet!" I smiled at the look of joy on her face. She wasn't used to the colors of sunrise and sunset, being born and raised in the smog. She was intent on watching every single one of them now. In her unimpeachable opinion, every new sky was more beautiful than the last.

"Then Daddy helped me practice my numbers and letters,

and we played cards all afternoon." She leaned into me and whispered, "I'm so bored with cards."

She'd grown up so much since I last saw her. It seemed like years instead of months. Her voice was still sweet and warm, but the words were more distinct now.

I laughed. "I'll see about stocking the house with some other things to play with, although you could probably find plenty to do down in the city, if your father was willing to take you there."

"No," Destin said instantly, looking between the two of us with a frown.

I sighed, shaking my head. Destin, whether from bitterness or reservation, had refused to visit the city yet. I suspected that was why Lana followed him everywhere now, insulting and intimidating him in equal measure. It was as if she wanted to drive him out of the house and into the city herself. So far, he'd resisted her aggressive charm.

Erlene gave me a big smile and grabbed my hand, holding it tightly between both of hers. "What did *you* do today?"

"Oh, you know, just a bit of hunting," I said quietly, and both Lana and Destin looked at me as I smiled and added, "Don't look at me like that. I didn't *catch* anything."

They weren't convinced. I had caught something after all, and I had the wonderful mood to prove it.

Erlene's next words ripped the air from my lungs and the joy from my heart. "What were you doing with those pins? Were you sewing something?"

For a moment, I could only stare at her, my breath caught somewhere in my throat.

Then, I sensed the eyes of Lana and Destin drilling into us, and I leaned forward to whisper, "Sweetheart, how do you know about that?"

Her brow furrowed. "I saw you holding a pin."

"No, you didn't." I hadn't brought those pins into the

house. I had melted all the evidence before returning to Sumner.

"Yes, I did," she insisted. "In my head."

An ominous silence fell across the room, and my ears started ringing. "What do you mean? *When* did you see it in your head?"

She shrugged. "When I was taking a walk with Daddy."

"Fuck," Destin whispered, and we all turned to him. He slid forward in his seat, gripping the armrest so hard that his knuckles turned white. "Erlene had a moment out in the garden. She stopped moving and just stared straight ahead for a whole minute. Wasn't responding to me."

"And you waited until *now* to tell any of us about that?" I snapped, my heart racing.

Were the sutilus getting to Erlene? Had they found out about her somehow and were launching a psychic attack into the capital?

But, if this was the sutilus' doing, then why had Erlene only seen me with those pins?

The sutilus couldn't have known about the pins either.

I quieted my spiraling logic and asked Destin, "When was this?"

"A few hours ago. We left right after breakfast."

My skin tingled. That would have been before I even entered the king's bedroom. Had Erlene seen something happen *before* it happened?

"What's wrong?" Destin demanded, seeing the worry on my face.

I quickly composed myself. I couldn't be sure what this was, but I didn't want any of us to panic about it quite yet. It could be nothing, even if I had a sneaking suspicion it was *something*.

"Nothing is wrong," I told him before looking at Erlene.

"But if you have another moment like that, I want you to tell me right away."

I relaxed as her sweet face nodded in agreement, but she returned to her initial question. "What about the pins?"

I didn't relish lying to her, but it had to be done. "You're right. I was sewing."

"Sewing what?"

Shit. "Oh. Uh…" Suddenly, I couldn't think of a single thing I might sew.

She gained a glassy kind of look in her eyes and tilted her head in thought. "Was it something with feathers? Were you sewing a wing onto an angel's back?"

My mouth flapped in shock. I didn't know how to respond to any of that.

What was she talking about?

Lana seemed to pick up on my alarm and sat up, slapping Destin with the edge of her wing as she perched on the edge of the couch. The corner of Destin's mouth twitched, but he shifted in his seat, batting her away.

"You know what? You should ask Lee about his old room down the hall," she said, nodding at the corridor leading to our bedroom. "There are a few toys stowed away in there. They should be in good enough shape for Erlene to play with, as long as the moths haven't discovered them."

"Toys?" Erlene perked up.

I smiled at her. "That sounds promising, doesn't it? Shall we go hunting for them together?"

She nodded, excitement radiating out of her bright gray-blue eyes.

Relieved by the change in activity, I slid her off my lap and leapt up, sprinting into the corridor. Her little feet chased after me.

Lana's voice followed us, harboring little bite. "I said you should *ask*, you wild vultures."

I took one side of the hall and Erlene took the other. We threw open door after door, racing each other to see who would find it first. When we were nearly at the end of the corridor, I revealed a small, bright room on my side of the hall.

The marble floor was softened by a thick blue rug embroidered with silk flowers. A small wooden rocking chair sat in the corner. Childish baubles were scattered across the dresser, and a single bed was dressed in pale blue linens on the far side of the room. A shelf beside the bed was stacked with books, and a chest sat at the foot of the bed with delicate iron fastenings.

Everything was covered in a layer of dust, even the walls, but I could see all the love Elona had poured into this room. Beautiful white stenciling crawled down from the ceiling, hand-painted on top of the blue walls. The swirls reminded me of Lee's markings, and I wondered if that had been precisely his mother's inspiration.

Erlene appeared beside me, her eyes lighting up. "You found them!"

She rushed past me, immediately hopping onto a wooden horse and pretending to ride it around the room. She was then quickly distracted by a collection of delicately painted figurines lined up on the windowsill.

I followed her in, smiling as I noticed the book lying on the dresser beneath a few paper blooms. The title burned into the leather was familiar; it was a collection of fables I'd read when I was a child myself.

Erlene would love them.

From far away, I heard the front door slam and a burble of voices. Gus or Lee must have just arrived home. They'd had some business to attend to with the troops today. A great number of soldiers had been recently recruited, and more were being sent out to patrol the coast. Lee wasn't leaving even a mile of shore neglected.

Joining Erlene at the window, I picked up a figurine and went along with the game she'd contrived, content just to listen to her voice.

I kept an ear turned to the hallway, so I heard the footsteps as they approached. It was absolutely absurd that I could recognize him by his stride alone. I twisted to greet Lee with a smile, but as he appeared on the threshold, he seemed dazed and a little bit angry.

"What are you doing in here?" he demanded.

Handing the figurine to Erlene, I stood from the floor and crossed the room to Lee. His chest rose and fell in a wild rhythm, his eyes flitting around the room as if blood was dripping down the walls.

"Erlene was asking about toys," I explained gently. "Is that alright?"

His gaze finally slid to me, swimming with so much emotion that I felt myself drowning right along with him. "Is it alright that you've opened the door to my childhood room without permission?" he clarified. He didn't say it harshly, just with the brutal honesty that conveyed his unrest.

His gaze slid past me again to survey the small room; he couldn't seem to help it.

I didn't think this would upset him. He'd told Destin and Erlene that they could take anything from the house they needed. Perhaps Lana had been right, though. I should have asked first.

I touched his arm. "Lee?"

After another moment of that glacial look, the corners of his eyes softened, and he looked down at me, his gaze a little warmer. "Yes, darling, it's alright. The toys might as well be enjoyed after being shut away for so long. I just wasn't expecting..." He couldn't finish his sentence.

I wrapped my arms around his waist and held him close, nuzzling the center of his chest. "I should have asked about it."

"No," he exhaled, squeezing me tight. "You never have to ask permission to roam about your own house. Everything I have is yours. Please, don't think twice about it."

Then, he walked us into the room, keeping his arm around my waist.

"It's been decades since I was last in here," he murmured. "Everything is exactly as I remember."

I leaned back, smiling at him. "Your mother obviously loved you very much."

His eyes turned a bit misty, his smile twisting to the side in consideration. "My fondest memories took place here, in this house. In this room particularly. I hated the palace. I think that was one of the worst things my father ever did to me— taking me away from Sumner House."

"It's okay," I whispered, taking his hand and placing it over my heart. "You're home now." I smiled and rested my palm against his chest. "We all are."

Lee leaned in slowly, pressing a kiss to my cheek. "Yes, we are."

"What's in here?" Erlene's little voice called.

We both turned to her. She stood in front of the little ornate chest, her hands perched on her hips and brow furrowed in determination. She would leave no stone unturned in this room. *Adorable.*

Lee ambled across the room, kneeling beside her in front of the chest. "*This,*" he said with a secretive air, "holds the prized possessions of my youth, Miss Erlene. It's filled with treasures."

"Oo, I want to see," she squealed, bouncing on her toes.

Satisfied with her interest, Lee reached down to unlatch the chest. Erlene leaned in close, her hands cradled against her chest and eyes bulging in anticipation. As the lid lifted,

Erlene gasped. She sat down next to him and removed the first item from the chest.

"A *cloak*," she breathed. "Oh, it's so pretty, and just my size."

Erlene wrapped the pale blue material around her neck, and Lee watched with a smile trembling on his lips, his eyes welling with tears he quickly blinked away.

As Erlene plucked a wooden sword and shield from the chest, Lee started digging through the contents himself, looking for something. When Lee pulled away, he held a plump little stuffed animal in his hands. He turned to Erlene with it, and her eyes immediately latched onto the handsome little bear.

"This was my plushy," Lee explained. "He's a bit dusty and old, but there's still a lot of love left in him, I think. Perhaps you would like to take care of him for me?"

"He's precious," she gasped, taking the stuffed bear from him with gentle hands. Her fingers traced the little patches on his hands and feet, the pretty red thread sewn over his heart. "Oh, thank you. I love him! Look at his sweet ears—and his wings! Lovely..."

Lee stood, roughly rubbing his eyes to drive the tears away.

My heart ached in my chest, overfull and bursting.

"I know you'll make him very happy, Erlene," he whispered, staggering back a step. "He needs a friend like you."

I grabbed Lee's hand and pulled him into me, looping my arms around his waist.

Lee surrendered to my embrace. He held me for a long while, his face buried in the crook of my neck as his breathing slowly evened out.

Then, he lifted his head and asked, "Hungry?"

I ran a hand through his hair, slowly rubbing the strands apart to hold him close for a moment longer. "Starved," I replied.

We left Erlene alone to enjoy her new toys and donned coats before departing the house, starting the walk down into the city. Lee preferred to walk through the streets rather than fly over them. The humans appreciated that, I think because it made him seem less scary, less like a ruler and more like a protector.

I was holding my breath as he held my hand.

I'd inserted myself between him and his father after he asked me not to. My head pounded with guilt—not because of what I'd done, but because I hadn't told him yet. I still wasn't sure if I should.

The sun was setting over the city, washing the buildings in a warm, rosy hue. Storm clouds hovered in the distance, and the orange light illuminated misty fingers of rain stretching down towards the earth. Rain had been slowly dissolving the snow around here for days. The dirt and grasslands were finally visible, even if they were still mostly frozen.

"What were you and Gus arguing about when you came home?" I ventured, watching the cobblestone road in front of us.

Lee sighed, running a hand through his hair. "The physicians believe my father has entered the final stage of deterioration before his passing. He fell asleep this afternoon and has yet to wake up. Most of my father's court are accepting of this news, had been anticipating it, but a few nobles are suspicious of the circumstances."

A needling sensation swept across my back. "What do you mean?"

"Apparently, he fell asleep during a visit from his acupuncturist."

"That's not so strange, is it?" I shrugged nonchalantly, but my wings trembled. "Acupuncture can have a relaxing effect."

Lee huffed a sharp laugh. "What's strange is how the healer reacted to our letter requesting her return for questioning. She said her appointment with the king had been canceled. She couldn't even tell us who had sent her away. According to the guards, *someone* attended to my father, and they thought it had been the usual female. No one knows what to believe."

I knew it had been risky, what I did, but the uncertainties of his court were exactly what I planned to exploit.

"Well, is there any evidence of the acupuncture supplies being tampered with?" I led. "If yes, then that would validate the nobles' concerns. If not, then perhaps the healer lied. Perhaps she was frightened that our court would try to punish her for being the last physician to touch him."

He glanced at me, his eyes narrowing.

"If this *was* treason," he said slowly, "then there's no trace of it. The salves and needles left behind were clean. Godfrey's court will yank on every last thread of power within their reach before they accept succession, though. They won't give up until he's truly dead."

"Sounds like that might not be so far off," I muttered.

Half of me wished I had given Godfrey enough poison to kill him outright, to avoid this waiting, but a quick death was too good for him. I wanted him to wake and realize he couldn't open his eyes. I wanted him to try and scream, only to realize no one would ever hear him. I wanted him to feel the same helplessness he had given his son.

I wanted him to die in the throes of fear.

"You don't understand my father. I'm not entirely sure he *can* die," Lee said bitterly.

We were just about to reach the city, so I squeezed Lee's hand and tugged him to a stop. I didn't want anyone else to hear what I had to say. "He's going to die, Lee. You need to prepare yourself for that."

He searched my face, frowning. "Do you know something about what happened today?"

I hesitated, considering his reaction. I couldn't read it.

Would he be happy with me? Relieved? Or was that look on his face the beginning of a storm? Destin hadn't understood when I told him about the baron. He thought I was a monster. The way he looked at me that day haunted me, but this... well, this was far worse, what I'd done.

I'd paralyzed Lee's father. *Tortured* him.

"How would you feel if I did?" I asked.

Lee's jaw slackened, his eyes widening. "I... I don't—" he stammered, trailing off as his gaze caught on some point beyond me. He cursed under his breath then hooked a hand around my waist, pushing me behind him.

Looking up, I saw Abaddon flying toward us, his white wings stark against the fading orange sky.

I shrugged Lee off, returning to his side. "Abaddon doesn't scare me." *Not anymore.*

He landed a few yards in front of us and stalked forward with heavy feet, eyes trained on Lee. "I sent for you over an hour ago. You're needed at the palace."

Lee slid a hand to the dip of my waist and angled himself in front of me.

"Not tonight, I'm not. I'm having dinner with my wife." Warm tingles spread like wildfire under my skin. "Any round table meeting you wish to call can be left for the morning."

Abaddon blinked, surprised at first, but then he lumbered closer with a glare. "You'll return to the palace at once, Alezandral, or else—"

"Or else what?" I cut him off, smirking when all eyes flew to me. "What are *you* going to do if he says no, Abaddon? I'll remind you that the king is in no state to punish my husband, and seeing as he can't order *you* to do it either, any threats you make could be seen as treason. You're only a Hand, and your king is silent."

Abaddon's chest expanded in a deep breath, his stare blackening. His upper lip curled back, and he took slow, menacing steps toward me. Lee tried to shield me, but I pushed him away and took a step forward of my own, tilting my chin up in defiance.

"I know you're the one to blame for what happened to the king today," he growled. "You did that to him."

I smiled and ambled closer. He had nothing on me. He had nothing, and that angered him. Perhaps it frightened him too.

"Prove it," I crooned before brushing past him.

Abaddon twisted to follow me, his face screwing up in a snarl.

"Traitorous whore," he hissed, and I recoiled as his spit flecked my face.

Then, I was stumbling away as Lee grabbed the front of Abaddon's tunic and slammed his other fist into the old bat's face. Abaddon stumbled back and tripped over his feet, landing hard on the damp, stone road. He flipped over to look at us, his eyes wide and enraged.

Then, Abaddon stiffly pushed himself up and brushed the dirt off his clothes. "You'll regret that, Alezandral," he muttered, wiping at his bloody lip.

"No, I don't think I will," Lee replied, his smile arrogant. "You're lucky it was my fist and not my sword, though that will be remedied quickly if you say even one more word about my wife. And I do mean *any* word."

Abaddon opened his mouth, presumably to spit something even more vile, but a murderous fog fell across Lee's expression, and the old bat wisely changed his mind.

He turned on his heel and took to the darkening sky. As he disappeared, Lee and I both exhaled, our conjoined hands pulsing as the blood rushed back into our fingers. We'd been holding onto each other for dear life. It was heavy, the truths left unspoken between us.

I waited for him to ask the question I knew he needed to ask. After a few heartbeats, he slowly turned to face me. "Is it true?"

My throat ached too powerfully to speak. My fear was too great.

I promised I would never allow anyone to hurt you again and I meant it, I said into his mind, rubbing the side of his pointer finger with my thumb. *If I can't prevent the hurt, then I will rip penance from your enemies' flesh instead. You will not stop me, husband.*

Husband, because he needed the reminder. I had every right to protect him. He was *mine*.

A thousand emotions fluttered across Lee's face, his confusion and surprise slightly more apparent than the others. *Is he going to die because of what you did?*

I spread my wings and lifted my chin, steeling my resolve. I wouldn't apologize, because I didn't feel sorry. All I could do was hope that, underneath his shock, he felt the slightest bit grateful. *No, Lee. He deserves to die, because he's an abusive sack of shit who hurt not only you, but your mother as well. He would get rid of me too if he felt I deserved it, which he does. You know that. I know that. Now we can both rest in the fact that he will never hurt anyone ever again. When he does give up the spirit, it will be his decision, even if I had to be the one to force his hand.*

Lee's lips parted on a soft sigh as he came to terms with my confession. For a moment, I worried that he would push me away, that I had gone too far, but then a certain twinkle danced across his features, and our bond flooded with a warm, heady feeling. Adoration. Respect. And something a little more.

Lee leaned in, pressing his forehead to mine as his blue eyes burned with passion. *No, wife, I won't stop you, but I'm going to worship at your altar if it's the last thing I do. You are my life. You are my everything.*

My chest squeezed, swelling with luminous relief. He didn't think I was a monster. He understood me, wanted me, even with my darkest urges laid bare. I looked between the busy city streets and Sumner House, biting my lip. I didn't want to spend the next hour in the city. I wanted to get him alone and all to myself, as soon as possible.

"Maybe we can stay home tonight?" I asked.

"A dinner at home sounds perfect," Lee said, smiling as he brushed a strand of hair out of my eyes. "You know, if we're quick, we might be able to talk Gus into cooking for us. I saw him digging through the pantry before we left. Had the experimental look in his eye."

All at once, the seriousness of our previous conversation was forgotten. We were moving forward, together, and happiness felt more than possible.

"Oh no," I laughed.

"Oh yes." He nodded solemnly, biting back a smile. "And there's only a forty-nine percent chance that it'll be burnt."

I shook my head. "I don't know whether to place a bet or run for the hills."

Lee tugged me closer, kissing the top of my head. "It won't

be that bad. We can always recruit Destin to keep him in line. He's a bit of a hardass, isn't he?"

The idea shot across my mind like a star—Destin and Gus skirting around each other in the kitchen, knives and mortal enemies colliding—and I laughed again. "Alright," I agreed. "I'd pay good coin to see that."

He chuckled, leading me back up the road to Sumner House. His knuckles caressed sweet lines between my wings as he murmured, "We'll definitely pay for it, one way or another."

CHAPTER 54

Destin and Gus did end up making dinner for the whole house, and they worked surprisingly well together.

Gus prepared the ingredients and Destin did the cooking. Destin surprised everyone by being pleasant. The General even made him smile a few times, though I was certain Destin would deny that if I pointed it out. I caught him casting furtive glances at Lana more than a few times, so maybe she'd threatened him into submission.

We gathered around the table in Lee's office to eat, which was as close to a dining room table as the house had. I'd have to see about fixing that soon.

The office was large enough to fit us all, but it was dim. This room didn't have windows. It was four walls of floor-to-ceiling bookshelves, and the faerie orbs shone with a soft, amber glow high up on the ceiling. They were old lights, losing their luster. We lit a few candelabras and placed them along the center of the table so everyone could see each other.

By the time I'd finished with my plate, Lee and Gus had

returned to working. They discussed a new arrangement for the troops that would hopefully spare a few men on the northern coast. Lana was showing Erlene how to rub beet juice on her lips to make them red, and Destin watched on in thinly-veiled horror. Poor man probably just had his daughter's whole adolescence flash in front of his eyes.

A maid came in and cleared the plates, then brought in some pastries she had fetched from the city for us. They were still warm, the centers a creamy lemon custard.

After devouring three pastries all by herself, Erlene passed out on Destin's lap, her arms clutching Lee's old plushy bear in her sleep.

I saw Lee's gaze drift to her, his eyes warm and tender. We were all hopeless when it came to this little girl, weren't we?

Destin soon excused himself from the table, bidding us a good night before carrying his daughter to bed.

Lana moved closer to Gus once they were gone, sitting in the chair next to him and propping her head up on one hand. She did her best to act like she was listening to Lee and Gus— who were now arguing over some conflict stirring up friction among the soldiers, an unveiled affair, from the sounds of it— but I could tell she was only here because it was better than being alone in some other part of the house.

After another few minutes of listening to them, my foot started tapping. Every heartbeat thumped heavily between my ears. I had far too much energy, with nowhere to put it.

Lee noticed and shot me an apologetic grin, reaching across the corner of the birchwood table to cover my hand with his own. "My apologies, darling."

I smiled in return, turning my palm over to squeeze his fingers. "It's alright. I'd rather talk about this now instead of later anyway."

I have other plans for you later, I sent down our bond.

His eyes darkened. *Oh really?*

Smirking, I tore my eyes away from Lee. "How are the newest recruits?" I asked Gus.

You beautiful, hot-blooded thing. Don't torture me. I can't bear it.

I continued ignoring him, biting back a grin.

His words sent me back to my time in the gnashing forest, when his notes were the only things I truly looked forward to. He had been more than a friend then. He had been my lifeline, the pulse in my veins and the hope in my heart.

That was only truer now.

Gus looked between the two of us before he answered, a knowing smile on his lips. "They're doing well enough to graduate. Abaddon has been dropping in on training more and more often over the last few months, though. I think he can sense most of his troops aren't really his own. With Godfrey's recent lean into The Veil, we have sides forming among nobility, but the army stands with us. My men are barely tolerating Abaddon's presence as it is."

"We should prepare for the worst," Lee muttered. "I think Abaddon has only just begun his reign of terror. We'll have a battle on our hands once my father's condition is officially declared."

Lana sighed. "They're going to try to pin it on you."

"There's not a chance they'll succeed in that," I asserted, squeezing Lee's hand.

I said it with such deep certainty that all three of them twisted to look at me. Lana and Gus pieced the truth together at that moment, and matching expressions of shock and awe rippled over their faces.

Lee chuckled under his breath. "No, they won't, but they'll still try." His fingertips wandered up my arm, softly swirling, drawing patterns on my skin, driving me absolutely fucking wild. The other three started discussing ways to divert the court's attention, but I wasn't hearing a word of it. I watched Lee's fingers dance across my arm, relishing the tingles flooding me with every caress. My toes curled, and a flutter stirred low in my belly.

I needed to feel more of him.

Carefully, I slipped my shoes off under the table. Then, I leaned over the corner of the table at the same time I extended my foot, my pointed toes searching blindly for Lee's leg.

When my foot connected with the cool silk of his trousers, Lee nearly jumped out of his seat. He stopped talking mid-sentence and looked at me, his eyebrows raised.

I smiled as my toes trailed up the line of his calf, then down again.

Lee's fingers wrapped around my forearm, squeezing firmly. I wasn't sure if he was asking me to stop or to keep going, but he wasn't whispering into my mind, so I took that as permission to keep stroking his leg.

"Lee?" Lana interjected. "You okay?"

He mumbled something under his breath.

"What was that, silly swan?" I crooned, turning in my seat for a better angle.

Lee smirked at me and repeated himself. "Nothing. *Yet.*"

Gus snorted, rubbing a palm over his mouth.

"You've got to be kidding me," Lana grumbled. "Could you two stop it?"

"What were you saying before that?" I prompted sweetly, tilting my head as my toes curled around the inside of his knee.

His legs fell apart as he sank back in his seat, his eyes shining.

Lee forced himself to return to the conversation, but a faint smile lingered on his face as I teased my toes up and down his leg. Every time I lifted my foot, I crept a little higher. I took my time, rubbing and prodding, and Lee pretended he couldn't feel it—at least until my foot was resting on the chair between his legs.

His thigh was thick, taut with hard muscle.

Goddess help me… I wanted to get on my knees and lick them.

So, I threw that imagining at him, me sitting between his legs beneath the table, exploring every ridge of his muscles and tendons with my tongue.

I stretched my toes a little farther, brushing against the hard bulge in his lap.

Lee's eyes flashed to me at the same time his hand seized my ankle, holding my foot in place against his twitching erection. There wasn't a trace of amusement on his face. His eyes burned with desire, his jaw feathering as he yanked me forward by my foot, and I nearly slid off my chair. I yelped in surprise and grabbed the armrests to catch myself, my soft stomach pressing into the edge of the table.

Lee barely glanced at the others. "Clear out, you two. We'll finish this conversation tomorrow."

"Good idea," Lana said haughtily as she rose from her seat. She leaned toward him to sneer, "Your *head* cleared out ten minutes ago."

I chuckled, but my gaze didn't waver. I couldn't look away from him.

"She's right," I muttered, pursing my lips to hide a smile. "I saw the thoughts flutter up and away myself."

"Did they look like silly little swans?" Lana asked blithely.

I shrugged, playing along. "They were *very* small."

"I'll never recover from the mockery you two subject me to daily," Lee muttered. "It's cruel, you know? My wife and my Hand, in cahoots against me."

"Cahoots?" I giggled.

Lana scoffed. "Boo hoo, cousin. Good night."

They fled the room, Gus stumbling at Lana's side from a glass too much of wine.

Lee and I looked at each other as the door shut behind them, and for a moment, we just stared at each other. Lee's eyes coasted slowly down my chest, his breath hitching as he eyed my breasts overflowing my gown and my soft curves pressed into the table.

"You're still holding my foot," I murmured.

His fingers flexed around my ankle. "I am."

"Is that all you're going to do?" I asked with a quirk of my brow.

Lee smirked, tilting his head in thought. "We haven't been training the way we should the last few days. I think we need to make up for that."

"What—right now?"

"Oh yes." He grinned. "I have a rather marvelous idea."

I mirrored his smile. "Let's hear it."

"I want to play with you," he said in a gravelly purr. "I want to lick your pretty pussy and teach you how to regulate your flame when your senses are overwhelmed."

I huffed a laugh, but the sound was strangled. Even as warmth trickled down my spine and pooled between my legs, a flash of fear speared through me. He wanted to train while fucking? That sounded... *dangerous*.

It was one thing to fight in the training ring, but something else entirely to bring our sparring into the bedroom. I didn't want to fuck this up.

I was only just beginning to realize how badly I wanted this to go right.

"Lee..."

He tugged on my ankle again, pressing the sole of my foot more firmly against his hardness. "Does it feel like I have a problem being the one to teach you, Sia?"

He'd heard my thoughts—not that I'd been shielding them. "No," I rasped.

"This isn't a burden to me. It's an honor, and it turns me on," he said gruffly. Then, his voice quieted to a soothing hum. "And besides, who else would you allow to see you so fully, to savor you so completely, if not *me*? I'm your handsome, powerful, and exceedingly clever husband, after all." He gave me a wink and let go of my ankle.

My skin prickled in the absence of his touch.

I wiggled upright in my seat—begrudgingly. I'd half expected him to drag me under the table and fuck me senseless. "Oh," I said flatly, biting the inside of my cheek, "is that all?"

Lee's eyes narrowed. "So vicious."

"Vicious enough to knock you on your ass," I agreed. "I might do it again."

"Make no mistake, darling, you might have gotten the upper hand down on the southern coast, but I am still your equal. I'm not afraid of your flame. The only thing I'm afraid of is dying before I get a taste of you."

My brow furrowed, my desire hesitating. "Why are you talking about dying?"

"Because that's how I feel every moment I'm away from you. I feel like I'm dying, like I'm wasting every breath that isn't taken at your side, and every breath that *is* fills me with new life. With one look, you revive me, again and again."

Heat surged like a sea within me, crashing against my ribs and foaming with desire. He had no right to make me love him this much.

"Are you sure you're the right person for the job?" I challenged him anyway, chewing on the inside of my lip to keep my smile hidden. "You didn't do much regulating yourself the other night when you snow-ploded all over the bedroom."

"I'm the *only* person for this job," he said sharply, his eyes narrowing in displeasure.

Obviously, he didn't like the idea of someone else *playing* with me.

Then, a smile tugged at one corner of his mouth as he added, "And you'll have to forgive the '*snow-ploding*.' I was a tad pent up."

"I didn't mind it," I said honestly.

"Yet you seem to assume that *I* will," he countered. "I'm not worried about you losing control while my mouth is between your thighs, Sia. I want you. All of you. In fact, I have every intention of tangling with your release in the future, to lose myself to your violence, but tonight… well, just consider this a lesson in *staying* power."

I considered his words, but I knew my decision had already been made. Any part of me he wanted, anywhere he wanted to take me, I would submit. I was *hungry* for surrender.

How had Lee become the only person capable of helping me feel safe and competent enough to wield my power masterfully? He'd been my teacher for many months now, and it felt no less vulnerable for me to rely on him now than it had been then.

I couldn't resist him, couldn't resist my own desires. He challenged me. He brought out the very best in me.

"Alright," I said softly.

The stillness of surprise rippled over him, but he quickly shook that away and rolled his shoulders back, preparing for what came next.

"Scoot your chair back." It was a gentle demand, but no less serious.

Without hesitation, I braced my feet on the floor and pushed myself away from the table. The chair vibrated as it scraped against the hard ground, imitating the tremble in my bones.

We were really doing this.

"A little more," he urged.

I loved when he got bossy, so I obeyed, stopping when he nodded. There was a good foot or so of space between me and the edge of the table now. Enough space for him.

I looked at him, but he didn't stand up yet.

He raised a hand to his chin, letting his fingertips trace the line of his lower lip as his eyes devoured my body. "Now, slide your underwear off and hand them to me."

I feigned a gasp of outrage. "You want me to give you my used lacy intimates? Golly jee! What are you going to do with them?"

Lee smiled at my game and leaned forward, bracing his forearms on the table. "Do what I say and find out, my sweet." His eyes slid down to where my thighs were pressed together beneath the table, like he could see straight through the wood.

I hitched my gown up to my thighs then slid my hands underneath, hooking my thumbs in the material. Lifting my hips, I pushed my undergarments down my legs. I lifted the dark fabric up between us, extending it across the table.

Lee just stared at them for a long moment, smirking, and my face grew hot.

The bastard was drawing this out for as long as possible. He was forcing his way underneath my skin, the way he always did, and it was making my pussy pulse like an artery. He finally took pity on me and reached forward, his cool fingers grazing mine as he took my underwear.

Lee brought the fabric to his nose and breathed in deep, soaking in my scent.

I shifted in my seat. I'd never seen anyone do that, male or female. It was like he couldn't help himself, like my scent was precious to him.

Lee opened his eyes into mine. They were dark, with a sliver of that ice blue glowing as he bit into the black lace, holding it between his teeth before he shoved his chair back, lowered himself to his knees, and *crawled* underneath the table.

My heart pounded wildly as he appeared at my feet.

Lee kneeled back in front of me and removed the lace from his mouth, reaching for my right hand. I gave it to him willingly, and with meticulous care, he wrapped the lace around my wrist, then around the armrest.

Goddess beside us… he was tying me down.

He positioned my arm so my elbow was flush with the side of the chair, leaving a few inches of space at the front of the armrest. It was a strange position, but not uncomfortable.

Lee plucked the cloth napkin from my lap and repeated the process with my other wrist. Then, he dropped his hands to my legs, and I parted them, giving him access.

He leaned in and buried his nose in my skirt, nuzzling gently, as if searching for my scent. Slowly, he pushed my gown up and out of his way. Peeling back an inch, his eyes glazed over as my pussy was exposed.

I couldn't quite see myself over my curves, thanks to being tied back and down, but I could tell he was pleased. The affectionate twinkle in his eyes made more luminous heat flood my center.

His body leaned in slightly, but he held back long enough to slide his hands underneath my knees, hooking each leg up on the ornamental knots of the adjacent armrests.

I could see myself now, spread open and wide, my arousal on full display.

Lee dragged his fingertips up the inside of my thighs then pressed on the lips between my legs, admiring my slick center.

A hard knot formed in my throat.

Why was I feeling the urge to cry?

When Lee finally spoke, his voice was rough and crackly—as if he was on the brink of tears too. This was more than sex for both of us. "I'm going to show you exactly how much and how long I have thirsted for you, my darling, my wife. You are exquisite."

"I am yours," I breathed. The words were out in the same instant I thought them.

Lee glanced up at me from beneath the furrowed ledge of his brow.

"Mine." The word was barely discernible through the rumble of his voice. He wasn't much of a man anymore. He was a wild animal, and he was starving.

I could feel my arousal weeping between my thighs and onto the chair. I could *smell* it, salty sweetness and raw need.

He kissed the inside of my knee, then the other. A nip of his teeth, and the soothing wet heat of his tongue joined his lips, those kisses growing sharper and fiercer as he worked his way towards my center. His soft savagery made me tremble.

I clutched the armrests with all my might.

Despite my attempt to hold on, vicious heat radiated out of my palms. Much more, and I would damage the upholstery.

Lee noticed at once. "You're burning up," he murmured. "Calm down, darling girl."

His lips slid up the last few inches to brush against my folds.

"That's impossible," I whimpered, my head kicking back.

Lee smiled wickedly against my center. "It's not impossible. Don't be afraid of what you're feeling. You push it out in moments of ecstasy because you don't want it to overwhelm you, but you must let it. Dig deep, let your flame fill you up. You are strong enough to hold it all without overflowing. You can do this."

Such sweet, gentle encouragement, even as he bit into my soft flesh, as his teeth ravaged my center while avoiding the place where my pulse thumped, tight and swollen. He teased my entrance, where I was heavy and aching.

I closed my eyes, focusing on his instruction.

Dig deep.

The depths were already yawning around me, so I let my power swallow me up instead of floating on the surface of it. As I sank into myself, I realized he was right. I was safe within the warm embrace of my flame, even as it bubbled and raged and licked around me with violent heat.

As his teeth shifted over my clit, he pressed his thumb against the hood, unsheathing the tender bundle in the center. I cried out as he licked and bit me, and my head emptied out as pleasure bloomed in my core, intense and delicious and *perfect.*

In my distraction, a few flames sputtered to life, licking at my arms.

Lee paused, raising his head and waiting for me to meet his gaze. My arousal glistened on his lips, and the sight only served to heighten my senses. "You can absorb it," he purred, his voice flush with authority. "Absorb it, and I'll let you come all over my tongue."

A soft moan tumbled from my mouth as I sank again into that boiling abyss.

He brushed tender kisses across my center, building the tension with his teeth and tongue. My hips tilted toward him as I absorbed my flame, and he rewarded me with a stinging bite, followed by a shallow thrust of his tongue into my core.

I was too full. There was no room for my thoughts, and so the words in my head poured out. "You're so fucking beautiful with your head between my legs," I cried. "Nothing is as beautiful as you like this."

His fingers dug into my flesh. "Fuck," he whimpered before he thrust his tongue deep into my channel.

"I love your sweet tongue," I whispered desperately. "You feel so good inside me."

"Sia," he growled in warning.

I couldn't stop. "I want to feast on you as you feast on me."

With a pained sound, he buried his face between my legs. He'd lost his focus and was truly feasting now, devouring with abandon. My back arched as I tried to bring his mouth back where I needed him, but I was at his mercy, his nails digging into my backside as he held me in place. Every roll of his tongue drove me closer to release, and I sank so far beneath my power that I could no longer see the surface.

I was burning, but at least *he* wasn't.

"*Please*," I sobbed.

"Eyes on me, my darling," he commanded as he pulled away. I forced myself to look down and found his eyes glittering with pride. He was drunk on my taste. He licked up my center again before murmuring, "Such a good girl. Now, when you come, I want you to hold onto your pleasure. Force it down into your toes."

I nodded, because I knew he was going to let me come now, and I would do anything for it.

He lowered his mouth to the crease of my thigh, kissing a line from one hip to the other before he blew gently on my center. The air was cold, torturous on my sensitive skin. Yet, I strained for more, my hips lifting off the chair.

A lick, hot and slick. Then, another blow.

Gooseflesh erupted all over my body. My legs shook, the heat of my orgasm building between them as his mouth closed over me and *sucked*.

The door to Lee's office slammed open, the interruption sudden and sobering.

Gus stood on the threshold, a letter clutched in his hand.

An urgent missive, then, one that couldn't wait until morning. I could have wept in disappointment.

Lee was beyond disappointment—a fury unlike any I'd ever seen before filled his eyes as he pulled my skirt down. "Someone had better be dying," he barked. He slid out from beneath the table, and the anger immediately dropped from his expression.

Because the regretful look in Gus' eyes told us that death had indeed descended, and the Halcyon seal on the letter announced who.

CHAPTER 55

Godfrey's funeral was a dreadful, silent affair. The priestesses and all of those who attended the procession wore white, and I was certain we were quite the vision, standing there on the dark stone shore as a summoned blizzard spun all around us.

The dead king was pushed out to sea at sunset, and the cannons that sunk his boat broke the unbearable emptiness with stunning finality.

Boom. Boom. Boom.

I glanced again at Lee, but he was still… somewhere else.

His blue eyes were hollow. He hadn't said a word to me in several hours, and he had barely mustered the presence of mind to make decisions concerning his father's passing last night, when the letter came. Lee had known his father's death was coming, but he hadn't been prepared.

My actions had not given him that mercy.

I did not know what to do except to hold his hand so tightly that I could barely feel my own. I couldn't bring him back to me. He wouldn't return until he was ready to face what had happened. I was bracing myself for that moment. I would be lying if I did not admit that I feared it. Would he feel resentment towards me? I had caused him this pain.

Even if it *had* been necessary.

The ride home was equally as tormenting. So much silence, silence that filled my bones and made me heavy and tired. I wished Lee could give me something, anything, a squeeze of his fingers or a sidelong glance, but he simply was not able. Even the bond was eerily quiet. Not like he was shutting me out, but more like there was nothing to be heard. He was not daring to even *think* a word too loudly.

Numbness had taken him. Perhaps he had needed that to face the funeral, to face this day. I would wait as long as he needed.

When we arrived at Sumner House, Lee fled the carriage before it came to a full stop, launching himself up the grand staircase. I followed more slowly, pausing as Lana and Gus emerged from the carriage behind ours. They'd seen Lee's mad dash for the house as well.

Gus approached me and set a compassionate hand on my arm. "It will be alright, Sia."

Lana stood at a distance, but her expression was kind. "Can we do anything?"

A shake of my head was all I managed before turning away and entering the house. The silence was here too. It was everywhere.

Lee was pacing our bedroom when I found him. He'd disposed of his tunic and shirt, walking around with his trousers hanging low on his hips, the laces loose. He barely acknowledged me as I entered our room.

I simply stood there on the threshold, watching him with my heart hammering against my ribs.

Lee's breath was coming fast and harsh, broken too. He was shaking his head, as if answering some question in his mind. *No. No. No. No.*

After what seemed like ages, he came to an abrupt halt, staring out the windows at the sea.

He took slow backward steps to the bed and perched on the edge of it, his wings spreading out behind him. Then, he started crying.

Deep, mournful sobs.

His hands fisted in his hair, and he tugged on the strands violently, like he was *punishing* himself. My heart throbbed with sorrow and anger, because I knew his father had driven him to this. His entire life, Lee had been taught that emotion was weakness, and today, the day of his father's passing, he was punishing himself for feeling grief over the man who had despised him. This punishment was all he knew, all he had of the father he'd lost.

My heart shattered into a thousand little pieces for him.

Crossing the room, I forced my hands into Lee's hair in an effort to replace his fists. At first, he would not relent, so I grabbed either side of his face and made him look at me through his tears. "I promised to never let anyone else hurt you," I said passionately, "and that includes yourself."

Agony rippled over his features as his hands fell. Then he reached out and grabbed my hips, pulling me in to bury his face against my belly.

"I hated him," he moaned.

I ran my fingers through his golden hair, holding him close. "I know."

Lee peered up at me, his cheeks shimmering with tears. "Then why do I feel this way?"

I kneeled between his legs and cradled his face. After a long while, I finally found the words I needed. "Because he was the only father you had, despite what he did to you. Grieve however you must, even if you are only mourning what you wish could have been. Children don't get a choice in where or to whom they're born, or who they learn to love, *how* they learn to love. But he didn't win, Lee. He didn't break you. You remained beautifully vulnerable despite him. What you feel for him now—it is pity. Because he did not have your heart. Don't be ashamed of feeling whatever you need to."

Tears streamed freely down his cheeks.

"I'm glad he's gone, because now, he can never hurt you again. He can never—" His throat worked around the profound words. "He can never hurt *me*."

"I know," I repeated.

He raised his hands to my shoulders, squeezing gently as his remorse surged between us. "Our heart bond is the best thing that ever happened to me, Sia. I regret many things in my life, the freedoms I have taken and roles I have played, but what I have with you has never been one of them. I'm sorry if I ever made you regret us."

I shook my head, caressing his cheeks. "I don't regret this."

Then, I brought my lips to his, sealing the words with a kiss. It was a light, comforting touch.

He welcomed it with surprise at first, then with wild enthusiasm. His grief bled into me like blood, bitter and tart.

I soothed it the best I could with my tongue. With every caress, I delved deeper into his agony, taking it into me so that he might not face it alone. I gave him my love, hoping it would be enough to close the wound, and he could finally start healing. This was the first kiss we'd shared alone, without anyone watching.

I wasn't sure how we'd made it so long without, because kissing him now, I never wanted to stop.

In a small way, I was also glad it had taken until this moment. It felt special to share this now, when I wanted to give him so much, but I had so little to offer. Only this. My kiss. My touch. I knew how quickly that comfort would fade once we stopped, so I kept going. If he needed me, I would continue kissing him like this forever.

When my lips were thoroughly swollen, Lee pulled away to gaze into my eyes. There were no words spoken, but we didn't need them.

He slid off the bed to kneel in front of me and dragged me back in, plundering my mouth again with a sure, eager tongue. He held me close, his arms wrapping around my waist and wings. My hands roamed his face and neck and bare chest, my fingers greedy.

There was contentment in our embrace, no urgency beyond staying in this moment with each other. The moment stretched until it encompassed many centuries, until I myself was forgotten. I lost track of how long we stayed there, kneeling on the floor together, but I was finally brought back by the ache in my knees.

The floor was hard beneath me, unforgiving.

Despite my best efforts to ignore it, I started shifting in his arms to lessen my discomfort, but that only made it worse. "Lee?"

He hummed in question, trailing kisses across my jaw.

"My knees hurt," I admitted.

Lee smiled against my neck. "Mine too."

"We should move to the bed."

"As long as I get to keep kissing you."

I wrapped my arms around his neck. "You'd better, or else I'm going to attack you in the middle of the night again."

"Always tempting me," he murmured as he stood, lifting me into his arms.

Lee's lips found mine again as he pulled me into bed. We settled on top of the covers, trading affection and comfort as the room darkened around us. The night finally fell, my oldest friend, the moon wrapping us in its silver arms.

The soft mattress pressed us closer together, aligning our bodies.

Lee's hands roamed, squeezing my curves through the

light, linen dress. He worshiped my jaw and neck with his kisses, returning to my mouth again and again to sip reverently from my lips.

The world spun behind my closed eyes. We could have been in another world entirely for all I knew, for all I cared.

As he grasped my leg under the knee and hooked it over his hip to draw us closer, the kiss changed. Our embrace grew more urgent, our lips hungry.

My fingers tangled in his hair, and a surge of warm pleasure filled my body, knowing I was free to touch him like this, that he wanted me to, even in this particularly raw and vulnerable state.

I absorbed his ragged exhales into my lungs, satisfying myself on the taste of his tongue… until even that wasn't enough. My breath quickened to sharp pants. My hips tilted and swiveled of its own volition, trying in vain to relieve the ache building between my legs. Within moments, Lee's thigh was pressed firmly between mine, and I was grinding myself against it with a shameless moan. As his arm wrapped around my lower back and his fingertips trailed leisurely along my backside before dipping between my legs from behind, I was certain I'd lost the ability to breathe at all.

He'd felt my desperation, and now, he either wished to ease it or torture me further.

Every cant of my hips forward brushed my clit against the bulging hardness in his breeches, and every withdrawal pushed his fingers closer to the place where I was *aching* for them. And yet, I was no closer to what I really wanted, no closer to what I needed.

I peeled back to look into Lee's eyes, smiling like a madwoman as his lips tried to follow mine. "I need you," I breathed.

The scorching desire that filled his gaze put my fire to shame.

He brushed his knuckles across my jaw, watching intently as my body reacted to that whisper of a touch. Savoring the way my eyes rolled and my hips rocked. His body throbbed against mine, moving like a tide at the mercy of the moon's pull. With a small smile, his other hand fisted in the skirt of my gown, hitching the thin material with purpose before pausing at the swell of my ass. He seemed to be waiting for my permission to continue.

I nodded softly, incapable of voicing how deeply I longed for this. My mouth was parched, my tongue thoroughly tied.

"Then you'll have me," he rasped before returning his lips to mine. In that kiss, I dissolved. I evaporated in the heat of his touch as his hands pushed my skirt to my hips and his fingers found the bundle of pleasure between my legs, circling my sensitive nerves and dragging my slick up from the entrance of my channel.

"So. Fucking. Wet." He pushed three digits in, stretching me with unyielding fierceness.

I clung to his shoulders as my back arched, groaning my approval.

We were in too much of a rush to bother dispensing with our clothes. I tore at his draw-strings as his warm palm swept my breasts up out of my bodice. He fondled and pinched my puckered flesh as his tongue plundered my mouth, the insistent organ demanding my full attention. I was so distracted that I didn't realize he had removed my lacy undergarments until his cock was notched at my entrance.

Then, he was pushing in, and after all our kissing and touching, I was more than ready for him. My fingers twisted in the back of his shirt as I tugged him half on top of me.

He hitched my knee higher on his hip and slid in deep, a smooth but forceful motion that made my sex flutter and my throat tighten. Then, he pulled back, easing the intense pressure for only a moment before snapping his hips forward to fill me further. He did it over and over until his hips collided with my soft flesh, the measured slaps mingling with my moans and the growls he made through gritted teeth.

When Lee banded an arm around the middle of my back, he lifted me slightly to latch his mouth onto my breast, and I cried out. I watched his golden hair dance across my skin, as he kissed and nibbled his way across my chest to my other breast. He lavished my nipple with sharp affection until I was beyond myself, until all I could see were the stars sparkling behind my eyes.

Lee slid a hand down my stomach, reaching between my thighs to flutter his fingertips over the bundle of nerves there.

My climax crashed over me with stunning clarity. It sheared through my spine, fizzling and twisting and bursting with delicious warmth. Vaguely, I was aware of Lee's hand on my jaw, knew he was watching as my body tightened and released. As the peak of my pleasure passed, Lee kissed either corner of my mouth—sweet, coaxing kisses—and I forced my eyes open.

Lee's eyes glowed a shockingly-bright blue. He'd stopped moving, and his swollen cock jerked restlessly inside me, soaking in the evidence of my pleasure.

But the smirk on his face was thoroughly gloating.

"Careful," I crooned. "That smug expression might get stuck on your face, and then no one in your kingdom will take you seriously."

Lee's lips twitched as he swiftly buried a hand in my hair, forcing my head back with a firm tug. Then, he leaned in to whisper on my neck, "You're still an exceptionally frustrating brat, and I *will* be reminding myself in the morning."

"What is that supposed to mean, *husband*?" I gave him a sweet, goading smile.

He offered me one slow thrust of his hips, laughing as I

gasped and writhed. "I plan to make you beg for it properly next time," he said lowly. "I'm a male of my word, you know."

I bit my lip, relishing the new spark of pleasure radiating up my spine. He was seated inside me, barely moving despite the promising fullness, and it made me want to scream, so I sharpened my words instead. "Right now, you're a male who is buried galaxies-deep inside me," I purred, "and there's only one word you need to heed."

When Lee's eyebrow piqued in curiosity, I brought my lips flush with his ear and whispered, *"Harder."*

He sighed against the shell of my ear, but then his hand found the back of my knee. He sat up far enough to stretch his wings flat beneath him, this new position spreading me wider, sinking him ever deeper. My legs now straddled his hips, my breasts crushed against his chest as he claimed my mouth again. His next thrust had me moaning against his lips. Those that followed were equally sharp and exquisitely rough, and he reached back between my legs to feel where we were connected. His fingers massaged my slick entrance, pushing in around his cock and making me pant.

Then, he grazed those fingers farther back, rubbing my arousal up between my ass cheeks, and I caught onto his intention a heartbeat before he forced a fingertip through the tight ring of muscle.

I yelped a bit, but he swallowed the sound, deepening our kiss as he pushed in a little further.

My entire body trembled, my mind already half blown from pleasure and scrambling to relax under his ministrations, but I knew what I wanted. I gave myself over to him completely.

His hips and fingers worked in tandem, taking turns creating luscious friction in my sex.

There was no possibility of holding back even an ounce of my pleasure at that point—my cries were as loud as the ocean crashing beyond the windows, and my fingers were making a mess of Lee's hair. Every drive of his hips pushed me further into our combined hunger until my consciousness was overcome in every way by hazy, luminous want. The bed was a cloud. We were two stars twinkling in the ether.

His voice reached through the darkness and consumed me. "Come undone for me, darling."

My body, of course, obeyed. How could it not?

I fisted the sheets to either side of us, barely present in the room as my flames burned twin holes through them.

This time, Lee followed after me into release, and his groan vibrated in my ear as his arms tightened to hold my hips in place. His warm seed filled me, overflowing and seeping between us as our bodies settled together.

I melted on top of him.

He did not allow me to move away, tightening one hand on the swell of my thigh to remain inside me as he brought his lips back to mine. For a long while, he simply reacquainted himself with the tangle of our tongues, riding out the aftershocks of our passion. And as our kisses slowed to a languid pull and sleep eventually came to claim us both, I could still feel his mouth on mine.

CHAPTER 56

Morning broke with a breathtaking sunrise. I watched the horizon fill with warm color, my mourning gown still tangled around my thighs. Lee snored softly in my ear.

It felt like only moments ago we'd been wrapped up in each other, joined at the lips. My mouth still tingled with the memory of his kisses. I skimmed my fingertips over my lip line, appreciating the tenderness he'd instilled there with his teeth, and heat filled my belly as I recounted the hours that had passed too quickly.

I couldn't remember when I'd last lost track of time and self like that, if I ever had. I'd been intoxicated by his touch.

As the sun finally crested the horizon and shone through the windows, I felt Lee's breathing hitch and deepen. He shifted, his strong arm tugging me closer as he nuzzled my neck. "Grand rising, darling."

His voice was thick with sleep, but his body was coming alive behind me. As his hips shifted at my backside, I felt his hard length stir.

"It seems we aren't the only ones rising," I said coyly, wiggling against his growing erection.

"Forgive me. You're far too beautiful in the morning." Lee started rolling away, having taken my teasing seriously, but I caught his arm.

"No." I pulled his arm back across my chest. "Don't you dare move."

He chuckled roughly, turning my face and dragging my lips back to his for a devastatingly gentle kiss. "Good. I have some unfinished business with you."

I hummed against his mouth.

That was as far as we got, though, because a knock sounded on the door to our room, light but insistent. I groaned in frustration, burying my face in my pillow as Lee pressed his forehead into the crook of my shoulder.

"Who is it?" he called, his deep tenor vibrating through me.

"It's me, cousin," Lana replied beyond the door, her lyrical voice muffled. "I've brought breakfast and much to discuss, I'm afraid. We've received another letter from the palace."

"Let us in so we can eat," Gus whined. "I have a raging headache."

He and Lana must have stayed up last night, drinking.

"Duty calls for us both." Lee sighed, disentangling himself from me to sit up against the headboard. He looked me over, and his eyes hardened. "Change out of that dress, darling. The time for mourning is at an end, and we must now prepare for a battle of court politics." Blatant disgust simmered in those last two words.

Lee waited for me to rise and abscond myself in the closet before he called the others in.

I heard very little of their murmuring voices as I undressed—nothing could be discerned beneath the sounds of breakfast being brought in—so I quickly gave up on listening and sifted through the dresses hanging on the clothes rack.

My gaze caught on a familiar swathe of pale blue, shimmering material hanging at the back of the closet.

I would need to look my part as Lee's queen, and I could think of nothing more fitting than the dress he'd given me so many months ago, the dress I'd stripped from my body and shoved into his arms the day I learned who he truly was.

He'd kept it, had sent it *here*, to this house that he loved, to the home that perhaps he'd always hoped we would share. My husband, my king, the dreamer.

I dressed, sighing in pleasure as the dress's magic formed to my body. Then, I ran my fingers through as many of the knots in my hair I could find and emerged from the closet.

Platters of dried fruit, roasted root vegetables, and baked goods had been placed on the bed. That was really the only surface with enough room for it all. Lana was stretched out on the mattress beside them, her head propped on one hand and her wings resting against the headboard, picking at the bowls with a fork.

Gus was tearing a pastry apart in front of the fire.

Lee paced in front of the windows, silhouetted by the golden light of dawn, his face pinched with worry. I came out as he growled, "Nothing good can come of this."

"Nothing good ever comes from that old bat," Lana retorted, stuffing a berry into her mouth.

Gus saw me first, his jaw slackening as he took me in. "*Sia*, by the Mother's design." His voice was filled with genuine, kind admiration.

I felt my cheeks warm.

Lee spun toward me. He scanned my body slowly, almost disbelieving at first, but that astonishment was soon replaced with smug satisfaction as he crossed the room to me. He took my hand in his, kissing each of my fingers. *Are you trying to undo me?*

"Definitely," I whispered.

Lana made a noise of disgust and flopped back on the mattress, throwing an arm over her eyes. "I'm going to dive headfirst into the sea. You guys are disgustingly cute."

I laughed at her. "Don't be jealous."

"Can we please return to the problem at hand?" she growled.

"What problem?" I demanded, turning back to Lee.

Lee grimaced. "My father's court has decided no further investigation is needed. We're moving forward with the coronation."

"That's a good thing, isn't it?"

"It's *suspicious*," he muttered, dropping my hand to return to his pacing. "We expected them to hold on to the seat of power, but they've dropped it into our laps without accusing any of us of anything. It doesn't make any sense. Abaddon is up to something."

"So we'll deal with him when the time comes and whatever it is he has planned."

"It might not be that simple," Lana argued. "especially if that plan has to do with the coronation tomorrow, which is almost certain. All the lords and ladies of the territory will be present, humans and seraphim both."

My brow furrowed. "What does that matter?"

"He intends to stir insurrection," Gus said softly, drawing our attention to where he sat in front of the hearth. He was staring intently at the flames, his eyes red and sunken. He looked like he had a rough night, and I wished for a moment that we were closer so I could ask why. "If Abaddon succeeds in his schemes, he'll turn the nobles against us, and then it won't matter who wears the crown. The city and all the progress we've made toward co-existence will be compromised. Our kin will consider us villains and traitors, and the humans will face grave peril."

Abaddon would have the seraphim turn on the humans. No. We couldn't have that.

"Then…" I hesitated. "We kill him, don't we?"

Gus glanced at me from across the room, a smile twisting his full lips.

Lana's laughter wrapped around us, musical and bright. "I think I rather like your wife after all, cousin. She's funny."

Lee smiled at the rising sun.

"Unfortunately," Gus interjected, "we'll need to tread more carefully than that here, my Queen. Abaddon has men loyal to him. They are few, but they are also old and strong-winged, and he'll be keeping them close after Godfrey's passing. He'll be prepared for such an attack."

After a long minute, Lee nodded to himself and turned toward us. "Gus is right. We can't kill Abaddon now, without public witnesses or transparent cause, but we can play his game in the meantime. Let him think we're none the wiser. We'll prepare for the coronation by bringing in an army of our own. Fill the grand hall with our soldiers, discreetly. When he pounces on me, we'll be ready for him, and we'll cut out his tongue before he utters a word if necessary. We'll bathe the entire room in his men's blood if we must."

"You would make a display of force to silence him?" Lana gasped, looking between all three of us. "That's risky, Alezandral."

"Not force," Lee replied with a smirk. "*Justice.*"

With a small smile aimed at me, he sat on the end of our wrinkled bed, clasping his hands between his knees. "If he makes his move at the coronation, we accuse him of treason. We tell the story of how Abaddon killed the king and now attempts to displace the rightful heir so he can take the throne for himself. The nobles will be easily swayed to our cause. The only thing his loyalists truly care about is power, and what better way to show them ours than a public execution?"

CHAPTER 57

The day passed swiftly as Lee and I were pulled in opposite directions.

I spent most of the day in the city, flitting from one shop to the next, hiring local businesses to decorate the ballroom Lee would be crowned in.

The coronation itself would take place at the palace, and I didn't want that old fortress to feel barren anymore. I wanted it to be warm and bright and full of life. I ended my day at those rusty iron gates that barred access to the palace and watched with a smile on my face as the city guardsmen wrenched them open.

Lee left the house shortly after breakfast, reporting to the barracks to gather soldiers for tomorrow's coronation. The debriefing took longer than he expected. He sent a letter late in the afternoon letting me know that he wouldn't be back in time for dinner, and Lana and Gus had been tasked with occupying the nobles and their many questions.

When I returned to Sumner House in the late afternoon, they were still gone.

So, I talked Destin into letting Erlene accompany me to a

restaurant down in the city, and as we were walking out the door, he decided to come with us.

It was nice, walking the streets with them.

Erlene's little hand clutched mine tightly, her bright eyes drinking in the bustle of bodies all around us. She pointed out items in the windows, and her excitement filled me with even more love and appreciation for the city. Where else could a human girl walk alongside seraphim without fear?

Not that Erlene would have ever been frightened. She thought every seraph who passed her by was the most beautiful being she'd ever laid eyes on, and she let them know it.

How lovely our cruel world seemed through the eyes of a little girl.

Destin kept his head down until we were seated at the restaurant, but then he lifted his gaze to our surroundings. The small tables were pushed close together in the candlelight. It was no different from the dineries and taverns his homeland had. This tavern in particular was human-owned, in fact.

By the time we finished eating and returned to the street, Destin was asking me questions.

Were humans living on the same streets as seraphim? *Yes.* Did humans have the right to shop and dine wherever they desired? *Absolutely.* Were there laws that protected them? *Many.* I felt him opening up to me more and more as we walked back home. I could see that he was finally seeing the truth: this city was only the beginning.

When we parted ways outside Erlene's room, he smiled at me, and I felt *forgiven*, if that was possible.

All the history between us—all that pain and disappointment—was forgotten for a brief moment, and I could see a future with him beside me. I knew how unusual that was, but even though this dream wasn't perfect, it was ours. I still loved him in the only way I could, and I knew he cared for me too. Everything would work out somehow, I just knew it.

As the sun set over Sumner House, I walked through the quiet corridor leading to Lee's office with a small silver chest in my arms.

The door to his office was open, and I peered through to find Lee behind his desk, poring over a disheveled stack of parchment. Dark circles had sunk into the skin beneath his blue eyes.

"It's getting late," I murmured.

He startled, his head snapping up to look at me. "I'm sorry," he sighed, glancing back down at the paperwork on his desk with a weary pinch in his brow. "There was more work to be done than I thought. I've been sent over a dozen letters today."

"Your father's court?"

He shook his head. "The nobles. They're taking this change in rulership as an opportunity to renegotiate land divides."

"That's presumptuous of them."

Lee leaned forward and scrubbed a hand over his face. "It's within their right," he muttered through his fingers. "The ones who favored my city plans believe I should reward them by taking land away from the ones who hesitated, but… I have to be careful. They are all powerful families. The only way I managed to convince my father's supporters in the first place was by reassuring them they wouldn't lose anything when the humans integrated. I have to do my best to make both sides happy, but I've yet to see a way to do that. Most of our land is claimed already."

I nodded, smiling as an idea struck me. "How much land does Abaddon's family own?"

He peered up at me, a smirk creasing one of his cheeks. "My ruthless lady."

Then, Lee returned his attention to the papers, dipping his

quill into the ink well and making a note before moving on to the next sheet.

I took a few steps into the room, and my gaze caught on a soft gleam emanating from the large table. There were several cushions arranged on the surface, polished rings of silver and gold sitting on them, inlaid with radiant gems of various colors—delicate crowns and diadems.

"Why are all these tiaras sitting here?" I paused at the edge of the table, inspecting them.

Lee didn't bother looking up. "A few belonged to my mother, but most are from the family coffers. I was going to show them to you in the morning, but now that you're here, I want you to choose a few to keep here at Sumner House. You'll need one for tomorrow, so pick a favorite."

My brow furrowed. "Why would *I* need one?"

"This coronation is as much yours as it is mine," he said easily, signing the next paper.

Confusion swirled through me like an icy dagger, and I set the chest down on the table, as if its weight was keeping me from understanding. How could this coronation be mine? I wouldn't be standing up there on the platforms, being blessed with holy oil and consecrated as king. *He* would.

"I'm just your consort." It was more a question than a statement.

Lee looked up at me, his eyes hard as stone. "Wrong. You are my queen, and you'll be theirs too after tomorrow."

Then, I understood.

Lee wanted to give me the official title, to share in all his authority, which meant I would be crowned tomorrow too. "You can't be serious," I gasped, balking at him.

He put aside his quill and folded his hands on the desk in front of him.

"Trust me," he murmured. "I take this matter *very* seriously."

"You shouldn't share this day with me, Lee," I insisted, glancing between him and the exquisite metalwork. "*You* were the one who changed this city. This is *your* country."

"Wrong again," he said firmly. "Everything I have, I most willingly share with you. This is the root of our bond. It's *our* city, *our* country, *our* throne. I won't have them any other way. Now, stop arguing with me and choose a fucking crown."

Would the country accept me, though? I was still a stranger to them.

The thought worried me, because my father had trained me to fear their opinion. I really did want Lee's people to like me. It would destroy us if they didn't. My future wasn't the only one at stake in this.

Warmth swelled in my chest anyway, because Lee was staring at me so sweetly right now, and his smile momentarily chased away my worry.

"You're mad," I murmured.

"Mad for *you*?" he said with a flash of his eyes. "Certainly."

I turned back to the arranged cushions on the table, trailing my fingertips over the diadems and crowns. This was a collection formed over many centuries, both silver and gold, dark and light. The amber orbs above my head reflected in the jewels, sparkling gently under my touch.

I gravitated toward a diadem with harshly-hewn silver leaving.

I was all too aware of Lee's stare burning into my back as I picked up the tiara and studied it closer. Dips within the metalwork had darkened from age, now near-black. Chains of shining silver dangled from each peak with small, dimpled pearls swinging at their ends. It was simple, but no less beautiful than the others.

"What do you think of this one?" I asked, showing it to him.

"Put it on," he commanded softly.

I perched the diadem on the crown of my head then laced my fingers behind my back and swayed from side to side. The nightgown I changed into after dinner twirled around my legs, ivory and sheer that left absolutely nothing to the imagination.

Lee's eyes devoured every lush curve of my body before returning to my face. "Stunning."

He hadn't even glanced at the tiara.

I reached up to remove it, but Lee shook his head and beckoned me forward with one finger. "Don't take the crown off. Come here."

After retrieving the silver chest, I walked to his desk.

Lee pushed his chair back and turned toward me as I rounded the desk to stand between his legs. His hands curled around the back of my thighs, his long fingers toying with my skirt. He leaned forward and nuzzled my belly with his nose.

Heat began pooling in my center, but I placed the chest on his desk and took a step back, encouraging him to open his eyes.

Lee frowned at me, irritated by the sudden space between us, before turning to stare at the chest. "What is this?"

"A present," I sang.

His face instantly lit up. "For *me?*"

I nodded and Lee perked up in his chair. He fisted a hand in my skirt to drag me down onto his lap, his smile radiant as he reached for the silver chest.

I'd have to make a point of surprising him with gifts more often.

Lee pushed the lid open, revealing blueish-silver steel on top of red velvet. His brow furrowed. "A helm?"

"Yes, made of sea steel."

"*Sea steel?*" His eyes snapped to mine, wide and disbelieving. "That's not possible."

I smiled broadly, finding great satisfaction in knowing

something he didn't—considering the know-it-all he was. As far as *he* was aware, sea steel was only a legend of his father's father and all the kings who came before him.

Sea steel had been used in Halcyon armor for many generations. They went to war with it. They were buried in it. Until Godfrey.

Lee's father was not given that honor.

"The helm was the only piece that would fit into this chest," I told him. "The rest of the armor will be delivered at first light."

He picked up the helm, leaning around me to admire it.

I grabbed the fabric that had been folded beneath the helm and turned it over to show him the black side of the red-lined cape, the purple and blue threads of magic glimmering throughout it. "This cloak isn't the traditional cloth. I had Kori weave your family crest into a fabric that shifts between blue and purple in the sunlight. It's you *and* me. I wanted to contribute in some way, but if you'd rather have the Halcyon colors, I understand. I've had one of those made too."

Lee kissed my arm, smiling as he shook his head. "I want what's ours."

"Good," I said brightly. "Then we'll match."

He chuckled then peered up at me. "In what deep, stormy sky did you find sea steel armor, Sia?"

I reached down into the bottom of the chest and withdrew Elona's journal. "I found the means to *make* it," I informed him, lifting the leather book between us, "with the help of your mother."

The warmth drained from Lee's face. He tentatively reached for the journal, and I set it in his hands.

I continued talking as he looked it over. "She wrote in this journal that she hoped you would wear the armor of your ancestors on the day the crown passed to you. She believed it was your birthright. Her writings were quite persuasive on the matter. In every matter, really."

And the journal? he asked silently. *Where did you find* this?

Revealed to me herself, I told him. Revealed by the memory of her. She knew that only someone who loved her or her son could have found that journal, and so it was mine by right. That was how she wanted it.

"No one has seen a scrap of sea steel in decades," he muttered, seemingly to himself.

"No one who *reported* it," I corrected him. "Your father did well in striking fear into the heart of this territory. So well, in fact, that those who possessed powerful means refused to strengthen your father with them. No one has seen sea steel in decades because it's been decades since a man ruled who was worthy of wearing it."

Lee gave me a shy smile, but his eyes were glittering with tears.

I ran my hands through his silky blond hair. "I tracked down the armor master your mother spoke with when you were born. He's an old armorer who lives by the sea north of the city. He died some years ago and passed his trade on to his son, but the family kept all the sea steel they had for you. I had to promise he wouldn't be arrested, so let's hope he isn't hiding something even more dangerous in his cellars."

"Knowing my territory, he might."

"Then may the Goddess be kind to us all," I said, laughing alongside him.

Lee's eyes drifted back to the helmet resting on my thigh. "Why did you do this for me?" he whispered.

"I told you—it's an engagement present. I owed you one."

You owe me nothing, he said down the bond. Out loud, he argued, "You could have given me any number of things, but you *chose* this."

"I just figured…" I sat back, smiling faintly as I caressed the runes etched into the helm. *Strength. Wisdom. Will.* "You have your own hurts to conquer, and this is a good place to start."

Lee leaned forward, dropping the helm and journal back into the chest before taking my face in his hands. He pulled me close and kissed me sweetly. Our lips danced and our tongues tangled as I twined my arms around his neck, melting against his chest.

Lee's fingers caressed my lower wings, finding all the spots that made my back arch and breath hitch. His laughter rumbled into me, and I writhed in his lap as he kissed me harder.

"Come to bed, husband," I said against his lips. "I can't sleep without you."

He inhaled sharply and stood, setting me on my feet before scooping the chest off the table. He relocated it to the shelf behind him then disappeared in a cloud of Materie. The click of a lock drew my attention to the door, and I saw Lee standing in front of it, sliding a bronze key back into the pocket of his tunic. He threw a smile over his shoulder before de-materialized again.

Rough hands circled my waist and turned me back around.

Black, shimmering Materie swirled to nothing around us as Lee lifted me off my feet and dropped me on top of the desk, his mouth closing over the side of my neck. He sucked on my flesh, and I felt the vessels bursting under my skin. The sharp ache bled into pleasure, and I hoped the mark he was leaving lingered for days—I'd wear it proudly.

Then, his mouth moved lower, biting and licking my breast over the nightgown.

He pressed a hand to my sternum and pushed me down until I was lying back on the desk, my head hanging over the edge. I felt the diadem slip out of my hair, colliding with the floor with a tinny clatter.

"What are you doing?" I gasped, threading my fingers through Lee's hair.

He kissed my belly and peered up the length of my body with a wicked darkness in his eyes. "Finishing the lesson we started. We can't have you burning through all the sheets in Sumner House."

A giggle bubbled out of me as he bit my stomach and spread my legs, shoving my skirt up around my hips. He kneeled, wasting no time latching his mouth around that throbbing bundle of nerves between my thighs. He kissed and licked with the perfect suction, and my back arched off the desk.

My head kicked back, swelling with a rush of arousal.

He didn't play with me this time.

This was a total assault of my senses, his mind wrapping around mine and his hoarfrost chilling the damp material over my breasts until I writhed against his sharp smile. His tongue stroked me to the brink of ecstasy in seconds. My moans echoed through the room, pitchy and desperate as his approval weaved through my scattered thoughts, praising me with honeyed words and raw desire.

I tipped into bliss, pleasure sweeping through my body in violent waves.

My flames trembled just beneath the surface, but I kept them contained as I tumbled down from that blinding peak. I pushed all of it down into my toes, holding it.

Lee's tongue started stroking faster. A low growl rumbled out of his lips as he sucked on my swollen flesh and rolled my clit between his teeth, and all at once, I was climbing again. My core was hot and achy, and I couldn't stop my hips from lifting off the edge of the desk, grinding myself more firmly against his mouth.

When his fingers prodded suddenly at my entrance, I groaned. *"Fuck yes."*

As he slid three broad fingers inside me, I detonated again. I gripped the edge of the desk next to my head as he worked me through to the end of my pleasure. I think I scorched a paper, but neither of us cared enough to stop. He turned predatory in the aftershocks, stimulating me with each receding wave until I cried out in breathy, wild moans.

I didn't realize I could sound like this. Then again, sex had never felt like this before.

He lifted his head only high enough to start brushing kisses over the creases of my thighs. The scruff on his jaw scraped me with every nibble, and I knew that was intentional. He was trying to kill me.

"I want more of you," I pleaded, tugging on his hair.

Lee chuckled mercilessly. "Oh, not a chance, darling. I want to see how swollen and wet this sweet pussy can get." Every word made his chin graze my clit, his stubble scratching the sensitive bud until I was kicking and fighting.

Mercy, mercy.

When he closed his mouth over the raw nerves, I screamed. I shoved at his shoulders, but he didn't budge. And then I was propping myself up on one elbow, looking down between my legs as Lee feasted on me like a wild animal.

Fresh arousal coursed through me, and I laughed. "Come up for air, you deviant."

He bit my clit before peeling back an inch, staring up at me with devotion or, maybe, obstinance. "I would happily drown in you, Sia."

His tongue slid smoothly between my lips, dropping his fingers to lick at my entrance.

"Fuck me," I rasped. "Please, fuck me now."

"I'm going to do more than fuck you, darling," he said as his hands squeezed my hips, hard enough to bruise. "I'm going to find a way to crawl across our bond into your tender fucking heart and build a home there. You won't be able to separate any piece of yourself from me. I will know every inch of you."

I nodded fervently. "Do it. I want you inside of me."

"I *am* inside of you," he whispers before plunging his tongue into my core, thrusting languidly into my wetness, his drool and my cum soaking the desk beneath me.

"*Lee...*" I dissolved into ecstasy a third time, forgetting my own name as I clawed at the hard surface beneath me.

Lee smiled at me when I finally returned to myself, his hands massaging my thighs. I could barely keep my eyes open, but all I cared about was feeling more of him. I wanted him to feel as good as I did.

When I reached for him, he caught my wrists and pinned them down at my sides, giving me a look that screamed, *stay right there.*

My heart sank as he pulled away.

Lee stood up and tugged my skirt down before stretching out on top of me, his hands bracing the desk to either side of my head. "Not tonight," he said affectionately.

"Why not?" I breathed, unable to keep the hurt from my voice.

Lee smirked and leaned down to whisper against my ear, "If I get inside of you now, we'll never get to sleep, and we both need to be well rested for the coronation."

I whimpered, hooking my legs around his waist. "I don't need sleep."

He chuckled, shaking his head even as his hips rocked against me. "We have no idea what's waiting for us tomorrow, and we *really* shouldn't risk nodding off during the ceremony. The priestess would be deeply offended. They'll refuse to anoint us, and then what will we do?"

"Whatever we want," I crooned.

Lee's smile grew, but it quickly faded as his eyes clouded over. "Everything except what I was born for," he said gently.

After a moment of contemplation, he asked, "Would you still want me if I wasn't a king?"

His gaze clashed with mine. There was something so very tragic about the way he asked that. He didn't bother hiding exactly how much that thought bothered him.

In another life, we might have never met. Never kissed. Never touched.

"I did not bind myself to a king in these woods," I murmured, brushing back the golden hair on his brow. "I bound myself to a boy with pale hair and a heart as broken as mine. I would want you if you were only a silly swan for the rest of your days, and I, a witch of my mother's bloodline. I believe we would have found each other in that life, in any life, just as we did in this one, but…" I smiled weakly, "we are not so unremarkable, you and I."

His eyes searched mine. "I don't know what I did to deserve you."

"Mmm. You must have done something truly vile."

"I disagree," he said, kissing my lips.

I mumbled back, "You often do."

"Well, stop saying preposterous things, and I won't have to."

I giggled then peeled back to look up into his eyes. "Take me to bed."

"That's more like it," he grinned.

He tucked one arm around my wings and the other under my knees as he scooped me up. A cool breeze tickled my back, and the smell of pine and mint curled in my nostril, so heady and familiar that I melted.

The twilight of sleep seized my bones, swift and vicious.

Lee was wrapping his magic around me, lulling me into a light, pleasant slumber—but it didn't smell the same as it had before.

I laughed weakly, already half gone from this realm.

At the sound of my amusement, Lee's magic lifted enough to keep me conscious for a few moments longer. "Let me in on the joke, darling."

"I don't smell poppy smoke anymore," I confessed, the words slurred.

"Oh? What do you smell, then?"

I nuzzled his chest. "Just more of *you.*"

Lee's arms tightened around me.

Before I surrendered my last thread of awareness, I heard his voice whispering somewhere between my mind and reality, "Sleep, my love."

CHAPTER 58

"Stop fussing," Lee murmured, removing my hand from the bodice of my dress and kissing each of my knuckles, smiling as his nose prodded the black opal on my finger. "You're perfect."

We'd spent the better part of the morning at Sumner House. His armor arrived, and we dressed each other in the dark blue light of dawn, before the sun even lifted over the ocean. I never realized what true intimacy was before Lee. Sex was nothing. His gentle touch, when it was dressing me rather than undressing, when it was cleansing instead of ravaging, was everything.

Now, we stood in a cold antechamber in the Halcyon palace, waiting for the ceremony to begin. Hundreds of voices burbled on the other side of that door, the drums beating, slow and resonant as a heartbeat.

He looked so handsome sealed into his pale blue armor, his shoulders broad and strong. His wings were splayed large behind him. The sea steel molded exquisitely to his long, lean abdomen and powerful legs. He was hard everywhere, and it made me want to wrap my soft body around him and succumb to the pull between us at last, right here in this musty room.

I shook my head to rid myself of that overwhelming desire. I'd been wanting for too long.

"I'm nervous," I confessed.

He looked into my eyes, his gaze soft. "Whatever for?"

I huffed a laugh. "I never imagined I would have any piece of your country, and now you want to share it all with me. I'm not equipped for this. What if—"

"You're not going to ruin anything," he said, cutting me off.

My nerves unraveled; I'd needed to hear that.

I clutched his hand between mine, bringing his palm to my cheek. The armor made his skin colder than I was used to. It was the influence of the sea steel; this metal drew his hoarfrost to the surface, intensifying it. At least I had the privilege of feeling his bare flesh. He'd left the gloves and helm of his armor at home; there was no use for them here today.

A horn blared from within the grand hall, and we both turned to face it.

We shared a tender look, and Lee took my hand as the doors were pulled open. Stunning daylight washed over us, beckoning us forward, and we emerged at the back of the room, behind the silver thrones that had been placed on a wide, white platform. Much like the ballroom at my father's palace, two paths of blue silk had been unfurled across the floor and around either side of the platform.

We would be separating here before joining back together in front of the thrones.

Lee gave me an encouraging smile, his fingers clinging to mine as we parted.

My empty hands tingled as I followed the blue silk, my skin turning a bit clammy, but it wasn't the crowd of nobles

sliding into view that was to blame. Abaddon was here somewhere. If we were right, he would strike any moment now. He
would try to hurt Lee.

This room was filled with our soldiers, and we were
prepared for an attack, but there was a dark sensation
crawling up my spine.

Deep down, I knew something wasn't right.

Rounding the front of the platform, I could see Lee again.
We turned toward each other, taking even steps to the rhythm
of the drumbeat, and I caught Lee's eyes drifting to the audience. He was searching for Abaddon among our witnesses.

But I hadn't seen him in the crowd.

Where the fuck was he? Why wasn't he ambushing Lee?

I halted mid-step when I heard a thick crackling behind
me, and I barely had time to turn before a hard mass slammed
into my side.

The world blurred as I tumbled across the hard marble.
My head collided with the edge of the platform, and my ears
rang as pain radiated through my skull. I groaned, pushing
myself up. A boot struck me in the stomach, and I buckled to
the ground with a cry. That boot kicked me, again and again,
until I was curled into myself.

A dark chuckle fluttered down around me.

I blinked through the pain, forcing my eyes to focus on my
surroundings. Abaddon stood above me, sneering. A thick ice
barrier surrounded us, closing us off from the rest of the
room. It was beyond freezing in here. Even as I reached for
my flame, my sparks sputtered and died in the air between us.
He was wielding the full depths of his hoarfrost against me.

I cursed under my breath as understanding dawned.

We'd been wrong. Abaddon had no intention of attacking
Lee today.

It was *me* he wanted.

He wanted to make sure Lee had no opportunity to sully the Halcyon bloodline, even if it was the last thing he did. Abaddon wanted me gone so Lee would marry someone else and strengthen his bloodline with a more suitable female. He was willing to die for that satisfaction.

But I wasn't going to take his betrayal lying down.

With my body curled into a tight ball, the dagger on my thigh was within reach. I withdrew it from the wrap of my dress and lunged forward as he kicked me again, sinking the blade into the side of his knee. He shouted, staggering back.

I twisted my body before he could recover and slammed my heel into his shin, snapping bone. Abaddon roared, the sound echoing off the ice around us as his blood-shot eyes met mine.

I reached back blindly and used the platform to pull myself upright, biting back a wince as a sharp ache pinched between my ribs.

He'd broken a bone in me too.

A look of pure hate settled over his features as he threw his hand out, and a spear of ice hurtled toward me. I dodged it, but he threw another one, so I summoned a wave of heat that carried just enough energy to knock it off course. I ran at him, knocking him to the ground before I straddled his stomach. Shards of ice scratched at my face, but I melted them before they could do any real damage. That was just about all the heat I could manage in here.

I tried to pin Abaddon's hands down, but he ripped free and smacked me across the face so hard that my ears started ringing. Then suddenly, he was on top of me.

His hands were around my neck, and I couldn't breathe. *I couldn't fucking breathe.*

I raked my fingernails across his hands and face, and then I saw the gleam of metal and blood at my side. I took hold of the dagger in his leg and twisted it, earning myself a gasp of precious air as he grabbed my hand and hit me in the face again.

Abaddon moved to wrench the blade out of his leg, and I used the opportunity to buck him off me.

I rolled out from under him and scrambled to my feet, my throat tight and breathing ragged. By the time he stood as well, I had my second dagger brandished.

Screams came from the other side of the barrier, someone ramming into the ice with all their strength, but it wasn't budging.

Abaddon smiled at me, lumbering forward. "You aren't leaving this room alive, you stupid fucking whore."

"You're closer to The Veil than I am right now," I rasped, "you old fucking bat." Every word was a lick of fire in my throat, and not the kind that was good for me—but it was worth it, seeing the offense sink deep.

He lurched forward with my dagger in his hand, but the ice at his side shattered as a wall of solid marble knocked him sideways before he could reach me.

Lana.

She leapt through the opening, and the marbled crystal wall she'd pulled up from the ground sank back down as she pounced on Abaddon. He managed one swipe at her before she struck the blade out of his hand, slicing a few of his fingers off in the process. A violent spray of blood hit the ice beside them. Lana must have found his one broken leg amusing, because as he clutched at his spurting fingers, she shoved his back against the wall, pressed her sword to his neck, and broke his other leg with the heel of her metal boot. She wrenched him forward by his hair, holding that blade against his neck as she turned him toward me.

An offering.

Lana's eyes met mine, and I saw none of the animosity

she'd once felt for me. Her gaze scanned my body, lingering on my neck and face, on the marks he'd left on me.

When her chin trembled, I knew: she cared for me. She'd *protected* me.

For her sake, I didn't show the pain every step gave me as I walked over to them. I leaned in, smirking an inch away from Abaddon's face. His breath sawed in and out, heavy from the pain. The cut on his brow bled angrily, and his teeth were bared, but he didn't dare move an inch. He knew Lana would slit his throat before he could lay another finger on me.

"You fucked up, Abaddon, and now, there's no one left to protect you."

"Go ahead," he snarled. "Kill me. You and the rest of our continent will join me in the Veil soon enough. Neither of you understand the reality of our position. We won't survive this war if Lee turns half the territory against him before the real fighting begins, and you are a fool if you believe my country will accept you as their queen. We're surrounded, we're vulnerable. You *need* me. If you get rid of me, the serpents will eat that boy alive."

My stomach churned as I leaned back, looking him over with furrowed brow. "War? What war? What are you talking about?"

"That's for the crown to know," he said with a crimson smile, "and I'll take it to my grave if he lets you wear it."

My hands trembled as rage swept through my body. "A grave is too good for you."

Lee materialized within the ice cage at that moment, only a few feet away. He turned in place, searching for me. His hands were bloody; someone had attacked him out there. His panicked blue eyes found mine, and then he re-materialized within my reach, Materie swirling out from him as his hands cradled my face. "Are you hurt?"

I shook my head, brushing Lee to the side as I addressed Lana. "Let him go."

Lana blinked once, but that was all the defiance she allowed herself before she dropped her sword from Abaddon's neck and let him sprawl on the ground in front of her.

I turned and threw my flames over the ice, watching it melt and pool across the white marble floor. The audience slowly came back into view. Whatever happened next, we would want witnesses for it. As Gus spotted us, he stalked forward from his place across the room. Several men were being held at sword point behind him—Abaddon's men.

Two soldiers were dead at his feet—I couldn't tell whether they were theirs or ours.

When I turned back to Lee, he was circling Abaddon, his face a frightening veil of control. As he returned to my side, I reached for him, alarmed by how cold the arm of his armor was—as crisp as a winter morning. *He knows something about the serpents, Lee. Something he's not telling us.*

His voice swept through my mind in response, sharp and blazing bright white. *I don't care.*

Lee walked past me and crouched in front of Abaddon with an ugly smile. There was no respect in that gesture of kneeling. He was showing Abaddon that he wasn't afraid of getting close to him, and I realized in that moment just how brave Lee truly was: brave and brutal and hungry for vengeance. All this time, he'd been waiting patiently for the chance to destroy the male at his feet, enduring his father's punishments and letting them both think they could control him.

They had never controlled Lee. The pain they put him through accomplished nothing, save for the hate in his eyes.

Lee's hand flexed around his sword as he looked the male up and down, his gaze simmering with disgust. "My wife reacted mercifully to your betrayal," he growled, only loud enough for Abaddon and me to hear him. "But what you have done today is unforgivable. You touched my wife, my beautiful wife, who loves this country so much that she cannot bear to hurt it, not even the rotten parts that I have allowed to fester for far too long. I no longer share her hesitation. The corruption in our territory must be expelled so that we may evolve."

He stood and waved the guards looming around us forward. "Restrain him."

Two guards surged forward, wrenching the male up off the floor, his legs bent unnaturally beneath him. Abaddon spat blood at Lee's feet, jerking against the arms holding him in place. "You're going to die for this, boy. Your bones will be scattered across this coast by the summer solstice."

"His wings too," Lee ordered.

Another pair of sentinels joined the first, their blue eyes glowing with delight beneath their helms.

Abaddon fought against the guards with renewed fervor. His eyes turned black. Fear—true fear—gripped him. "No," he protested, his voice building to a scream. "No, no, no you can't do this. Traitor! Fucking kin-killer!"

Lee threw a hard look at someone behind me. "Silence him."

Gus stepped around me, removing the belt from his tunic, and shoved the strip of leather between Abaddon's teeth.

The old bat continued screaming as the belt was tightened, his screams now muffled.

There was only one way this would end. He couldn't be allowed to endure in this territory, not even as a prisoner. Abaddon was a danger to this country and to my husband, and if he was given the opportunity, he would destroy us all for the sake of his twisted morals. He would rather see us die than live in peace with the humans. Delusions of power had blinded him. He thought he was better than them, better than us.

I would show him exactly how wrong he was.

"Strip him," I whispered viciously. "Those colors no longer belong to him."

A few gasps echoed through the room behind me, but they were laced with hunger. We weren't the only ones who wanted to see this male humiliated.

Lana stepped forward and slid her sword beneath Abaddon's tunic. She tore it open, her face a cold mask of duty as silver tears tracked down the male's cheeks. His protests softened—he could see there was no way out.

He'd overestimated his men. They weren't fighting to free him. Loyalty was a fickle god without any love to bind it.

Lana ripped the blue material away from his wings, baring the vulnerable roots, and then moved on to the bloody trousers. I looked away as he was exposed from the waist down, meeting Lee's fierce stare instead.

We have to, he said down the bond. It was almost like he was searching for approval, for permission. Equals, even in this.

I nodded solemnly. *I know.*

Once Abaddon was naked, Lee beckoned the guards forward, and they dragged him up onto the staircase to the platform. Lee followed them up, standing on the top step as he pulled his sword out of its sheath. I stood to the side, watching as he directed the guards, having them shove Abaddon down to his busted knees and stretch all four of his white wings back. Then, he pointed the blade around the room.

His declaration was rich and deep, woven with velvety danger. "Let this be a warning to anyone who mistakes my wife's mercy for weakness."

Then, Lee lifted his sword and brought it down, and I felt

the entire room hold its breath as that blade sliced through the delicate knuckles on Abaddon's back. Those pristine white wings were severed away, falling to either side of his writhing body. The leather belt in Abaddon's mouth was not enough to silence his scream. His agony ripped through the room as blood gushed from the wounds, decorating Lee's armor with crimson red flecks.

The guards let him collapse in a heap on the floor.

Red coursed like twin rivers from his back, staining his pale skin and pooling under his belly, soaking into the wings that no longer belonged to him. He crawled to them, moaning mournfully as his fingers fisted in the feathers.

The wings were still twitching. Their nerves were still alive, if only for a few moments more.

I swallowed the acidic bile creeping up my throat.

This punishment was difficult to watch, but I kept my eyes open. I absorbed every moment. We had a responsibility not to shy from the grotesqueness of this, Lee and me. This was our legacy, being bathed in the blood of our enemies. We would not hide from it.

Shimmering white scales started bursting from the skin surrounding Abaddon's open wounds and down the length of his legs.

He screamed again, a cry of desperation and loss.

Lee returned his bloody sword to its sheath and addressed the guards. "Drop him at least a mile off-shore. If he surfaces anywhere near the coast, drive a dagger into his heart."

The guards dragged Abaddon out of the hall, and he didn't fight them. Why would he fight it now? We'd already taken everything he cared about. His crooked legs were already sealing together. The white scales shimmered like pearls in the sunlight, a dark trail of blood following after him as they carried him up the aisle and out the door.

Lee's burning gaze slid to mine as he stepped off the platform, returning to his position on the blue carpet runner across from me, acting as though the interruption had never occurred.

The blood between us reminded the witnesses otherwise.

He nodded at the musicians, and a horn rang out with chilling expectancy. The drums started up again. *Thump. Thump. Thump.*

Keep walking, darling. Hold your head high.

The rest of the ceremony continued without incident. We were anointed with oil by the priestess and knelt in front of our respective thrones. The throne in front of me had belonged to Lee's mother. Before her, no female had ruled in equal capacity in the Halcyon territory, and perhaps that was partly why Lee was so adamant about me ruling alongside him. He honored his mother by crowning his wife.

Lee's court knelt below the platform behind us and were anointed as well: Lana and Gus and a couple other young seraphim I hadn't met yet.

They recited their vows first, and then Lana and Gus were called forward to place the circlets of silver on our heads. I knew it was Lana at my back by the feel of her delicate fingers running down the length of my hair, her hands settling on my shoulders and squeezing before slipping away. Her gentle encouragement brought tears to my eyes.

The priestess led us into our oath, and I tried to keep my voice steady.

They were the same promises Godfrey had made and

eventually broke. *To govern the Halcyon people with honor and devotion. To rule justly, for the greater good of our kind and all others who have been granted sanctuary within our boundaries.*

I heard the heaviness in Lee's voice as those words slithered under our skin, settling deep enough to scrape over our bones. Once it was spoken, Lee and I stood to face the witnesses.

The musicians slammed into their drums, and horns blared to either side of us. Some of the nobles stood, cheering and whistling, while others clapped meekly in their seats.

A sliver of pride speared through me, but I knew we were a long way from earning the trust of the territory. Word of the violence that occurred here today would spread through the city. Abaddon's loyalists were on edge, and the humans would be frightened.

As tradition directed, the nobles of the territory brought forward offerings and laid them in front of us, all symbolic—fur pelts to keep us warm, braided rope to strengthen our alliances, herbal tonics to bless our bodies. The parade of gifts dragged on for an hour or so before, slowly, the witnesses each paid their respects and filed out of the grand hall.

When Lana and Gus were the only ones left, Gus ordered the guards to leave, and Lana climbed the stairs to us with a bundle of bound parchment in her hands. She'd opted for a full set of black and iron leathers today instead of a dress.

She extended the stack to me, and I took the yellowed paper, my brow furrowing as I flicked through them.

The letters were wrinkled, the ink watery.

"We found letters in Abaddon's tunic," Lana explained. "It seems to be correspondence with the serpent king himself. He'd been meeting with them behind your father's back."

Lee sat back, his arms spread wide to either armrest. "Any hint as to why?"

"None," she sighed. "The letters only name a place and time."

Gus joined us up on the platform, reaching for the letters as he leaned against the back of my throne. I let Gus have them and turned to Lee.

His fingers were rapping anxiously against the armrest. After a moment, they fell still. "I guess the only way to find out what they've been talking about is to send a letter of our own." His gaze slid to Gus. "Send messengers out to the serpents' usual haunts. I want an audience with their leader as soon as possible. Tell them the continuation of our treaty relies on it."

Lana stepped forward. "Abaddon made it sound like they have plans for you, cousin. Maybe meeting with the *snake king* right now isn't the best idea."

"It's the only idea we have." Gus peeled himself away from my throne and stalked to the front of the platform, looking down at the pool of Abaddon's blood oxidizing in the sun. He looked handsome and crisp in a fine navy tunic, the sides of his head freshly buzzed.

He tore the stack of letters in half and threw them into the ichor. The yellowed parchment quickly soaked the crimson up until the words were no longer decipherable.

I inched to the edge of my seat. "The longer we wait, the more time we give them to plan an attack. For all we know, Abaddon could have been lying in the hopes that we would spare him. We have no reason to believe they bear ill will towards Lee. Beyond what their nature encourages, of course."

Lee returned my stare. "Your Queen is right. Send the messengers."

Lana rolled her eyes and muttered something under her breath as she stalked down the staircase, stepping around Abaddon's blood with a curled lip.

I couldn't hide my smile as she slammed the door to the hall shut behind her.

"I'm off to see to the traitors we arrested," Gus announced. "Perhaps one of them can give us keener insight into Abaddon's meetings—I doubt he convened with the serpents without bringing along protection."

Lee was lost to his thoughts, barely managing a nod in Gus' direction.

I left my throne, smiling as I placed a hand on the General's arm. "We'll wait for you and Lana to finish before heading home. Lock the doors on your way out, would you?"

He bowed at the waist, winking. "As you wish, my Queen."

I turned to Lee as the door snapped shut, my smile twisting into a smirk.

Lee straightened in his seat, his deep blue eyes roaming the length of my body. "What are you up to now, darling?"

"I have an offering for the king," I said sweetly.

He chuckled, his head tilting to one side. "Do you?"

I nodded slowly, pulling at the ties on my dress until the layers fell open, baring myself to his crazed stare. Reaching up, I loosened the flaps around my wings and shrugged the fabric off my shoulders. The gown landed heavily on the floor around my feet.

Then, I did the most vulnerable thing I could: I sank to my knees.

Lee hummed in appreciation, his eyes sparkling. "This is a most splendid offering indeed. Is this you begging, my sweet?"

I shivered at his loving tone.

"Yes," I said without hesitation, letting my surrender course through me. It was a soft warmth filling my limbs, tingling down into my fingers and toes, so unlike my flame but still familiar.

He spread his legs and tapped the inside of his thigh. "Then be a good girl and crawl to me."

Every pretense fell away, and I saw the real him. He was at ease like this: smug and aroused, affection in his eyes. I wanted him like this every day.

I placed my hands on the cold marble in front of me, moving toward him, but then something seemed to change his mind, and he lifted a hand to stop me.

"Wait."

I frowned, but Lee only brushed his fingers down the front of his chest, and Materie shimmered to life, the glittering ether curling down his body as his armor disappeared. As the Materie dropped away from his pale flesh, the dark tendrils traveled across the floor between us. The fur pelts that had been given to us materialized across the marble floor, cushioning it.

"Very thoughtful of you," I teased. "My knees thank you."

He smiled. "That won't be the only part of your body singing my praises once I'm done with you. Do you scream just as pretty?"

"Never mind," I said flatly. "You're an arrogant bastard."

That made him laugh. "Yes, and this arrogant bastard is telling you to crawl. Don't deny me. I already know how much you want to obey, how much you want to be my good girl." Then, he crooked a slender finger at me, and my body lit up with need.

I crawled to him, letting my hips sway and my breasts swing with each pull forward.

He absorbed every moment of the show I was putting on, his breathing measured but heavy. His cock stood at attention, long and hard and pulsing. He had an intellectual's mind, but his body was pure warrior.

As I pressed myself between his legs, I shuddered at the feel of his bare skin on mine, my flesh tightening as he slid his hands into my hair.

He tugged my head back, and I gasped, arching into him.

Lee kissed me, the faintest brush of his lips, before pulling away. When I tried to follow him, his hands tightened in my hair, holding me in place as his eyes darkened. "This is the last time you'll get on your knees for anyone, Sia. Do you understand me?"

"What if I like getting on my knees for you?" I whispered, the words small but true.

He leaned in and kissed me again, deeper this time. "Then that will be our little secret," he murmured against my lips.

Lee wrapped his hands around my upper arms and dragged me into his lap. I straddled him, shuffling forward until I molded myself to him, my soft curves to his lean muscle. Our kiss deepened again, and I ran my fingertips across the stubble on his cheeks before burying my hands in his hair, moaning softly as he licked my open mouth.

"That's it, darling." The head of his erection pressed against my slick core, and he reached down to wrap a hand around his cock, sliding it up and down between my lips, teasing my clit with the hot head before notching himself at my entrance. "My beautiful, clever girl."

The words sent a bolt of lightning straight to my core, and I opened my legs wider, lowering myself into his lap.

His eyes burned with blue light as he entered me.

My body only managed an inch or two before I had to pause, his thickness stretching me right past the point of discomfort. I teetered there, on the fine edge of pain and pleasure.

I dropped my forehead to his, inhaling shakily.

"Take me." His hands slid up over my hips, and he thrusted up at the same time he pulled my body down, impaling me the rest of the way. It was delicious agony.

Lee's mouth covered mine, devouring my cry as his tongue swept in. Groaning, he rolled his hips, circling one direction and then the other, stretching my tight channel.

My tongue tangled with his, but then his hips fell still.

The only movement left between us was the dance of our mouths and his cock twitching inside me as he allowed my body to acclimate. Every caress of his tongue slithered through my core, flooding my sex with luminous arousal. All my nerves came alive, given breath by our connection.

My hips tilted against his, driven forward by instinct.

Lee growled, and his fingers dug into the flesh of my hips. He withdrew nearly to his tip and pushed back in, his hips lifting off the throne, rocking my body up against his. His eyes dropped to my bare chest, watching as my breasts swayed from the rough motion. I gasped for air, my head kicking back as his cock jerked inside me.

Smiling, he lifted my hips between his palms and wrenched me back down again, fucking me hard and slow, his eyes swimming with delight at the way my body responded to his touch.

"Do I feel good inside you, darling?" he purred, nuzzling my neck. "Because you feel incredible to me."

He pistoned into me, sharp and fevered, and my core fluttered around him with every push, pleasure bleeding through every inch. My body greedily accepted him, and his hips collided with my softness, our flesh slapping together in a raw, erotic beat. Moans tumbled over my tongue as I anchored my hands to the throne behind him, holding tight as his thrusts grew more forceful.

My legs started shaking.

"*Fuck*," I whimpered.

His chest rumbled against mine, and then his hands slid under my thighs as he hooked both of my knees over his shoulders, driving into me deeper, so deep that I could feel every plunge of his cock in my throat. It brought out something ancient in me—whining moans and growls I didn't realize I could make.

I ground myself against him, needing more, needing *all of him.*

Just as I was cresting the peak of my pleasure, Lee gripped me hard around the waist and stood from the throne. My fingers were ripped free from the crystal headrest, so I buried them in Lee's hair instead. He held himself inside me as he took two steps forward and knelt on the fur blanket, gently laying me down between his thick thighs.

He skimmed his hands over my curves, drinking me in before his gaze trained on the place we were connected, giving one, slow thrust. "I love your body, Sia. You are so fucking beautiful."

Then, one of his hands moved to my wing, pinning it to the floor, and I gasped.

He'd placed his weight in the perfect spot, avoiding bone and joint so that he didn't hurt me. It was only a small discomfort. I didn't expect the surge of arousal between my legs, the sparkling pleasure it triggered deep inside me.

Lee started thrumming my clit, fast and rough, a breath-taking contrast to the slow strokes of his hips.

My back arched, drawing more attention to his hand on my wing. The wet slap of our flesh colliding and our combined moans filled my ears, and a pull stirred low in my belly.

For whatever reason, being held down was really turning me on.

Perhaps I liked being pinned down for the same reason Lee liked pain. There was a familiarity to the things that once used to hurt us, control us, and there was power in taking those memories and replacing them with other moments, moments we chose.

We could replace them with each other.

There was a trust I'd never had before. It felt like healing. It didn't need to make sense. I just needed it.

I trusted Lee with every part of me, my body and my heart and my mind. Some of it I couldn't help, but in all of it, I was grateful. He found that little girl I used to be, so full of hope and love, and he turned me back into a dreamer. He showed me new ways of fighting and fucking and *living*. I was no longer frightened of losing myself in the dark, the way I was with Tova, the way I was with Destin. I was ready to be a glimmer of light in that darkness with *him*.

My body ignited with pleasure.

I shattered around him, my legs stiffening and slipping off his shoulders. He caught me under the knees with his arms, holding me open, angling himself as deep as possible.

I scratched at his arms, trying to pull him down to me.

He only moaned and kicked his head back, relishing the violence of my fingertips. So, I dug my nails in deeper. I drew a masterpiece across his shoulders and down his chest.

His scored flesh bloomed a delicious shade of pink.

As I slid my nails over the scar across his heart, his thrusts hastened, growing rough and wild. He leaned down with a growl and bit my heart scar, and a soft after-wave of bliss sharpened to a peak between my legs, tossing me back under the haze of ecstasy. I think I screamed, but I couldn't hear it. I scraped my nails across his chest, harder than before, and he fell after me into pleasure, groaning breathlessly against my breast.

Lee dropped to the fur pelt beside me, resting his cheek on my shoulder. His every exhale caressed my bare skin, and I could still feel the phantom of his teeth on my scar, pinching and pulling.

I played with his hair, pulling the strands between my fingers.

"You're the best thing that ever happened to me too," I confessed.

He didn't reply to that, only tugged me closer and draped

my leg over his waist so we were facing each other. His eyes searched mine as he trailed a knuckle across my cheek.

I wondered what he was looking for.

Before I could ask, he embraced me tightly, tucking my face against his neck. The fur pelt beneath us tickled my sensitive skin, but we laid there like that for a long while, breathing each other in. His hands leisurely traveled up and down my body, massaging and worshiping every inch of my torso, then my arms, my shoulders and neck.

The blood in my veins pumped a little hotter, and my limbs grew heavy.

At some point, my eyes fluttered shut and I drifted to sleep, but I woke when I felt something rough wrapping around my wrist.

Lee was kneeling over me, a rope in his hands.

"What are you doing?" I asked groggily.

"Playing with you a little more," he answered, leaning in to taste my lips. "Do you want me to stop?"

He'd warned me that he wanted to tie me up.

My pulse quickened as those words dropped into my belly, stirring my sex back to life. I really shouldn't want this so badly, but then, my feelings were my own. My healing was my own. There was no one who could keep me from it except myself.

I shook my head. "Keep going."

Lee kissed my wrist, where the evidence of my previous imprisonment still lingered, before he continued tying the rope up my arm, tight enough to feel but not enough to lose feeling. He was utterly calm as he worked, but I could feel his desire for me in every knot he made. His eyes held mine, the blue depths shining with adoration as he moved on to my torso and my wings, cinching each tier with care. My legs were last, and he pressed a kiss to the inside of each ankle before crawling up over me again.

I couldn't move.

My arms were tied behind my back and my legs were bound open by four separate ropes that weaved into the lattice work covering my abdomen. Lee grabbed me by the hip and neck, pulling me astride him before his Materie wrapped around us.

A second of blindness, a cocoon of stars, and suddenly, we weren't on the ground anymore.

His arms released me, there was a slight drop, and my heart leapt into my throat, but my body snapped to a stop almost immediately. The ropes wrapped around my body pulled taut as the ceiling came into view above me, considerably closer than it had been a second ago.

I gasped for air, disoriented by the sudden shift in place.

Lee leaned in over me, his white wings beating evenly behind him. He was flying freely at my side, but I was immobilized, hanging at the mercy of several ropes.

The ropes were tied to the beams near the peak of the ceiling. Clearly, his Materie was capable of doing more than moving items or people from one place to the next. It could *do* things, like tying rope and unrolling pelts. If Lee could do this with only a fraction of Quintessential power, what else could their people do?

"How do you feel?" he demanded. "Are you in any pain?"

His hands slid down my body, testing the ropes.

"No," I breathed.

"If you feel pain at any point, or you lose feeling in any part of your body, you tell me immediately. Do you understand?" He looked at me seriously, and I nodded, wondering how I could possibly feel pain when his hands were on me.

He didn't allow me any more time to think about it.

Lee lowered his mouth to my chest, licking my breasts and tugging on my nipples with his teeth as my body tightened. It was agony not being able to touch him, not being able to move to release that tension. My frustration tumbled out in short, sharp gasps and needy moans. He kissed my stomach and my thick thighs, then settled between my legs with a gentle nip to my clit.

I wanted to writhe, but I couldn't.

"I want to taste you again—taste *us*." He dragged his tongue up my center, groaning loudly. "After last night, I think I'm addicted. I want to lick you until you're crying again."

Delirious laughter bubbled out of me. "You're trying to kill me, aren't you?"

Grinning fiendishly, Lee buried his head between my thighs again, and he didn't stop until my screams echoed through the rafters.

CHAPTER 60

By the time we settled into the carriage across from Gus and Lee, the sky was leaning into dusk. I'd spent most of the afternoon tangled up with Lee as he massaged and kissed the rope marks all over my body with an herbal tonic, which led to more needy rutting on my hands and knees, my face buried in fur pelts and his massive wings trembling around us both.

The oil, the rope, the pelts. Every offering, he made brilliant use of.

It made me think Lee had been planning this day for quite a while. He was an imaginative lover, I'd give him that. I smiled as the memory of his strong body crumbling on top of me surfaced.

Alright, I could give him more than that. I was utterly consumed by him. I couldn't keep my eyes or my hands off him. I smiled like a love-sick dove when he tucked me under his arm, his wing curling protectively behind mine.

Lana smirked at us from across the cab. She was leaning up against the corner of the cab, one long leg bent in front of her chest. "You two are practically levitating. Was the ride that good?"

Gus barked a laugh at the ceiling.

Lee's smile faltered. "I'm not having this conversation with you, cousin."

"It had to be good," Gus interjected, biting his lip to banish a smile. "They were locked up in that throne room for hours. I thought they were waiting on us, not the other way around." He and Lana shared a weighty look, barely-contained amusement building between them.

Lee glared at his general. "Not you too."

"Oh, come on," Lana said emphatically. "You know I have to tease you at least a little bit. It's my right as your kin. I obviously can't trust your wife to do it properly anymore."

I gasped, feeling somewhat slighted. "And why not?" She quirked a brow at me, and I narrowed my eyes in return. "I hope you're not implying I'm now some doe-eyed waif who can't formulate a proper insult. His dick doesn't muzzle me."

Lana and Gus erupted into a fit of raucous laughter.

I slapped my hands over my face with a groan. "Ugh. Forget I said that."

Lee snickered, rubbing a palm across his jaw as his fingers played over my waist. *Doesn't it, though?*

I poked a finger in his face, glaring at him with an amused grin. "Quiet, you."

He wiggled his eyebrows. *Not a chance. You'll have to muzzle me.*

I just might.

Lee licked his lips. *Promise?*

Rolling my eyes, I nuzzled into Lee's side and looked over at Gus, who was finally regaining a bit of his composure. Despite the general's history with Lee, he seemed sincerely happy to see us, simply happy that we were happy. I hoped that could be Destin and me someday. "Did Abaddon's men have anything to say?"

Gus scoffed. "Oh, plenty. Nothing of use to us, though. The soldiers who accompanied him are the ones we were forced to execute during the ceremony."

"And now our territory is three zealots fewer," Lee muttered, staring out the window.

I sat with the anger in Lee's voice for a long moment, bristling under the weight of their deaths. "We should reach out to their families," I said softly. "Make sure they're being looked after. We took their fathers and sons and brothers from them today."

Gus looked at me as his eyebrows raised. "I think that's a very good idea, my Queen. We'll send healers."

Lana withdrew a quill and parchment from her long tunic. "And we best send an elder too. The families will be angry." Her jaw tightened as she scrawled instructions on the paper. She must have been angry when she heard about her brother. I could see the burning pain in her eyes.

I glanced at Lee.

His lips were pressed together in a slight grimace as his gaze wandered outside the window.

I touched his chin and gently turned his face toward mine. *What's wrong?*

Lee's eyes simmered with regret. *I should have thought of that. Their families.* He dropped his gaze to my chest, squinting as if he could see through my clothes to the scar above my breast. He wasn't angry with me for speaking up—I knew that —but he *was* agitated. With himself, probably.

I slid a hand over his and squeezed. *You've been doing this on your own for a long time, but you have me to help you now. Don't be so hard on yourself.*

He turned his hand over and threaded his fingers with mine, smiling weakly.

A moment after the letter evaporated above Lana's palm, another folded sheet of parchment slipped into the atmosphere between us.

We all shared a look of confusion as it fell.

"That was quick," Lana muttered, reaching out.

Instead of the paper drifting towards her hand, though, it twirled and veered the opposite direction, right into Lee's lap, the paper wrinkled and slightly damp. He unfolded the letter and read it, his face paling as he slowly lowered it.

Delicate script filled the page, the ink still bleeding.

Lee crumpled the paper in his hands before I could read it, a rough edge to the movement. "It's the serpent king," he growled. "They responded to our summons—he's ready to meet, but it has to be tonight. *Now.*"

WE ARRIVED at the rendezvous as the sun slipped past the horizon.

The serpent king had summoned us to the Halcyon temple, although it was really just a staircase descending into the sea. It was currently high tide, and every angry wave crashed against the top step of the staircase, swelling out over the stretch of golden sand between us and them. They were out there, watching us. I could feel their eyes bearing down on me. Fear prickled across my back, shuddering through my wings.

We halted just beyond the reach of the waves.

Darkness swirled above our heads, an all-consuming blanket of night. Storm clouds muted the stars and moon as rain drizzled sleepily all around us. Two long rows of charmed braziers burned on either side, painting us and our path in firelight.

I held on tightly to Lee's hand, but he'd gone cold and distant. This time, I knew it had nothing to do with me.

His mind was an open door right now—either from the consummation of our bond, or the weight of our surroundings—and his thoughts ran through me like a shiver. He'd been here before, when he was younger, used to sit on this staircase at low tide and watch the ocean breathe. The memories were fleeting and gray, faded by time.

This was where the last traces of his mother had been found—her feathers scattering the beach and her clothes abandoned on the stairs. This was where she'd walked into the sea.

This was where she'd left him.

Gus and Lana flanked us, and a handful of sentinels stood watch a few yards behind them, armed to the teeth with iron. We took every precaution, and yet, my skin still buzzed in anticipation.

As the ocean crashed into the staircase again, a soft silver glow split through the foam.

A dark figure clutched to the top step, holding on as the water receded. They crawled forward, then slowly, they rolled upright. Dark eyes reflected the fire. Dark brown skin and silver scales glistened softly.

With a growing smirk, the creature unsteadily pushed himself to his feet.

His *feet.*

This was the serpent king.

Four more bodies crawled up the stairs behind him. They struggled with the shakiness of their temporary legs, but eventually, they pushed themselves upright as well.

The serpent king strolled toward us with alarming grace.

Serpents could walk on two legs for short periods of time if they possessed the magical means required for such a spell, but only ever within reach of the ocean's embrace. Everywhere the sand was wet, they were allowed to roam.

They must have a former Impundulu in their ranks, one with witch's blood.

Lightning sprites were trapped in the vials hanging around each of their necks. The sprites' chaotic, transformative energy rattled inside the glass, softly tinkling as it flowed into the feathers stuffed in alongside them. Every serpent had dragged a portion of their wings into the ocean with them, to be used for this precise purpose. The feathers were conduits, transferring the sprites' magic to the serpents, temporarily disrupting the ancient sorcery that forced them to grow tails and fins.

Once the lightning sprites ran out of light, though, they would have to return to the water.

After meeting with the Wight, I couldn't help but wonder if the serpents were under a curse too. Why was our world the way it was? The belief that it was all by the Divine Mother's design no longer sated me. How much meddling did the gods and elves do before our time, and how much did they continue to meddle now?

Perhaps there was no such thing as fate.

There was only life, with all its sorrow and joy. We were the product of ancient curses and reluctant bonds. We all lived, and then we died, and those who lived beyond us housed our ghosts for a little while in the shape of blurry memories.

These serpents endured a kind of death too. Who they used to be died the instant their wings were severed, and I imagine they mourned themselves.

The serpent king didn't look mournful, though.

I could see him better now that the firelight surrounded him. He was naked, but streams of water slid like curling snakes around his legs and hips. It didn't seem like he was in control of them—the water had a mind of its own, lingering on his skin like the ocean reminding us of its claim over him. The silvery scales on his brown skin were still visible, some of them having receded only far enough to free his legs.

His hair was as white as the moon.

"A new frost lord has ascended the silver throne," he said as he ambled to a stop, his dark brown eyes finding Lee. "I suppose congratulations are in order. Step forward, boy. Let us get a good look at you." He reached a hand out, beckoning Lee forward.

Lee grimaced. "I'm fine here."

The serpent king stepped forward with an irreverent grin. "Come now, Alezandral. You wouldn't want to disappoint your maker, would you?" Then he glanced over his shoulder at three of the serpents he'd brought with him.

Two males crowded a tall, curvy female.

Lee's eyes landed on her, and I felt the barriers around his mind slam shut. He wasn't quick enough, though. I had already felt his surprise and confusion and fear. As I turned to him, his hand squeezed mine so hard, my joints started aching.

"Lee, what's going on?"

He wasn't blinking, wasn't breathing. He couldn't look away from her—that pale, naked female. "It's *her*," he finally rasped.

I looked at her, *really* looked.

And I realized with a start that I recognized her. Lush curves and a serious brow, the collection of freckles across her nose now a stark contrast to her pallid complexion. White hair covered her shoulders where there had once been light brown.

Lee's mother didn't die a decade ago.

She'd been *transformed*.

There she stood, alive and as cold and unfathomable as the ocean…next to her king.

A sharp pang of panic reverberated through me. The last time Lee had seen his mother, she'd had wings—she'd been warm and full of color. I knew without reading his thoughts that this revelation was as much a shock to him as it was to me. He'd been told his mother was dead, but his whole life, he'd been searching for a reason.

"Lee," Lana seethed under her breath. "You need to snap out of it. *Please.*"

He couldn't. I knew Lee wasn't here. He was somewhere far away, trapped in that phantom of the past standing in front of him, her blue eyes drilling into his.

I knew what I had to do.

With one last comforting squeeze, I pulled my hand out of Lee's and stepped forward, drawing the attention of the serpents. "I'll be speaking on behalf of the Halcyon people today," I declared.

The serpent king's brow furrowed. "Who are *you*?"

Gus' voice growled to life behind me. "Sabrina is our queen."

"And you will address her with respect," Lana added in an equally harsh tone.

The serpent king rocked back a step, surprise blooming over his features. A smug sort of charm twinkled in his eyes. "*Queen* Sabrina, is it?"

I ignored the derisive lilt to his voice. Donning my regal mask was too easy. "As of today, I have as much authority over this territory and its affairs as my husband. If you wish to parlay, you will do so with me."

He laughed, and the three male serpents behind him chuckled along. "My Elona's little prince finally met his match. Isn't she lovely, pet?"

The serpent king glanced at Lee's mother.

Elona looked away from her son for what might have been the first time since she surfaced, and those piercing blue eyes met mine. On the outside, everything about her was cold and still, but there was something in that stare…

She only nodded once in what might have been approval and returned her gaze to Lee.

Not a word. I got the grim feeling she wasn't *allowed* to speak.

"I don't want your flattery," I snapped. "I want to know why you've been meeting with Abaddon behind Godfrey's back."

The serpent king dropped his smile. "I'm not inclined to flattery, *sky dweller*—only truth. I heard the runaway princess was a shy, skittish girl, but I can see now that was a careful lie. Believe me, I'm glad for that. Perhaps you will be more apt to listen than the last king. He was a coward." He tilted his head in thought. "His sniveling Hand started seeing the direness of our situation and met with me several times, but he was ultimately useless. I suppose you know that. I have you to blame for his presence in my ocean, after all. I wish you had killed him instead."

"Why were you meeting with them?" I demanded. "What do you want?"

"Only what belongs to me." He lifted his arms to either side in a vague gesture. "The ocean. It has been my home and hunting grounds for as long as your kind have filled the sky. Until recently, we have existed side-by-side in relative peace."

"Sure," I scoffed. "If by relative peace you mean we live in separate worlds and despise each other at a distance. We don't want your bloody ocean. Keep it."

The serpent's chin lowered until he was looking at me from beneath the ledge of his brow. "I wish it was that simple, but the circumstances have forced my hand. My people desire true peace again. For decades now, we have suffered for the mistakes of your forefathers, and we grow tired of it." He hesitated, then said slowly, "We are prepared for war."

The hair on my arms and the nape of my neck lifted. A stone of dread formed in the pit of my stomach, and I had to gulp down air as his words rattled around my mind. *War.* Abaddon had used that word too, back in the throne room.

"I'll have you know," I said darkly, "that I don't respond well to threats."

A laugh rasped out of the serpent king as he shook his head. "You think that was a threat? Little girl, if I wanted to kill you, I would have done so already. We aren't declaring war on the Halcyon."

That should have soothed me, but the look in his eyes told me that the reality was far worse.

"The war is already upon us," he continued. "It is in our oceans, surrounding your nations—and if we don't act soon, the flesh thieves will harvest us all."

CHAPTER 61

Our carriage flew fast and furious over the gnashing forest.

Lee and I were traveling to my father's territory. After the conversation we had with the serpent king, it was clear we didn't have time to waste. We had to gather our allies and call a meeting of the territories. If the serpent king had been telling the truth, then we'd seen only a fraction of the sutilus' army so far, but we would be seeing more of it soon. *Much more.*

The serpents had been fighting them off for more than a century—the invasion had never been stopped, only slowed.

And all this time, we'd seen them as our enemies.

Murderous natures and appetites aside, we had a mutual crisis on our hands, and the serpents wanted to be our allies against it, against the sutilus, or *flesh thieves*, as the snake king called them.

I stopped pacing in the center of the carriage and turned to look at Lee. He hadn't so much as blinked in several minutes, his hands fisted on top of his steel-plated thighs. He was staring at the ground in front of him, the depths of his gaze dark and burning.

"Lee, look at me," I whispered as I slid in front of him.

When he didn't move, I cradled his chin in my hand and tilted his face toward mine. His eyes were desolate, and I buried my hands in his hair as I inched closer, forcing him to lean back.

"Talk to me."

Lee's eyes squeezed shut, and his brow pinched in the semblance of pain. "I can't get it out of my mind. I keep seeing her, like *that.*"

I rubbed the silky strands of his hair between my fingers.

"Your mother meant a lot to you," I reasoned. "You were lied to. Of course you're upset."

His hands tightened on my hips and pushed me back. "I'm not upset," he said vehemently. "I'm fucking *angry.* And I can't stop *thinking* about it. I'm driving myself crazy." His voice broke on the last word.

I knew he wasn't angry with his mother. He was angry with the circumstances, because nothing would fix this. Elona was a serpent now, and Lee had to live with the fact that his mother existed in a place just beyond his reach, in a place far more dangerous than the Veil. She was still alive, but she could be suffering under the surface for all we knew. There was no peace for him.

There were worse things than true death. Half-life, for instance. Half-love.

I cradled his cheeks and bent at the waist, pressing my forehead to his. "Then let me help. Let me help you forget for a while."

"*How?*"

I smiled and kissed him, shuddering as he dragged me close again. His touch traveled up my back to my lower wings, caressing them reverently. His hands were gentle, but I knew he needed more. He didn't want to think anymore—he just wanted to feel, and I knew how to make him feel.

I bit his lower lip, tugging his flesh between my teeth until he gasped and jerked back.

Lee's eyes were intensely dark, rimmed with a sliver of pale blue light. "Sia?"

"Take what you need from me," I whispered, nibbling on his parted lips, licking into his mouth without succumbing to another kiss. He growled at the way I teased him, and his kisses grew sharp and hungry along my jaw—*ravenous*.

A moan escaped my lips.

Lee surged forward, claiming my mouth as he took me into his arms. We staggered backwards until I fell into the opposite bench seat. Lee's palm caught my lower back, arching my spine toward him as his other hand slid between the skirts of my dress, finding my slick heat with a groan.

I sucked on his neck, and he plunged two fingers inside me, thrusting as his tongue plundered my mouth, every stroke rough but controlled. Oblivion danced around the edges of my vision, every sensation another step into madness. His scruff scratched my face raw, the feeling so savage that my core trembled around his fingers.

I fisted a hand in his hair and tugged his head back to look at him

Lee smirked at me down the length of his nose. There was something about his smug face in a full suit of armor—the power it had over me was insane. I was already coming undone, but *he* was the one who needed to come undone right now.

"You can do better than that," I taunted.

His eyes darkened a heartbeat before he ripped me up into his arms and swung me around. My wings snapped into my back with the help of his Materie, and he swallowed my gasp of surprise as he lowered me into the footwell of the carriage.

His large wings flared above the seats to either side of us, and his lips left mine only long enough for him to remove his weapon belt along with the steel plates around his hips. Then, he freed his hard length and hauled me toward him by my thighs.

Lee sank into me with one powerful thrust, his hands holding my hips in place as I writhed in his lap. He withdrew slowly, only to snap his hips forward again while tilting my sex up, hitting a transcendent spot deep inside me.

My lips parted in a moan as I leaned up, digging my nails into his neck as an anchor.

He continued thrusting into me, manipulating my body weight, our bodies sliding up the aisle of the foot well.

Every plunge, every slam into the deepest parts of me... fuck, I was about to fly right out of my skin. Lee was unleashed, and I was nearly gone too. His thrusts came faster, fiercer, as if he'd felt the desperation in my body, or maybe he'd read it in my mind.

This was perfect, him filling me. His armor glinted in the moonlight, that lock of blond hair bouncing against his furrowed brow.

Our eyes met, and the corner of his mouth curled arrogantly.

I lurched forward and wrapped my arms around Lee's neck, pulling him down for a kiss as my body detonated.

He lifted me in the same heartbeat and slammed me up against the carriage door, thrusting into me with violent force. I rode out my pleasure, unaware of the words falling out of my mouth. Lee groaned in my ear as he picked up speed.

The wooden panels behind my head shuddered from the might of his thrusts, and for a moment, I feared the door would swing open on us and I would tumble out—but then Lee braced his hands on either side of me, and I clung to his forearms as he drove into me a few more times, spilling himself with a breathless moan.

I slumped against the door and slowly peeled my eyes open, smiling when I saw the calmness on Lee's face. He'd needed that just as much as I did.

I twirled the lock of hair on his forehead between my forefingers. It was damp, darkened with sweat, but I could still see strands of pure gold glistening under my touch. He was still buried inside me, and I wasn't eager to move. I liked feeling this close to him, bonded in more ways than one.

Lee opened his eyes, looking into mine, his hands squeezing my waist. "What is that pretty smile for?"

Without hesitation, I told him the truth. "I love you, Alezandral." I ran both my hands through his hair. "I'm perfectly mad for you."

He stared at me, aghast by my confession.

I ignored his silence and kissed him deeply, my lips trembling with the overwhelming desire to laugh. I'd rendered him speechless, and a warm satisfaction stirred within my chest. I would take my victories where I could.

That delicious warmth bled away as Lee grasped my upper arms and peeled himself back.

His hands were shaking. He was paler than usual, and there was something in his gaze that absolutely terrified me, because I could see he was afraid of what I'd said.

"Are you sure?" he said softly.

My heart sank. What kind of response was that? Of course I was sure. I'd never been surer of anything else in my entire life. I hadn't confessed my love expecting him to say it back. I had prepared myself for a variety of different reactions, and I would have readily accepted any of them. Teasing, distraction, even silence. Him doubting my feelings, though? That was cruel.

Unless… he honestly didn't feel the same way and knew he never would.

I thought he did. I thought I had felt it. In every touch, every kiss, I felt it. Was I that deluded, that desperate for love that I had imagined he fell for me? Perhaps I should have known better. Seraphim were born to fly, not fall. Falling from the heights we flew to was fatal.

A terrible thought burrowed its way into my heart and grew claws.

Maybe he wasn't capable of love. Maybe I wasn't either. Maybe we were both just a little too fucked up, and Lee knew that. He'd promised friendship and companionship when he proposed to me, not love.

I pushed him away and tugged the sides of my dress closed, needing to shield myself somehow from his blistering rejection. There was nowhere to hide, though, so he saw the tears in my eyes as they welled up. I was certain he heard the whisper of my thoughts, too. The pain I felt in this moment was too great, too deep, and our bond was too strong.

Our connection wasn't mere water and spirit anymore. A river of steel flowed between us that I couldn't sever.

Lee grabbed my wrists, wrenching my hands away from the bodice of my dress. When I lifted my gaze to his, I saw that his expression was panicked, simmering with guilt. "Please stop," he rasped. "I didn't mean it like that."

I fought his grip, and he let go—so easily, he let me go.

"Then how did you mean it?" I shouted, on the brink of violence. "Tell me."

Just cut my chest open and rip my fucking heart out, I thought. *That would hurt less.*

Anger flashed across his features, and he grabbed the underside of my chin, forcing me to hold his stare. "You will not push me away after telling me you love me. Do you understand? You will keep me. You will not be afraid, because you are mine. And if you're mine, then I am yours, Sia. I'm yours."

It was as if he'd lit a match inside me, calling my magic to the surface with his words.

Black ash swirled in the air around us as I reached for him, but a thud echoed outside our carriage, loud enough to make us both jump and turn toward the window.

Lee pulled out of me and leapt to his feet. "What the fuck was *that?*"

He scrambled up onto the bench and peered through the glass panel, his eyes widening as a cacophony of sounds erupted nearby and distant screams sliced into our cab. Before I could ask, Lee lurched for his weapons belt and the silver plates he'd removed earlier.

"We're under attack, Sia."

"*What?*" I staggered to my feet to look out the window for myself.

I barely caught a glimpse of a burning carriage as it plummeted into the gnashing forest below. The pegasi had been cut free from the cab, flying as a pair in and out of the storm clouds in a panic. That had been the carriage I was supposed to take, but I'd refused it. I hoped the driver had escaped with his life, but if he did, I couldn't see him in the sky.

The door on the other side of our carriage opened, and the unsettling chaos infiltrated our cab. It was so loud, thump after deafening thump echoing through the night, like a songless drum. Sentinels were shouting, and the pegasi leading our carriage whinnied and cried as the driver roared directions at them in the elven tongue. A sentinel appeared in the open doorway, holding himself there against the pummeling wind.

He looked between the two of us with a mixture of relief and dread. "Your Majesties, we need to take to the sky. Your carriages have been targeted."

Lee was still reattaching the plates around his hips. "By *who?*" he spat.

The sentinel shook his head; he didn't know. "They're firing shells that detonate upon impact."

Another thud sounded, and I fell against the door again as the carriage weaved sharply. The cannonball must have connected with something beside us—a sentinel, perhaps—because an explosion rocked our vehicle forward, sending me sprawling over the bench at the front of the cab. The driver had successfully dodged whatever was thrown at us, but I knew we were losing control of the carriage. Pegasi were only obedient to a point.

Lee's head whipped back and forth between me and the sentinel before he stalked toward me with outstretched arms.

"You go first," he commanded.

I knew what he was thinking. He was going to use his Materie to get us away from the line of fire, but he didn't intend to come with me right away. Me first, then the sentinel.

I shook my head, tears springing to my eyes. "Lee, don't you *dare—*"

"Don't be afraid. I'll be with you soon," he said gruffly.

Then he touched my hip, and I plummeted, squeezed through his Materie into the starry sky on the other side. The sounds of the aerial attack were muted now, far away.

I couldn't see much. I was tumbling too wildly, and my eyes were veiled with dark tears.

Lee had released my wings for me, so I twisted in midair to right myself, willing my wings to spread and catch the chilling wind.

I managed to slow my descent enough not to completely impale myself on a tree, but I still collided with it. The sulfur-tinged air was knocked out of my lungs, and I gasped for a new breath, my senses filling with pine and sweet sap as I turned my attention to the sky.

Fire billowed in sharp bursts through the storm clouds— the explosive shells hitting our men. The carriage was dodging them, swell after swell.

We'd been ambushed.

Someone in the forest had known we were coming.

Cannons were being fired in an organized pattern, forming a cage to keep our parade contained, herding our carriage away from safety.

Where was Lee? *Where was he?*

I launched myself off the tree at the same moment that I saw a set of two cannonballs whistling through the air. The first clipped the edge of the cab and exploded, turning it upside down, but the second hit true, detonating like a thunderclap through my soul.

CHAPTER 62

LEE

Somewhere in the dark recesses of my mind, I heard Sia scream.

I knew she wasn't there with me. I'd thrown her as far as my Materie allowed before reaching for the sentinel in the doorway.

That had been a mistake. The worst of my life.

I could still see the sentinel's body bursting apart in a shower of blood and feathers as the cannonball slammed into his back, could still feel the vicious guilt that had stalled my heart. Another death on my hands. I could still feel the heat of the incendiaries as the ball collided with the ceiling and flipped the cab upside down. My prickling dread as the ground slid out from under my feet.

Sheer luck had spared me. I fell through the open door into the sky at the same moment the second explosive hit the carriage, shattering it from the inside out.

That luck hadn't saved me from getting caught in the wreckage, though.

Even broken into pieces, the carriage was heavier than me —it fell faster. It had all happened so quickly. I hadn't been given a chance to dematerialize before the first beam of debris slammed into me. That was how I found myself crashing through the canopy of the forest, ripping up my palms as I grappled desperately for something, *anything*, to slow my fall. I could only assume I'd been successful, because I was still alive. Pinned beneath a few smoldering beams of lumber with a mouthful of dirt... but alive.

The sea steel armor had kept my body from being crushed.

This enormous, heart-wrenching gift from my wife had saved me just as completely as *she* had a decade ago, on that day when we'd promised ourselves to one another in the forest behind my father's palace. Even through the punishments and the brainwashing that came afterward, the constant torture my father subjected me to, she had always been my protection.

I had held onto her like one might hold on to their gods.

She'd been taken away from me, but my memories of that day—her screaming for me, demanding that my father stop dragging that icy knife through my back—had followed me around for years. It was a reminder of the pure, unconditional love that I hadn't believed existed before I met her.

Sia had plucked me like a flower and pressed me inside the vicious sinews of her heart, and I was never able to forget it.

And now... she was screaming for me again.

I forced my eyes open, ignoring the burn of smoke as it filled my nostrils. I was alive, and I had to get out of here. Voices echoed through the forest somewhere close by— muffled shouts of victory. The attackers had human voices and spoke in the common tongue. Rebels? Random vigilantes? It didn't matter. Soon enough, they would track down this wreckage, and I needed to be ready for them.

My wife. My heartmate. I needed to get back to her. I would crawl if I had to.

She had to be so scared, so worried, and my heart just

couldn't bear that knowledge. I could feel her heart breaking in tandem with mine, and I instantly despised myself for it.

I dug my fingers into the dirt, trying to drag myself out of the debris.

The movement sent a deep blade of pain piercing through my back and I paused, craning my neck to look over my shoulder. My stomach roiled when I saw the damage.

A shard of metal from the shattered carriage had hit me in the back, embedding itself in the soft tissues around the root of my upper wing, where the armor couldn't protect me. I reached toward it with my Materie, attempting to send the wings into my back until I could deal with them properly—but I stopped as the pain intensified, radiating through my ribcage, making it impossible to breathe.

The metal had severed something inside me.

My heartbeat slowed to a sluggish crawl as the reality of my situation dawned. I was losing my wings.

The irony of this was not lost on me, not after I'd taken Abaddon's wings earlier that day. Fate seemed insistent that I spend the last few moments of my life clinging desperately to the forest floor, listening to the stampede of soldiers closing in around me. I knew my life would be at an end even if I triumphed over them.

But for *her*, for my girl, I would do my best.

She would come searching for me, and Goddess be damned if I let her find a corpse. Goddess be damned if I let her lose even one more person without the privilege of a goodbye.

I had been falling my whole life—falling for lies and dreams and the ghost of a bond I feared just as deeply as I longed for it. And now, I'd finally hit the ground. It was a pity I had to let go of it all now, just when those dreams had finally turned into something real.

I should have taken the opportunity in that carriage to

voice the words blazing so brightly in my heart, the words that belonged to her. The words that were true and that she deserved.

Gritting my teeth, I closed my eyes and dug my fingers deeper into the earth, knowing that this next part would really fucking hurt. I hoped she could hear my confession now... now that it was too late.

I love you too, Sia. I always have.

I will love you until I can love no longer.

ACKNOWLEDGMENTS

This story has been a labor of both love and grief. And I couldn't have done it without my people.

To my husband, thank you for being my rock when I need stability and the soft place for me to rest when the world is too brutal.

To my readers, thank you for taking this journey with me, for reading my stories and loving them, for sharing your love of my characters with others and showing me day after day that this adventure is worth it.

To Shannon, Erin, Michaela, and the rest of my writer friends who beta read this book, TOB would not be the same without you, and I cherish each of you—for your intelligence, your encouragement and advice, and especially your friendship.

To my editor, Alexa, and my sensitivity reader, Lo, your professional expertise is invaluable to me. Project after project, you provide such incredible support. Thank you for helping me make this book the best it could possibly be.

THANK YOU.

And to my brother, James, thank you for 27 years of the best sibling relationship in the world. Thank you for being a brother, a father figure, and a friend.

Rest In Peace.

ABOUT THE AUTHOR

Beka Westrup is a genre-hopping author of fantasy and romance. The Obsidian Blaze is her fifth full-length novel. She lives in the PNW with her husband and two children, collecting more books than she'll ever be able to read and drinking copious amounts of iced coffee.

Stay in the know with Beka's Newsletter:
https://www.bekawestrup.com/coming-soon-03

facebook.com/bekawestrup

x.com/bekawestrup

instagram.com/bekaboowrites

tiktok.com/@bekabooauthor